SHANNON HALE

FRiENDS FOREVER

Artwork by
LeUYEN PHAM

Color by **HILARY SYCAMORE** and **LeUYEN PHAM**

First Second
New York

First Second

PUBLISHED BY FIRST SECOND
FIRST SECOND IS AN IMPRINT OF ROARING BROOK PRESS,
A DIVISION OF HOLTZBRINCK PUBLISHING HOLDINGS LIMITED PARTNERSHIP
120 BROADWAY, NEW YORK, NY 10271
FIRSTSECONDBOOKS.COM
MACKIDS.COM

LIBRARY OF CONGRESS CONTROL NUMBER: 2021906613

OUR BOOKS MAY BE PURCHASED IN BULK FOR PROMOTIONAL, EDUCATIONAL, OR BUSINESS USE.
PLEASE CONTACT YOUR LOCAL BOOKSELLER OR THE MACMILLAN CORPORATE AND PREMIUM SALES DEPARTMENT AT
(800) 221-7945 EXT. 5442 OR BY EMAIL AT MACMILLANSPECIALMARKETS@MACMILLAN.COM.

FIRST EDITION, 2021
EDITED BY CONNIE HSU
COVER AND INTERIOR BOOK DESIGN BY MOLLY JOHANSON
COLOR BY HILARY SYCAMORE AND LEUYEN PHAM

THE ART IN THIS BOOK WAS RENDERED IN CROQUILLE AND INDIA BLACK INK AND DIGITALLY COLORED.

PRINTED IN THE UNITED STATES OF AMERICA BY WORZALLA, STEVENS POINT, WISCONSIN

ISBN 978-1-250-31756-8 (PAPERBACK)
1 3 5 7 9 10 8 6 4 2

ISBN 978-1-250-31755-1 (HARDCOVER)
1 3 5 7 9 10 8 6 4 2

DON'T MISS YOUR NEXT FAVORITE BOOK FROM FIRST SECOND! FOR THE LATEST UPDATES GO TO
FIRSTSECONDNEWSLETTER.COM AND SIGN UP FOR OUR ENEWSLETTER.

For Mom and Dad,
Happy days to you!
I love you so much.
w/B, Shannon

FoR Dinah, WReN, Max,
Maggie, Leo, and Adrien--
You've kept us going all year...
w/B, UyEN

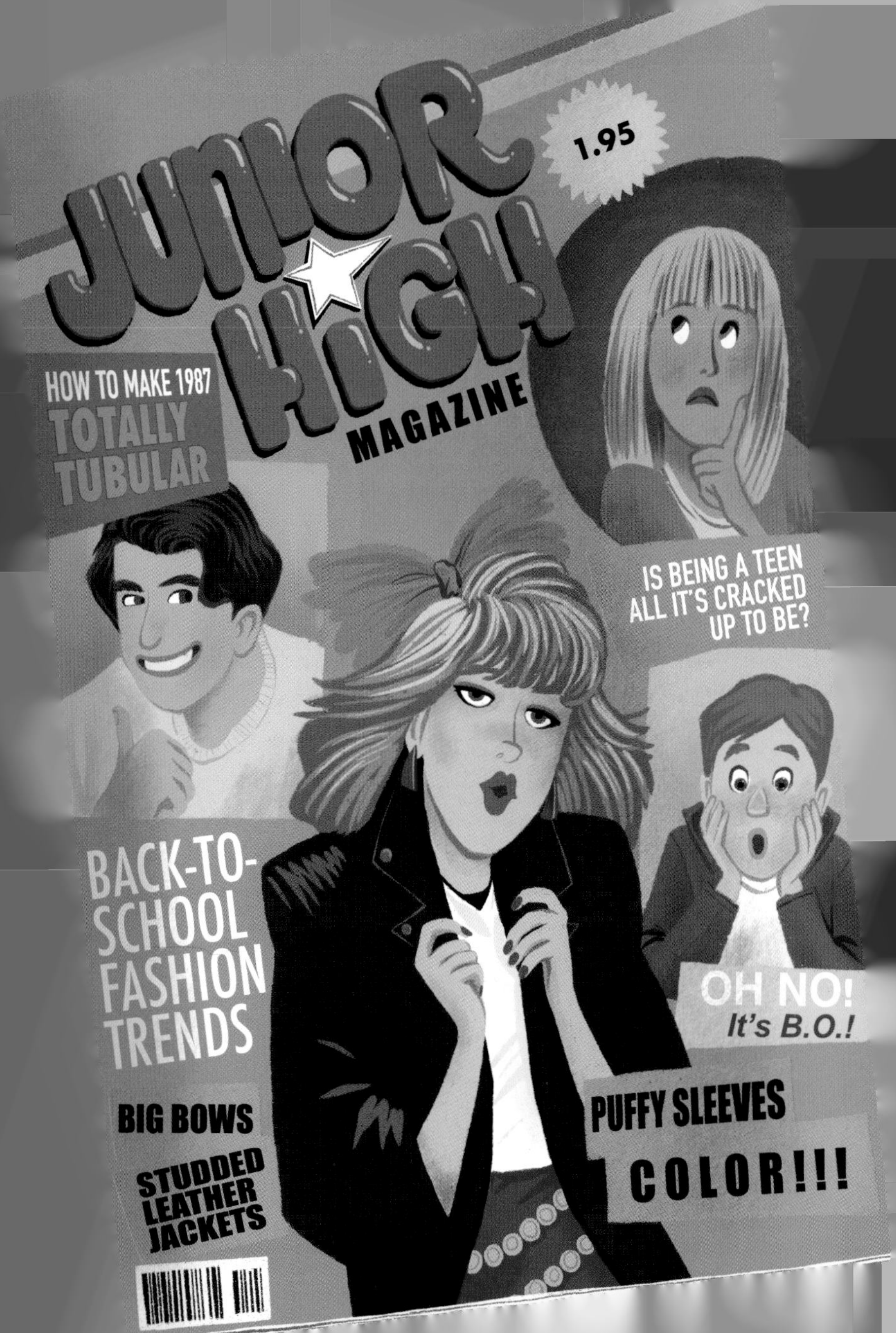

1.95
JUNIOR HIGH
MAGAZINE
HOW TO MAKE 1987
TOTALLY
TUBULAR
IS BEING A TEEN
ALL IT'S CRACKED
UP TO BE?
BACK-TO-
SCHOOL
FASHION
TRENDS
OH NO!
It's B.O.!
BIG BOWS
PUFFY SLEEVES
STUDDED
LEATHER
JACKETS
COLOR!!!

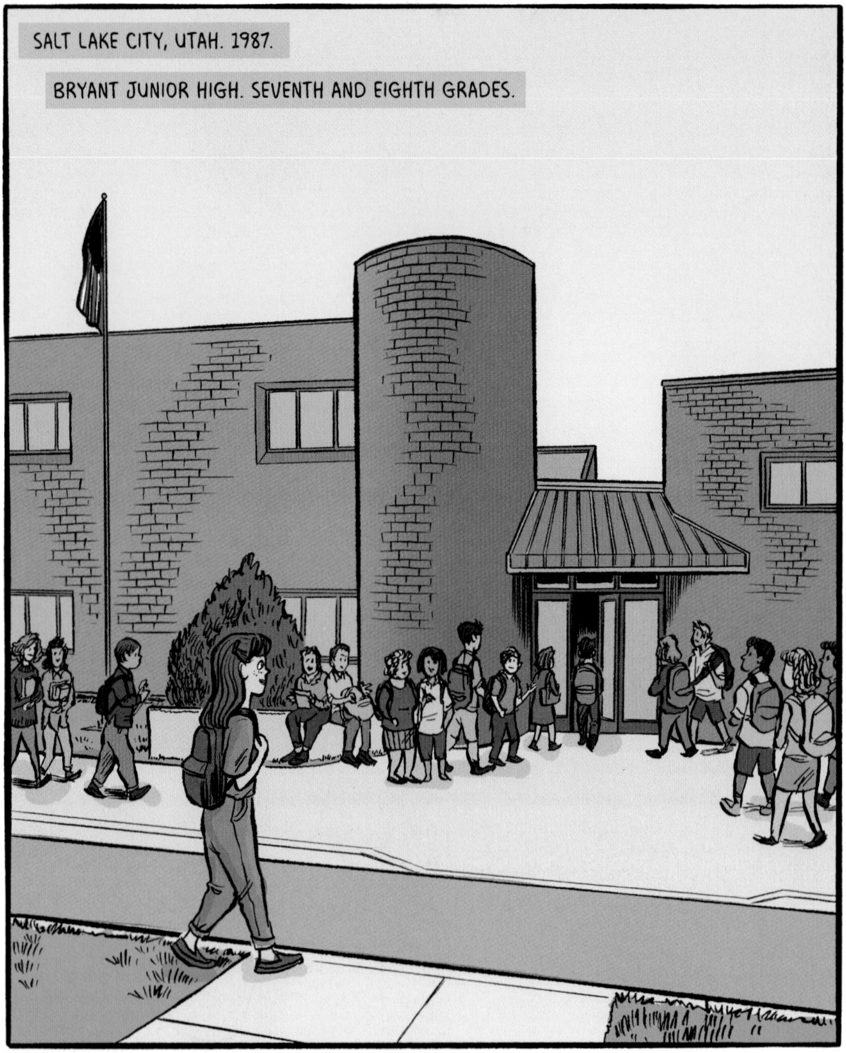
SALT LAKE CITY, UTAH. 1987.
BRYANT JUNIOR HIGH. SEVENTH AND EIGHTH GRADES.

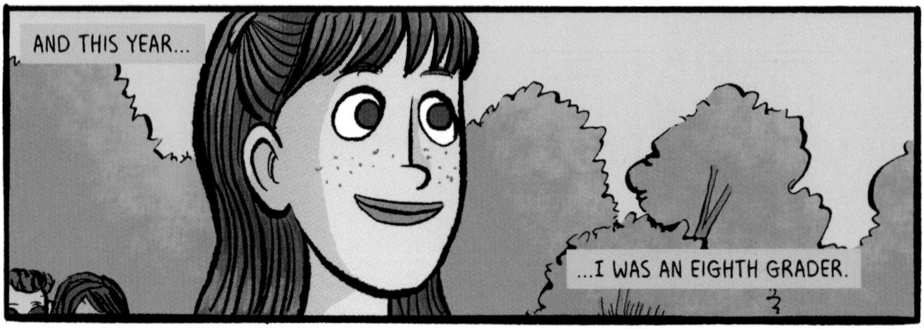
AND THIS YEAR...
...I WAS AN EIGHTH GRADER.

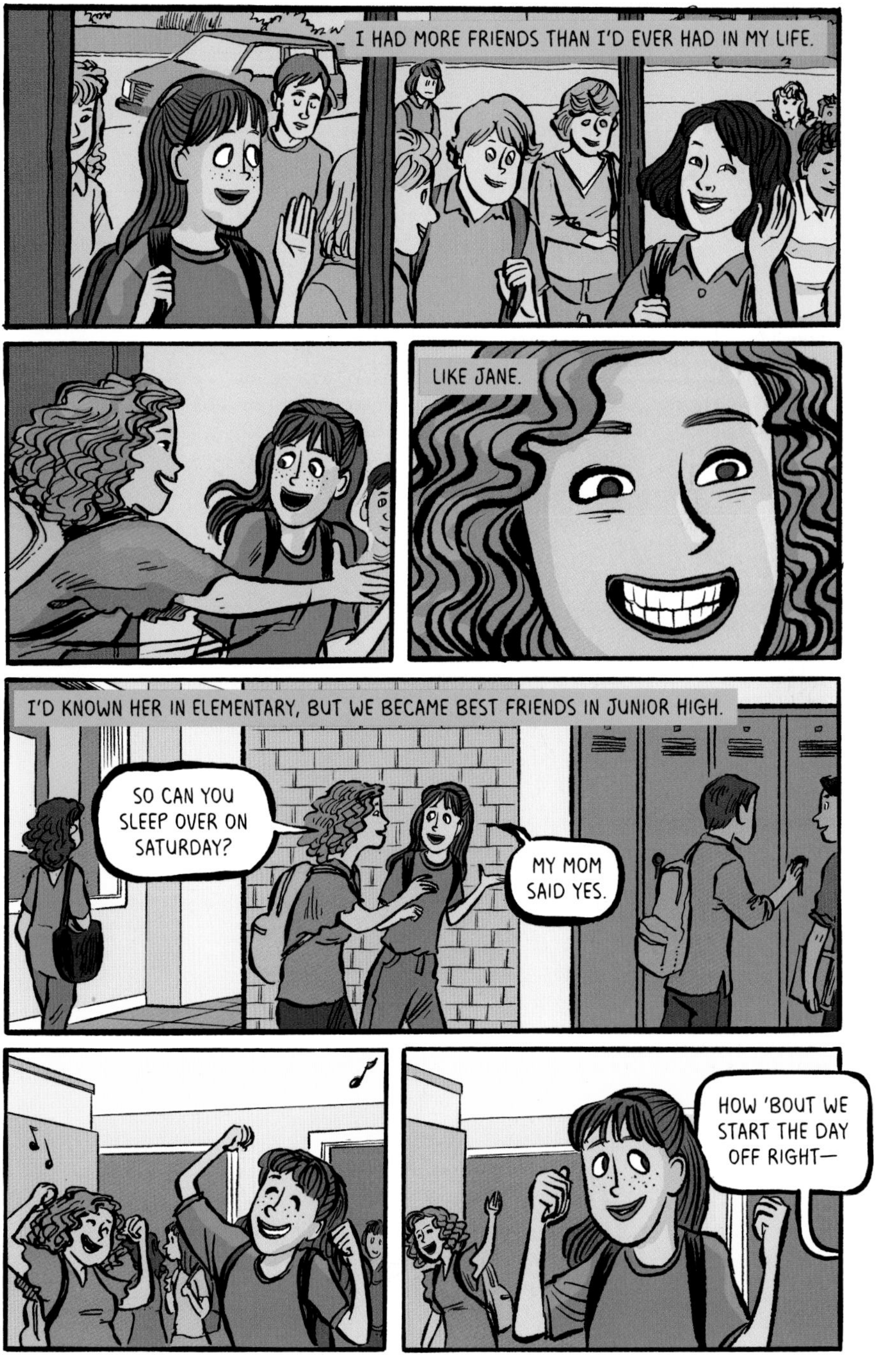
I HAD MORE FRIENDS THAN I'D EVER HAD IN MY LIFE.
LIKE JANE.
I'D KNOWN HER IN ELEMENTARY, BUT WE BECAME BEST FRIENDS IN JUNIOR HIGH.
SO CAN YOU SLEEP OVER ON SATURDAY?
MY MOM SAID YES.
HOW 'BOUT WE START THE DAY OFF RIGHT—

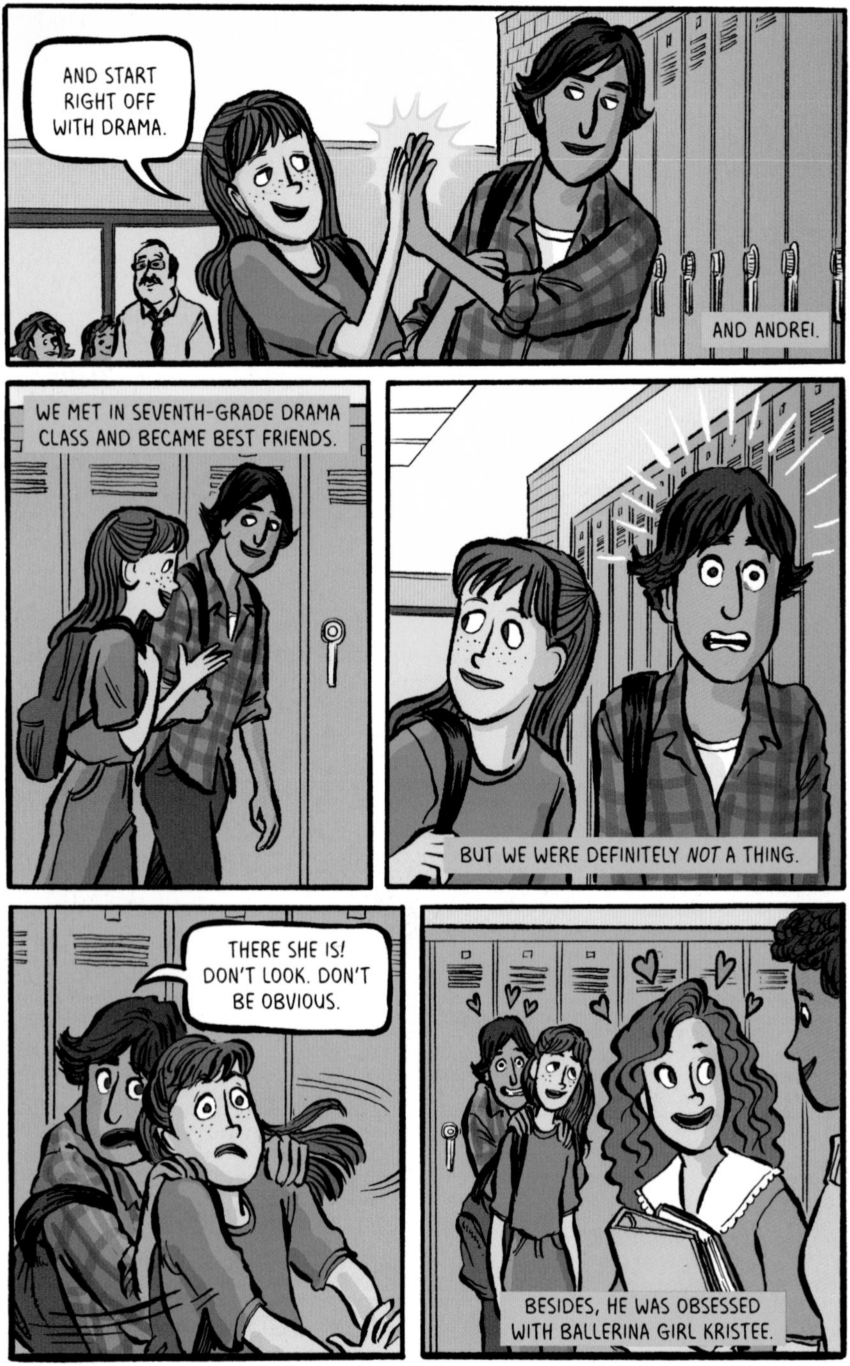
AND START RIGHT OFF WITH DRAMA.
AND ANDREI.
WE MET IN SEVENTH-GRADE DRAMA CLASS AND BECAME BEST FRIENDS.
BUT WE WERE DEFINITELY *NOT* A THING.
THERE SHE IS! DON'T LOOK. DON'T BE OBVIOUS.
BESIDES, HE WAS OBSESSED WITH BALLERINA GIRL KRISTEE.

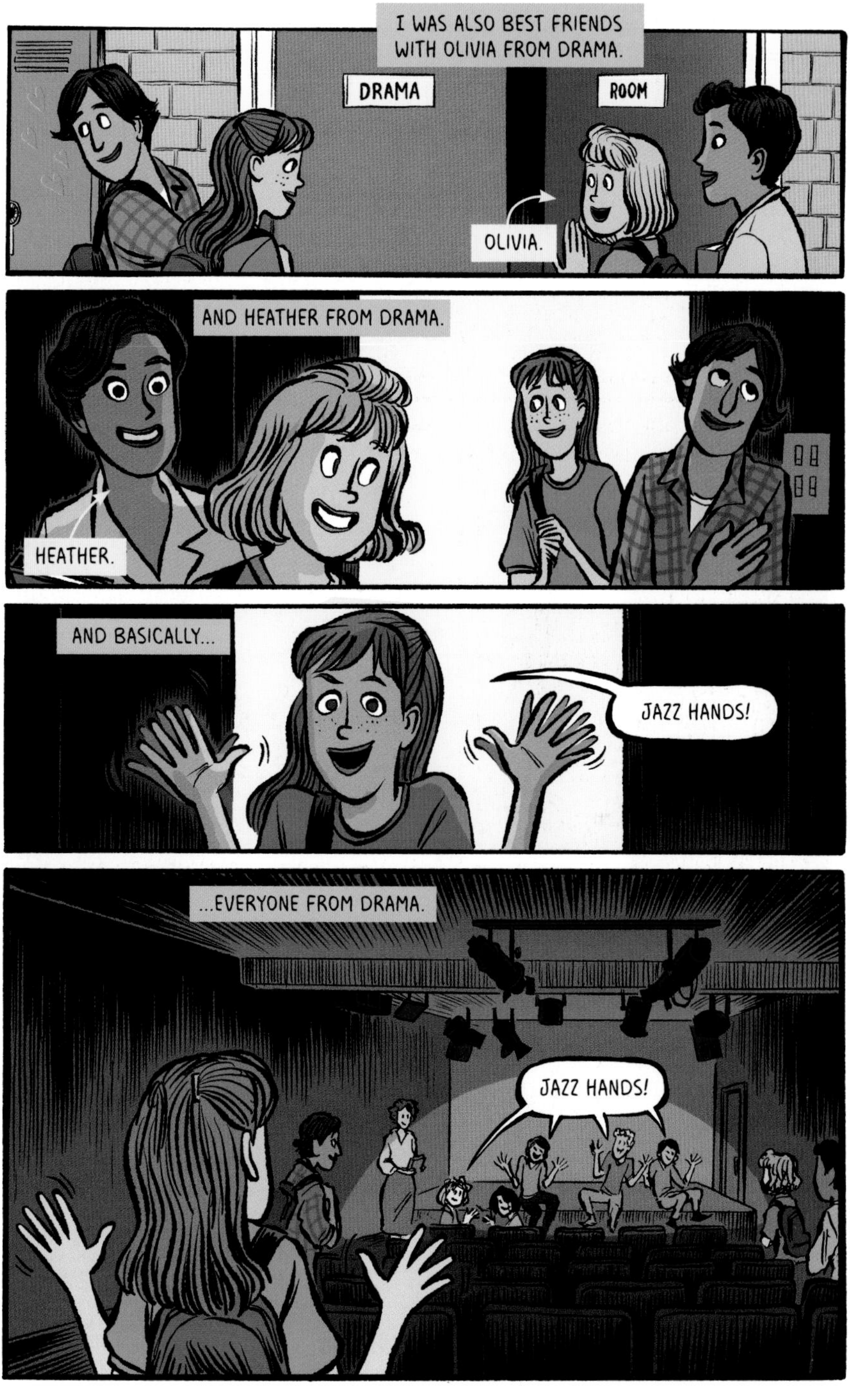
I WAS ALSO BEST FRIENDS WITH OLIVIA FROM DRAMA.
DRAMA
ROOM
OLIVIA.
AND HEATHER FROM DRAMA.
HEATHER.
AND BASICALLY...
JAZZ HANDS!
...EVERYONE FROM DRAMA.
JAZZ HANDS!

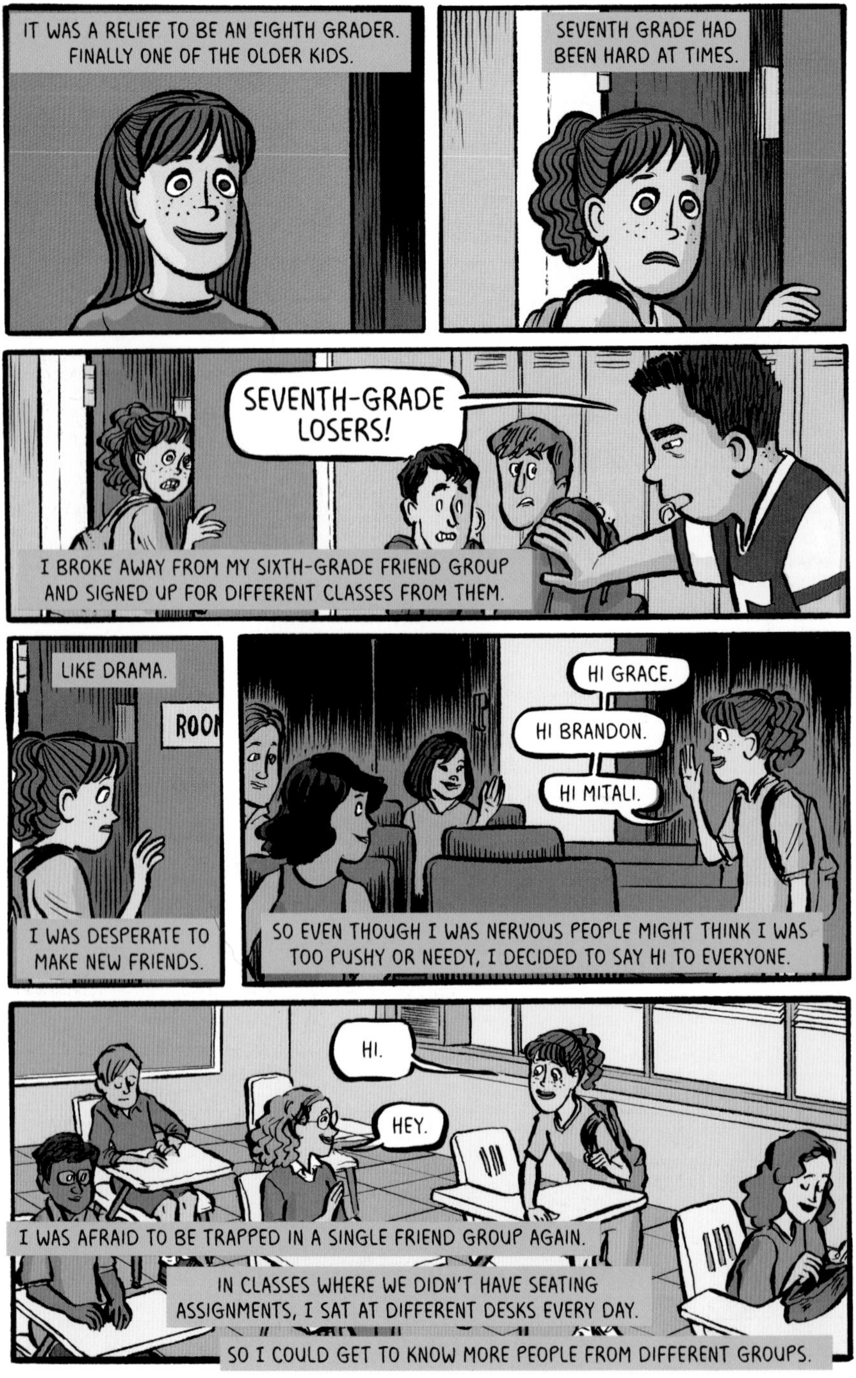
IT WAS A RELIEF TO BE AN EIGHTH GRADER. FINALLY ONE OF THE OLDER KIDS.
SEVENTH GRADE HAD BEEN HARD AT TIMES.
SEVENTH-GRADE LOSERS!
I BROKE AWAY FROM MY SIXTH-GRADE FRIEND GROUP AND SIGNED UP FOR DIFFERENT CLASSES FROM THEM.
LIKE DRAMA.
ROOM
I WAS DESPERATE TO MAKE NEW FRIENDS.
HI GRACE.
HI BRANDON.
HI MITALI.
SO EVEN THOUGH I WAS NERVOUS PEOPLE MIGHT THINK I WAS TOO PUSHY OR NEEDY, I DECIDED TO SAY HI TO EVERYONE.
HI.
HEY.
I WAS AFRAID TO BE TRAPPED IN A SINGLE FRIEND GROUP AGAIN.
IN CLASSES WHERE WE DIDN'T HAVE SEATING ASSIGNMENTS, I SAT AT DIFFERENT DESKS EVERY DAY.
SO I COULD GET TO KNOW MORE PEOPLE FROM DIFFERENT GROUPS.

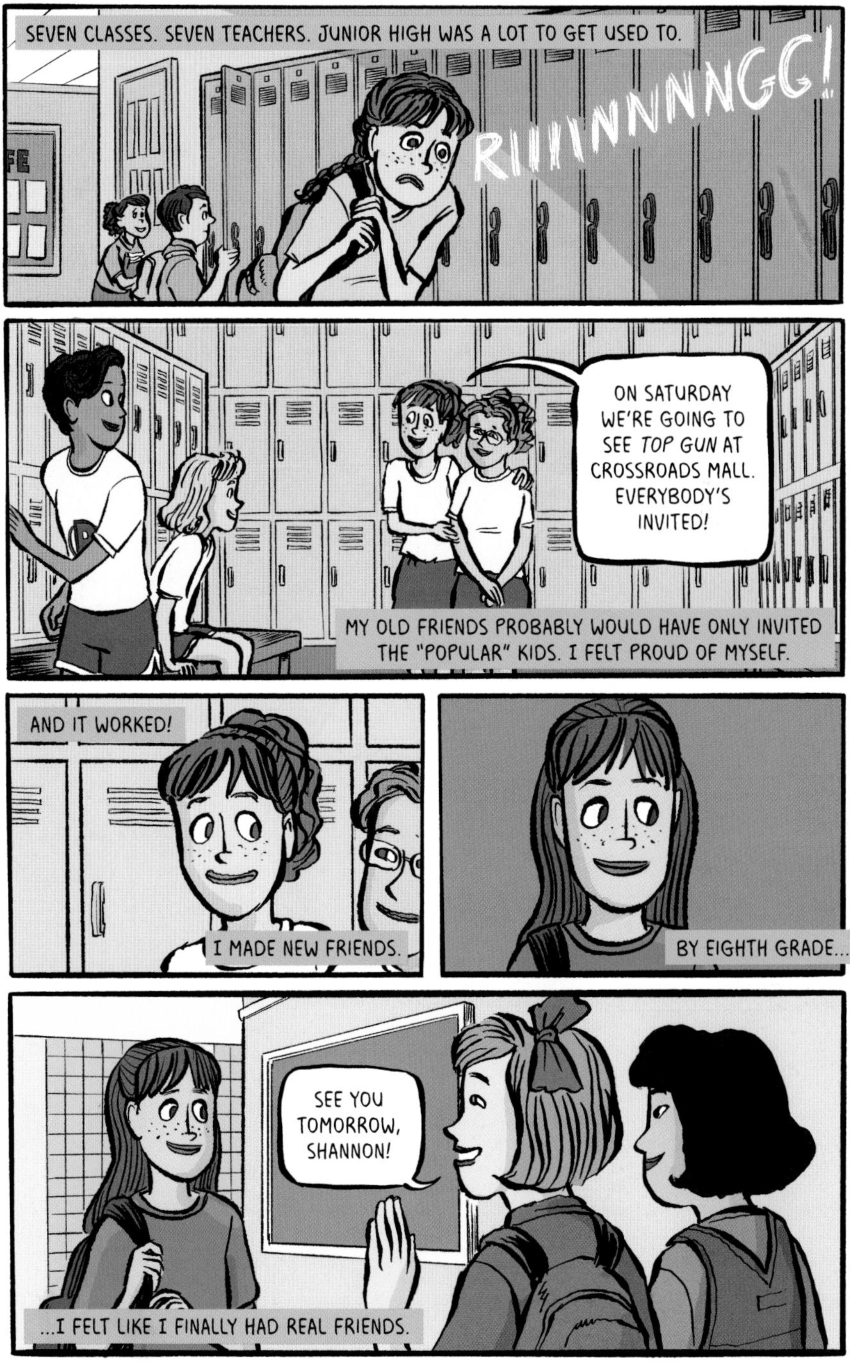
SEVEN CLASSES. SEVEN TEACHERS. JUNIOR HIGH WAS A LOT TO GET USED TO.
RIIIINNNNGG!
ON SATURDAY WE'RE GOING TO SEE *TOP GUN* AT CROSSROADS MALL. EVERYBODY'S INVITED!
MY OLD FRIENDS PROBABLY WOULD HAVE ONLY INVITED THE "POPULAR" KIDS. I FELT PROUD OF MYSELF.
AND IT WORKED!
I MADE NEW FRIENDS.
BY EIGHTH GRADE...
SEE YOU TOMORROW, SHANNON!
...I FELT LIKE I FINALLY HAD REAL FRIENDS.

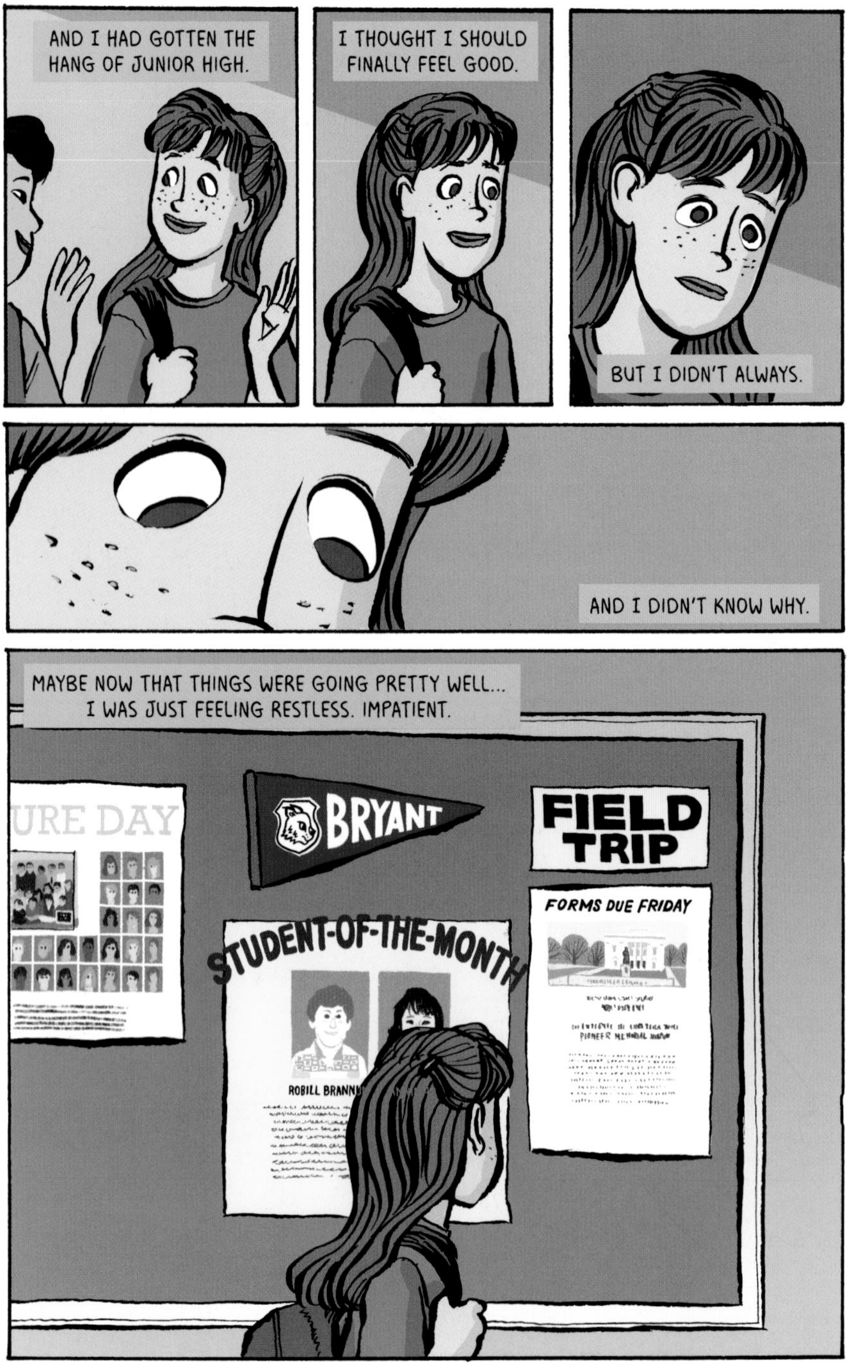
AND I HAD GOTTEN THE HANG OF JUNIOR HIGH.
I THOUGHT I SHOULD FINALLY FEEL GOOD.
BUT I DIDN'T ALWAYS.
AND I DIDN'T KNOW WHY.
MAYBE NOW THAT THINGS WERE GOING PRETTY WELL... I WAS JUST FEELING RESTLESS. IMPATIENT.
BRYANT
FIELD TRIP
FORMS DUE FRIDAY
STUDENT-OF-THE-MONTH

IN EIGHTH GRADE, THERE WERE SO MANY THINGS I WANTED TO DO...AND DO WELL!

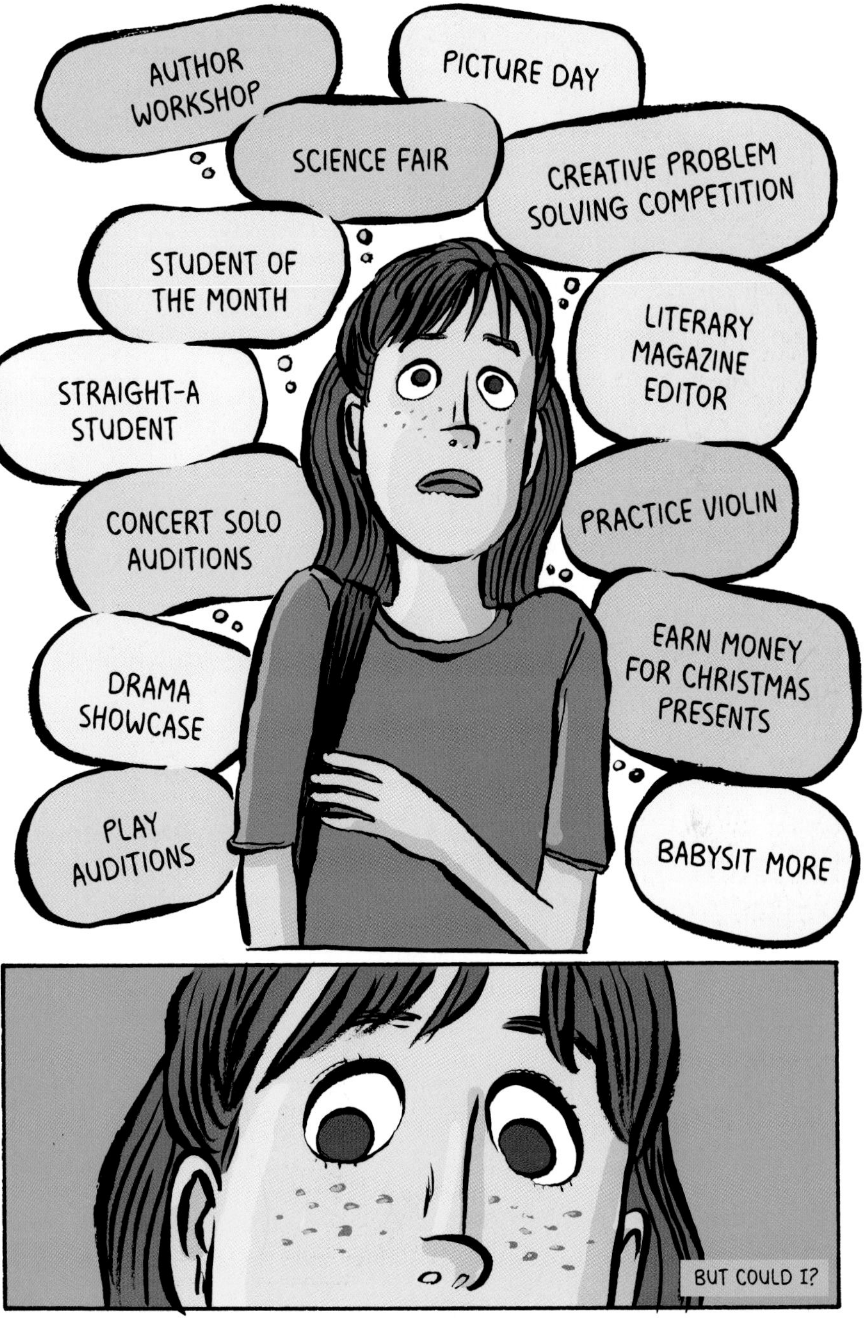
AUTHOR WORKSHOP
PICTURE DAY
SCIENCE FAIR
CREATIVE PROBLEM SOLVING COMPETITION
STUDENT OF THE MONTH
LITERARY MAGAZINE EDITOR
STRAIGHT-A STUDENT
CONCERT SOLO AUDITIONS
PRACTICE VIOLIN
DRAMA SHOWCASE
EARN MONEY FOR CHRISTMAS PRESENTS
PLAY AUDITIONS
BABYSIT MORE
BUT COULD I?

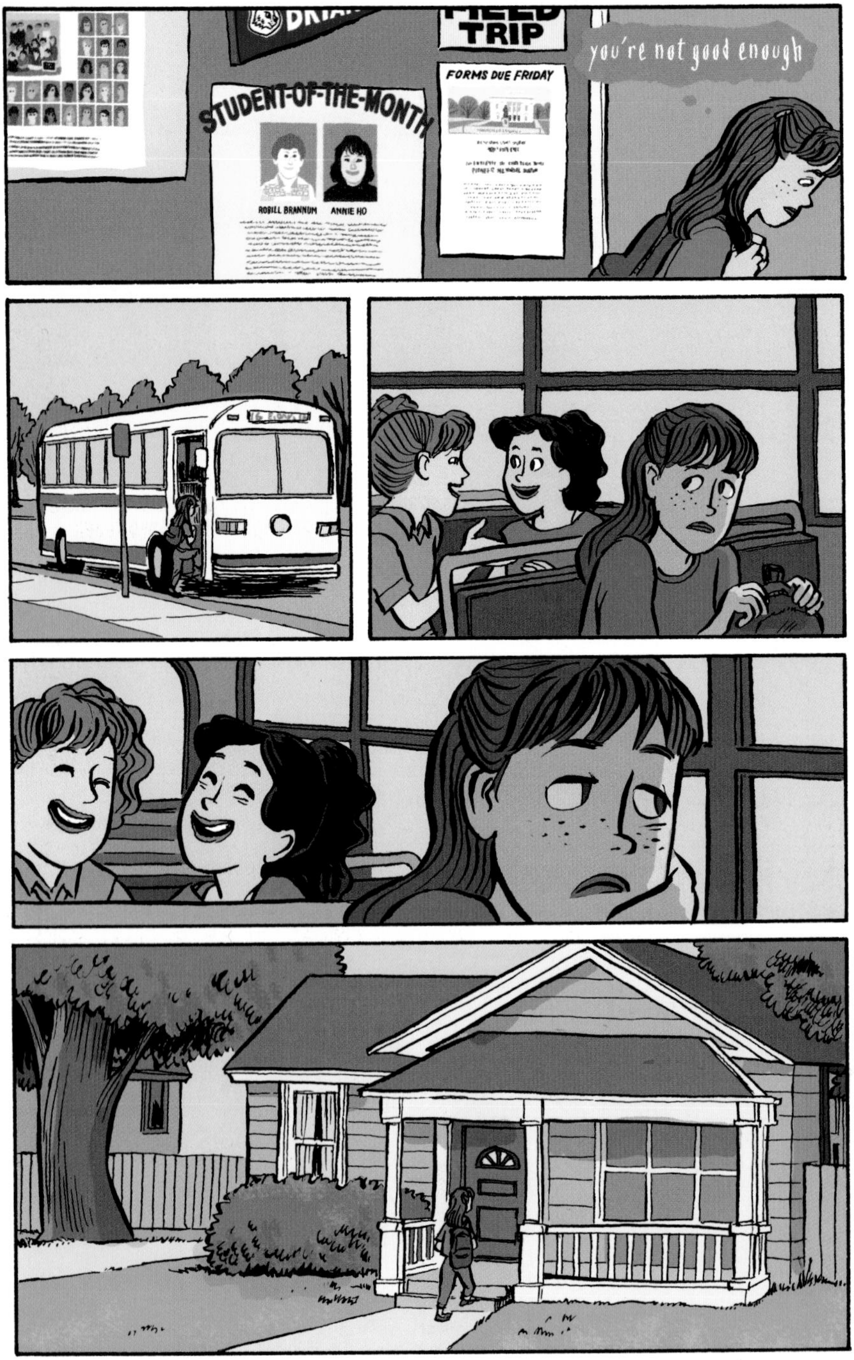
TRIP
FORMS DUE FRIDAY
you're not good enough
STUDENT-OF-THE-MONTH
ROBILL BRANNUM
ANNIE HO

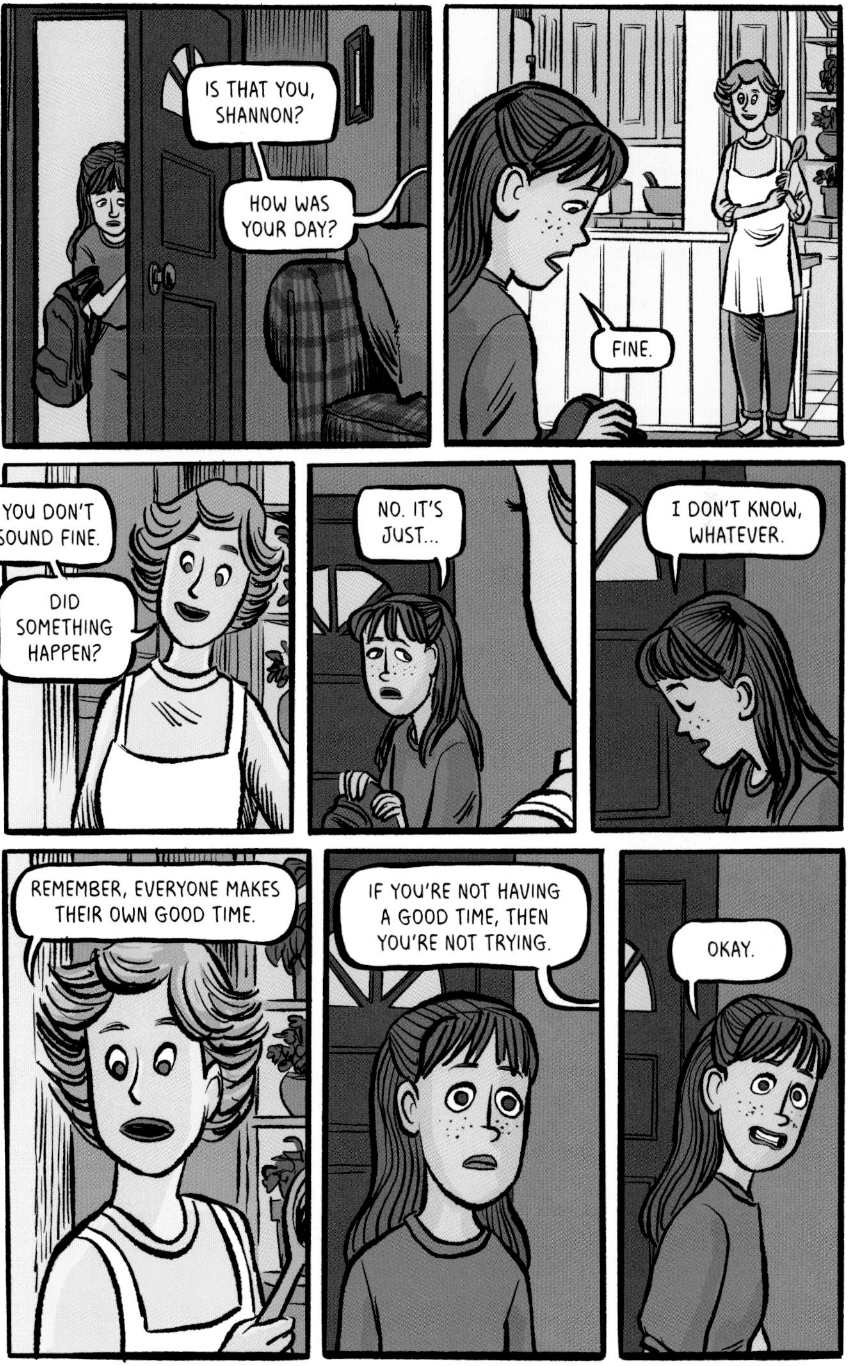
IS THAT YOU, SHANNON?
HOW WAS YOUR DAY?
FINE.
YOU DON'T SOUND FINE.
DID SOMETHING HAPPEN?
NO. IT'S JUST...
I DON'T KNOW, WHATEVER.
REMEMBER, EVERYONE MAKES THEIR OWN GOOD TIME.
IF YOU'RE NOT HAVING A GOOD TIME, THEN YOU'RE NOT TRYING.
OKAY.

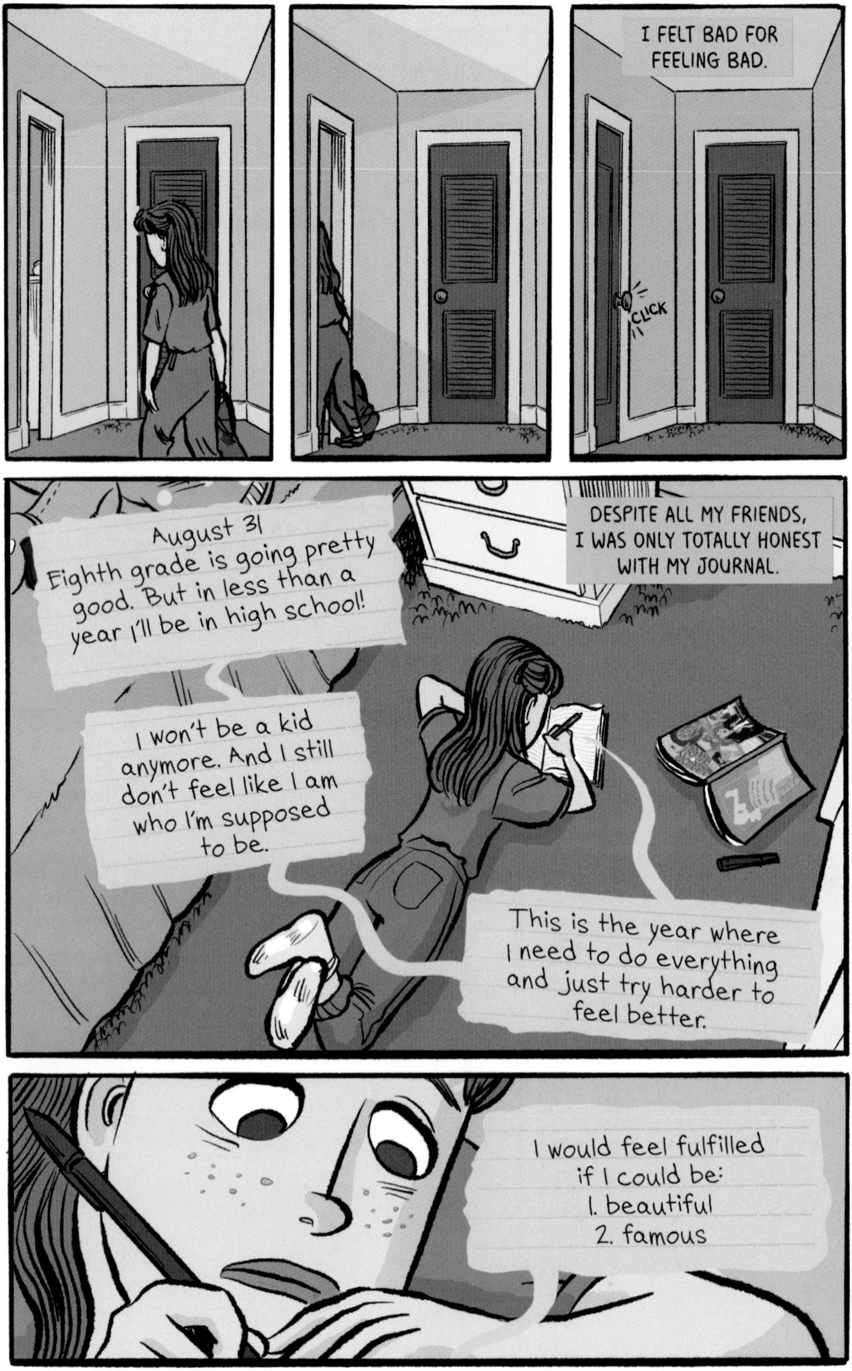
I FELT BAD FOR FEELING BAD.
CLICK
DESPITE ALL MY FRIENDS, I WAS ONLY TOTALLY HONEST WITH MY JOURNAL.
August 31
Eighth grade is going pretty good. But in less than a year I'll be in high school!
I won't be a kid anymore. And I still don't feel like I am who I'm supposed to be.
This is the year where I need to do everything and just try harder to feel better.
I would feel fulfilled if I could be:
1. beautiful
2. famous

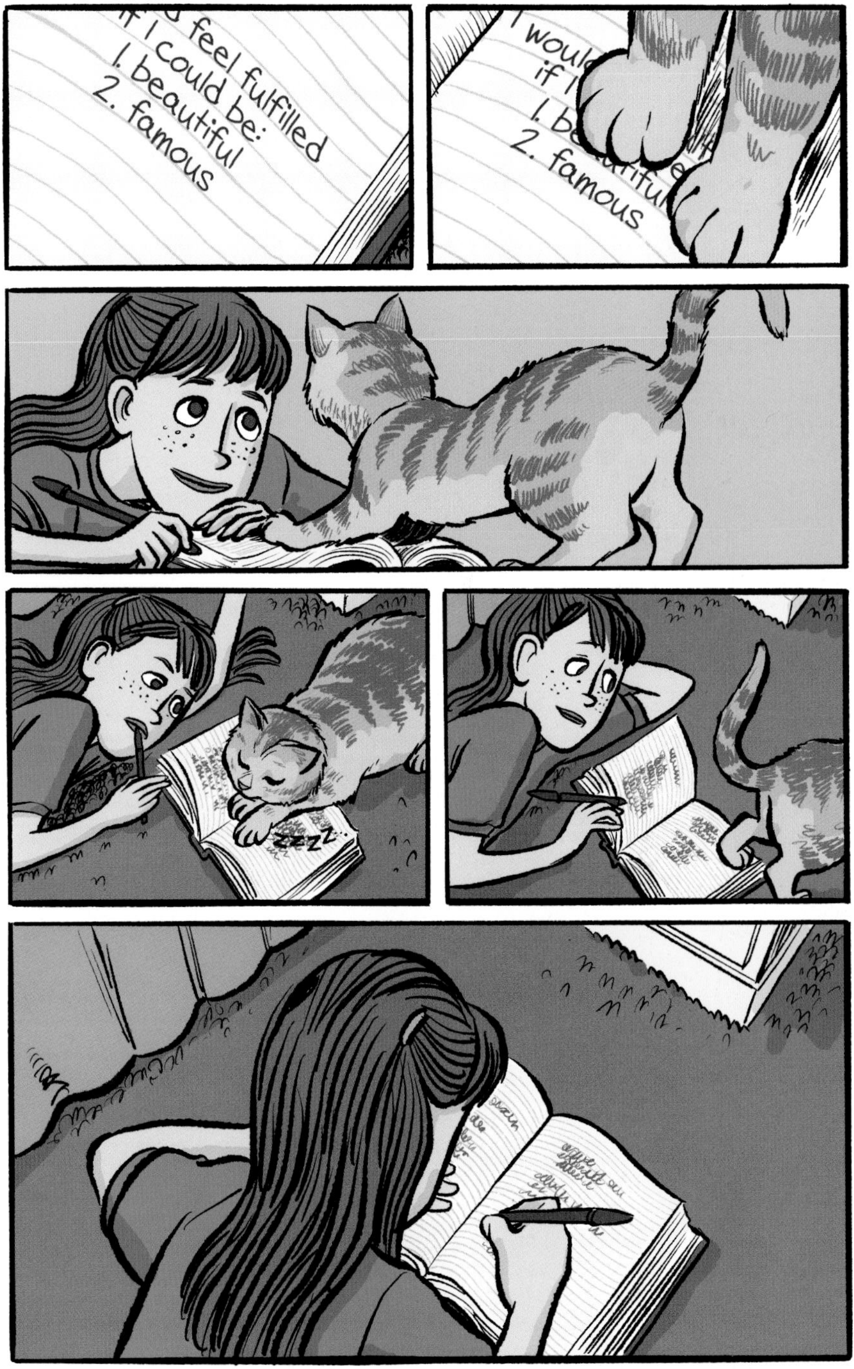
feel fulfilled
if I could be:
1. beautiful
2. famous
2. famous
ZZZ

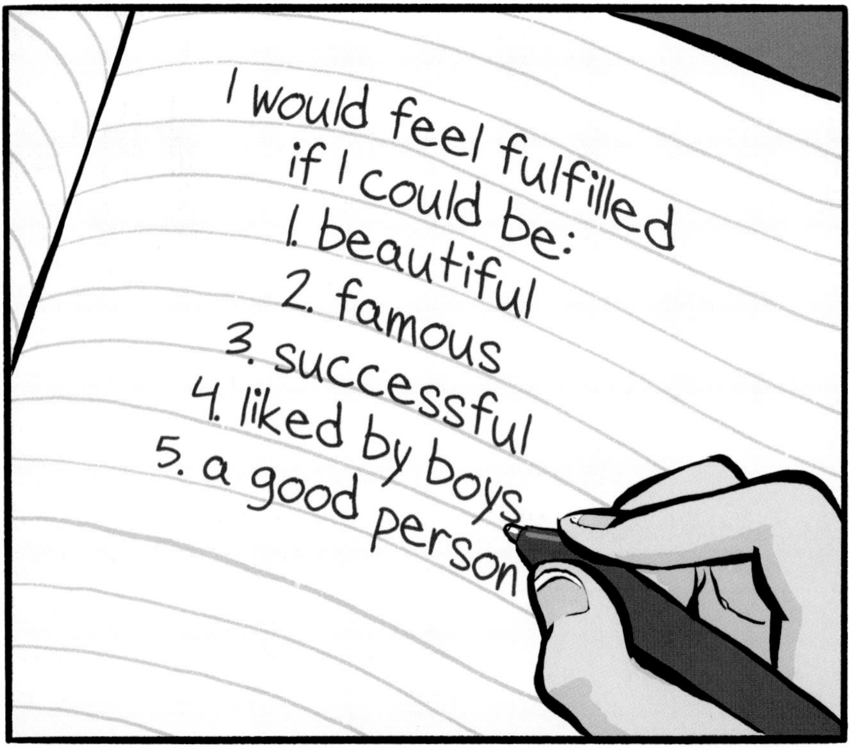
I would feel fulfilled
if I could be:
1. beautiful
2. famous
3. successful
4. liked by boys
5. a good person

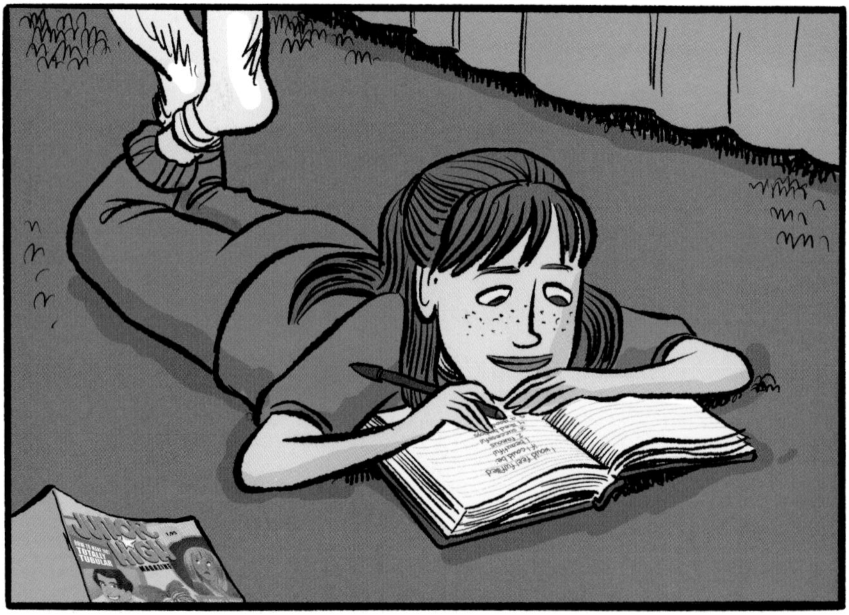

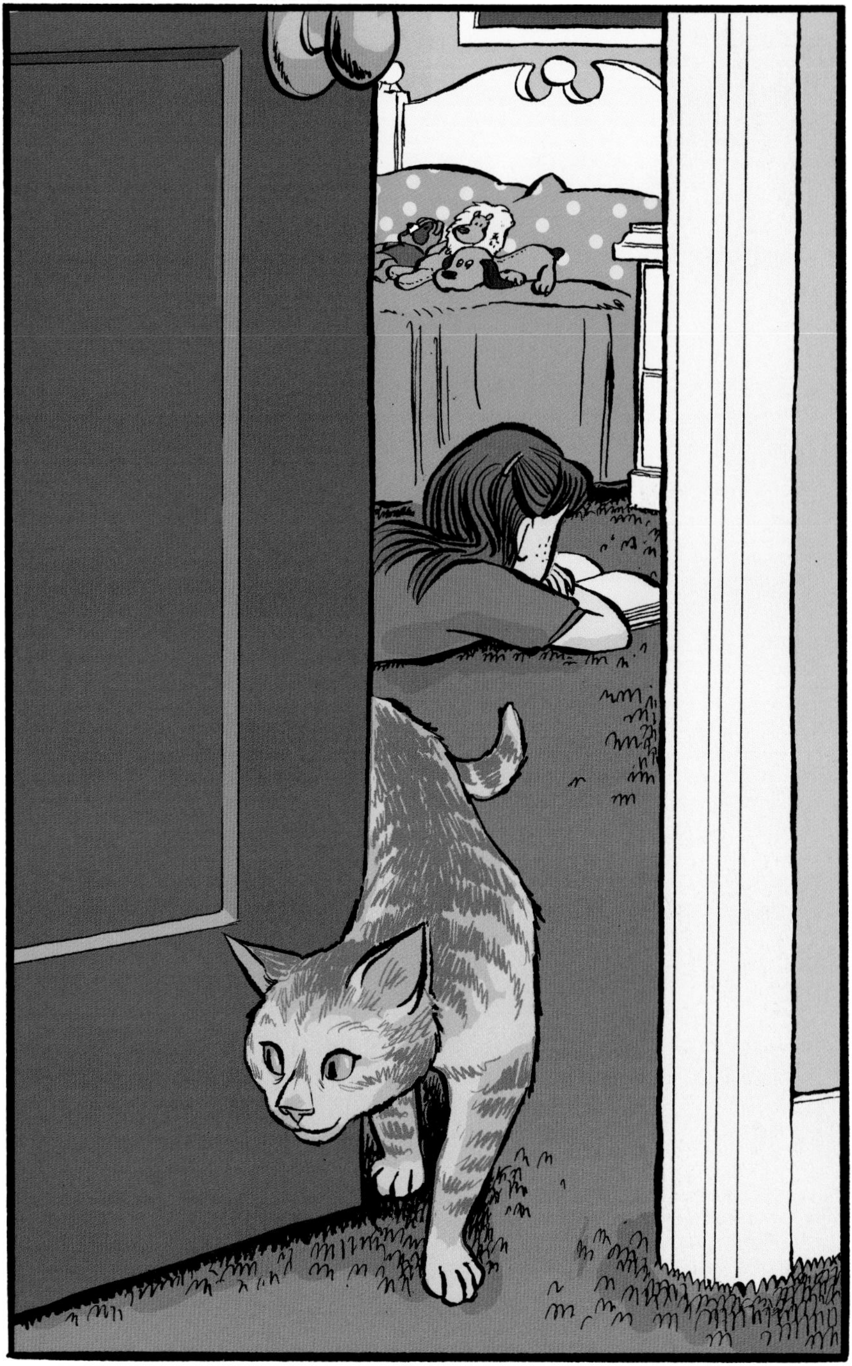

CHAPTER 1

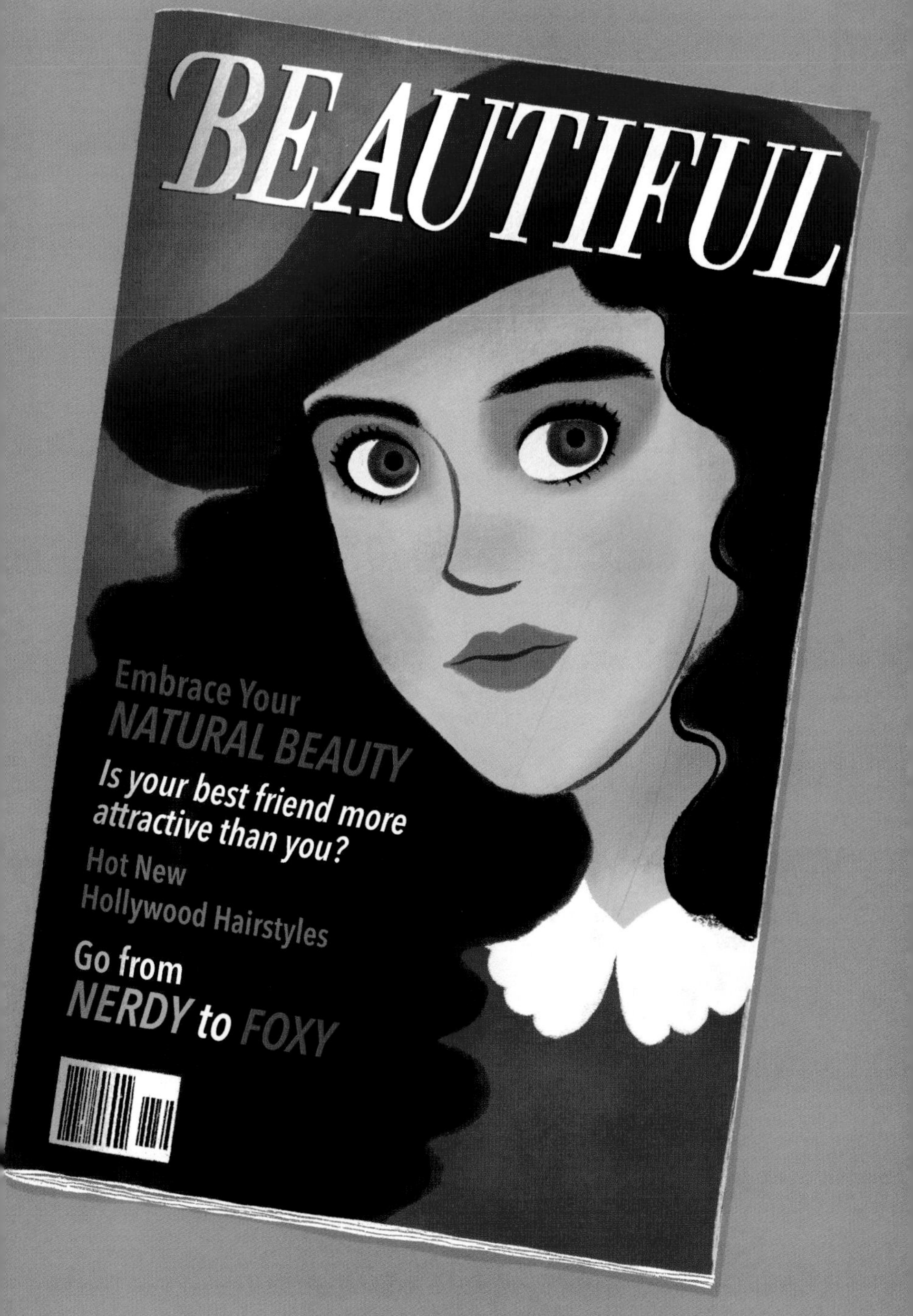
BEAUTIFUL
Embrace Your
NATURAL BEAUTY
Is your best friend more attractive than you?
Hot New
Hollywood Hairstyles
Go from
NERDY to FOXY

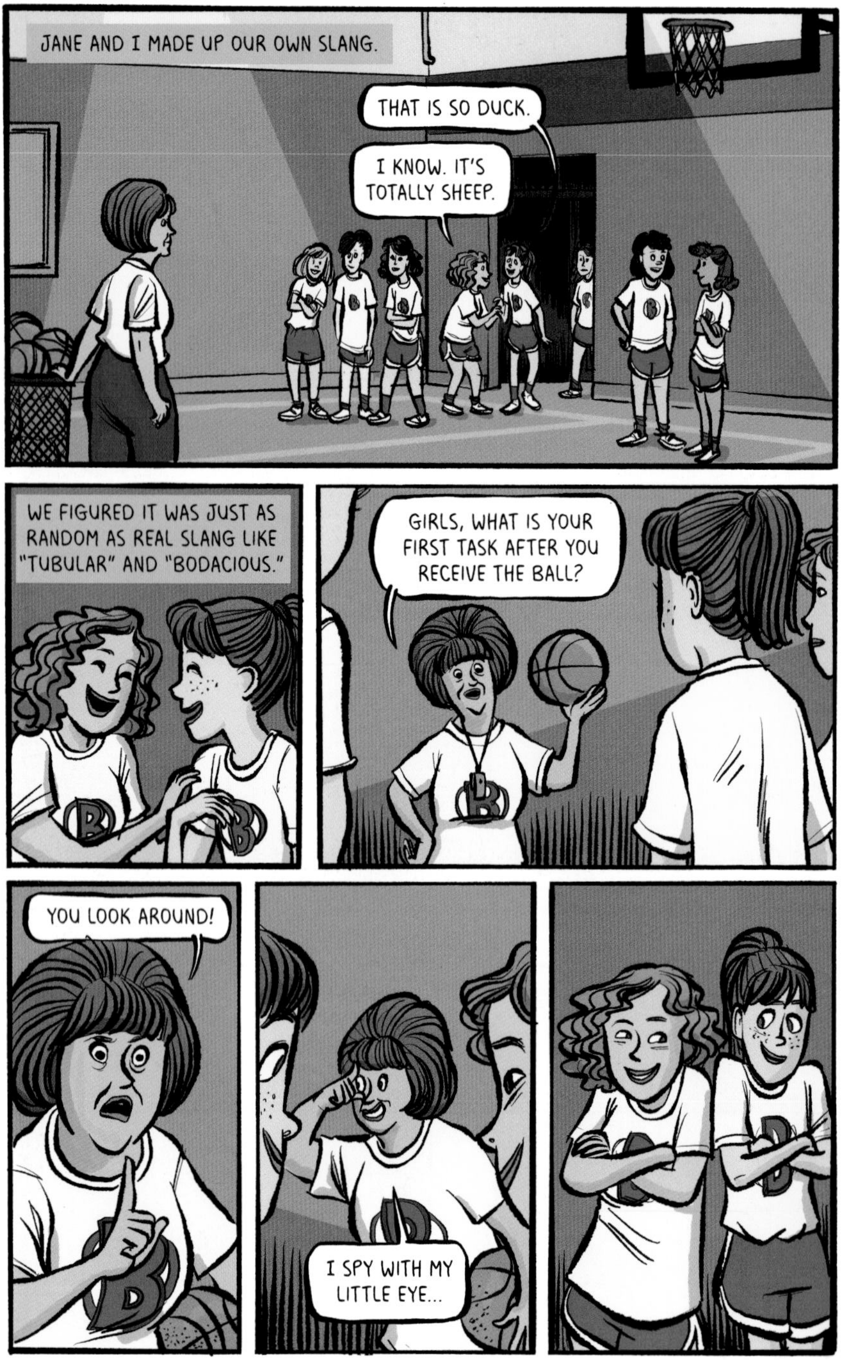
JANE AND I MADE UP OUR OWN SLANG.
THAT IS SO DUCK.
I KNOW. IT'S TOTALLY SHEEP.
WE FIGURED IT WAS JUST AS RANDOM AS REAL SLANG LIKE "TUBULAR" AND "BODACIOUS."
GIRLS, WHAT IS YOUR FIRST TASK AFTER YOU RECEIVE THE BALL?
YOU LOOK AROUND!
I SPY WITH MY LITTLE EYE...

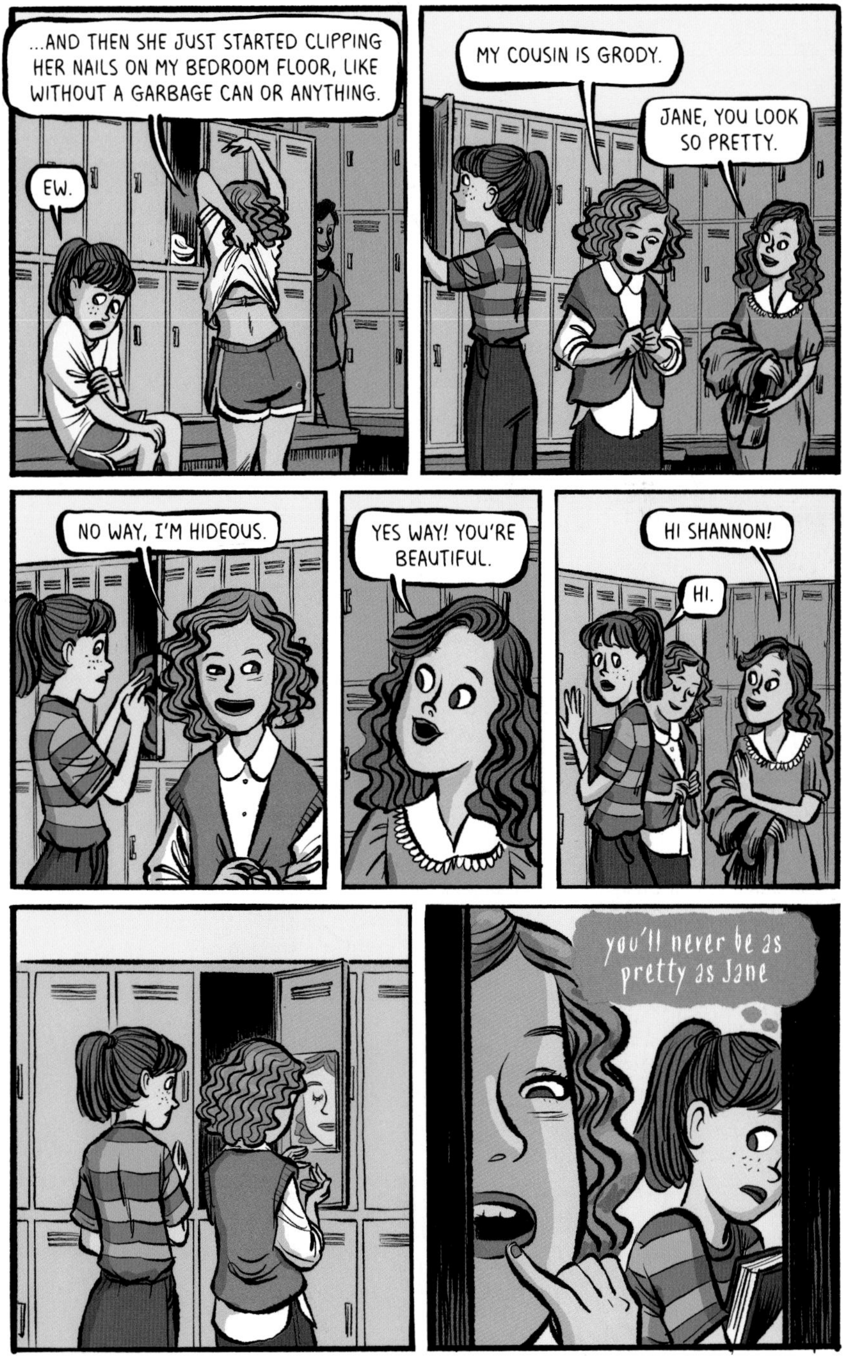
...AND THEN SHE JUST STARTED CLIPPING HER NAILS ON MY BEDROOM FLOOR, LIKE WITHOUT A GARBAGE CAN OR ANYTHING.
EW.
MY COUSIN IS GRODY.
JANE, YOU LOOK SO PRETTY.
NO WAY, I'M HIDEOUS.
YES WAY! YOU'RE BEAUTIFUL.
HI SHANNON!
HI.
you'll never be as pretty as Jane

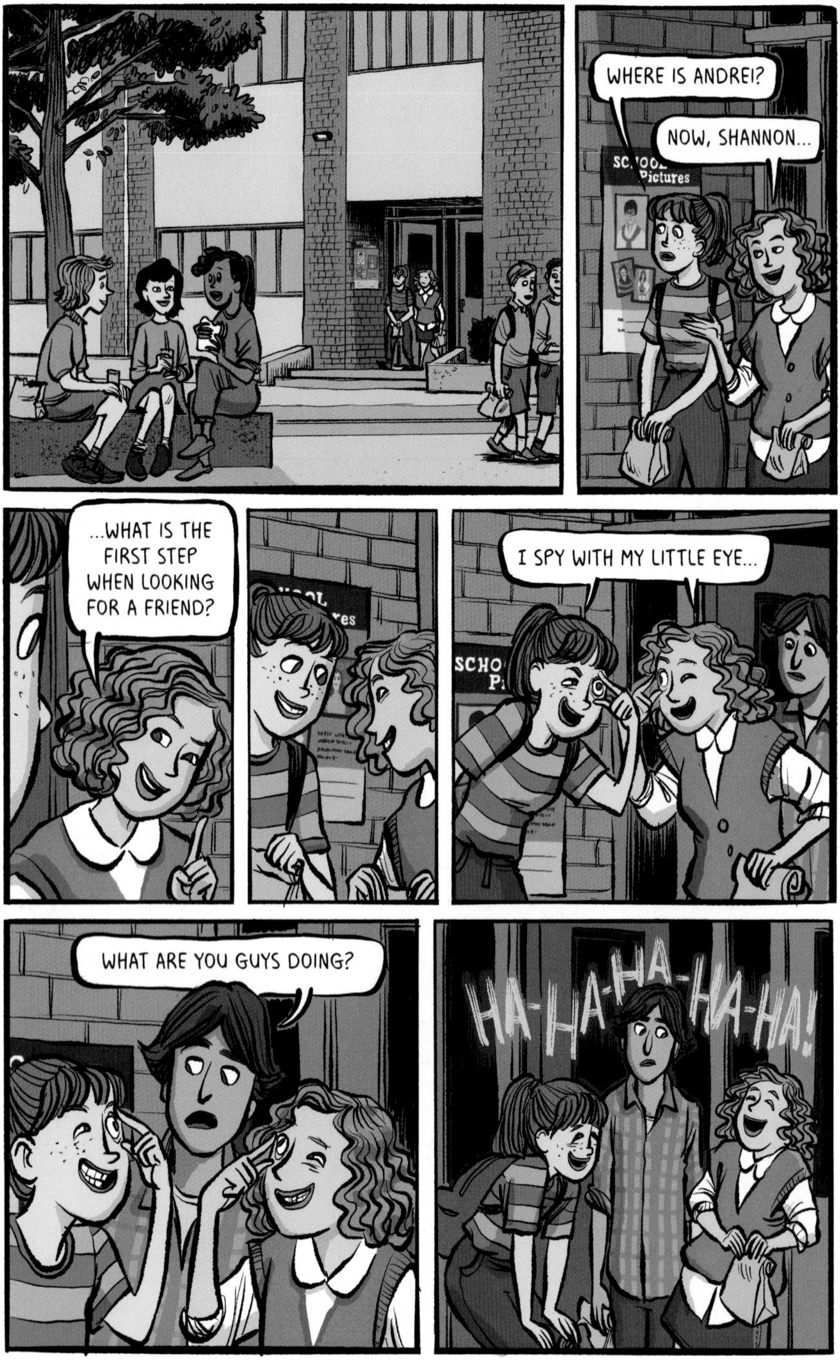

WHERE IS ANDREI?
NOW, SHANNON...
SCHOOL Pictures
...WHAT IS THE FIRST STEP WHEN LOOKING FOR A FRIEND?
I SPY WITH MY LITTLE EYE...
WHAT ARE YOU GUYS DOING?
HA-HA-HA-HA-HA!

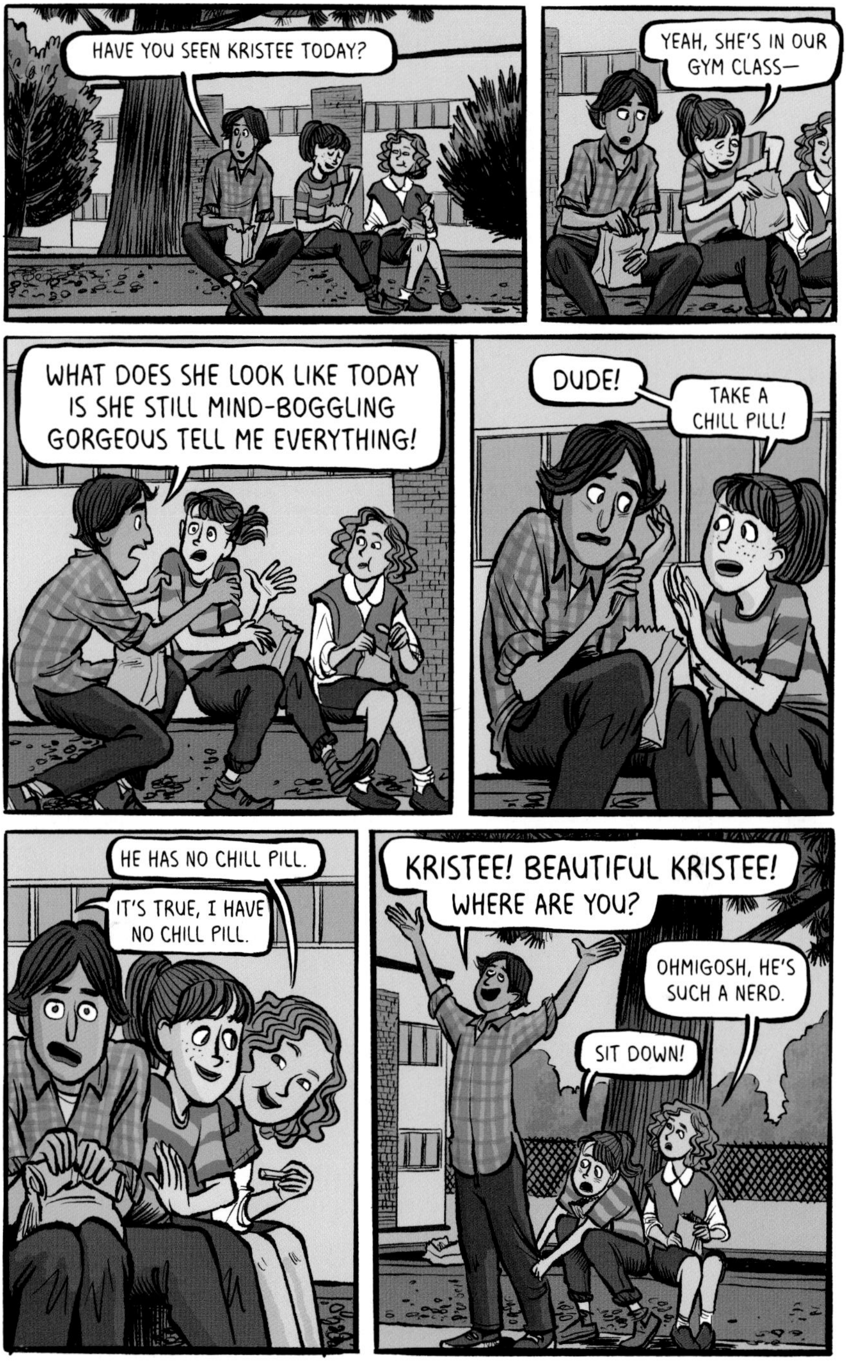
HAVE YOU SEEN KRISTEE TODAY?
YEAH, SHE'S IN OUR GYM CLASS—
WHAT DOES SHE LOOK LIKE TODAY IS SHE STILL MIND-BOGGLING GORGEOUS TELL ME EVERYTHING!
DUDE!
TAKE A CHILL PILL!
HE HAS NO CHILL PILL.
IT'S TRUE, I HAVE NO CHILL PILL.
KRISTEE! BEAUTIFUL KRISTEE! WHERE ARE YOU?
OHMIGOSH, HE'S SUCH A NERD.
SIT DOWN!

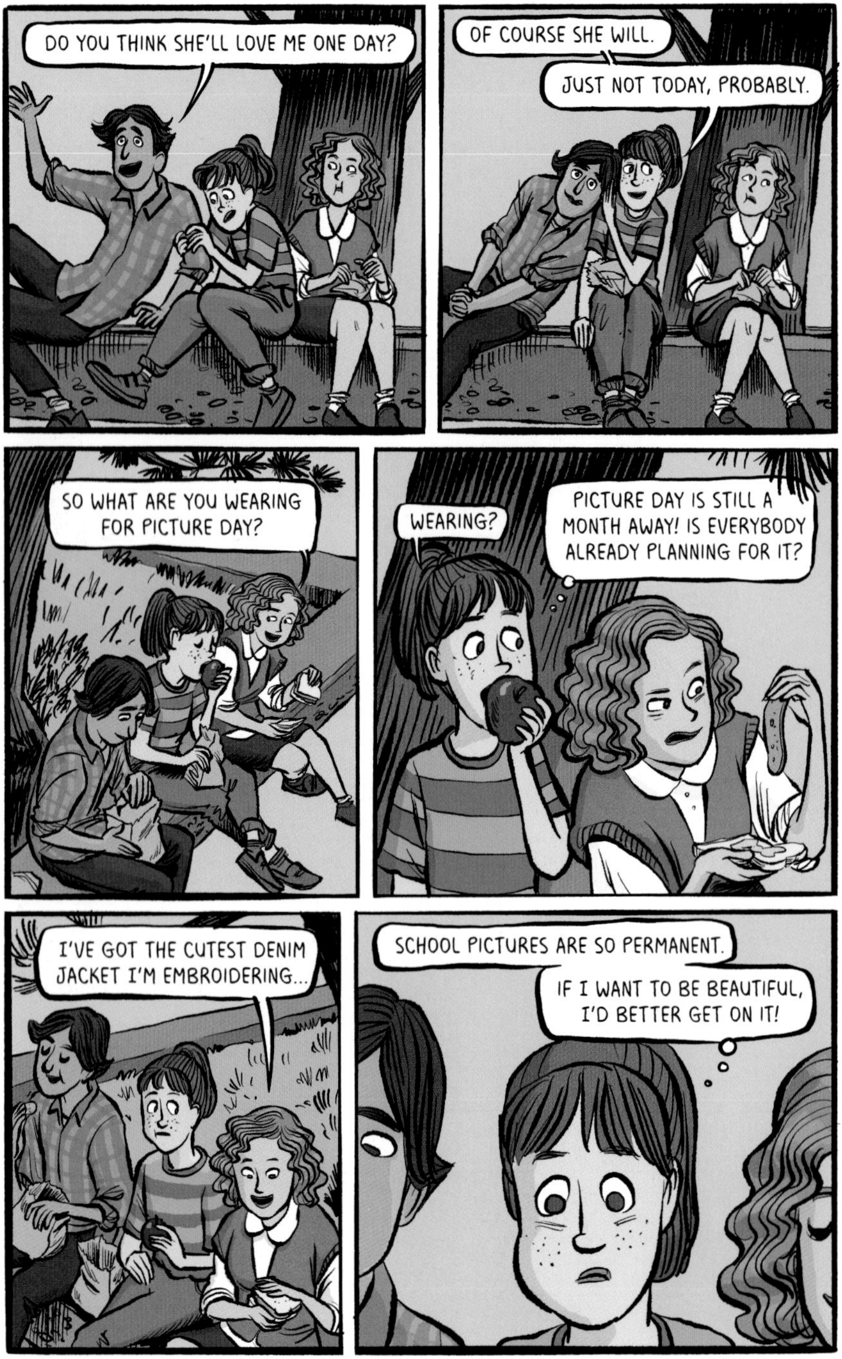
DO YOU THINK SHE'LL LOVE ME ONE DAY?
OF COURSE SHE WILL.
JUST NOT TODAY, PROBABLY.
SO WHAT ARE YOU WEARING FOR PICTURE DAY?
WEARING?
PICTURE DAY IS STILL A MONTH AWAY! IS EVERYBODY ALREADY PLANNING FOR IT?
I'VE GOT THE CUTEST DENIM JACKET I'M EMBROIDERING...
SCHOOL PICTURES ARE SO PERMANENT.
IF I WANT TO BE BEAUTIFUL, I'D BETTER GET ON IT!

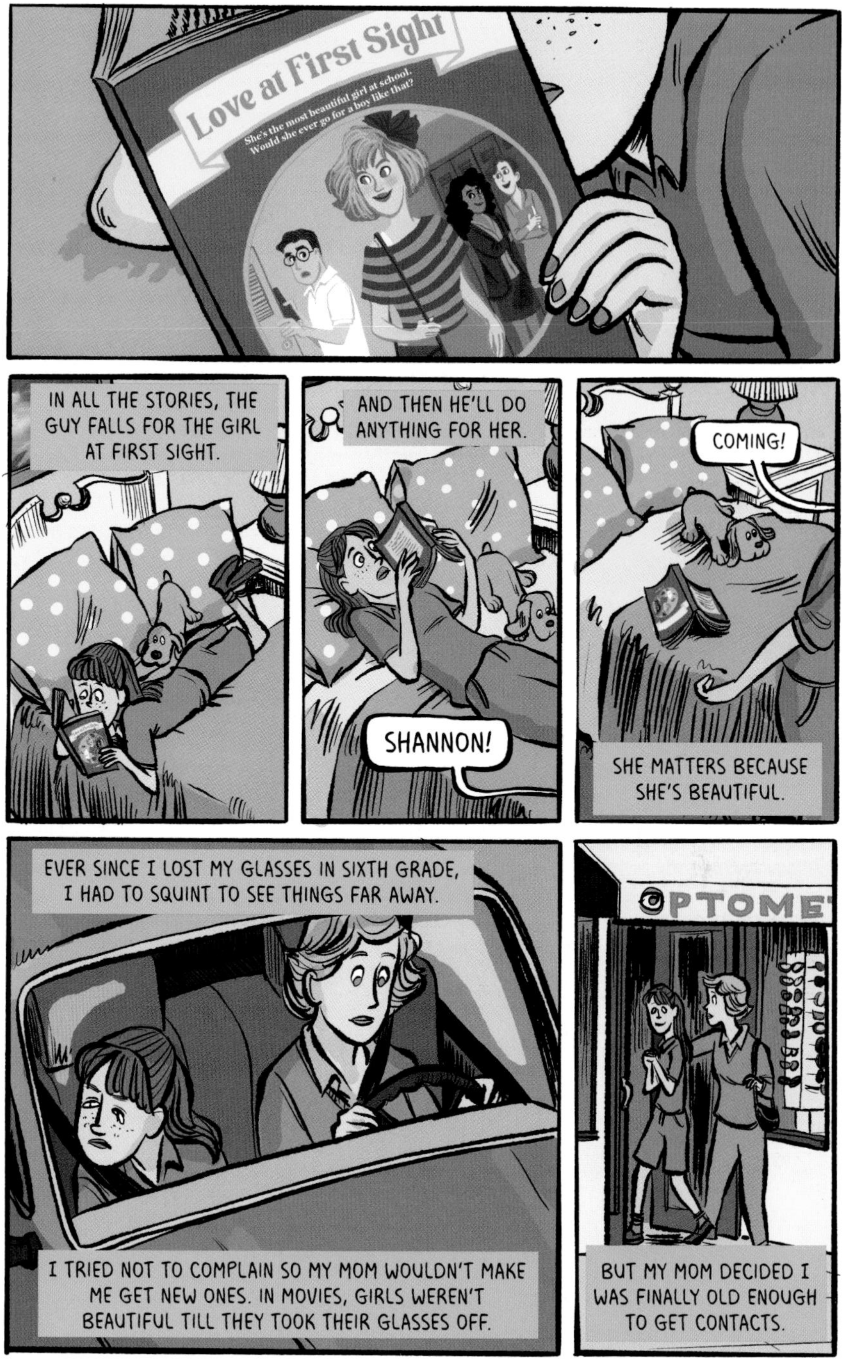
Love at First Sight
She's the most beautiful girl at school. Would she ever go for a boy like that?
IN ALL THE STORIES, THE GUY FALLS FOR THE GIRL AT FIRST SIGHT.
AND THEN HE'LL DO ANYTHING FOR HER.
SHANNON!
COMING!
SHE MATTERS BECAUSE SHE'S BEAUTIFUL.
EVER SINCE I LOST MY GLASSES IN SIXTH GRADE, I HAD TO SQUINT TO SEE THINGS FAR AWAY.
I TRIED NOT TO COMPLAIN SO MY MOM WOULDN'T MAKE ME GET NEW ONES. IN MOVIES, GIRLS WEREN'T BEAUTIFUL TILL THEY TOOK THEIR GLASSES OFF.
OPTOMET
BUT MY MOM DECIDED I WAS FINALLY OLD ENOUGH TO GET CONTACTS.

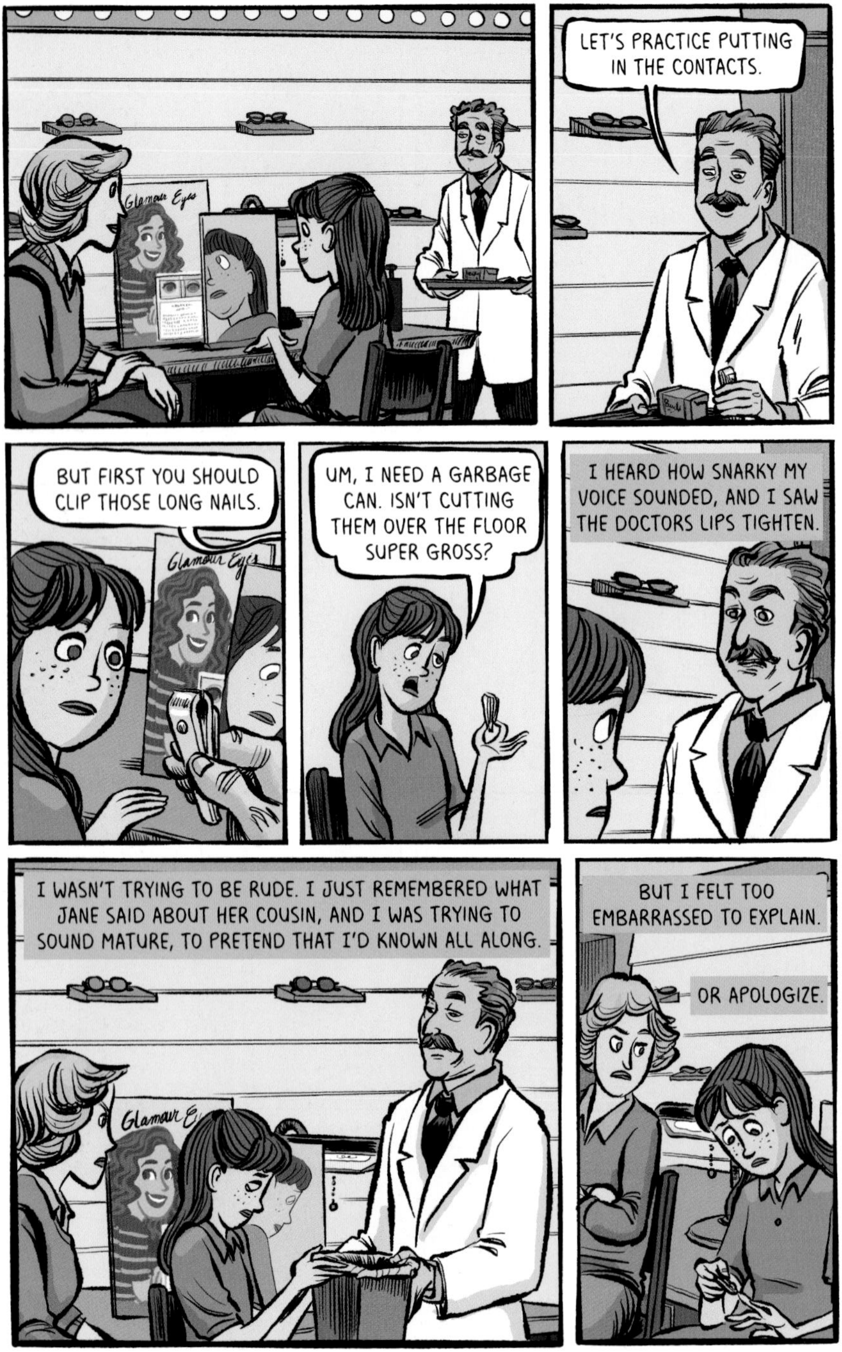

Glamour Eyes
LET'S PRACTICE PUTTING IN THE CONTACTS.
BUT FIRST YOU SHOULD CLIP THOSE LONG NAILS.
Glamour Eyes
UM, I NEED A GARBAGE CAN. ISN'T CUTTING THEM OVER THE FLOOR SUPER GROSS?
I HEARD HOW SNARKY MY VOICE SOUNDED, AND I SAW THE DOCTORS LIPS TIGHTEN.
I WASN'T TRYING TO BE RUDE. I JUST REMEMBERED WHAT JANE SAID ABOUT HER COUSIN, AND I WAS TRYING TO SOUND MATURE, TO PRETEND THAT I'D KNOWN ALL ALONG.
BUT I FELT TOO EMBARRASSED TO EXPLAIN.
OR APOLOGIZE.

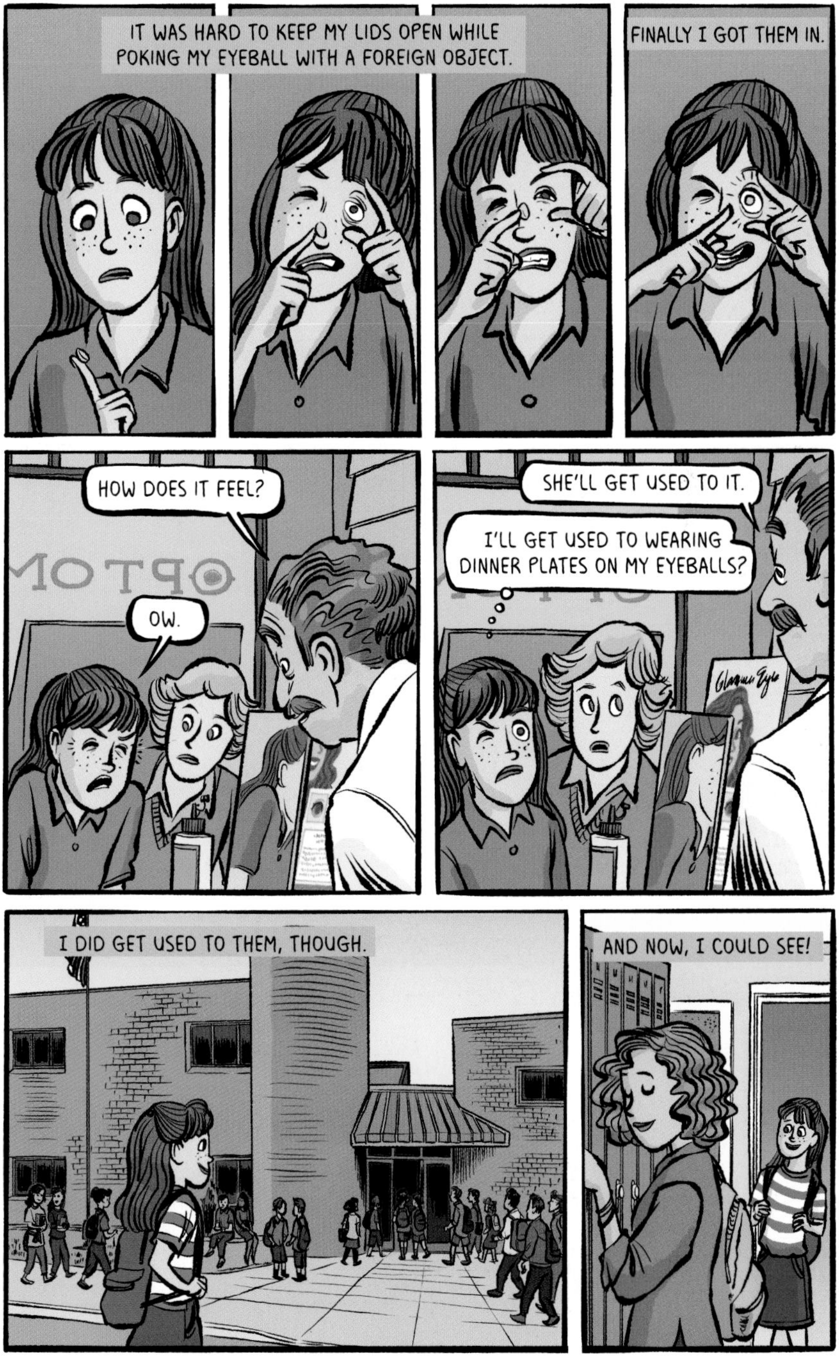
IT WAS HARD TO KEEP MY LIDS OPEN WHILE POKING MY EYEBALL WITH A FOREIGN OBJECT.
FINALLY I GOT THEM IN.
HOW DOES IT FEEL?
OW.
OPTOM
SHE'LL GET USED TO IT.
I'LL GET USED TO WEARING DINNER PLATES ON MY EYEBALLS?
I DID GET USED TO THEM, THOUGH.
AND NOW, I COULD SEE!

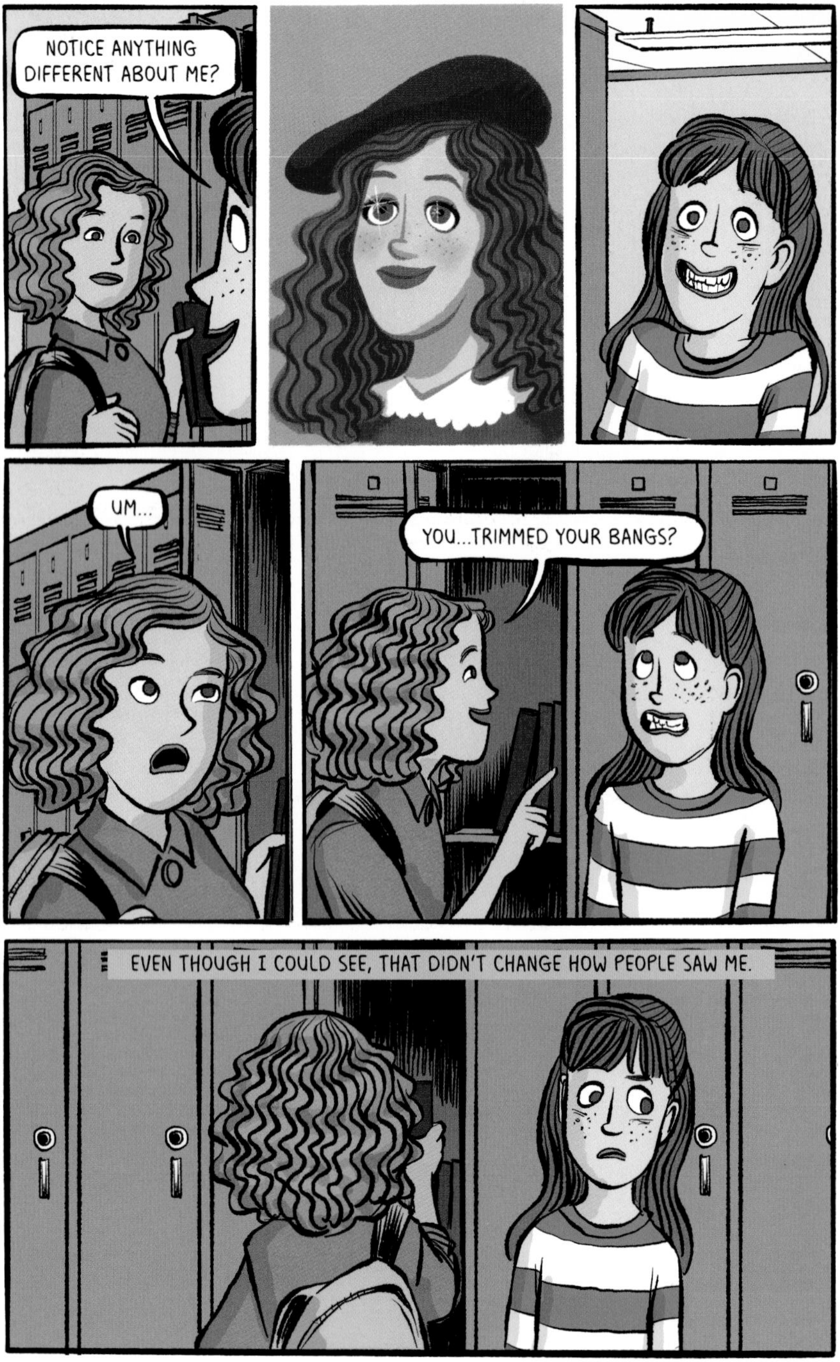
NOTICE ANYTHING DIFFERENT ABOUT ME?
UM...
YOU...TRIMMED YOUR BANGS?
EVEN THOUGH I COULD SEE, THAT DIDN'T CHANGE HOW PEOPLE SAW ME.

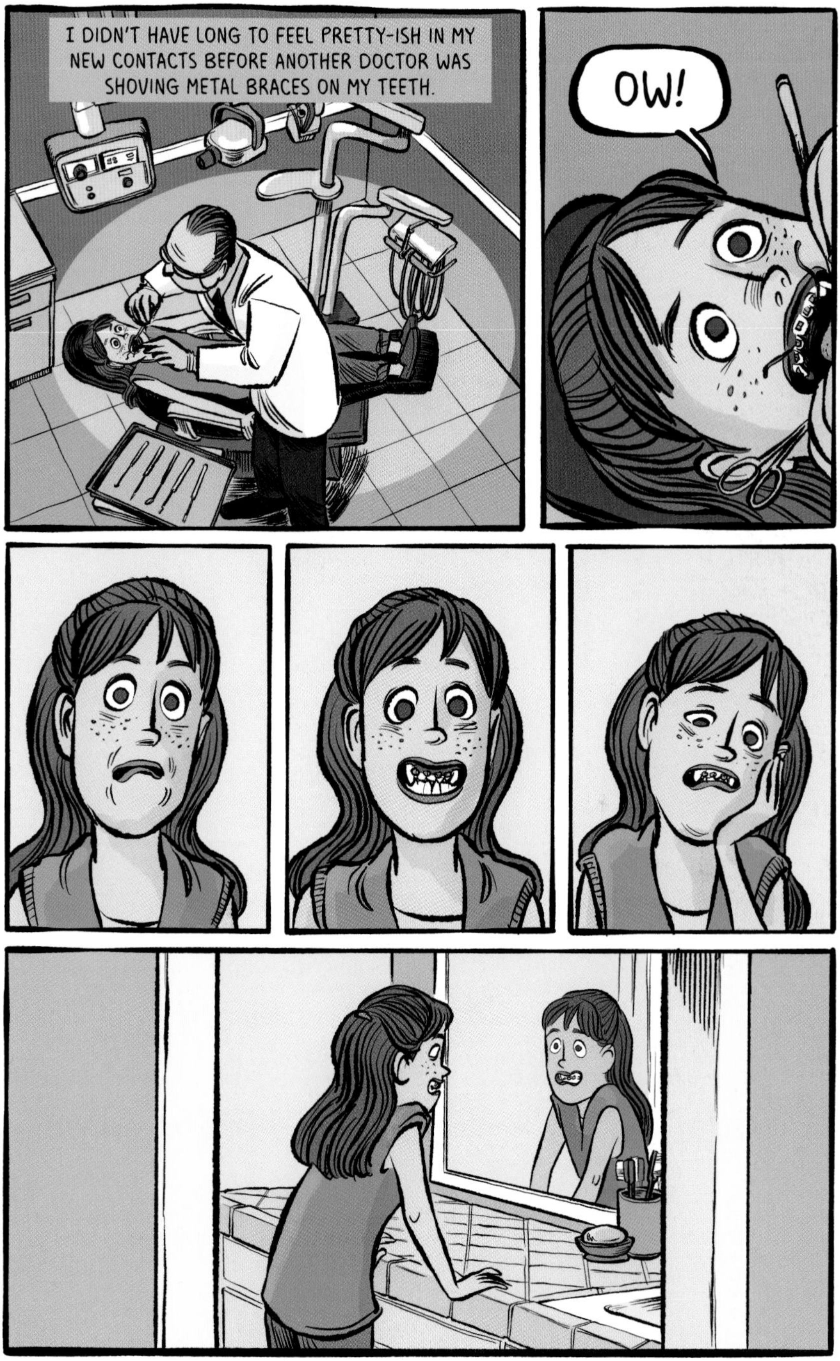
I DIDN'T HAVE LONG TO FEEL PRETTY-ISH IN MY NEW CONTACTS BEFORE ANOTHER DOCTOR WAS SHOVING METAL BRACES ON MY TEETH.
OW!

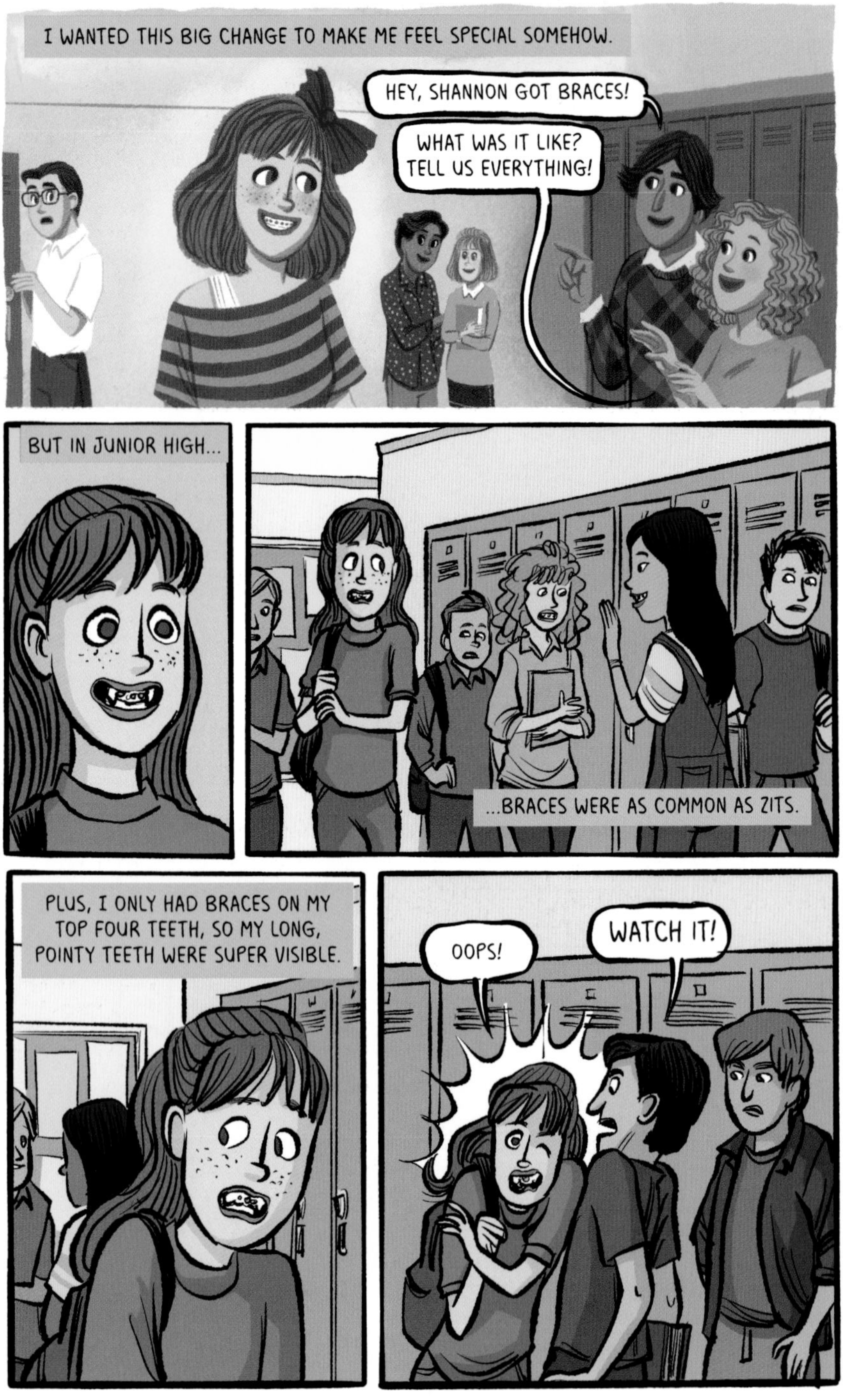
I WANTED THIS BIG CHANGE TO MAKE ME FEEL SPECIAL SOMEHOW.
HEY, SHANNON GOT BRACES!
WHAT WAS IT LIKE? TELL US EVERYTHING!
BUT IN JUNIOR HIGH...
...BRACES WERE AS COMMON AS ZITS.
PLUS, I ONLY HAD BRACES ON MY TOP FOUR TEETH, SO MY LONG, POINTY TEETH WERE SUPER VISIBLE.
OOPS!
WATCH IT!

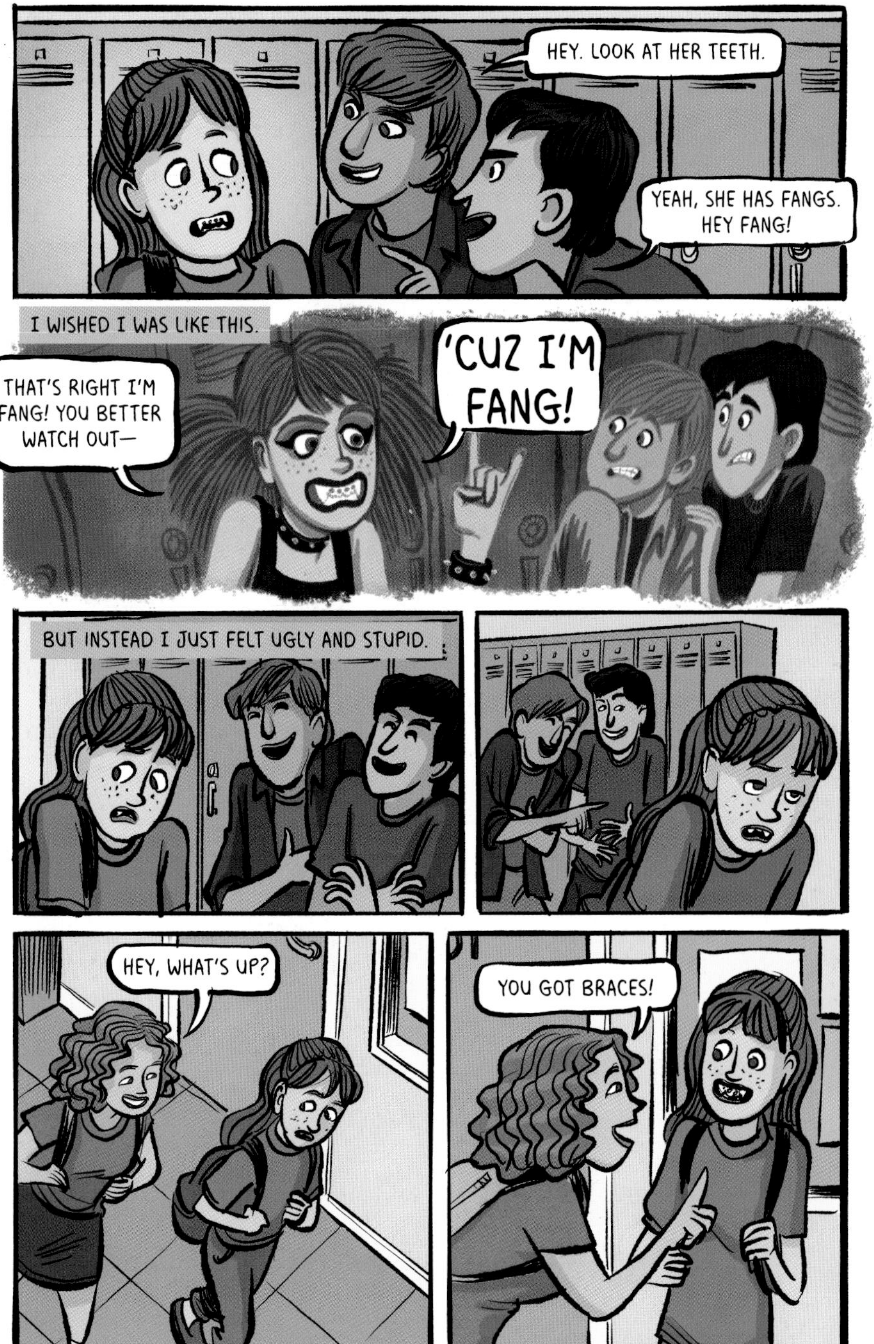
HEY. LOOK AT HER TEETH.
YEAH, SHE HAS FANGS. HEY FANG!
I WISHED I WAS LIKE THIS.
THAT'S RIGHT I'M FANG! YOU BETTER WATCH OUT—
'CUZ I'M FANG!
BUT INSTEAD I JUST FELT UGLY AND STUPID.
HEY, WHAT'S UP?
YOU GOT BRACES!

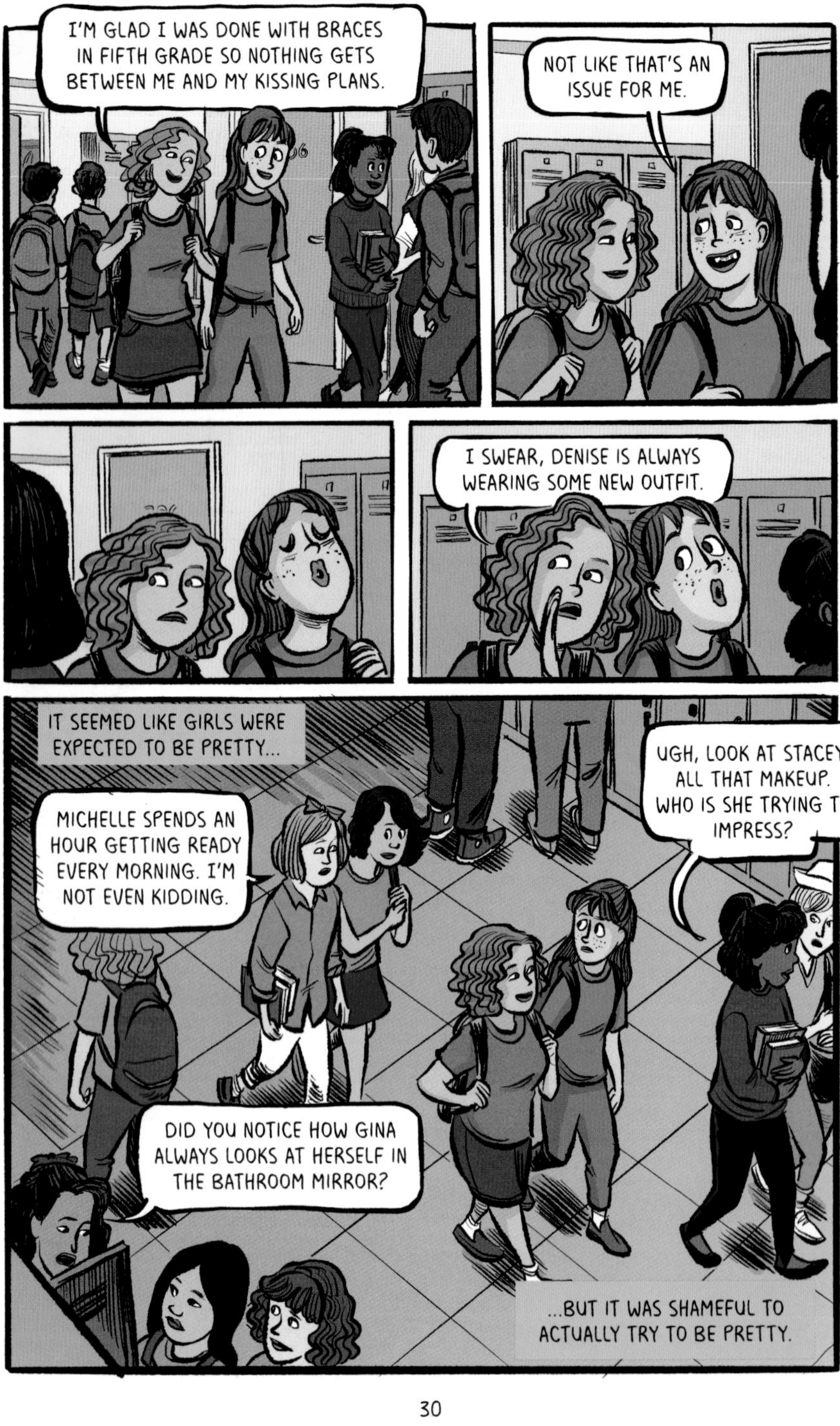
I'M GLAD I WAS DONE WITH BRACES IN FIFTH GRADE SO NOTHING GETS BETWEEN ME AND MY KISSING PLANS.
NOT LIKE THAT'S AN ISSUE FOR ME.
I SWEAR, DENISE IS ALWAYS WEARING SOME NEW OUTFIT.
IT SEEMED LIKE GIRLS WERE EXPECTED TO BE PRETTY...
UGH, LOOK AT STACEY. ALL THAT MAKEUP. WHO IS SHE TRYING TO IMPRESS?
MICHELLE SPENDS AN HOUR GETTING READY EVERY MORNING. I'M NOT EVEN KIDDING.
DID YOU NOTICE HOW GINA ALWAYS LOOKS AT HERSELF IN THE BATHROOM MIRROR?
...BUT IT WAS SHAMEFUL TO ACTUALLY TRY TO BE PRETTY.

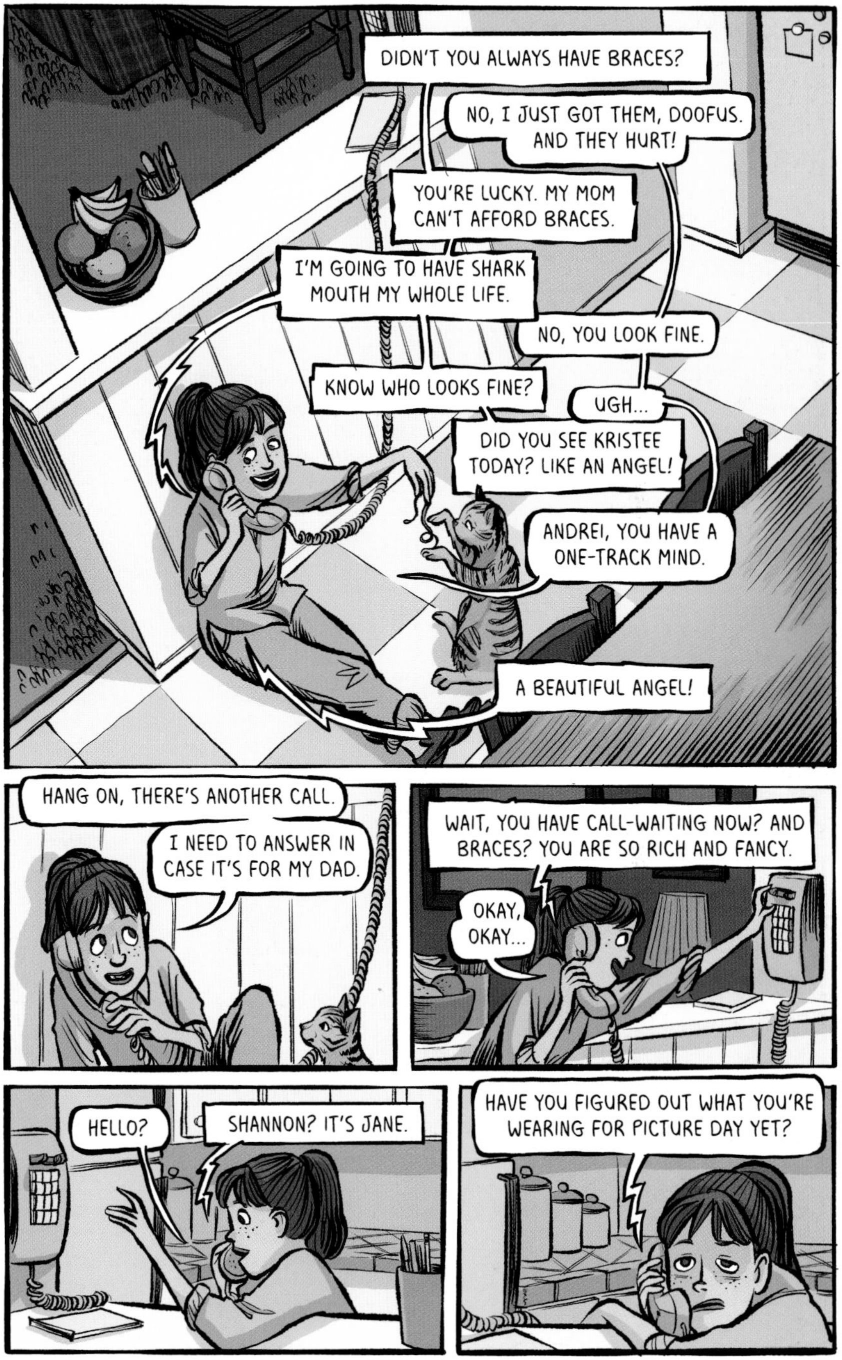
DIDN'T YOU ALWAYS HAVE BRACES?
NO, I JUST GOT THEM, DOOFUS. AND THEY HURT!
YOU'RE LUCKY. MY MOM CAN'T AFFORD BRACES.
I'M GOING TO HAVE SHARK MOUTH MY WHOLE LIFE.
NO, YOU LOOK FINE.
KNOW WHO LOOKS FINE?
UGH...
DID YOU SEE KRISTEE TODAY? LIKE AN ANGEL!
ANDREI, YOU HAVE A ONE-TRACK MIND.
A BEAUTIFUL ANGEL!
HANG ON, THERE'S ANOTHER CALL.
I NEED TO ANSWER IN CASE IT'S FOR MY DAD.
WAIT, YOU HAVE CALL-WAITING NOW? AND BRACES? YOU ARE SO RICH AND FANCY.
OKAY, OKAY...
HELLO?
SHANNON? IT'S JANE.
HAVE YOU FIGURED OUT WHAT YOU'RE WEARING FOR PICTURE DAY YET?

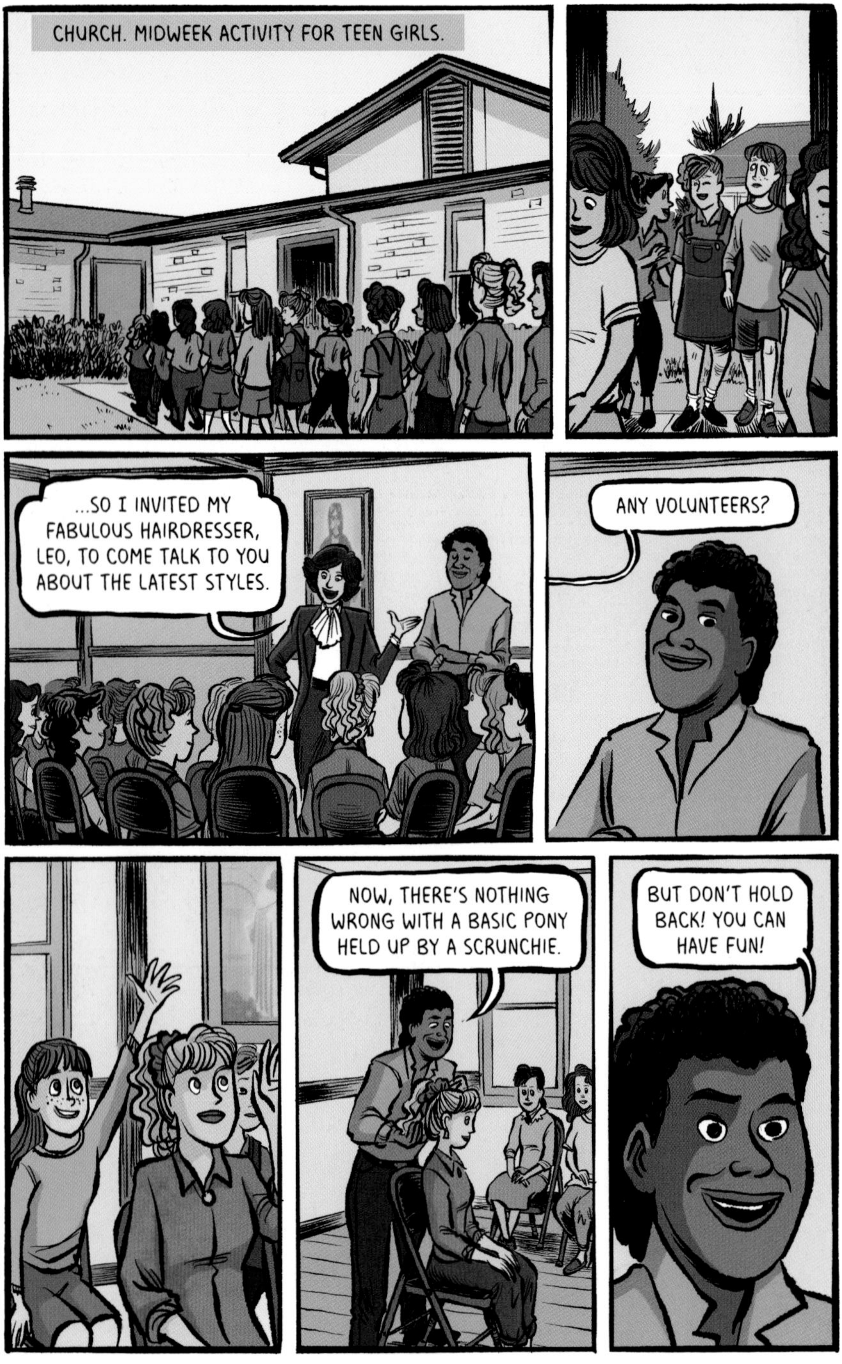
CHURCH. MIDWEEK ACTIVITY FOR TEEN GIRLS.
...SO I INVITED MY FABULOUS HAIRDRESSER, LEO, TO COME TALK TO YOU ABOUT THE LATEST STYLES.
ANY VOLUNTEERS?
NOW, THERE'S NOTHING WRONG WITH A BASIC PONY HELD UP BY A SCRUNCHIE.
BUT DON'T HOLD BACK! YOU CAN HAVE FUN!

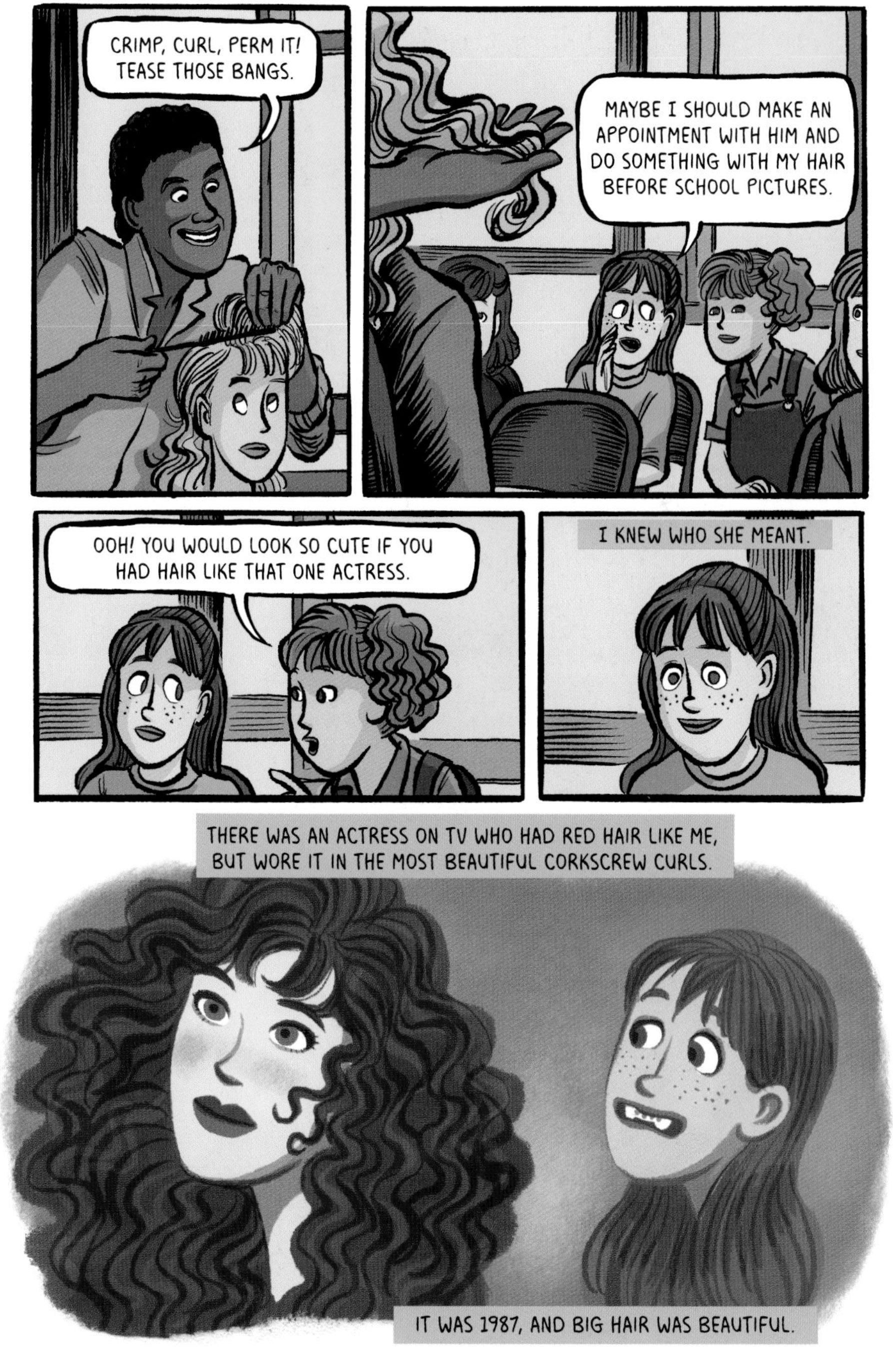
CRIMP, CURL, PERM IT! TEASE THOSE BANGS.
MAYBE I SHOULD MAKE AN APPOINTMENT WITH HIM AND DO SOMETHING WITH MY HAIR BEFORE SCHOOL PICTURES.
OOH! YOU WOULD LOOK SO CUTE IF YOU HAD HAIR LIKE THAT ONE ACTRESS.
I KNEW WHO SHE MEANT.
THERE WAS AN ACTRESS ON TV WHO HAD RED HAIR LIKE ME, BUT WORE IT IN THE MOST BEAUTIFUL CORKSCREW CURLS.
IT WAS 1987, AND BIG HAIR WAS BEAUTIFUL.

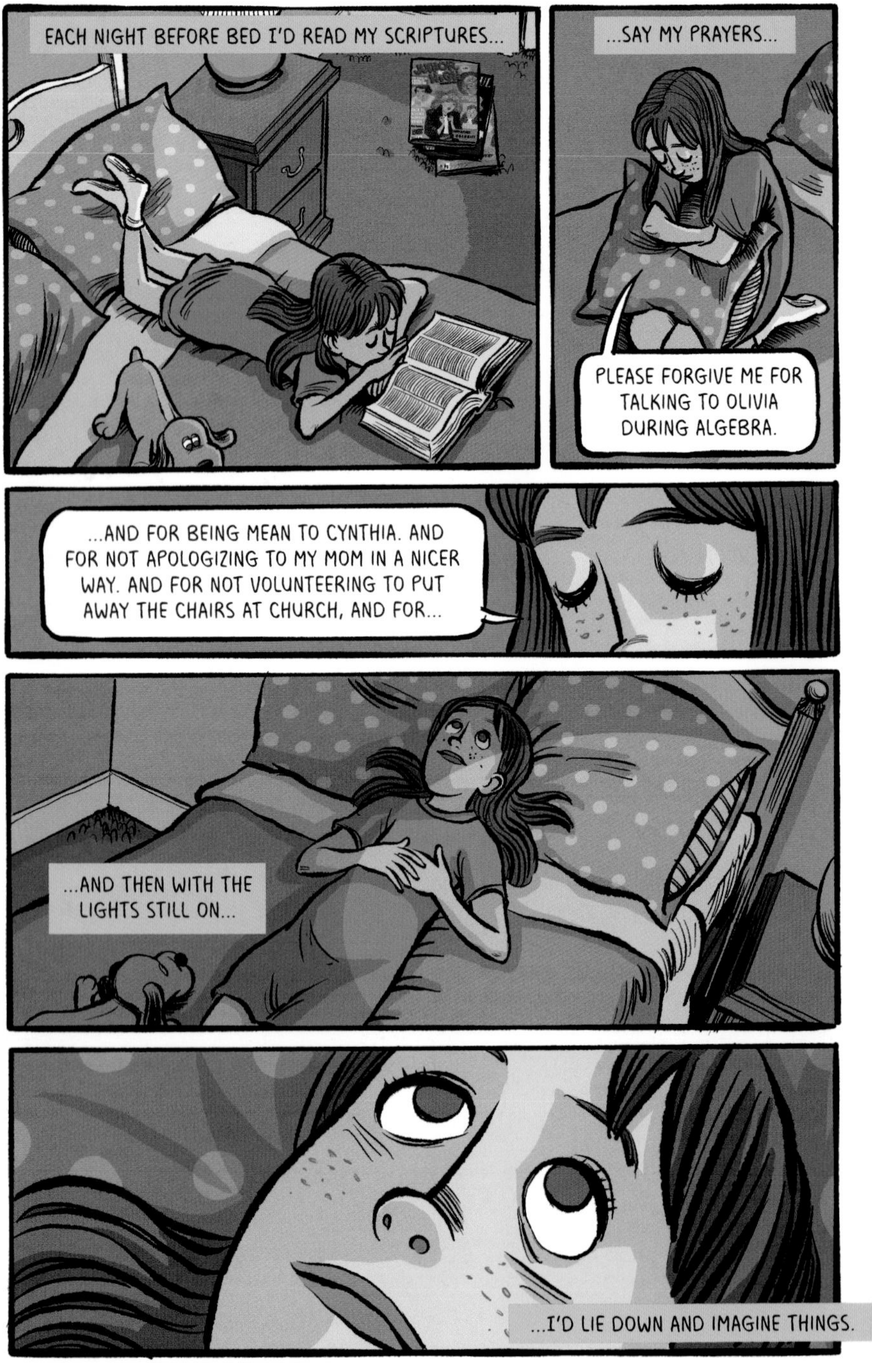
EACH NIGHT BEFORE BED I'D READ MY SCRIPTURES...
...SAY MY PRAYERS...
PLEASE FORGIVE ME FOR TALKING TO OLIVIA DURING ALGEBRA.
...AND FOR BEING MEAN TO CYNTHIA. AND FOR NOT APOLOGIZING TO MY MOM IN A NICER WAY. AND FOR NOT VOLUNTEERING TO PUT AWAY THE CHAIRS AT CHURCH, AND FOR...
...AND THEN WITH THE LIGHTS STILL ON...
...I'D LIE DOWN AND IMAGINE THINGS.

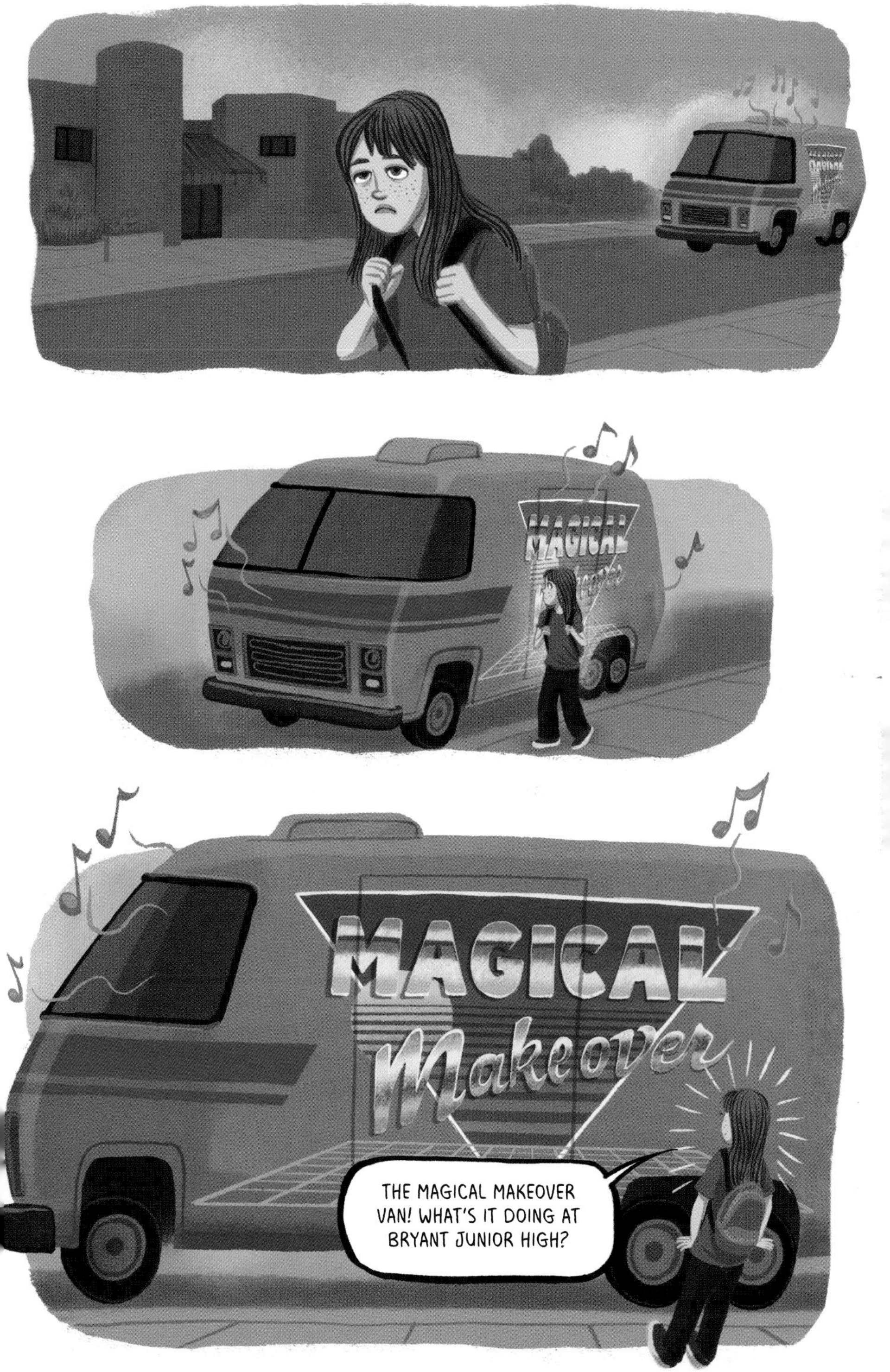
MAGICAL
Makeover
MAGICAL
Makeover
THE MAGICAL MAKEOVER VAN! WHAT'S IT DOING AT BRYANT JUNIOR HIGH?

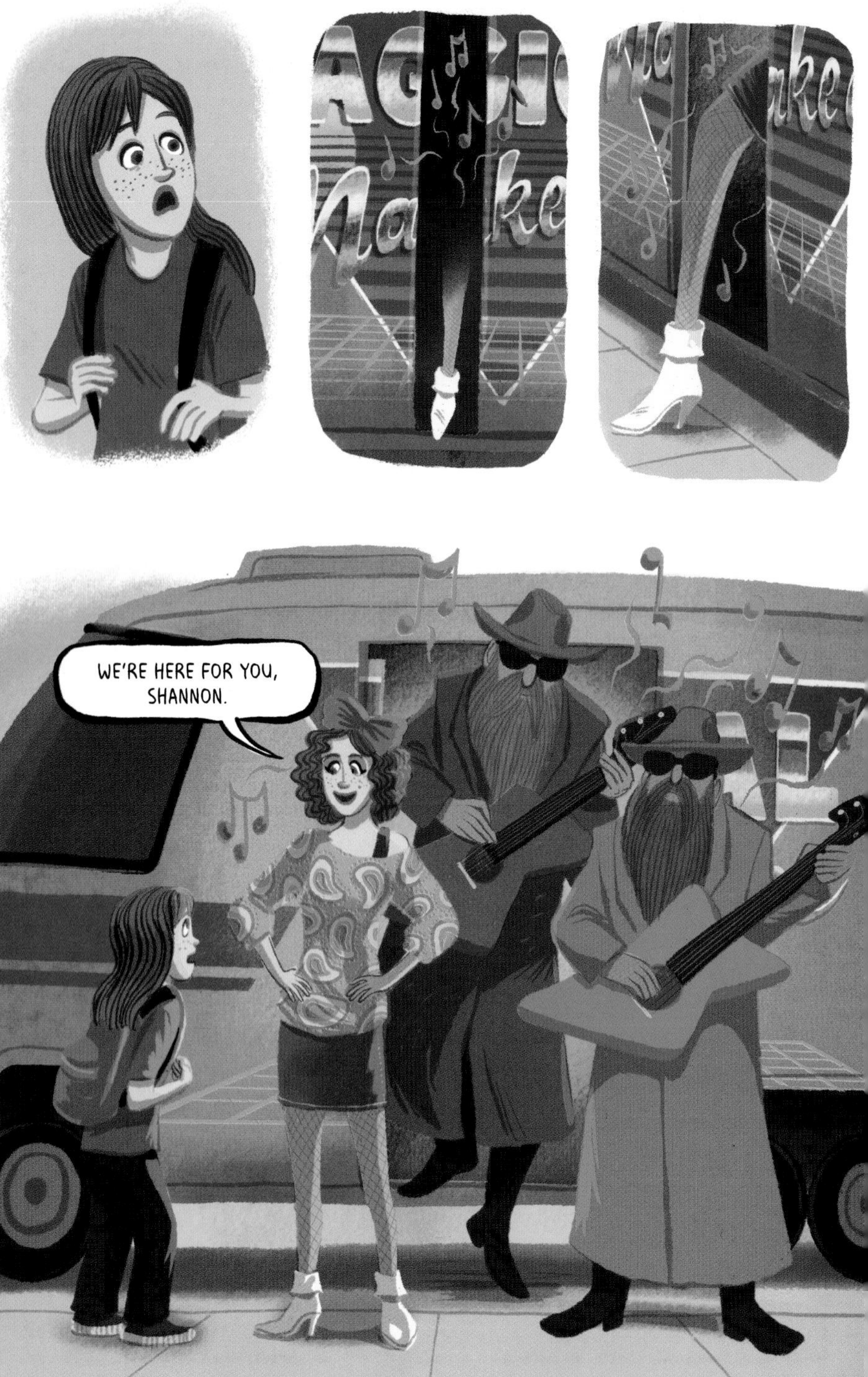
WE'RE HERE FOR YOU, SHANNON.

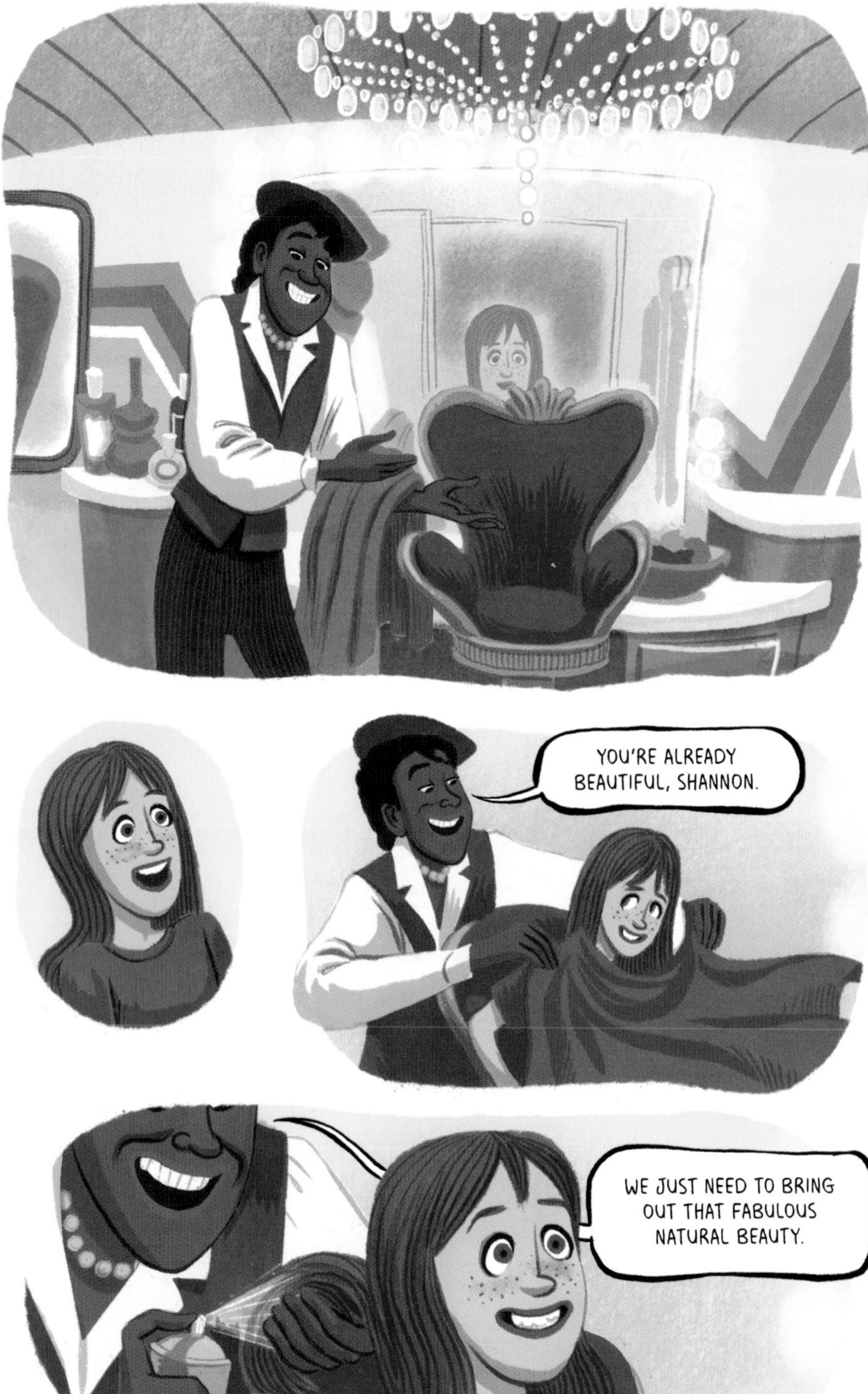
YOU'RE ALREADY BEAUTIFUL, SHANNON.
WE JUST NEED TO BRING OUT THAT FABULOUS NATURAL BEAUTY.

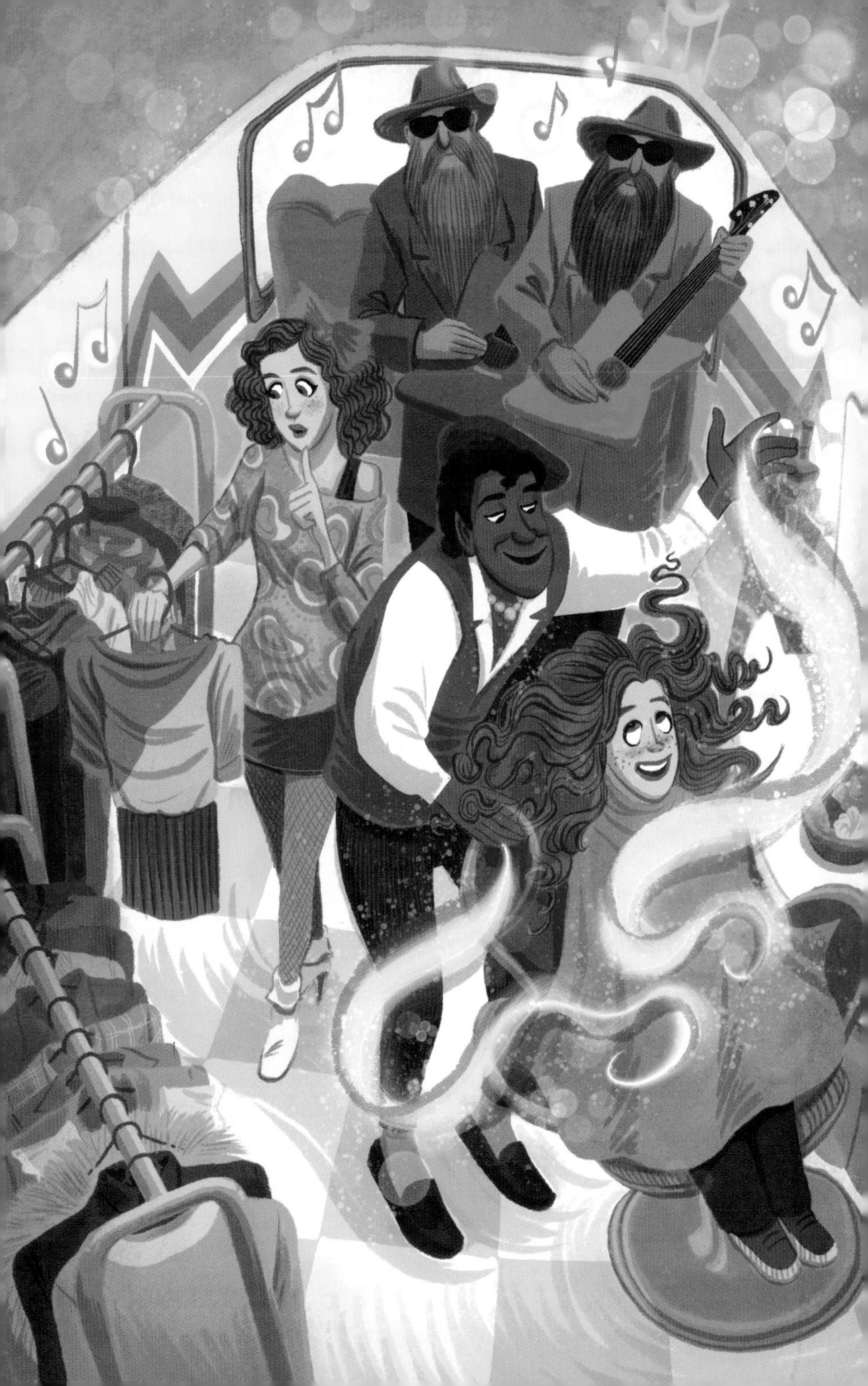

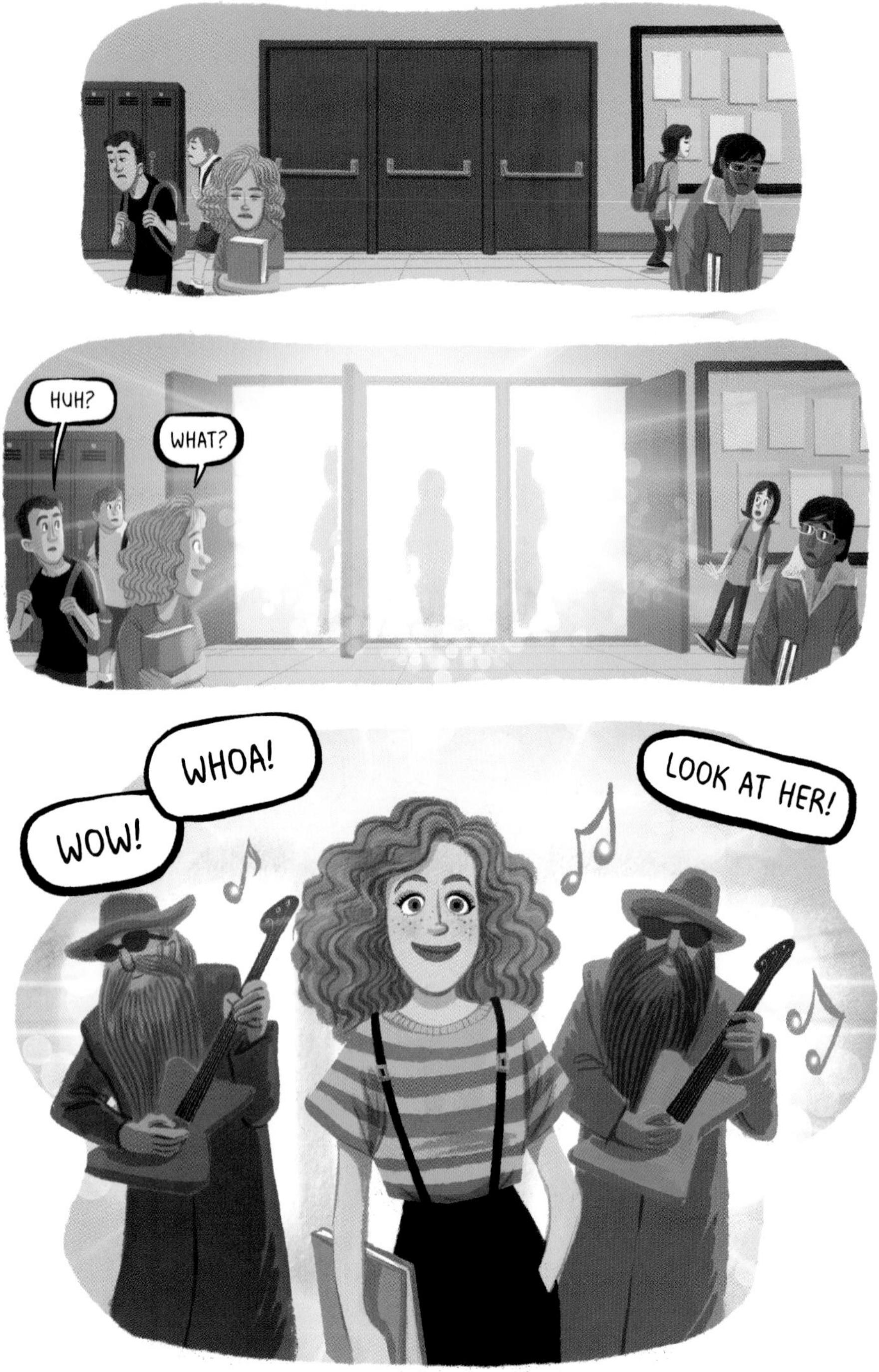
HUH?
WHAT?
WOW!
WHOA!
LOOK AT HER!

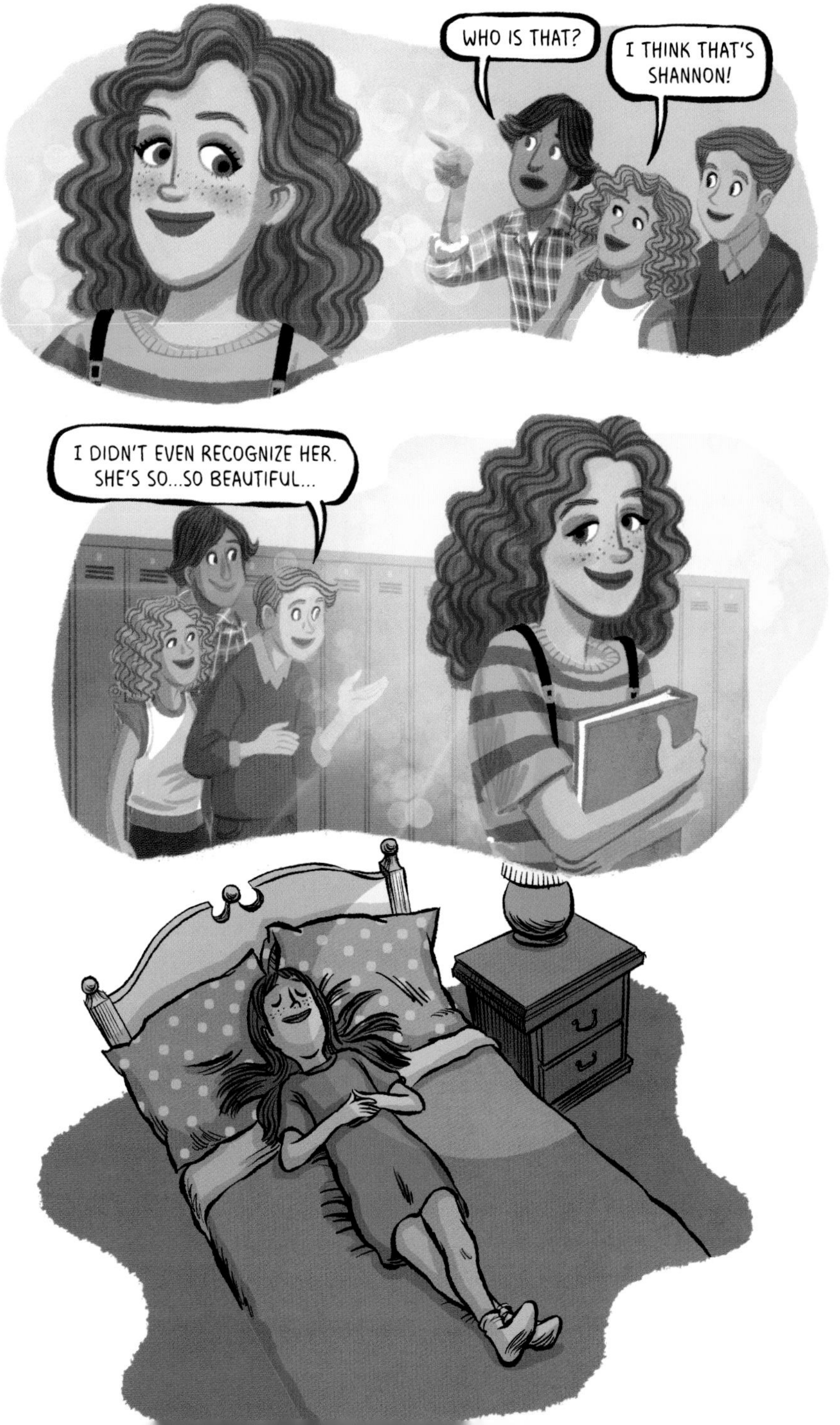
WHO IS THAT?
I THINK THAT'S SHANNON!
I DIDN'T EVEN RECOGNIZE HER. SHE'S SO...SO BEAUTIFUL...

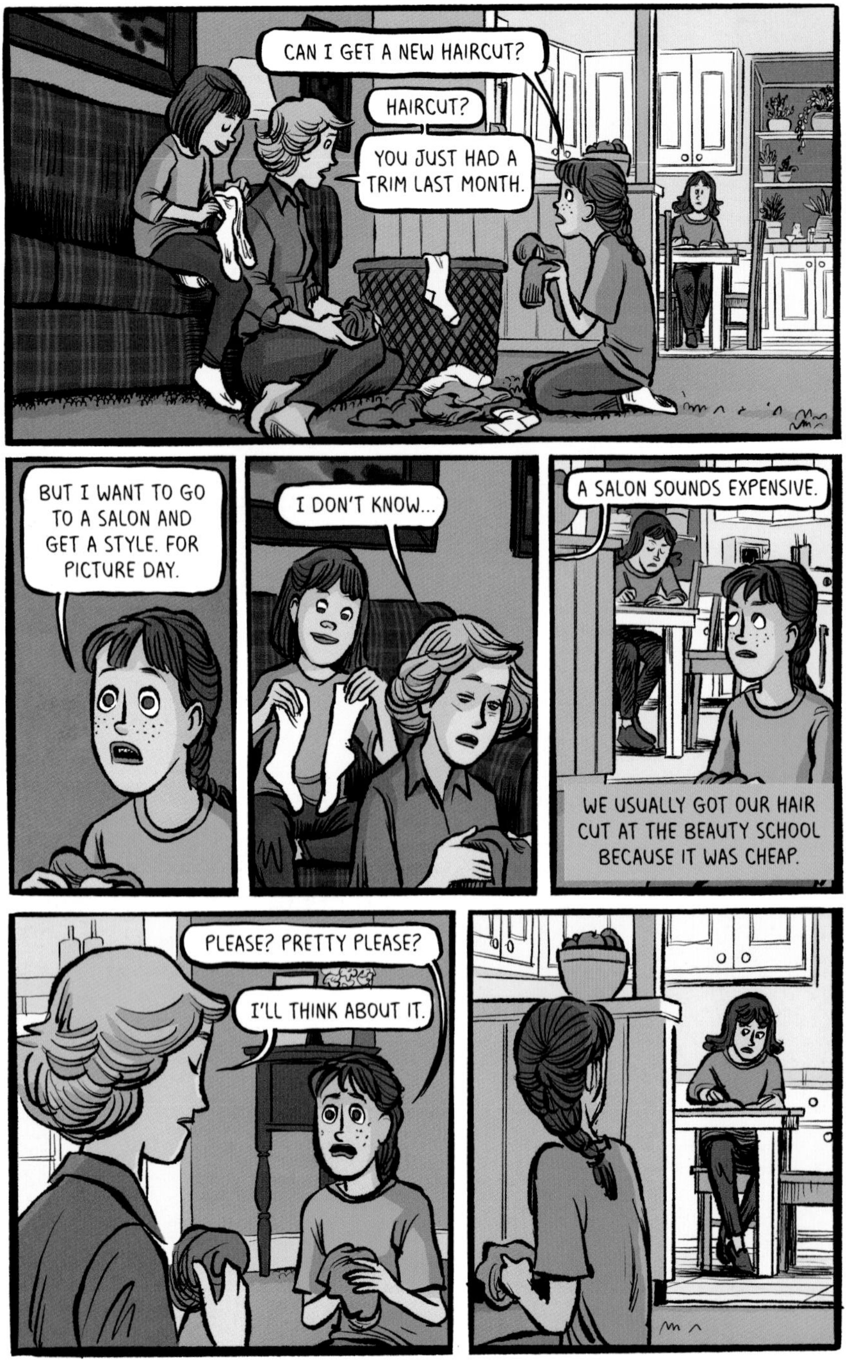
CAN I GET A NEW HAIRCUT?
HAIRCUT?
YOU JUST HAD A TRIM LAST MONTH.
BUT I WANT TO GO TO A SALON AND GET A STYLE. FOR PICTURE DAY.
I DON'T KNOW...
A SALON SOUNDS EXPENSIVE.
WE USUALLY GOT OUR HAIR CUT AT THE BEAUTY SCHOOL BECAUSE IT WAS CHEAP.
PLEASE? PRETTY PLEASE?
I'LL THINK ABOUT IT.

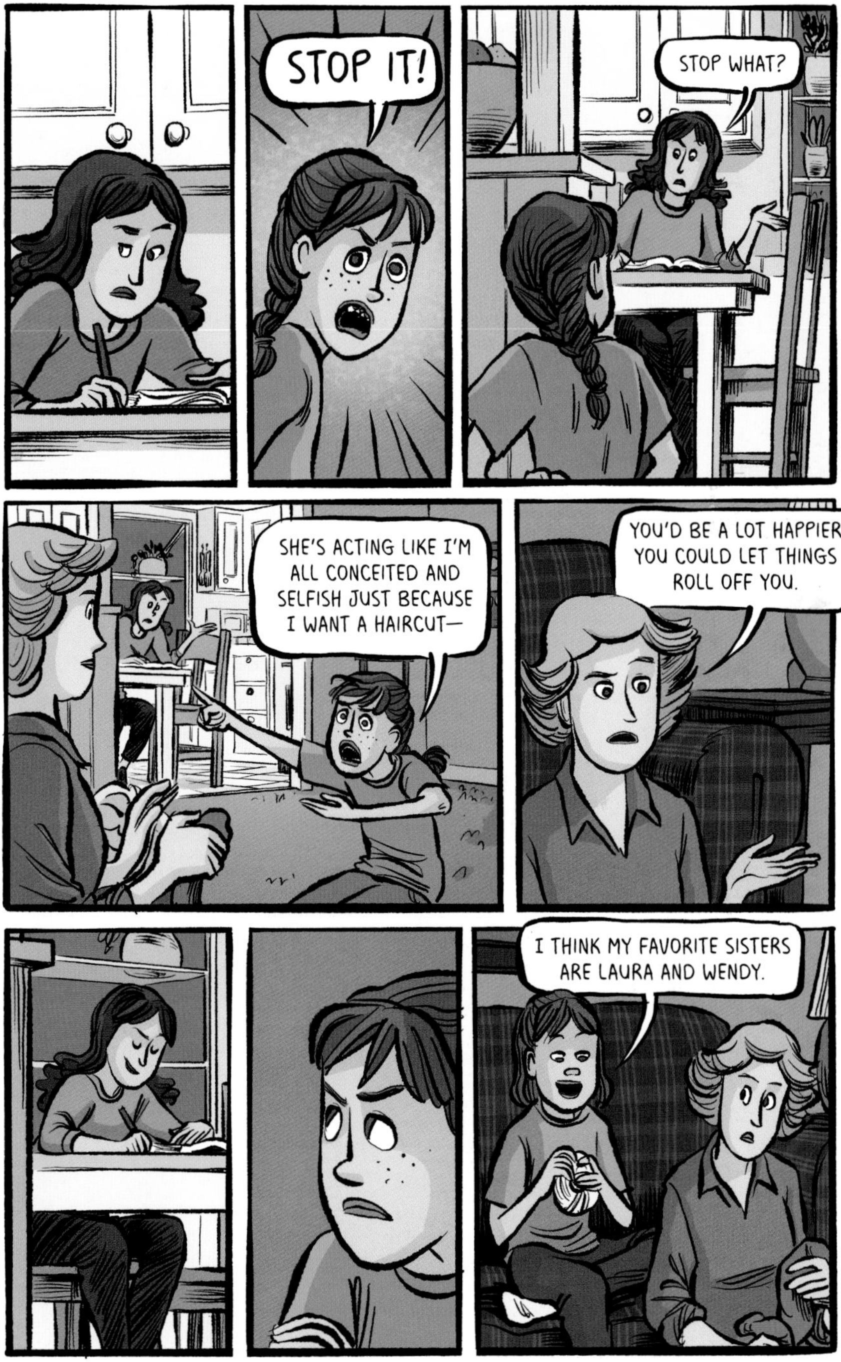
STOP IT!
STOP WHAT?
SHE'S ACTING LIKE I'M ALL CONCEITED AND SELFISH JUST BECAUSE I WANT A HAIRCUT—
YOU'D BE A LOT HAPPIER IF YOU COULD LET THINGS ROLL OFF YOU.
I THINK MY FAVORITE SISTERS ARE LAURA AND WENDY.

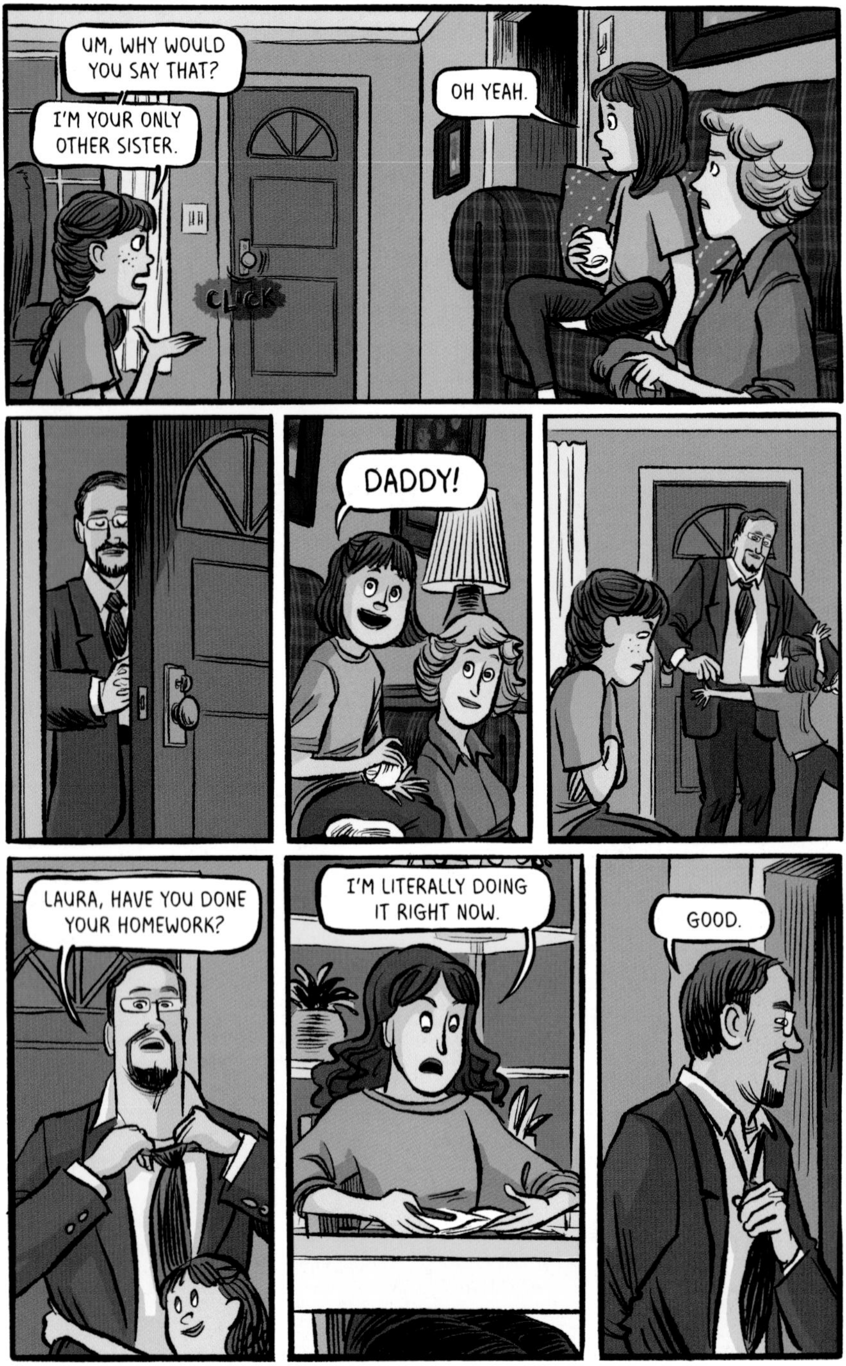
UM, WHY WOULD YOU SAY THAT?
I'M YOUR ONLY OTHER SISTER.
CLICK
OH YEAH.
DADDY!
LAURA, HAVE YOU DONE YOUR HOMEWORK?
I'M LITERALLY DOING IT RIGHT NOW.
GOOD.

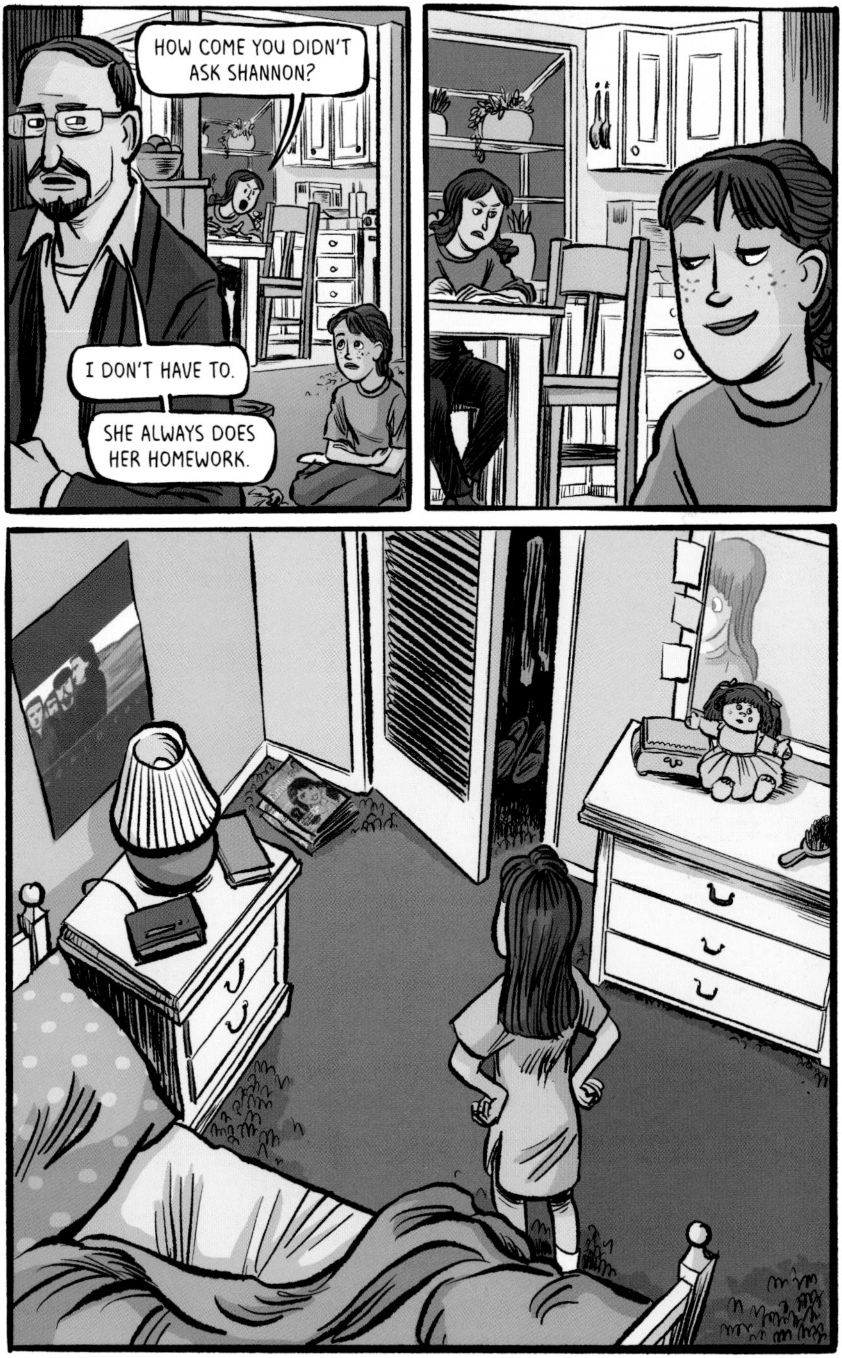
HOW COME YOU DIDN'T ASK SHANNON?
I DON'T HAVE TO.
SHE ALWAYS DOES HER HOMEWORK.

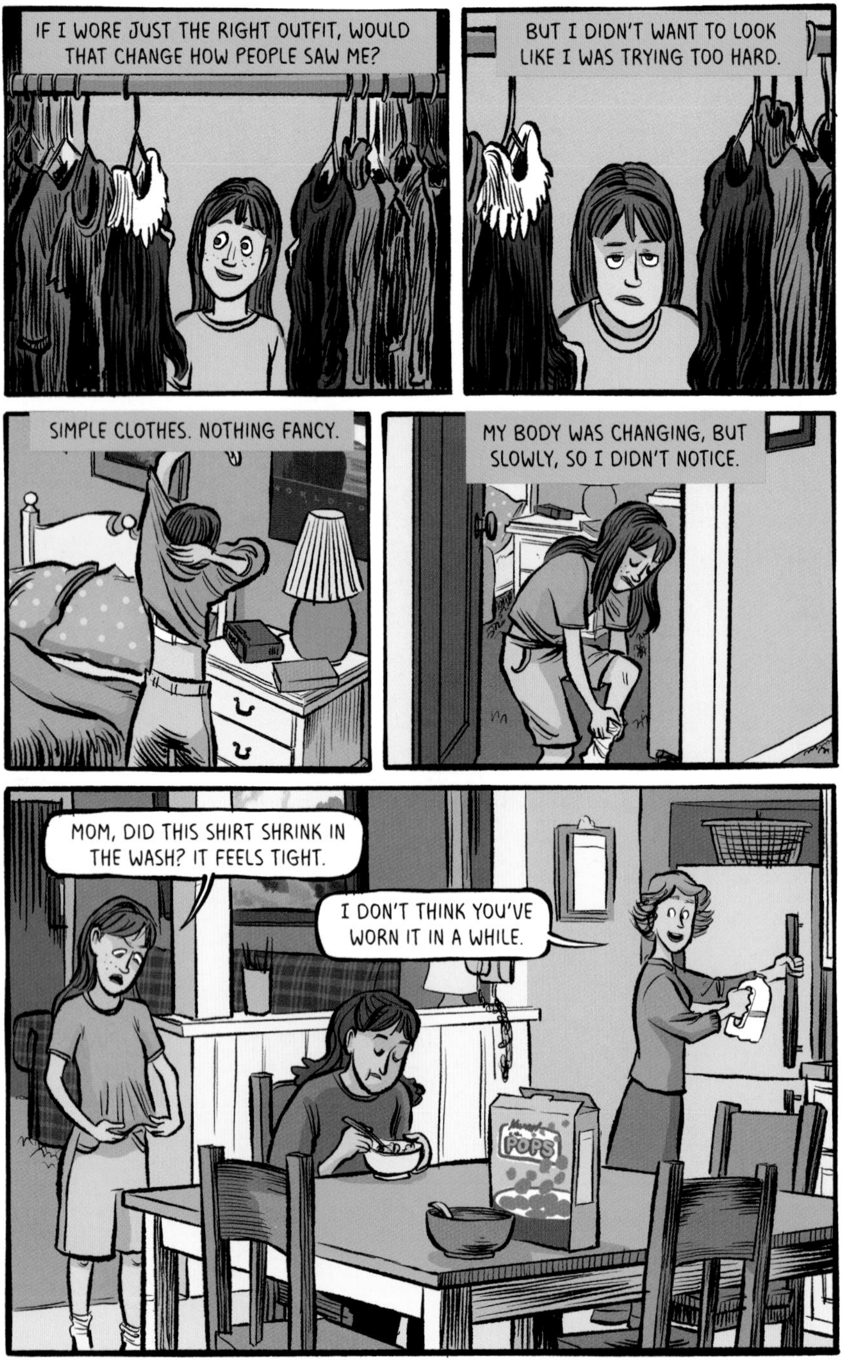
IF I WORE JUST THE RIGHT OUTFIT, WOULD THAT CHANGE HOW PEOPLE SAW ME?
BUT I DIDN'T WANT TO LOOK LIKE I WAS TRYING TOO HARD.
SIMPLE CLOTHES. NOTHING FANCY.
MY BODY WAS CHANGING, BUT SLOWLY, SO I DIDN'T NOTICE.
MOM, DID THIS SHIRT SHRINK IN THE WASH? IT FEELS TIGHT.
I DON'T THINK YOU'VE WORN IT IN A WHILE.
POPS

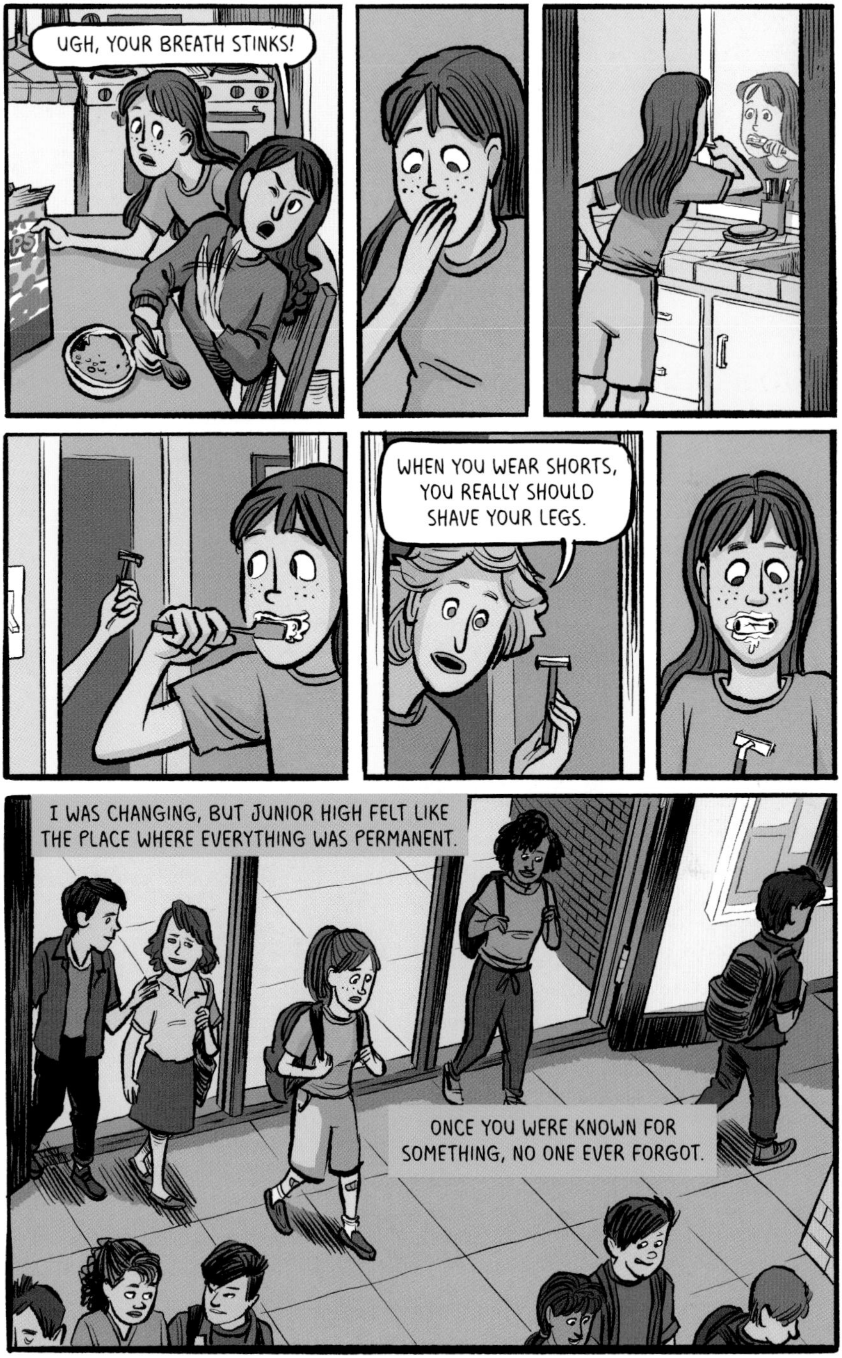
UGH, YOUR BREATH STINKS!
WHEN YOU WEAR SHORTS, YOU REALLY SHOULD SHAVE YOUR LEGS.
I WAS CHANGING, BUT JUNIOR HIGH FELT LIKE THE PLACE WHERE EVERYTHING WAS PERMANENT.
ONCE YOU WERE KNOWN FOR SOMETHING, NO ONE EVER FORGOT.

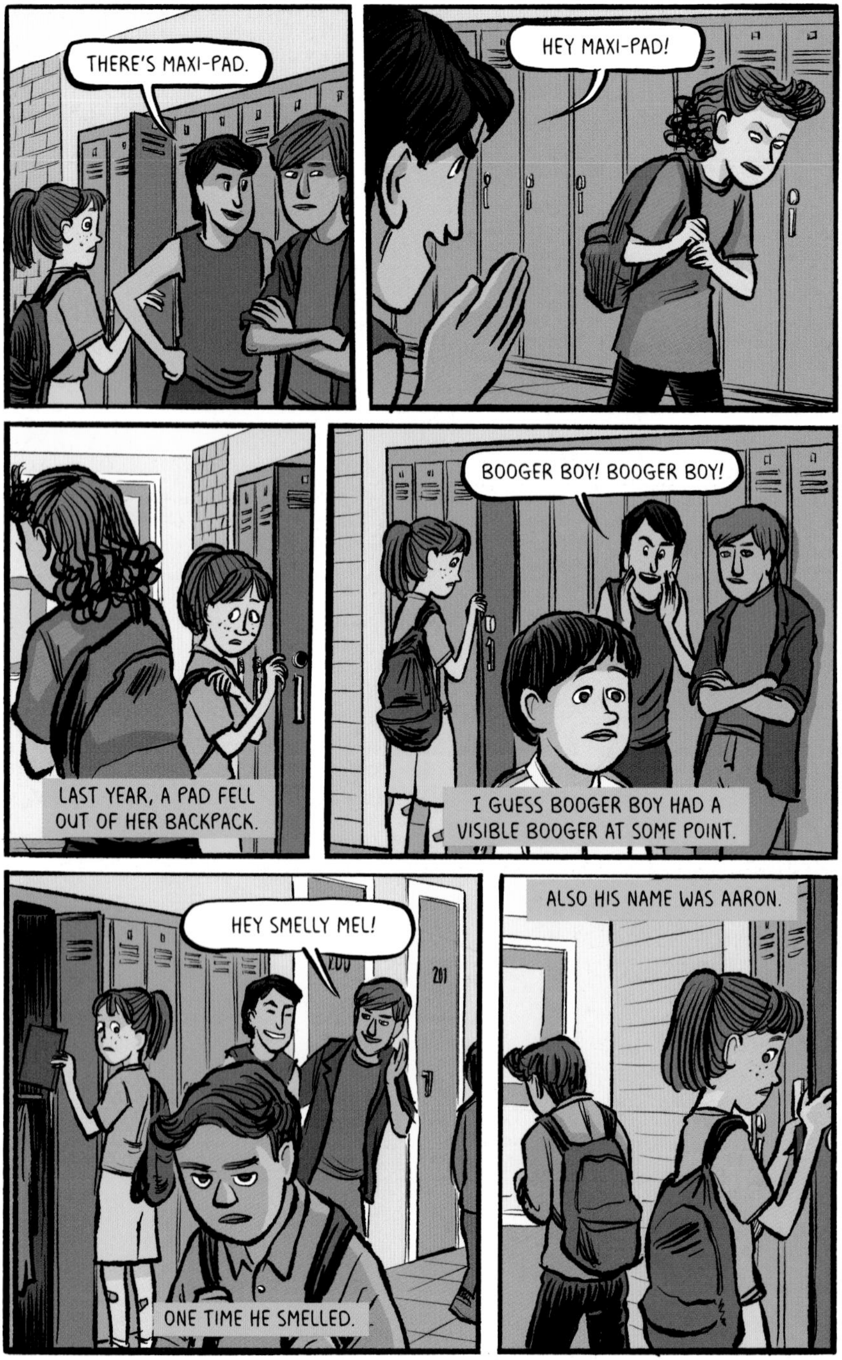
THERE'S MAXI-PAD.
HEY MAXI-PAD!
LAST YEAR, A PAD FELL OUT OF HER BACKPACK.
BOOGER BOY! BOOGER BOY!
I GUESS BOOGER BOY HAD A VISIBLE BOOGER AT SOME POINT.
HEY SMELLY MEL!
ONE TIME HE SMELLED.
ALSO HIS NAME WAS AARON.

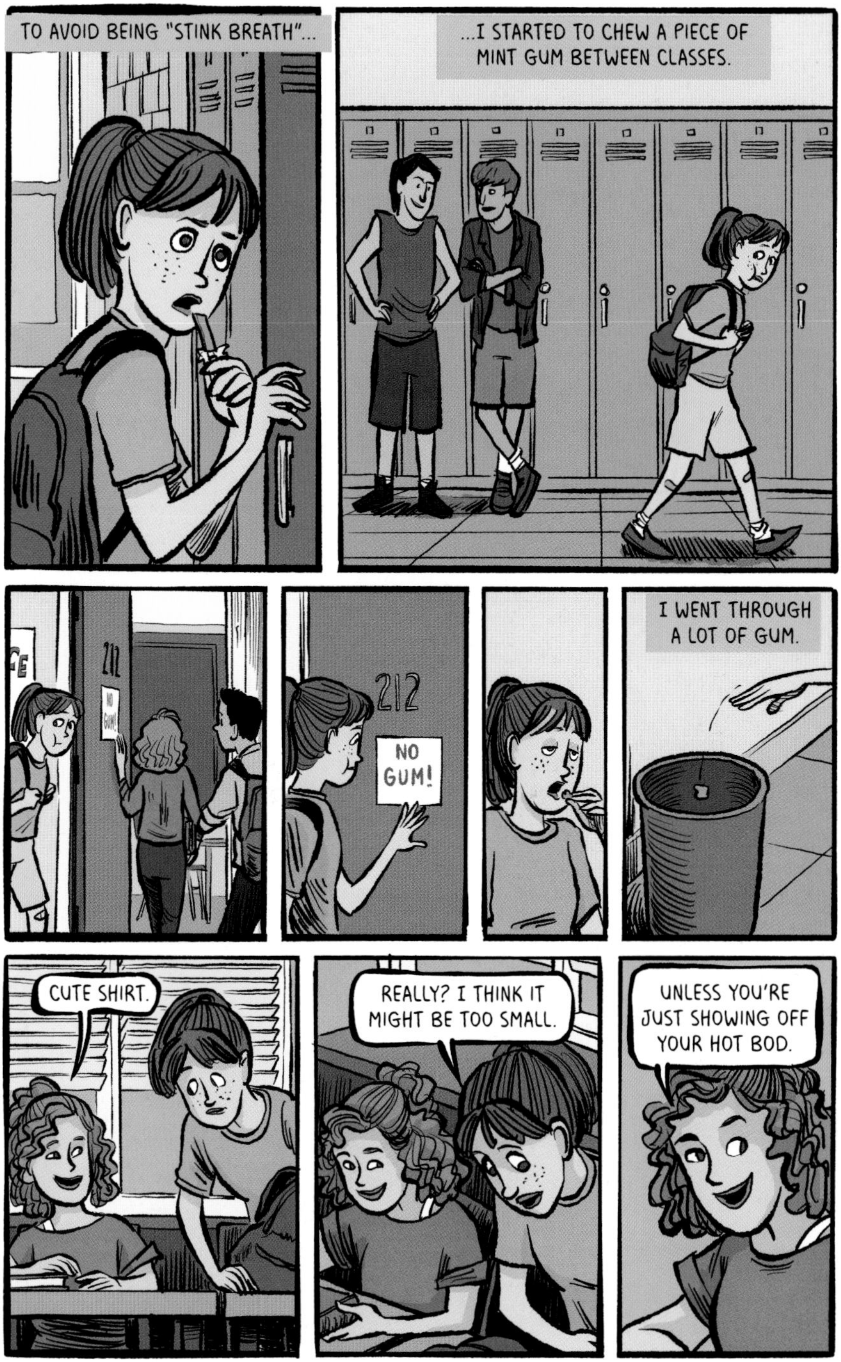
TO AVOID BEING "STINK BREATH"...
...I STARTED TO CHEW A PIECE OF MINT GUM BETWEEN CLASSES.
212
NO GUM!
212
NO GUM!
I WENT THROUGH A LOT OF GUM.
CUTE SHIRT.
REALLY? I THINK IT MIGHT BE TOO SMALL.
UNLESS YOU'RE JUST SHOWING OFF YOUR HOT BOD.

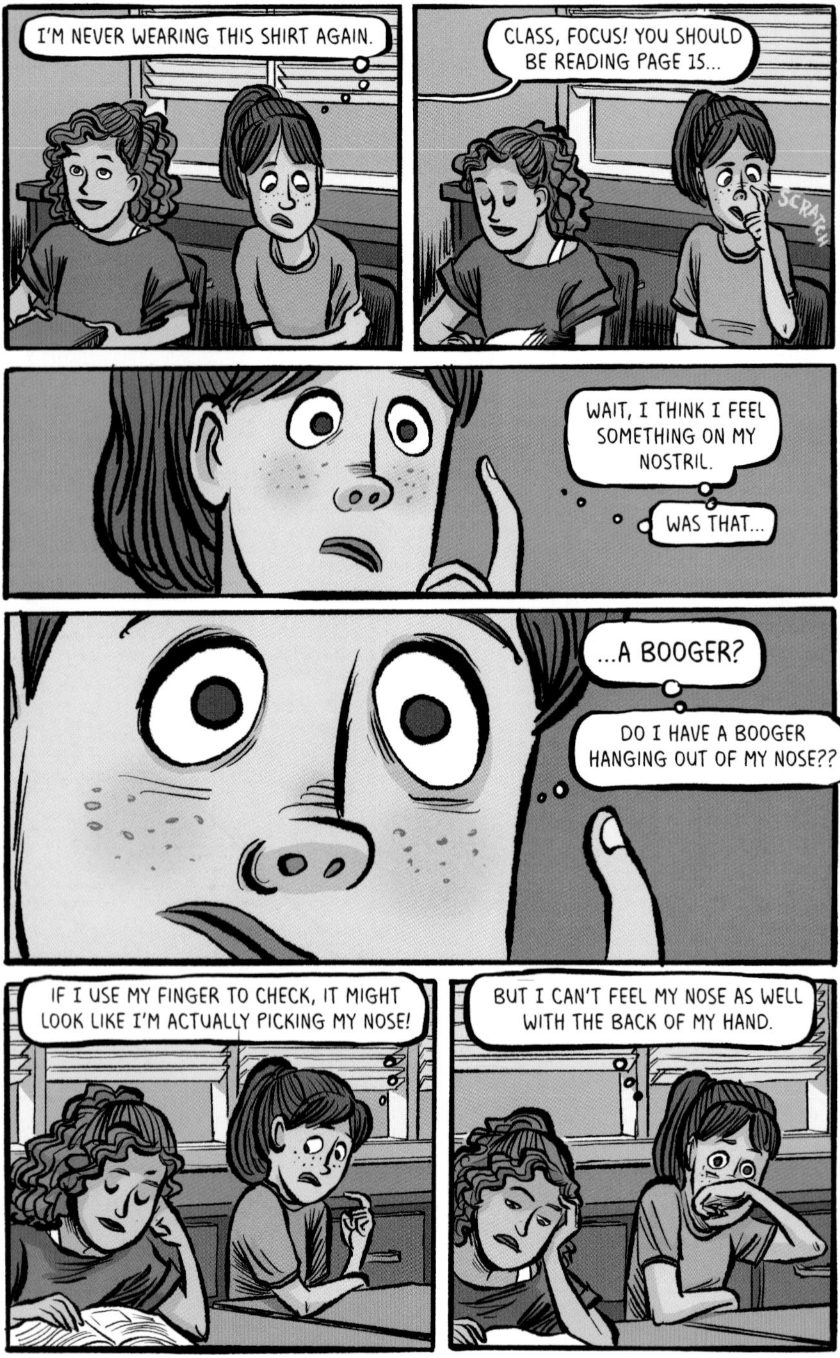
I'M NEVER WEARING THIS SHIRT AGAIN.
CLASS, FOCUS! YOU SHOULD BE READING PAGE 15...
SCRATCH
WAIT, I THINK I FEEL SOMETHING ON MY NOSTRIL.
WAS THAT...
...A BOOGER?
DO I HAVE A BOOGER HANGING OUT OF MY NOSE??
IF I USE MY FINGER TO CHECK, IT MIGHT LOOK LIKE I'M ACTUALLY PICKING MY NOSE!
BUT I CAN'T FEEL MY NOSE AS WELL WITH THE BACK OF MY HAND.

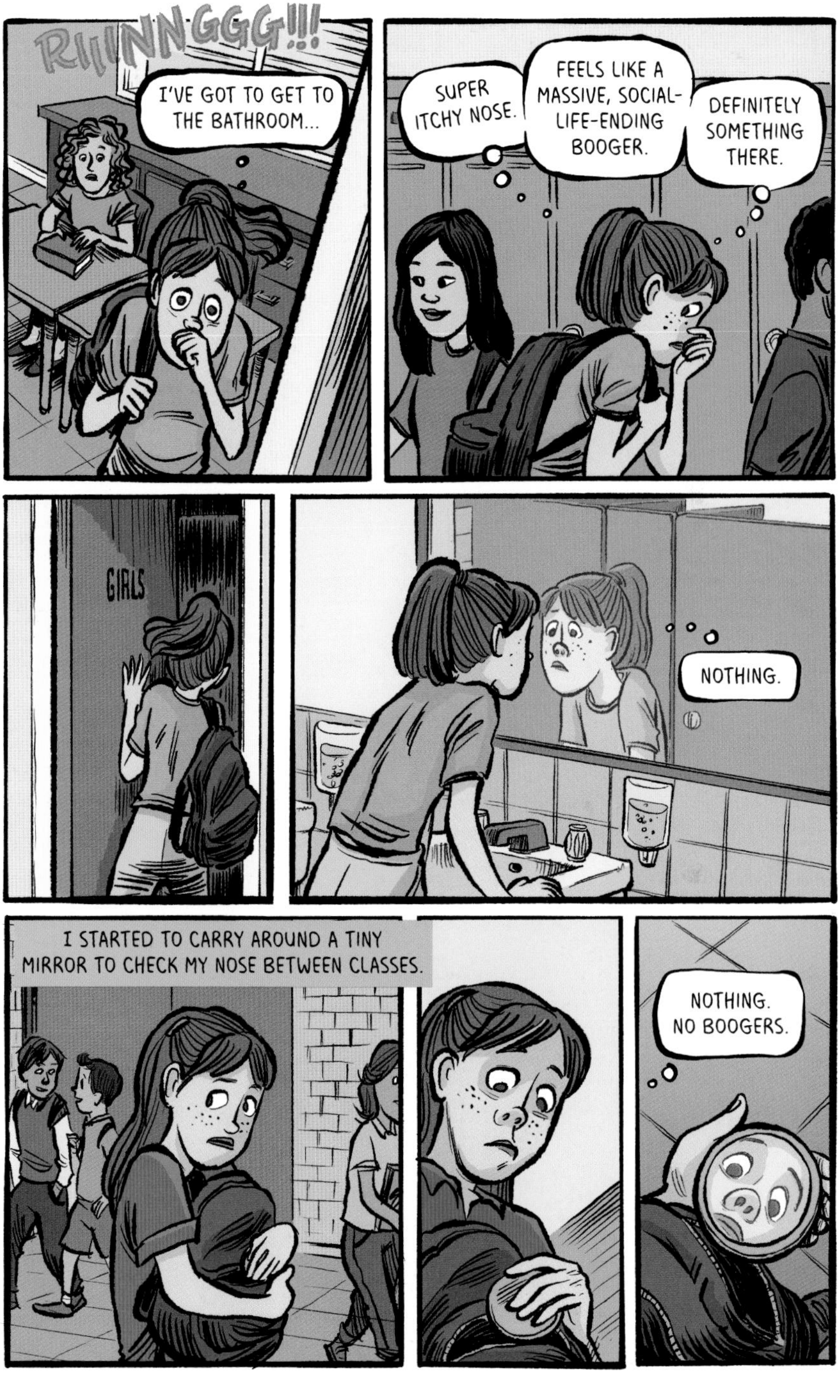
RIIINNGGG!!!
I'VE GOT TO GET TO THE BATHROOM...
SUPER ITCHY NOSE.
FEELS LIKE A MASSIVE, SOCIAL-LIFE-ENDING BOOGER.
DEFINITELY SOMETHING THERE.
GIRLS
NOTHING.
I STARTED TO CARRY AROUND A TINY MIRROR TO CHECK MY NOSE BETWEEN CLASSES.
NOTHING. NO BOOGERS.

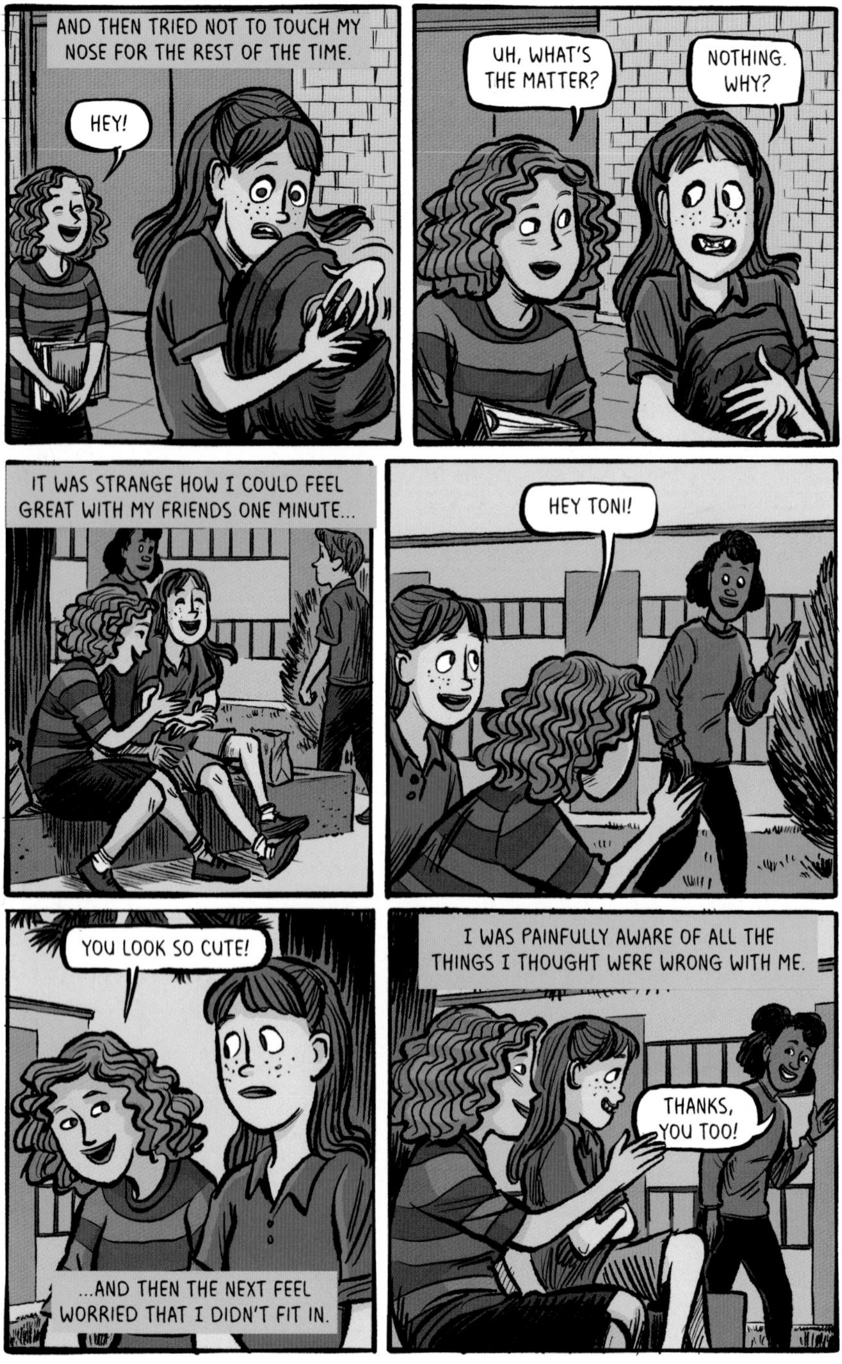
AND THEN TRIED NOT TO TOUCH MY NOSE FOR THE REST OF THE TIME.
HEY!
UH, WHAT'S THE MATTER?
NOTHING. WHY?
IT WAS STRANGE HOW I COULD FEEL GREAT WITH MY FRIENDS ONE MINUTE...
HEY TONI!
YOU LOOK SO CUTE!
...AND THEN THE NEXT FEEL WORRIED THAT I DIDN'T FIT IN.
I WAS PAINFULLY AWARE OF ALL THE THINGS I THOUGHT WERE WRONG WITH ME.
THANKS, YOU TOO!

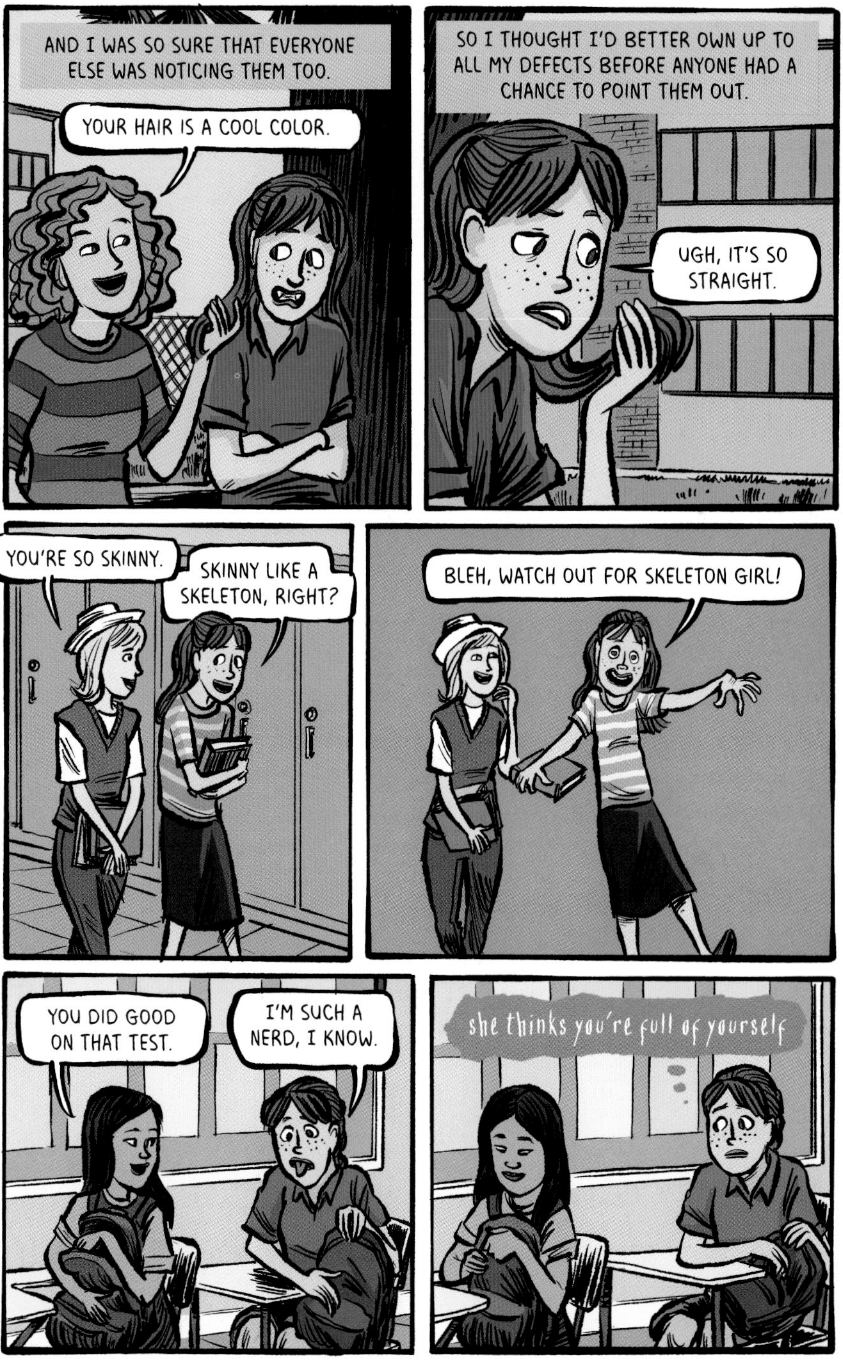
AND I WAS SO SURE THAT EVERYONE ELSE WAS NOTICING THEM TOO.
YOUR HAIR IS A COOL COLOR.
SO I THOUGHT I'D BETTER OWN UP TO ALL MY DEFECTS BEFORE ANYONE HAD A CHANCE TO POINT THEM OUT.
UGH, IT'S SO STRAIGHT.
YOU'RE SO SKINNY.
SKINNY LIKE A SKELETON, RIGHT?
BLEH, WATCH OUT FOR SKELETON GIRL!
YOU DID GOOD ON THAT TEST.
I'M SUCH A NERD, I KNOW.
she thinks you're full of yourself

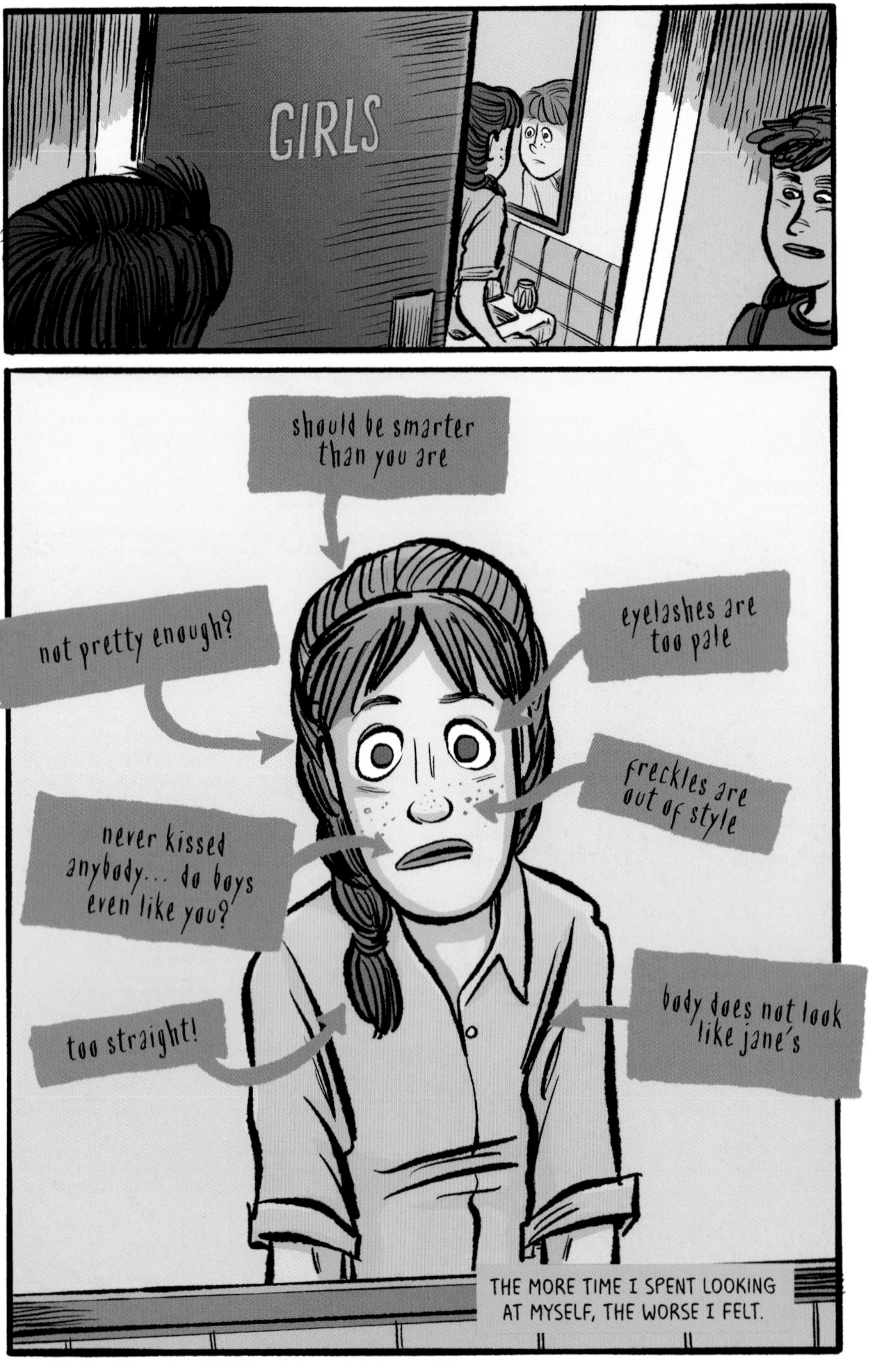
GIRLS
should be smarter than you are
not pretty enough?
eyelashes are too pale
freckles are out of style
never kissed anybody... do boys even like you?
too straight!
body does not look like jane's
THE MORE TIME I SPENT LOOKING AT MYSELF, THE WORSE I FELT.

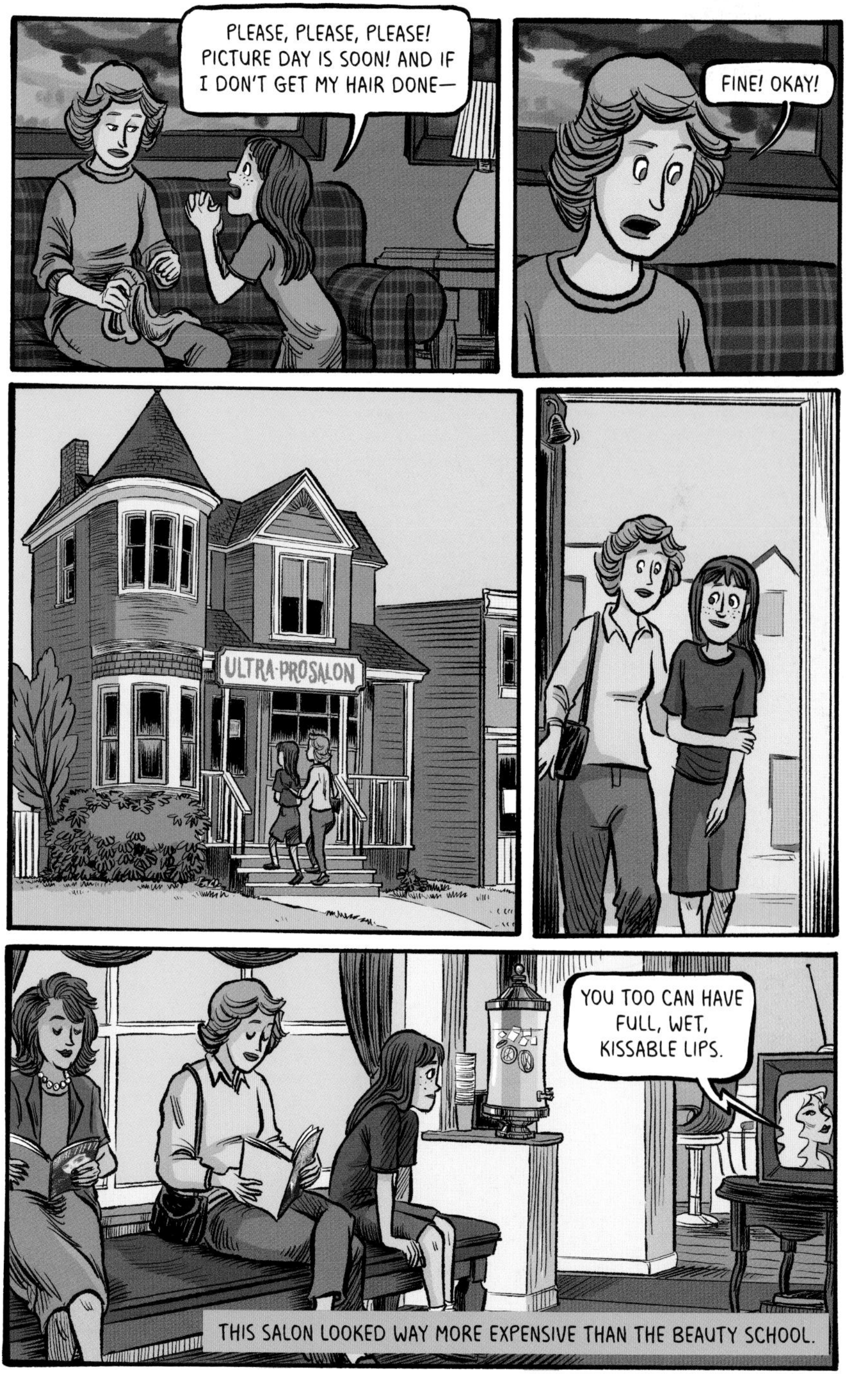
PLEASE, PLEASE, PLEASE! PICTURE DAY IS SOON! AND IF I DON'T GET MY HAIR DONE—
FINE! OKAY!
ULTRA-PROSALON
YOU TOO CAN HAVE FULL, WET, KISSABLE LIPS.
THIS SALON LOOKED WAY MORE EXPENSIVE THAN THE BEAUTY SCHOOL.

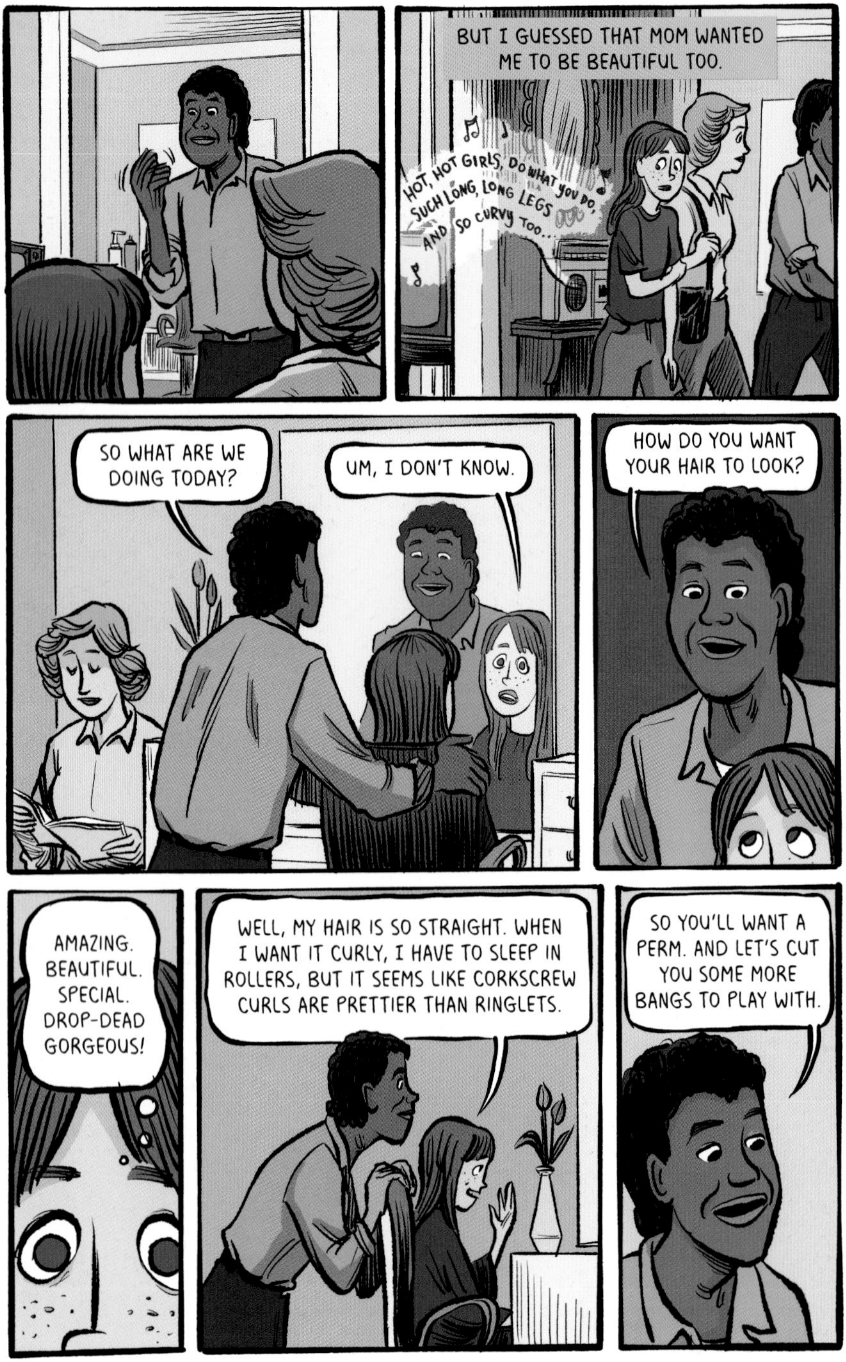
BUT I GUESSED THAT MOM WANTED ME TO BE BEAUTIFUL TOO.
HOT, HOT GIRLS, DO WHAT YOU DO, SUCH LONG, LONG LEGS AND SO CURVY TOO...
SO WHAT ARE WE DOING TODAY?
UM, I DON'T KNOW.
HOW DO YOU WANT YOUR HAIR TO LOOK?
AMAZING. BEAUTIFUL. SPECIAL. DROP-DEAD GORGEOUS!
WELL, MY HAIR IS SO STRAIGHT. WHEN I WANT IT CURLY, I HAVE TO SLEEP IN ROLLERS, BUT IT SEEMS LIKE CORKSCREW CURLS ARE PRETTIER THAN RINGLETS.
SO YOU'LL WANT A PERM. AND LET'S CUT YOU SOME MORE BANGS TO PLAY WITH.

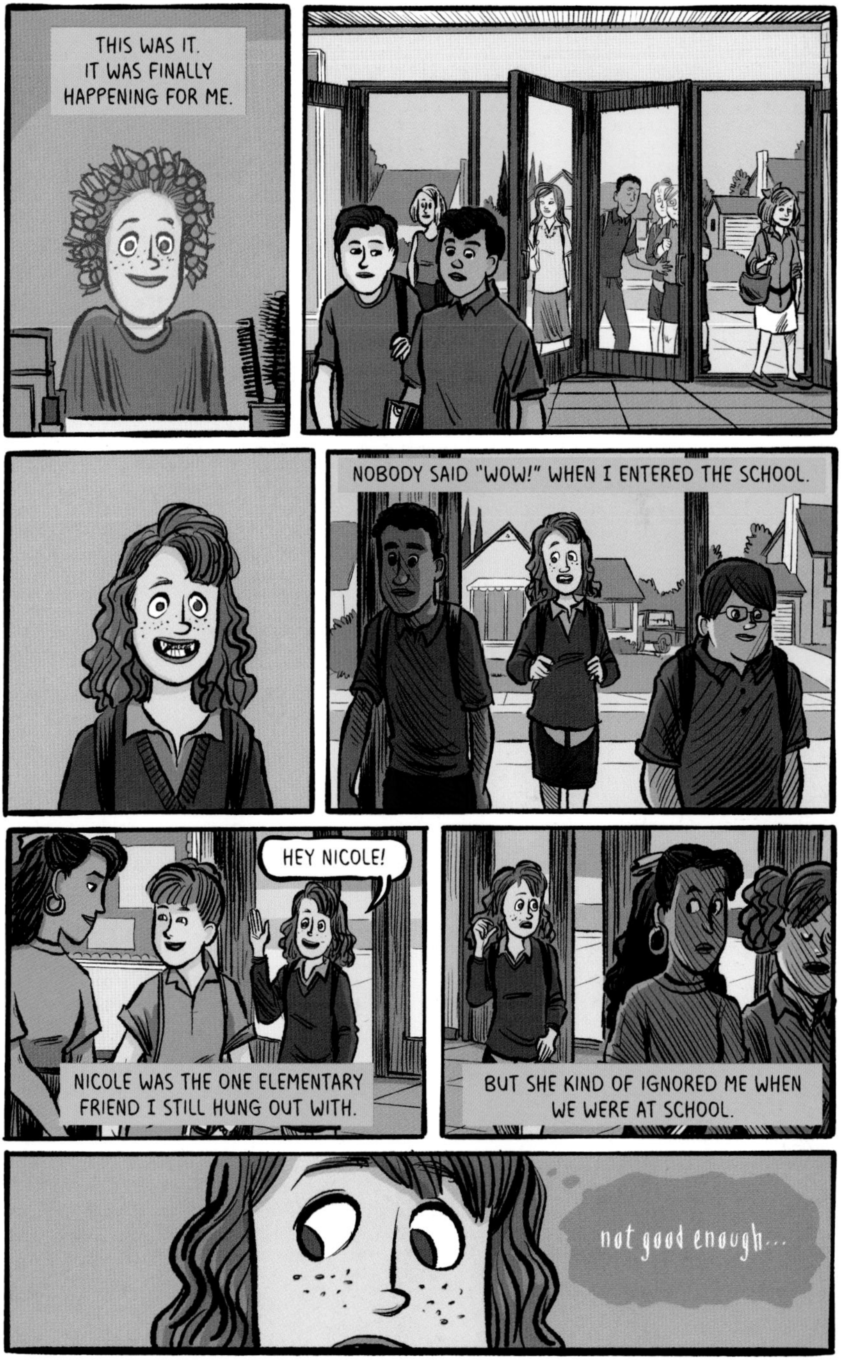
THIS WAS IT. IT WAS FINALLY HAPPENING FOR ME.
NOBODY SAID "WOW!" WHEN I ENTERED THE SCHOOL.
HEY NICOLE!
NICOLE WAS THE ONE ELEMENTARY FRIEND I STILL HUNG OUT WITH.
BUT SHE KIND OF IGNORED ME WHEN WE WERE AT SCHOOL.
not good enough...

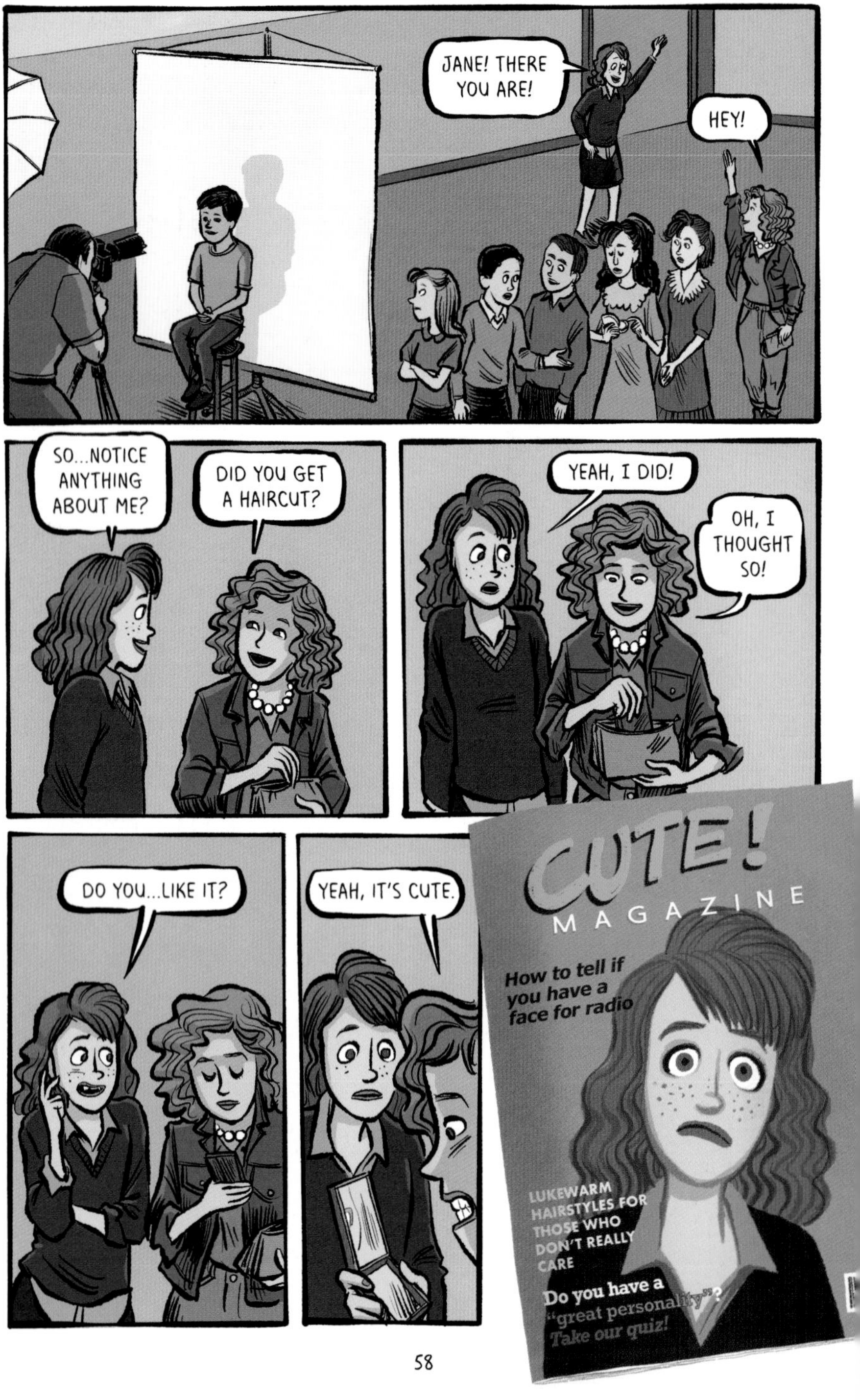
JANE! THERE YOU ARE!
HEY!
SO...NOTICE ANYTHING ABOUT ME?
DID YOU GET A HAIRCUT?
YEAH, I DID!
OH, I THOUGHT SO!
DO YOU...LIKE IT?
YEAH, IT'S CUTE.
CUTE!
MAGAZINE
How to tell if you have a face for radio
LUKEWARM HAIRSTYLES FOR THOSE WHO DON'T REALLY CARE
Do you have a "great personality"? Take our quiz!

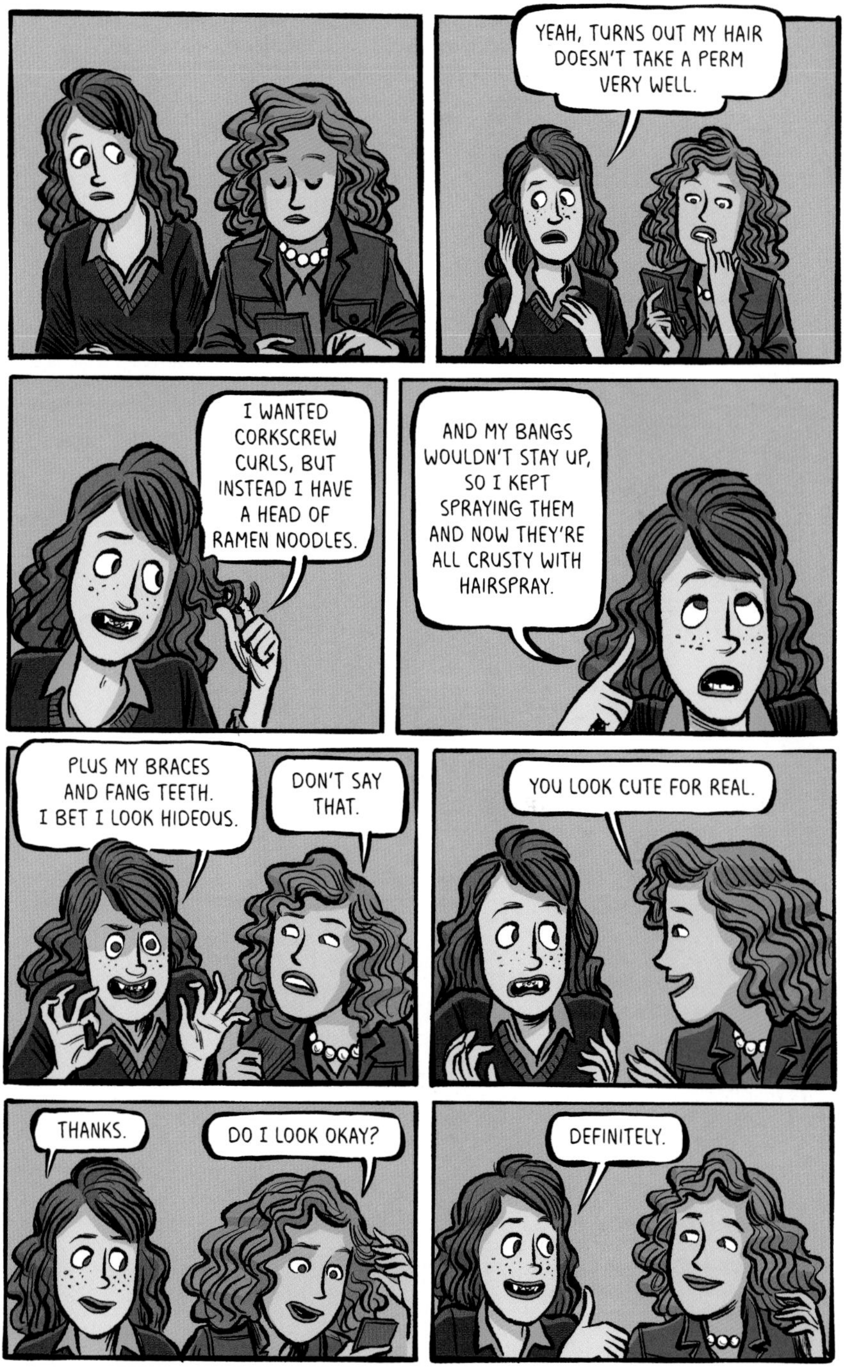
YEAH, TURNS OUT MY HAIR DOESN'T TAKE A PERM VERY WELL.
I WANTED CORKSCREW CURLS, BUT INSTEAD I HAVE A HEAD OF RAMEN NOODLES.
AND MY BANGS WOULDN'T STAY UP, SO I KEPT SPRAYING THEM AND NOW THEY'RE ALL CRUSTY WITH HAIRSPRAY.
PLUS MY BRACES AND FANG TEETH. I BET I LOOK HIDEOUS.
DON'T SAY THAT.
YOU LOOK CUTE FOR REAL.
THANKS.
DO I LOOK OKAY?
DEFINITELY.

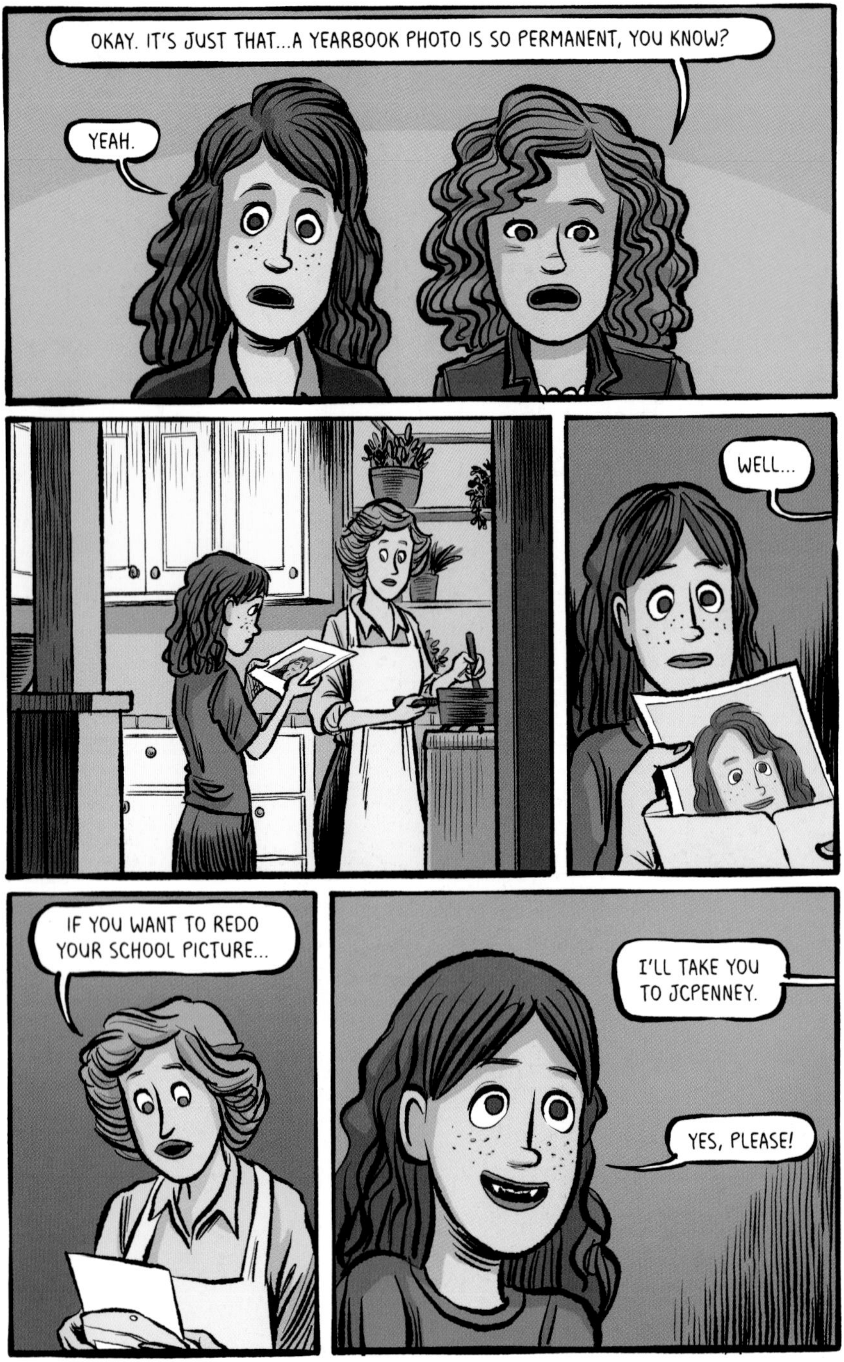
OKAY. IT'S JUST THAT...A YEARBOOK PHOTO IS SO PERMANENT, YOU KNOW?
YEAH.
WELL...
IF YOU WANT TO REDO YOUR SCHOOL PICTURE...
I'LL TAKE YOU TO JCPENNEY.
YES, PLEASE!

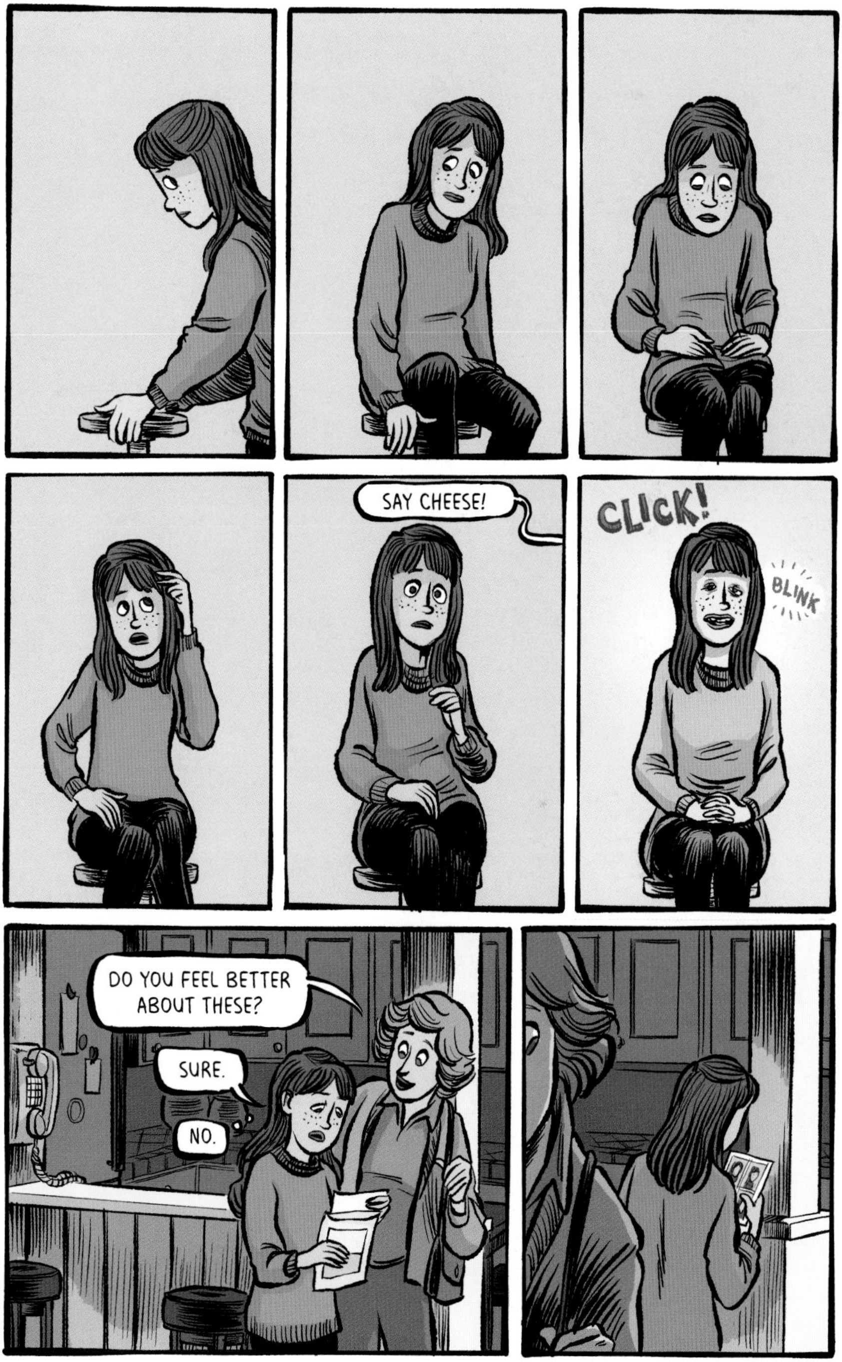
SAY CHEESE!
CLICK!
BLINK
DO YOU FEEL BETTER ABOUT THESE?
SURE.
NO.

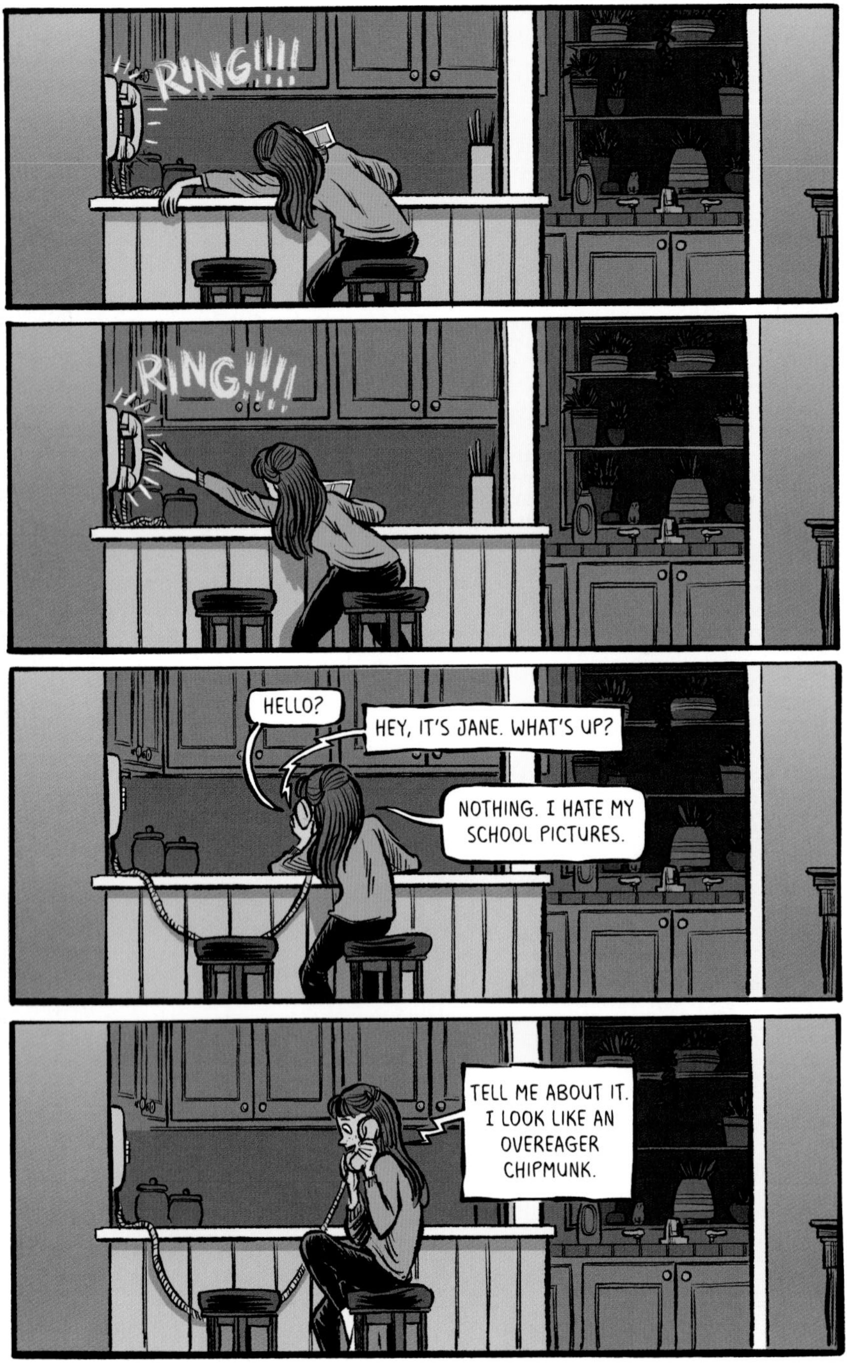
RING!!!!
RING!!!!
HELLO?
HEY, IT'S JANE. WHAT'S UP?
NOTHING. I HATE MY SCHOOL PICTURES.
TELL ME ABOUT IT. I LOOK LIKE AN OVEREAGER CHIPMUNK.

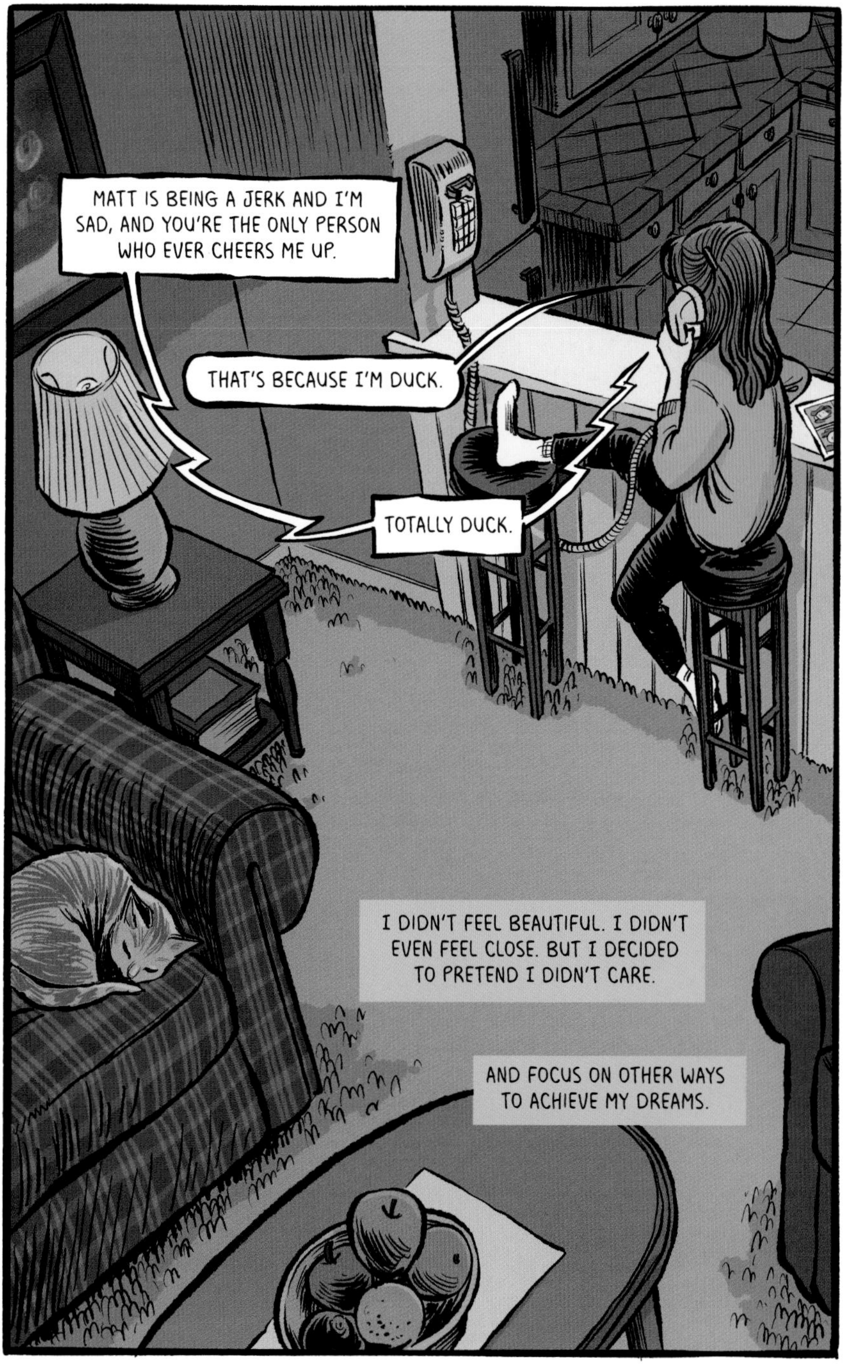
MATT IS BEING A JERK AND I'M SAD, AND YOU'RE THE ONLY PERSON WHO EVER CHEERS ME UP.
THAT'S BECAUSE I'M DUCK.
TOTALLY DUCK.
I DIDN'T FEEL BEAUTIFUL. I DIDN'T EVEN FEEL CLOSE. BUT I DECIDED TO PRETEND I DIDN'T CARE.
AND FOCUS ON OTHER WAYS TO ACHIEVE MY DREAMS.

CHAPTER 2

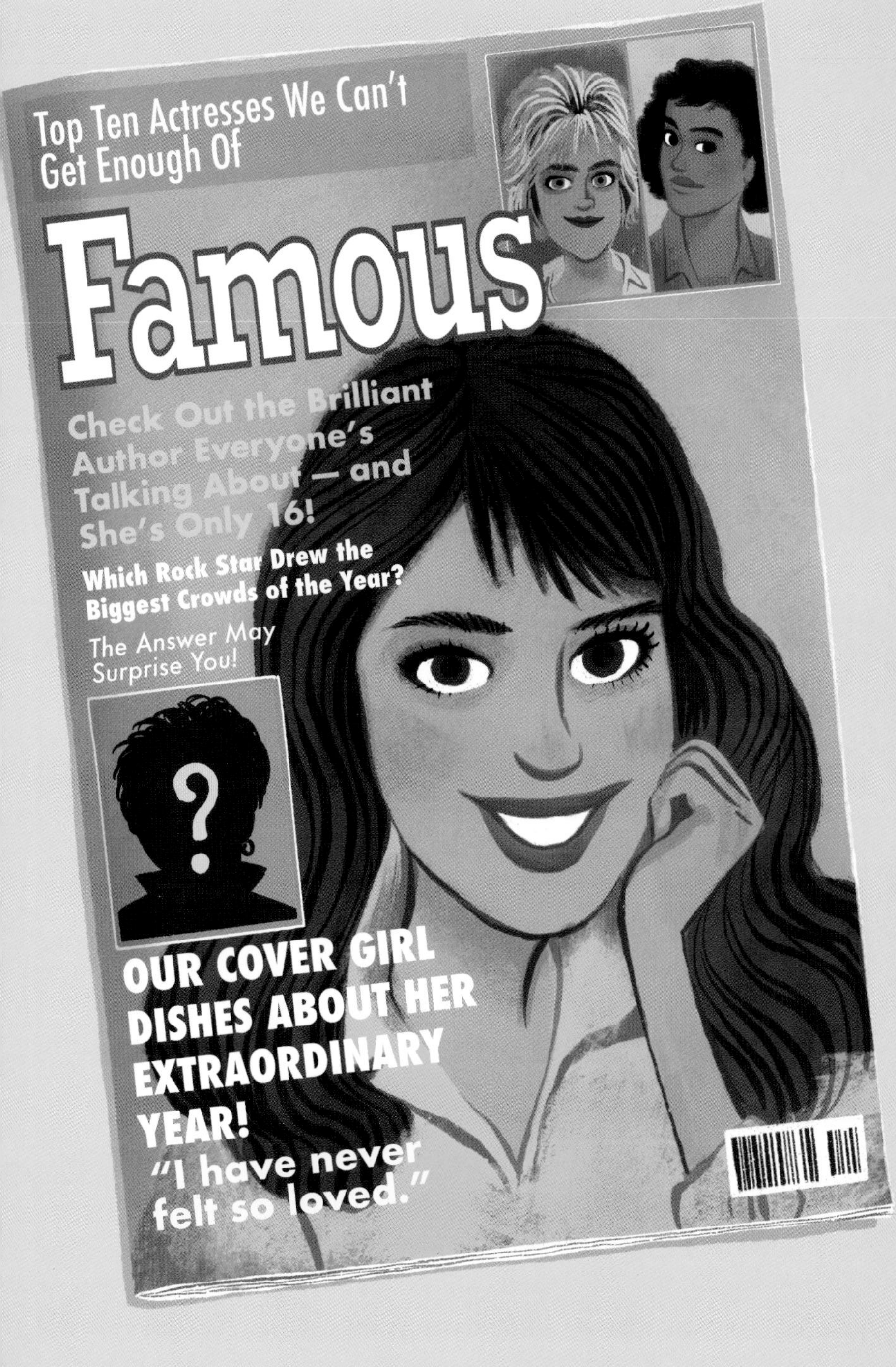
Top Ten Actresses We Can't Get Enough Of
Famous
Check Out the Brilliant Author Everyone's Talking About — and She's Only 16!
Which Rock Star Drew the Biggest Crowds of the Year?
The Answer May Surprise You!
?
OUR COVER GIRL DISHES ABOUT HER EXTRAORDINARY YEAR!
"I have never felt so loved."

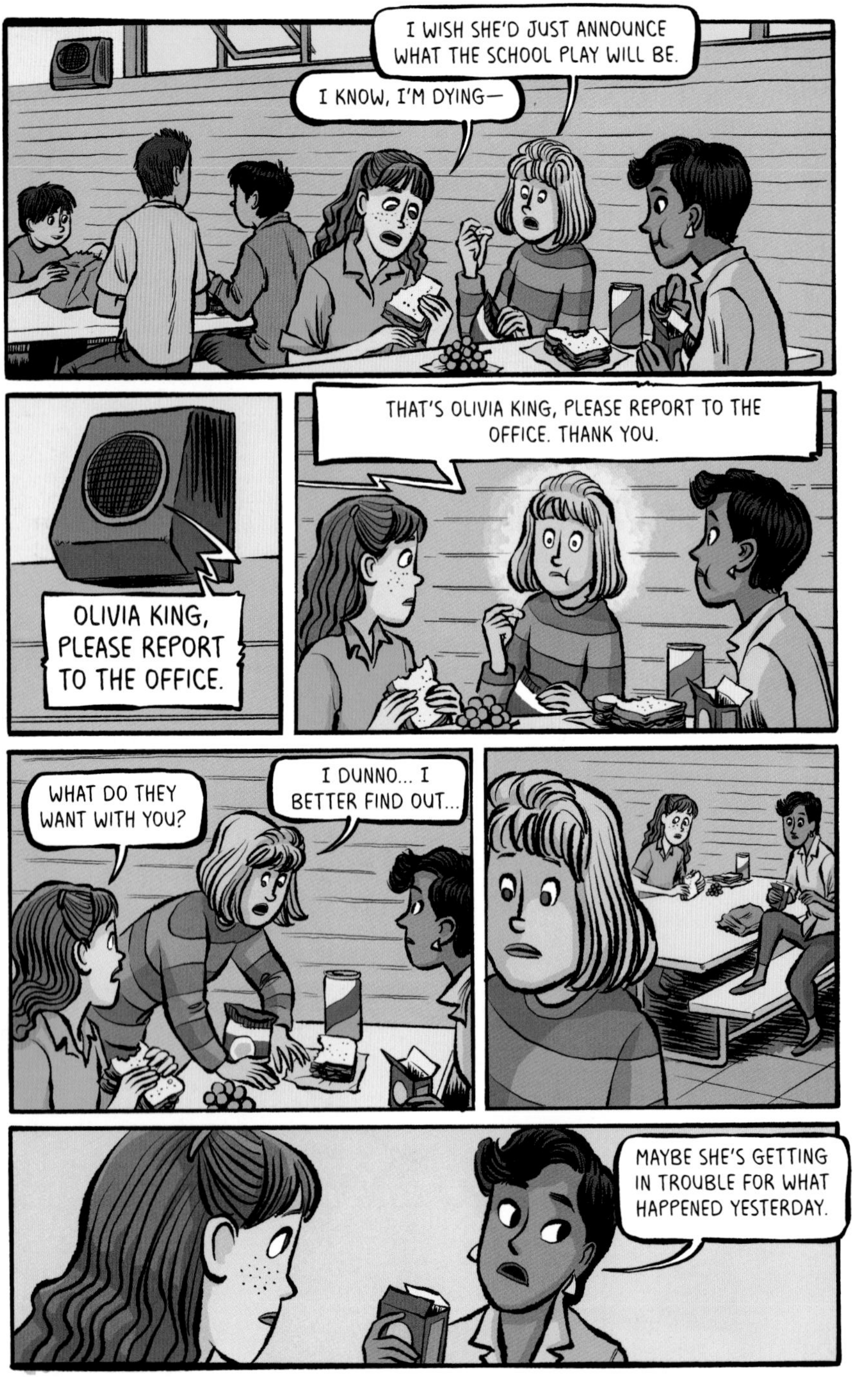
I WISH SHE'D JUST ANNOUNCE WHAT THE SCHOOL PLAY WILL BE.
I KNOW, I'M DYING—
OLIVIA KING, PLEASE REPORT TO THE OFFICE.
THAT'S OLIVIA KING, PLEASE REPORT TO THE OFFICE. THANK YOU.
WHAT DO THEY WANT WITH YOU?
I DUNNO... I BETTER FIND OUT...
MAYBE SHE'S GETTING IN TROUBLE FOR WHAT HAPPENED YESTERDAY.

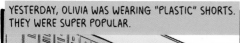

YESTERDAY, OLIVIA WAS WEARING "PLASTIC" SHORTS. THEY WERE SUPER POPULAR.

BUT THEY HAD ELASTIC WAISTBANDS...

YOUNG LADY, THAT IS INAPPROPRIATE!

BUT IT WASN'T HER FAULT! I CAN'T BELIEVE HE YELLED AT HER FOR GETTING PANTSED.

HEY, IT WASN'T NICE WHEN YOU PANTSED OLIVIA.

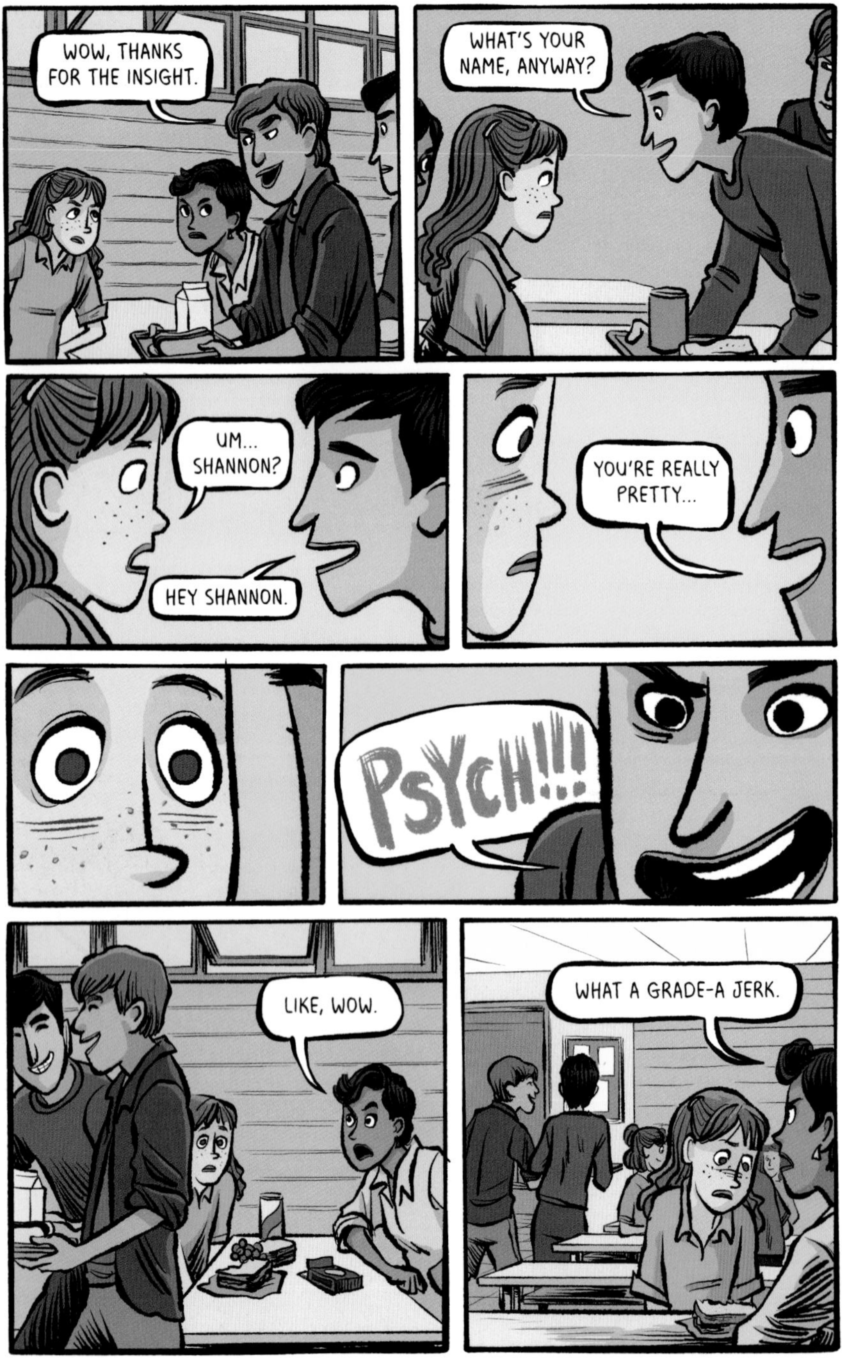
WOW, THANKS FOR THE INSIGHT.
WHAT'S YOUR NAME, ANYWAY?
UM... SHANNON?
HEY SHANNON.
YOU'RE REALLY PRETTY...
PSYCH!!!
LIKE, WOW.
WHAT A GRADE-A JERK.

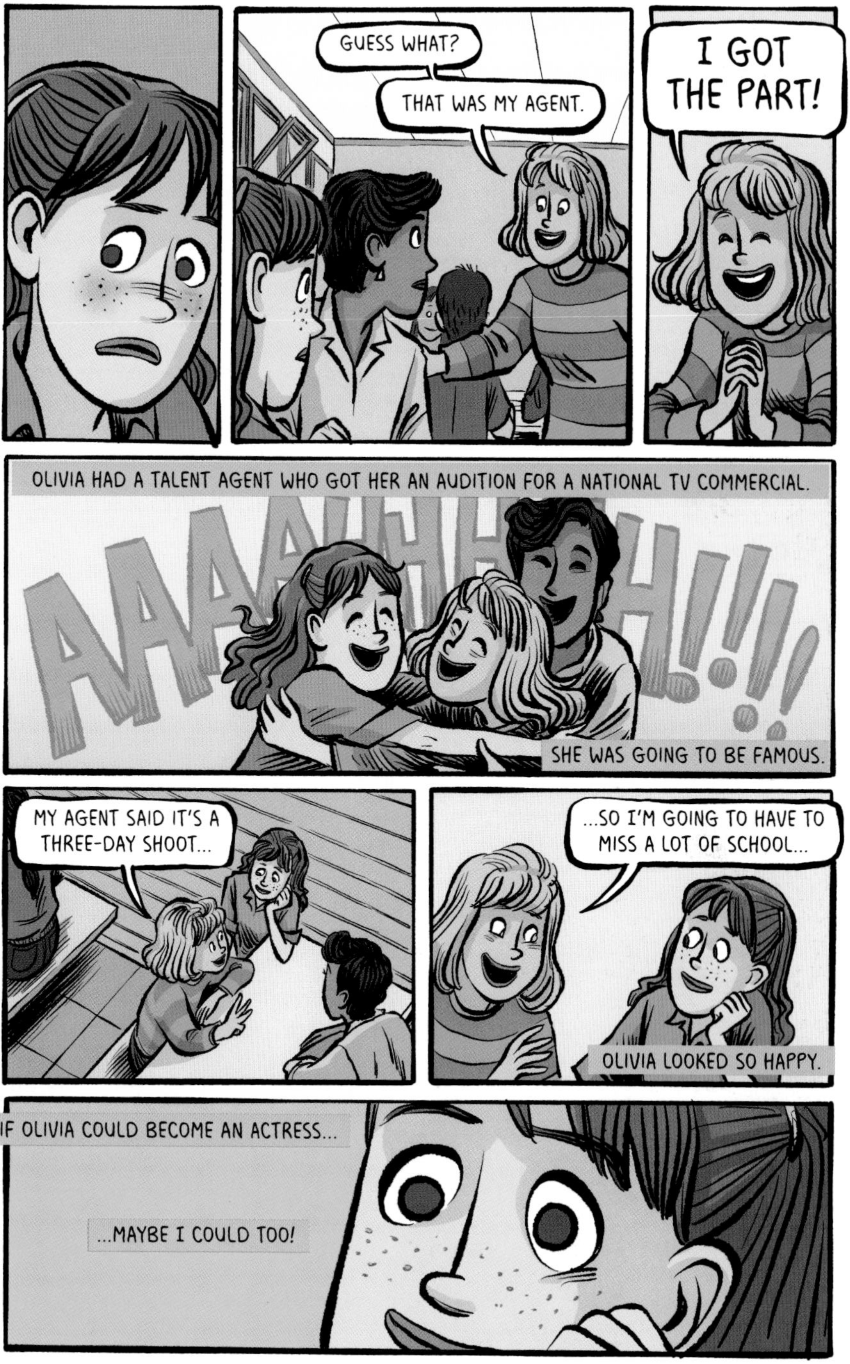
GUESS WHAT?
THAT WAS MY AGENT.
I GOT THE PART!
OLIVIA HAD A TALENT AGENT WHO GOT HER AN AUDITION FOR A NATIONAL TV COMMERCIAL.
AAAAHHHHH!!!!
SHE WAS GOING TO BE FAMOUS.
MY AGENT SAID IT'S A THREE-DAY SHOOT...
...SO I'M GOING TO HAVE TO MISS A LOT OF SCHOOL...
OLIVIA LOOKED SO HAPPY.
IF OLIVIA COULD BECOME AN ACTRESS...
...MAYBE I COULD TOO!

IF I WAS FAMOUS, I'D FEEL CONFIDENT, LIKE I WAS COVERED IN ARMOR.

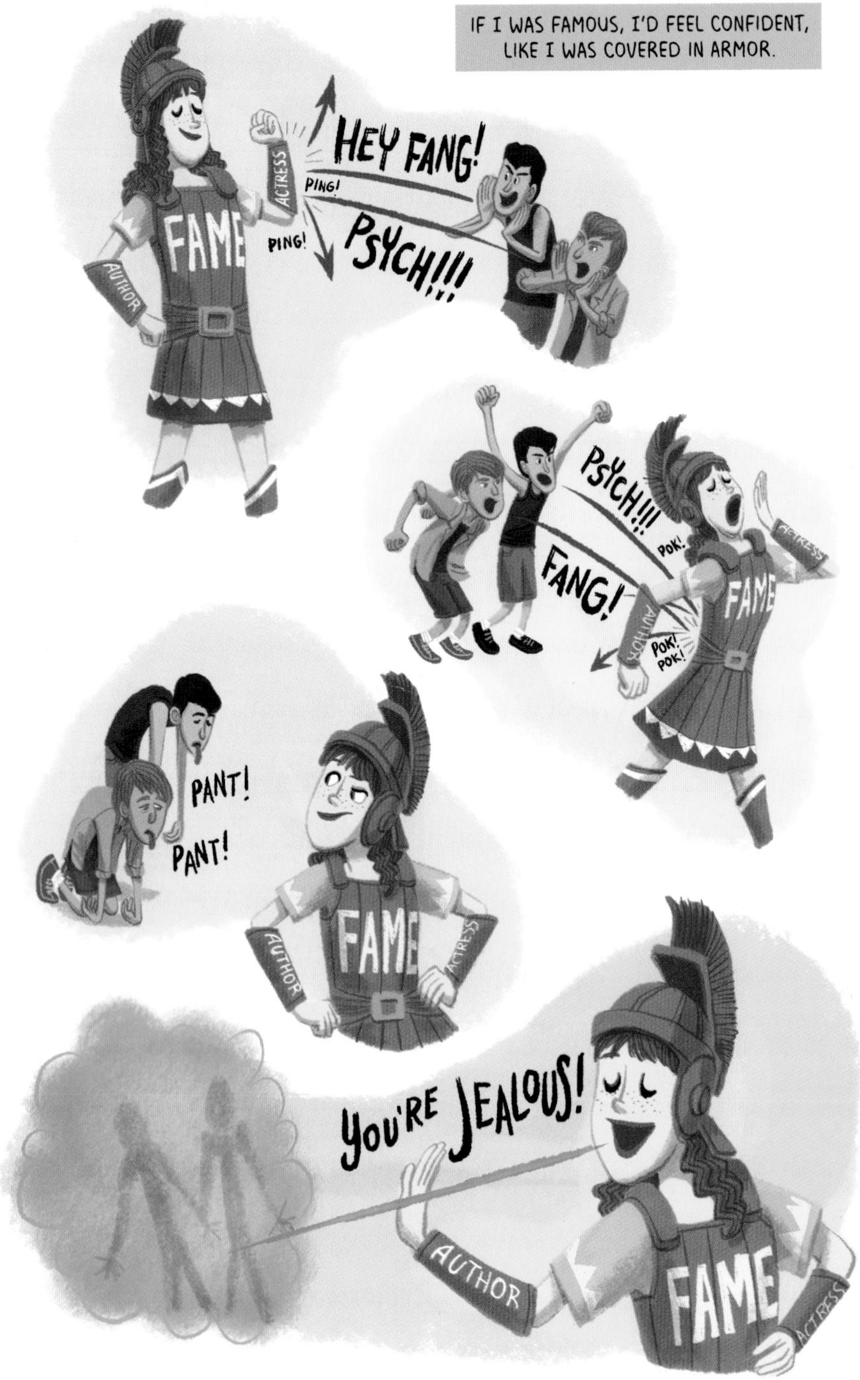
ACTRESS
FAME
AUTHOR
HEY FANG!
PING!
PING!
PSYCH!!!
PSYCH!!!
POK!
FANG!
POK! POK!
ACTRESS
FAME
AUTHOR
PANT!
PANT!
FAME
AUTHOR
ACTRESS
YOU'RE JEALOUS!
AUTHOR
FAME
ACTRESS

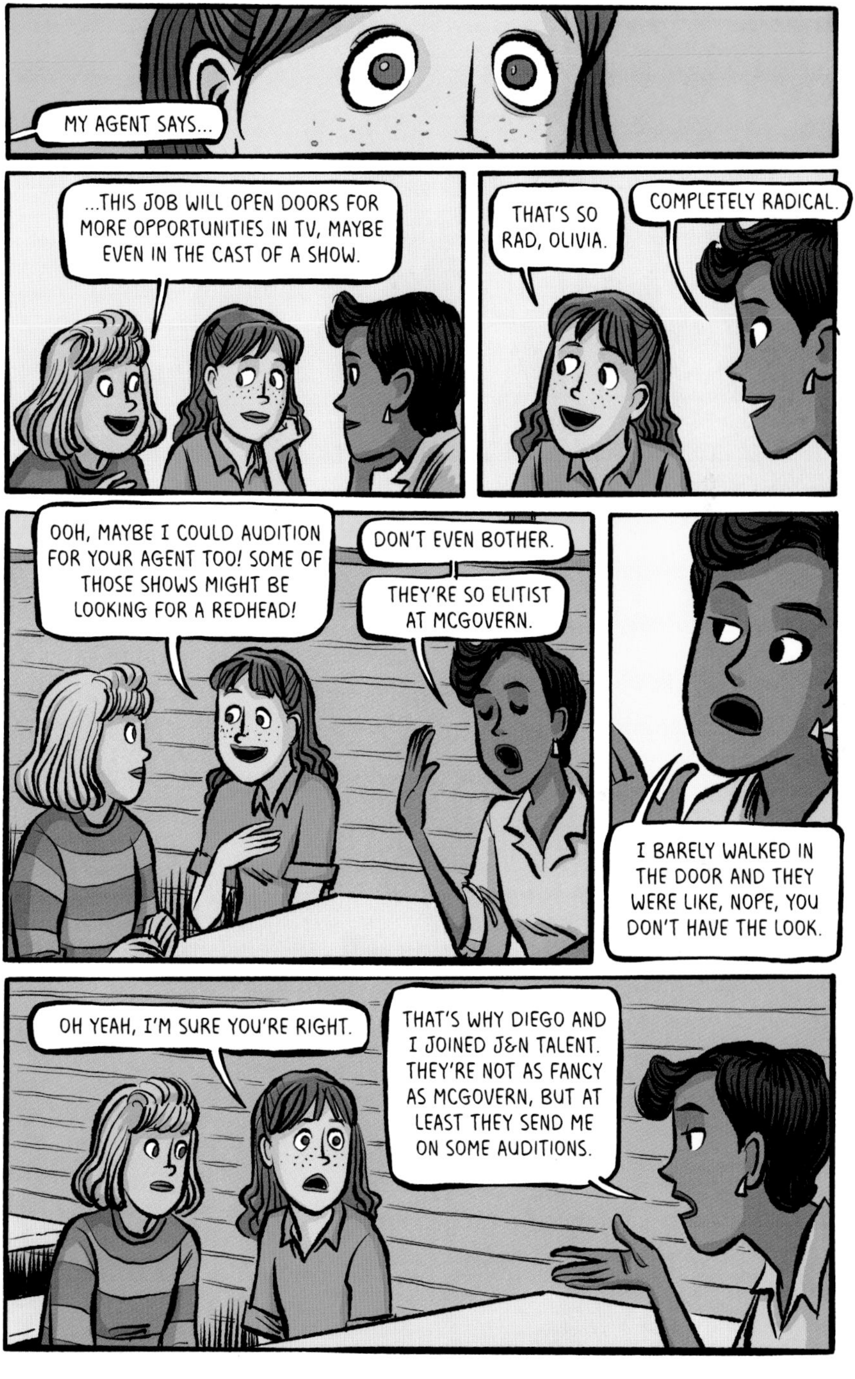
MY AGENT SAYS...
...THIS JOB WILL OPEN DOORS FOR MORE OPPORTUNITIES IN TV, MAYBE EVEN IN THE CAST OF A SHOW.
THAT'S SO RAD, OLIVIA.
COMPLETELY RADICAL.
OOH, MAYBE I COULD AUDITION FOR YOUR AGENT TOO! SOME OF THOSE SHOWS MIGHT BE LOOKING FOR A REDHEAD!
DON'T EVEN BOTHER.
THEY'RE SO ELITIST AT MCGOVERN.
I BARELY WALKED IN THE DOOR AND THEY WERE LIKE, NOPE, YOU DON'T HAVE THE LOOK.
OH YEAH, I'M SURE YOU'RE RIGHT.
THAT'S WHY DIEGO AND I JOINED J&N TALENT. THEY'RE NOT AS FANCY AS MCGOVERN, BUT AT LEAST THEY SEND ME ON SOME AUDITIONS.

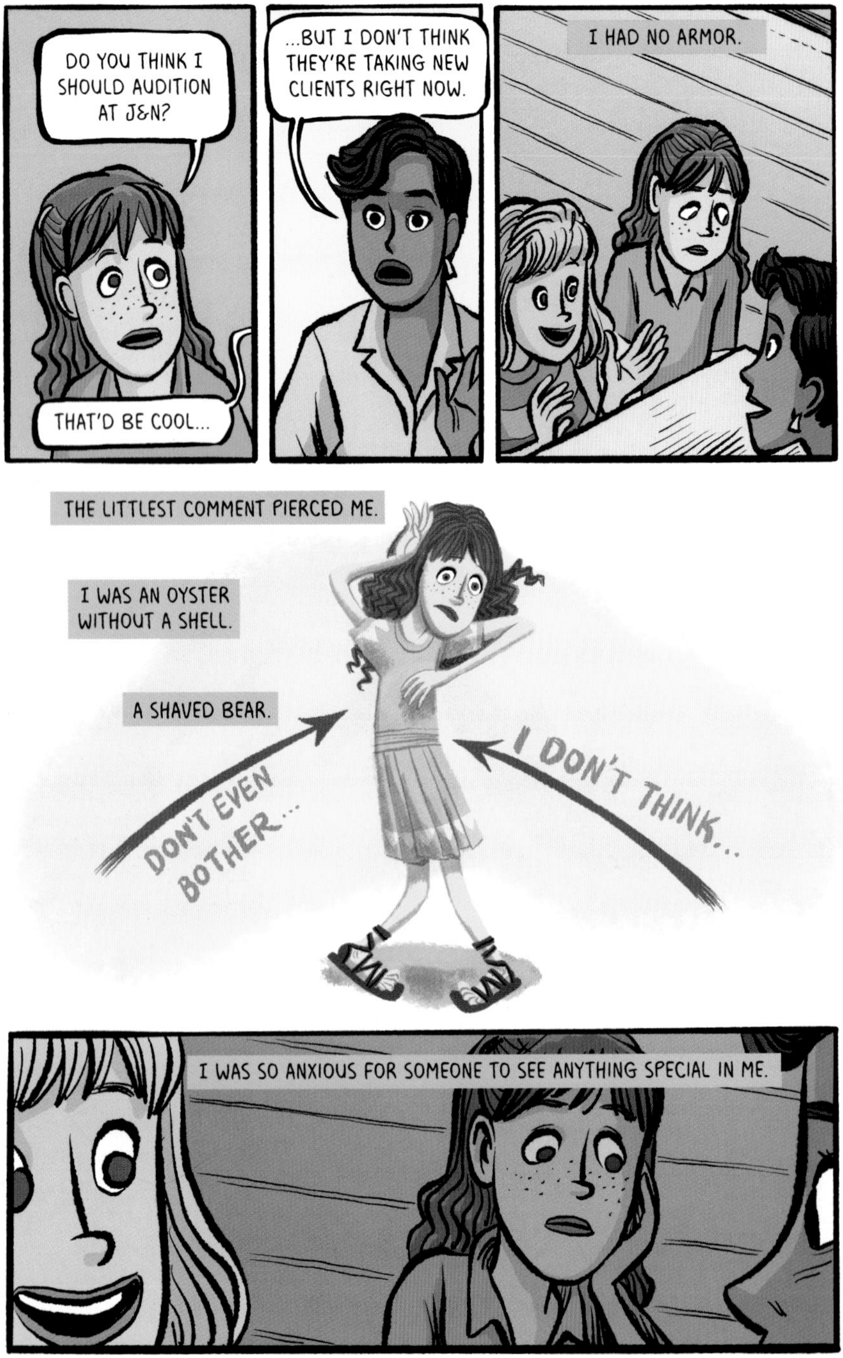
DO YOU THINK I SHOULD AUDITION AT J&N?
THAT'D BE COOL...
...BUT I DON'T THINK THEY'RE TAKING NEW CLIENTS RIGHT NOW.
I HAD NO ARMOR.
THE LITTLEST COMMENT PIERCED ME.
I WAS AN OYSTER WITHOUT A SHELL.
A SHAVED BEAR.
DON'T EVEN BOTHER...
I DON'T THINK...
I WAS SO ANXIOUS FOR SOMEONE TO SEE ANYTHING SPECIAL IN ME.

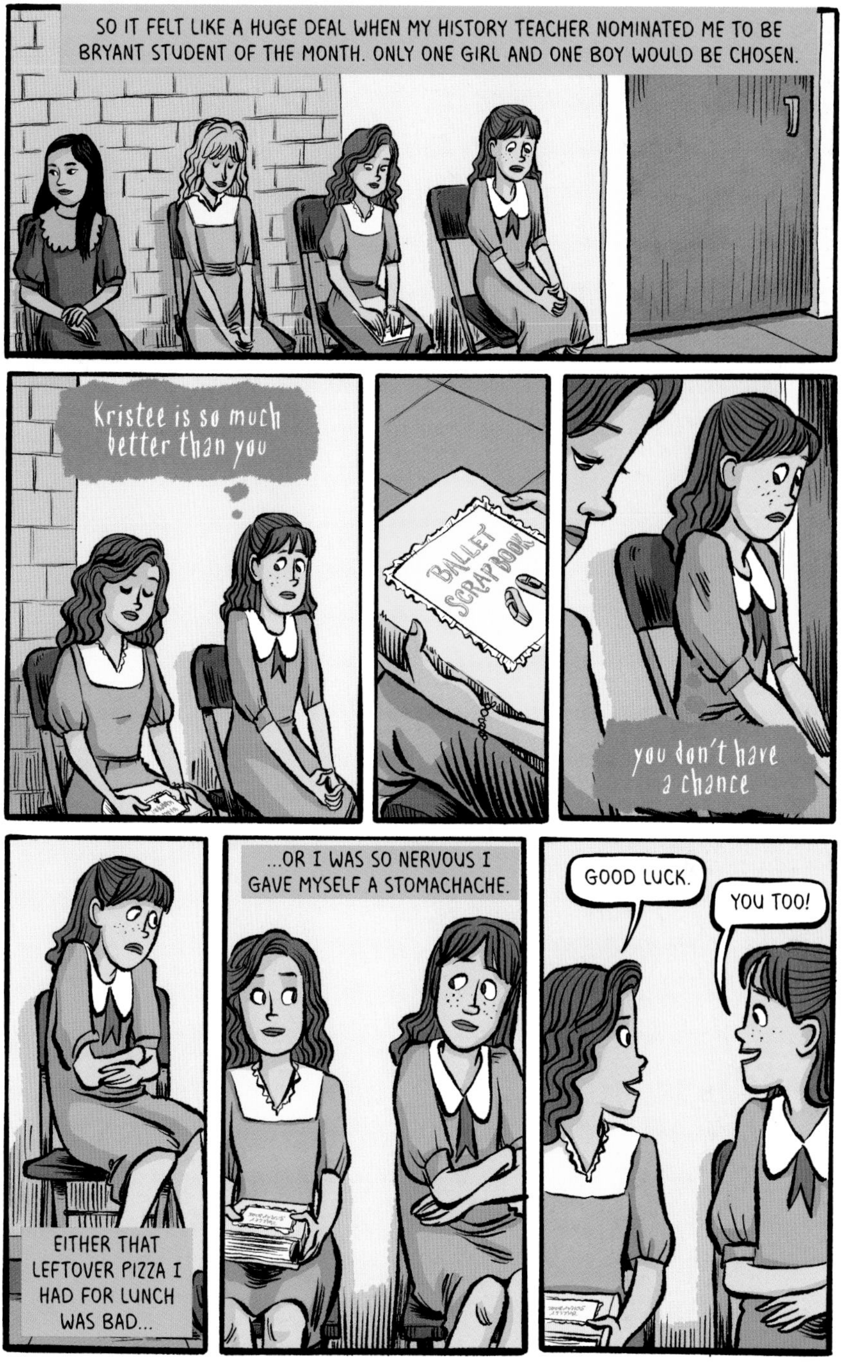
SO IT FELT LIKE A HUGE DEAL WHEN MY HISTORY TEACHER NOMINATED ME TO BE BRYANT STUDENT OF THE MONTH. ONLY ONE GIRL AND ONE BOY WOULD BE CHOSEN.
Kristee is so much better than you
BALLET SCRAPBOOK
you don't have a chance
EITHER THAT LEFTOVER PIZZA I HAD FOR LUNCH WAS BAD...
...OR I WAS SO NERVOUS I GAVE MYSELF A STOMACHACHE.
GOOD LUCK.
YOU TOO!

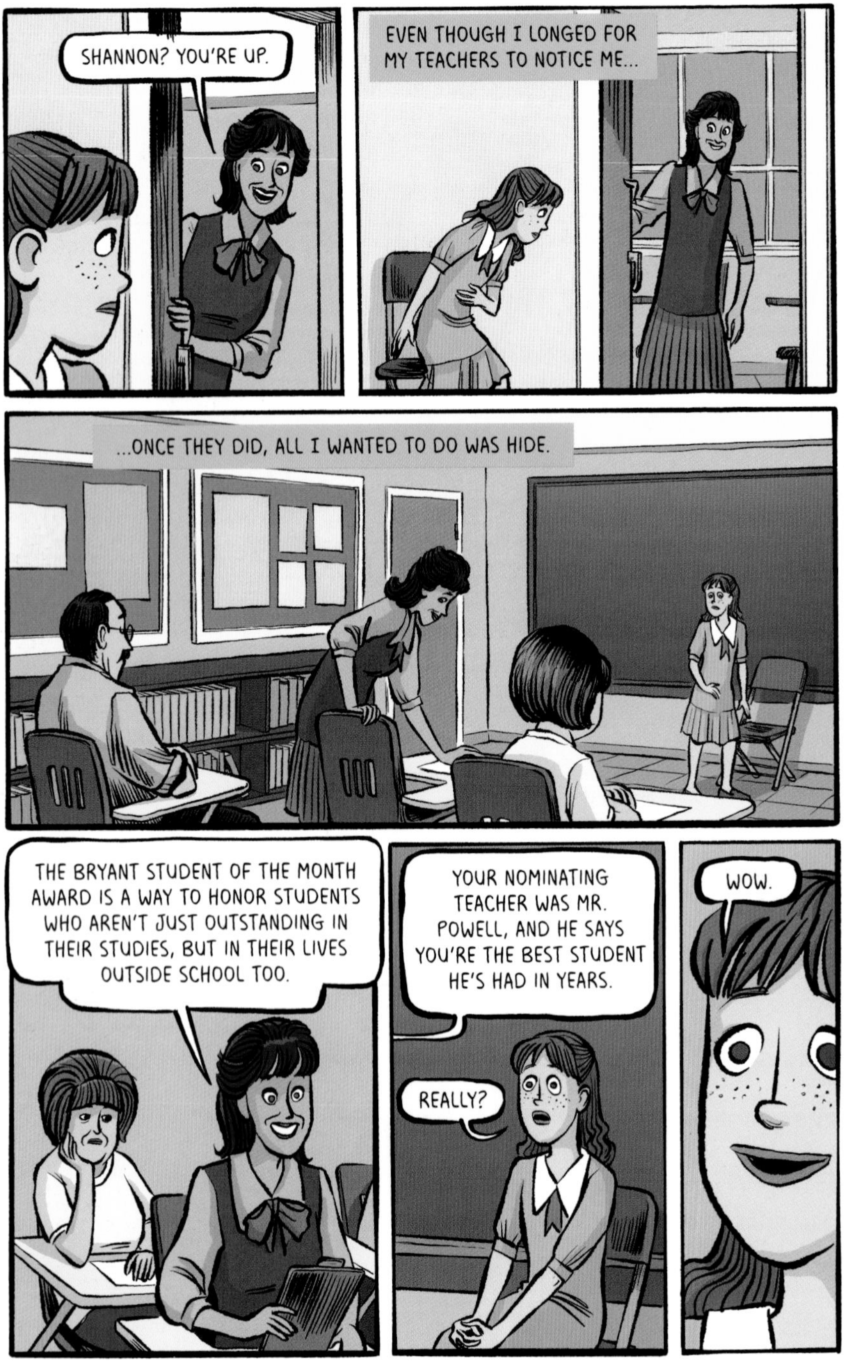
SHANNON? YOU'RE UP.
EVEN THOUGH I LONGED FOR MY TEACHERS TO NOTICE ME...
...ONCE THEY DID, ALL I WANTED TO DO WAS HIDE.
THE BRYANT STUDENT OF THE MONTH AWARD IS A WAY TO HONOR STUDENTS WHO AREN'T JUST OUTSTANDING IN THEIR STUDIES, BUT IN THEIR LIVES OUTSIDE SCHOOL TOO.
YOUR NOMINATING TEACHER WAS MR. POWELL, AND HE SAYS YOU'RE THE BEST STUDENT HE'S HAD IN YEARS.
REALLY?
WOW.

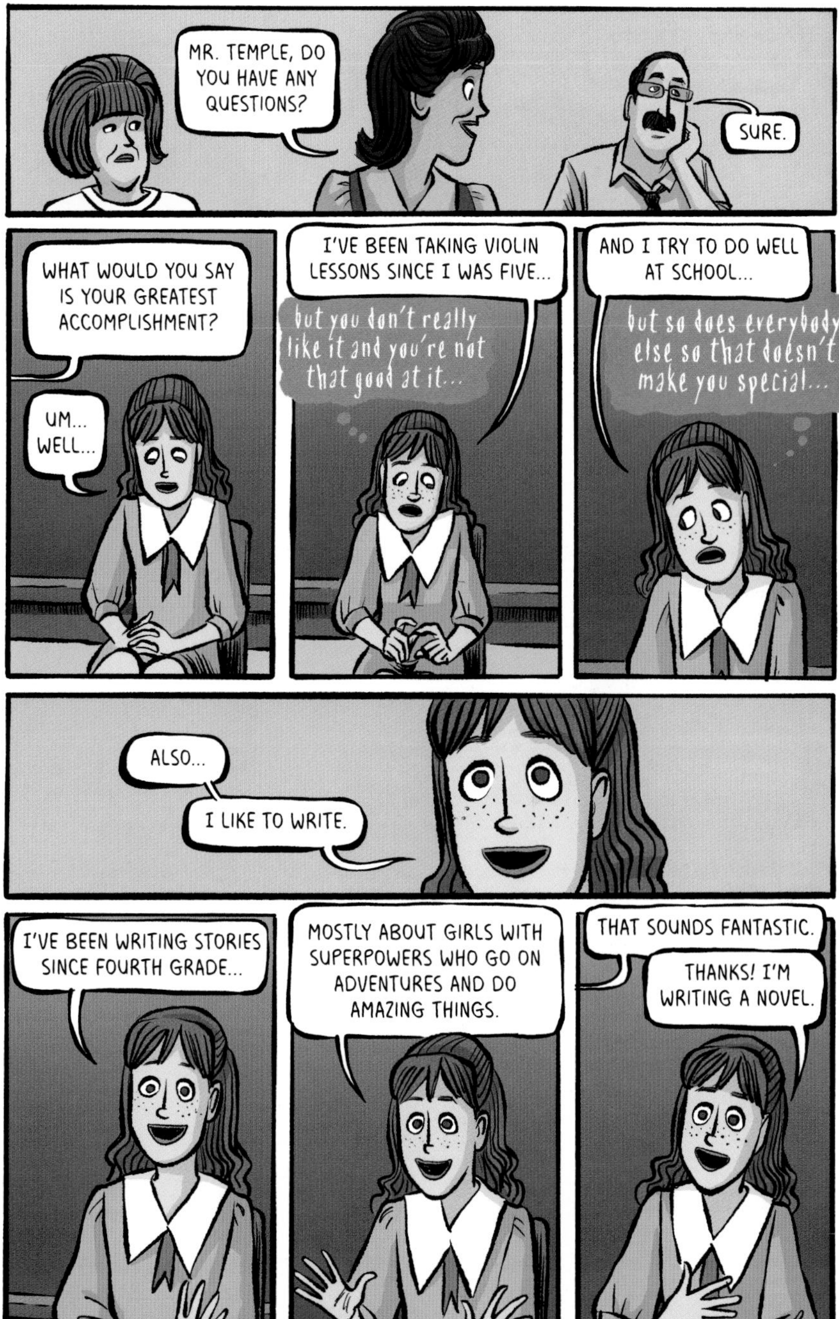
MR. TEMPLE, DO YOU HAVE ANY QUESTIONS?
SURE.
WHAT WOULD YOU SAY IS YOUR GREATEST ACCOMPLISHMENT?
UM... WELL...
I'VE BEEN TAKING VIOLIN LESSONS SINCE I WAS FIVE...
but you don't really like it and you're not that good at it...
AND I TRY TO DO WELL AT SCHOOL...
but so does everybody else so that doesn't make you special...
ALSO...
I LIKE TO WRITE.
I'VE BEEN WRITING STORIES SINCE FOURTH GRADE...
MOSTLY ABOUT GIRLS WITH SUPERPOWERS WHO GO ON ADVENTURES AND DO AMAZING THINGS.
THAT SOUNDS FANTASTIC.
THANKS! I'M WRITING A NOVEL.

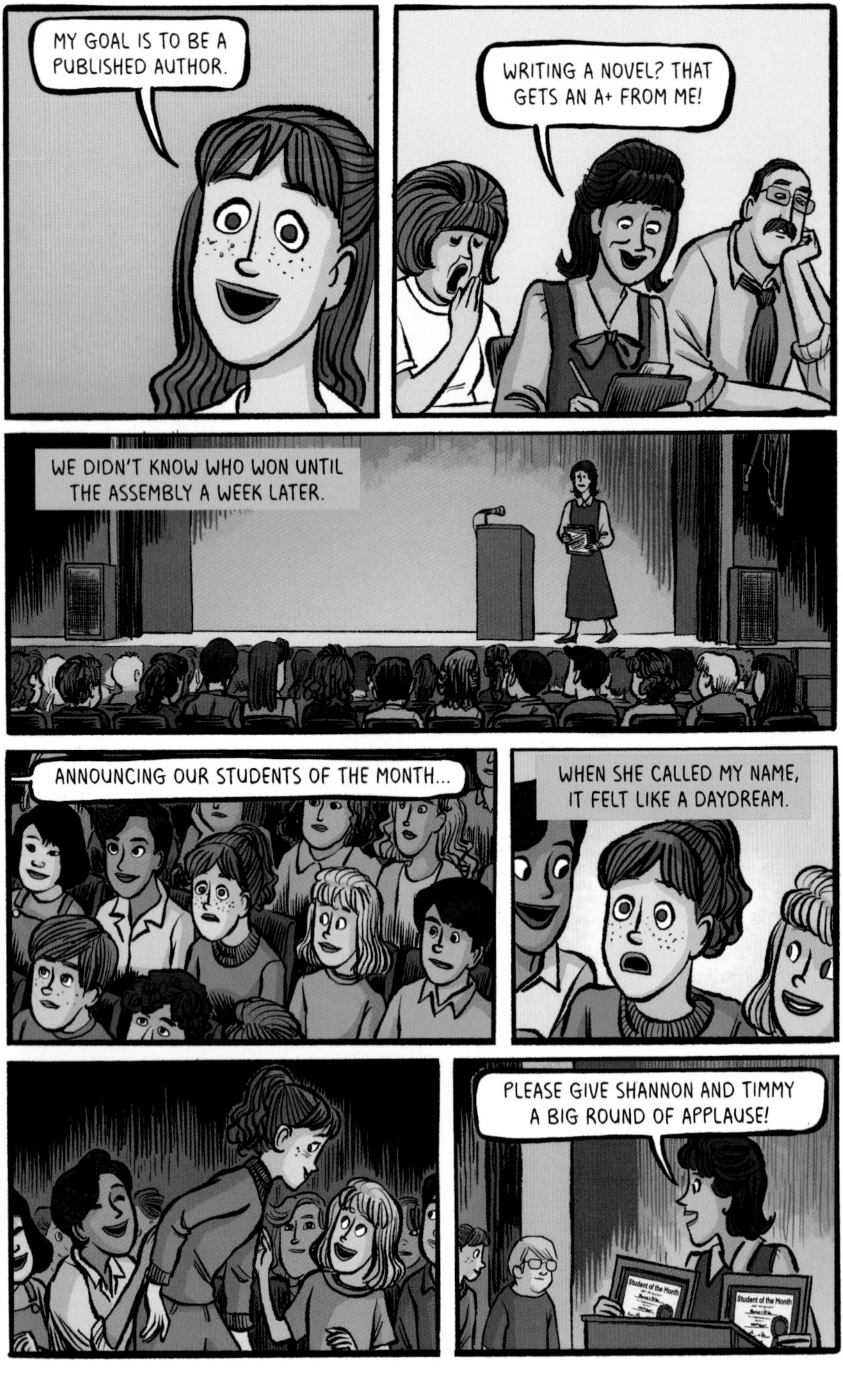
MY GOAL IS TO BE A PUBLISHED AUTHOR.
WRITING A NOVEL? THAT GETS AN A+ FROM ME!
WE DIDN'T KNOW WHO WON UNTIL THE ASSEMBLY A WEEK LATER.
ANNOUNCING OUR STUDENTS OF THE MONTH...
WHEN SHE CALLED MY NAME, IT FELT LIKE A DAYDREAM.
PLEASE GIVE SHANNON AND TIMMY A BIG ROUND OF APPLAUSE!
Student of the Month
Student of the Month

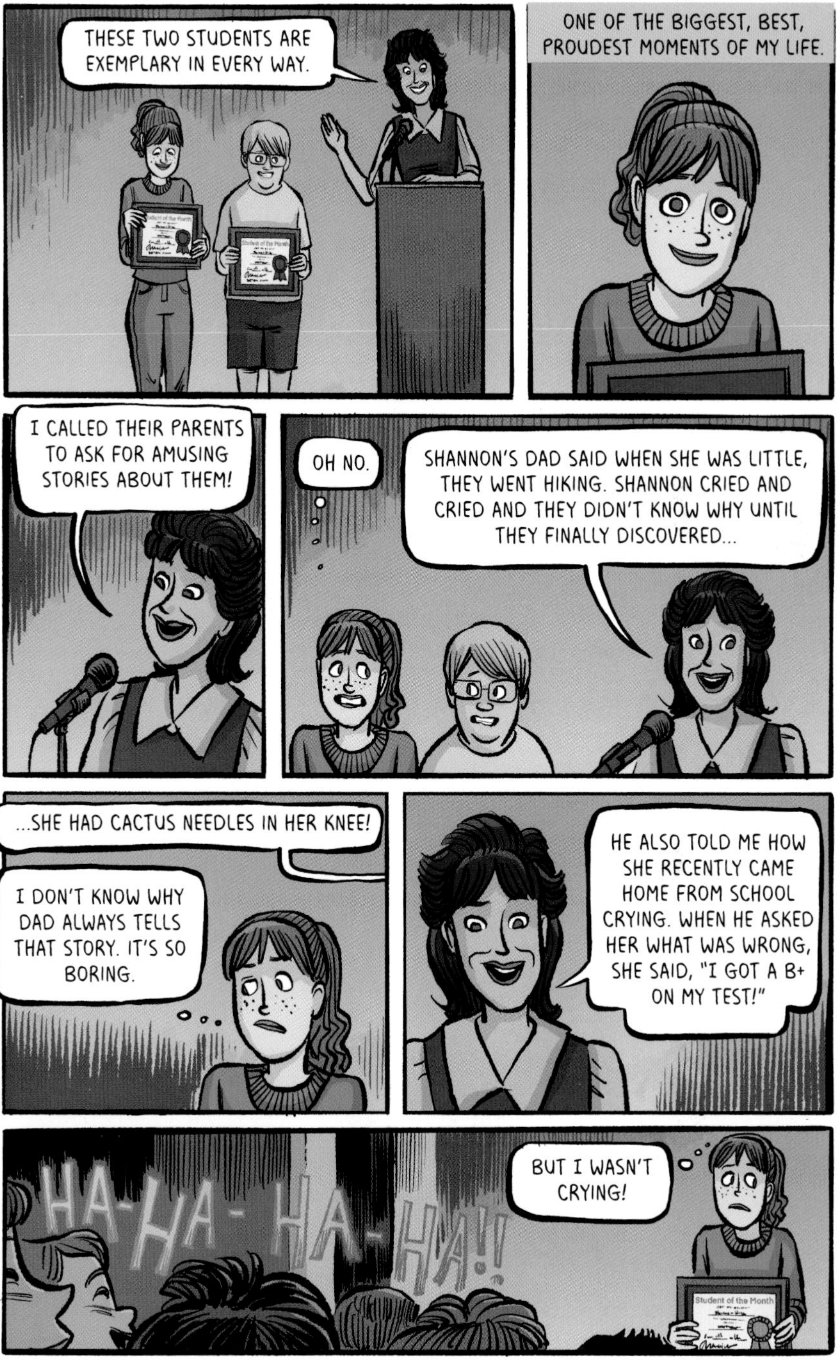
THESE TWO STUDENTS ARE EXEMPLARY IN EVERY WAY.
ONE OF THE BIGGEST, BEST, PROUDEST MOMENTS OF MY LIFE.
I CALLED THEIR PARENTS TO ASK FOR AMUSING STORIES ABOUT THEM!
OH NO.
SHANNON'S DAD SAID WHEN SHE WAS LITTLE, THEY WENT HIKING. SHANNON CRIED AND CRIED AND THEY DIDN'T KNOW WHY UNTIL THEY FINALLY DISCOVERED...
...SHE HAD CACTUS NEEDLES IN HER KNEE!
I DON'T KNOW WHY DAD ALWAYS TELLS THAT STORY. IT'S SO BORING.
HE ALSO TOLD ME HOW SHE RECENTLY CAME HOME FROM SCHOOL CRYING. WHEN HE ASKED HER WHAT WAS WRONG, SHE SAID, "I GOT A B+ ON MY TEST!"
HA-HA-HA-HA!!
BUT I WASN'T CRYING!
Student of the Month

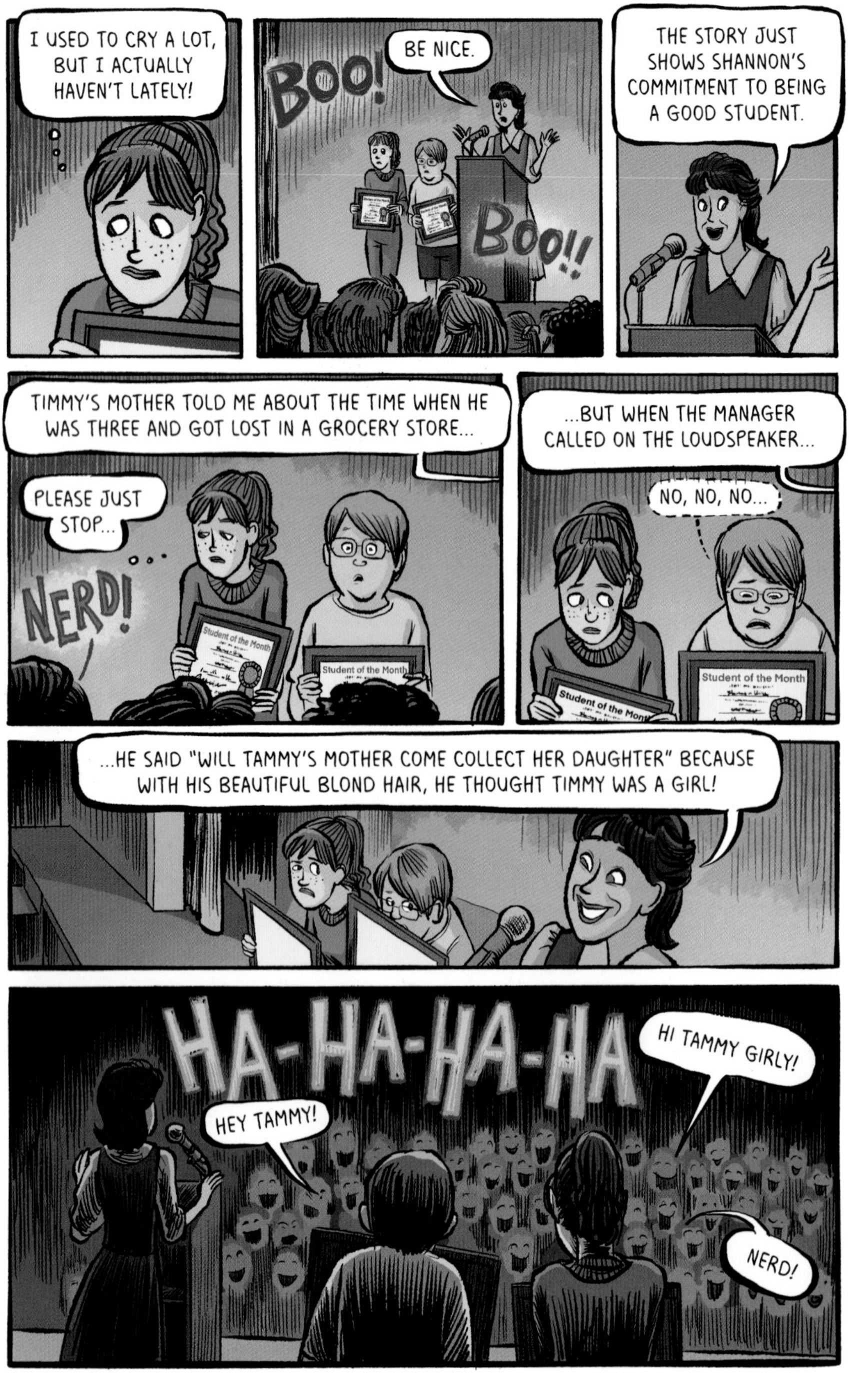
I USED TO CRY A LOT, BUT I ACTUALLY HAVEN'T LATELY!
BOO!
BE NICE.
BOO!!
THE STORY JUST SHOWS SHANNON'S COMMITMENT TO BEING A GOOD STUDENT.
TIMMY'S MOTHER TOLD ME ABOUT THE TIME WHEN HE WAS THREE AND GOT LOST IN A GROCERY STORE...
PLEASE JUST STOP...
NERD!
Student of the Month
Student of the Month
...BUT WHEN THE MANAGER CALLED ON THE LOUDSPEAKER...
NO, NO, NO...
Student of the Month
Student of the Month
...HE SAID "WILL TAMMY'S MOTHER COME COLLECT HER DAUGHTER" BECAUSE WITH HIS BEAUTIFUL BLOND HAIR, HE THOUGHT TIMMY WAS A GIRL!
HA-HA-HA-HA
HI TAMMY GIRLY!
HEY TAMMY!
NERD!

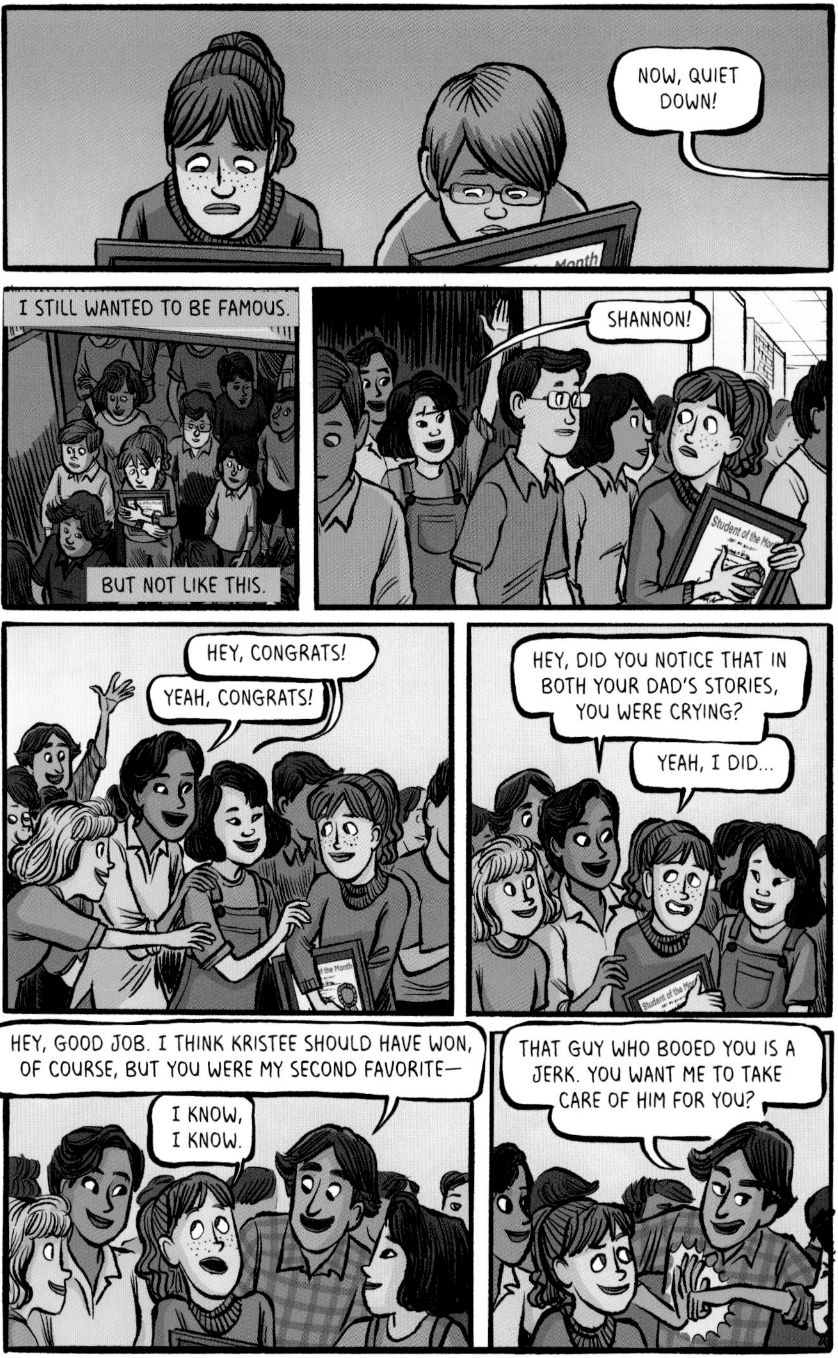
NOW, QUIET DOWN!
I STILL WANTED TO BE FAMOUS.
BUT NOT LIKE THIS.
SHANNON!
Student of the Month
HEY, CONGRATS!
YEAH, CONGRATS!
HEY, DID YOU NOTICE THAT IN BOTH YOUR DAD'S STORIES, YOU WERE CRYING?
YEAH, I DID...
HEY, GOOD JOB. I THINK KRISTEE SHOULD HAVE WON, OF COURSE, BUT YOU WERE MY SECOND FAVORITE—
I KNOW, I KNOW.
THAT GUY WHO BOOED YOU IS A JERK. YOU WANT ME TO TAKE CARE OF HIM FOR YOU?

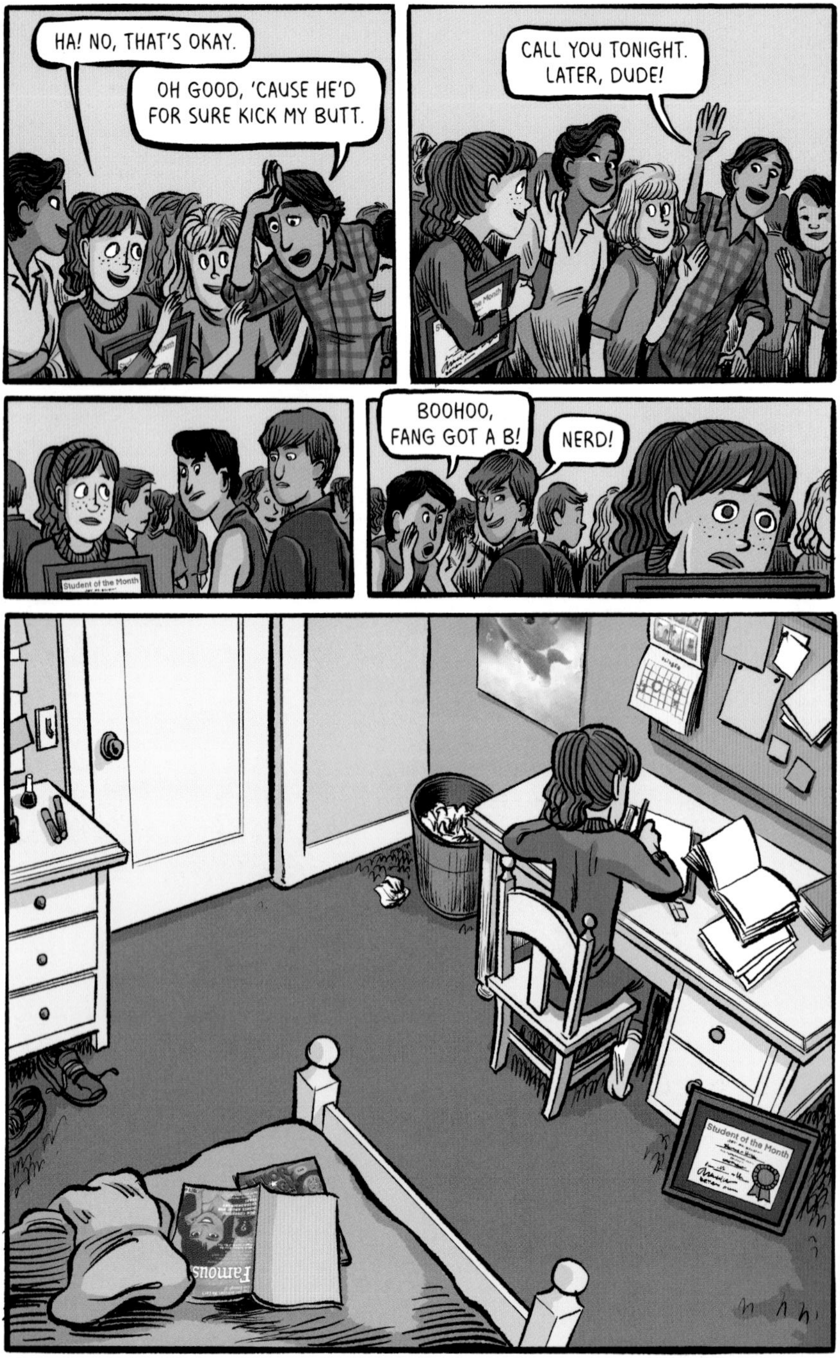
HA! NO, THAT'S OKAY.
OH GOOD, 'CAUSE HE'D FOR SURE KICK MY BUTT.
CALL YOU TONIGHT. LATER, DUDE!
Student of the Month
BOOHOO, FANG GOT A B!
NERD!
Student of the Month
Famous

EVEN THOUGH I FELT LIKE MY NOVEL WAS MY GREATEST ACCOMPLISHMENT...

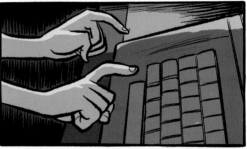

don't write a word unless it's perfect

write better if you want to be a famous author

if you mess up everyone will laugh at you

...I HADN'T BEEN ABLE TO WRITE A NEW CHAPTER FOR A LONG TIME.

INSTEAD I WORKED ON A SHORT STORY FOR CREATIVE WRITING CLASS.

The buzz of the school crowd was almost too much for the frail, fair-haired thirteen-year-old girl...

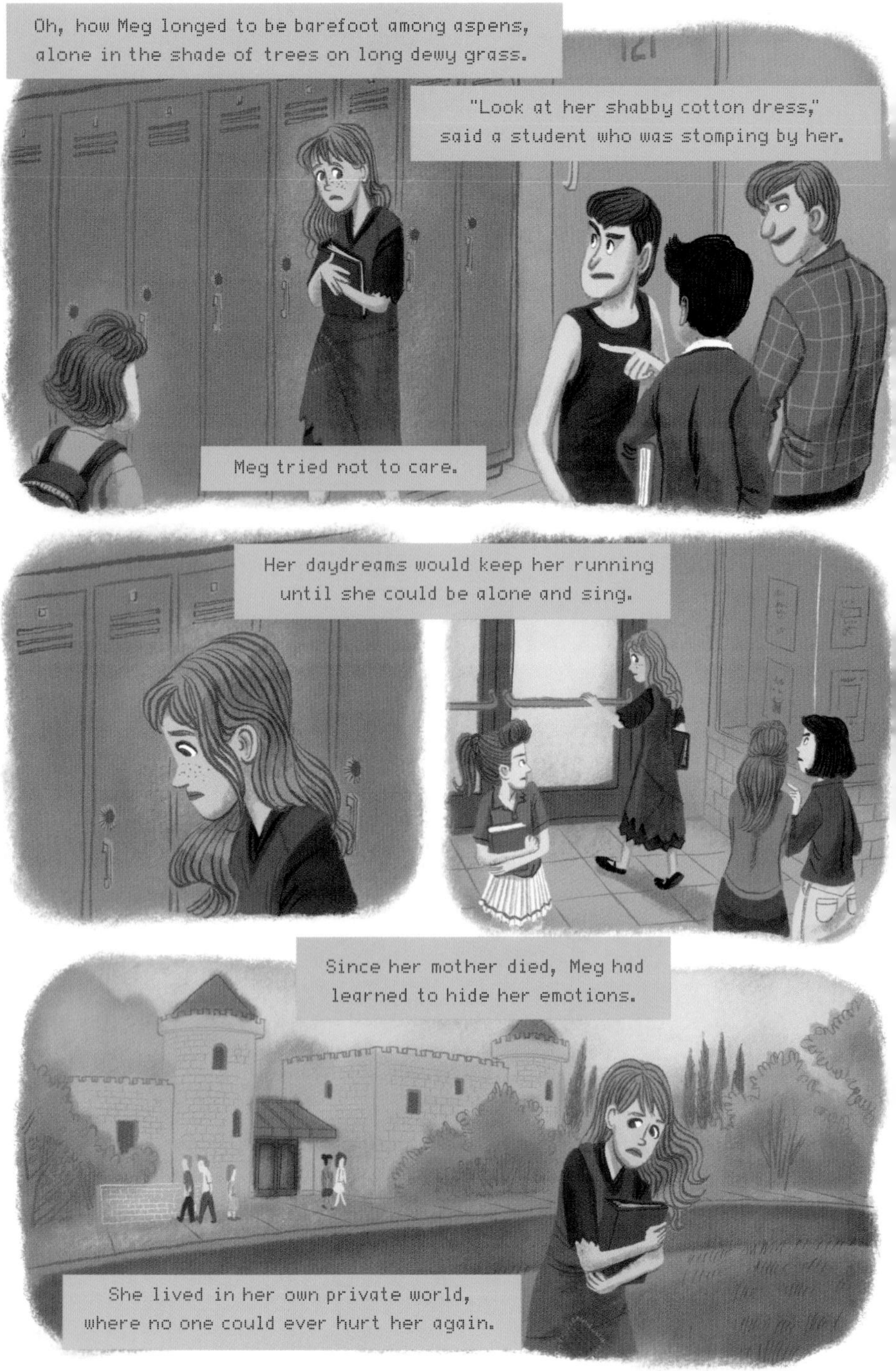
Oh, how Meg longed to be barefoot among aspens, alone in the shade of trees on long dewy grass.
"Look at her shabby cotton dress," said a student who was stomping by her.
Meg tried not to care.
Her daydreams would keep her running until she could be alone and sing.
Since her mother died, Meg had learned to hide her emotions.
She lived in her own private world, where no one could ever hurt her again.

When school was out, Meg ran as fast as she could, and then slowly, cautiously, entered a park.

She was so happy to be surrounded by aspens again, she did the only thing that she could to let out her emotions.

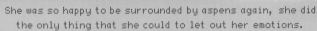

Her voice rang out above the canopy of treetops.

"I'm sorry," said the girl. "I didn't mean to intrude, but that was the most beautiful sound that I have ever heard!"

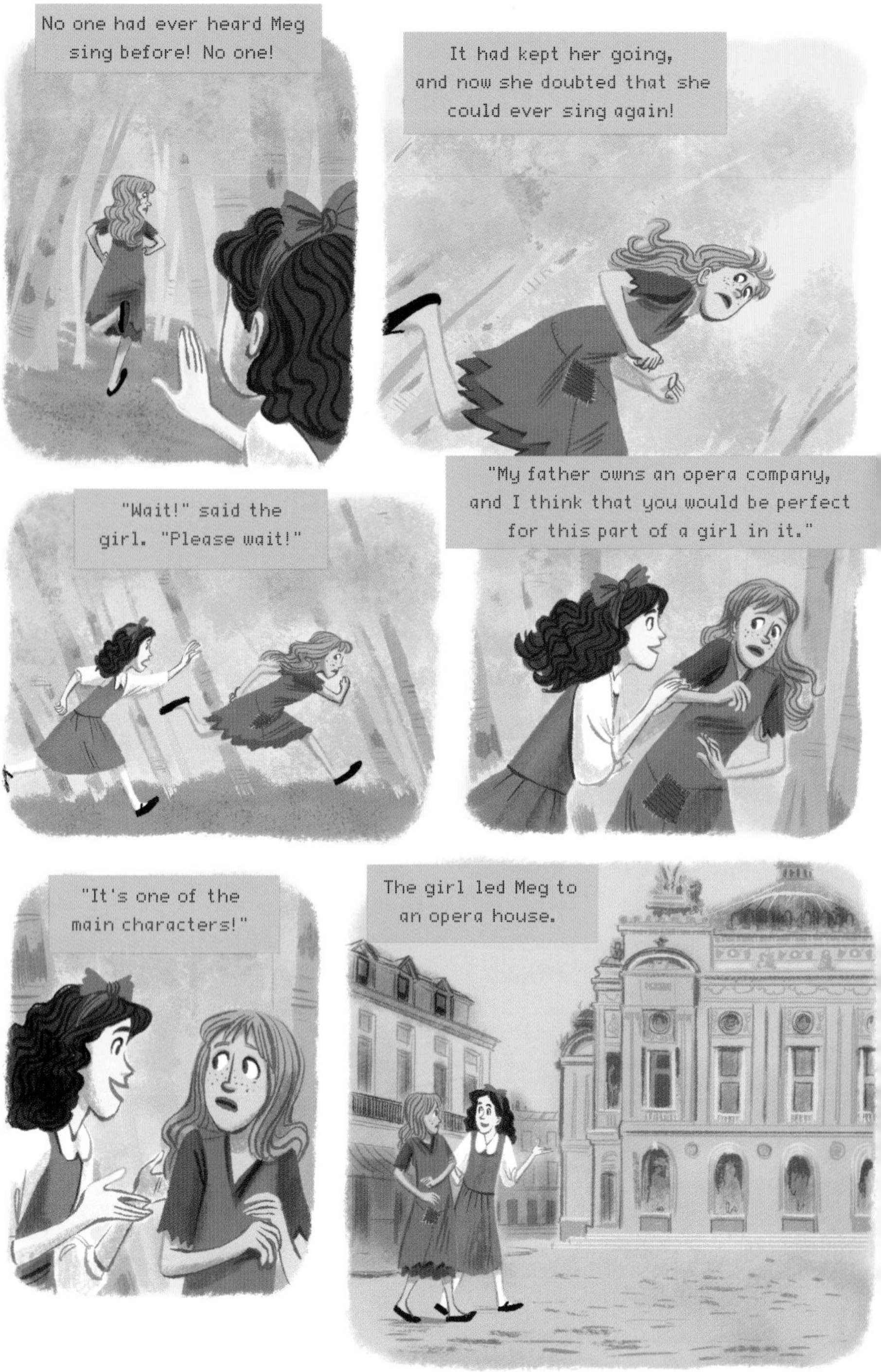
No one had ever heard Meg sing before! No one!
It had kept her going, and now she doubted that she could ever sing again!
"Wait!" said the girl. "Please wait!"
"My father owns an opera company, and I think that you would be perfect for this part of a girl in it."
"It's one of the main characters!"
The girl led Meg to an opera house.

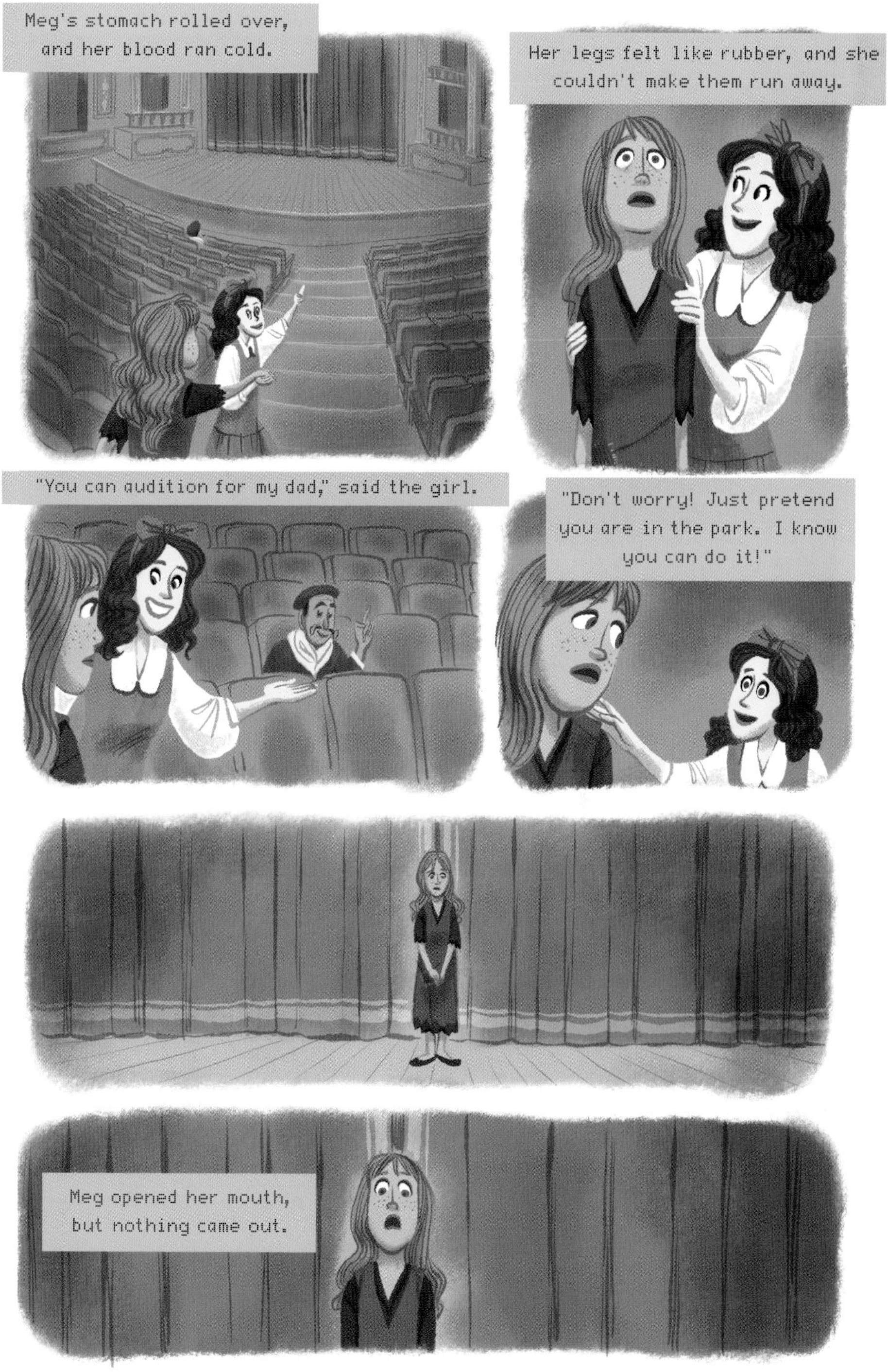
Meg's stomach rolled over, and her blood ran cold.
Her legs felt like rubber, and she couldn't make them run away.
"You can audition for my dad," said the girl.
"Don't worry! Just pretend you are in the park. I know you can do it!"
Meg opened her mouth, but nothing came out.

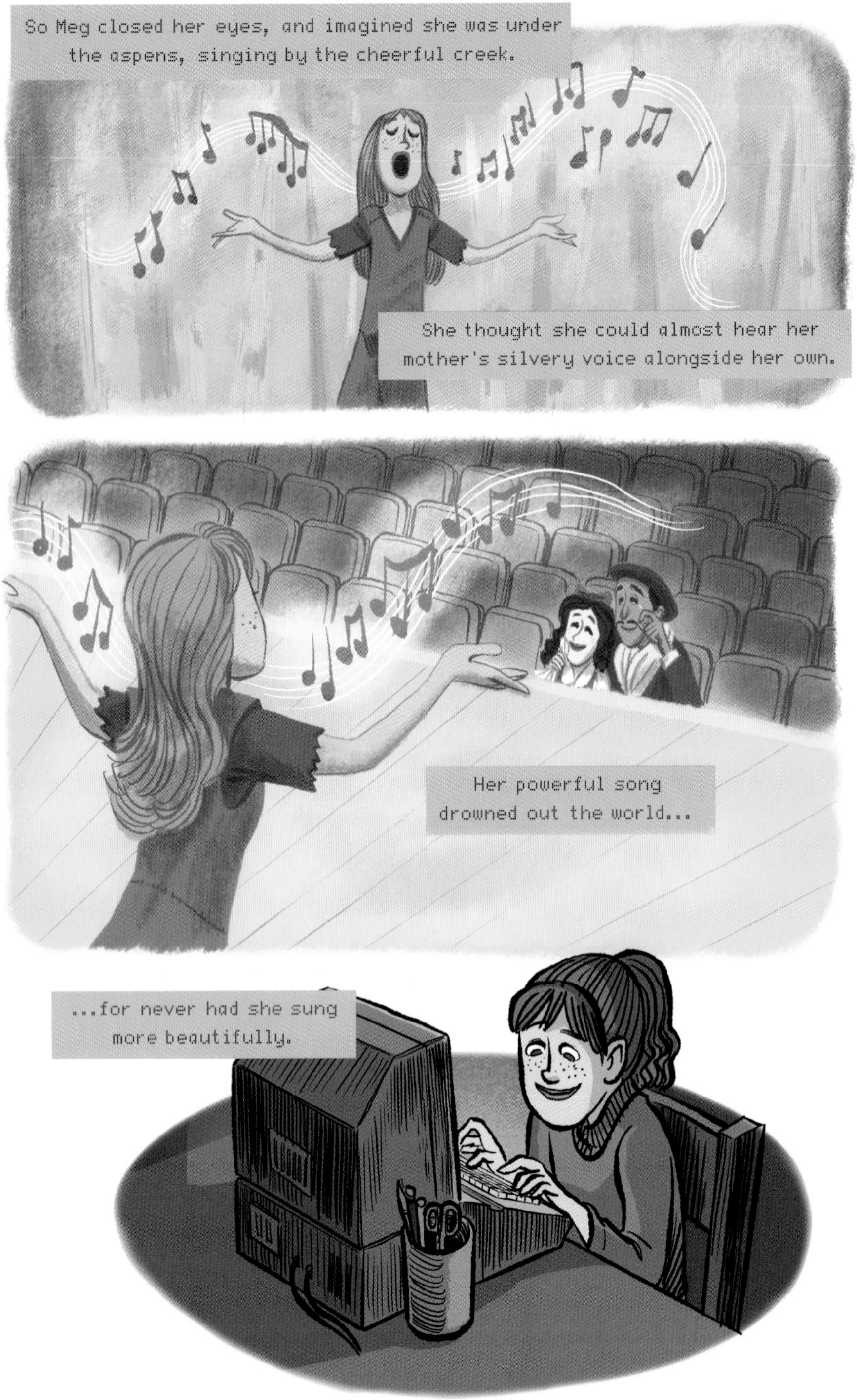
So Meg closed her eyes, and imagined she was under the aspens, singing by the cheerful creek.
She thought she could almost hear her mother's silvery voice alongside her own.
Her powerful song drowned out the world...
...for never had she sung more beautifully.

BESIDES CREATIVE WRITING, DRAMA WAS MY SAFE HAVEN.

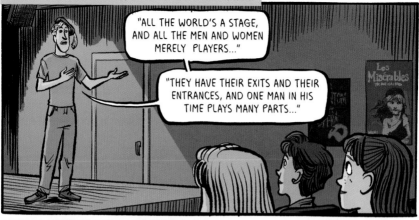

"ALL THE WORLD'S A STAGE, AND ALL THE MEN AND WOMEN MERELY PLAYERS..."

"THEY HAVE THEIR EXITS AND THEIR ENTRANCES, AND ONE MAN IN HIS TIME PLAYS MANY PARTS..."

THANK YOU, BILLY. YOU'VE PASSED YOUR SHAKESPEARE SOLILOQUY.

NEXT UP IS SHANNON DOING THE ASSIGNMENT OF A WORDLESS HUMOR SCENE.

HAPPY BIRTHDAY...

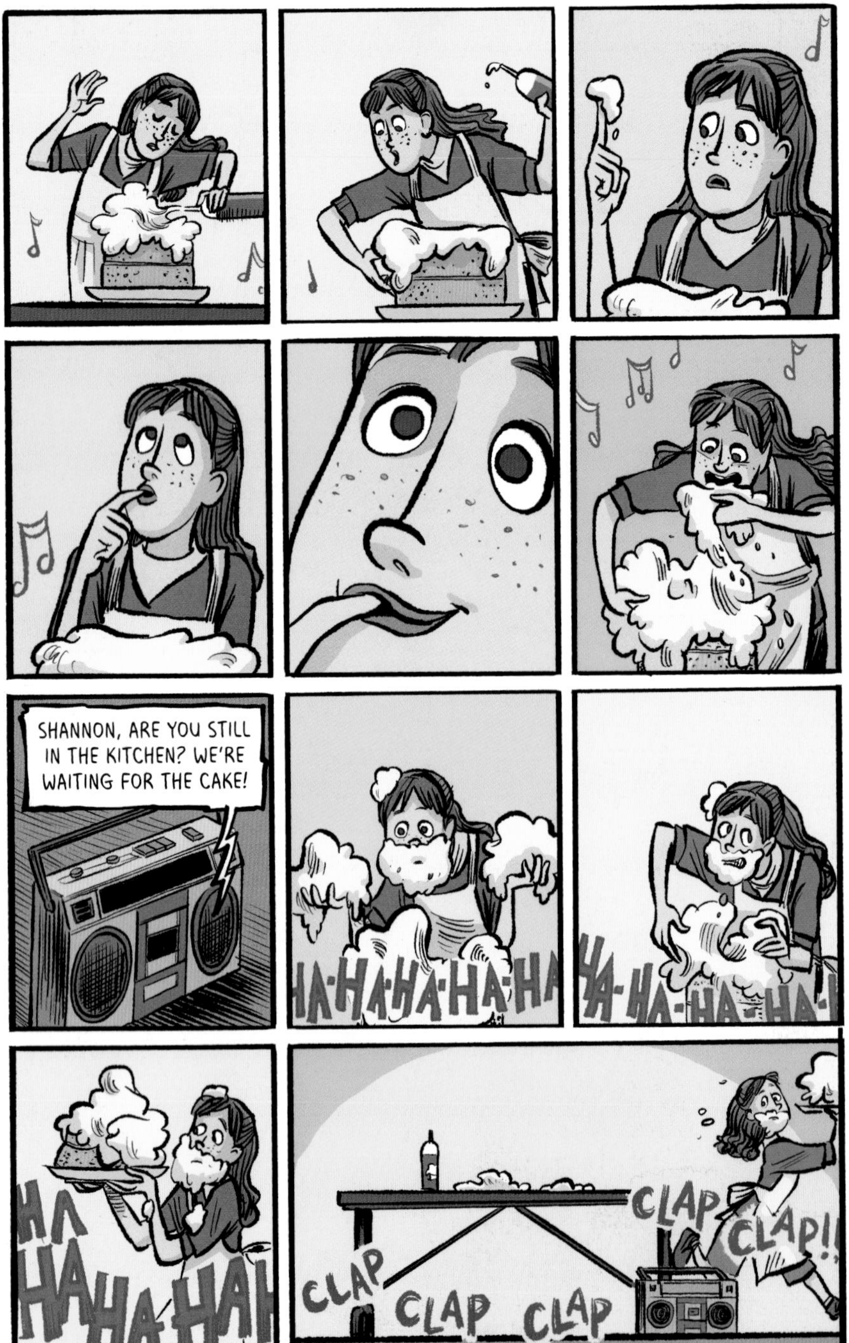
SHANNON, ARE YOU STILL IN THE KITCHEN? WE'RE WAITING FOR THE CAKE!
HA-HA-HA-HA-HA-HA
HA-HA-HA-HA-HA
HA HAHAHAHAH
CLAP
CLAP
CLAP
CLAP
CLAP!!

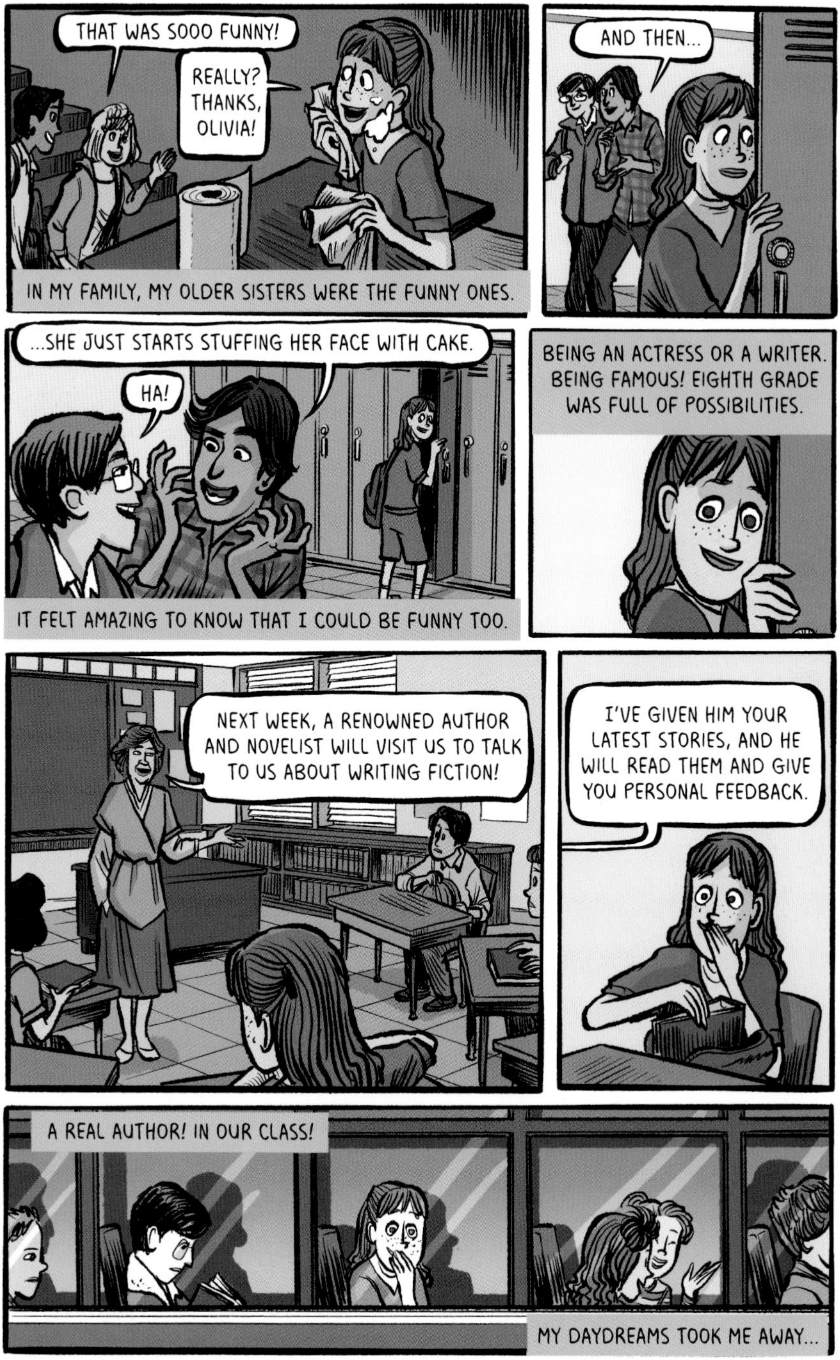
THAT WAS SOOO FUNNY!
REALLY? THANKS, OLIVIA!
IN MY FAMILY, MY OLDER SISTERS WERE THE FUNNY ONES.
AND THEN...
...SHE JUST STARTS STUFFING HER FACE WITH CAKE.
HA!
IT FELT AMAZING TO KNOW THAT I COULD BE FUNNY TOO.
BEING AN ACTRESS OR A WRITER. BEING FAMOUS! EIGHTH GRADE WAS FULL OF POSSIBILITIES.
NEXT WEEK, A RENOWNED AUTHOR AND NOVELIST WILL VISIT US TO TALK TO US ABOUT WRITING FICTION!
I'VE GIVEN HIM YOUR LATEST STORIES, AND HE WILL READ THEM AND GIVE YOU PERSONAL FEEDBACK.
A REAL AUTHOR! IN OUR CLASS!
MY DAYDREAMS TOOK ME AWAY...

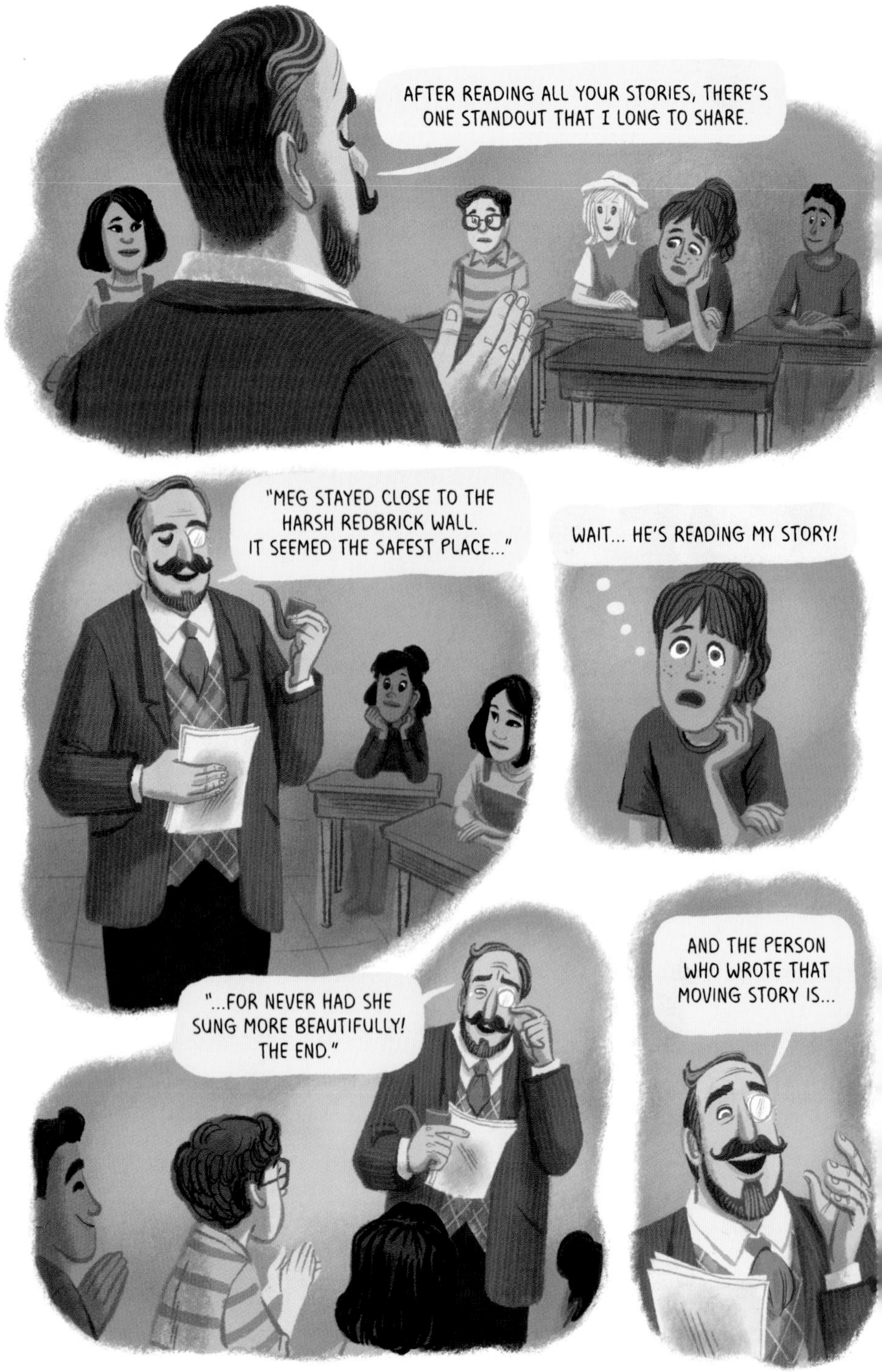
AFTER READING ALL YOUR STORIES, THERE'S ONE STANDOUT THAT I LONG TO SHARE.
"MEG STAYED CLOSE TO THE HARSH REDBRICK WALL. IT SEEMED THE SAFEST PLACE..."
WAIT... HE'S READING MY STORY!
"...FOR NEVER HAD SHE SUNG MORE BEAUTIFULLY! THE END."
AND THE PERSON WHO WROTE THAT MOVING STORY IS...

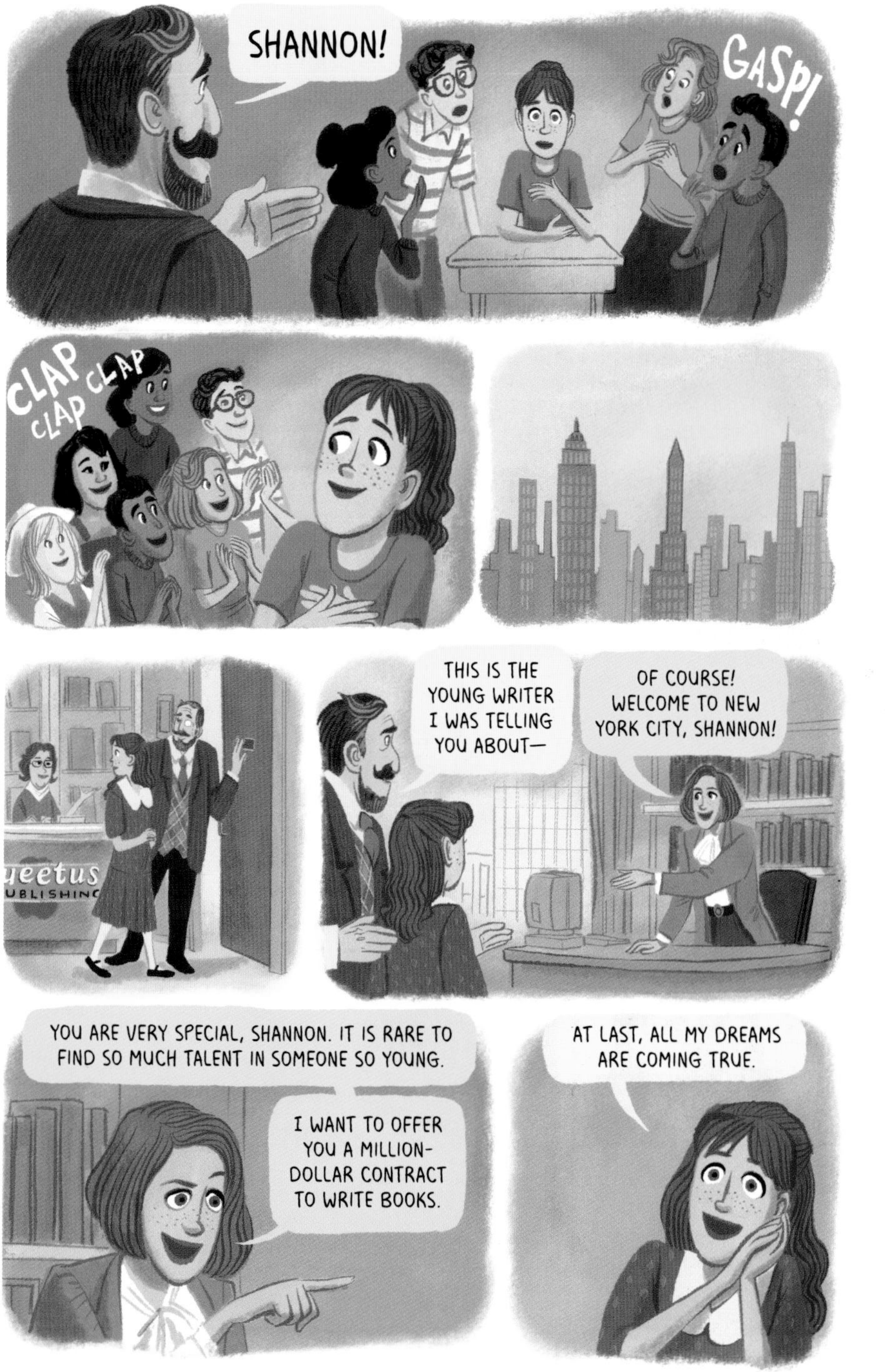
SHANNON!
GASP!
CLAP CLAP CLAP
THIS IS THE YOUNG WRITER I WAS TELLING YOU ABOUT—
OF COURSE! WELCOME TO NEW YORK CITY, SHANNON!
YOU ARE VERY SPECIAL, SHANNON. IT IS RARE TO FIND SO MUCH TALENT IN SOMEONE SO YOUNG.
I WANT TO OFFER YOU A MILLION-DOLLAR CONTRACT TO WRITE BOOKS.
AT LAST, ALL MY DREAMS ARE COMING TRUE.

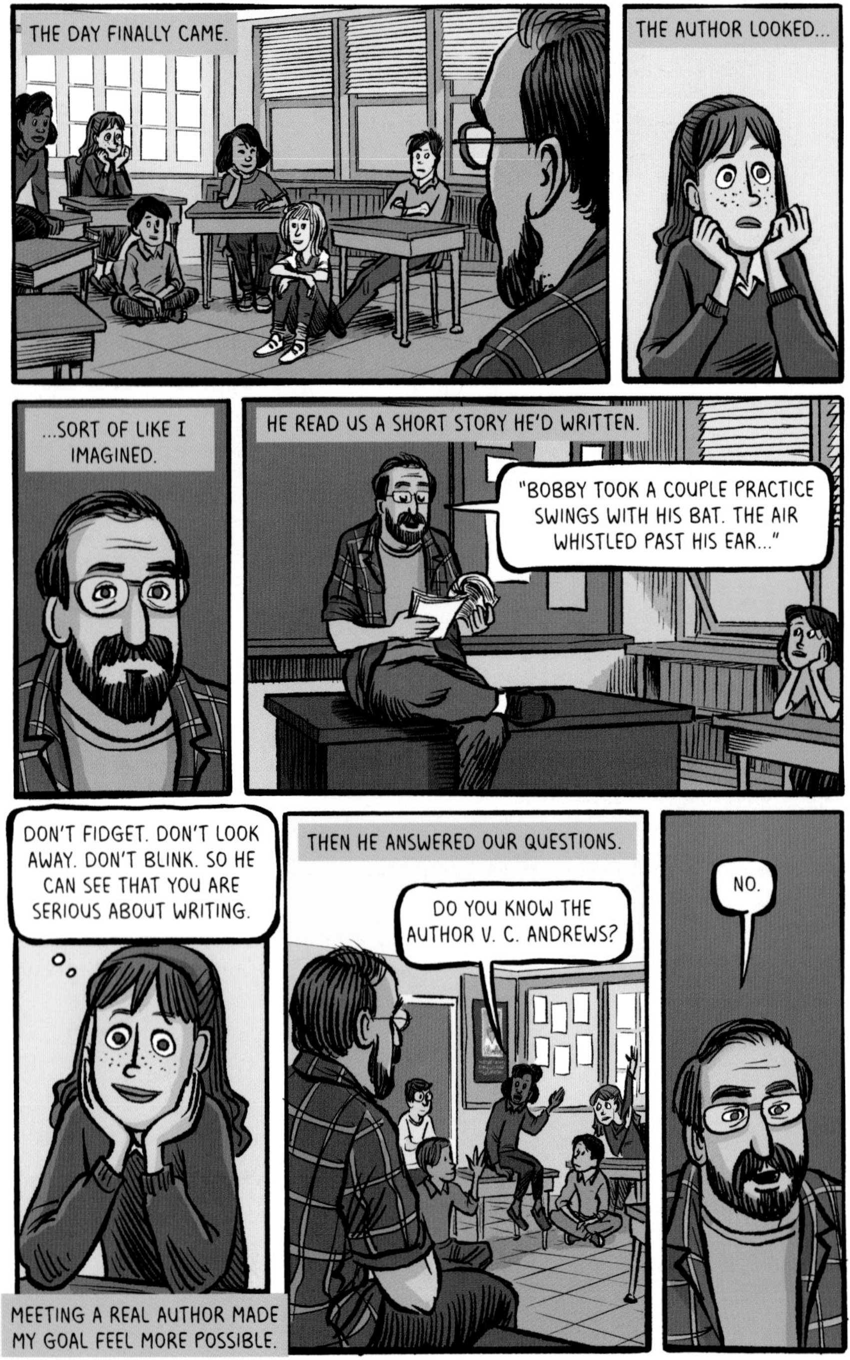
THE DAY FINALLY CAME.
THE AUTHOR LOOKED...
...SORT OF LIKE I IMAGINED.
HE READ US A SHORT STORY HE'D WRITTEN.
"BOBBY TOOK A COUPLE PRACTICE SWINGS WITH HIS BAT. THE AIR WHISTLED PAST HIS EAR..."
DON'T FIDGET. DON'T LOOK AWAY. DON'T BLINK. SO HE CAN SEE THAT YOU ARE SERIOUS ABOUT WRITING.
MEETING A REAL AUTHOR MADE MY GOAL FEEL MORE POSSIBLE.
THEN HE ANSWERED OUR QUESTIONS.
DO YOU KNOW THE AUTHOR V. C. ANDREWS?
NO.

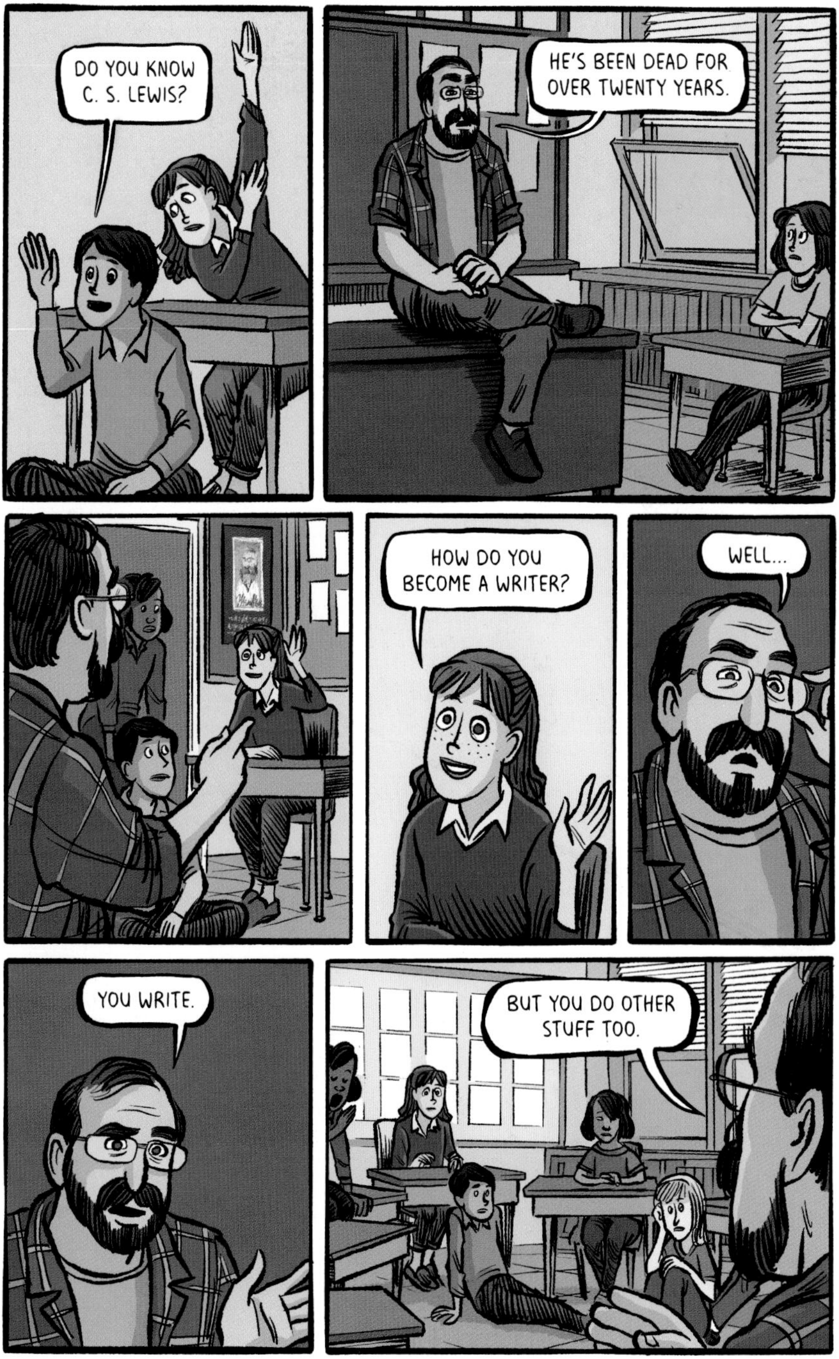
DO YOU KNOW C. S. LEWIS?
HE'S BEEN DEAD FOR OVER TWENTY YEARS.
HOW DO YOU BECOME A WRITER?
WELL...
YOU WRITE.
BUT YOU DO OTHER STUFF TOO.

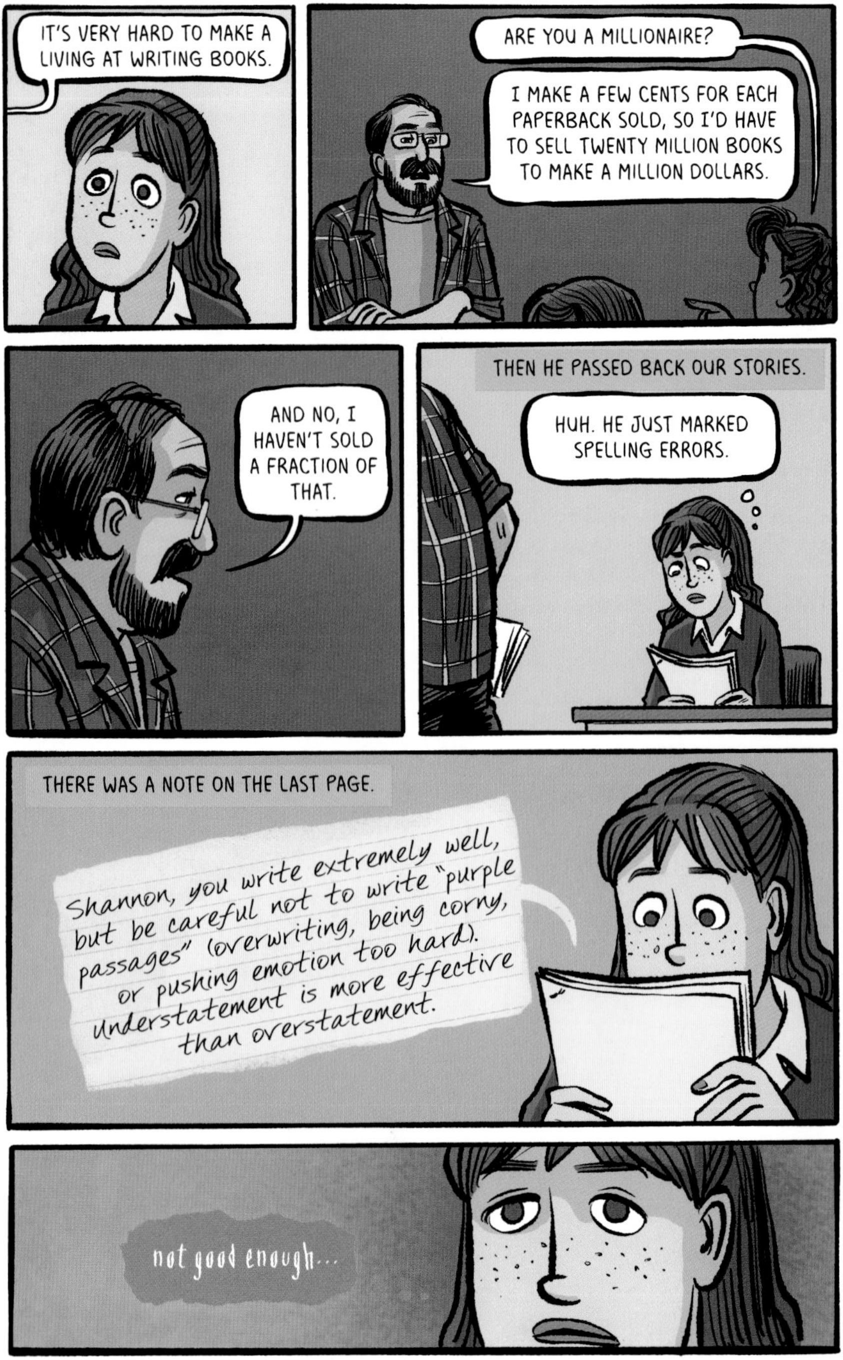
IT'S VERY HARD TO MAKE A LIVING AT WRITING BOOKS.
ARE YOU A MILLIONAIRE?
I MAKE A FEW CENTS FOR EACH PAPERBACK SOLD, SO I'D HAVE TO SELL TWENTY MILLION BOOKS TO MAKE A MILLION DOLLARS.
AND NO, I HAVEN'T SOLD A FRACTION OF THAT.
THEN HE PASSED BACK OUR STORIES.
HUH. HE JUST MARKED SPELLING ERRORS.
THERE WAS A NOTE ON THE LAST PAGE.
Shannon, you write extremely well, but be careful not to write "purple passages" (overwriting, being corny, or pushing emotion too hard). Understatement is more effective than overstatement.
not good enough...

...I KNOW I SHOULDN'T FEEL BAD.

HE DID SAY I WRITE WELL, AND IT'S NOT LIKE I EXPECTED HIM TO SAY I WAS THE BEST WRITER EVER OR ANYTHING.

IT'S JUST THAT... IT'S MY DREAM.

I USED TO WANT TO BE A WRITER TOO.

YEAH, EVERYBODY DOES. THEN WE GROW UP.

I KNEW HEATHER WASN'T TRYING TO BE MEAN. SHE ALWAYS SAID THE FIRST THING SHE THOUGHT.

AND I WAS LEARNING TO PLAY THE PART I THOUGHT I SHOULD—

A COOL GIRL WHO DIDN'T GET OFFENDED AND NEVER FELT BAD.

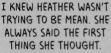

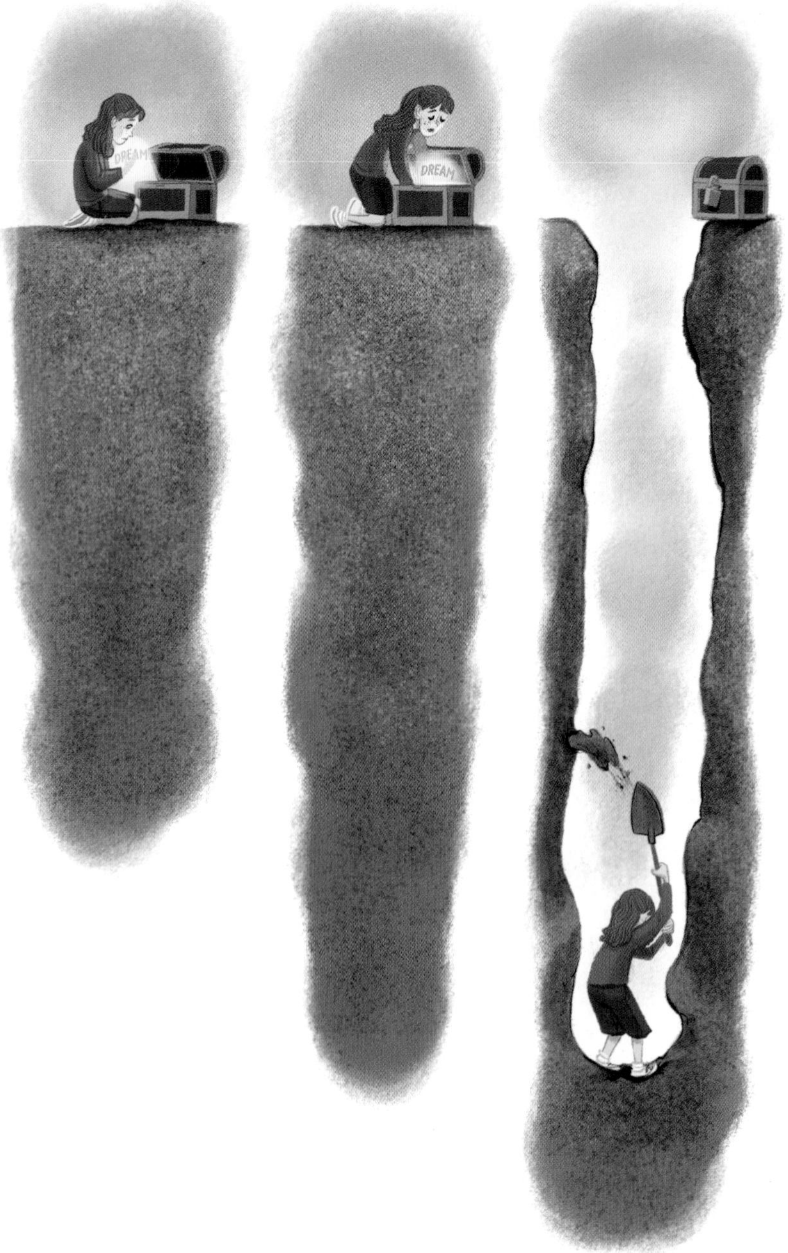
DREAM
DREAM

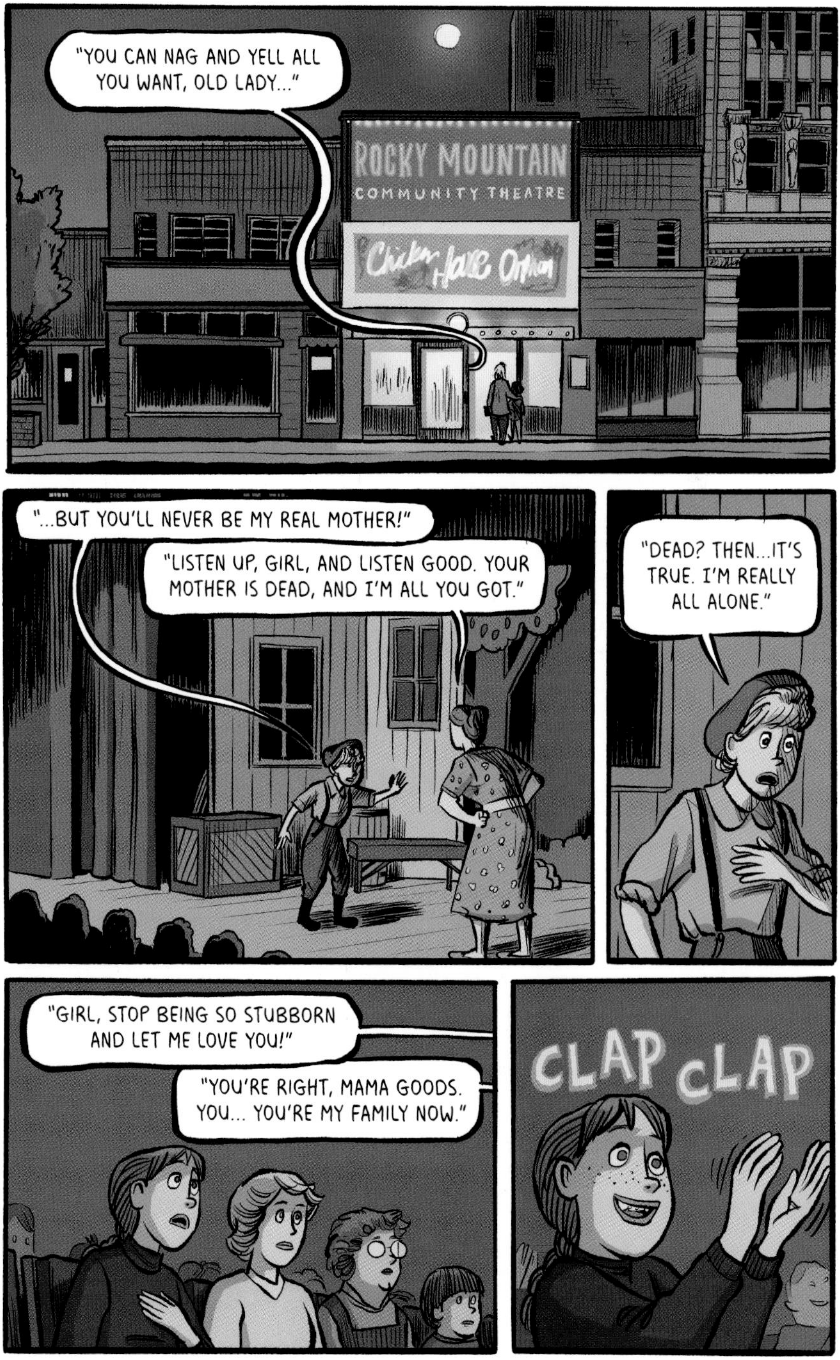
"YOU CAN NAG AND YELL ALL YOU WANT, OLD LADY..."
ROCKY MOUNTAIN
COMMUNITY THEATRE
"...BUT YOU'LL NEVER BE MY REAL MOTHER!"
"LISTEN UP, GIRL, AND LISTEN GOOD. YOUR MOTHER IS DEAD, AND I'M ALL YOU GOT."
"DEAD? THEN...IT'S TRUE. I'M REALLY ALL ALONE."
"GIRL, STOP BEING SO STUBBORN AND LET ME LOVE YOU!"
"YOU'RE RIGHT, MAMA GOODS. YOU... YOU'RE MY FAMILY NOW."
CLAP CLAP

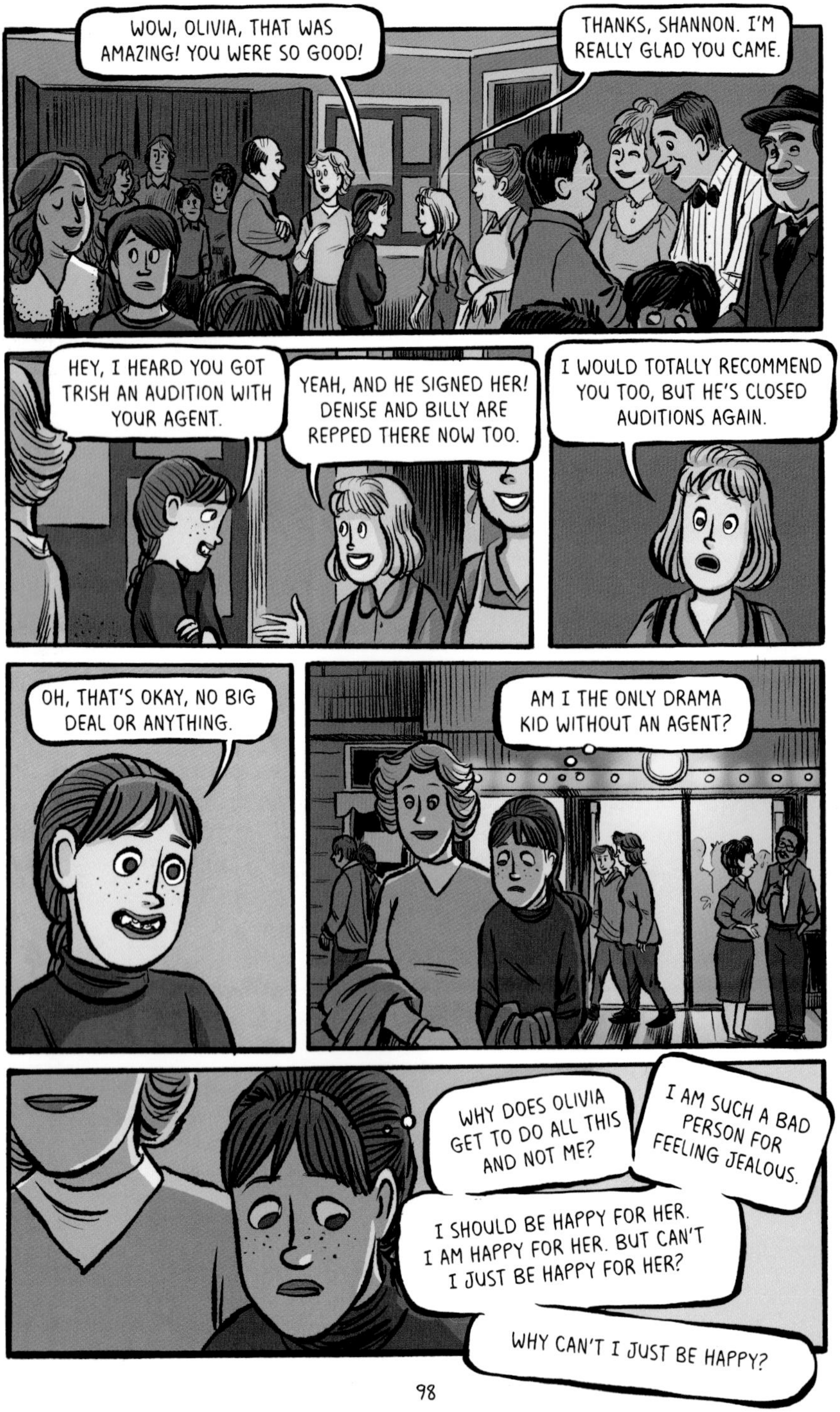
WOW, OLIVIA, THAT WAS AMAZING! YOU WERE SO GOOD!
THANKS, SHANNON. I'M REALLY GLAD YOU CAME.
HEY, I HEARD YOU GOT TRISH AN AUDITION WITH YOUR AGENT.
YEAH, AND HE SIGNED HER! DENISE AND BILLY ARE REPPED THERE NOW TOO.
I WOULD TOTALLY RECOMMEND YOU TOO, BUT HE'S CLOSED AUDITIONS AGAIN.
OH, THAT'S OKAY, NO BIG DEAL OR ANYTHING.
AM I THE ONLY DRAMA KID WITHOUT AN AGENT?
WHY DOES OLIVIA GET TO DO ALL THIS AND NOT ME?
I AM SUCH A BAD PERSON FOR FEELING JEALOUS.
I SHOULD BE HAPPY FOR HER. I AM HAPPY FOR HER. BUT CAN'T I JUST BE HAPPY FOR HER?
WHY CAN'T I JUST BE HAPPY?

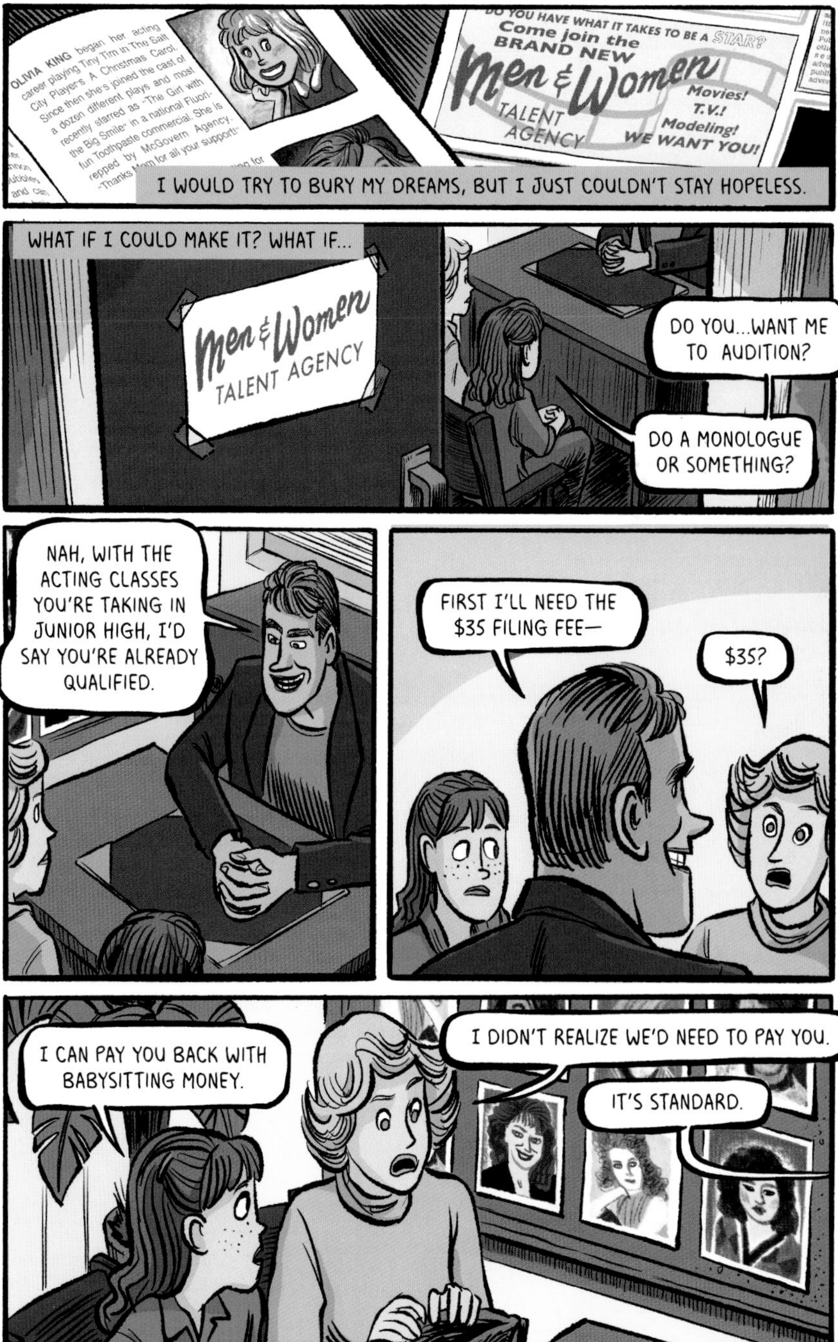
OLIVIA KING began her acting career playing Tiny Tim in The Salt City Player's A Christmas Carol. Since then she's joined the cast of a dozen different plays and most recently starred as "The Girl with the Big Smile" in a national Fluori-fun Toothpaste commercial. She is repped by McGovern Agency. -Thanks Mom for all your support!-
DO YOU HAVE WHAT IT TAKES TO BE A STAR? Come join the BRAND NEW
Men & Women TALENT AGENCY
Movies! T.V.! Modeling! WE WANT YOU!
I WOULD TRY TO BURY MY DREAMS, BUT I JUST COULDN'T STAY HOPELESS.
WHAT IF I COULD MAKE IT? WHAT IF...
Men & Women TALENT AGENCY
DO YOU...WANT ME TO AUDITION?
DO A MONOLOGUE OR SOMETHING?
NAH, WITH THE ACTING CLASSES YOU'RE TAKING IN JUNIOR HIGH, I'D SAY YOU'RE ALREADY QUALIFIED.
FIRST I'LL NEED THE $35 FILING FEE—
$35?
I CAN PAY YOU BACK WITH BABYSITTING MONEY.
I DIDN'T REALIZE WE'D NEED TO PAY YOU.
IT'S STANDARD.

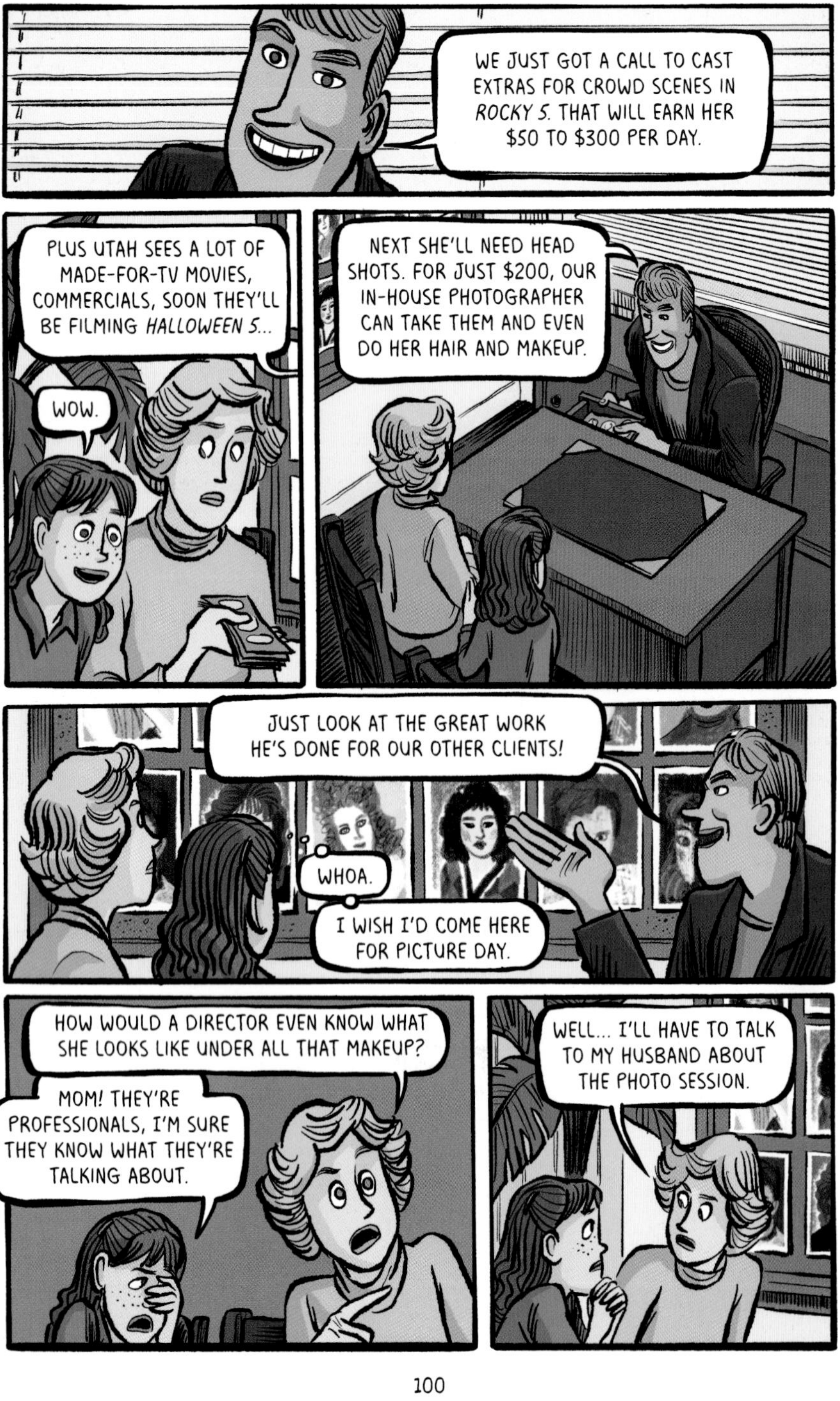
WE JUST GOT A CALL TO CAST EXTRAS FOR CROWD SCENES IN *ROCKY 5*. THAT WILL EARN HER $50 TO $300 PER DAY.
PLUS UTAH SEES A LOT OF MADE-FOR-TV MOVIES, COMMERCIALS, SOON THEY'LL BE FILMING *HALLOWEEN 5*...
WOW.
NEXT SHE'LL NEED HEAD SHOTS. FOR JUST $200, OUR IN-HOUSE PHOTOGRAPHER CAN TAKE THEM AND EVEN DO HER HAIR AND MAKEUP.
JUST LOOK AT THE GREAT WORK HE'S DONE FOR OUR OTHER CLIENTS!
WHOA.
I WISH I'D COME HERE FOR PICTURE DAY.
HOW WOULD A DIRECTOR EVEN KNOW WHAT SHE LOOKS LIKE UNDER ALL THAT MAKEUP?
MOM! THEY'RE PROFESSIONALS, I'M SURE THEY KNOW WHAT THEY'RE TALKING ABOUT.
WELL... I'LL HAVE TO TALK TO MY HUSBAND ABOUT THE PHOTO SESSION.

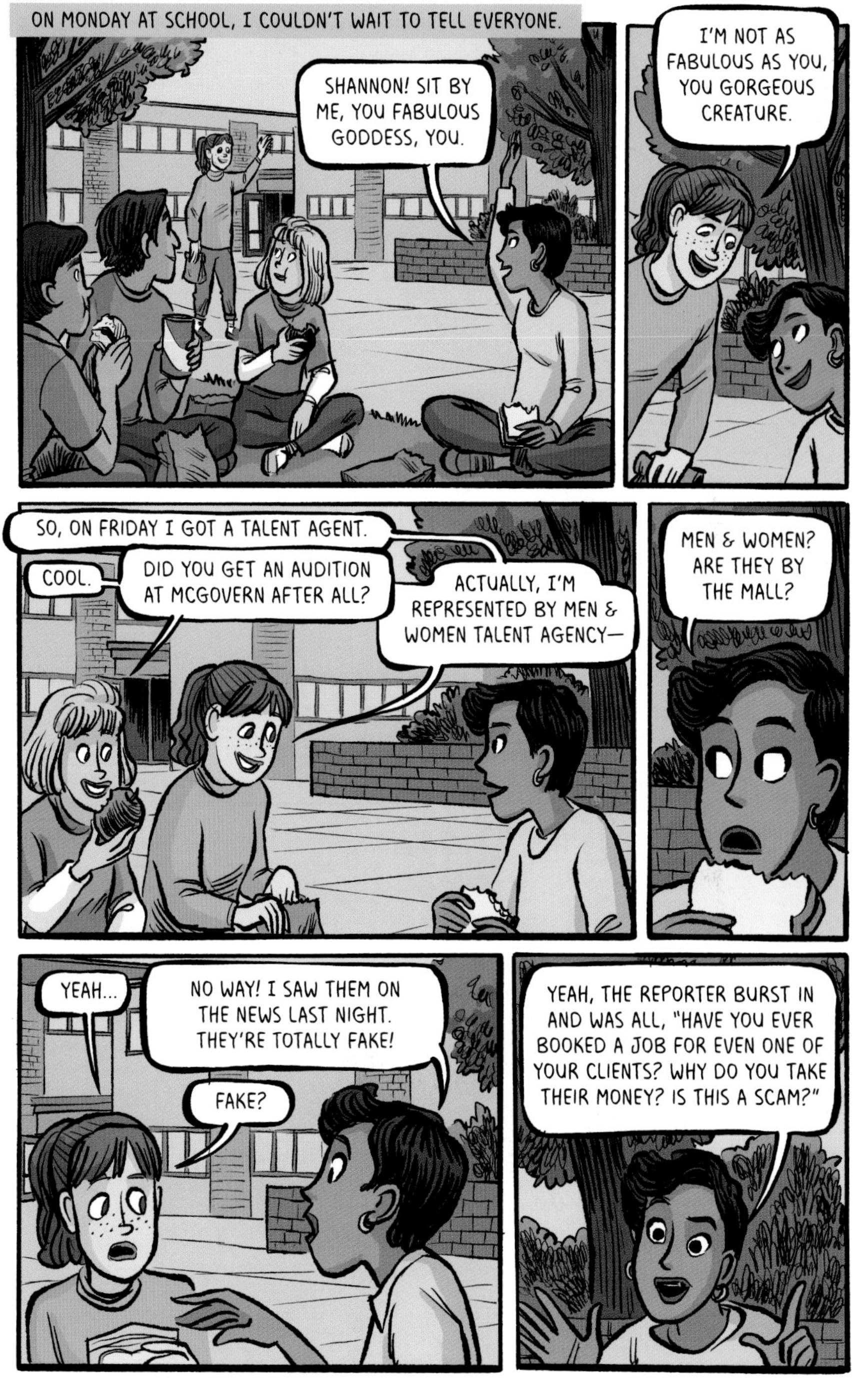
ON MONDAY AT SCHOOL, I COULDN'T WAIT TO TELL EVERYONE.
SHANNON! SIT BY ME, YOU FABULOUS GODDESS, YOU.
I'M NOT AS FABULOUS AS YOU, YOU GORGEOUS CREATURE.
SO, ON FRIDAY I GOT A TALENT AGENT.
COOL.
DID YOU GET AN AUDITION AT MCGOVERN AFTER ALL?
ACTUALLY, I'M REPRESENTED BY MEN & WOMEN TALENT AGENCY—
MEN & WOMEN? ARE THEY BY THE MALL?
YEAH...
NO WAY! I SAW THEM ON THE NEWS LAST NIGHT. THEY'RE TOTALLY FAKE!
FAKE?
YEAH, THE REPORTER BURST IN AND WAS ALL, "HAVE YOU EVER BOOKED A JOB FOR EVEN ONE OF YOUR CLIENTS? WHY DO YOU TAKE THEIR MONEY? IS THIS A SCAM?"

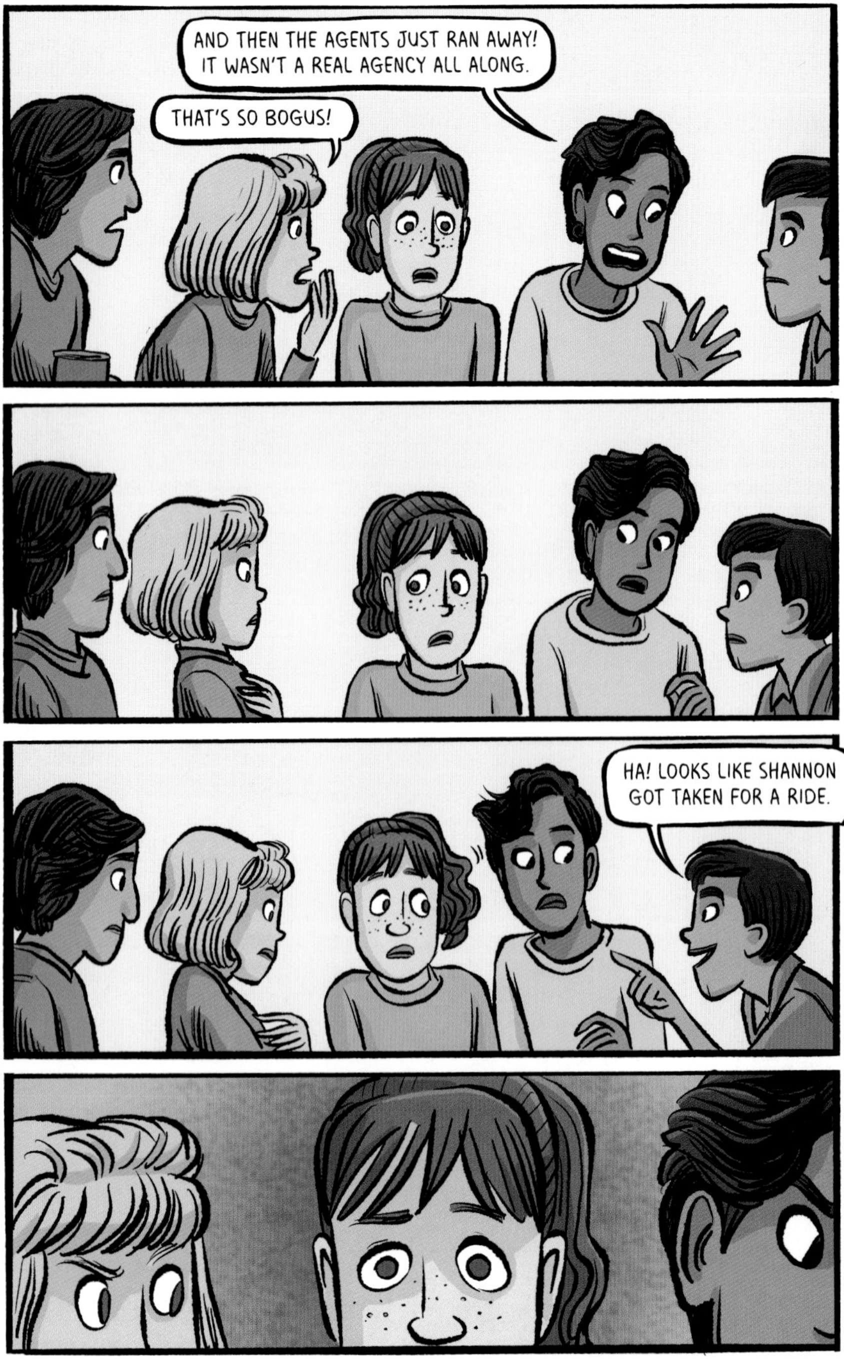
AND THEN THE AGENTS JUST RAN AWAY! IT WASN'T A REAL AGENCY ALL ALONG.
THAT'S SO BOGUS!
HA! LOOKS LIKE SHANNON GOT TAKEN FOR A RIDE.

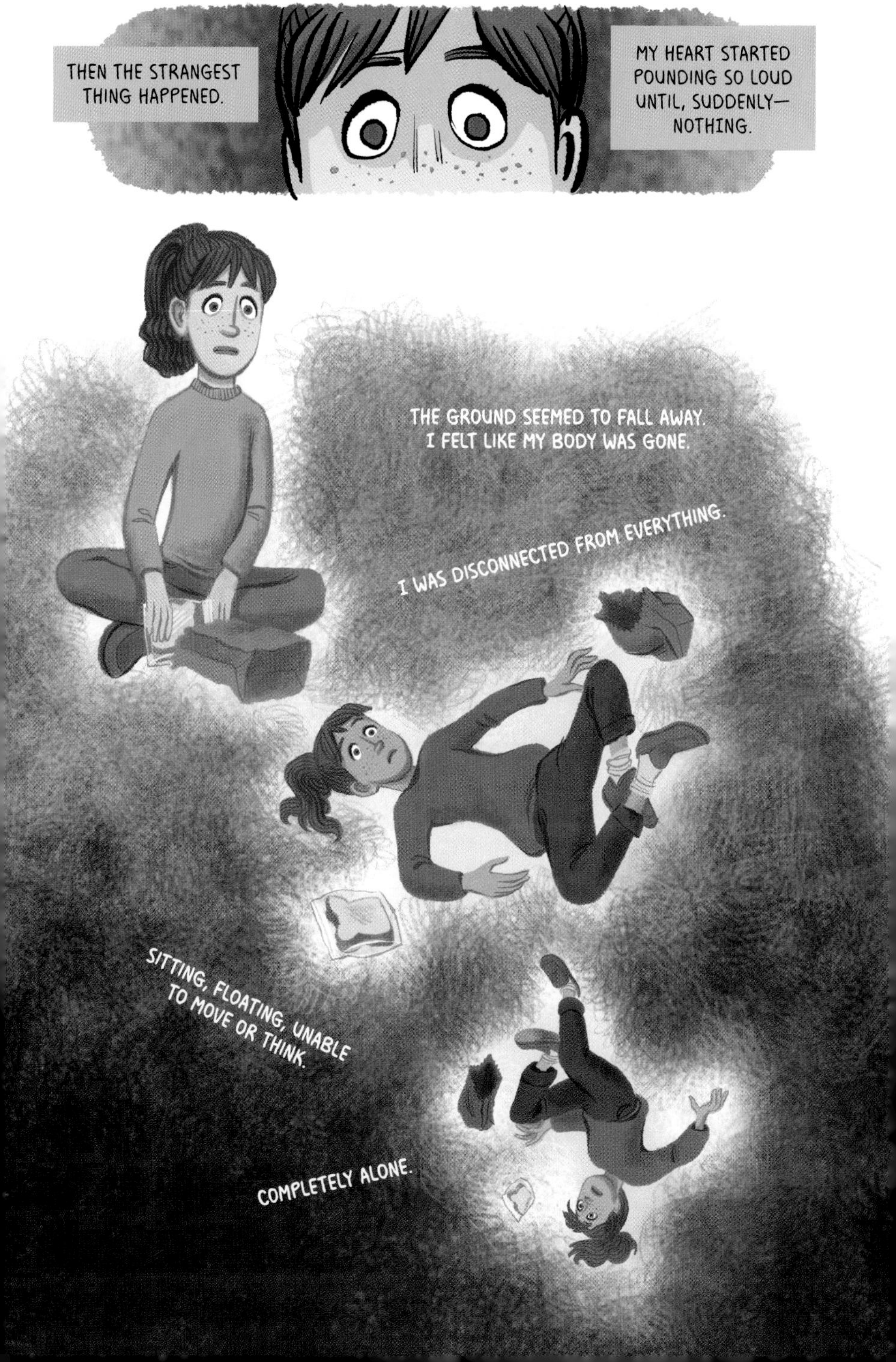
THEN THE STRANGEST THING HAPPENED.
MY HEART STARTED POUNDING SO LOUD UNTIL, SUDDENLY—NOTHING.
THE GROUND SEEMED TO FALL AWAY. I FELT LIKE MY BODY WAS GONE.
I WAS DISCONNECTED FROM EVERYTHING.
SITTING, FLOATING, UNABLE TO MOVE OR THINK.
COMPLETELY ALONE.

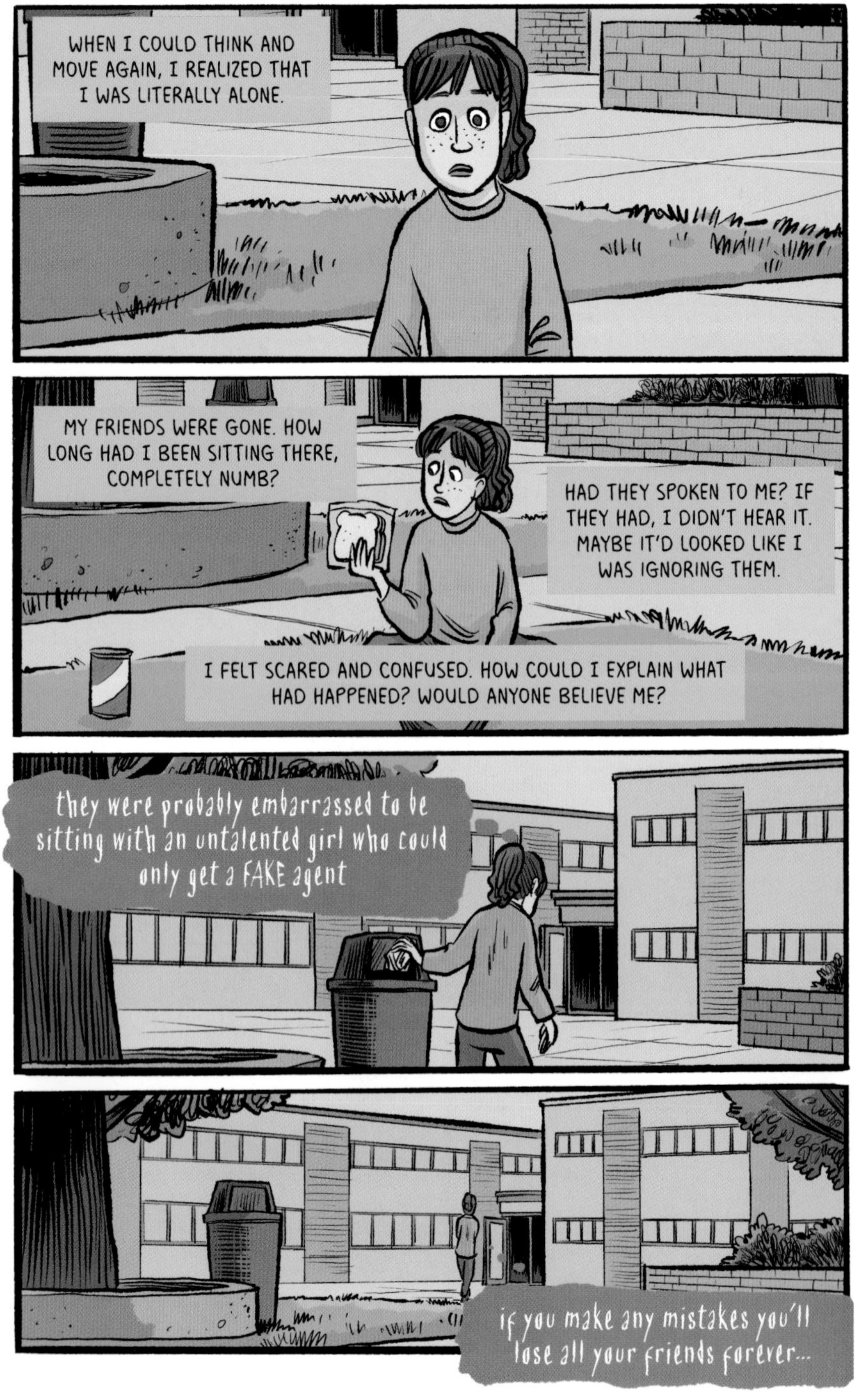
WHEN I COULD THINK AND MOVE AGAIN, I REALIZED THAT I WAS LITERALLY ALONE.
MY FRIENDS WERE GONE. HOW LONG HAD I BEEN SITTING THERE, COMPLETELY NUMB?
HAD THEY SPOKEN TO ME? IF THEY HAD, I DIDN'T HEAR IT. MAYBE IT'D LOOKED LIKE I WAS IGNORING THEM.
I FELT SCARED AND CONFUSED. HOW COULD I EXPLAIN WHAT HAD HAPPENED? WOULD ANYONE BELIEVE ME?
they were probably embarrassed to be sitting with an untalented girl who could only get a FAKE agent
if you make any mistakes you'll lose all your friends forever...

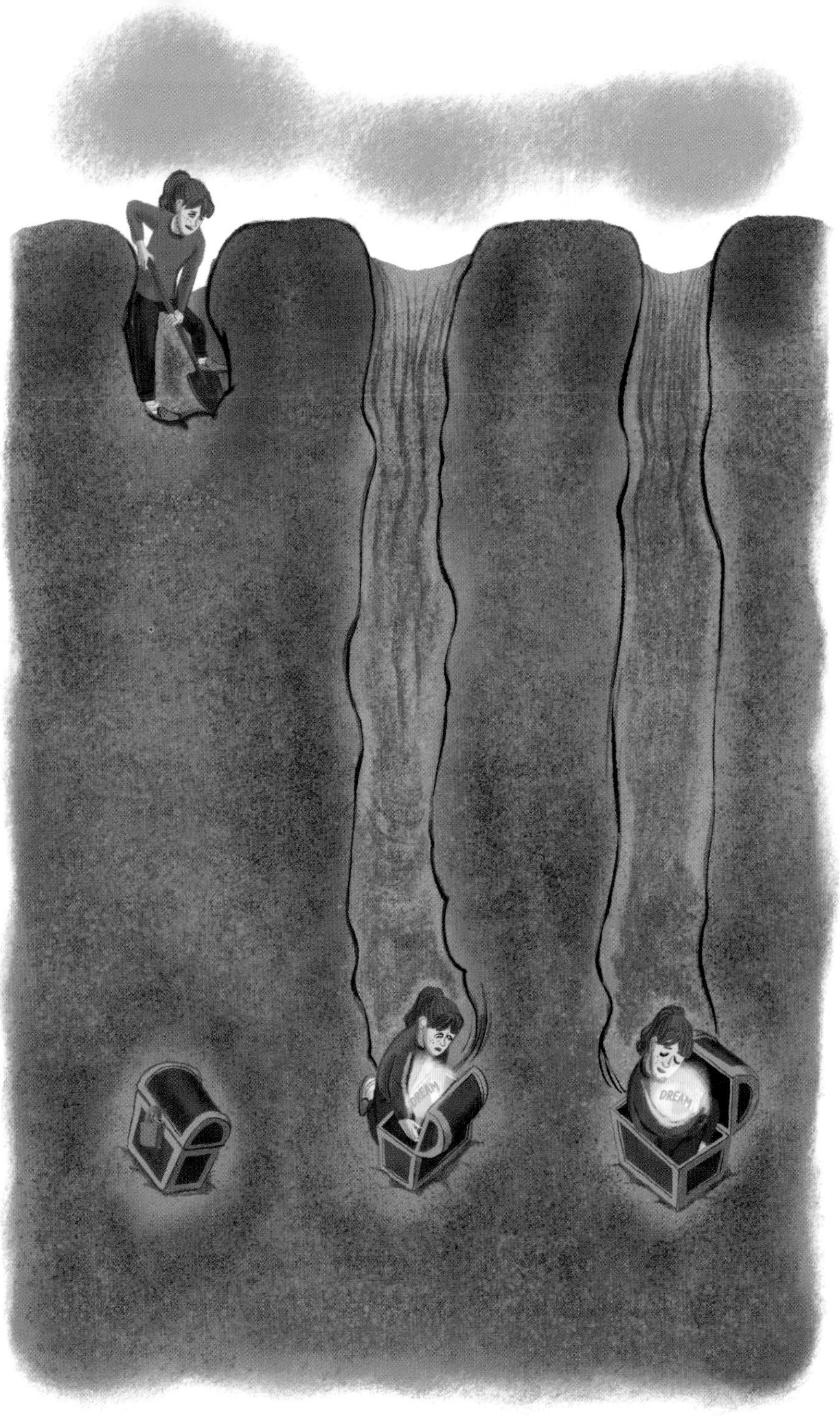
DREAM
DREAM

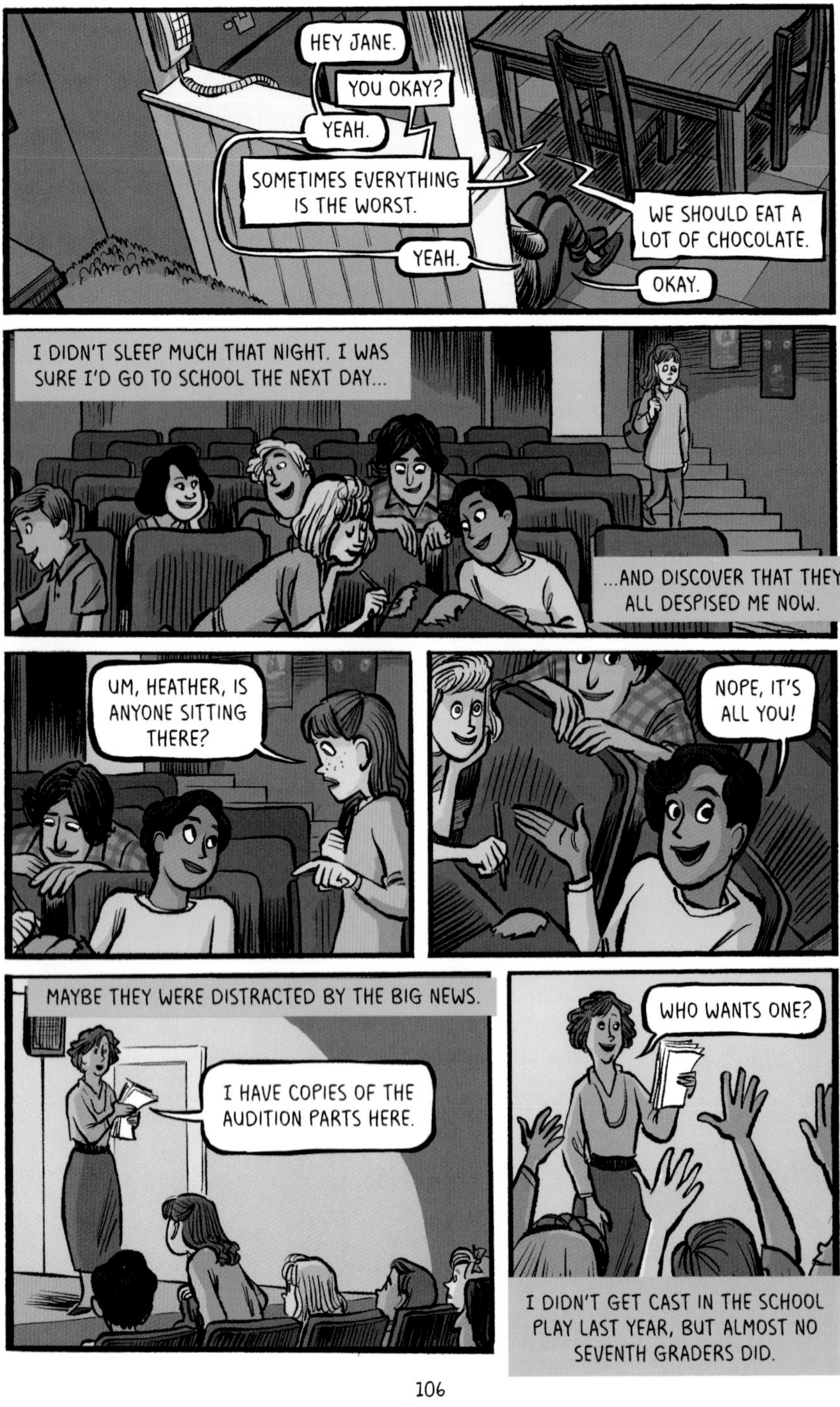
HEY JANE.
YOU OKAY?
YEAH.
SOMETIMES EVERYTHING IS THE WORST.
YEAH.
WE SHOULD EAT A LOT OF CHOCOLATE.
OKAY.
I DIDN'T SLEEP MUCH THAT NIGHT. I WAS SURE I'D GO TO SCHOOL THE NEXT DAY...
...AND DISCOVER THAT THEY ALL DESPISED ME NOW.
UM, HEATHER, IS ANYONE SITTING THERE?
NOPE, IT'S ALL YOU!
MAYBE THEY WERE DISTRACTED BY THE BIG NEWS.
I HAVE COPIES OF THE AUDITION PARTS HERE.
WHO WANTS ONE?
I DIDN'T GET CAST IN THE SCHOOL PLAY LAST YEAR, BUT ALMOST NO SEVENTH GRADERS DID.

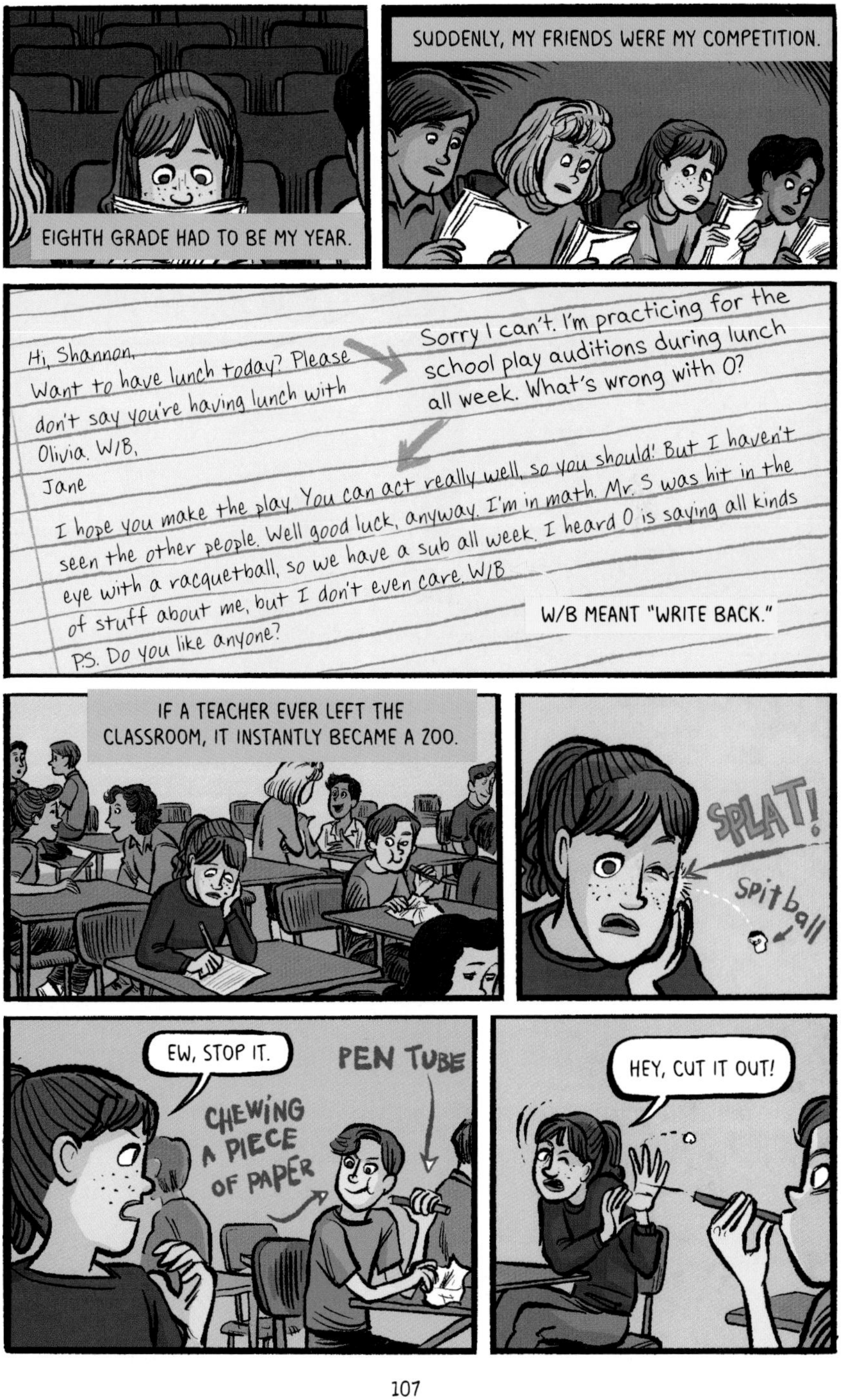
EIGHTH GRADE HAD TO BE MY YEAR.
SUDDENLY, MY FRIENDS WERE MY COMPETITION.
Hi, Shannon,
Want to have lunch today? Please don't say you're having lunch with Olivia. W/B,
Jane
Sorry I can't. I'm practicing for the school play auditions during lunch all week. What's wrong with O?
I hope you make the play. You can act really well, so you should! But I haven't seen the other people. Well good luck, anyway. I'm in math. Mr. S was hit in the eye with a racquetball, so we have a sub all week. I heard O is saying all kinds of stuff about me, but I don't even care. W/B
P.S. Do you like anyone?
W/B MEANT "WRITE BACK."
IF A TEACHER EVER LEFT THE CLASSROOM, IT INSTANTLY BECAME A ZOO.
SPLAT!
Spitball
EW, STOP IT.
CHEWING A PIECE OF PAPER
PEN TUBE
HEY, CUT IT OUT!

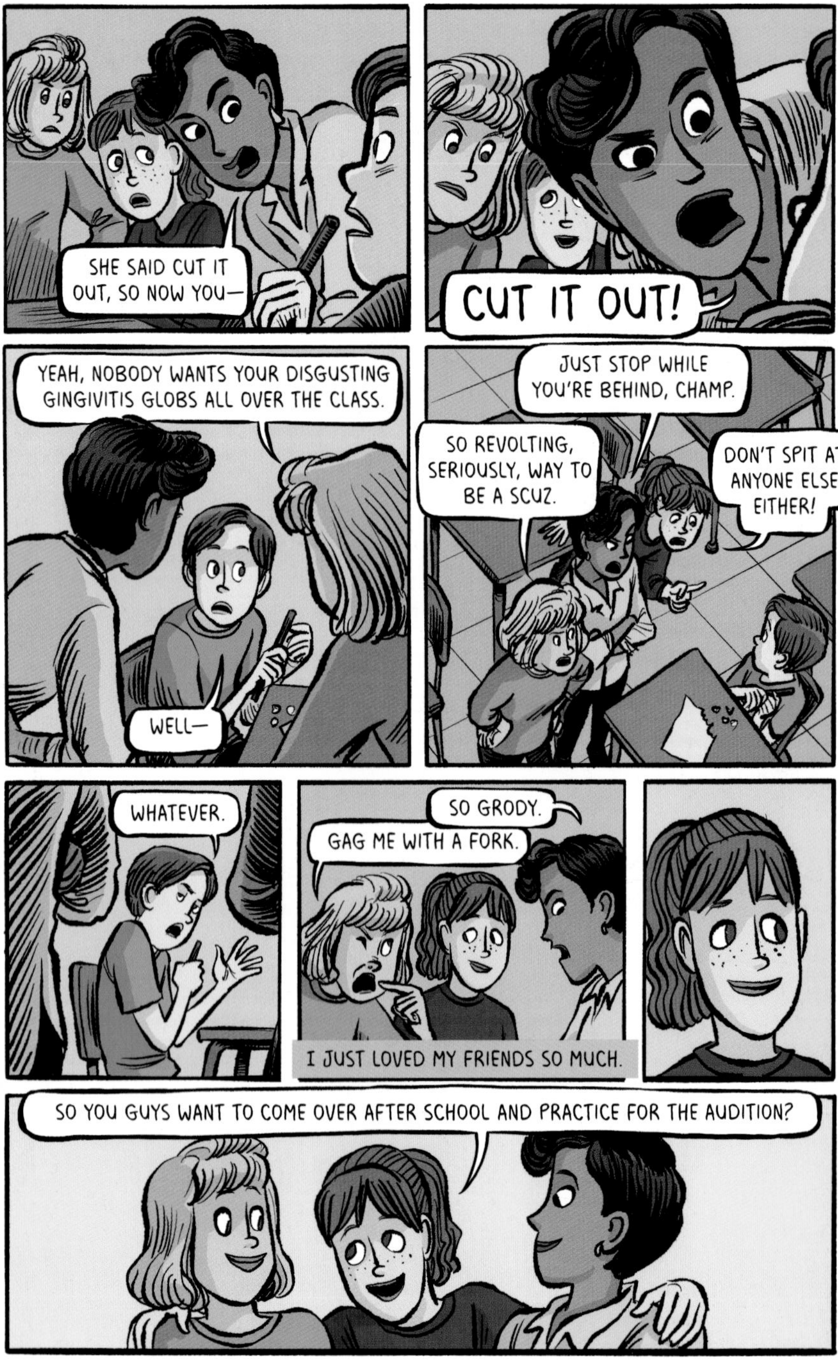
SHE SAID CUT IT OUT, SO NOW YOU—
CUT IT OUT!
YEAH, NOBODY WANTS YOUR DISGUSTING GINGIVITIS GLOBS ALL OVER THE CLASS.
WELL—
JUST STOP WHILE YOU'RE BEHIND, CHAMP.
SO REVOLTING, SERIOUSLY, WAY TO BE A SCUZ.
DON'T SPIT AT ANYONE ELSE EITHER!
WHATEVER.
SO GRODY.
GAG ME WITH A FORK.
I JUST LOVED MY FRIENDS SO MUCH.
SO YOU GUYS WANT TO COME OVER AFTER SCHOOL AND PRACTICE FOR THE AUDITION?

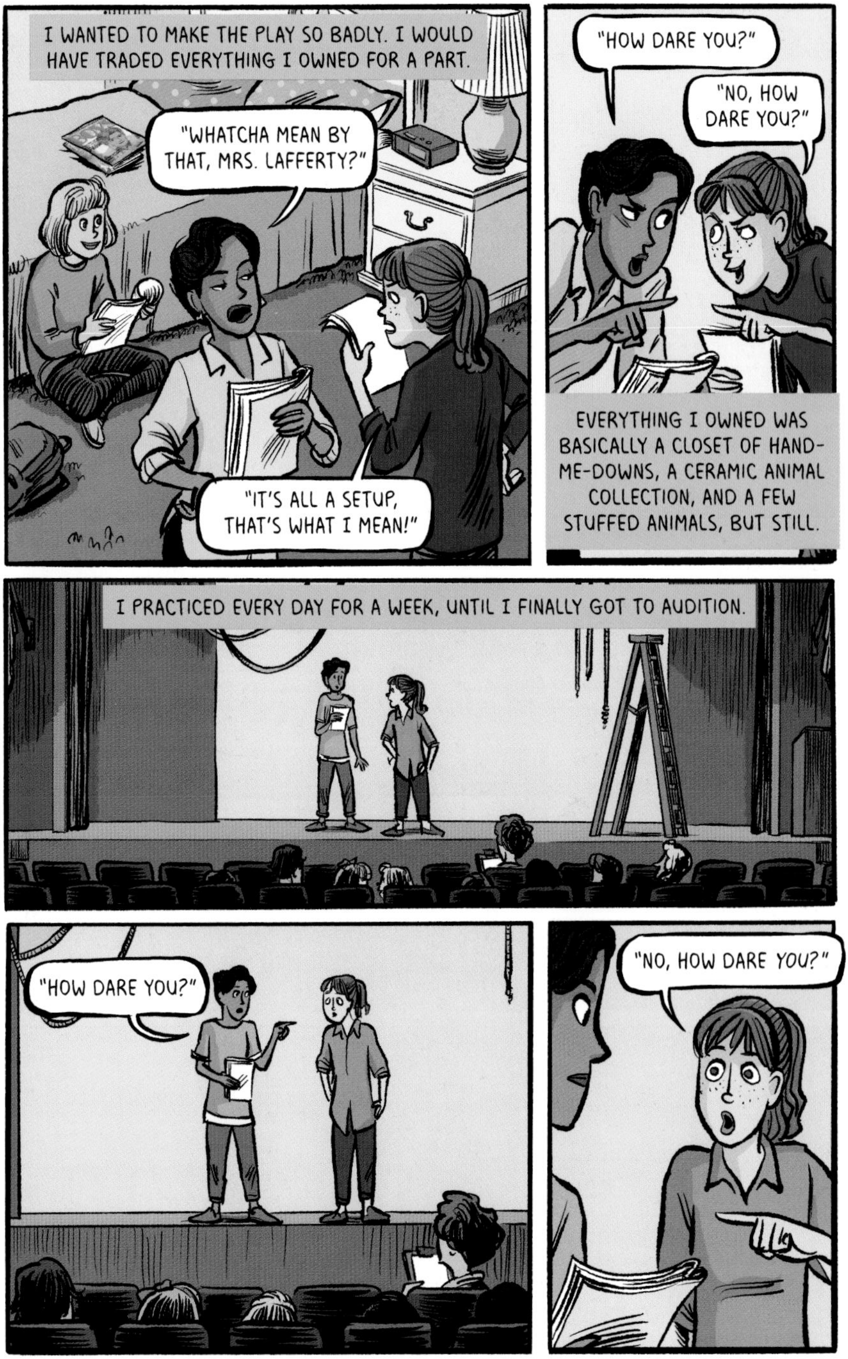
I WANTED TO MAKE THE PLAY SO BADLY. I WOULD HAVE TRADED EVERYTHING I OWNED FOR A PART.
"WHATCHA MEAN BY THAT, MRS. LAFFERTY?"
"IT'S ALL A SETUP, THAT'S WHAT I MEAN!"
"HOW DARE YOU?"
"NO, HOW DARE YOU?"
EVERYTHING I OWNED WAS BASICALLY A CLOSET OF HAND-ME-DOWNS, A CERAMIC ANIMAL COLLECTION, AND A FEW STUFFED ANIMALS, BUT STILL.
I PRACTICED EVERY DAY FOR A WEEK, UNTIL I FINALLY GOT TO AUDITION.
"HOW DARE YOU?"
"NO, HOW DARE *YOU*?"

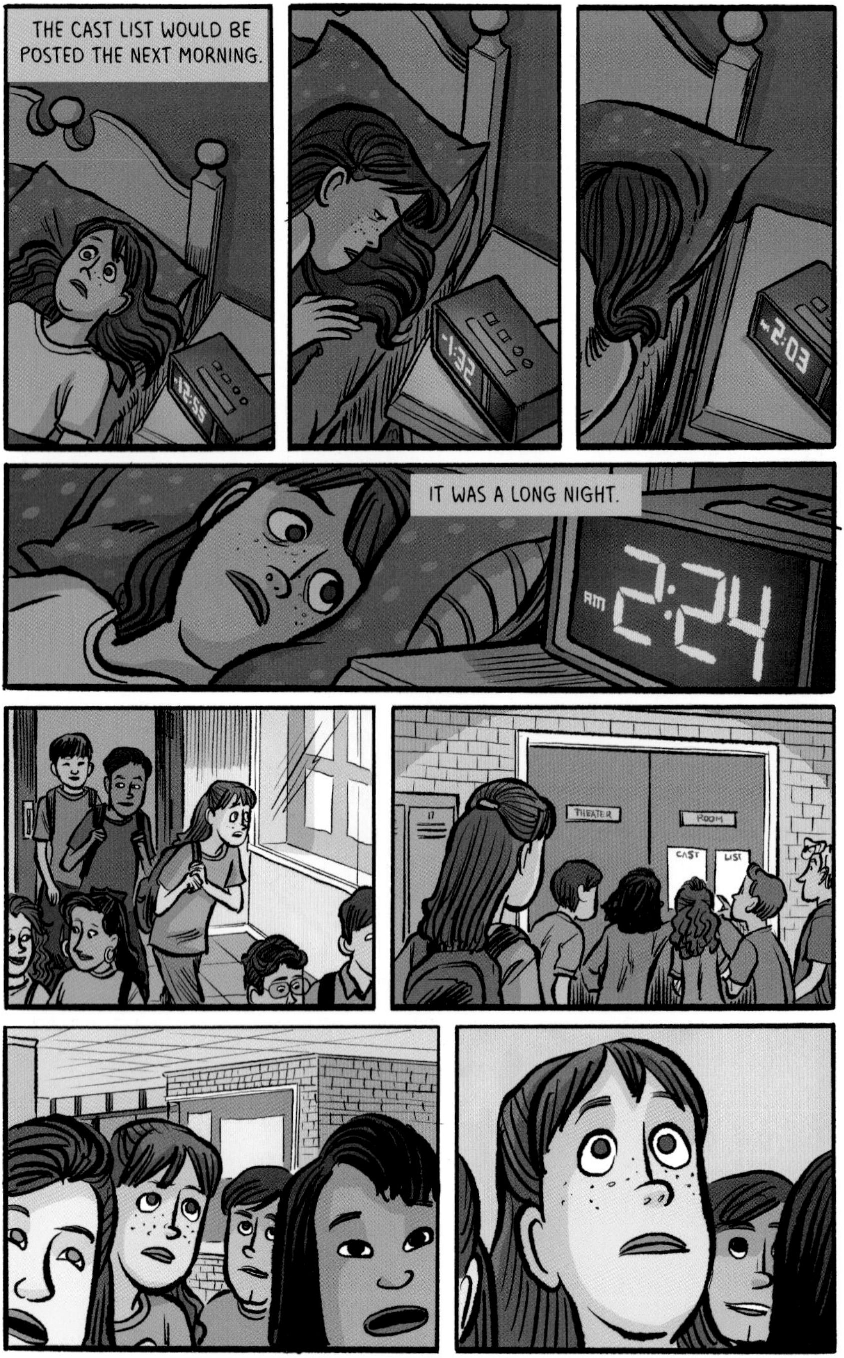
THE CAST LIST WOULD BE POSTED THE NEXT MORNING.
12:55
1:32
2:03
IT WAS A LONG NIGHT.
AM 2:24
THEATER
ROOM
CAST
LIST

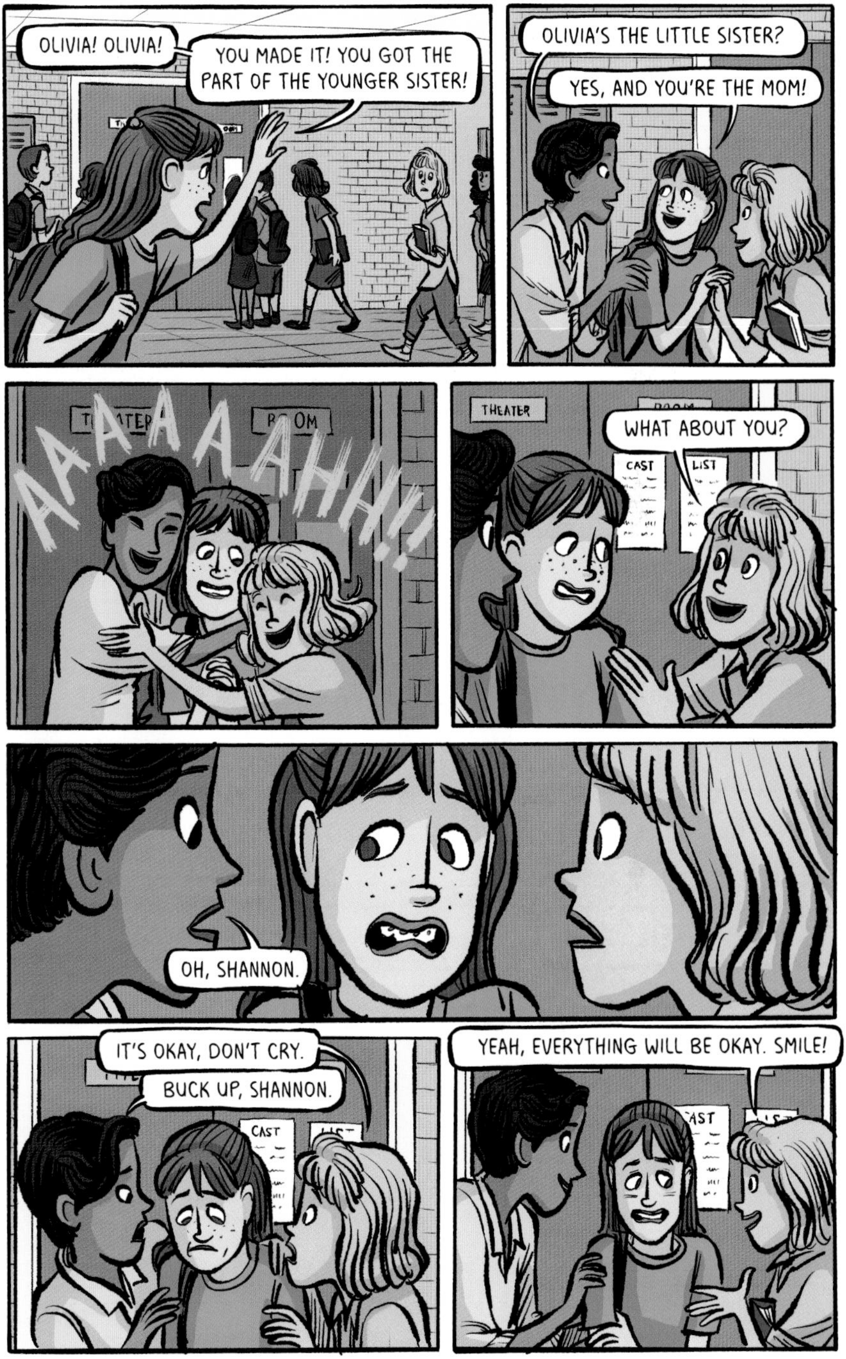
OLIVIA! OLIVIA!
YOU MADE IT! YOU GOT THE PART OF THE YOUNGER SISTER!
OLIVIA'S THE LITTLE SISTER?
YES, AND YOU'RE THE MOM!
AAAAAAAHH!!
THEATER
WHAT ABOUT YOU?
CAST
LIST
OH, SHANNON.
IT'S OKAY, DON'T CRY.
BUCK UP, SHANNON.
CAST
YEAH, EVERYTHING WILL BE OKAY. SMILE!

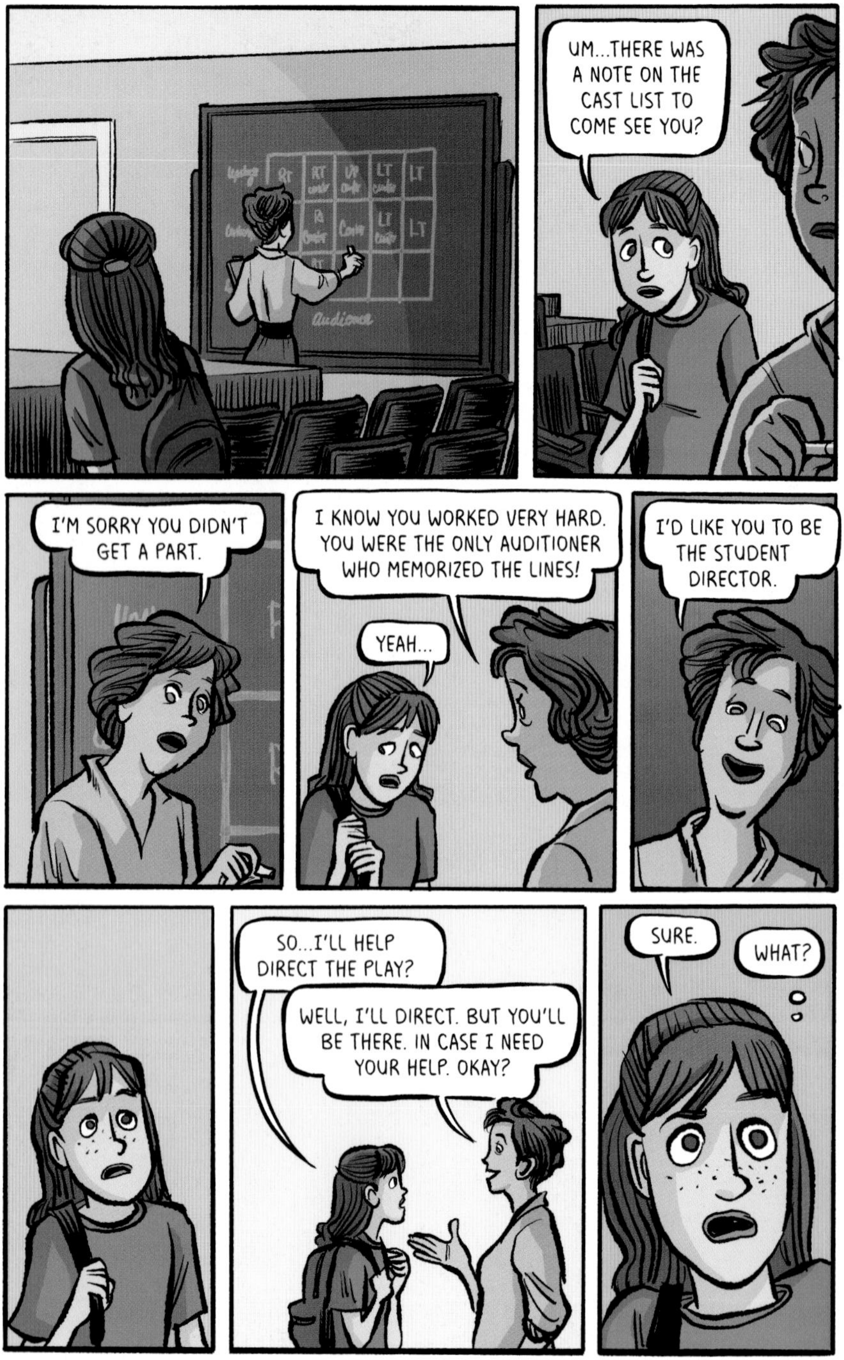
UM...THERE WAS A NOTE ON THE CAST LIST TO COME SEE YOU?
I'M SORRY YOU DIDN'T GET A PART.
I KNOW YOU WORKED VERY HARD. YOU WERE THE ONLY AUDITIONER WHO MEMORIZED THE LINES!
YEAH...
I'D LIKE YOU TO BE THE STUDENT DIRECTOR.
SO...I'LL HELP DIRECT THE PLAY?
WELL, I'LL DIRECT. BUT YOU'LL BE THERE. IN CASE I NEED YOUR HELP. OKAY?
SURE.
WHAT?

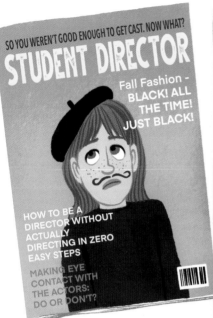

SO YOU WEREN'T GOOD ENOUGH TO GET CAST. NOW WHAT?

STUDENT DIRECTOR

Fall Fashion -
BLACK! ALL
THE TIME!
JUST BLACK!

HOW TO BE A
DIRECTOR WITHOUT
ACTUALLY
DIRECTING IN ZERO
EASY STEPS

MAKING EYE
CONTACT WITH
THE ACTORS:
DO OR DON'T?

BEING STUDENT DIRECTOR MEANT
GOING TO EARLY MORNING REHEARSALS.

THANKS, DAD.

JUST DON'T LET ALL THESE REHEARSALS
GET IN THE WAY OF YOUR HOMEWORK.

I WON'T.

AND THE AFTER-SCHOOL REHEARSALS.

"HORACE! YOU DIDN'T..."

UM...LINE?

"YOU DIDN'T STASH THE
BAGS WHERE—"

"YOU DIDN'T
STASH THE BAGS
WHERE I SAID!"

HOW DID THAT
SCENE LOOK?

"AND WHAT'S THIS, THEN?"

GREAT! YOU'RE
SO FUNNY.

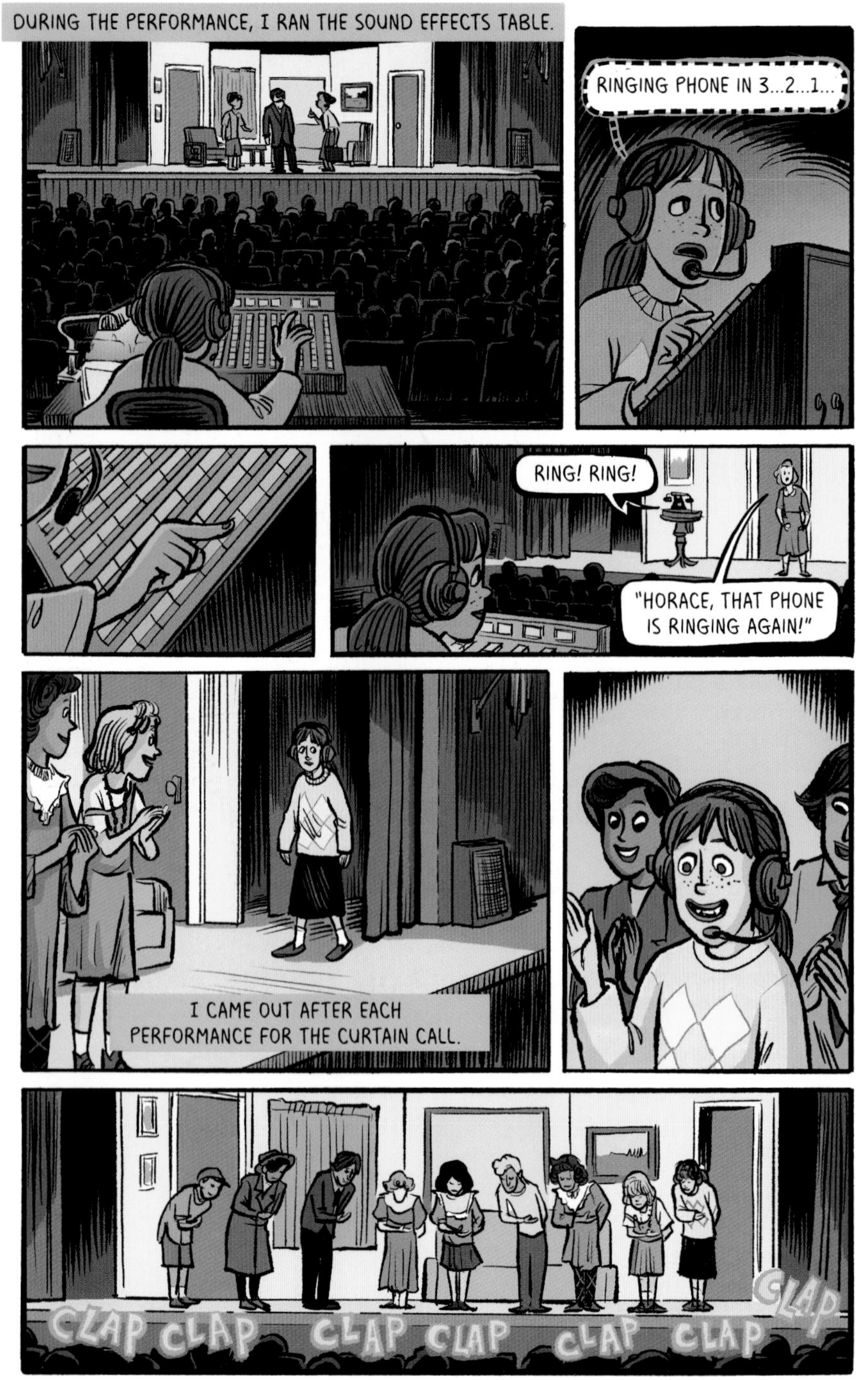
DURING THE PERFORMANCE, I RAN THE SOUND EFFECTS TABLE.
RINGING PHONE IN 3...2...1...
RING! RING!
"HORACE, THAT PHONE IS RINGING AGAIN!"
I CAME OUT AFTER EACH PERFORMANCE FOR THE CURTAIN CALL.
CLAP CLAP CLAP CLAP CLAP CLAP CLAP

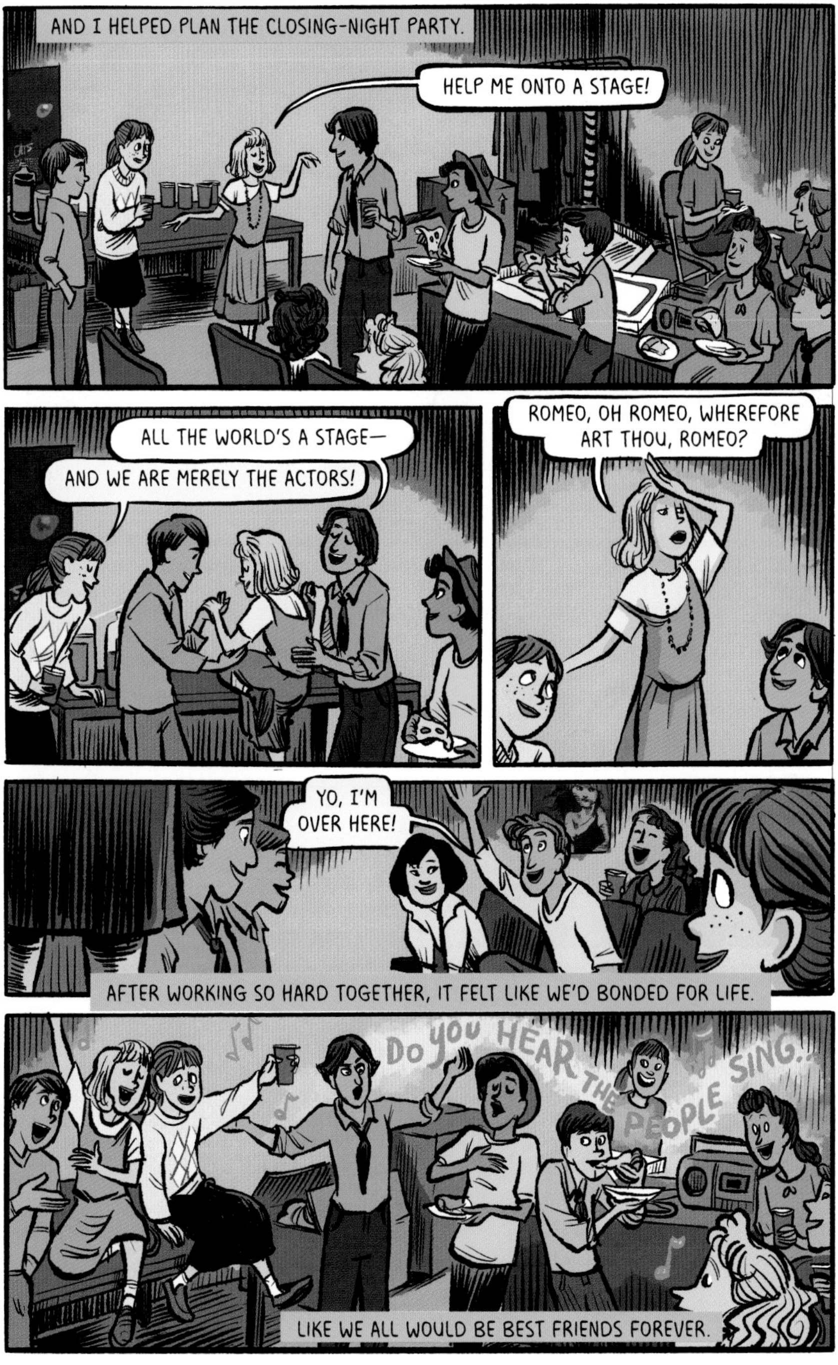
AND I HELPED PLAN THE CLOSING-NIGHT PARTY.
HELP ME ONTO A STAGE!
ALL THE WORLD'S A STAGE—
AND WE ARE MERELY THE ACTORS!
ROMEO, OH ROMEO, WHEREFORE ART THOU, ROMEO?
YO, I'M OVER HERE!
AFTER WORKING SO HARD TOGETHER, IT FELT LIKE WE'D BONDED FOR LIFE.
DO YOU HEAR THE PEOPLE SING...
LIKE WE ALL WOULD BE BEST FRIENDS FOREVER.

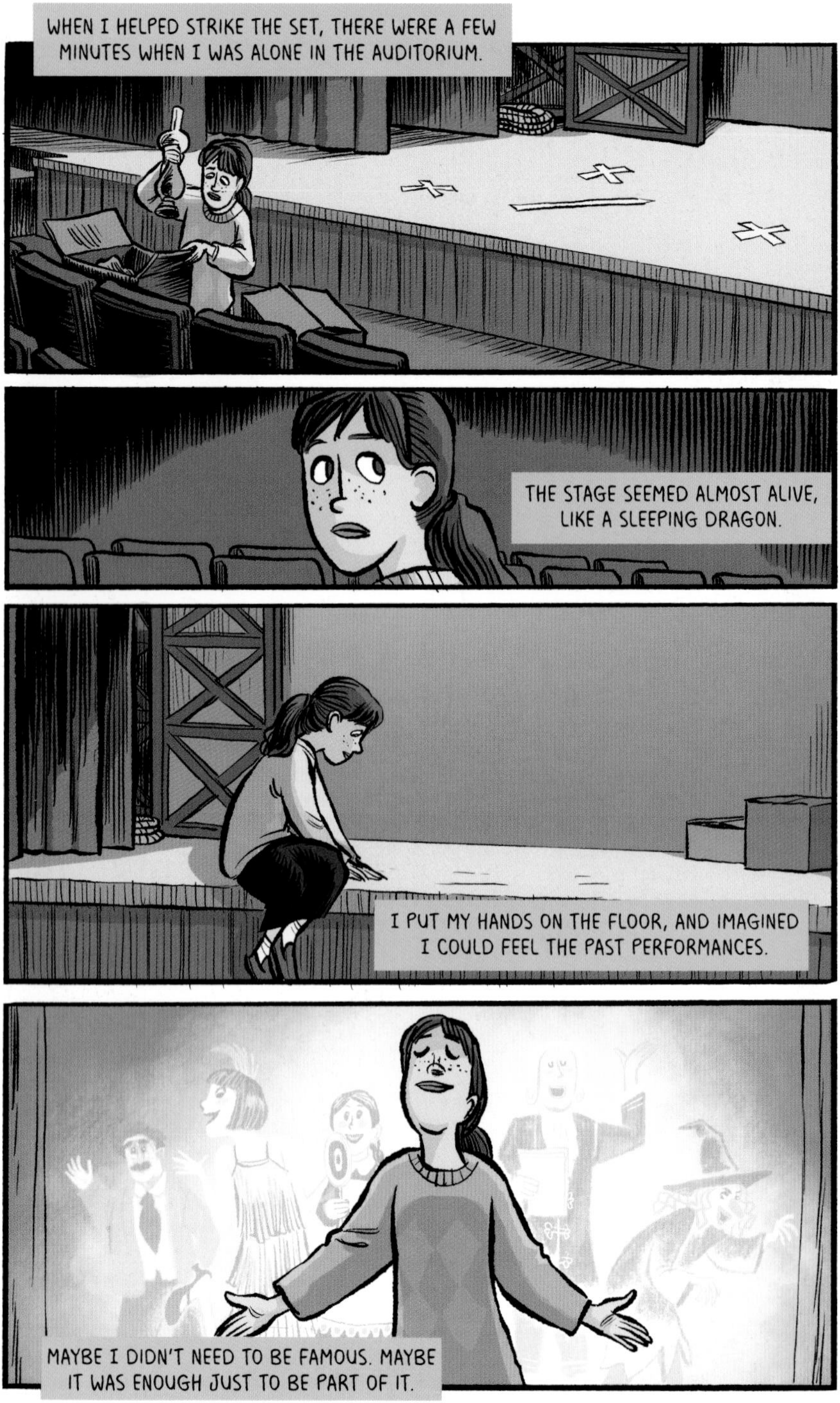
WHEN I HELPED STRIKE THE SET, THERE WERE A FEW MINUTES WHEN I WAS ALONE IN THE AUDITORIUM.
THE STAGE SEEMED ALMOST ALIVE, LIKE A SLEEPING DRAGON.
I PUT MY HANDS ON THE FLOOR, AND IMAGINED I COULD FEEL THE PAST PERFORMANCES.
MAYBE I DIDN'T NEED TO BE FAMOUS. MAYBE IT WAS ENOUGH JUST TO BE PART OF IT.

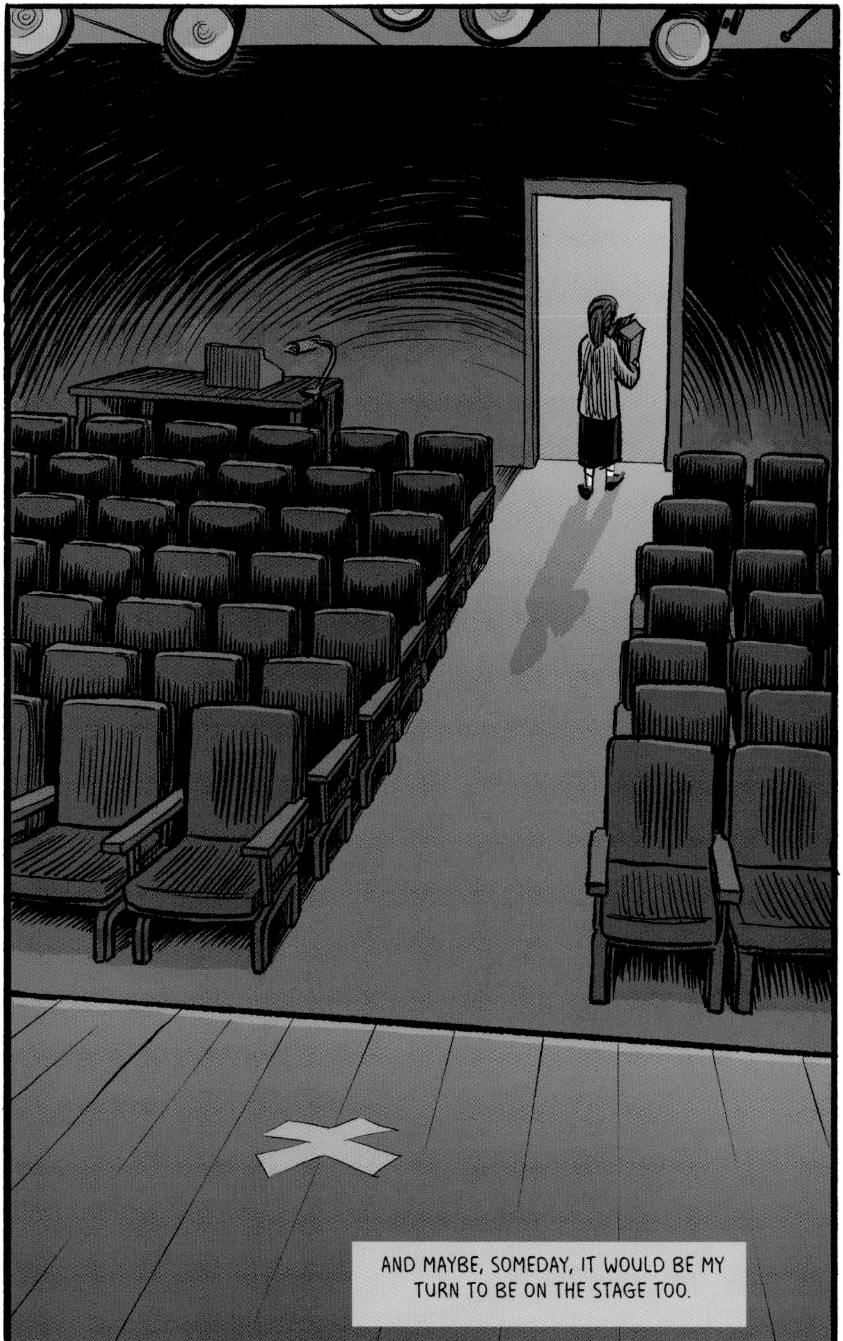
AND MAYBE, SOMEDAY, IT WOULD BE MY TURN TO BE ON THE STAGE TOO.

CHAPTER 3

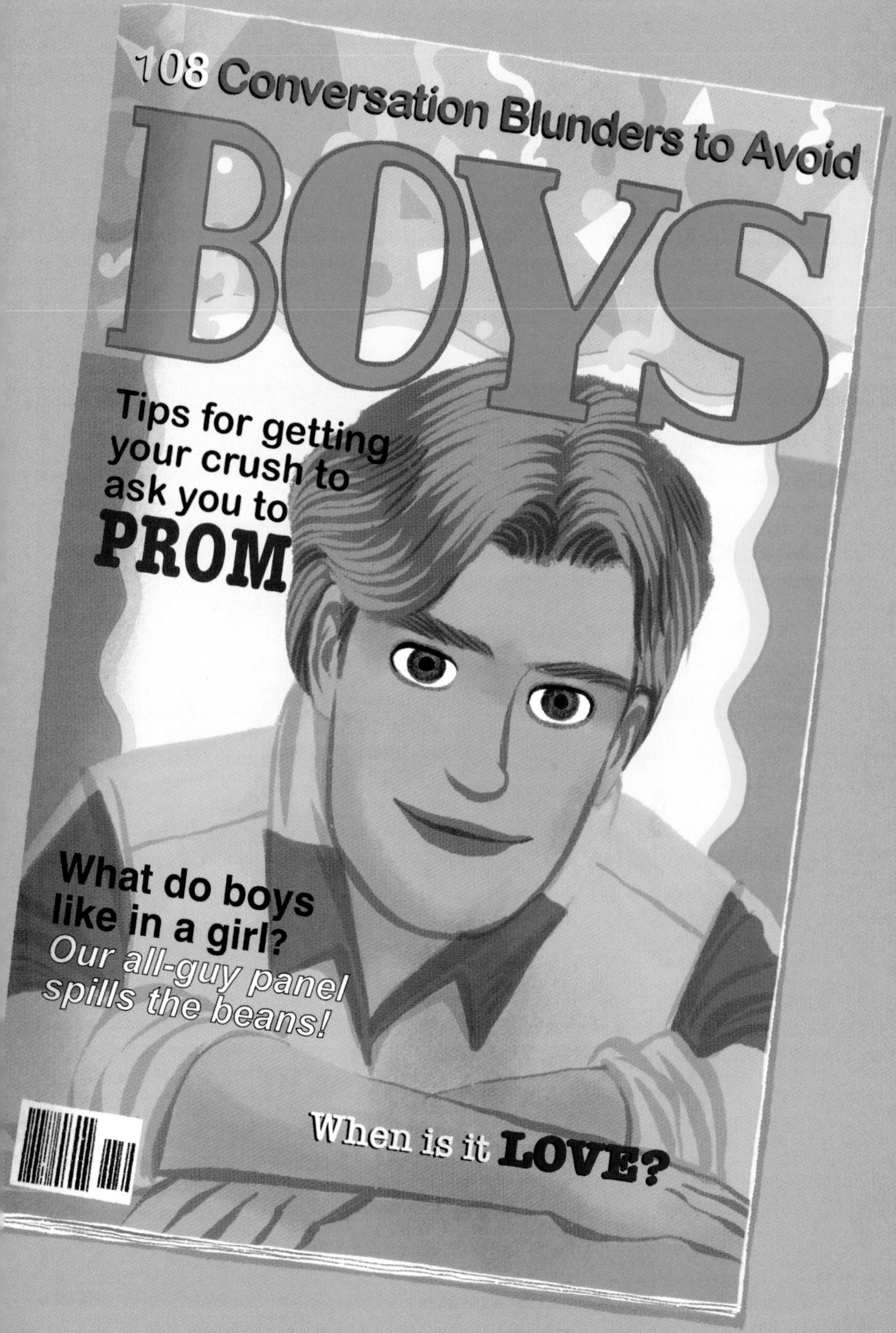
108 Conversation Blunders to Avoid
BOYS
Tips for getting your crush to ask you to PROM
What do boys like in a girl?
Our all-guy panel spills the beans!
When is it LOVE?

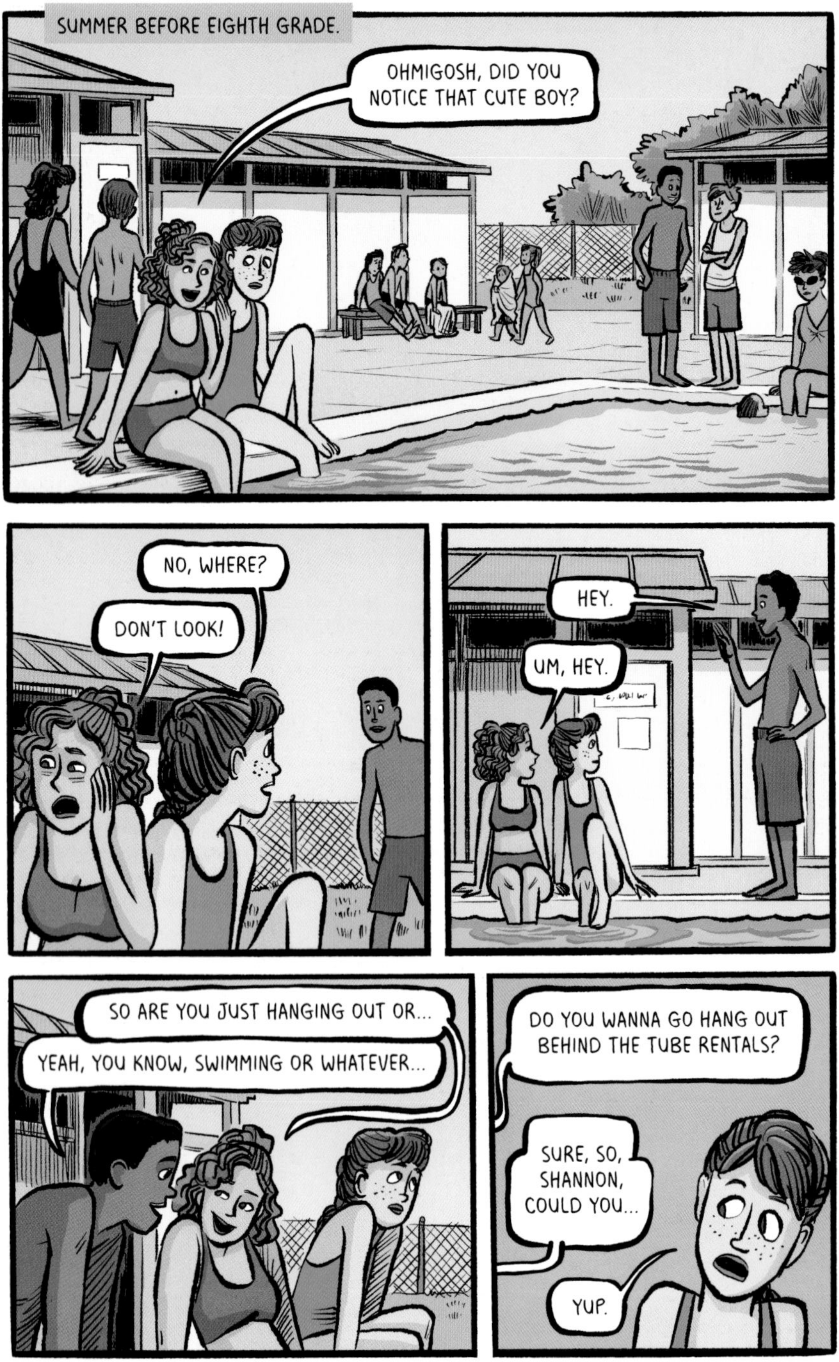
SUMMER BEFORE EIGHTH GRADE.
OHMIGOSH, DID YOU NOTICE THAT CUTE BOY?
NO, WHERE?
DON'T LOOK!
HEY.
UM, HEY.
SO ARE YOU JUST HANGING OUT OR...
YEAH, YOU KNOW, SWIMMING OR WHATEVER...
DO YOU WANNA GO HANG OUT BEHIND THE TUBE RENTALS?
SURE, SO, SHANNON, COULD YOU...
YUP.

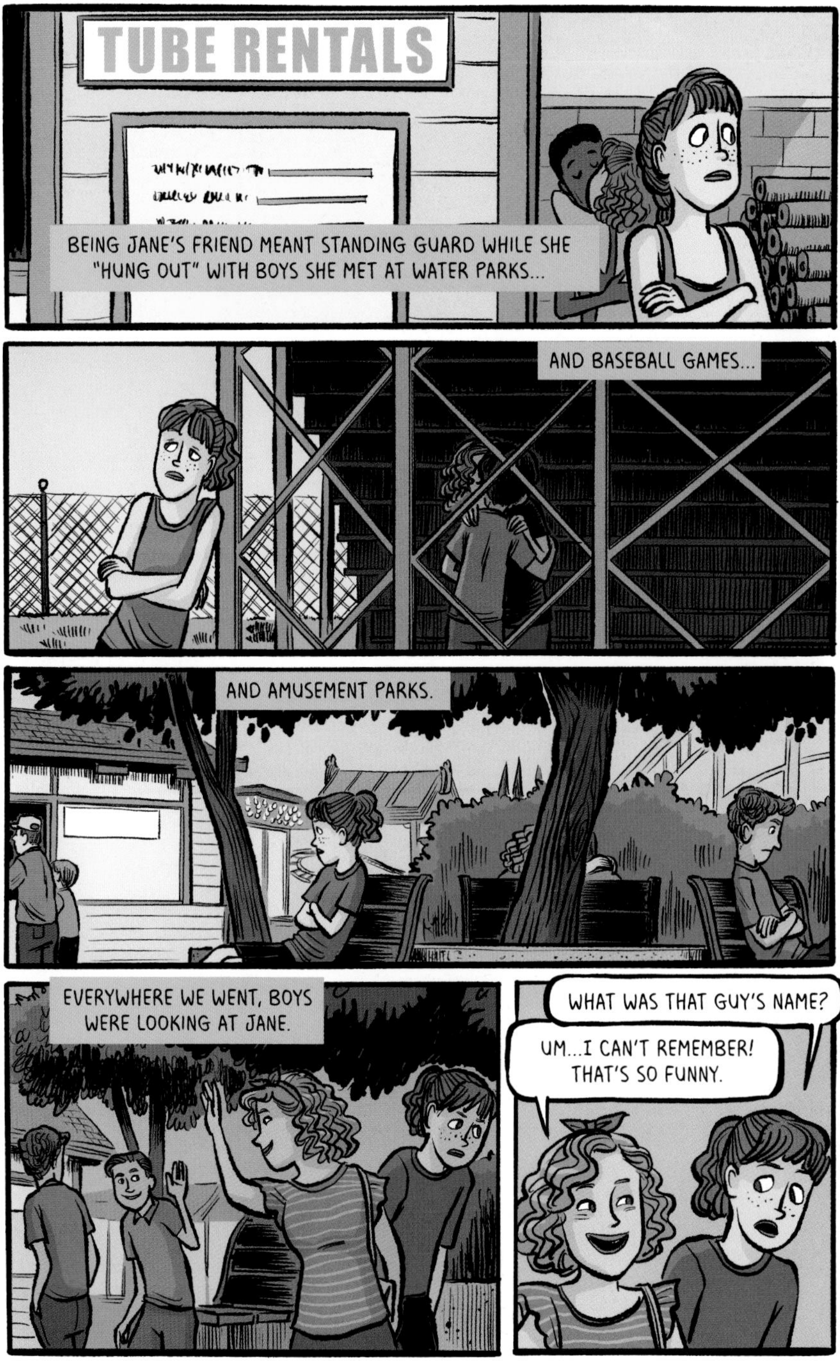
TUBE RENTALS
BEING JANE'S FRIEND MEANT STANDING GUARD WHILE SHE "HUNG OUT" WITH BOYS SHE MET AT WATER PARKS...
AND BASEBALL GAMES...
AND AMUSEMENT PARKS.
EVERYWHERE WE WENT, BOYS WERE LOOKING AT JANE.
WHAT WAS THAT GUY'S NAME?
UM...I CAN'T REMEMBER! THAT'S SO FUNNY.

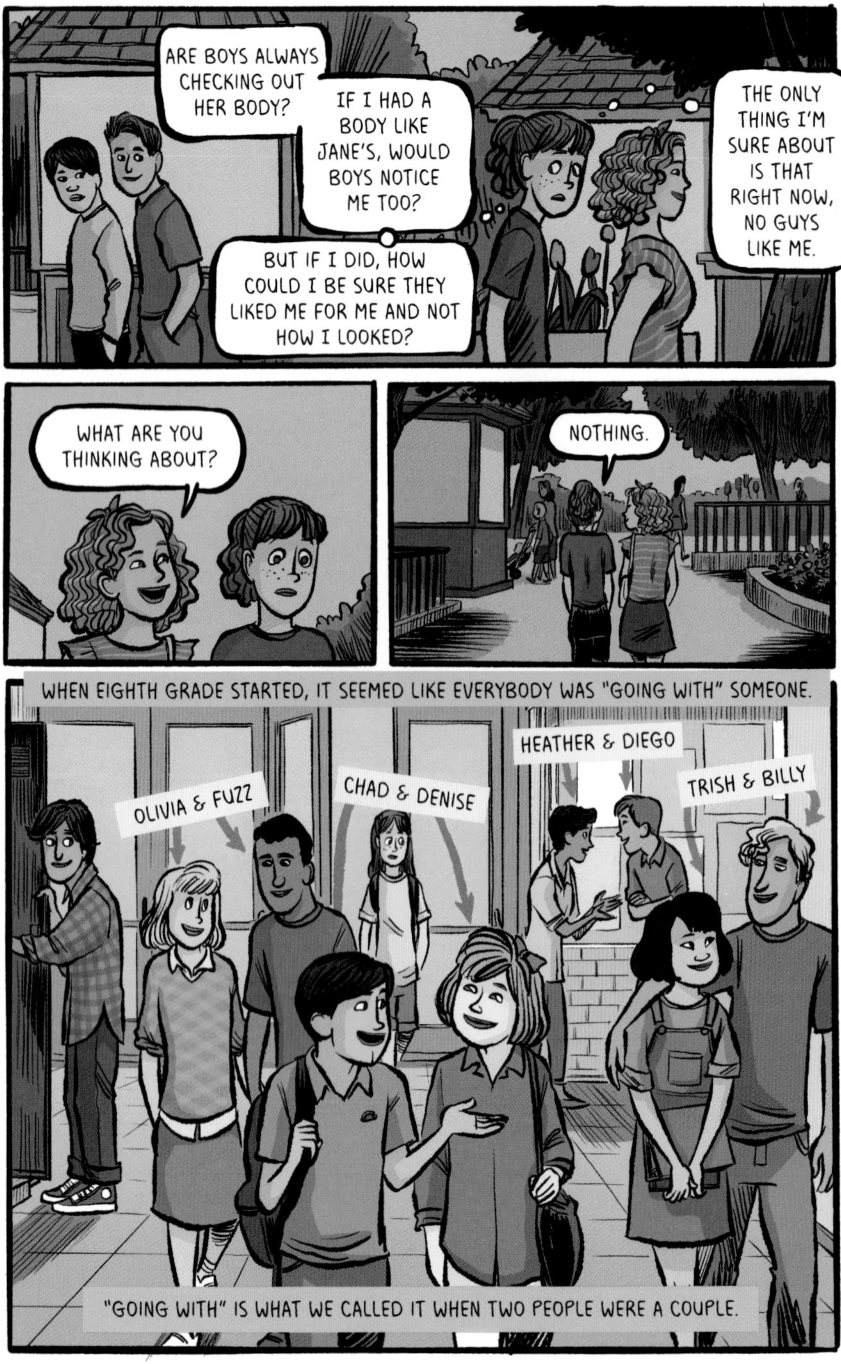
ARE BOYS ALWAYS CHECKING OUT HER BODY?
IF I HAD A BODY LIKE JANE'S, WOULD BOYS NOTICE ME TOO?
BUT IF I DID, HOW COULD I BE SURE THEY LIKED ME FOR ME AND NOT HOW I LOOKED?
THE ONLY THING I'M SURE ABOUT IS THAT RIGHT NOW, NO GUYS LIKE ME.
WHAT ARE YOU THINKING ABOUT?
NOTHING.
WHEN EIGHTH GRADE STARTED, IT SEEMED LIKE EVERYBODY WAS "GOING WITH" SOMEONE.
OLIVIA & FUZZ
CHAD & DENISE
HEATHER & DIEGO
TRISH & BILLY
"GOING WITH" IS WHAT WE CALLED IT WHEN TWO PEOPLE WERE A COUPLE.

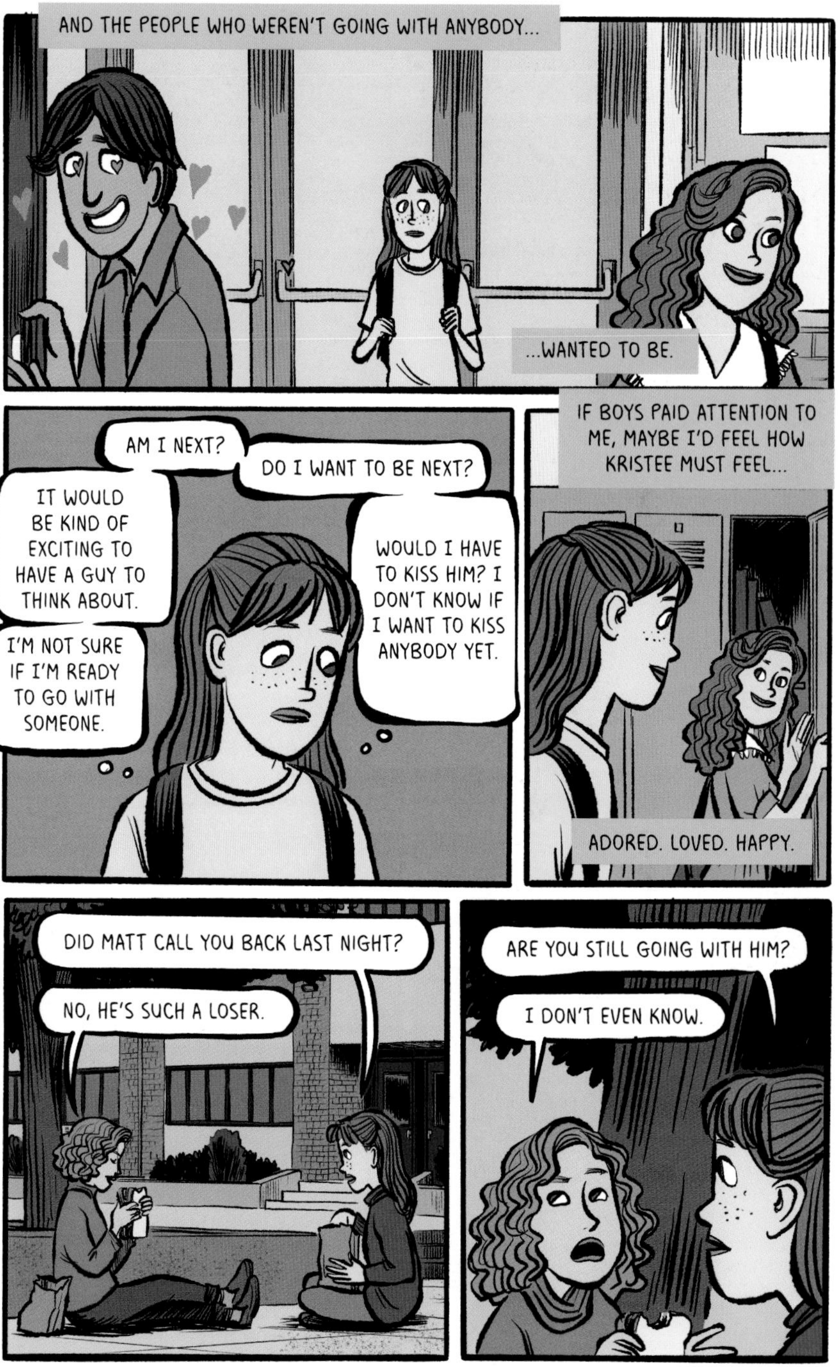
AND THE PEOPLE WHO WEREN'T GOING WITH ANYBODY...
...WANTED TO BE.
AM I NEXT?
DO I WANT TO BE NEXT?
IT WOULD BE KIND OF EXCITING TO HAVE A GUY TO THINK ABOUT.
WOULD I HAVE TO KISS HIM? I DON'T KNOW IF I WANT TO KISS ANYBODY YET.
I'M NOT SURE IF I'M READY TO GO WITH SOMEONE.
IF BOYS PAID ATTENTION TO ME, MAYBE I'D FEEL HOW KRISTEE MUST FEEL...
ADORED. LOVED. HAPPY.
DID MATT CALL YOU BACK LAST NIGHT?
NO, HE'S SUCH A LOSER.
ARE YOU STILL GOING WITH HIM?
I DON'T EVEN KNOW.

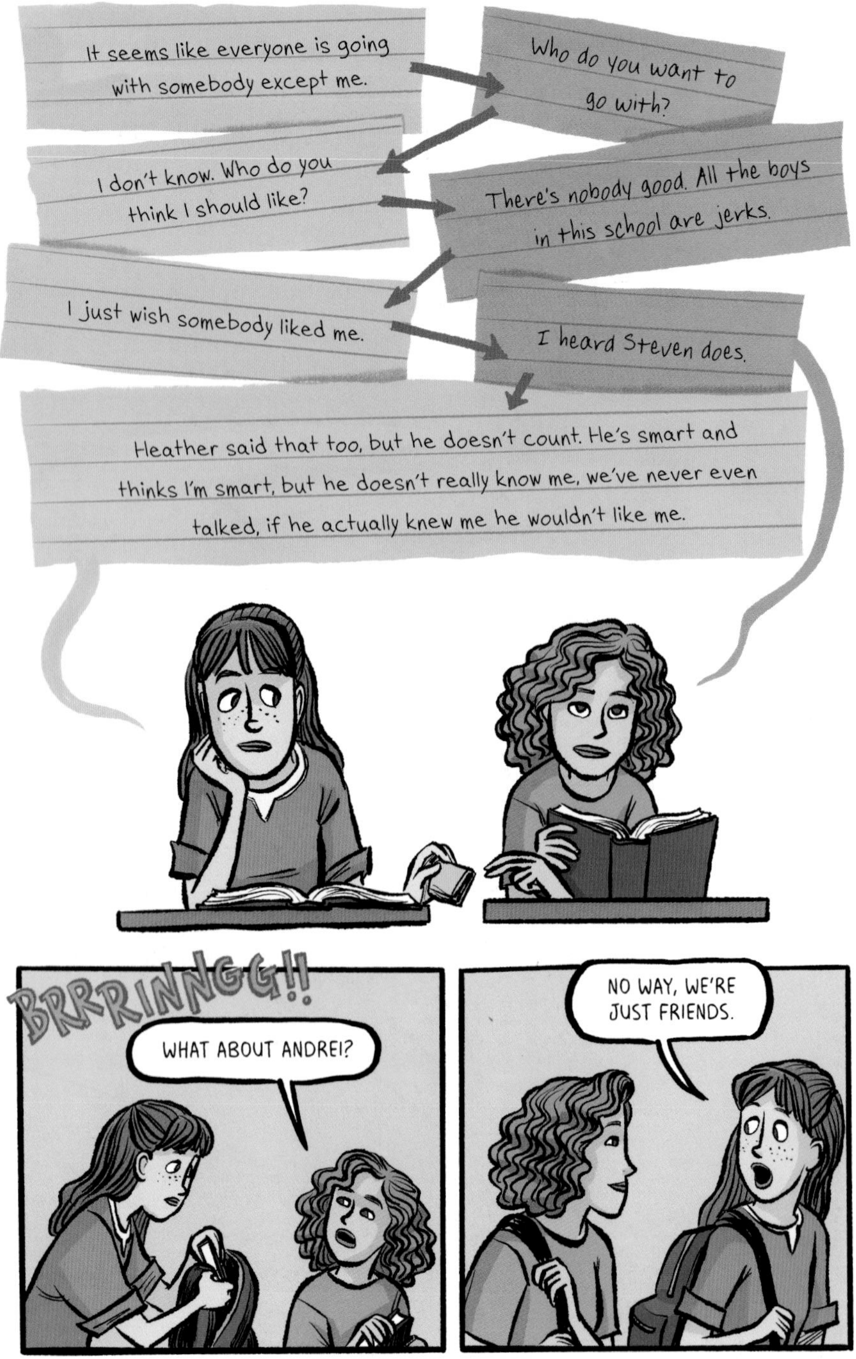
It seems like everyone is going with somebody except me.
Who do you want to go with?
I don't know. Who do you think I should like?
There's nobody good. All the boys in this school are jerks.
I just wish somebody liked me.
I heard Steven does.
Heather said that too, but he doesn't count. He's smart and thinks I'm smart, but he doesn't really know me, we've never even talked, if he actually knew me he wouldn't like me.
BRRRINNGG!!
WHAT ABOUT ANDREI?
NO WAY, WE'RE JUST FRIENDS.

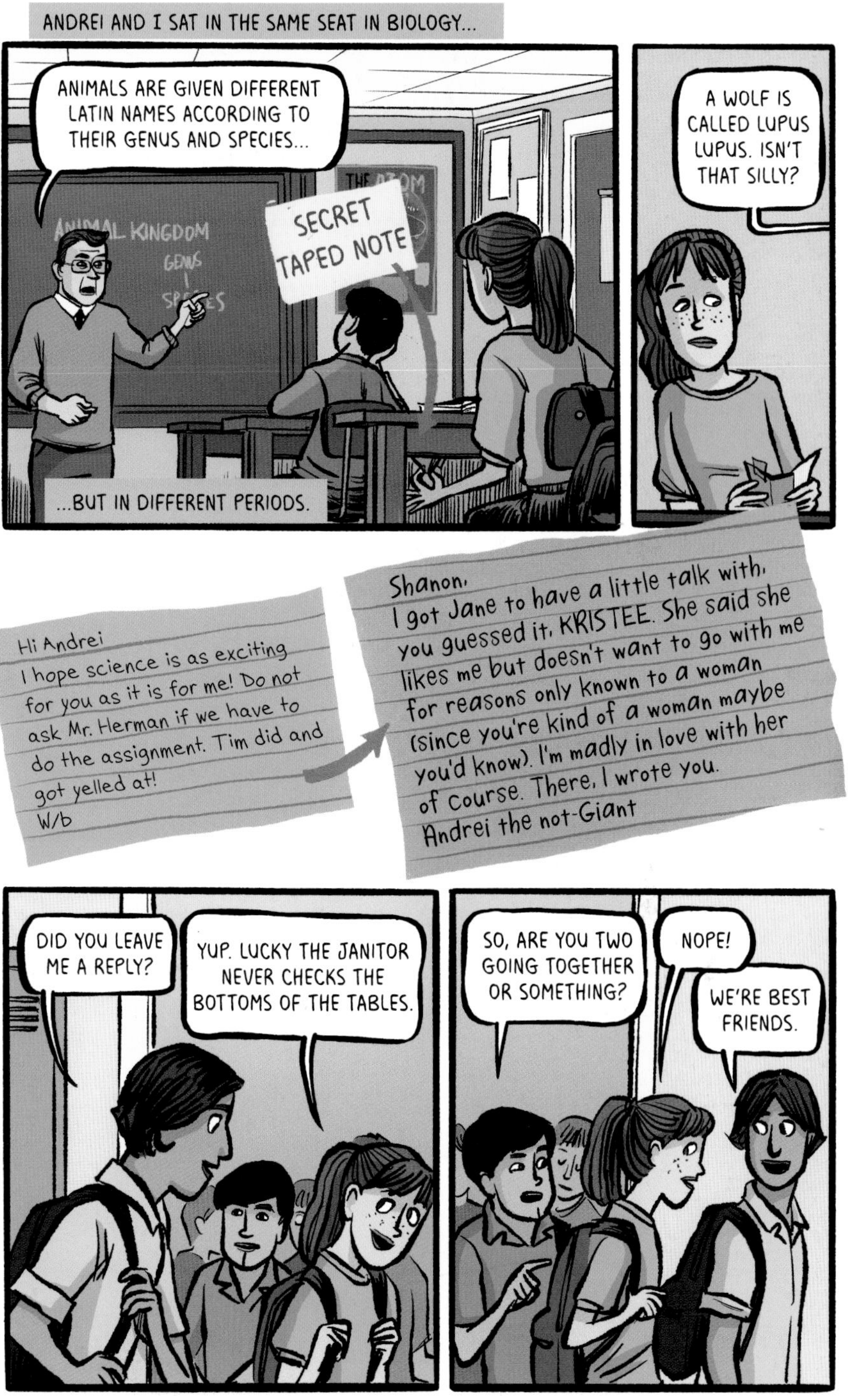
ANDREI AND I SAT IN THE SAME SEAT IN BIOLOGY...
ANIMALS ARE GIVEN DIFFERENT LATIN NAMES ACCORDING TO THEIR GENUS AND SPECIES...
ANIMAL KINGDOM
GENUS
SPECIES
THE ATOM
SECRET TAPED NOTE
...BUT IN DIFFERENT PERIODS.
A WOLF IS CALLED LUPUS LUPUS. ISN'T THAT SILLY?
Hi Andrei
I hope science is as exciting for you as it is for me! Do not ask Mr. Herman if we have to do the assignment. Tim did and got yelled at!
W/b
Shanon,
I got Jane to have a little talk with, you guessed it, KRISTEE. She said she likes me but doesn't want to go with me for reasons only known to a woman (since you're kind of a woman maybe you'd know). I'm madly in love with her of course. There, I wrote you.
Andrei the not-Giant
DID YOU LEAVE ME A REPLY?
YUP. LUCKY THE JANITOR NEVER CHECKS THE BOTTOMS OF THE TABLES.
SO, ARE YOU TWO GOING TOGETHER OR SOMETHING?
NOPE!
WE'RE BEST FRIENDS.

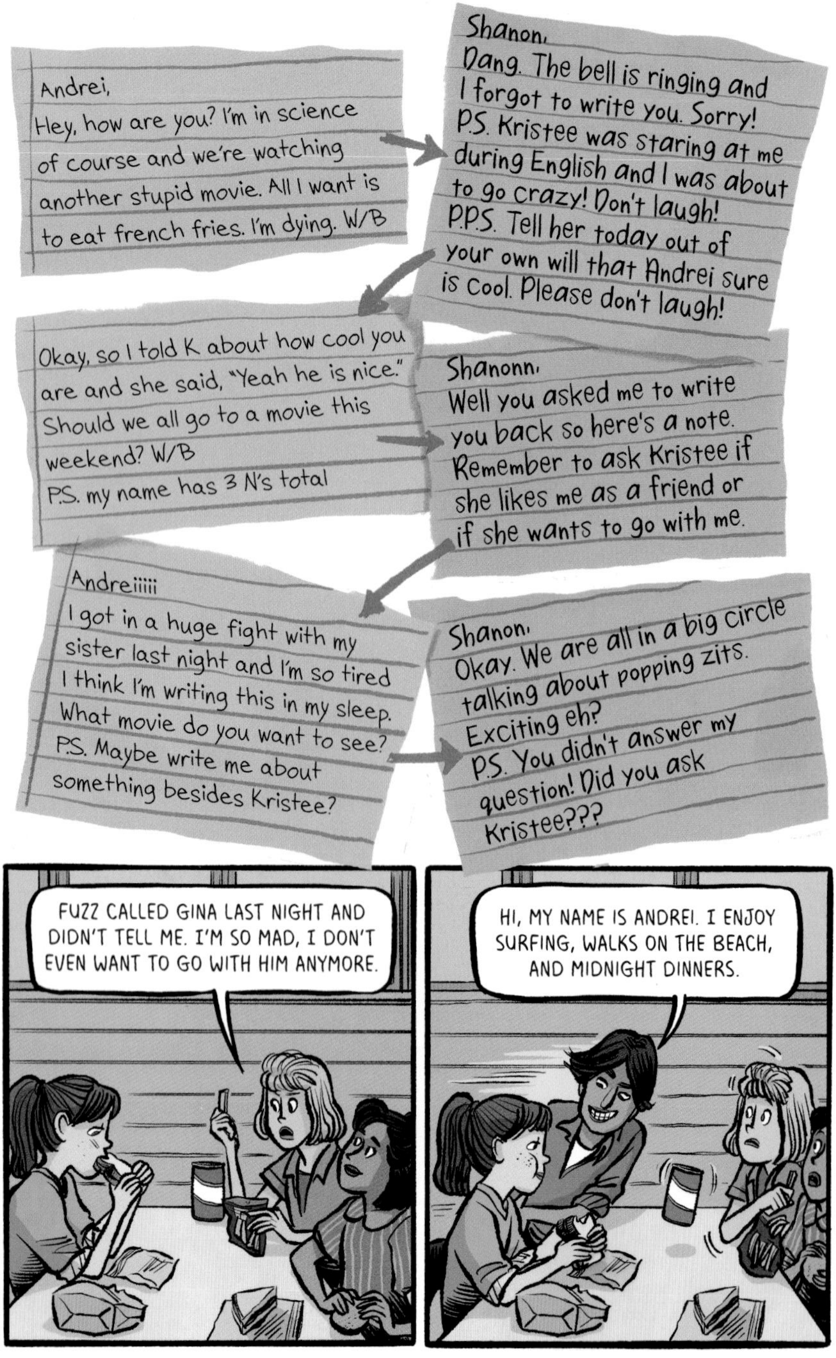

Andrei,
Hey, how are you? I'm in science of course and we're watching another stupid movie. All I want is to eat french fries. I'm dying. W/B
Shanon,
Dang. The bell is ringing and I forgot to write you. Sorry!
P.S. Kristee was staring at me during English and I was about to go crazy! Don't laugh!
P.P.S. Tell her today out of your own will that Andrei sure is Cool. Please don't laugh!
Okay, so I told K about how cool you are and she said, "Yeah he is nice." Should we all go to a movie this weekend? W/B
P.S. my name has 3 N's total
Shanonn,
Well you asked me to write you back so here's a note. Remember to ask Kristee if she likes me as a friend or if she wants to go with me.
Andreiiiii
I got in a huge fight with my sister last night and I'm so tired I think I'm writing this in my sleep. What movie do you want to see?
P.S. Maybe write me about something besides Kristee?
Shanon,
Okay. We are all in a big circle talking about popping zits. Exciting eh?
P.S. You didn't answer my question! Did you ask Kristee???
FUZZ CALLED GINA LAST NIGHT AND DIDN'T TELL ME. I'M SO MAD, I DON'T EVEN WANT TO GO WITH HIM ANYMORE.
HI, MY NAME IS ANDREI. I ENJOY SURFING, WALKS ON THE BEACH, AND MIDNIGHT DINNERS.

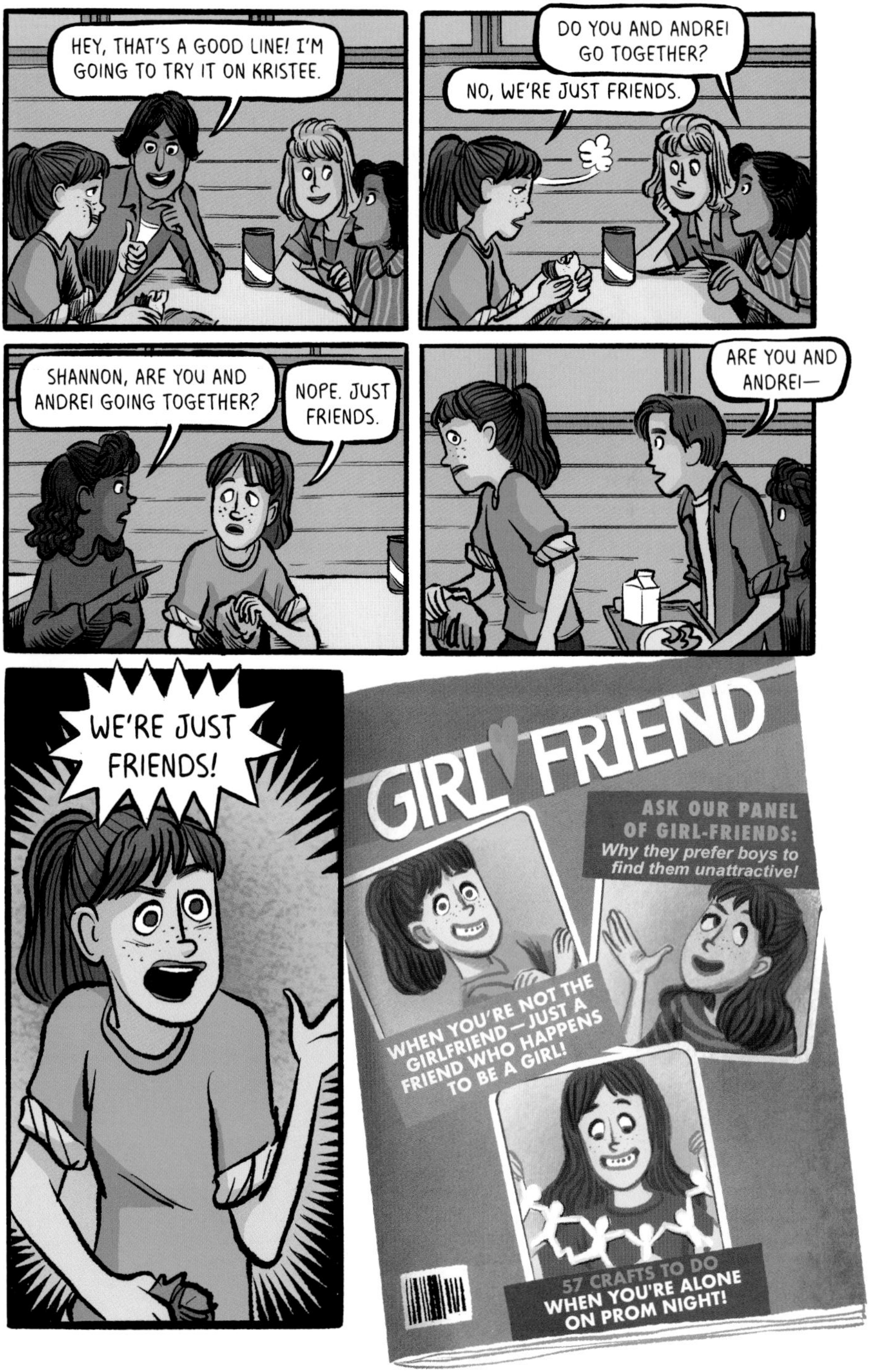
HEY, THAT'S A GOOD LINE! I'M GOING TO TRY IT ON KRISTEE.
DO YOU AND ANDREI GO TOGETHER?
NO, WE'RE JUST FRIENDS.
SHANNON, ARE YOU AND ANDREI GOING TOGETHER?
NOPE. JUST FRIENDS.
ARE YOU AND ANDREI—
WE'RE JUST FRIENDS!
GIRL FRIEND
ASK OUR PANEL OF GIRL-FRIENDS:
Why they prefer boys to find them unattractive!
WHEN YOU'RE NOT THE GIRLFRIEND—JUST A FRIEND WHO HAPPENS TO BE A GIRL!
57 CRAFTS TO DO WHEN YOU'RE ALONE ON PROM NIGHT!

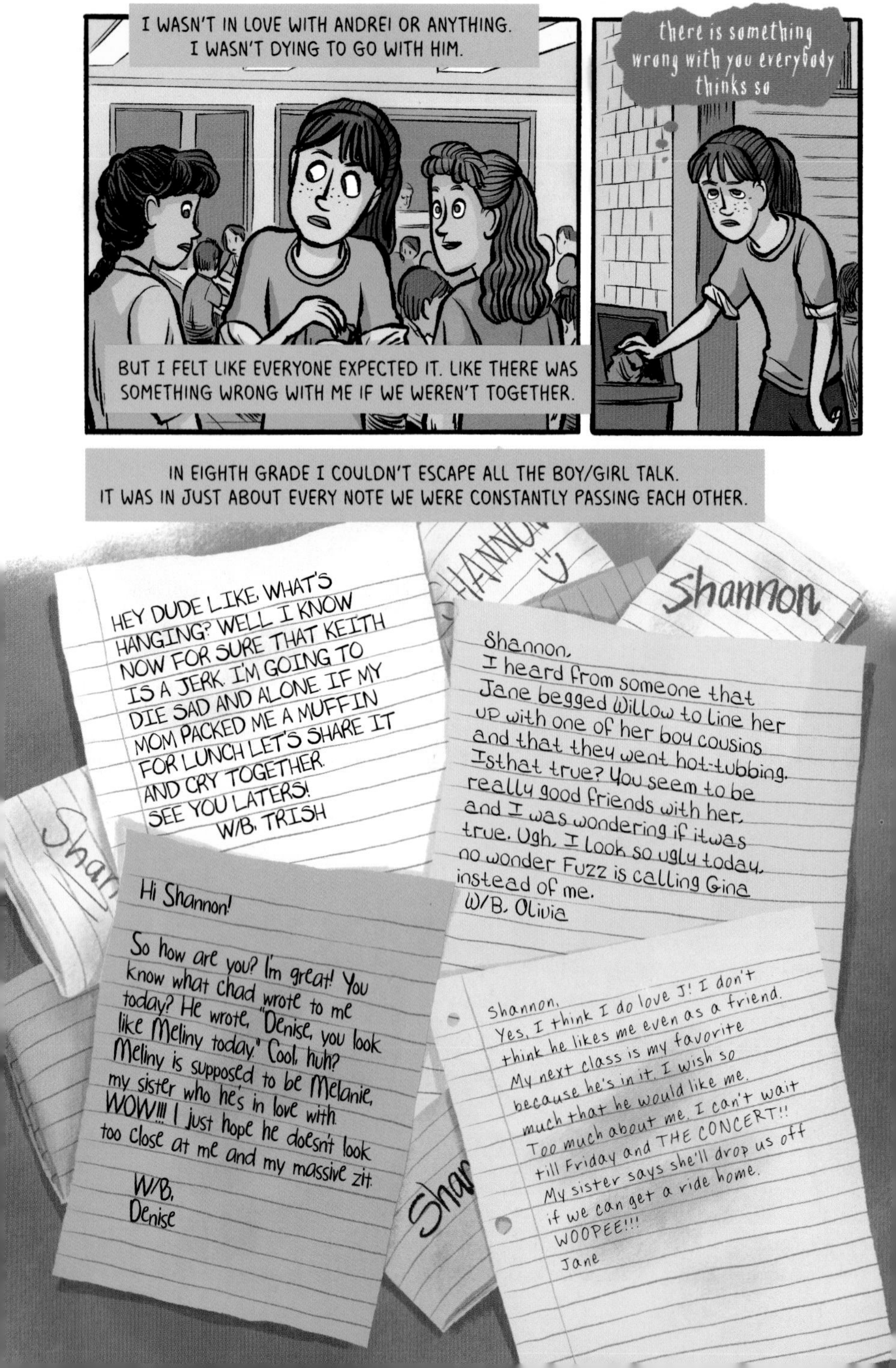
I WASN'T IN LOVE WITH ANDREI OR ANYTHING. I WASN'T DYING TO GO WITH HIM.
BUT I FELT LIKE EVERYONE EXPECTED IT. LIKE THERE WAS SOMETHING WRONG WITH ME IF WE WEREN'T TOGETHER.
there is something wrong with you everybody thinks so
IN EIGHTH GRADE I COULDN'T ESCAPE ALL THE BOY/GIRL TALK. IT WAS IN JUST ABOUT EVERY NOTE WE WERE CONSTANTLY PASSING EACH OTHER.
Shannon
HEY DUDE LIKE, WHAT'S HANGING? WELL I KNOW NOW FOR SURE THAT KEITH IS A JERK. I'M GOING TO DIE SAD AND ALONE. IF MY MOM PACKED ME A MUFFIN FOR LUNCH LET'S SHARE IT AND CRY TOGETHER. SEE YOU LATERS! W/B, TRISH
Shannon, I heard from someone that Jane begged Willow to line her up with one of her boy cousins and that they went hot-tubbing. Isthat true? You seem to be really good friends with her, and I was wondering if itwas true. Ugh, I look so ugly today, no wonder Fuzz is calling Gina instead of me. W/B, Olivia
Hi Shannon! So how are you? I'm great! You know what chad wrote to me today? He wrote, "Denise, you look like Meliny today." Cool, huh? Meliny is supposed to be Melanie, my sister who he's in love with. WOW!!! I just hope he doesn't look too close at me and my massive zit. W/B, Denise
Shannon, Yes, I think I do love J! I don't think he likes me even as a friend. My next class is my favorite because he's in it. I wish so much that he would like me. Too much about me. I can't wait till Friday and THE CONCERT!! My sister says she'll drop us off if we can get a ride home. WOOPEE!!! Jane

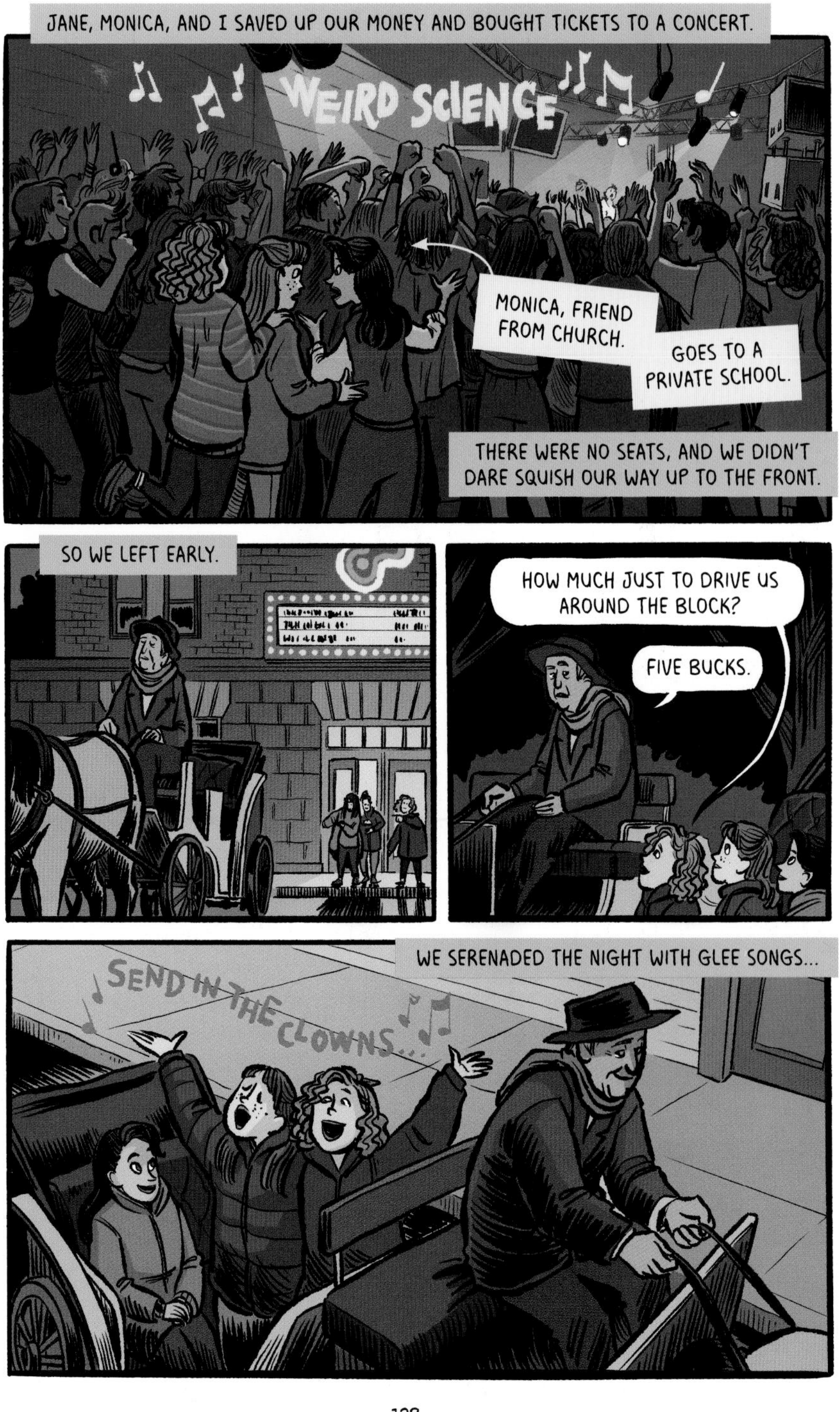
JANE, MONICA, AND I SAVED UP OUR MONEY AND BOUGHT TICKETS TO A CONCERT.
WEIRD SCIENCE
MONICA, FRIEND FROM CHURCH.
GOES TO A PRIVATE SCHOOL.
THERE WERE NO SEATS, AND WE DIDN'T DARE SQUISH OUR WAY UP TO THE FRONT.
SO WE LEFT EARLY.
HOW MUCH JUST TO DRIVE US AROUND THE BLOCK?
FIVE BUCKS.
WE SERENADED THE NIGHT WITH GLEE SONGS...
SEND IN THE CLOWNS...

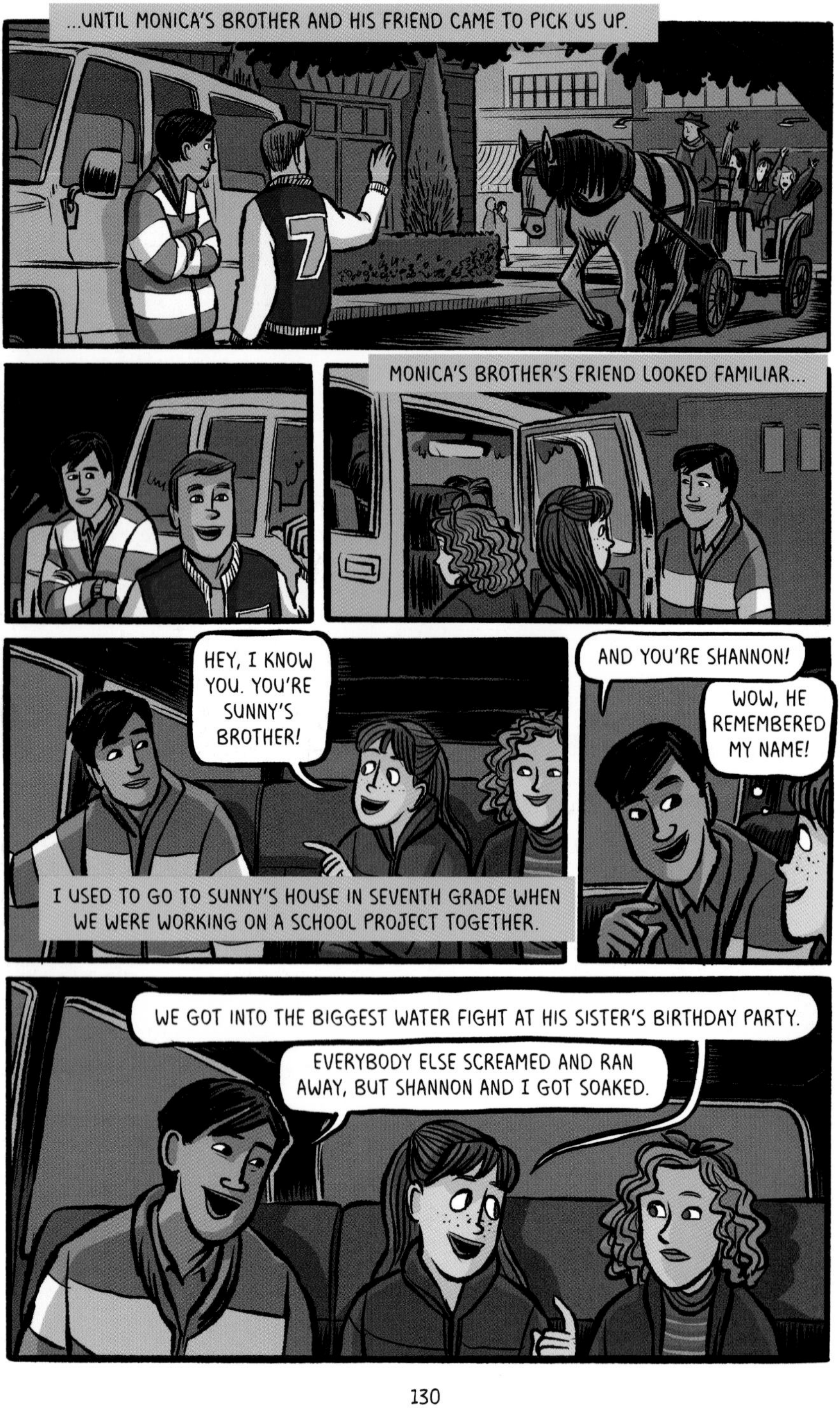
...UNTIL MONICA'S BROTHER AND HIS FRIEND CAME TO PICK US UP.
MONICA'S BROTHER'S FRIEND LOOKED FAMILIAR...
HEY, I KNOW YOU. YOU'RE SUNNY'S BROTHER!
I USED TO GO TO SUNNY'S HOUSE IN SEVENTH GRADE WHEN WE WERE WORKING ON A SCHOOL PROJECT TOGETHER.
AND YOU'RE SHANNON!
WOW, HE REMEMBERED MY NAME!
WE GOT INTO THE BIGGEST WATER FIGHT AT HIS SISTER'S BIRTHDAY PARTY.
EVERYBODY ELSE SCREAMED AND RAN AWAY, BUT SHANNON AND I GOT SOAKED.

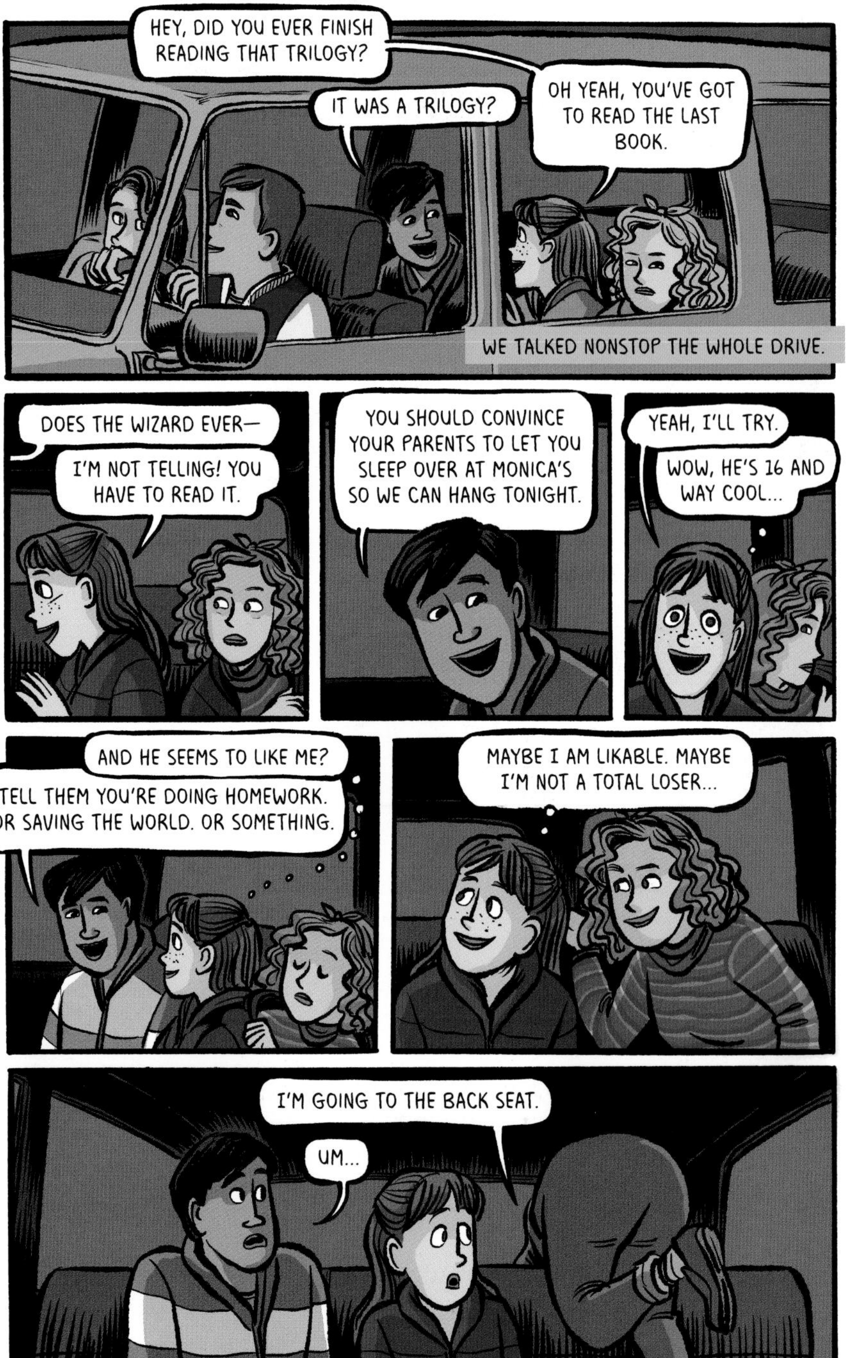
HEY, DID YOU EVER FINISH READING THAT TRILOGY?
IT WAS A TRILOGY?
OH YEAH, YOU'VE GOT TO READ THE LAST BOOK.
WE TALKED NONSTOP THE WHOLE DRIVE.
DOES THE WIZARD EVER—
I'M NOT TELLING! YOU HAVE TO READ IT.
YOU SHOULD CONVINCE YOUR PARENTS TO LET YOU SLEEP OVER AT MONICA'S SO WE CAN HANG TONIGHT.
YEAH, I'LL TRY.
WOW, HE'S 16 AND WAY COOL...
AND HE SEEMS TO LIKE ME?
TELL THEM YOU'RE DOING HOMEWORK. OR SAVING THE WORLD. OR SOMETHING.
MAYBE I AM LIKABLE. MAYBE I'M NOT A TOTAL LOSER...
I'M GOING TO THE BACK SEAT.
UM...

DOES ANYBODY WANT TO JOIN ME BACK HERE? PREFERABLY A BOY?

I'LL TAKE YOU UP ON THAT.

HAHAHA!

YOU'RE SUCH A GOOF.

WHAT ABOUT THIS? IS THIS BETTER?

HA, NICE SULTRY VOICE.

YOU CAN DROP ME OFF FIRST.

HAHAHAHA!

SLAM!!

YOU CAN DROP ME OFF FIRST.

HAHAHA!

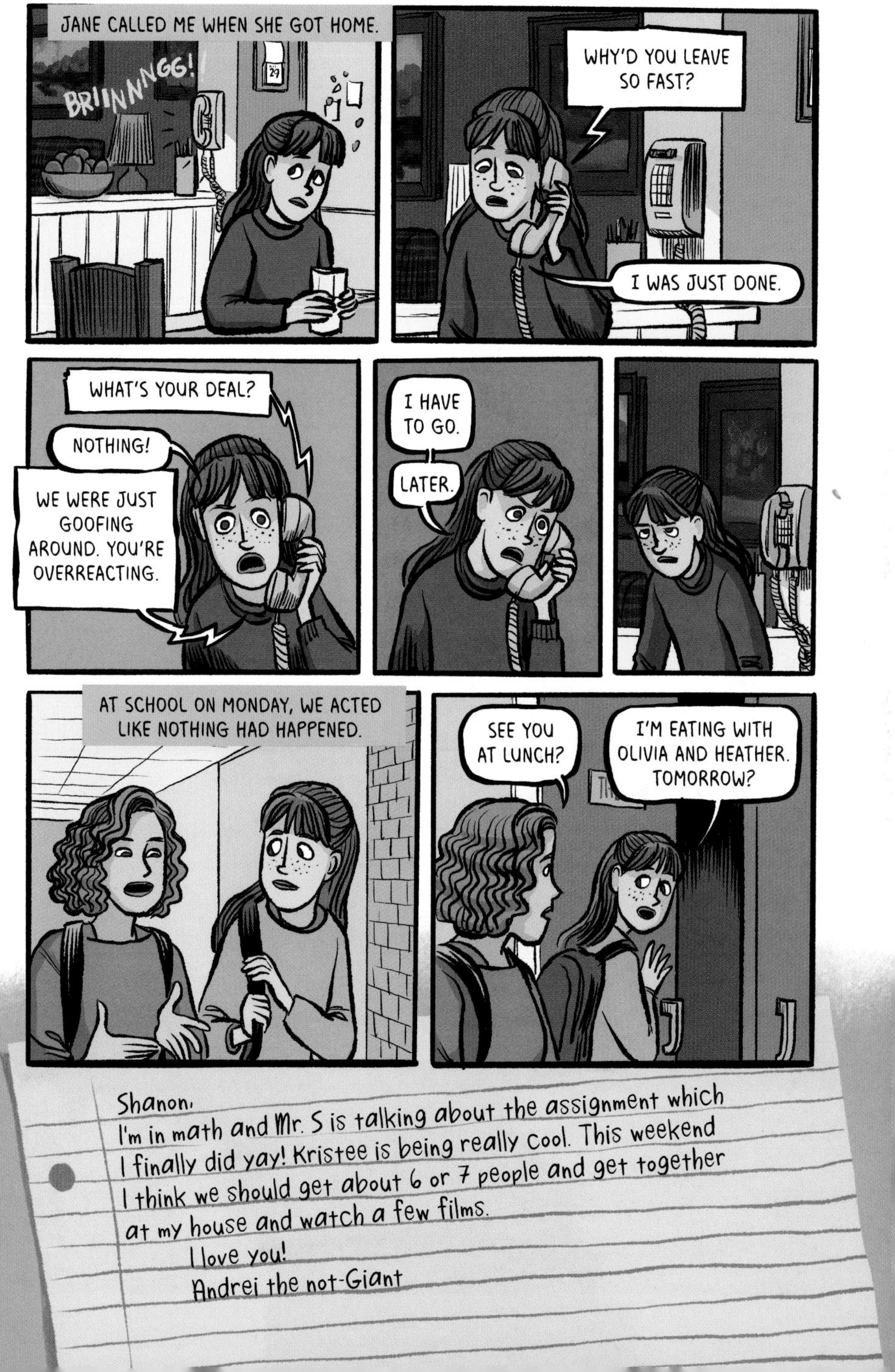
JANE CALLED ME WHEN SHE GOT HOME.
BRIINNNGG!!
WHY'D YOU LEAVE SO FAST?
I WAS JUST DONE.
WHAT'S YOUR DEAL?
NOTHING!
WE WERE JUST GOOFING AROUND. YOU'RE OVERREACTING.
I HAVE TO GO.
LATER.
AT SCHOOL ON MONDAY, WE ACTED LIKE NOTHING HAD HAPPENED.
SEE YOU AT LUNCH?
I'M EATING WITH OLIVIA AND HEATHER. TOMORROW?
Shanon,
I'm in math and Mr. S is talking about the assignment which
I finally did yay! Kristee is being really cool. This weekend
I think we should get about 6 or 7 people and get together
at my house and watch a few films.
I love you!
Andrei the not-Giant

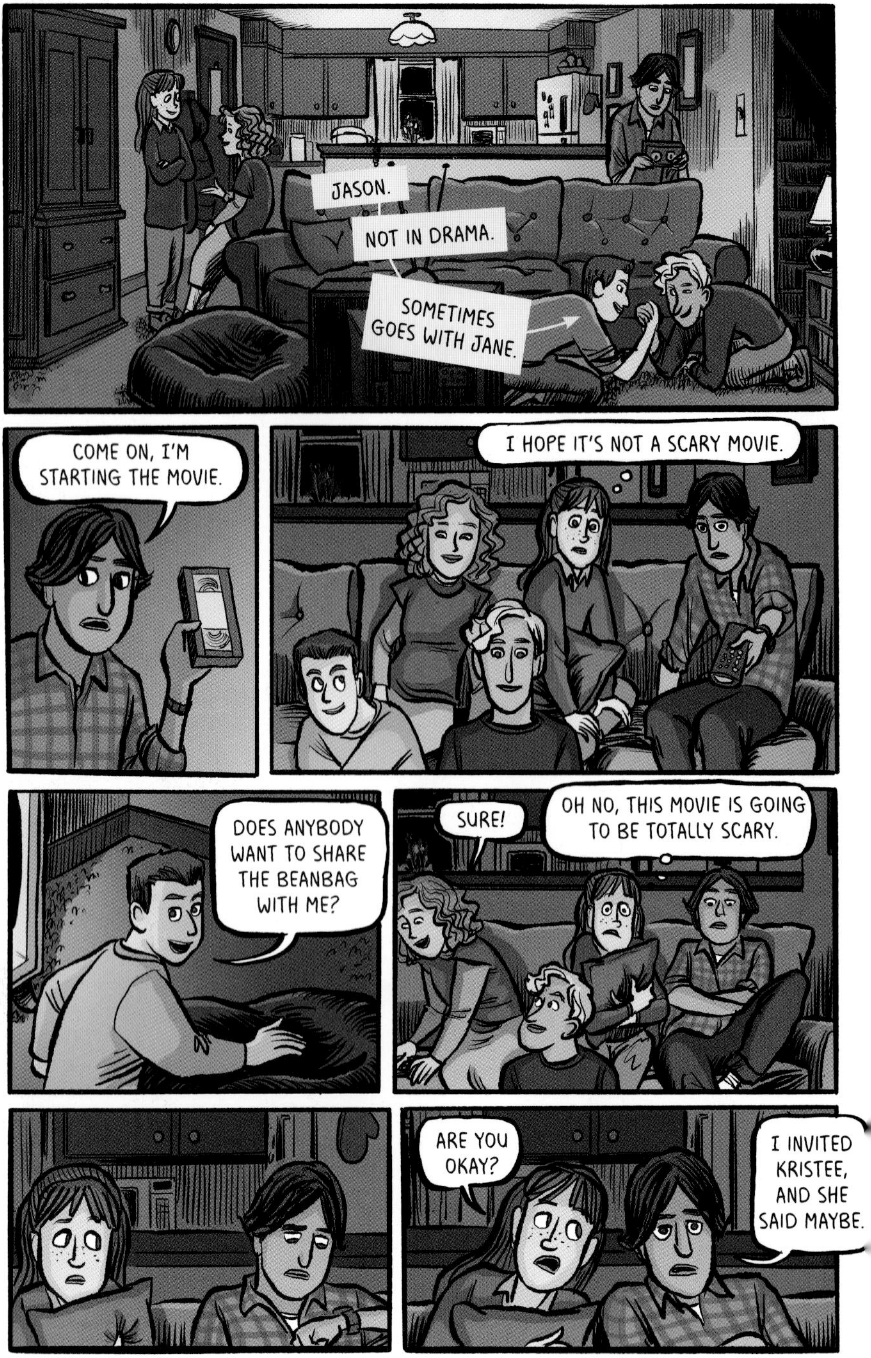
JASON.
NOT IN DRAMA.
SOMETIMES GOES WITH JANE.
COME ON, I'M STARTING THE MOVIE.
I HOPE IT'S NOT A SCARY MOVIE.
DOES ANYBODY WANT TO SHARE THE BEANBAG WITH ME?
SURE!
OH NO, THIS MOVIE IS GOING TO BE TOTALLY SCARY.
ARE YOU OKAY?
I INVITED KRISTEE, AND SHE SAID MAYBE.

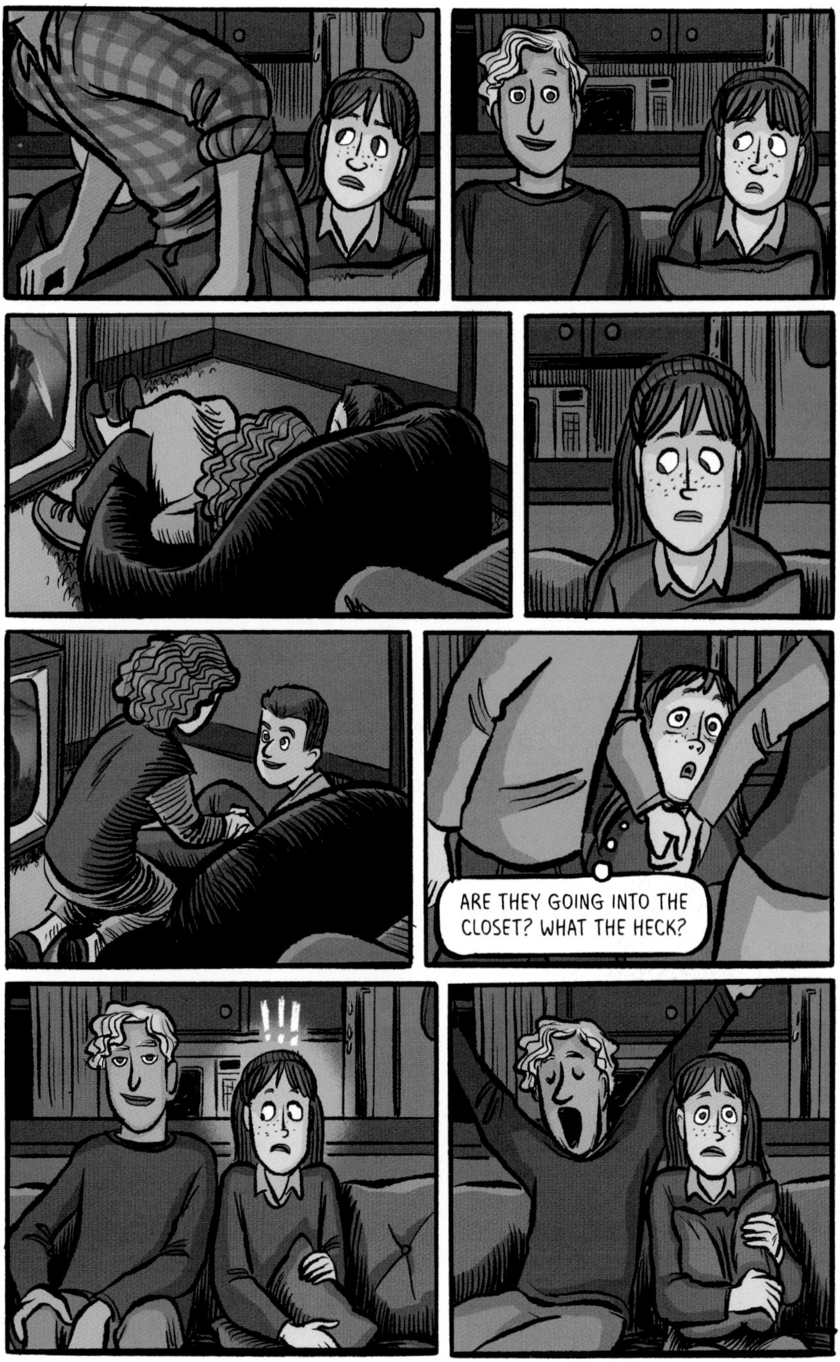
!!
ARE THEY GOING INTO THE CLOSET? WHAT THE HECK?

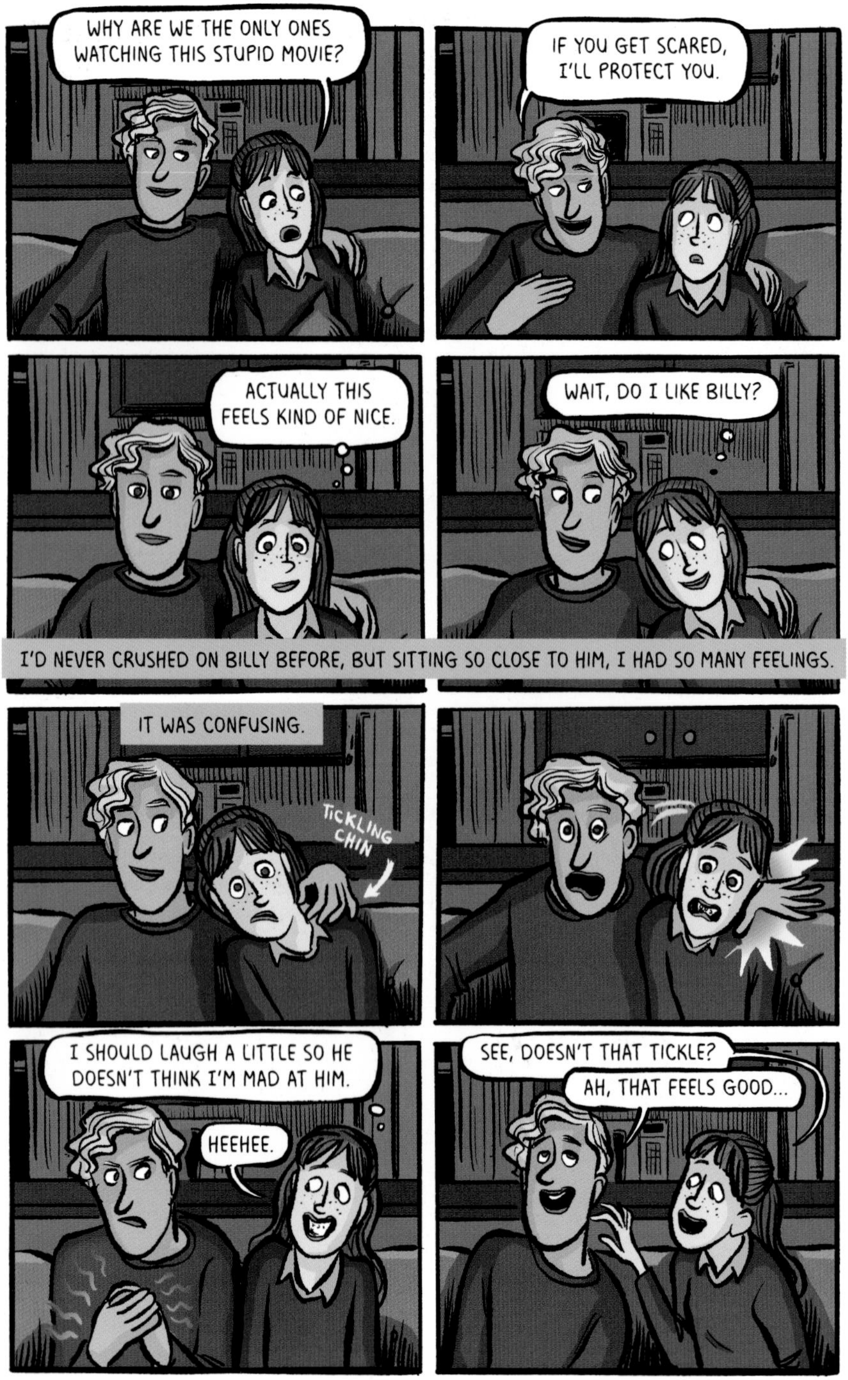
WHY ARE WE THE ONLY ONES WATCHING THIS STUPID MOVIE?
IF YOU GET SCARED, I'LL PROTECT YOU.
ACTUALLY THIS FEELS KIND OF NICE.
WAIT, DO I LIKE BILLY?
I'D NEVER CRUSHED ON BILLY BEFORE, BUT SITTING SO CLOSE TO HIM, I HAD SO MANY FEELINGS.
IT WAS CONFUSING.
TICKLING CHIN
I SHOULD LAUGH A LITTLE SO HE DOESN'T THINK I'M MAD AT HIM.
HEEHEE.
SEE, DOESN'T THAT TICKLE?
AH, THAT FEELS GOOD...

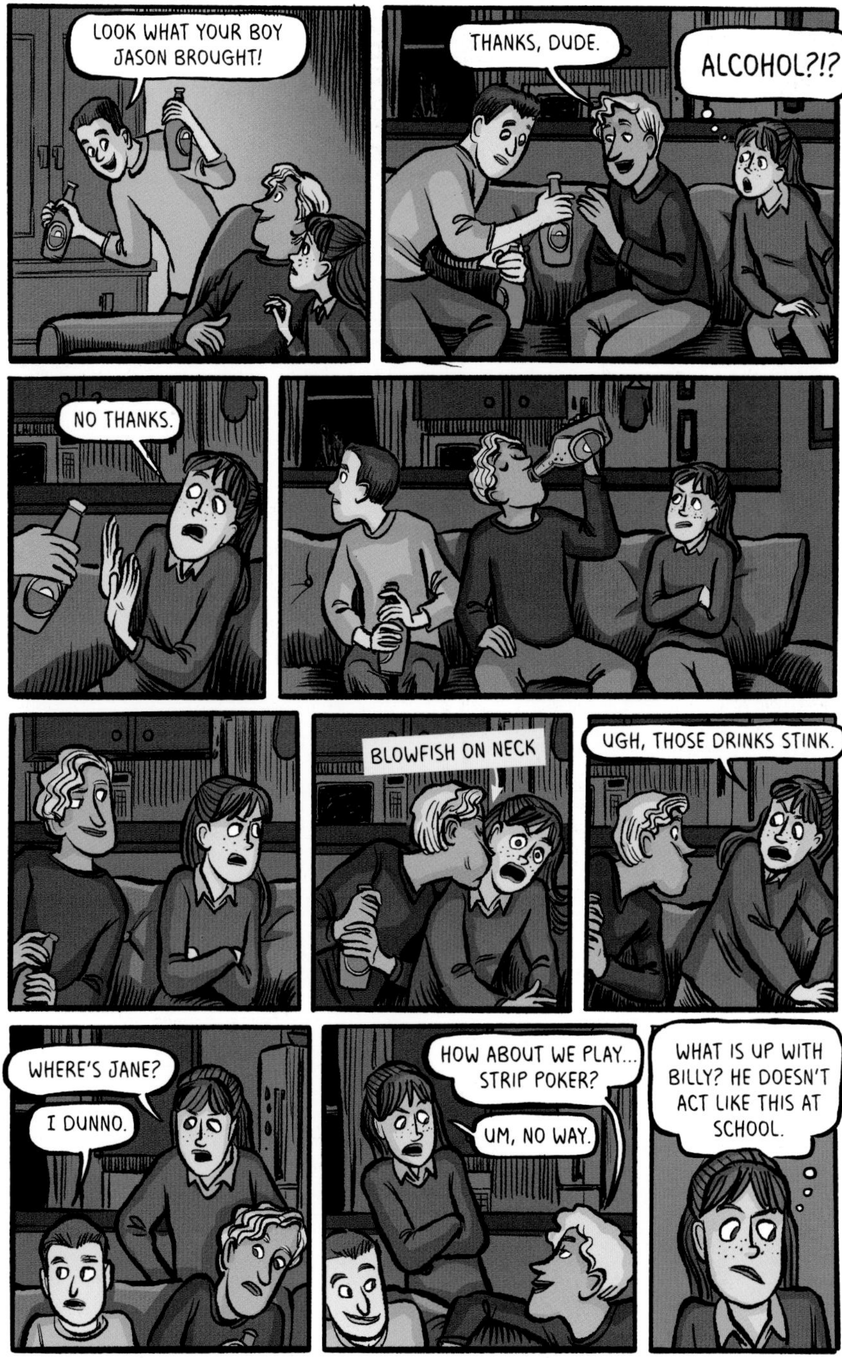
LOOK WHAT YOUR BOY JASON BROUGHT!
THANKS, DUDE.
ALCOHOL?!?
NO THANKS.
BLOWFISH ON NECK
UGH, THOSE DRINKS STINK.
WHERE'S JANE?
I DUNNO.
HOW ABOUT WE PLAY... STRIP POKER?
UM, NO WAY.
WHAT IS UP WITH BILLY? HE DOESN'T ACT LIKE THIS AT SCHOOL.

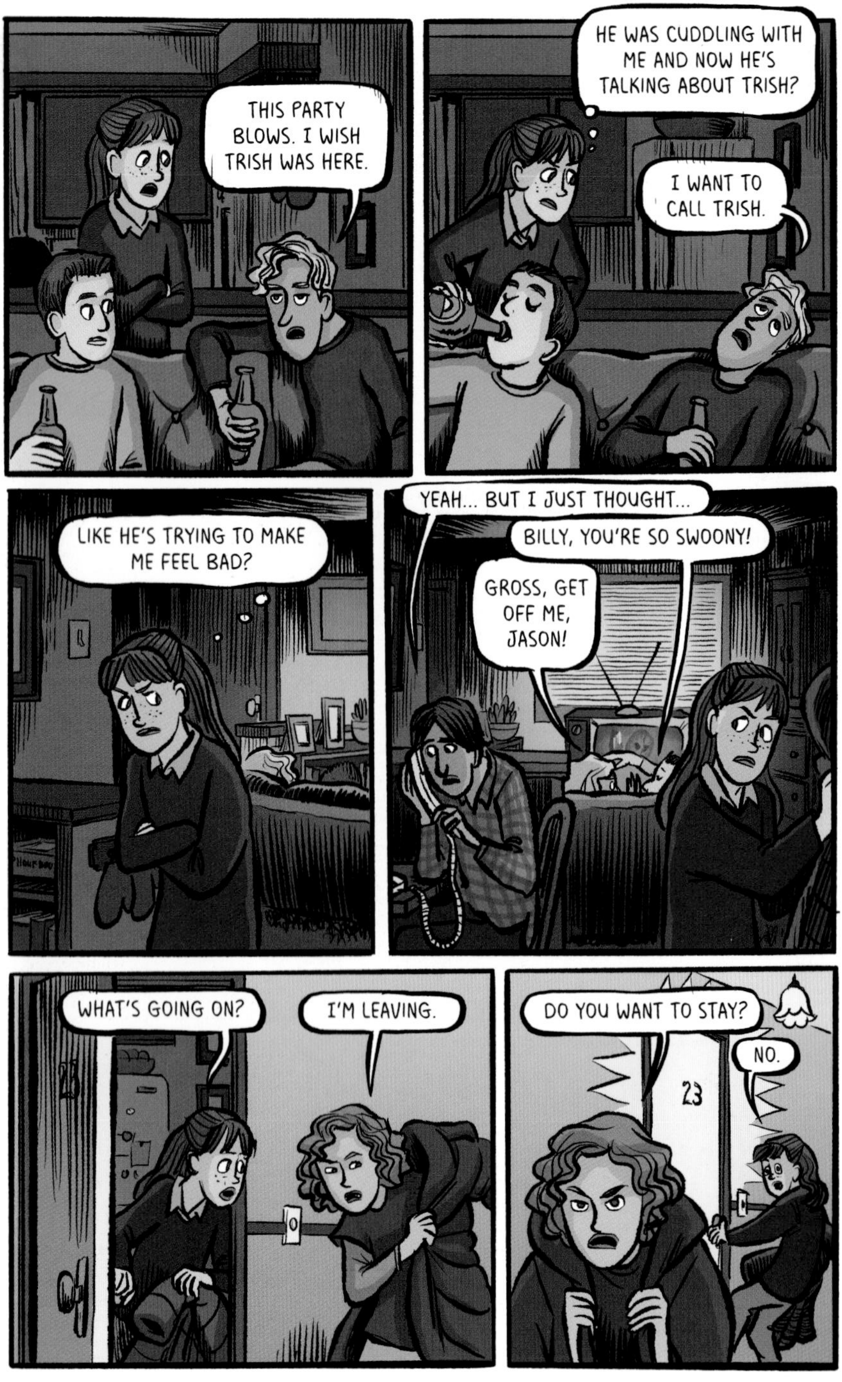
THIS PARTY BLOWS. I WISH TRISH WAS HERE.
HE WAS CUDDLING WITH ME AND NOW HE'S TALKING ABOUT TRISH?
I WANT TO CALL TRISH.
LIKE HE'S TRYING TO MAKE ME FEEL BAD?
YEAH... BUT I JUST THOUGHT...
BILLY, YOU'RE SO SWOONY!
GROSS, GET OFF ME, JASON!
WHAT'S GOING ON?
I'M LEAVING.
DO YOU WANT TO STAY?
NO.
23

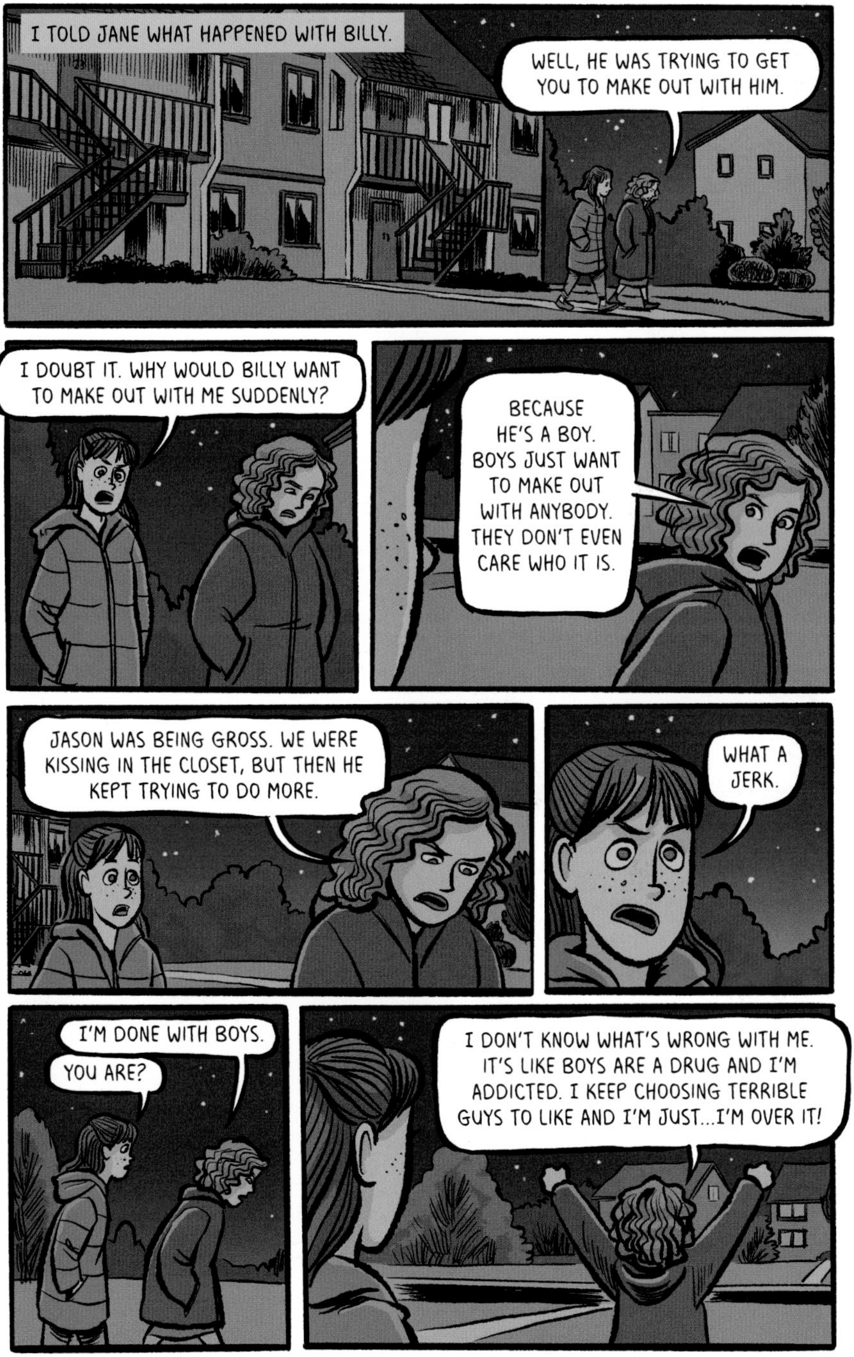
I TOLD JANE WHAT HAPPENED WITH BILLY.
WELL, HE WAS TRYING TO GET YOU TO MAKE OUT WITH HIM.
I DOUBT IT. WHY WOULD BILLY WANT TO MAKE OUT WITH ME SUDDENLY?
BECAUSE HE'S A BOY. BOYS JUST WANT TO MAKE OUT WITH ANYBODY. THEY DON'T EVEN CARE WHO IT IS.
JASON WAS BEING GROSS. WE WERE KISSING IN THE CLOSET, BUT THEN HE KEPT TRYING TO DO MORE.
WHAT A JERK.
I'M DONE WITH BOYS.
YOU ARE?
I DON'T KNOW WHAT'S WRONG WITH ME. IT'S LIKE BOYS ARE A DRUG AND I'M ADDICTED. I KEEP CHOOSING TERRIBLE GUYS TO LIKE AND I'M JUST...I'M OVER IT!

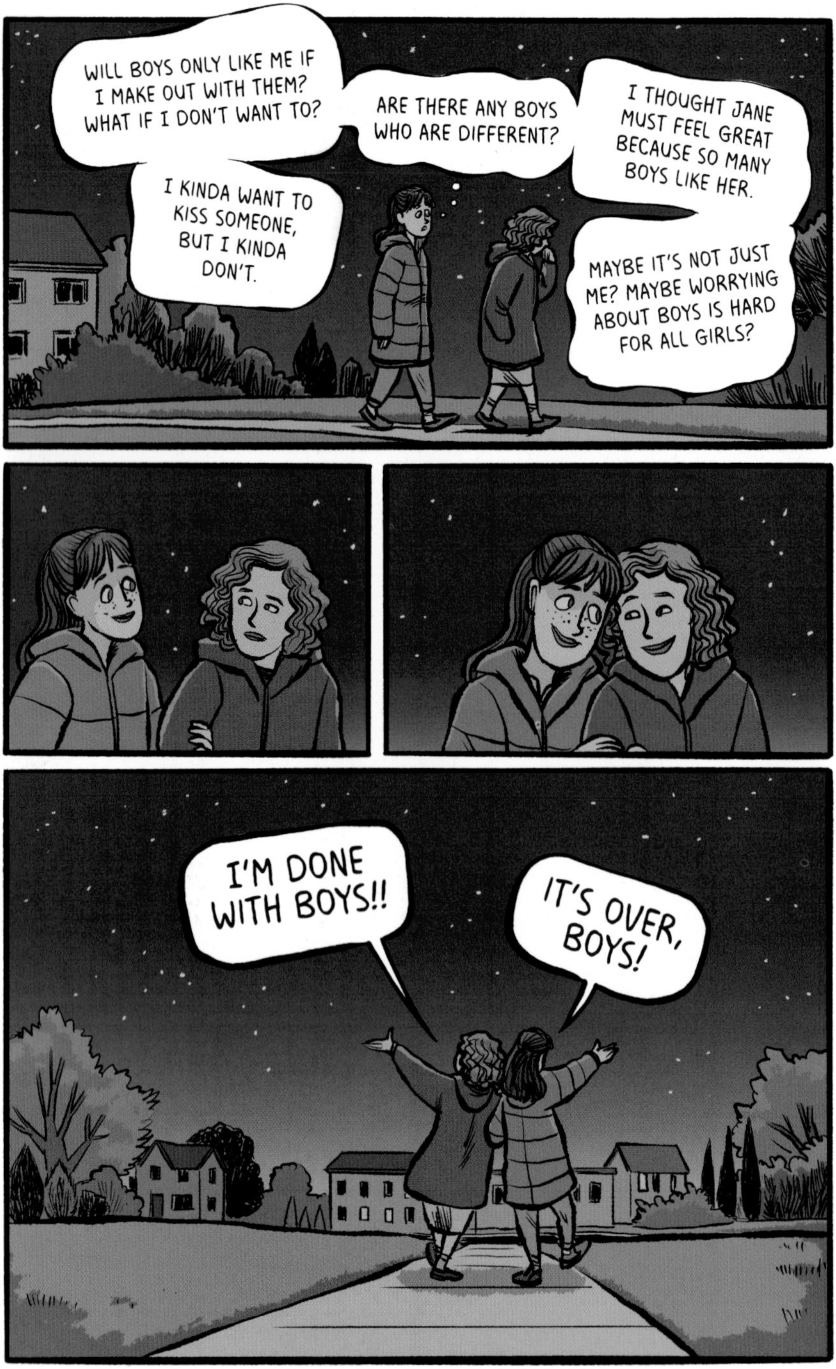
WILL BOYS ONLY LIKE ME IF I MAKE OUT WITH THEM? WHAT IF I DON'T WANT TO?
I KINDA WANT TO KISS SOMEONE, BUT I KINDA DON'T.
ARE THERE ANY BOYS WHO ARE DIFFERENT?
I THOUGHT JANE MUST FEEL GREAT BECAUSE SO MANY BOYS LIKE HER.
MAYBE IT'S NOT JUST ME? MAYBE WORRYING ABOUT BOYS IS HARD FOR ALL GIRLS?
I'M DONE WITH BOYS!!
IT'S OVER, BOYS!

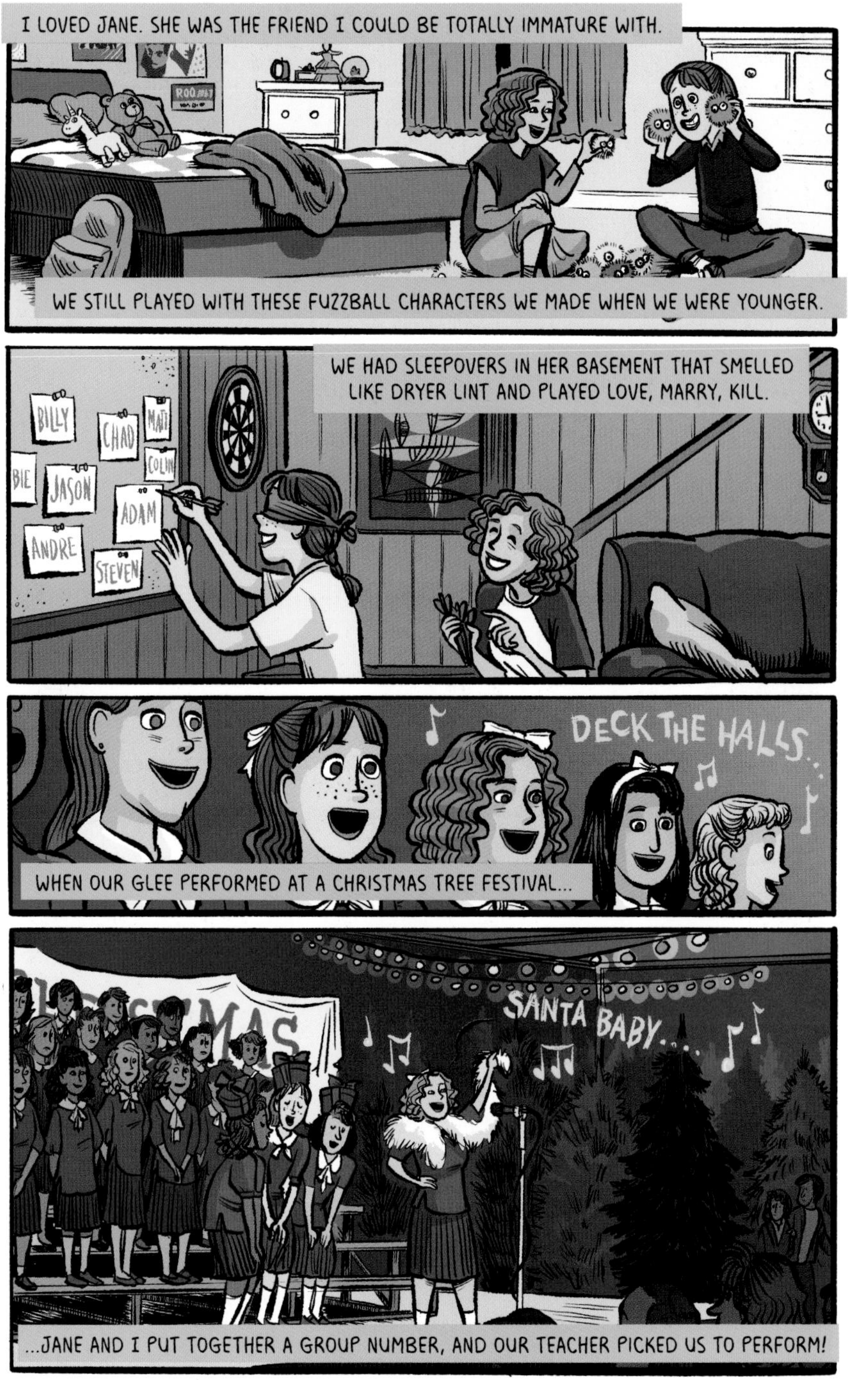
I LOVED JANE. SHE WAS THE FRIEND I COULD BE TOTALLY IMMATURE WITH.
WE STILL PLAYED WITH THESE FUZZBALL CHARACTERS WE MADE WHEN WE WERE YOUNGER.
WE HAD SLEEPOVERS IN HER BASEMENT THAT SMELLED LIKE DRYER LINT AND PLAYED LOVE, MARRY, KILL.
BILLY
CHAD
MATT
COLIN
JASON
ADAM
ANDRE
STEVEN
DECK THE HALLS...
WHEN OUR GLEE PERFORMED AT A CHRISTMAS TREE FESTIVAL...
SANTA BABY....
...JANE AND I PUT TOGETHER A GROUP NUMBER, AND OUR TEACHER PICKED US TO PERFORM!

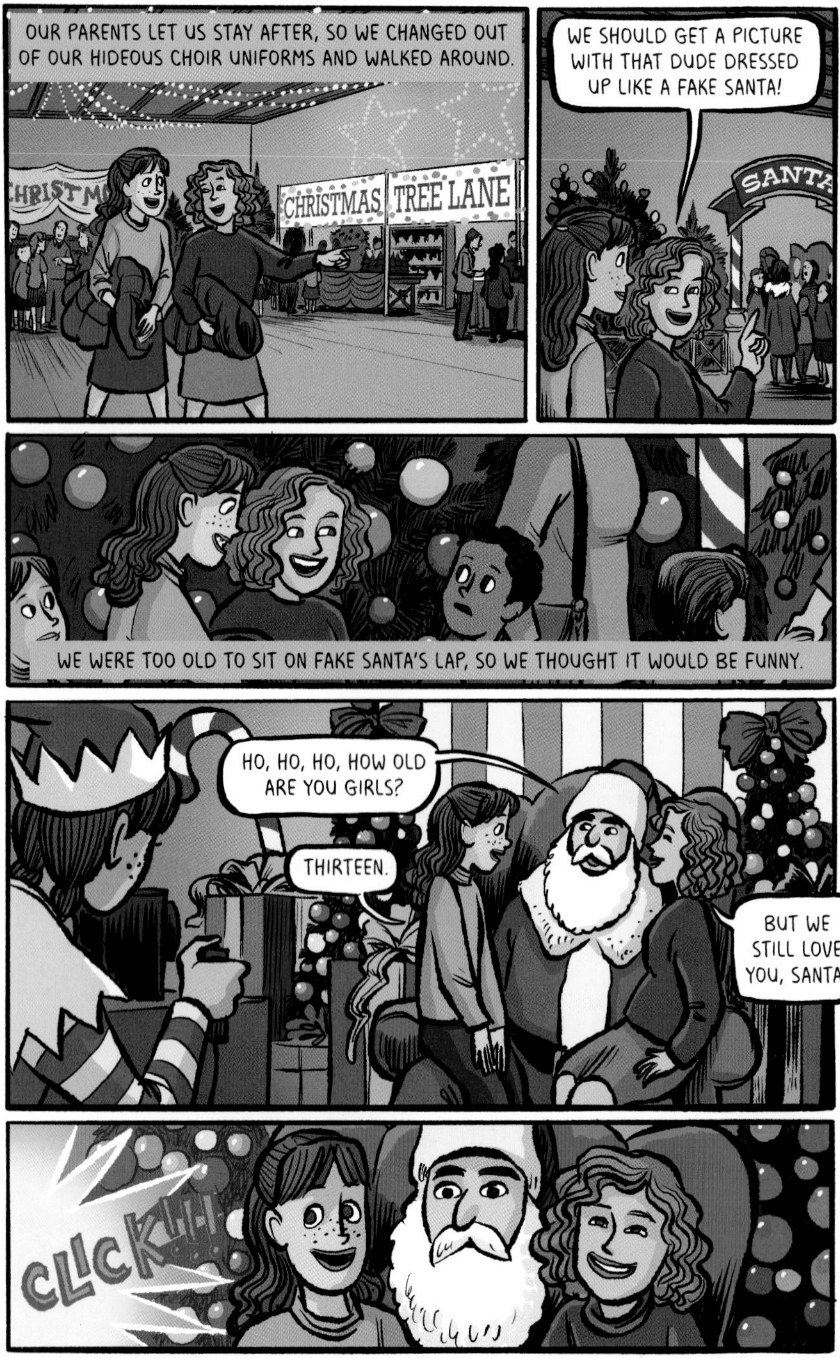
OUR PARENTS LET US STAY AFTER, SO WE CHANGED OUT OF OUR HIDEOUS CHOIR UNIFORMS AND WALKED AROUND.
CHRISTMAS TREE LANE
WE SHOULD GET A PICTURE WITH THAT DUDE DRESSED UP LIKE A FAKE SANTA!
SANTA
WE WERE TOO OLD TO SIT ON FAKE SANTA'S LAP, SO WE THOUGHT IT WOULD BE FUNNY.
HO, HO, HO, HOW OLD ARE YOU GIRLS?
THIRTEEN.
BUT WE STILL LOVE YOU, SANTA!
CLICKHH

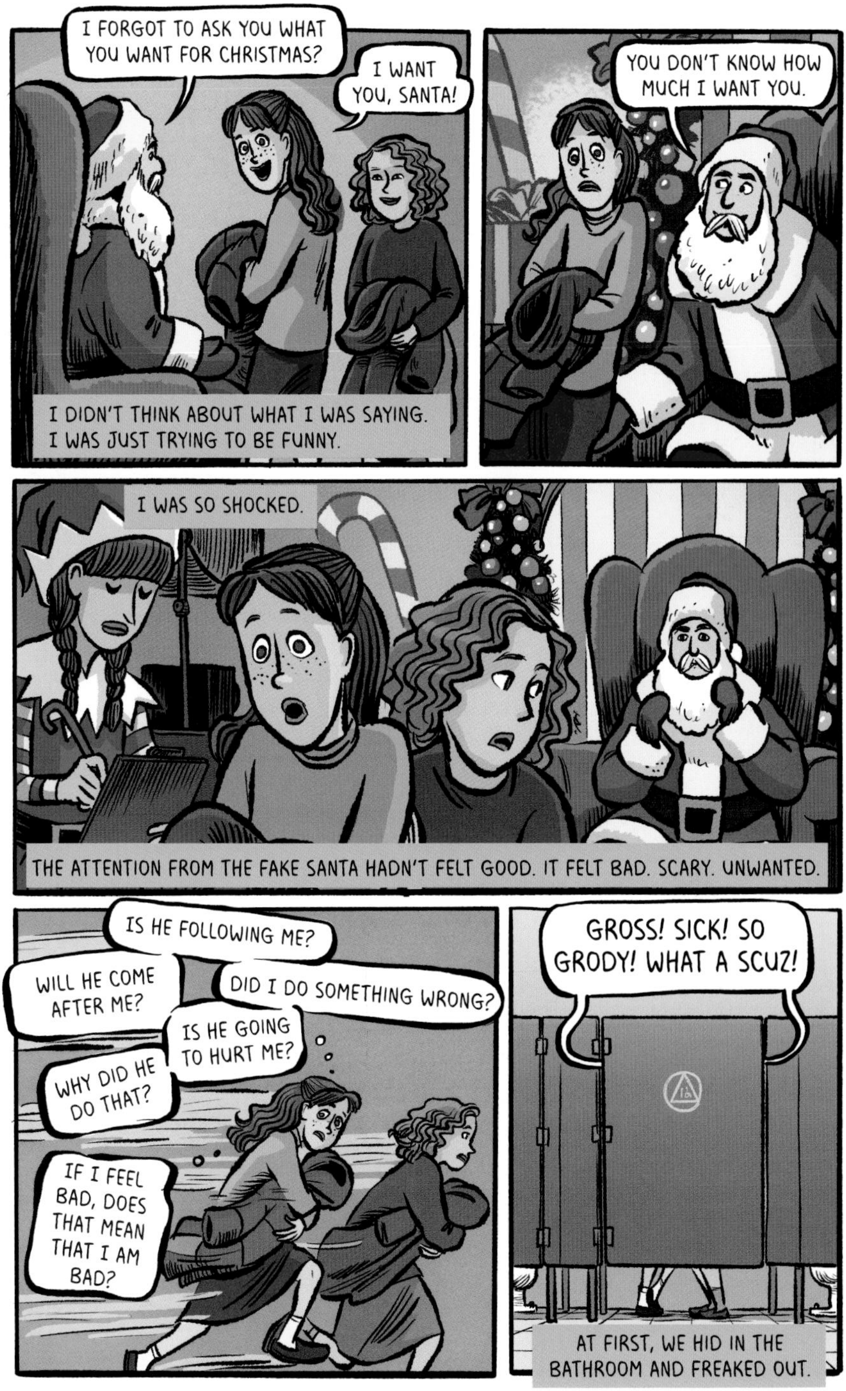
I FORGOT TO ASK YOU WHAT YOU WANT FOR CHRISTMAS?
I WANT YOU, SANTA!
I DIDN'T THINK ABOUT WHAT I WAS SAYING. I WAS JUST TRYING TO BE FUNNY.
YOU DON'T KNOW HOW MUCH I WANT YOU.
I WAS SO SHOCKED.
THE ATTENTION FROM THE FAKE SANTA HADN'T FELT GOOD. IT FELT BAD. SCARY. UNWANTED.
IS HE FOLLOWING ME?
WILL HE COME AFTER ME?
DID I DO SOMETHING WRONG?
IS HE GOING TO HURT ME?
WHY DID HE DO THAT?
IF I FEEL BAD, DOES THAT MEAN THAT I AM BAD?
GROSS! SICK! SO GRODY! WHAT A SCUZ!
AT FIRST, WE HID IN THE BATHROOM AND FREAKED OUT.

WHEN WE CALLED JANE'S MOM TO COME GET US, WE DIDN'T TELL HER WHAT HAPPENED.

I DON'T KNOW WHY. IT WASN'T OUR FAULT THAT THE FAKE SANTA WAS A CREEP.

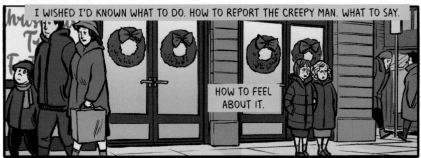
I WISHED I'D KNOWN WHAT TO DO. HOW TO REPORT THE CREEPY MAN. WHAT TO SAY.

HOW TO FEEL ABOUT IT.

BY THE NEXT DAY, MOSTLY I JUST FELT ANGRY.

IF YOU WANT TO GET BY, YOU HAVE TO LET ME SPANK YOU.

YOU'RE SUCH A DIRTBAG.

IS THAT WHAT YOU THINK? WELL, I THINK—

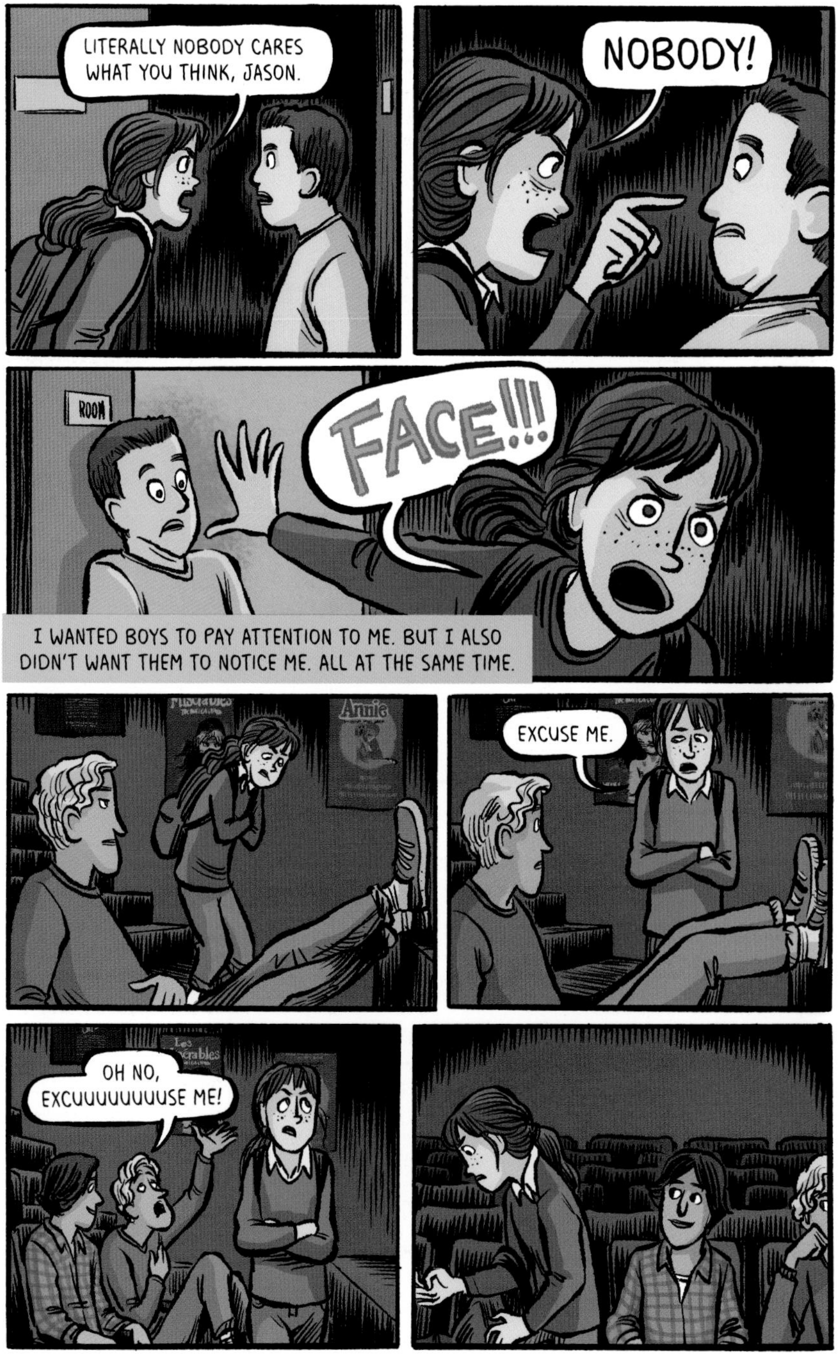
LITERALLY NOBODY CARES WHAT YOU THINK, JASON.
NOBODY!
ROOM
FACE!!!
I WANTED BOYS TO PAY ATTENTION TO ME. BUT I ALSO DIDN'T WANT THEM TO NOTICE ME. ALL AT THE SAME TIME.
Annie
EXCUSE ME.
OH NO, EXCUUUUUUUUSE ME!

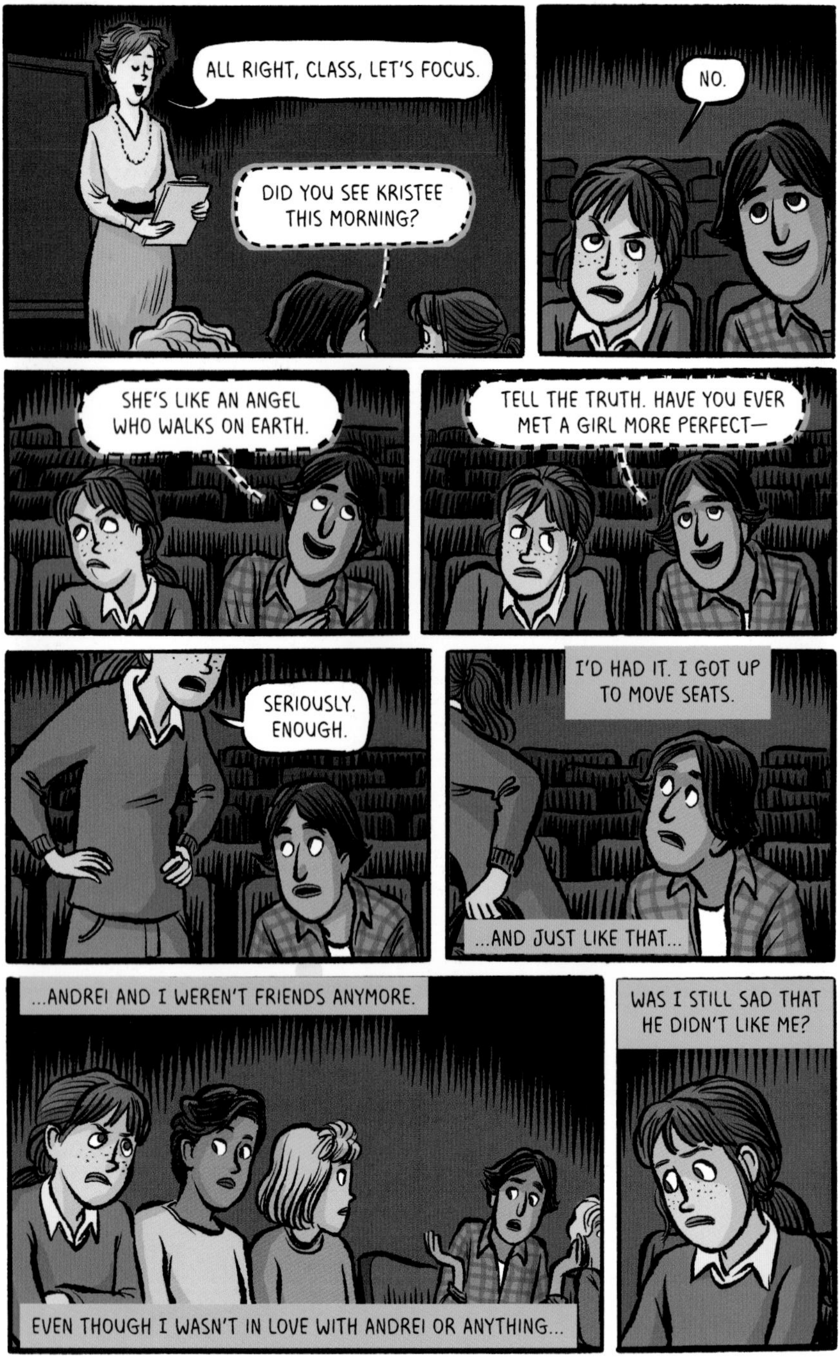
ALL RIGHT, CLASS, LET'S FOCUS.
DID YOU SEE KRISTEE THIS MORNING?
NO.
SHE'S LIKE AN ANGEL WHO WALKS ON EARTH.
TELL THE TRUTH. HAVE YOU EVER MET A GIRL MORE PERFECT—
SERIOUSLY. ENOUGH.
I'D HAD IT. I GOT UP TO MOVE SEATS.
...AND JUST LIKE THAT...
...ANDREI AND I WEREN'T FRIENDS ANYMORE.
EVEN THOUGH I WASN'T IN LOVE WITH ANDREI OR ANYTHING...
WAS I STILL SAD THAT HE DIDN'T LIKE ME?

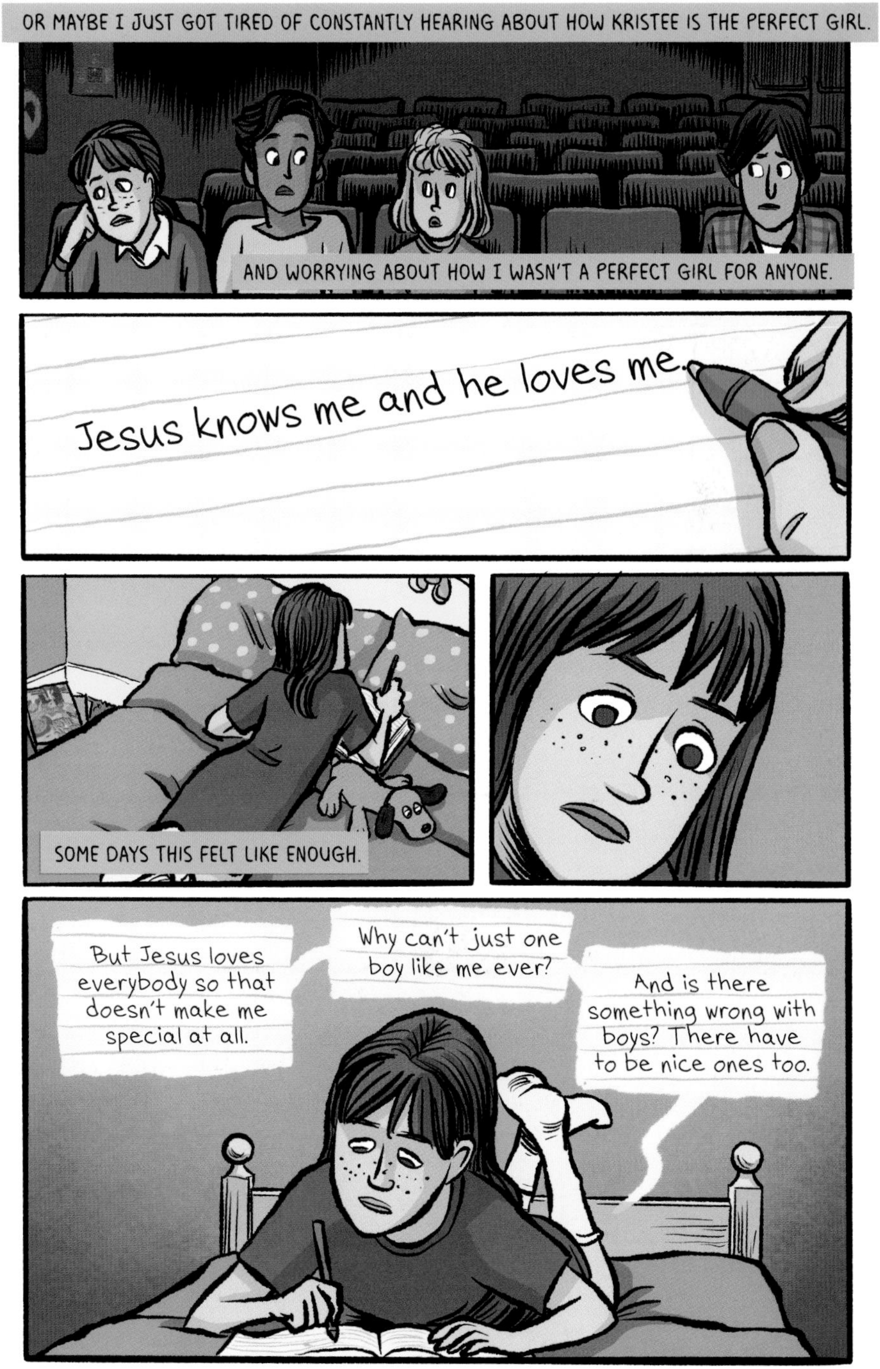
OR MAYBE I JUST GOT TIRED OF CONSTANTLY HEARING ABOUT HOW KRISTEE IS THE PERFECT GIRL.
AND WORRYING ABOUT HOW I WASN'T A PERFECT GIRL FOR ANYONE.
Jesus knows me and he loves me.
SOME DAYS THIS FELT LIKE ENOUGH.
But Jesus loves everybody so that doesn't make me special at all.
Why can't just one boy like me ever?
And is there something wrong with boys? There have to be nice ones too.

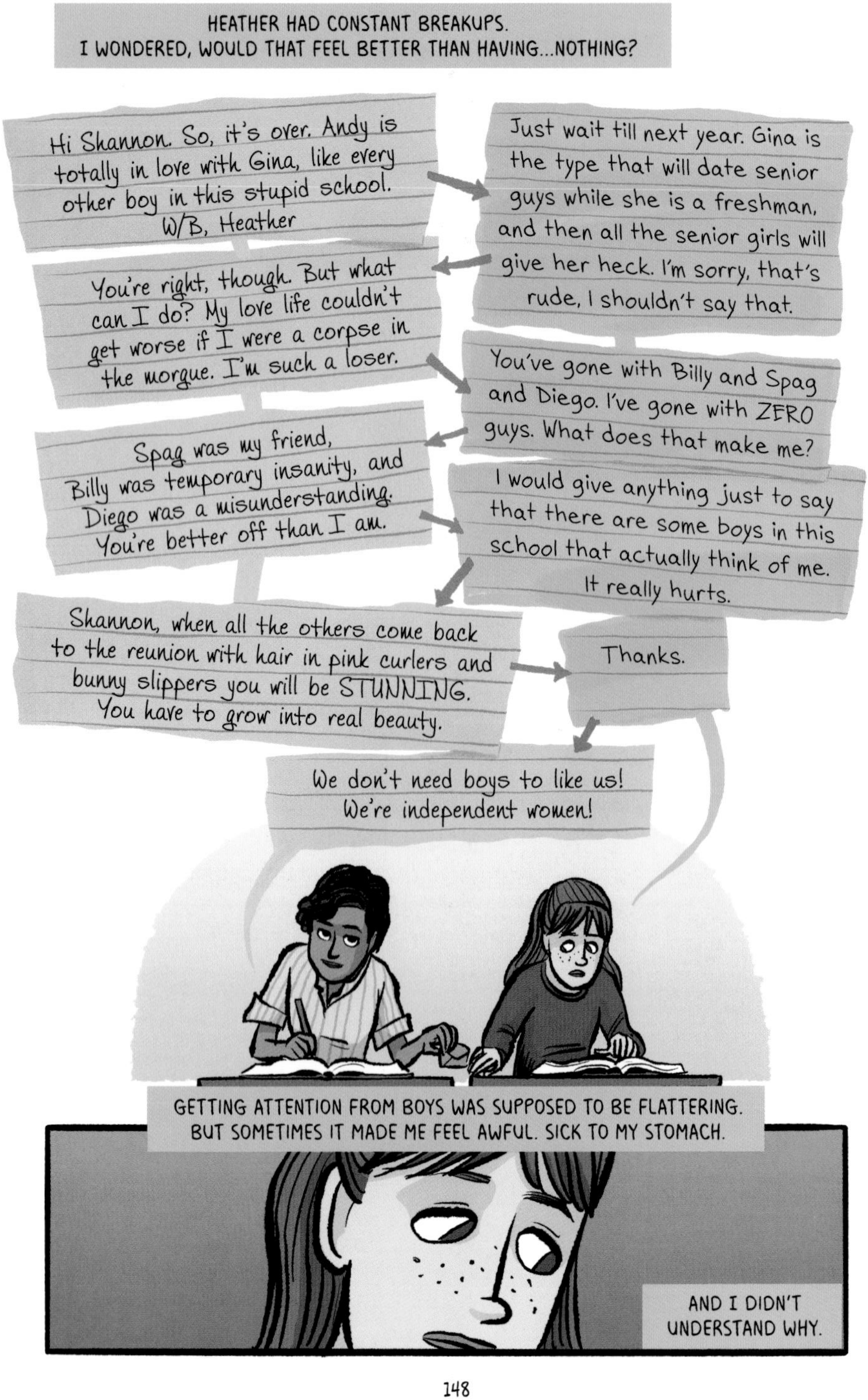
HEATHER HAD CONSTANT BREAKUPS. I WONDERED, WOULD THAT FEEL BETTER THAN HAVING...NOTHING?
Hi Shannon. So, it's over. Andy is totally in love with Gina, like every other boy in this stupid school. W/B, Heather
Just wait till next year. Gina is the type that will date senior guys while she is a freshman, and then all the senior girls will give her heck. I'm sorry, that's rude, I shouldn't say that.
You're right, though. But what can I do? My love life couldn't get worse if I were a corpse in the morgue. I'm such a loser.
You've gone with Billy and Spag and Diego. I've gone with ZERO guys. What does that make me?
Spag was my friend, Billy was temporary insanity, and Diego was a misunderstanding. You're better off than I am.
I would give anything just to say that there are some boys in this school that actually think of me. It really hurts.
Shannon, when all the others come back to the reunion with hair in pink curlers and bunny slippers you will be STUNNING. You have to grow into real beauty.
Thanks.
We don't need boys to like us! We're independent women!
GETTING ATTENTION FROM BOYS WAS SUPPOSED TO BE FLATTERING. BUT SOMETIMES IT MADE ME FEEL AWFUL. SICK TO MY STOMACH.
AND I DIDN'T UNDERSTAND WHY.

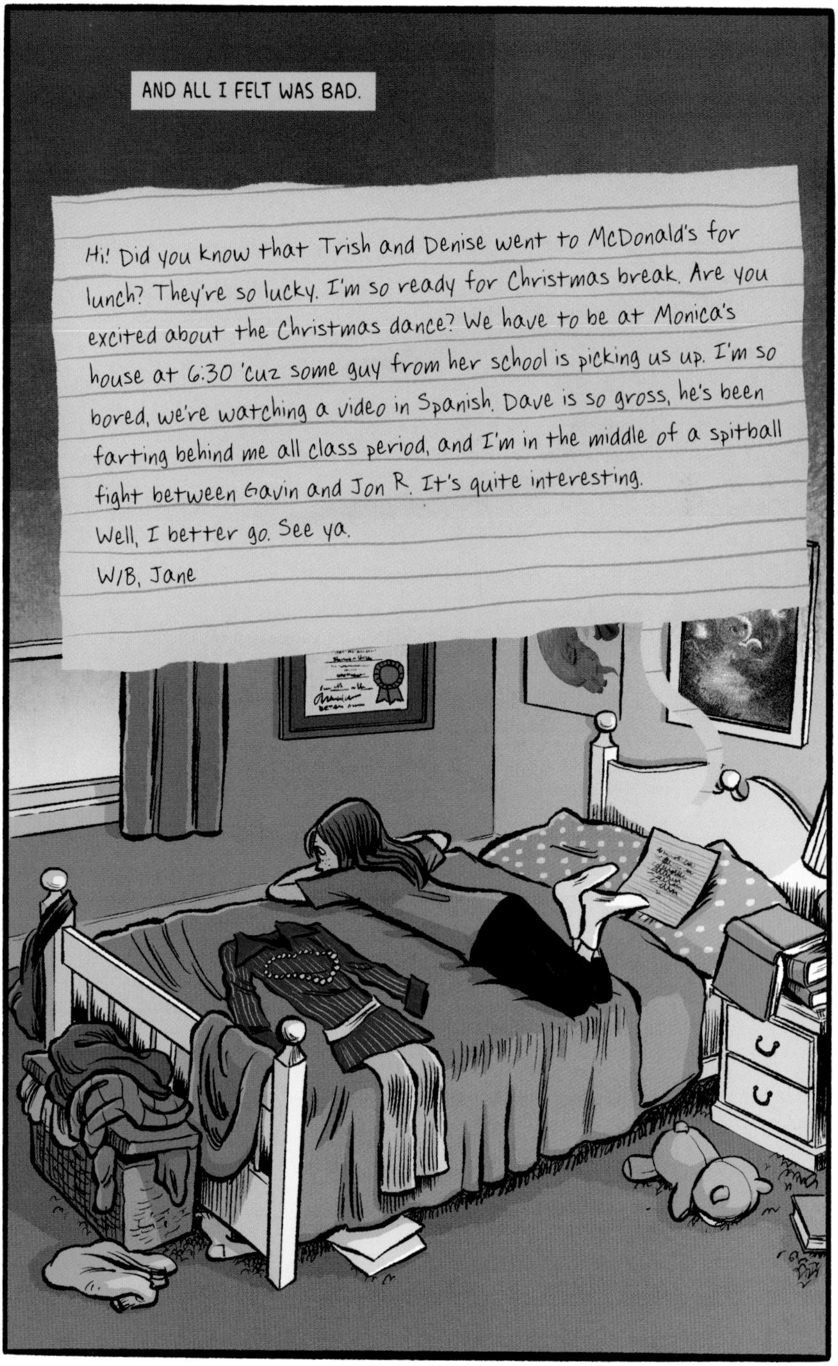
AND ALL I FELT WAS BAD.
Hi! Did you know that Trish and Denise went to McDonald's for lunch? They're so lucky. I'm so ready for Christmas break. Are you excited about the Christmas dance? We have to be at Monica's house at 6:30 'cuz some guy from her school is picking us up. I'm so bored, we're watching a video in Spanish. Dave is so gross, he's been farting behind me all class period, and I'm in the middle of a spitball fight between Gavin and Jon R. It's quite interesting.
Well, I better go. See ya.
W/B, Jane

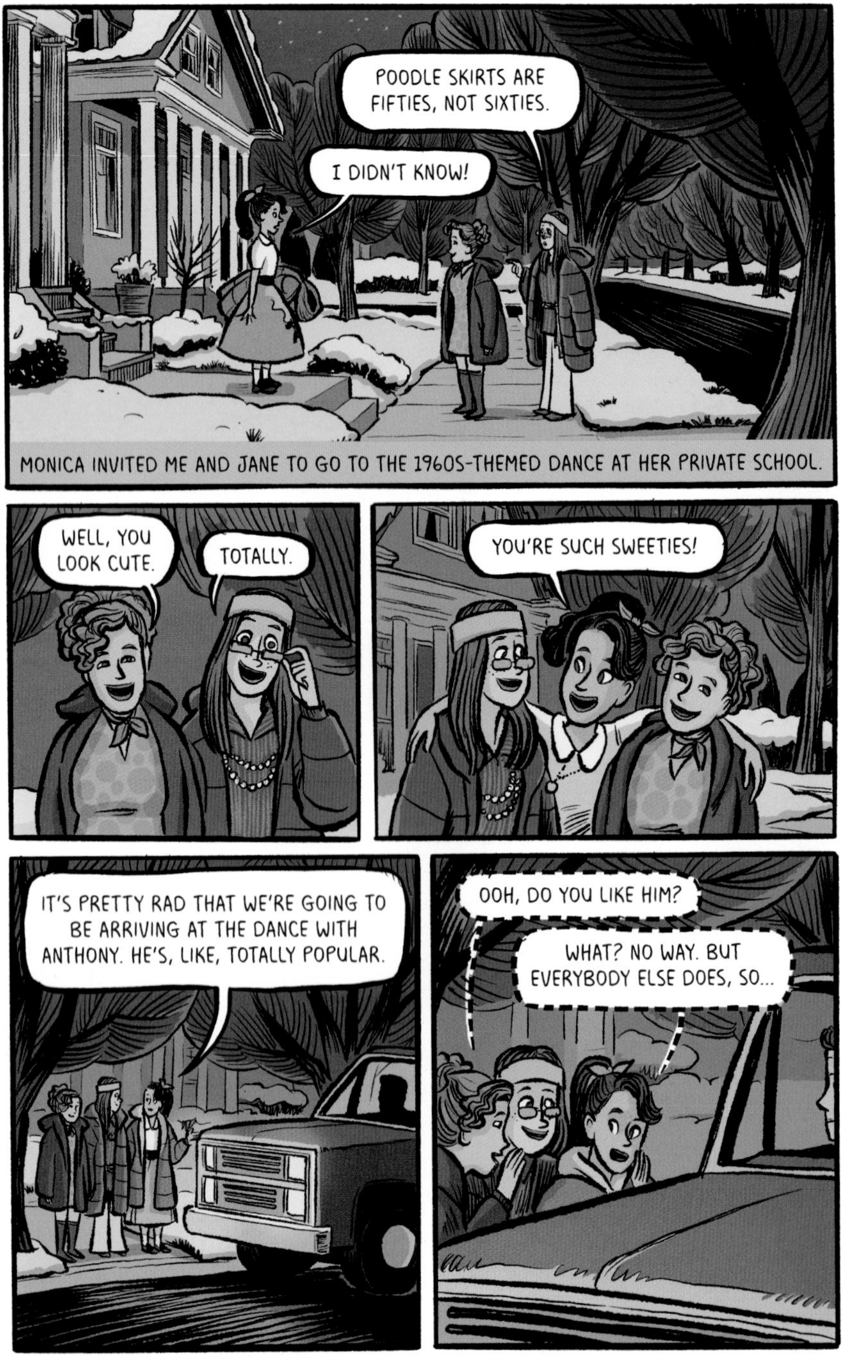
POODLE SKIRTS ARE FIFTIES, NOT SIXTIES.
I DIDN'T KNOW!
MONICA INVITED ME AND JANE TO GO TO THE 1960S-THEMED DANCE AT HER PRIVATE SCHOOL.
WELL, YOU LOOK CUTE.
TOTALLY.
YOU'RE SUCH SWEETIES!
IT'S PRETTY RAD THAT WE'RE GOING TO BE ARRIVING AT THE DANCE WITH ANTHONY. HE'S, LIKE, TOTALLY POPULAR.
OOH, DO YOU LIKE HIM?
WHAT? NO WAY. BUT EVERYBODY ELSE DOES, SO...

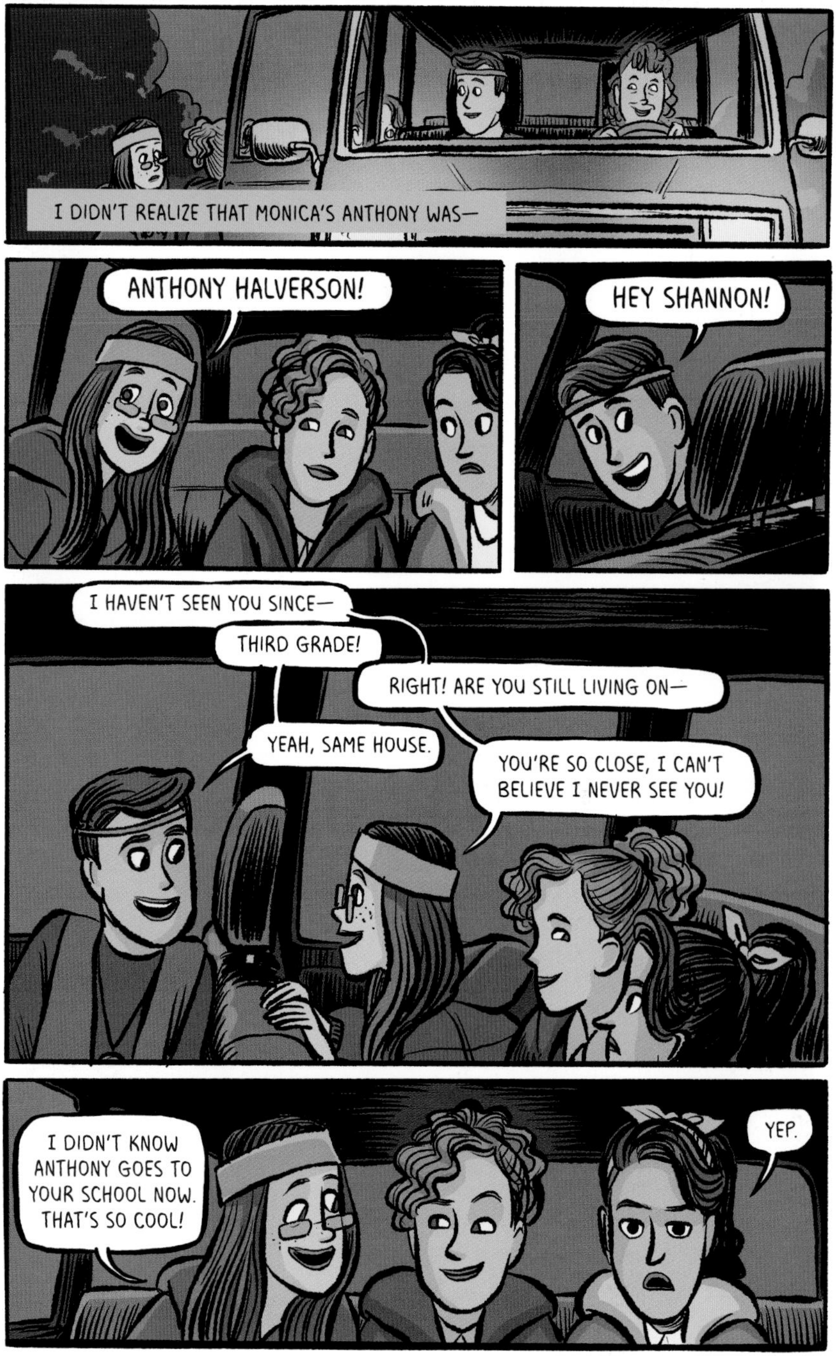

I DIDN'T REALIZE THAT MONICA'S ANTHONY WAS—
ANTHONY HALVERSON!
HEY SHANNON!
I HAVEN'T SEEN YOU SINCE—
THIRD GRADE!
RIGHT! ARE YOU STILL LIVING ON—
YEAH, SAME HOUSE.
YOU'RE SO CLOSE, I CAN'T BELIEVE I NEVER SEE YOU!
I DIDN'T KNOW ANTHONY GOES TO YOUR SCHOOL NOW. THAT'S SO COOL!
YEP.

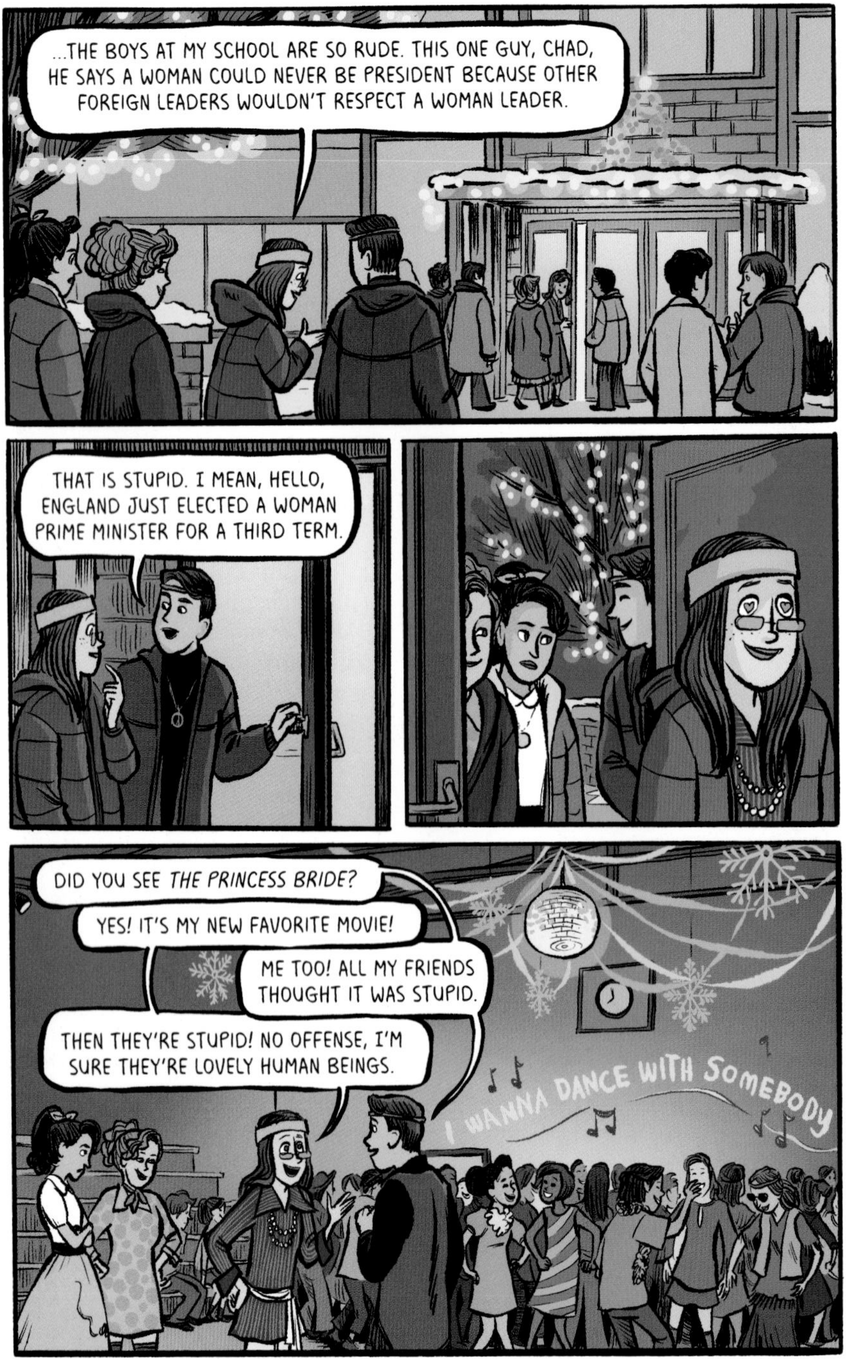
...THE BOYS AT MY SCHOOL ARE SO RUDE. THIS ONE GUY, CHAD, HE SAYS A WOMAN COULD NEVER BE PRESIDENT BECAUSE OTHER FOREIGN LEADERS WOULDN'T RESPECT A WOMAN LEADER.
THAT IS STUPID. I MEAN, HELLO, ENGLAND JUST ELECTED A WOMAN PRIME MINISTER FOR A THIRD TERM.
DID YOU SEE *THE PRINCESS BRIDE?*
YES! IT'S MY NEW FAVORITE MOVIE!
ME TOO! ALL MY FRIENDS THOUGHT IT WAS STUPID.
THEN THEY'RE STUPID! NO OFFENSE, I'M SURE THEY'RE LOVELY HUMAN BEINGS.
I WANNA DANCE WITH SOMEBODY

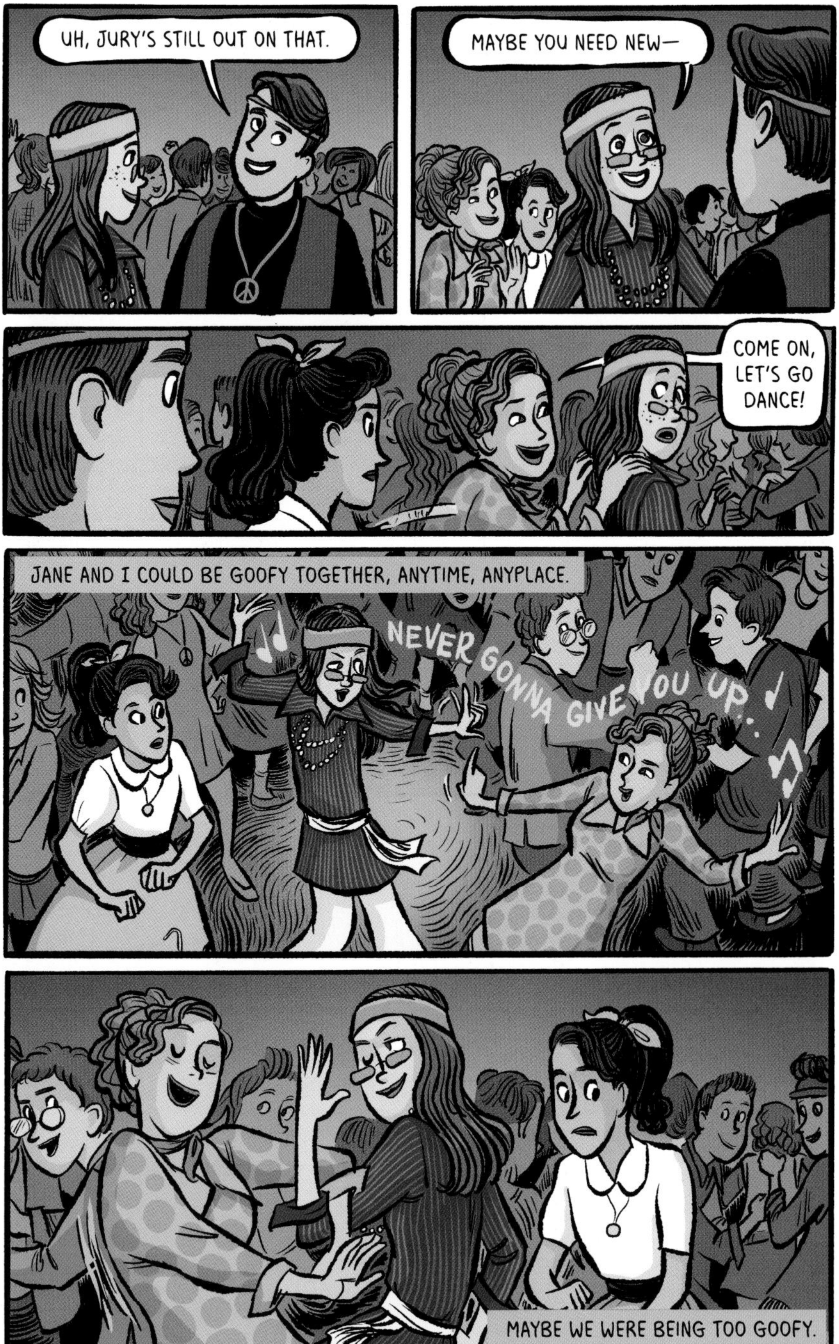
UH, JURY'S STILL OUT ON THAT.
MAYBE YOU NEED NEW—
COME ON, LET'S GO DANCE!
JANE AND I COULD BE GOOFY TOGETHER, ANYTIME, ANYPLACE.
NEVER GONNA GIVE YOU UP...
MAYBE WE WERE BEING TOO GOOFY.

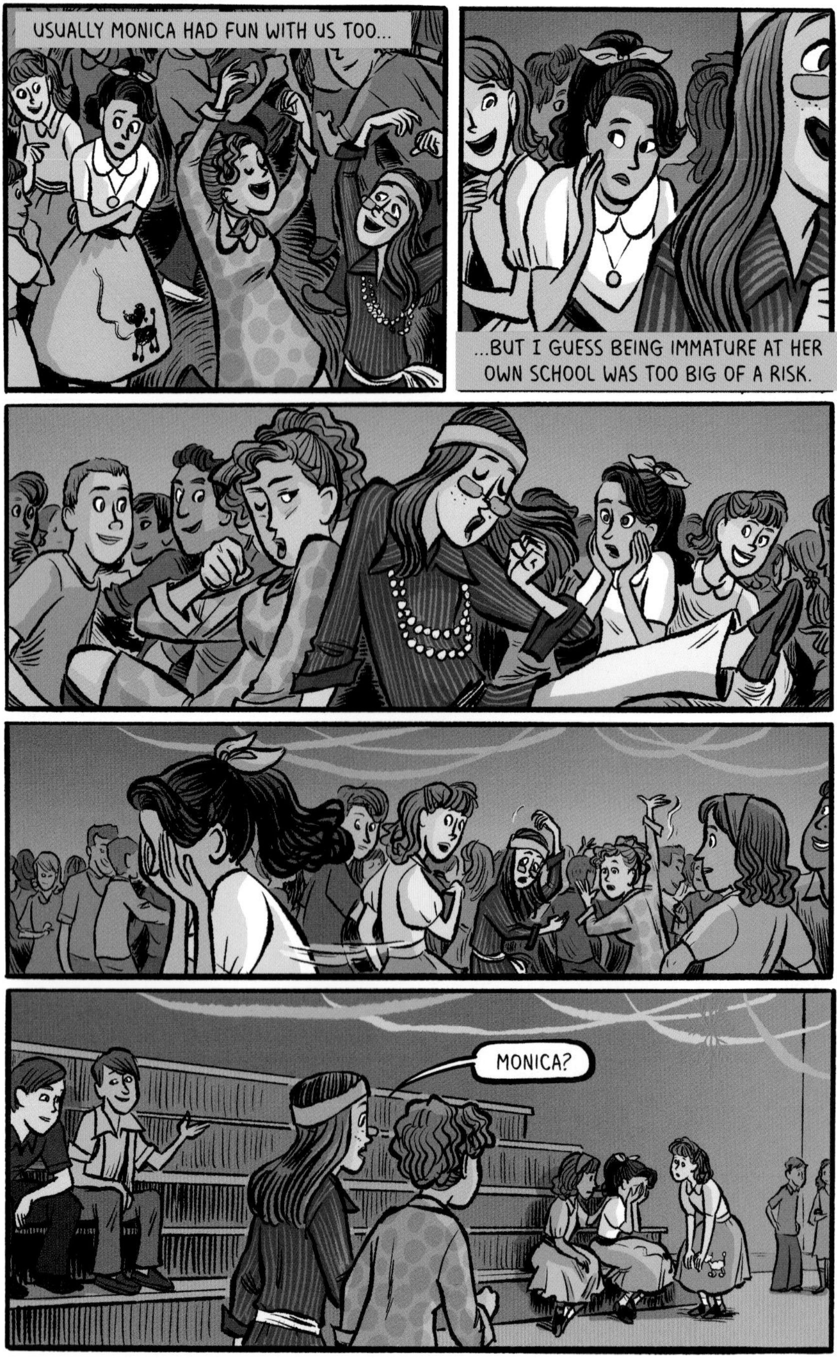
USUALLY MONICA HAD FUN WITH US TOO...
...BUT I GUESS BEING IMMATURE AT HER OWN SCHOOL WAS TOO BIG OF A RISK.
MONICA?

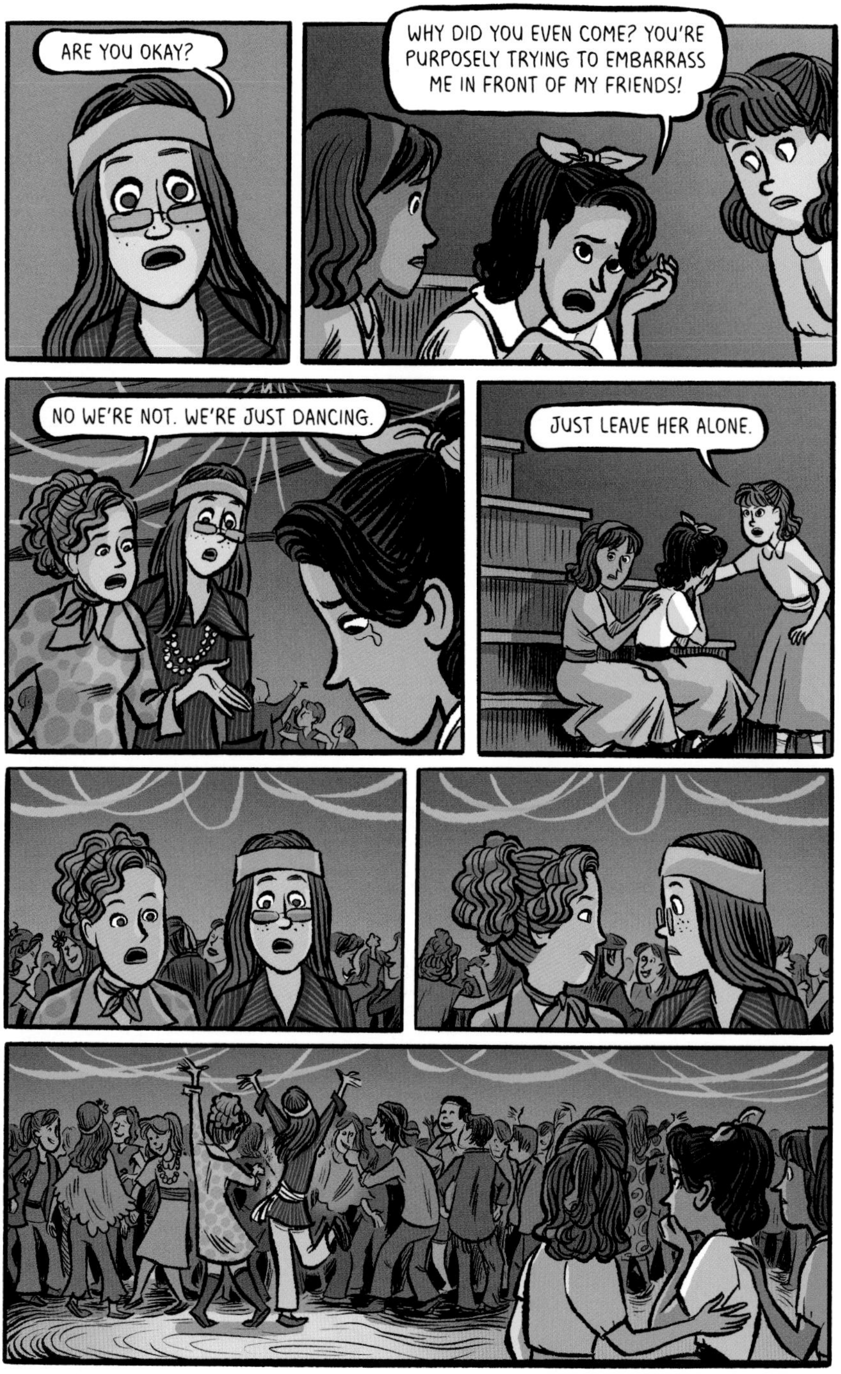
ARE YOU OKAY?
WHY DID YOU EVEN COME? YOU'RE PURPOSELY TRYING TO EMBARRASS ME IN FRONT OF MY FRIENDS!
NO WE'RE NOT. WE'RE JUST DANCING.
JUST LEAVE HER ALONE.

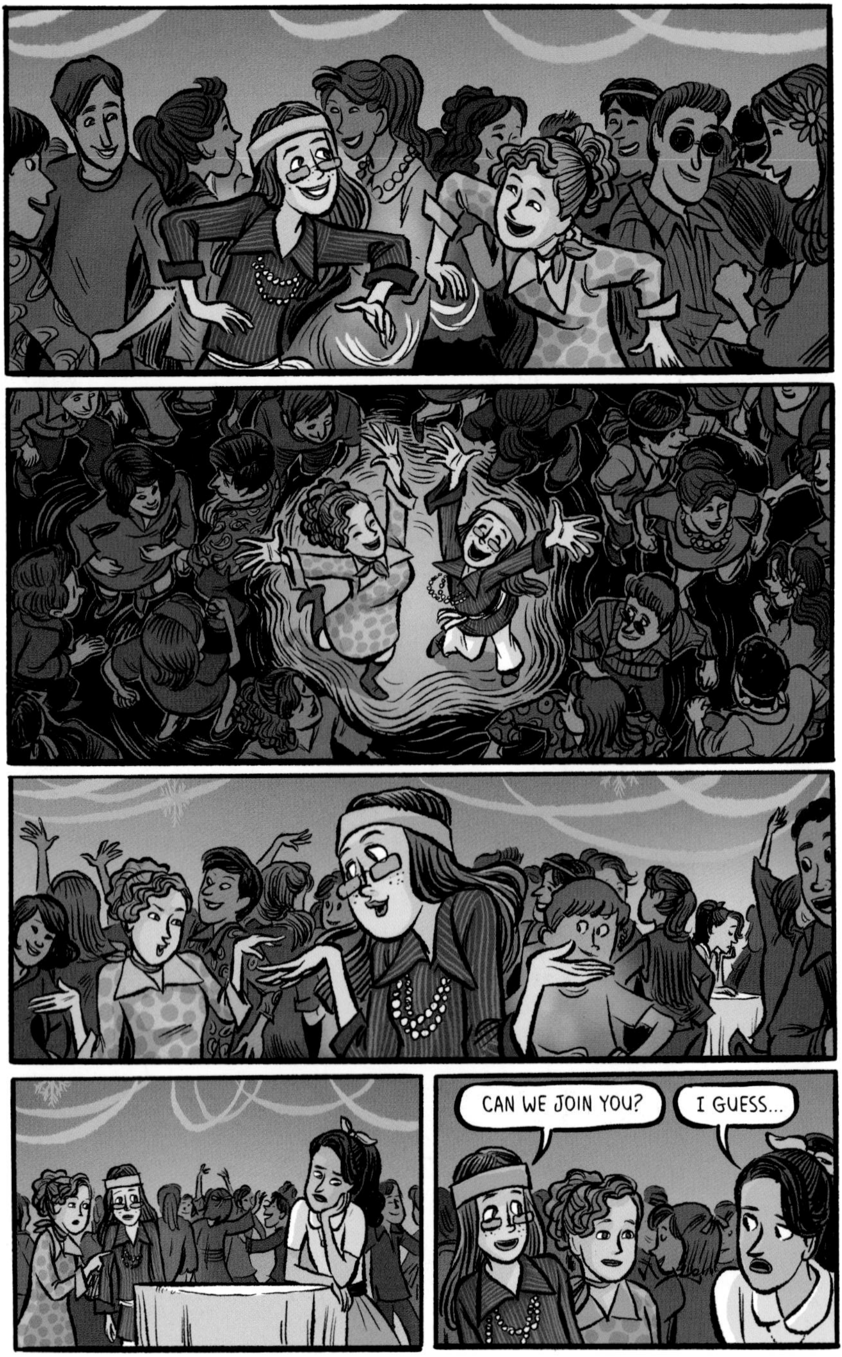
CAN WE JOIN YOU?
I GUESS...

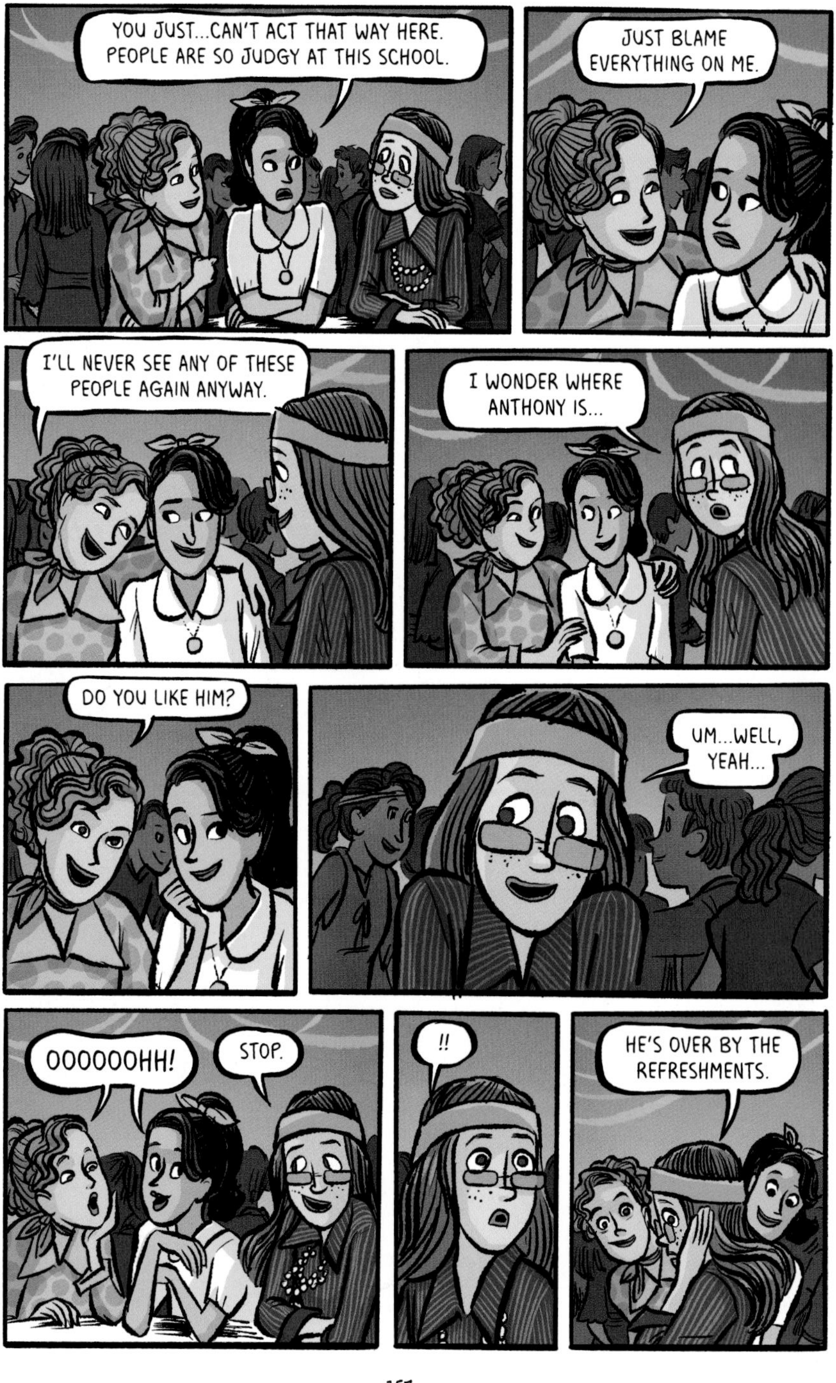
YOU JUST...CAN'T ACT THAT WAY HERE. PEOPLE ARE SO JUDGY AT THIS SCHOOL.
JUST BLAME EVERYTHING ON ME.
I'LL NEVER SEE ANY OF THESE PEOPLE AGAIN ANYWAY.
I WONDER WHERE ANTHONY IS...
DO YOU LIKE HIM?
UM...WELL, YEAH...
OOOOOOHH!
STOP.
!!
HE'S OVER BY THE REFRESHMENTS.

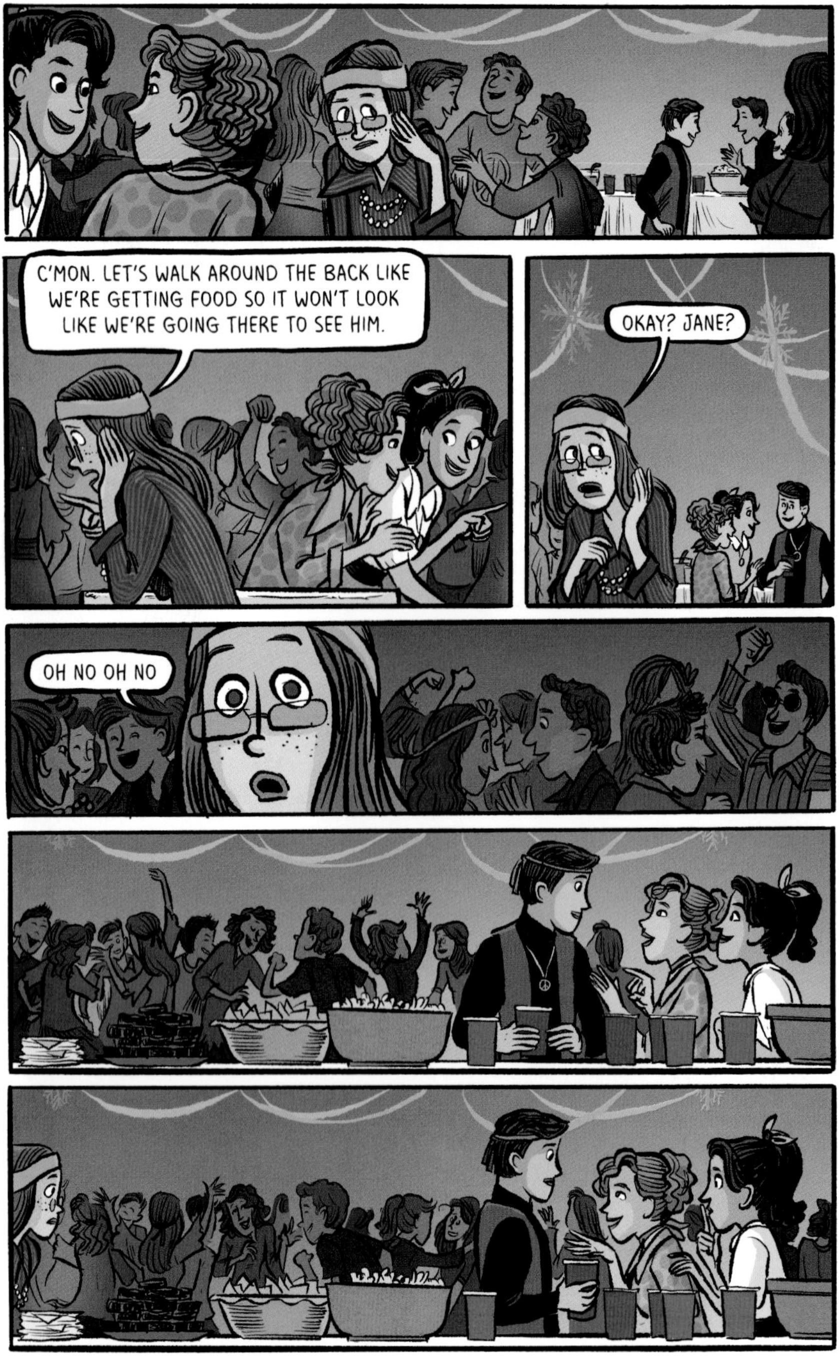
C'MON. LET'S WALK AROUND THE BACK LIKE WE'RE GETTING FOOD SO IT WON'T LOOK LIKE WE'RE GOING THERE TO SEE HIM.
OKAY? JANE?
OH NO OH NO

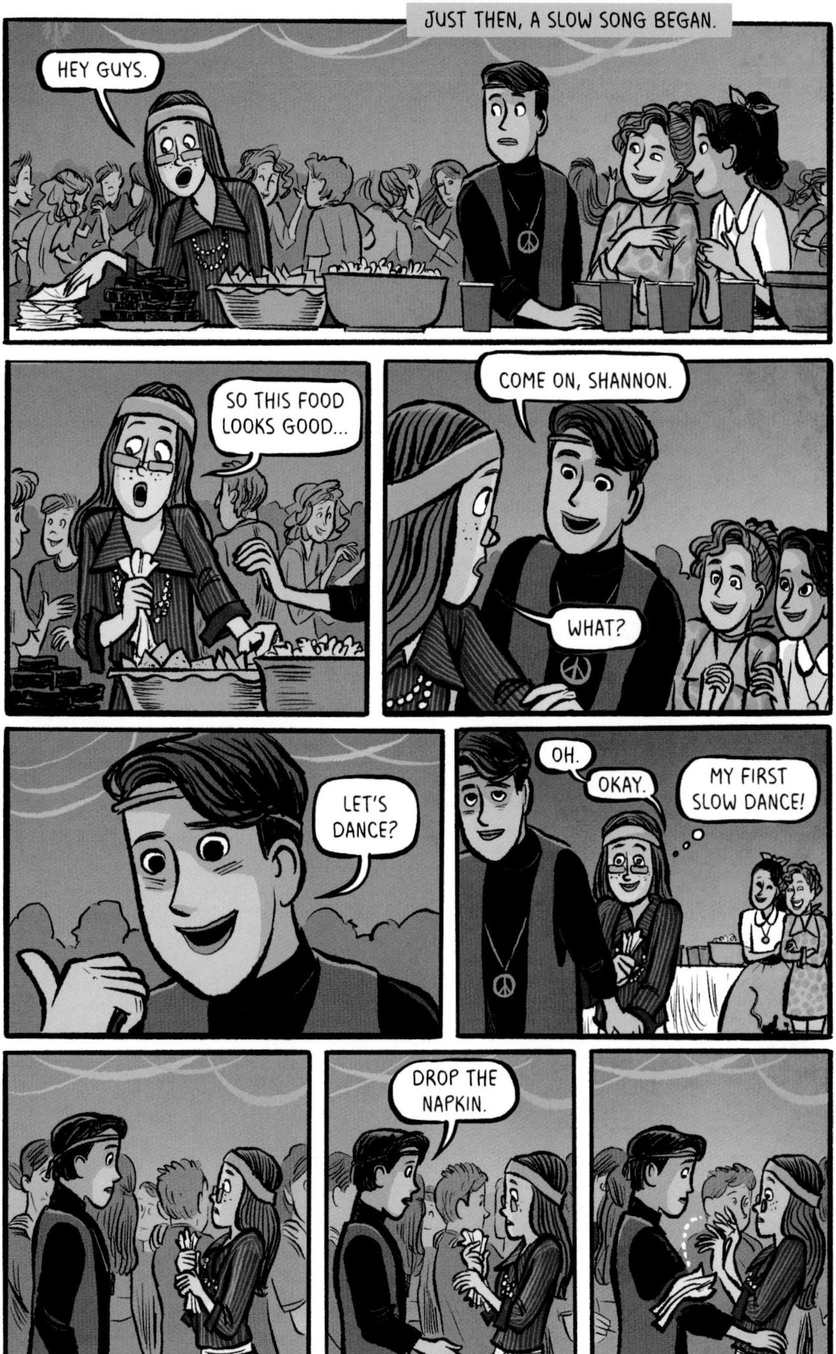
JUST THEN, A SLOW SONG BEGAN.
HEY GUYS.
SO THIS FOOD LOOKS GOOD...
COME ON, SHANNON.
WHAT?
LET'S DANCE?
OH.
OKAY.
MY FIRST SLOW DANCE!
DROP THE NAPKIN.

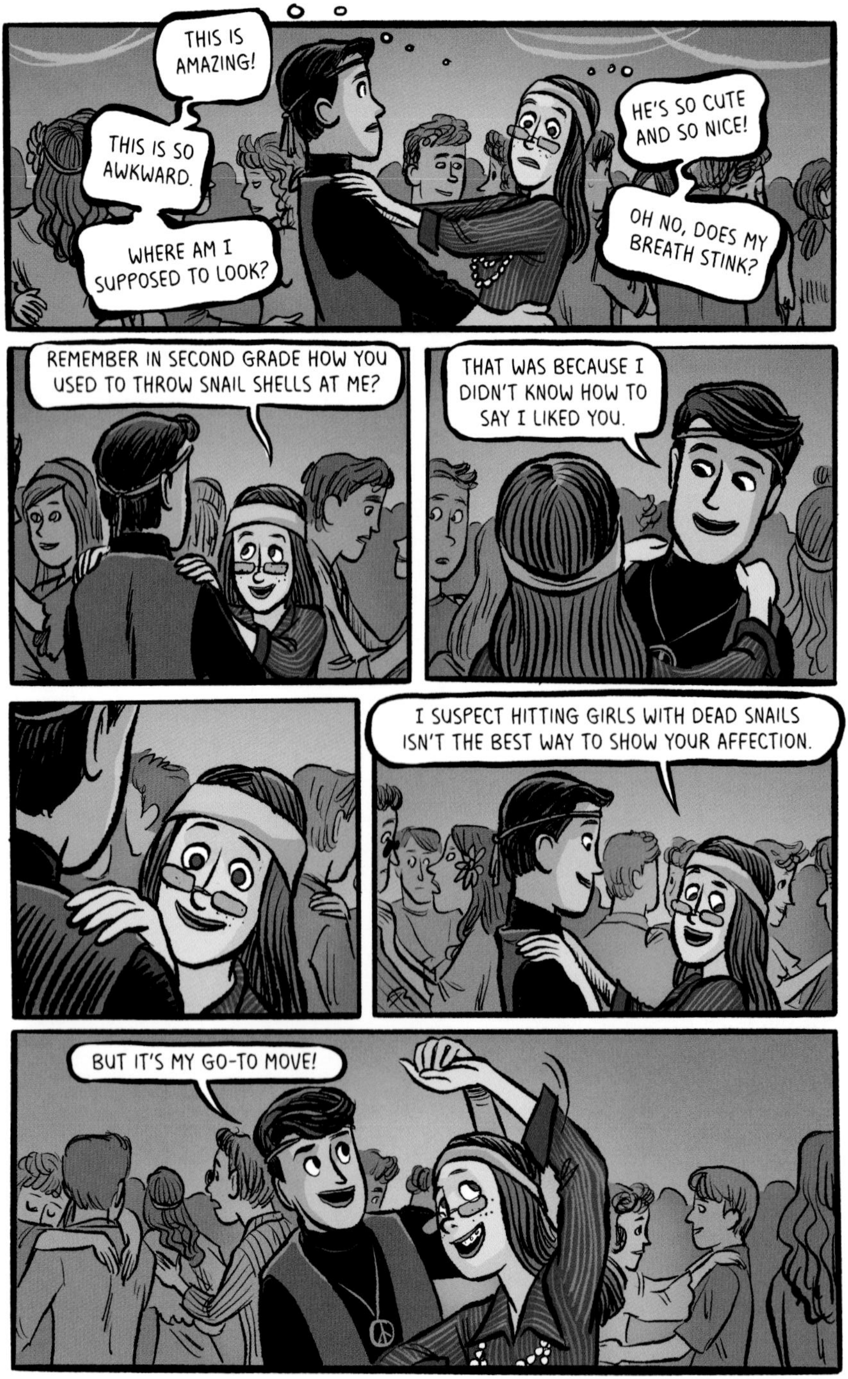
THIS IS AMAZING!
THIS IS SO AWKWARD.
WHERE AM I SUPPOSED TO LOOK?
HE'S SO CUTE AND SO NICE!
OH NO, DOES MY BREATH STINK?
REMEMBER IN SECOND GRADE HOW YOU USED TO THROW SNAIL SHELLS AT ME?
THAT WAS BECAUSE I DIDN'T KNOW HOW TO SAY I LIKED YOU.
I SUSPECT HITTING GIRLS WITH DEAD SNAILS ISN'T THE BEST WAY TO SHOW YOUR AFFECTION.
BUT IT'S MY GO-TO MOVE!

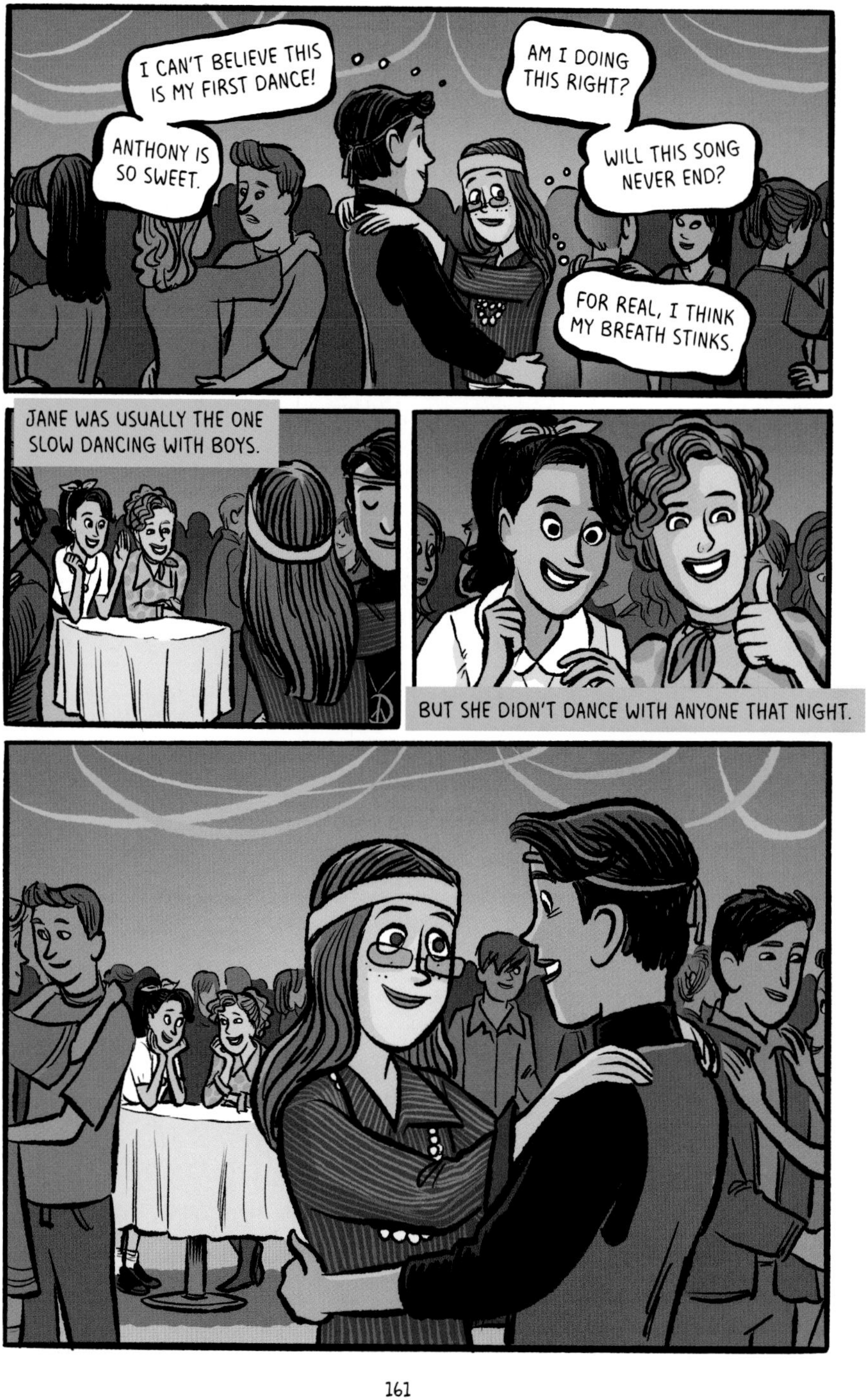
I CAN'T BELIEVE THIS IS MY FIRST DANCE!
ANTHONY IS SO SWEET.
AM I DOING THIS RIGHT?
WILL THIS SONG NEVER END?
FOR REAL, I THINK MY BREATH STINKS.
JANE WAS USUALLY THE ONE SLOW DANCING WITH BOYS.
BUT SHE DIDN'T DANCE WITH ANYONE THAT NIGHT.

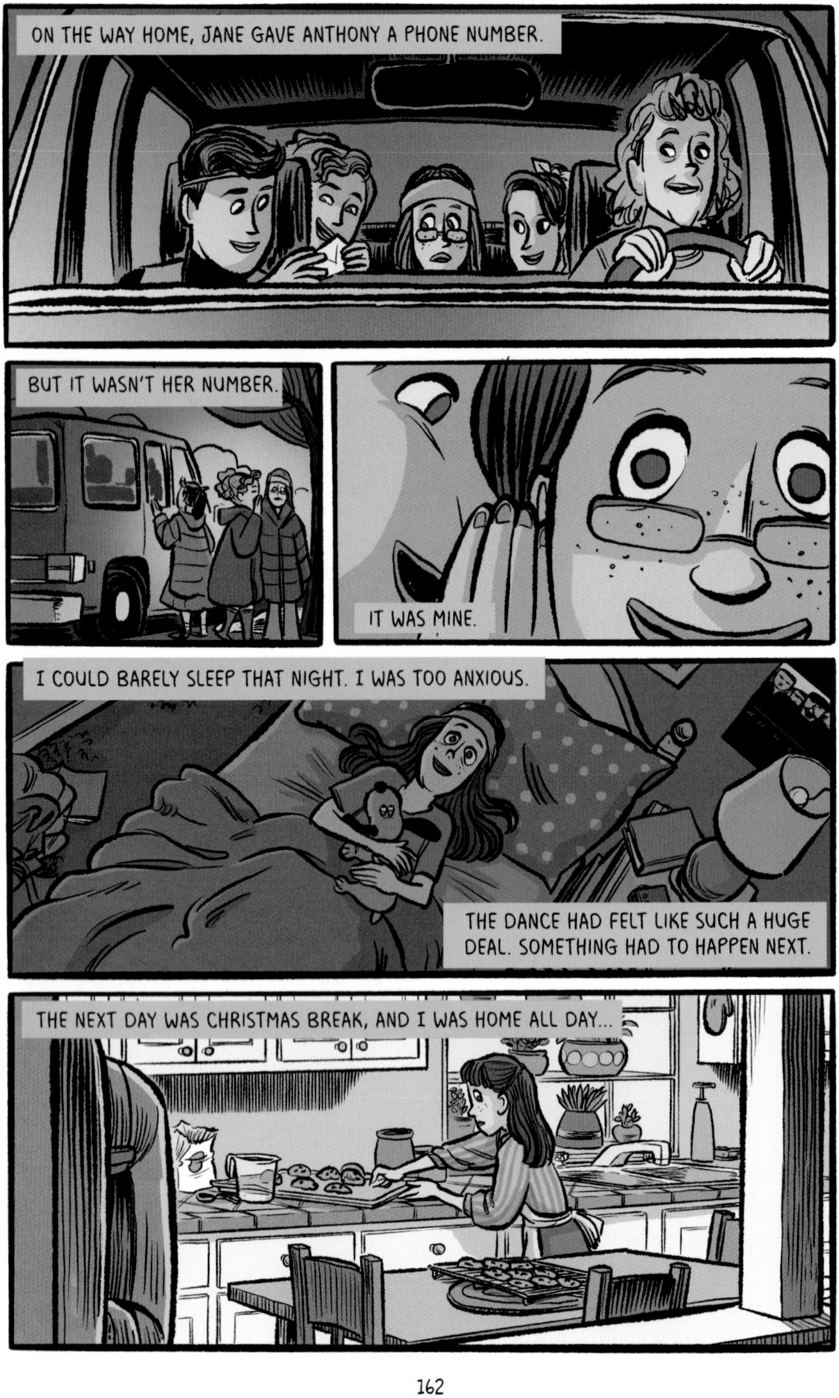
ON THE WAY HOME, JANE GAVE ANTHONY A PHONE NUMBER.
BUT IT WASN'T HER NUMBER.
IT WAS MINE.
I COULD BARELY SLEEP THAT NIGHT. I WAS TOO ANXIOUS.
THE DANCE HAD FELT LIKE SUCH A HUGE DEAL. SOMETHING HAD TO HAPPEN NEXT.
THE NEXT DAY WAS CHRISTMAS BREAK, AND I WAS HOME ALL DAY...

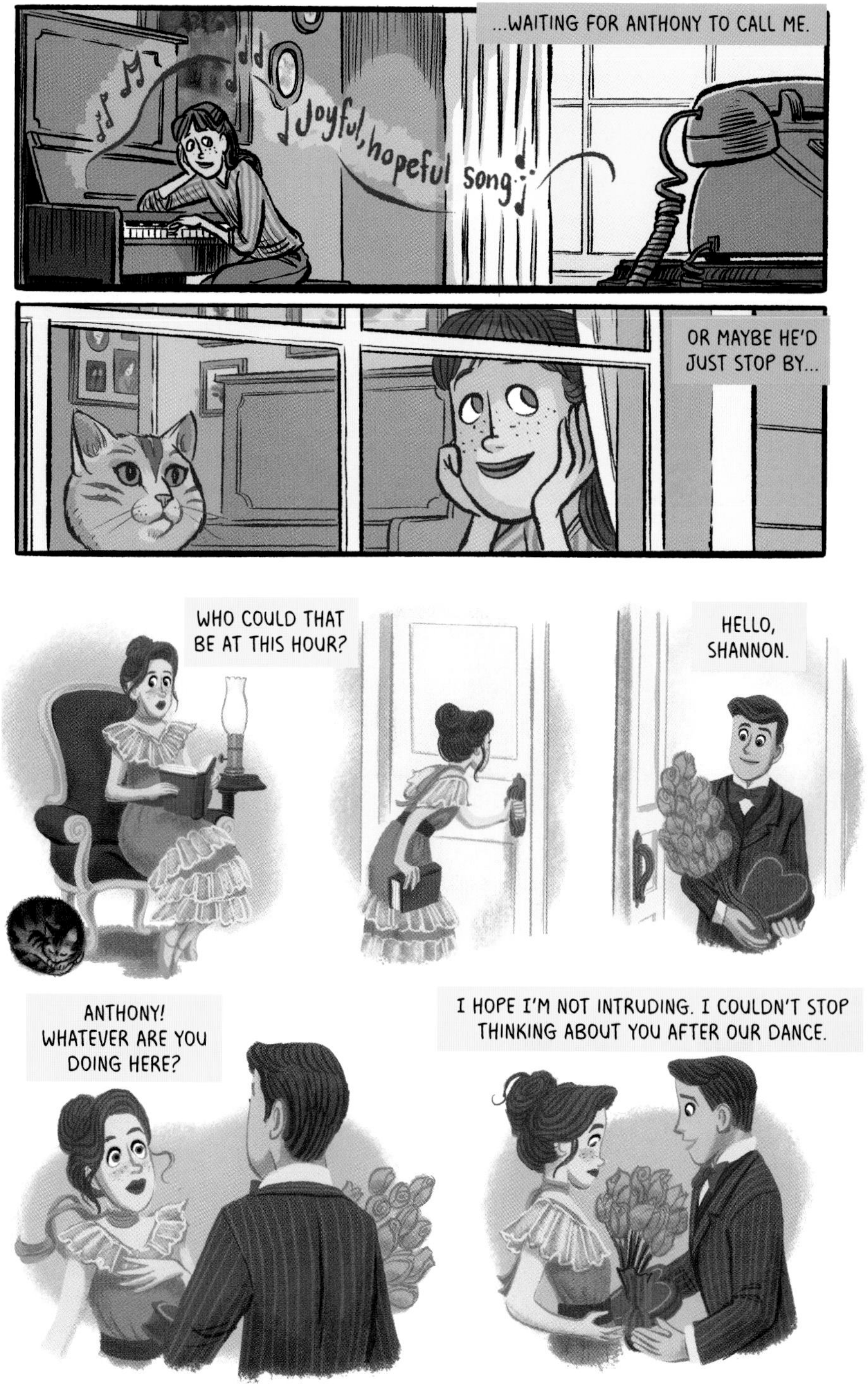
...WAITING FOR ANTHONY TO CALL ME.
Joyful, hopeful song
OR MAYBE HE'D JUST STOP BY...
WHO COULD THAT BE AT THIS HOUR?
HELLO, SHANNON.
ANTHONY! WHATEVER ARE YOU DOING HERE?
I HOPE I'M NOT INTRUDING. I COULDN'T STOP THINKING ABOUT YOU AFTER OUR DANCE.

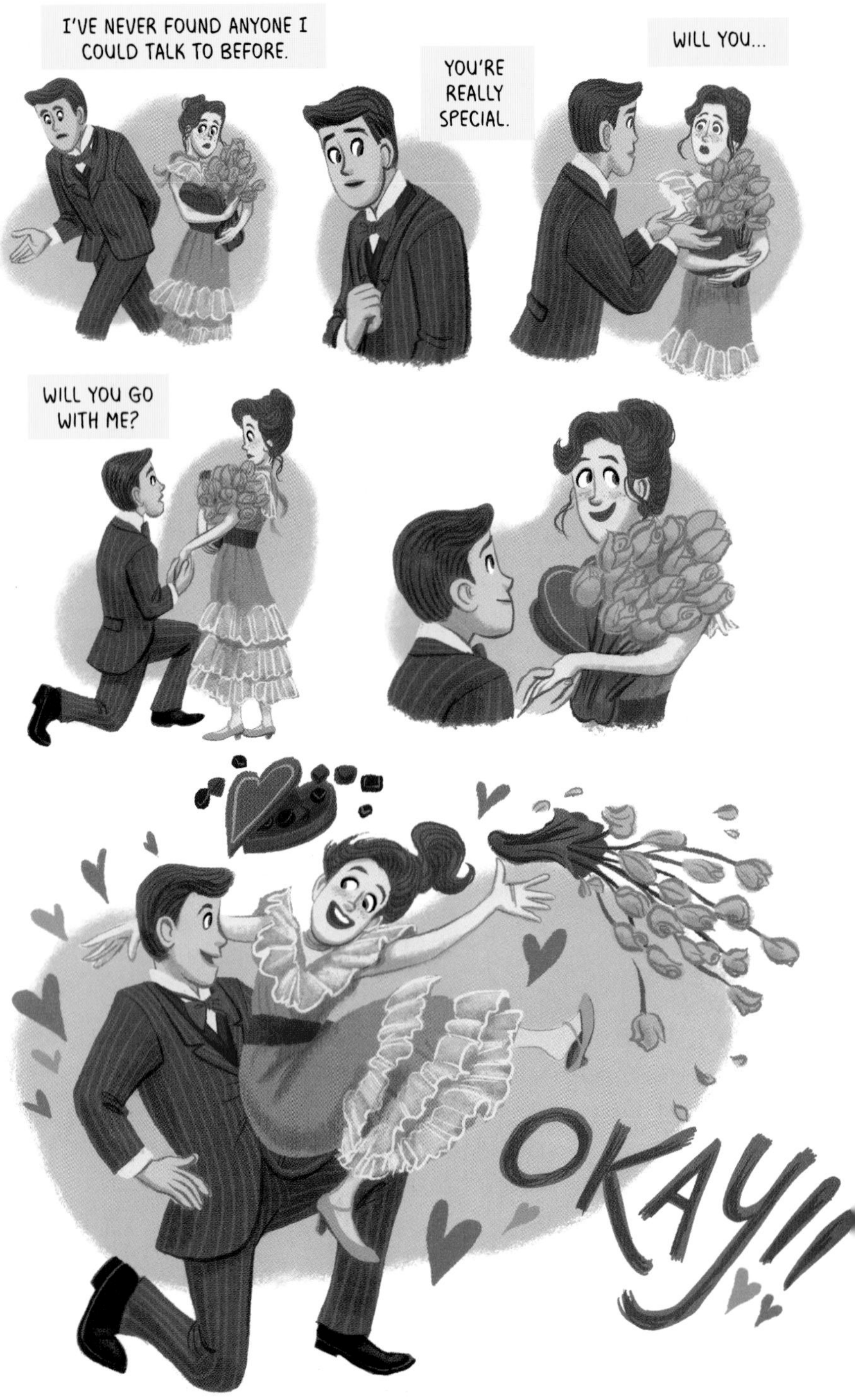
I'VE NEVER FOUND ANYONE I COULD TALK TO BEFORE.
YOU'RE REALLY SPECIAL.
WILL YOU...
WILL YOU GO WITH ME?
OKAY!!

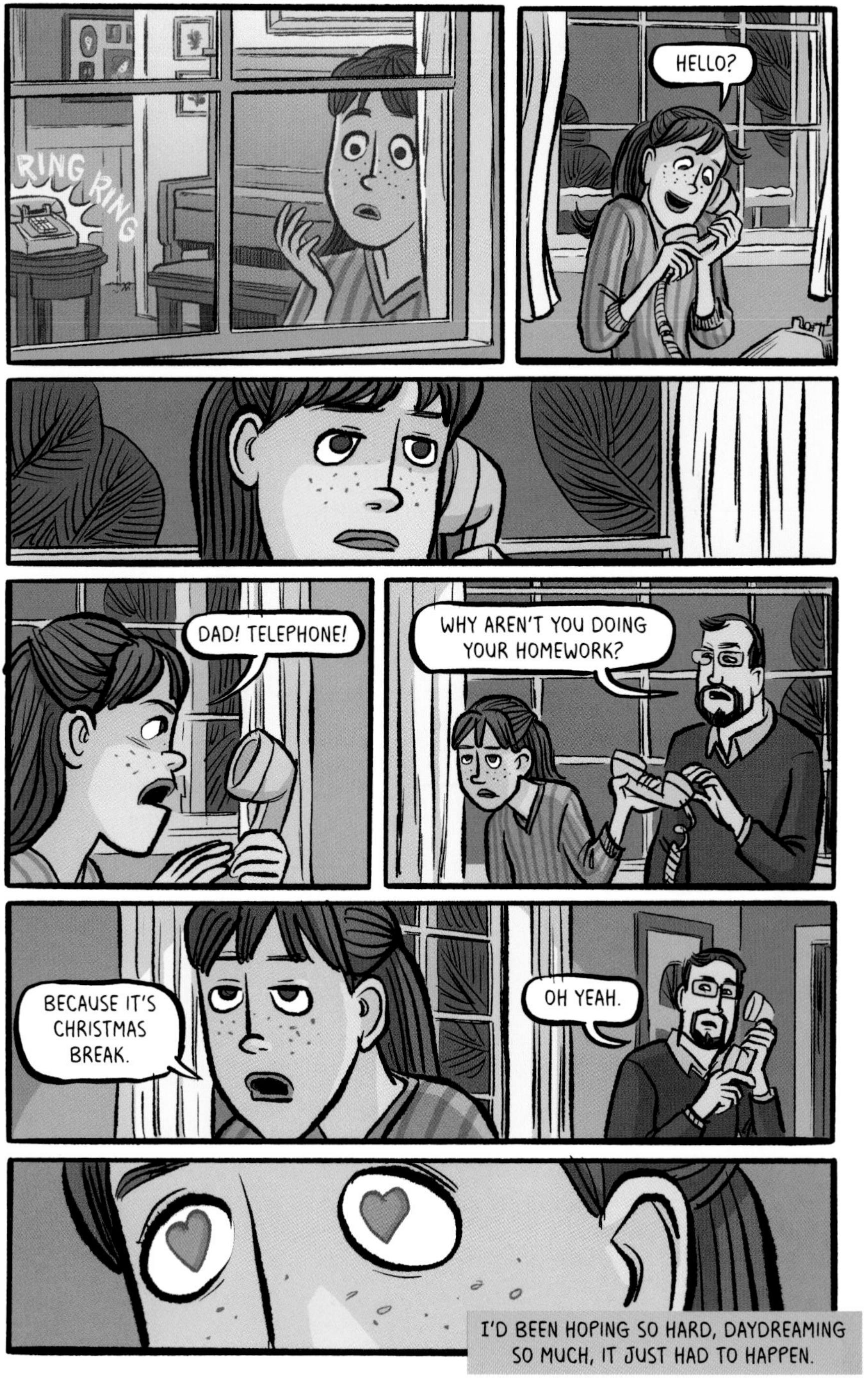

RING RING
HELLO?
DAD! TELEPHONE!
WHY AREN'T YOU DOING YOUR HOMEWORK?
BECAUSE IT'S CHRISTMAS BREAK.
OH YEAH.
I'D BEEN HOPING SO HARD, DAYDREAMING SO MUCH, IT JUST HAD TO HAPPEN.

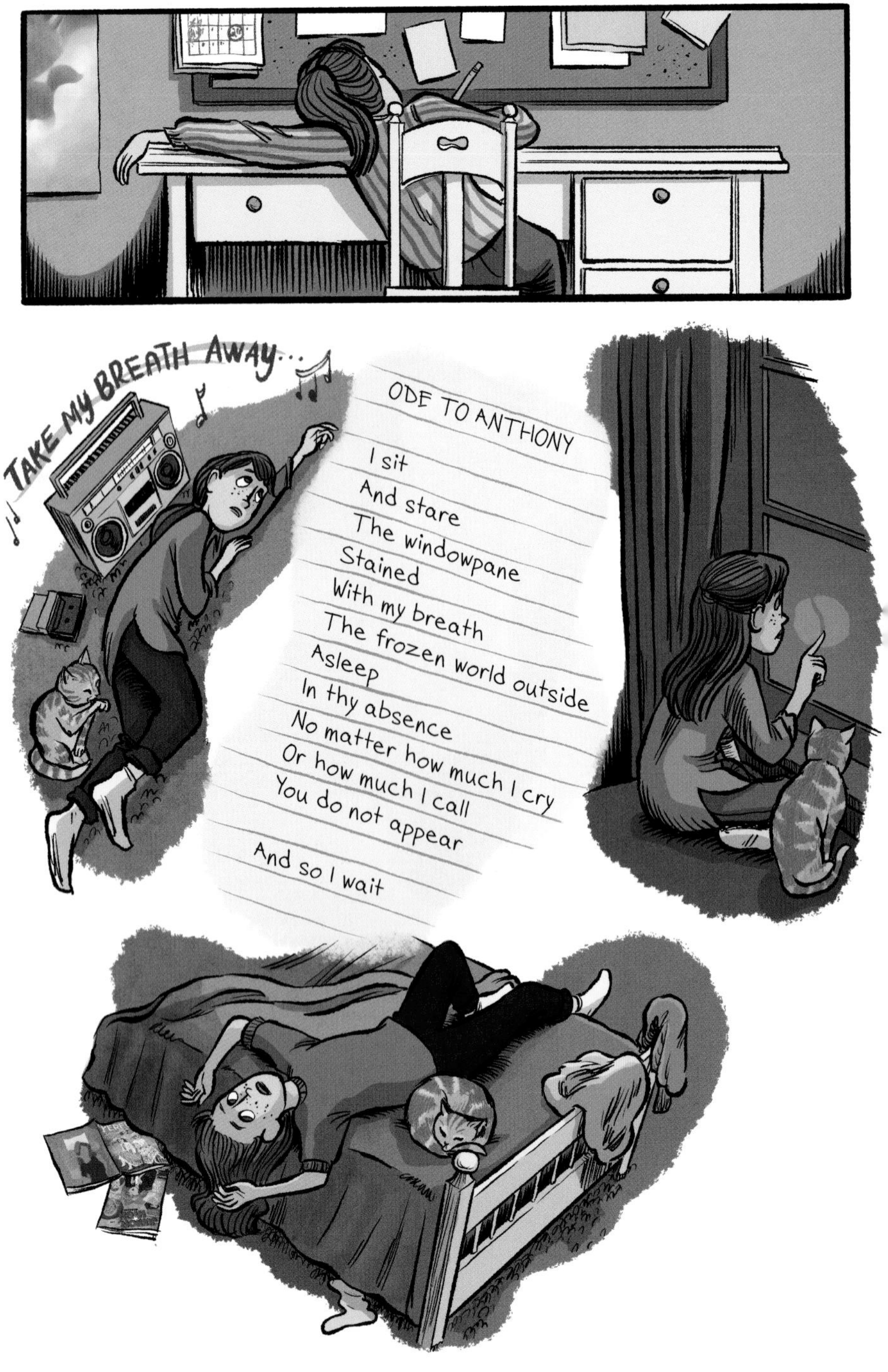
TAKE MY BREATH AWAY...
ODE TO ANTHONY
I sit
And stare
The windowpane
Stained
With my breath
The frozen world outside
Asleep
In thy absence
No matter how much I cry
Or how much I call
You do not appear
And so I wait

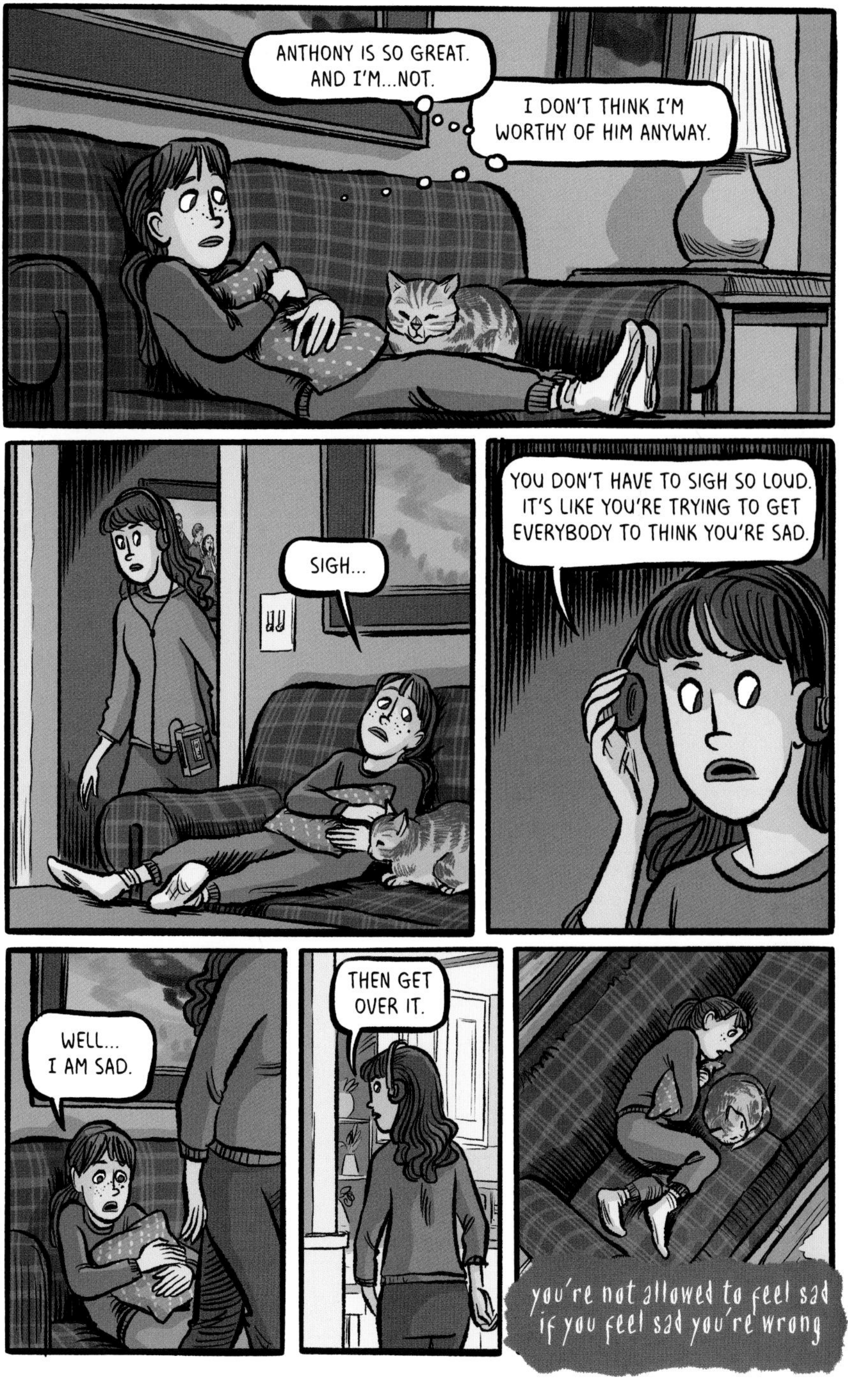
ANTHONY IS SO GREAT. AND I'M...NOT.
I DON'T THINK I'M WORTHY OF HIM ANYWAY.
SIGH...
YOU DON'T HAVE TO SIGH SO LOUD. IT'S LIKE YOU'RE TRYING TO GET EVERYBODY TO THINK YOU'RE SAD.
WELL... I AM SAD.
THEN GET OVER IT.
you're not allowed to feel sad
if you feel sad you're wrong

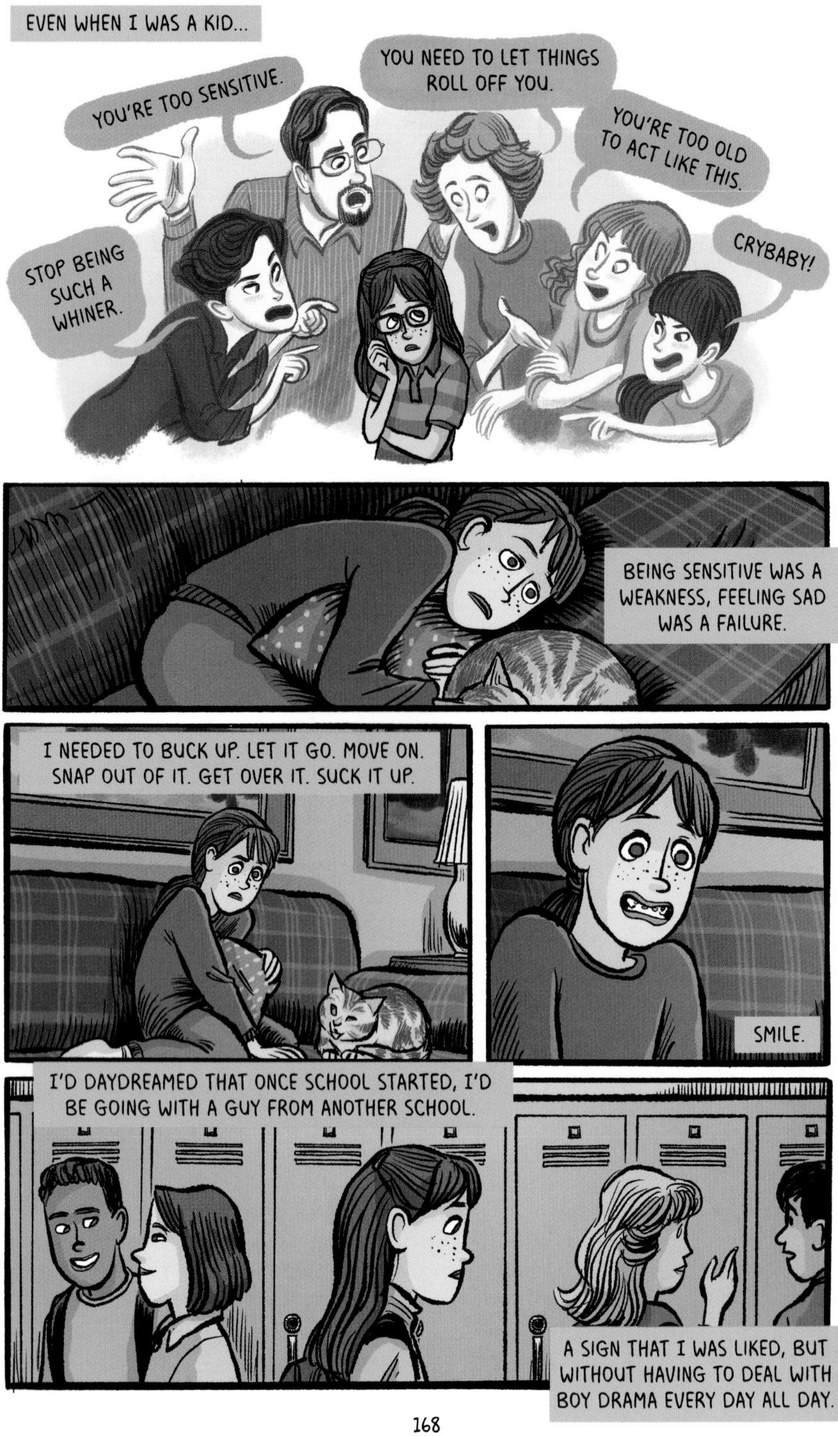
EVEN WHEN I WAS A KID...
YOU'RE TOO SENSITIVE.
YOU NEED TO LET THINGS ROLL OFF YOU.
YOU'RE TOO OLD TO ACT LIKE THIS.
STOP BEING SUCH A WHINER.
CRYBABY!
BEING SENSITIVE WAS A WEAKNESS, FEELING SAD WAS A FAILURE.
I NEEDED TO BUCK UP. LET IT GO. MOVE ON. SNAP OUT OF IT. GET OVER IT. SUCK IT UP.
SMILE.
I'D DAYDREAMED THAT ONCE SCHOOL STARTED, I'D BE GOING WITH A GUY FROM ANOTHER SCHOOL.
A SIGN THAT I WAS LIKED, BUT WITHOUT HAVING TO DEAL WITH BOY DRAMA EVERY DAY ALL DAY.

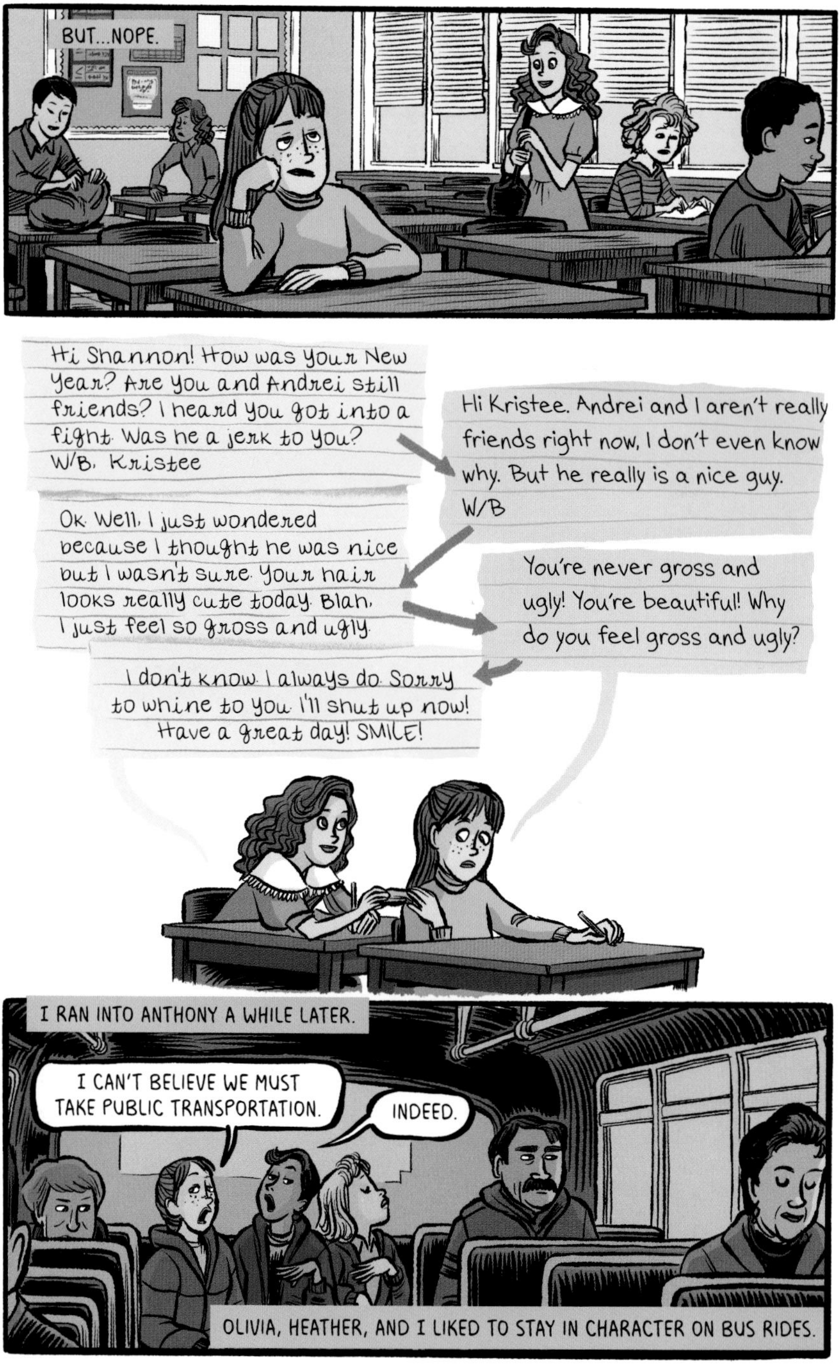
BUT...NOPE.
Hi Shannon! How was your New Year? Are you and Andrei still friends? I heard you got into a fight. Was he a jerk to you? W/B, Kristee
Hi Kristee. Andrei and I aren't really friends right now, I don't even know why. But he really is a nice guy. W/B
Ok. Well, I just wondered because I thought he was nice but I wasn't sure. Your hair looks really cute today. Blah, I just feel so gross and ugly.
You're never gross and ugly! You're beautiful! Why do you feel gross and ugly?
I don't know. I always do. Sorry to whine to you. I'll shut up now! Have a great day! SMILE!
I RAN INTO ANTHONY A WHILE LATER.
I CAN'T BELIEVE WE MUST TAKE PUBLIC TRANSPORTATION.
INDEED.
OLIVIA, HEATHER, AND I LIKED TO STAY IN CHARACTER ON BUS RIDES.

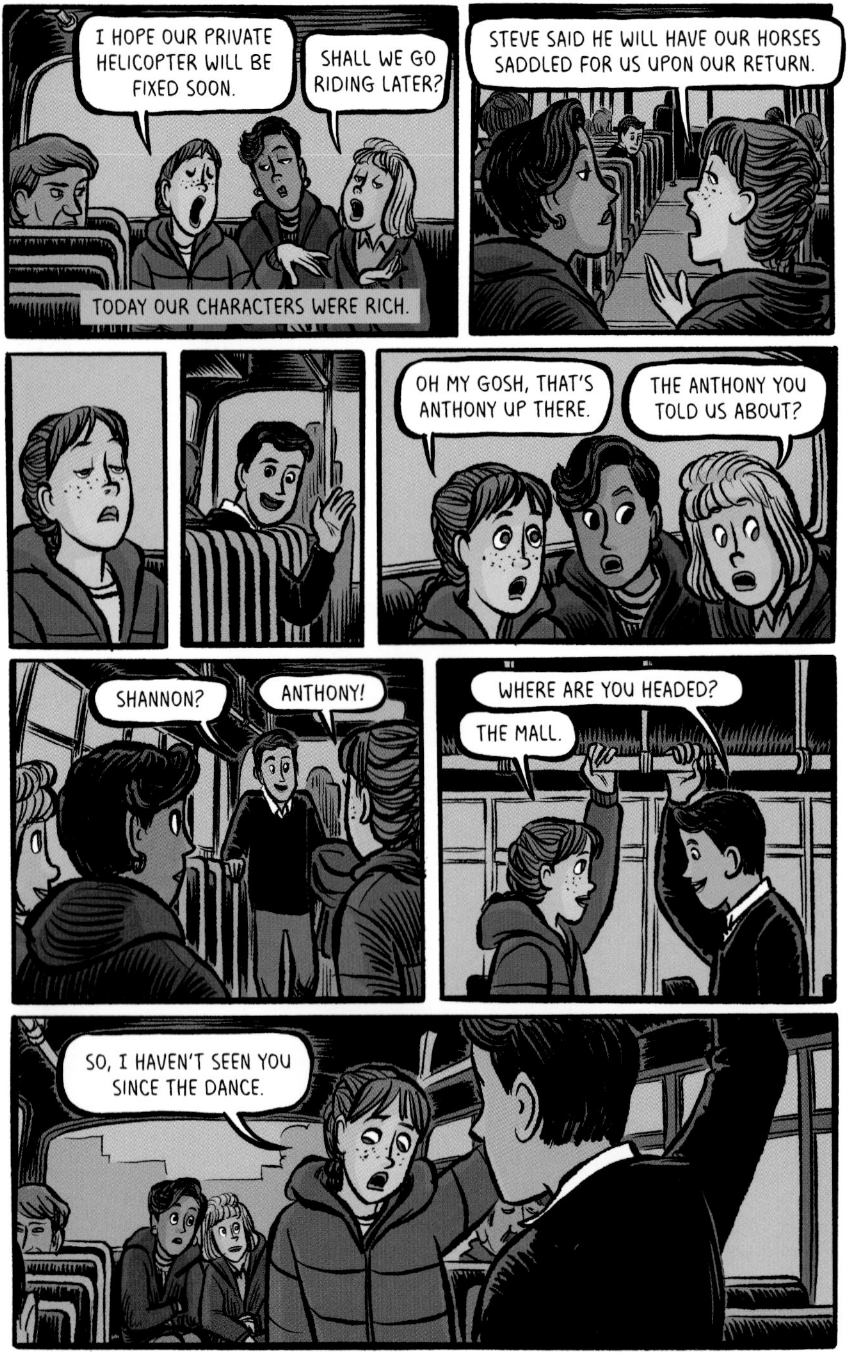
I HOPE OUR PRIVATE HELICOPTER WILL BE FIXED SOON.
SHALL WE GO RIDING LATER?
TODAY OUR CHARACTERS WERE RICH.
STEVE SAID HE WILL HAVE OUR HORSES SADDLED FOR US UPON OUR RETURN.
OH MY GOSH, THAT'S ANTHONY UP THERE.
THE ANTHONY YOU TOLD US ABOUT?
SHANNON?
ANTHONY!
WHERE ARE YOU HEADED?
THE MALL.
SO, I HAVEN'T SEEN YOU SINCE THE DANCE.

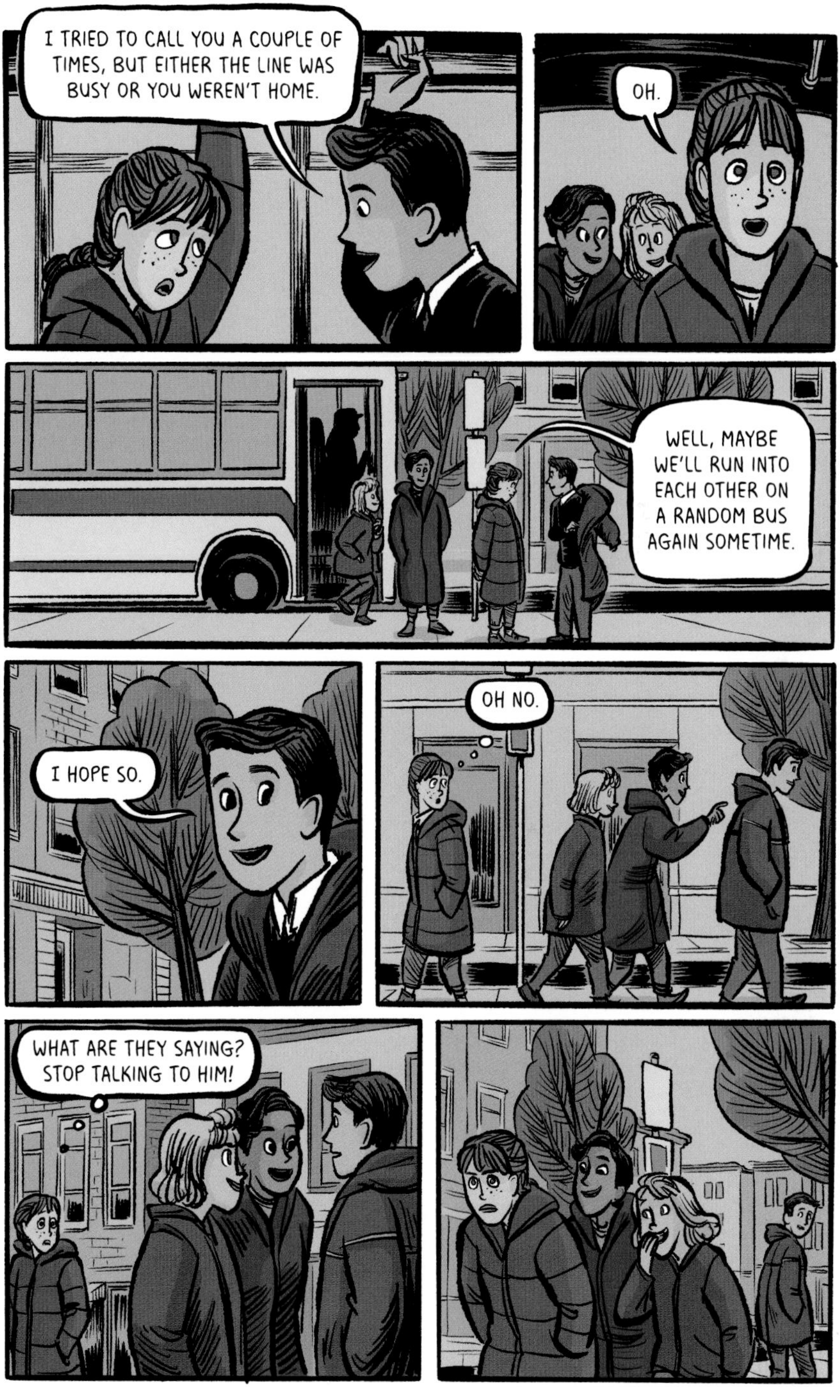
I TRIED TO CALL YOU A COUPLE OF TIMES, BUT EITHER THE LINE WAS BUSY OR YOU WEREN'T HOME.
OH.
WELL, MAYBE WE'LL RUN INTO EACH OTHER ON A RANDOM BUS AGAIN SOMETIME.
I HOPE SO.
OH NO.
WHAT ARE THEY SAYING? STOP TALKING TO HIM!

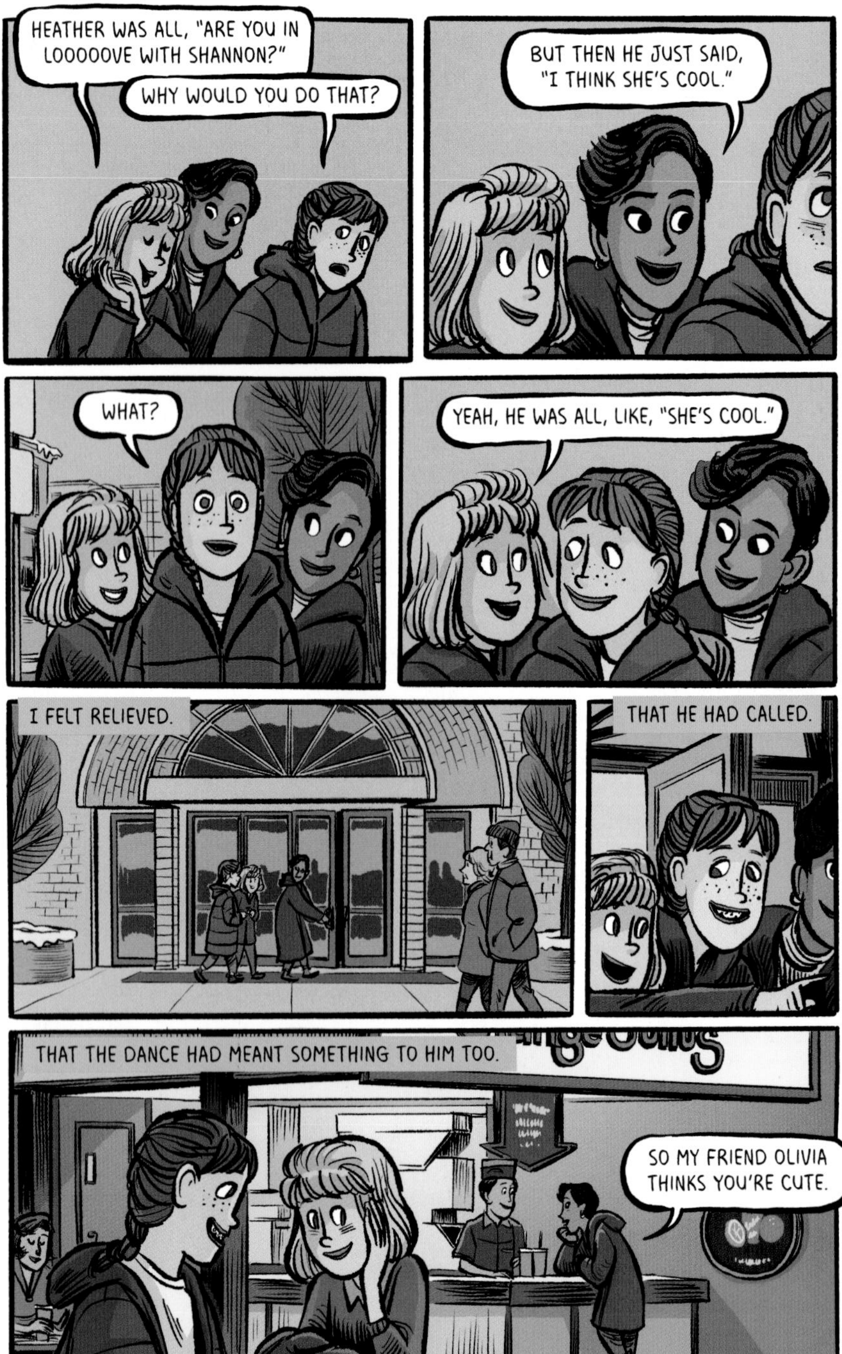
HEATHER WAS ALL, "ARE YOU IN LOOOOOVE WITH SHANNON?"
WHY WOULD YOU DO THAT?
BUT THEN HE JUST SAID, "I THINK SHE'S COOL."
WHAT?
YEAH, HE WAS ALL, LIKE, "SHE'S COOL."
I FELT RELIEVED.
THAT HE HAD CALLED.
THAT THE DANCE HAD MEANT SOMETHING TO HIM TOO.
SO MY FRIEND OLIVIA THINKS YOU'RE CUTE.

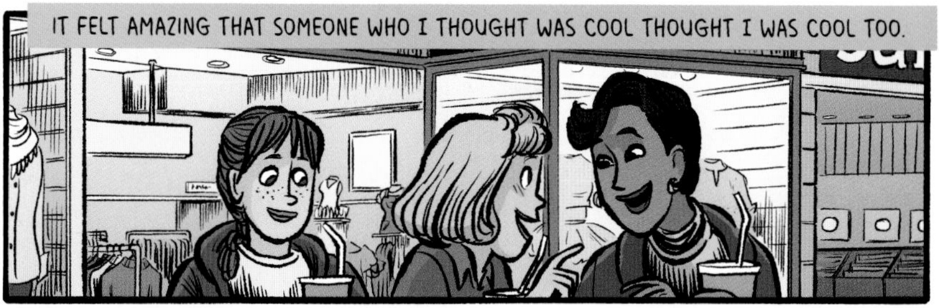
IT FELT AMAZING THAT SOMEONE WHO I THOUGHT WAS COOL THOUGHT I WAS COOL TOO.

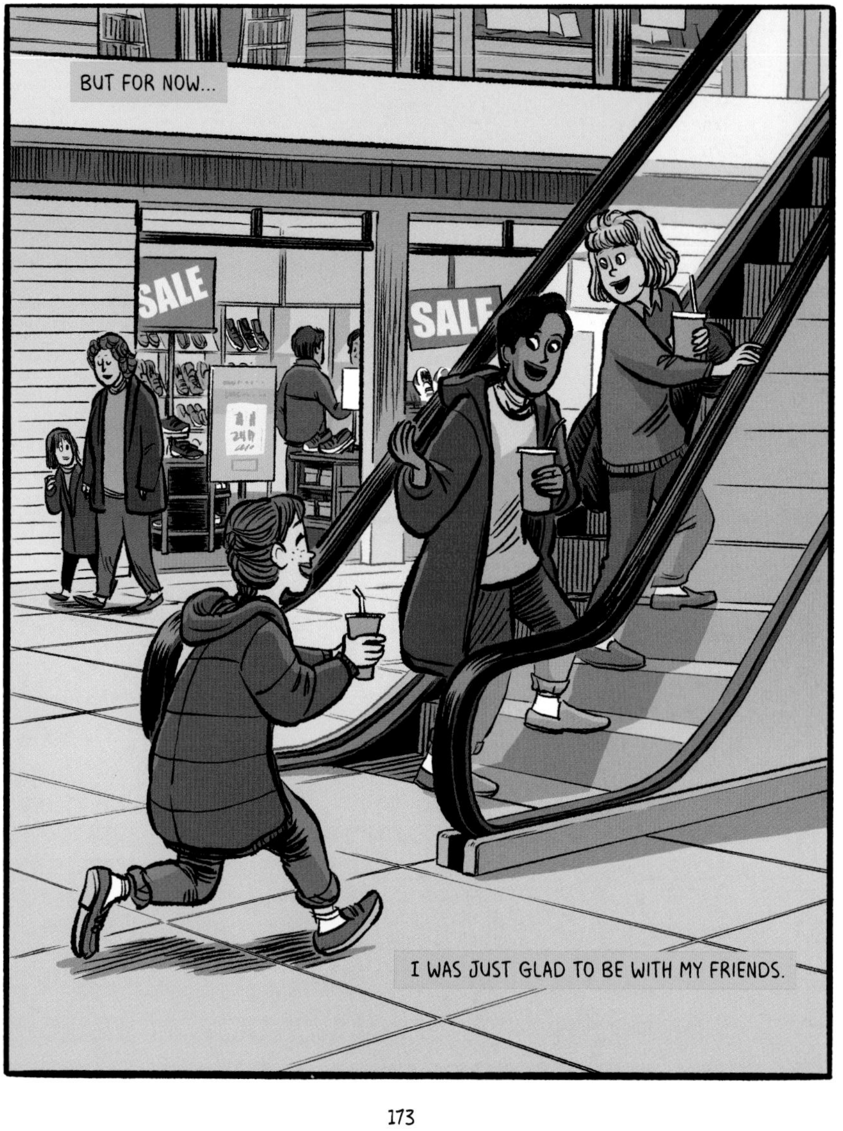
BUT FOR NOW...
SALE
SALE
I WAS JUST GLAD TO BE WITH MY FRIENDS.

CHAPTER 4

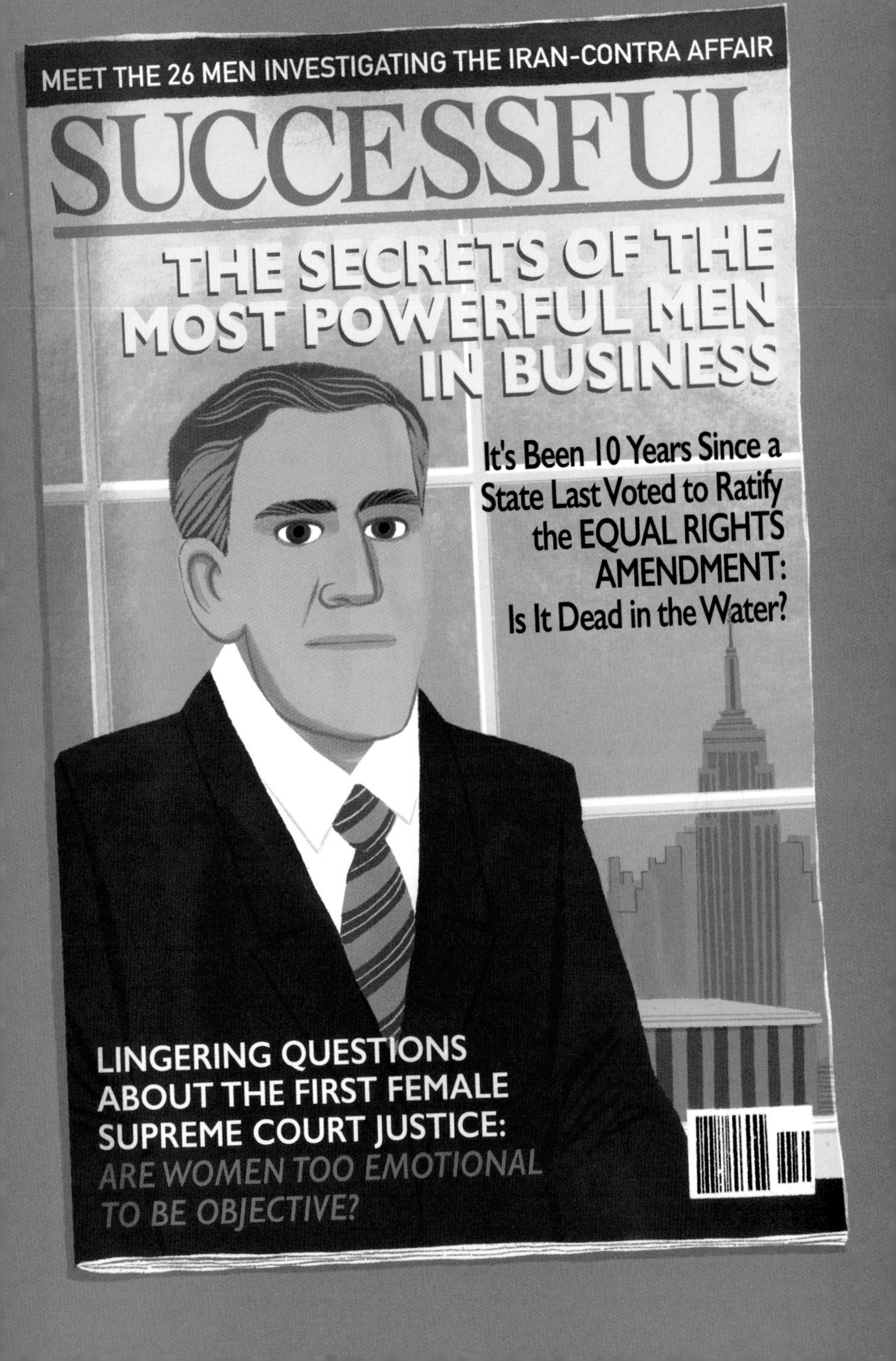
MEET THE 26 MEN INVESTIGATING THE IRAN-CONTRA AFFAIR
SUCCESSFUL
THE SECRETS OF THE MOST POWERFUL MEN IN BUSINESS
It's Been 10 Years Since a State Last Voted to Ratify the EQUAL RIGHTS AMENDMENT: Is It Dead in the Water?
LINGERING QUESTIONS ABOUT THE FIRST FEMALE SUPREME COURT JUSTICE:
ARE WOMEN TOO EMOTIONAL TO BE OBJECTIVE?

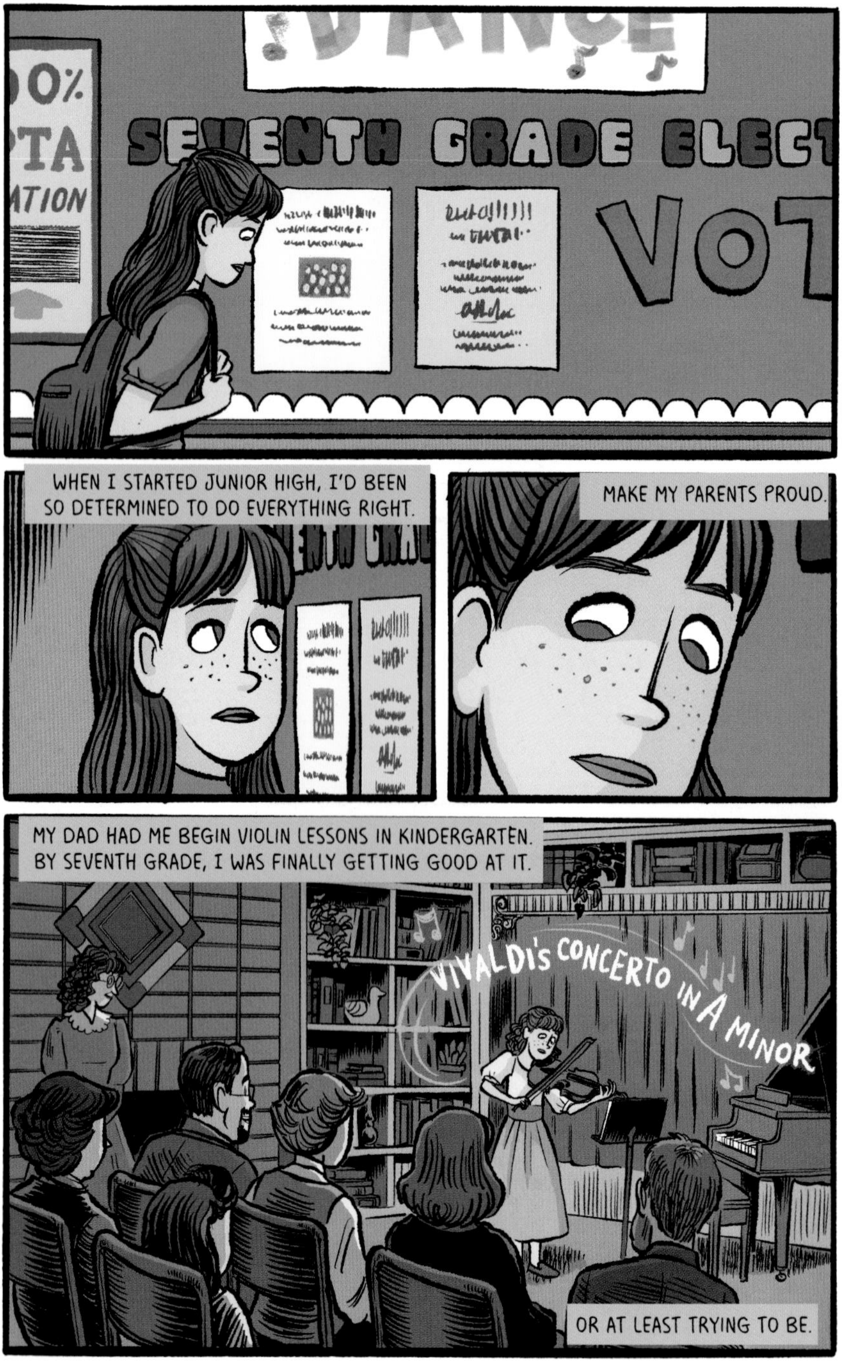
DANCE
SEVENTH GRADE ELECT
VOT
WHEN I STARTED JUNIOR HIGH, I'D BEEN SO DETERMINED TO DO EVERYTHING RIGHT.
MAKE MY PARENTS PROUD.
MY DAD HAD ME BEGIN VIOLIN LESSONS IN KINDERGARTEN. BY SEVENTH GRADE, I WAS FINALLY GETTING GOOD AT IT.
VIVALDI'S CONCERTO IN A MINOR
OR AT LEAST TRYING TO BE.

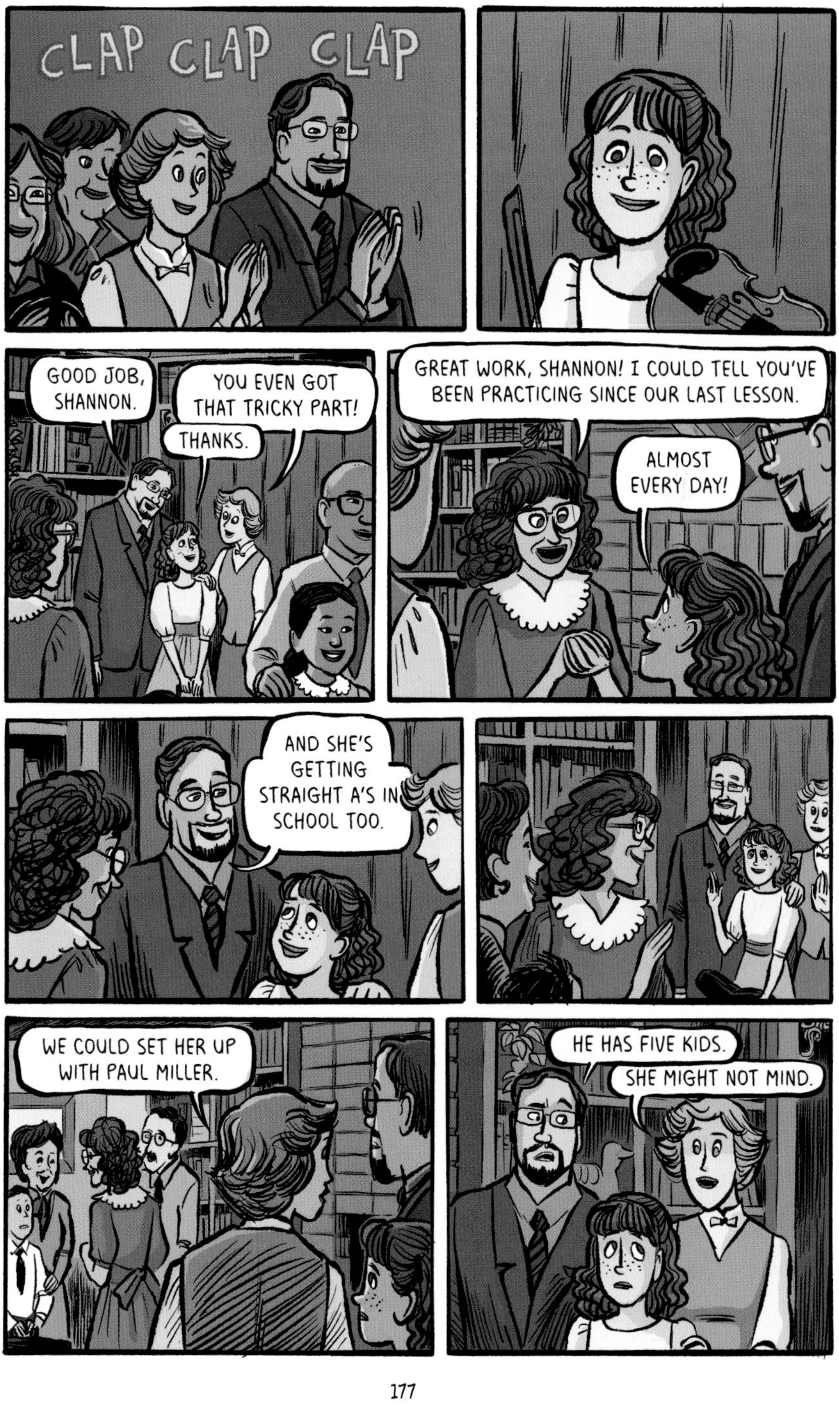
CLAP CLAP CLAP
GOOD JOB, SHANNON.
YOU EVEN GOT THAT TRICKY PART!
THANKS.
GREAT WORK, SHANNON! I COULD TELL YOU'VE BEEN PRACTICING SINCE OUR LAST LESSON.
ALMOST EVERY DAY!
AND SHE'S GETTING STRAIGHT A'S IN SCHOOL TOO.
WE COULD SET HER UP WITH PAUL MILLER.
HE HAS FIVE KIDS.
SHE MIGHT NOT MIND.

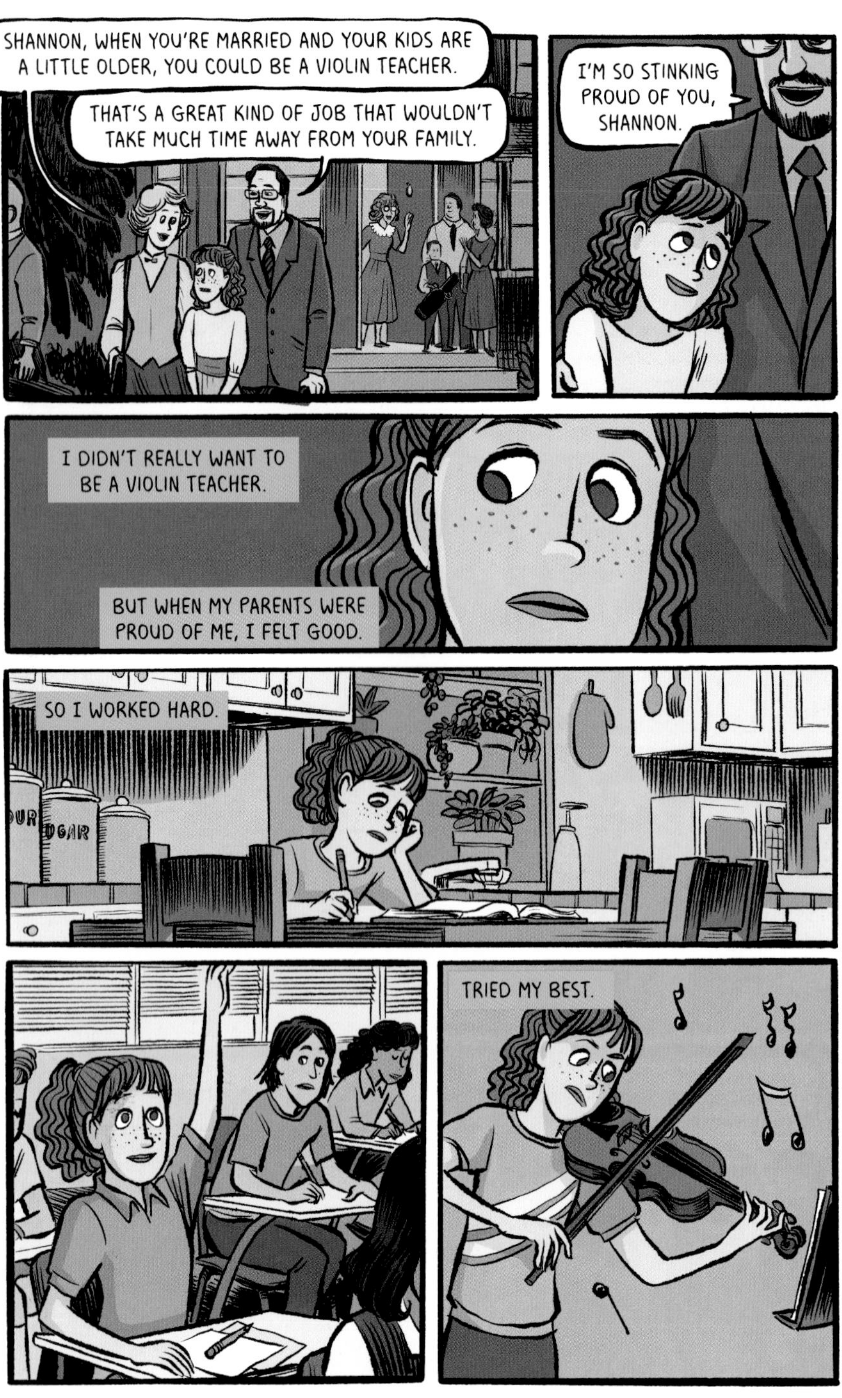
SHANNON, WHEN YOU'RE MARRIED AND YOUR KIDS ARE A LITTLE OLDER, YOU COULD BE A VIOLIN TEACHER.
THAT'S A GREAT KIND OF JOB THAT WOULDN'T TAKE MUCH TIME AWAY FROM YOUR FAMILY.
I'M SO STINKING PROUD OF YOU, SHANNON.
I DIDN'T REALLY WANT TO BE A VIOLIN TEACHER.
BUT WHEN MY PARENTS WERE PROUD OF ME, I FELT GOOD.
SO I WORKED HARD.
OUR
UGAR
TRIED MY BEST.

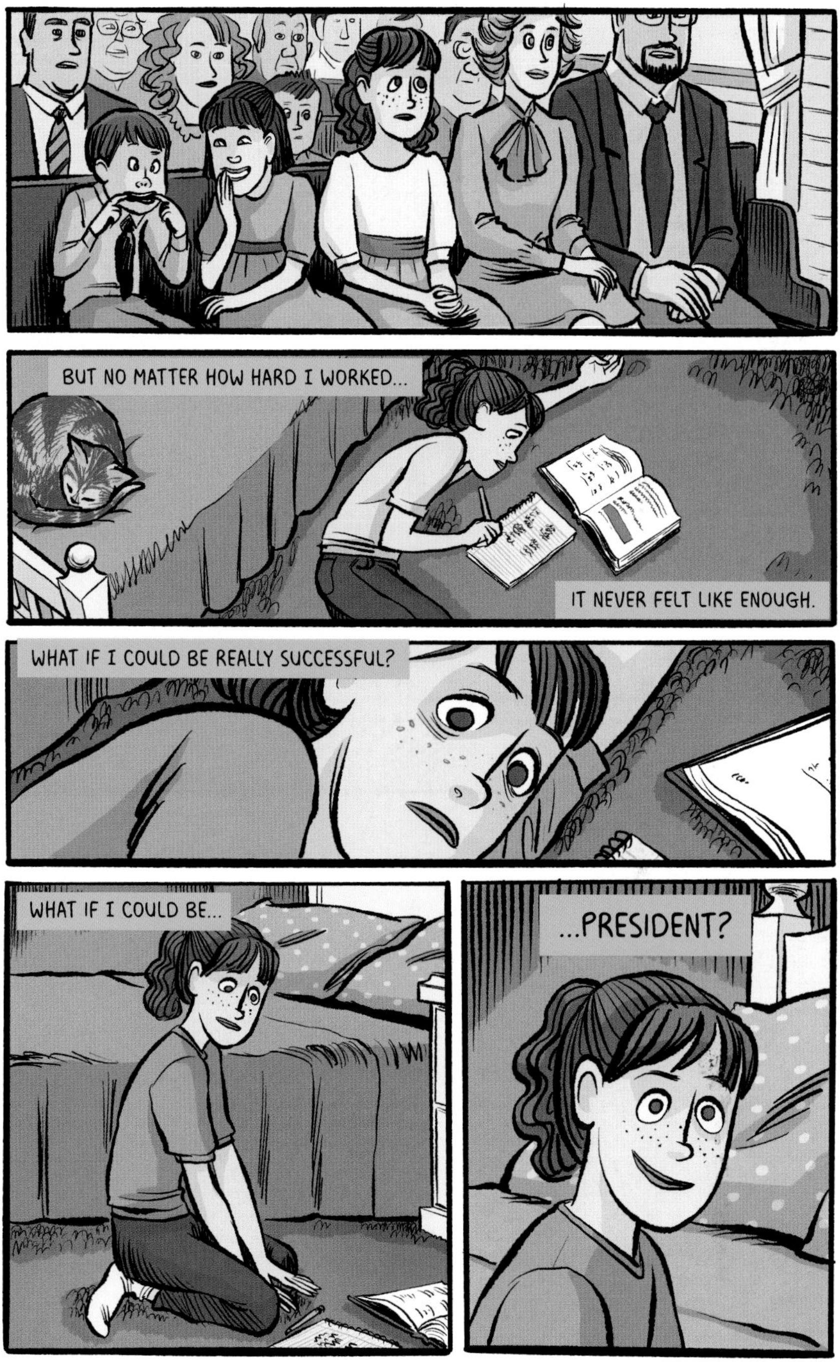
BUT NO MATTER HOW HARD I WORKED...
IT NEVER FELT LIKE ENOUGH.
WHAT IF I COULD BE REALLY SUCCESSFUL?
WHAT IF I COULD BE...
...PRESIDENT?

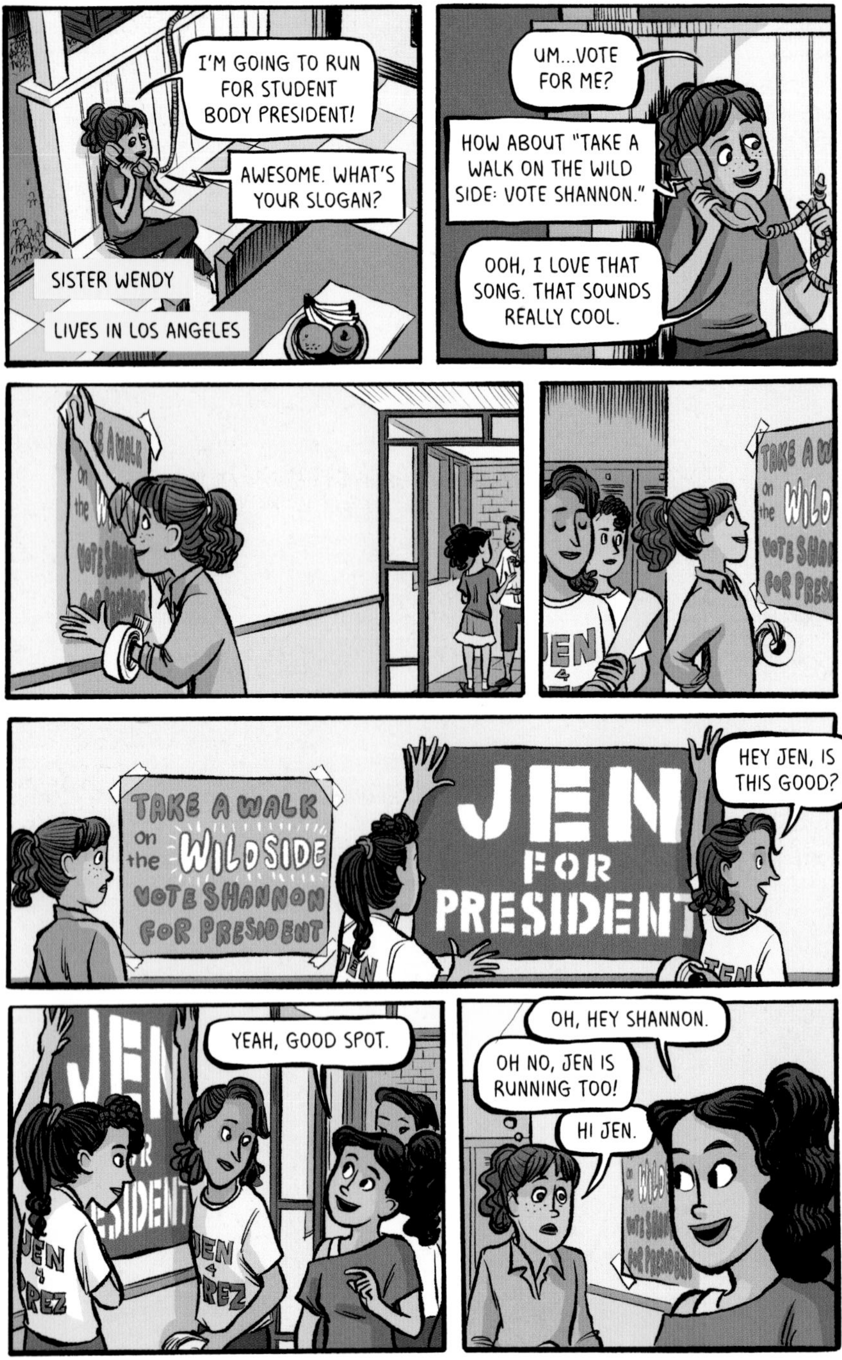
I'M GOING TO RUN FOR STUDENT BODY PRESIDENT!
AWESOME. WHAT'S YOUR SLOGAN?
SISTER WENDY
LIVES IN LOS ANGELES
UM...VOTE FOR ME?
HOW ABOUT "TAKE A WALK ON THE WILD SIDE: VOTE SHANNON."
OOH, I LOVE THAT SONG. THAT SOUNDS REALLY COOL.
TAKE A WALK on the WILDSIDE VOTE SHANNON FOR PRESIDENT
JEN FOR PRESIDENT
HEY JEN, IS THIS GOOD?
YEAH, GOOD SPOT.
JEN 4 PREZ
OH, HEY SHANNON.
OH NO, JEN IS RUNNING TOO!
HI JEN.

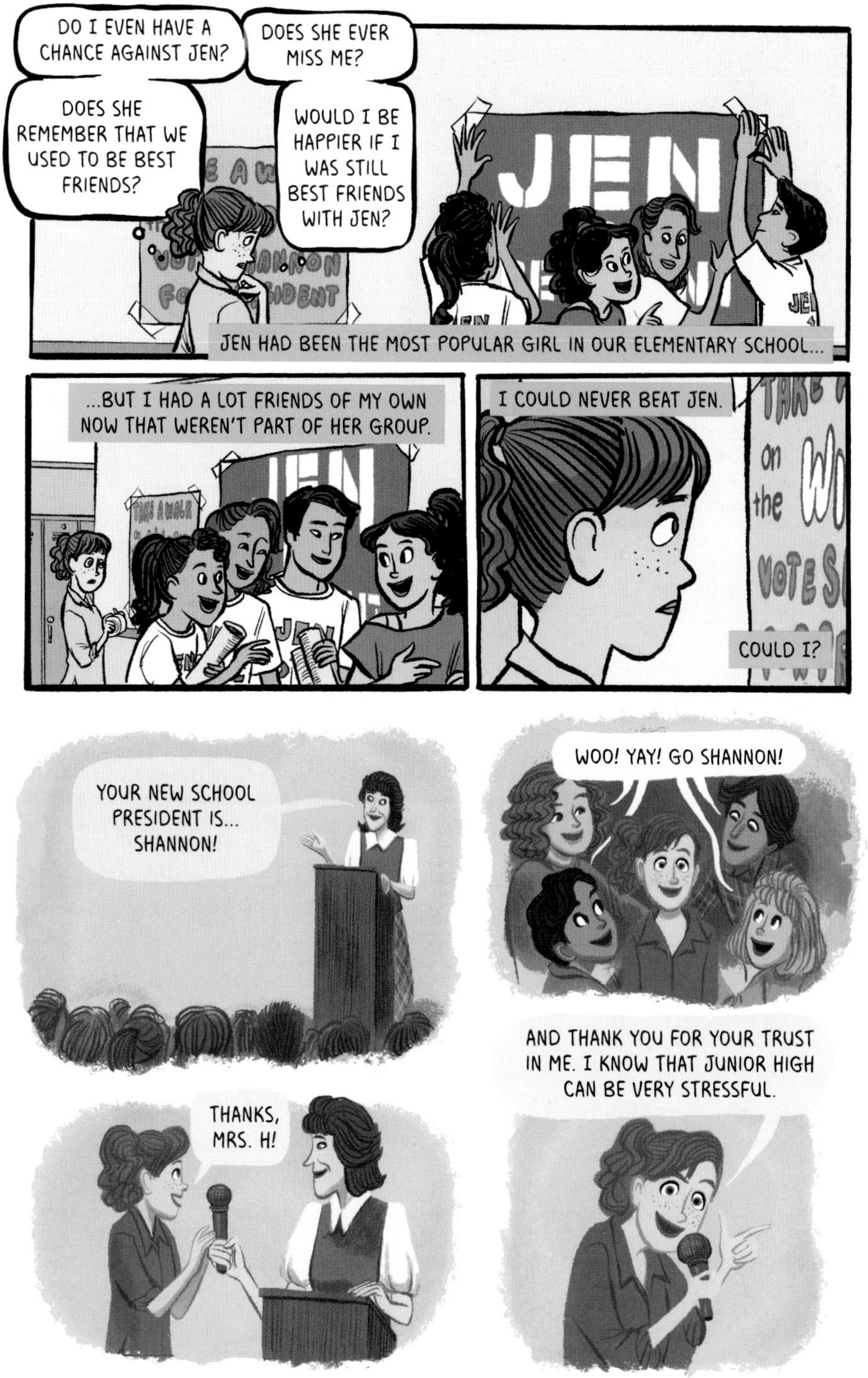
DO I EVEN HAVE A CHANCE AGAINST JEN?
DOES SHE REMEMBER THAT WE USED TO BE BEST FRIENDS?
DOES SHE EVER MISS ME?
WOULD I BE HAPPIER IF I WAS STILL BEST FRIENDS WITH JEN?
JEN
VOTE SHANNON FOR PRESIDENT
JEN HAD BEEN THE MOST POPULAR GIRL IN OUR ELEMENTARY SCHOOL...
...BUT I HAD A LOT FRIENDS OF MY OWN NOW THAT WEREN'T PART OF HER GROUP.
TAKE A WALK
I COULD NEVER BEAT JEN.
on the
VOTE
COULD I?
YOUR NEW SCHOOL PRESIDENT IS... SHANNON!
WOO! YAY! GO SHANNON!
THANKS, MRS. H!
AND THANK YOU FOR YOUR TRUST IN ME. I KNOW THAT JUNIOR HIGH CAN BE VERY STRESSFUL.

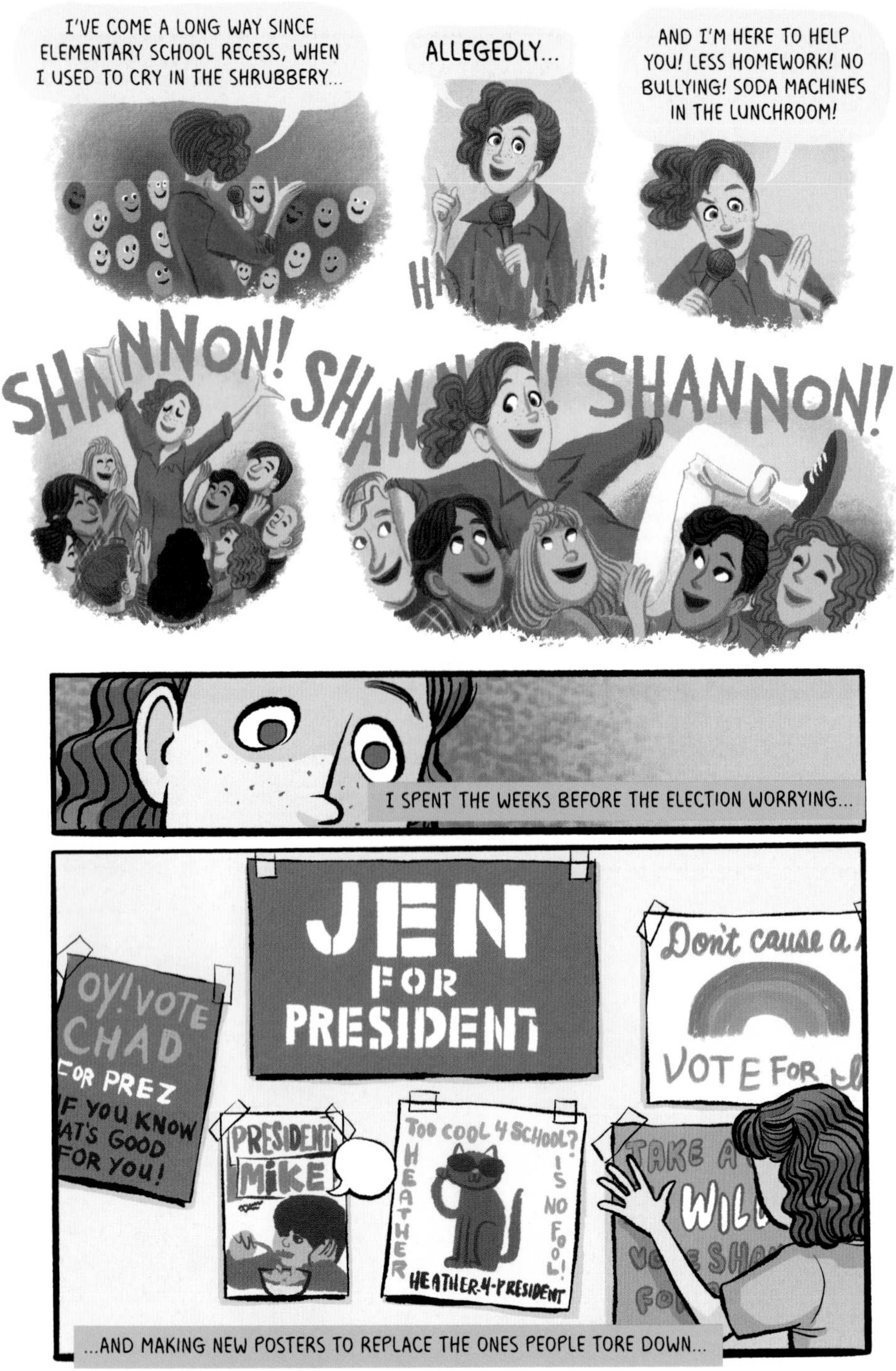
I'VE COME A LONG WAY SINCE ELEMENTARY SCHOOL RECESS, WHEN I USED TO CRY IN THE SHRUBBERY...
ALLEGEDLY...
AND I'M HERE TO HELP YOU! LESS HOMEWORK! NO BULLYING! SODA MACHINES IN THE LUNCHROOM!
SHANNON!
I SPENT THE WEEKS BEFORE THE ELECTION WORRYING...
JEN FOR PRESIDENT
OY! VOTE CHAD
PRESIDENT MIKE
TOO COOL 4 SCHOOL?
HEATHER IS NO FOOL!
HEATHER-4-PRESIDENT
...AND MAKING NEW POSTERS TO REPLACE THE ONES PEOPLE TORE DOWN...

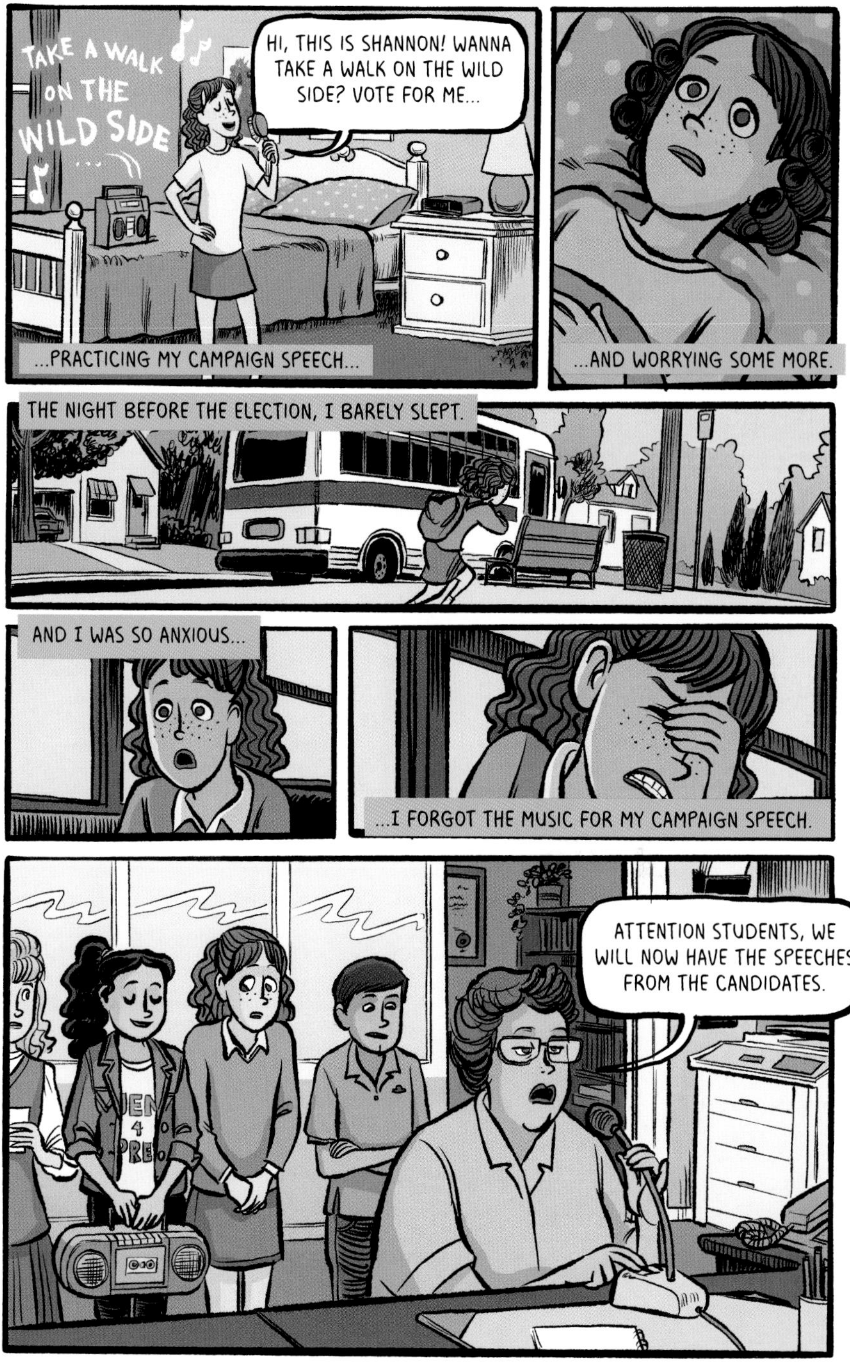
TAKE A WALK ON THE WILD SIDE
HI, THIS IS SHANNON! WANNA TAKE A WALK ON THE WILD SIDE? VOTE FOR ME...
...PRACTICING MY CAMPAIGN SPEECH...
...AND WORRYING SOME MORE.
THE NIGHT BEFORE THE ELECTION, I BARELY SLEPT.
AND I WAS SO ANXIOUS...
...I FORGOT THE MUSIC FOR MY CAMPAIGN SPEECH.
ATTENTION STUDENTS, WE WILL NOW HAVE THE SPEECHES FROM THE CANDIDATES.

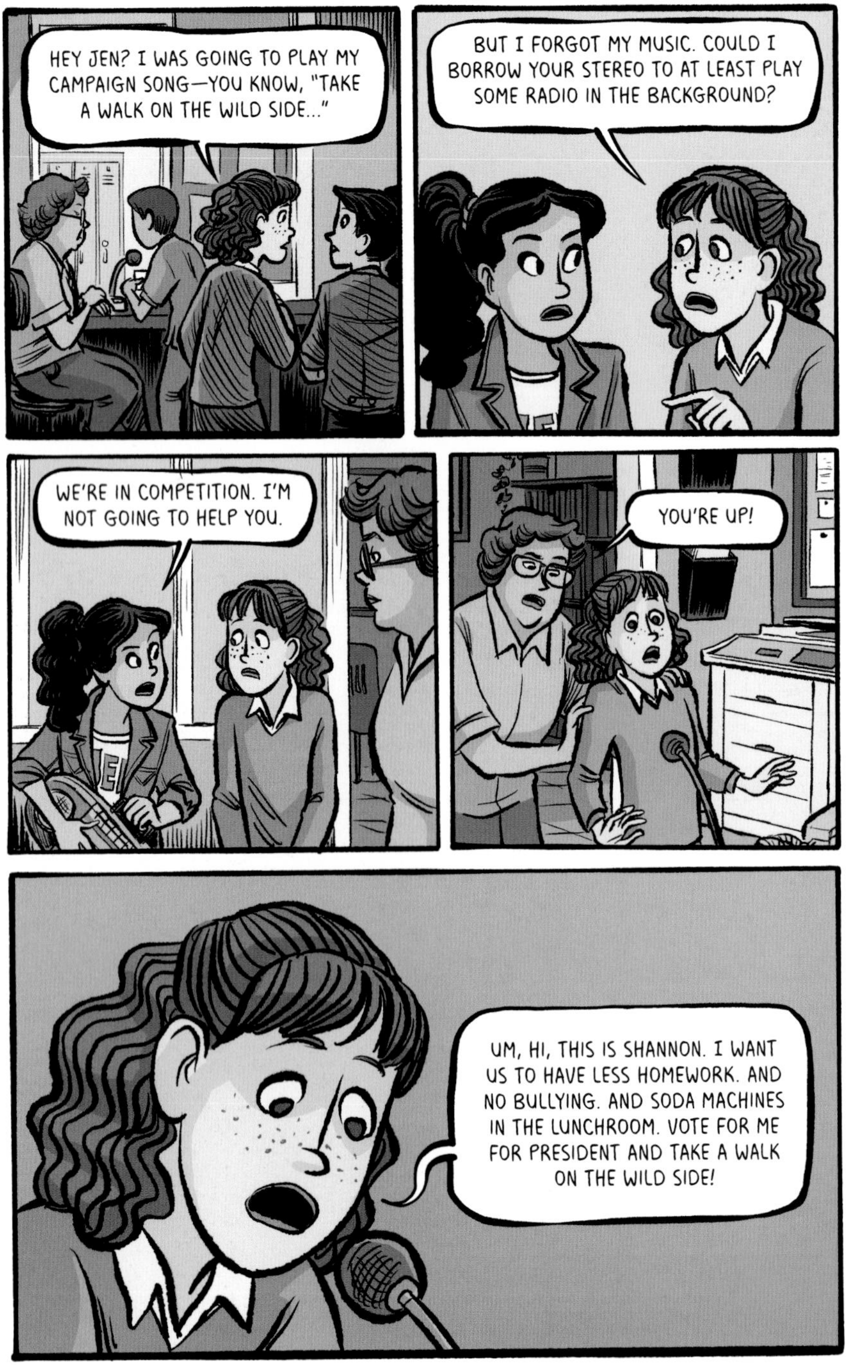
HEY JEN? I WAS GOING TO PLAY MY CAMPAIGN SONG—YOU KNOW, "TAKE A WALK ON THE WILD SIDE..."
BUT I FORGOT MY MUSIC. COULD I BORROW YOUR STEREO TO AT LEAST PLAY SOME RADIO IN THE BACKGROUND?
WE'RE IN COMPETITION. I'M NOT GOING TO HELP YOU.
YOU'RE UP!
UM, HI, THIS IS SHANNON. I WANT US TO HAVE LESS HOMEWORK. AND NO BULLYING. AND SODA MACHINES IN THE LUNCHROOM. VOTE FOR ME FOR PRESIDENT AND TAKE A WALK ON THE WILD SIDE!

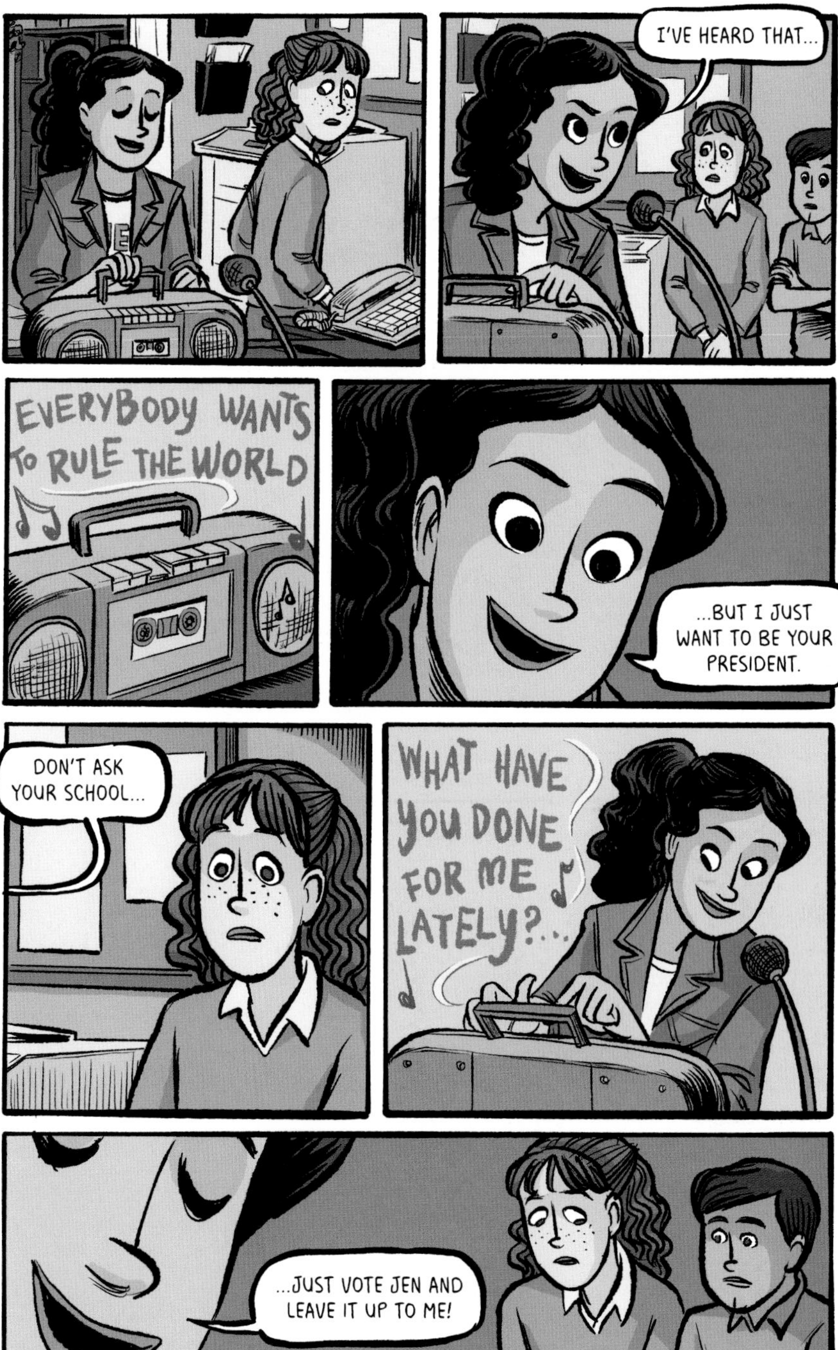
I'VE HEARD THAT...
EVERYBODY WANTS TO RULE THE WORLD
...BUT I JUST WANT TO BE YOUR PRESIDENT.
DON'T ASK YOUR SCHOOL...
WHAT HAVE YOU DONE FOR ME LATELY?...
...JUST VOTE JEN AND LEAVE IT UP TO ME!

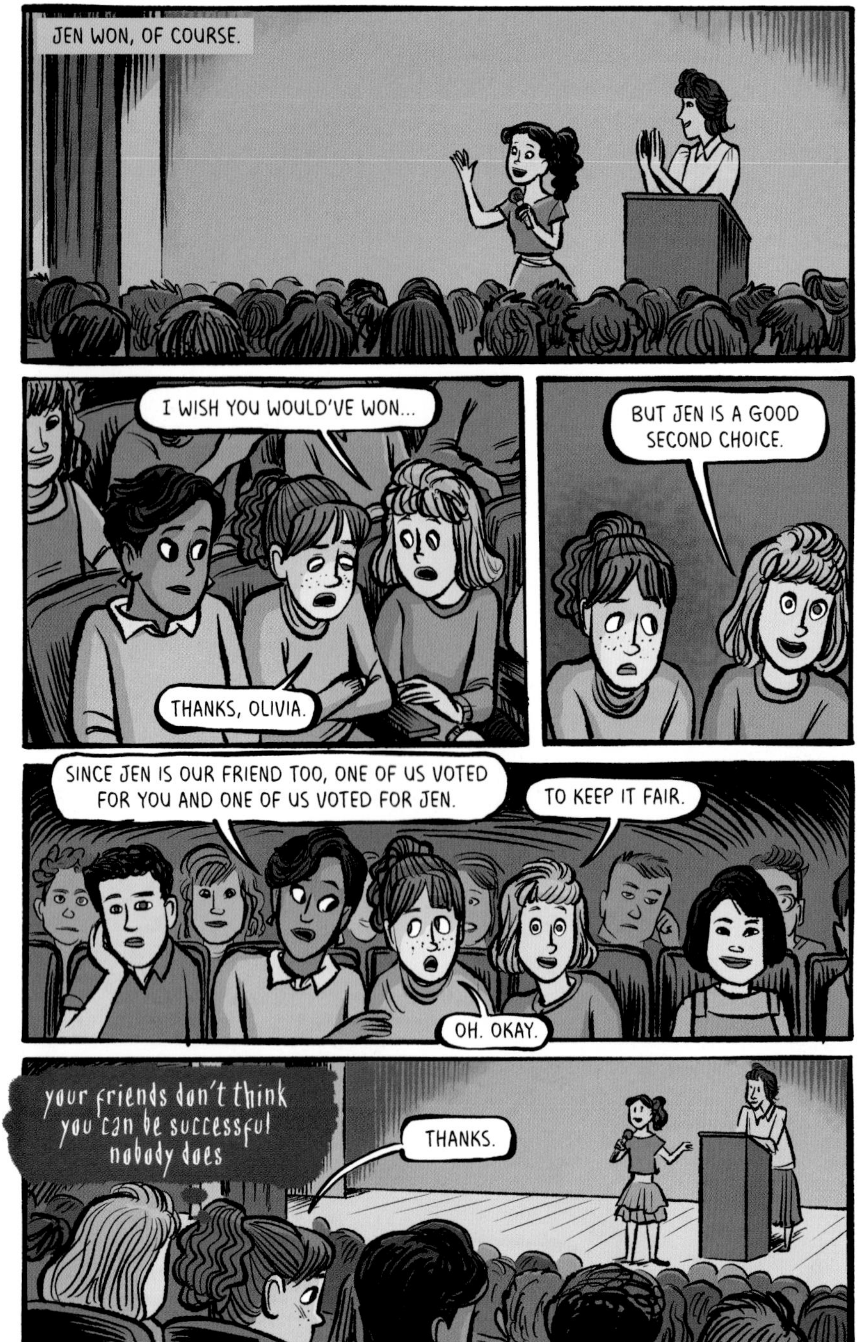

JEN WON, OF COURSE.
I WISH YOU WOULD'VE WON...
THANKS, OLIVIA.
BUT JEN IS A GOOD SECOND CHOICE.
SINCE JEN IS OUR FRIEND TOO, ONE OF US VOTED FOR YOU AND ONE OF US VOTED FOR JEN.
TO KEEP IT FAIR.
OH. OKAY.
your friends don't think you can be successful nobody does
THANKS.

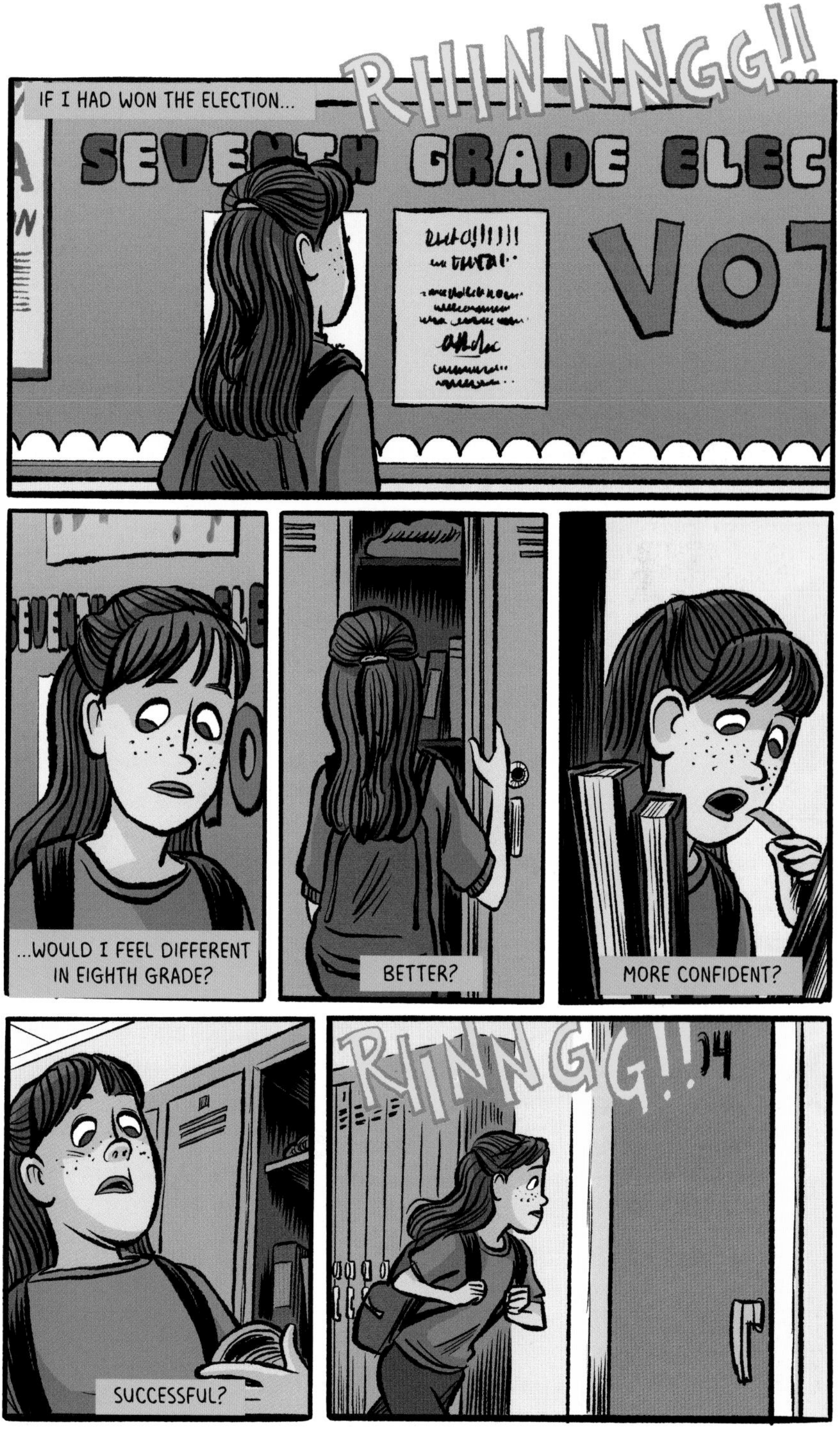
IF I HAD WON THE ELECTION...
RIIINNNGG!!
SEVENTH GRADE ELEC
VOT
...WOULD I FEEL DIFFERENT IN EIGHTH GRADE?
BETTER?
MORE CONFIDENT?
SUCCESSFUL?
RINNGG!!

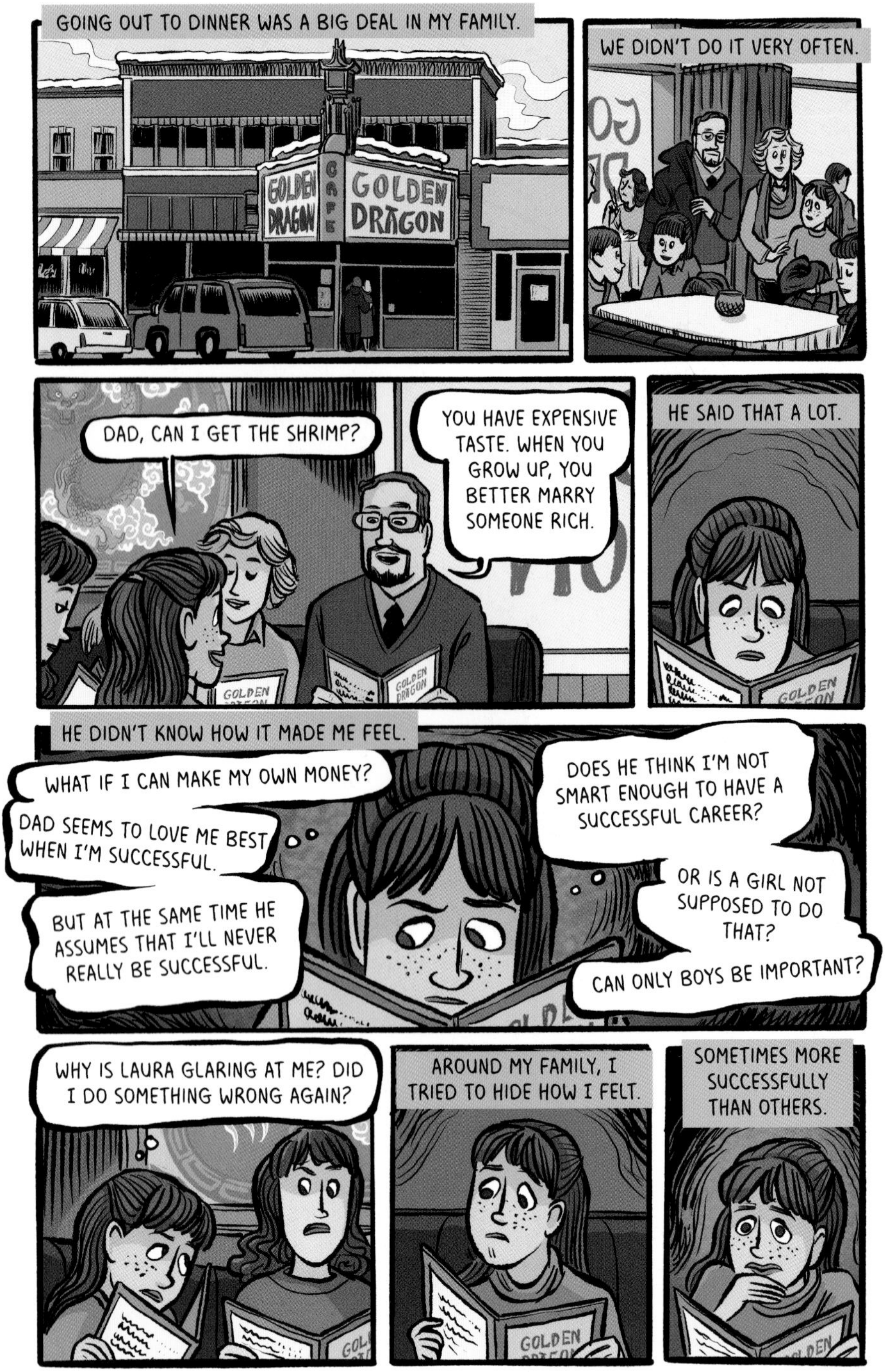
GOING OUT TO DINNER WAS A BIG DEAL IN MY FAMILY.
GOLDEN DRAGON
CAFE
GOLDEN DRAGON
WE DIDN'T DO IT VERY OFTEN.
DAD, CAN I GET THE SHRIMP?
YOU HAVE EXPENSIVE TASTE. WHEN YOU GROW UP, YOU BETTER MARRY SOMEONE RICH.
GOLDEN
GOLDEN DRAGON
HE SAID THAT A LOT.
HE DIDN'T KNOW HOW IT MADE ME FEEL.
WHAT IF I CAN MAKE MY OWN MONEY?
DAD SEEMS TO LOVE ME BEST WHEN I'M SUCCESSFUL.
BUT AT THE SAME TIME HE ASSUMES THAT I'LL NEVER REALLY BE SUCCESSFUL.
DOES HE THINK I'M NOT SMART ENOUGH TO HAVE A SUCCESSFUL CAREER?
OR IS A GIRL NOT SUPPOSED TO DO THAT?
CAN ONLY BOYS BE IMPORTANT?
WHY IS LAURA GLARING AT ME? DID I DO SOMETHING WRONG AGAIN?
AROUND MY FAMILY, I TRIED TO HIDE HOW I FELT.
GOLDEN
SOMETIMES MORE SUCCESSFULLY THAN OTHERS.

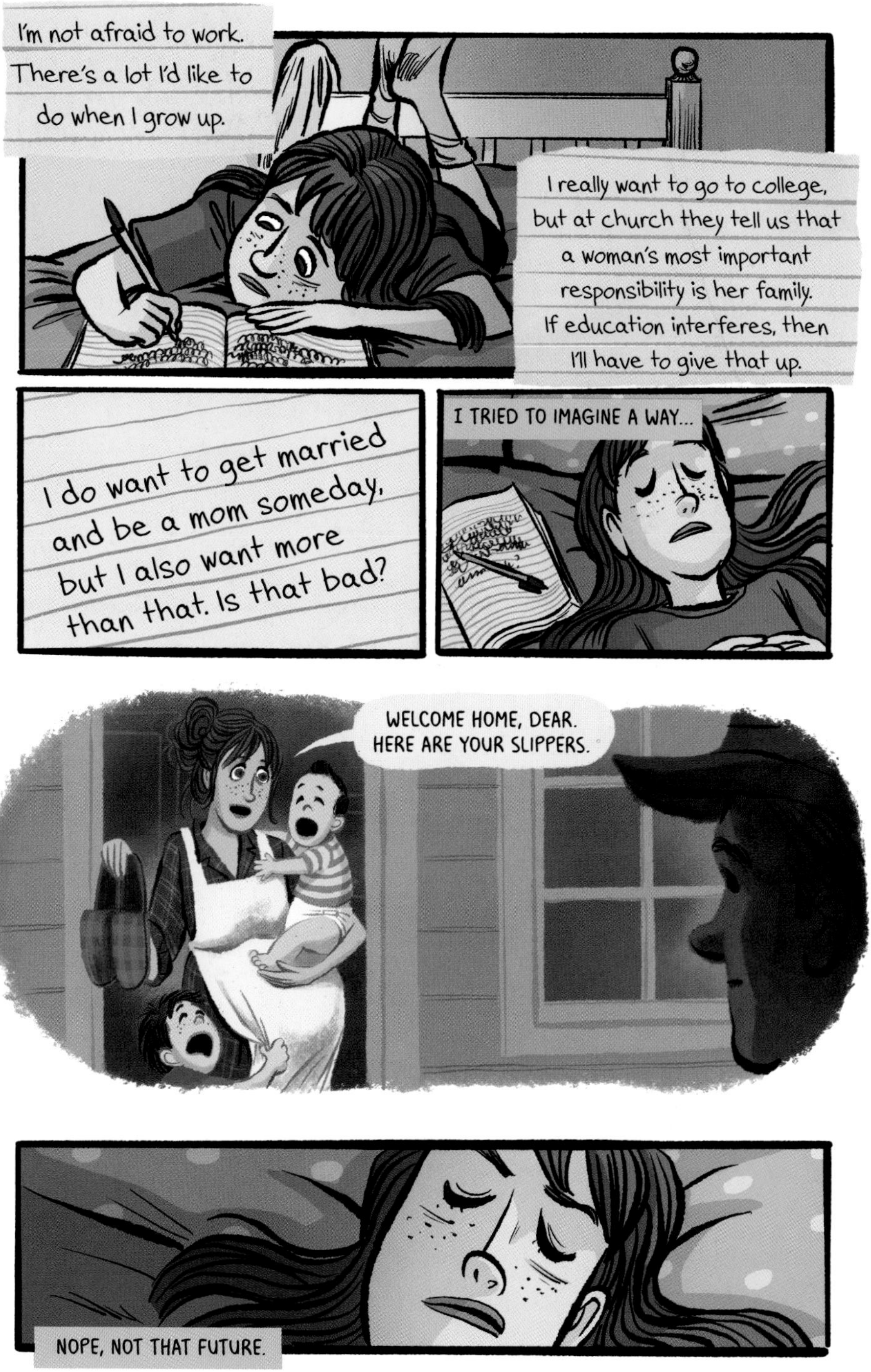
I'm not afraid to work. There's a lot I'd like to do when I grow up.
I really want to go to college, but at church they tell us that a woman's most important responsibility is her family. If education interferes, then I'll have to give that up.
I do want to get married and be a mom someday, but I also want more than that. Is that bad?
I TRIED TO IMAGINE A WAY...
WELCOME HOME, DEAR. HERE ARE YOUR SLIPPERS.
NOPE, NOT THAT FUTURE.

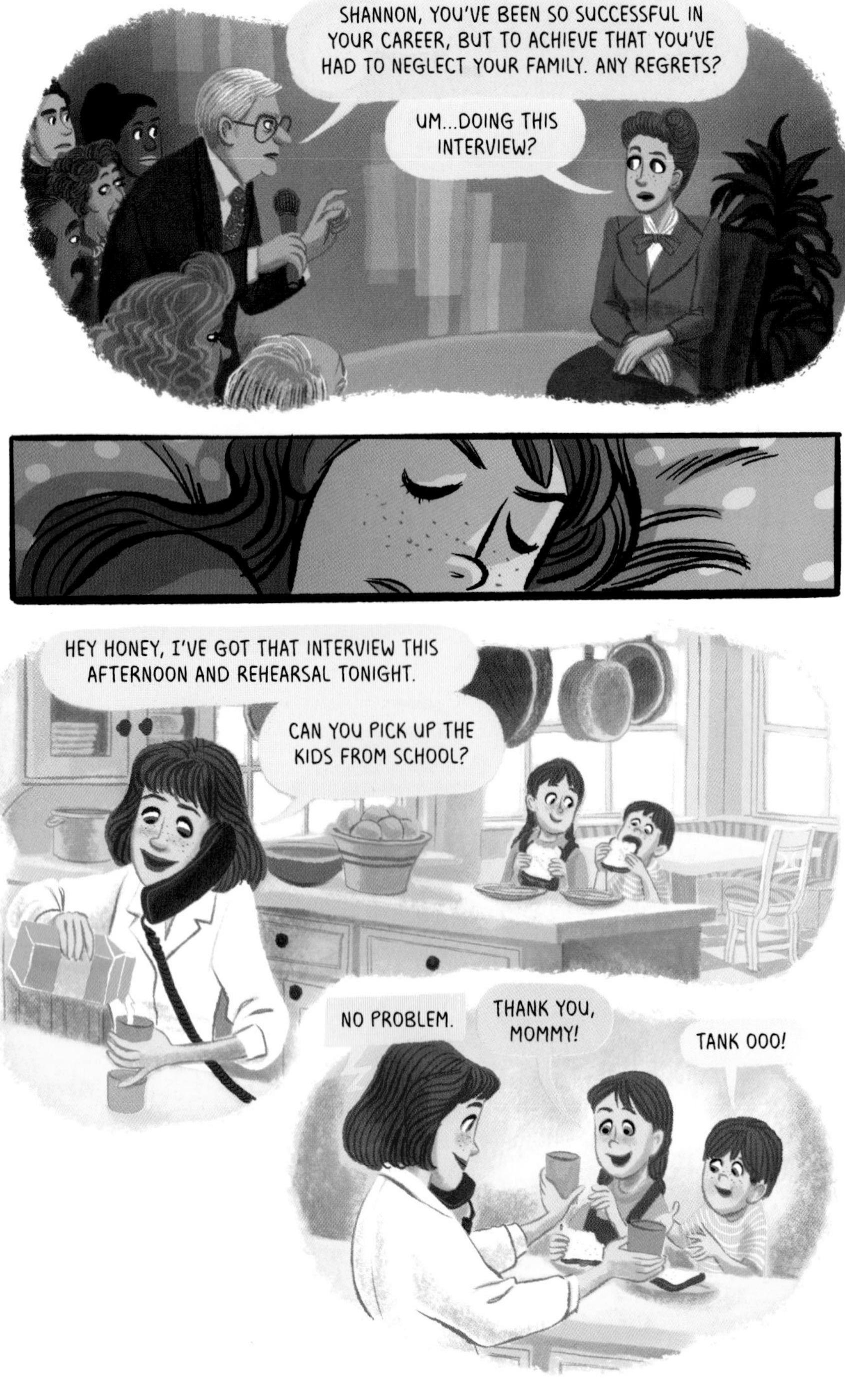
SHANNON, YOU'VE BEEN SO SUCCESSFUL IN YOUR CAREER, BUT TO ACHIEVE THAT YOU'VE HAD TO NEGLECT YOUR FAMILY. ANY REGRETS?
UM...DOING THIS INTERVIEW?
HEY HONEY, I'VE GOT THAT INTERVIEW THIS AFTERNOON AND REHEARSAL TONIGHT.
CAN YOU PICK UP THE KIDS FROM SCHOOL?
NO PROBLEM.
THANK YOU, MOMMY!
TANK OOO!

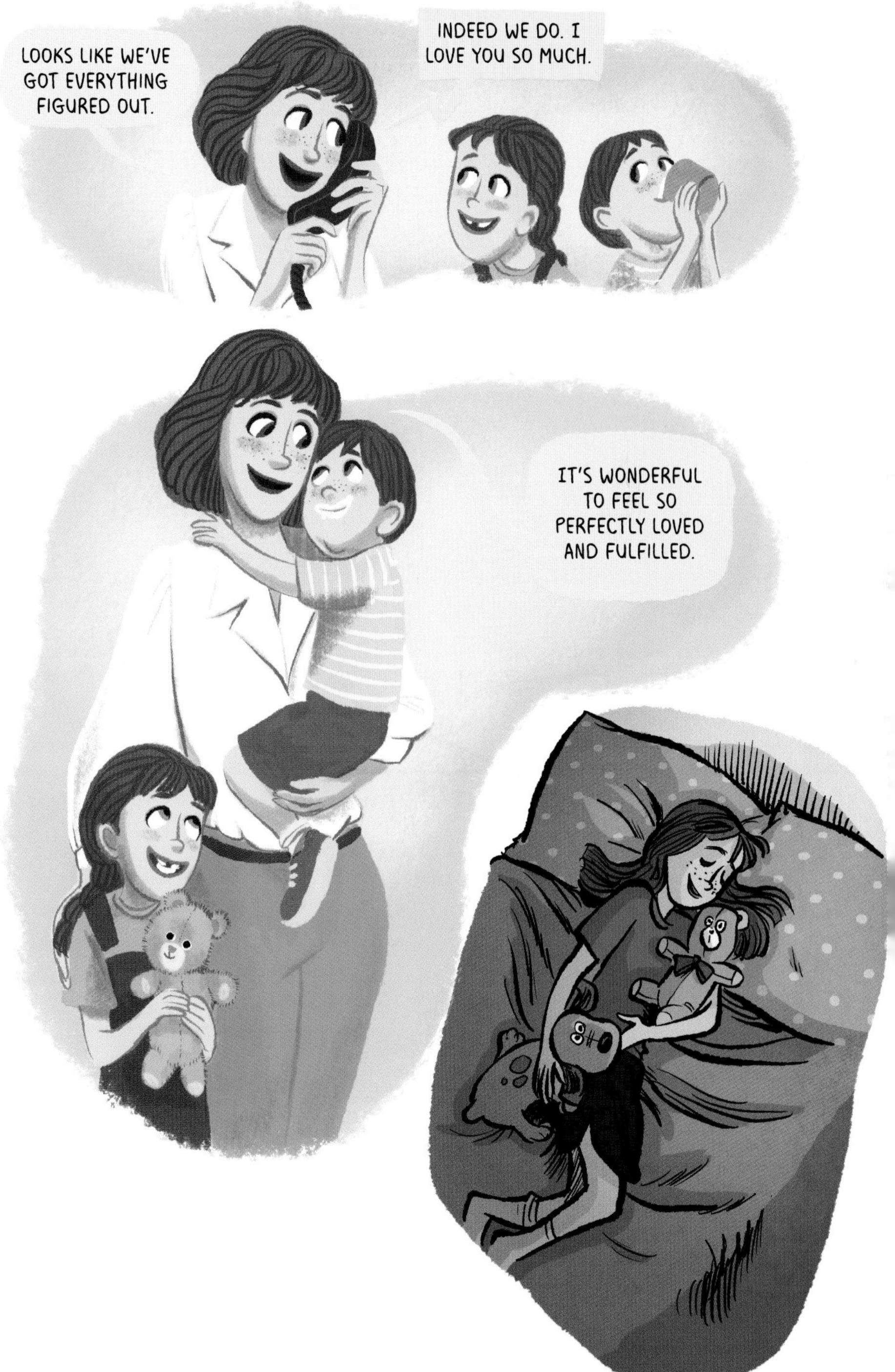
LOOKS LIKE WE'VE GOT EVERYTHING FIGURED OUT.
INDEED WE DO. I LOVE YOU SO MUCH.
IT'S WONDERFUL TO FEEL SO PERFECTLY LOVED AND FULFILLED.

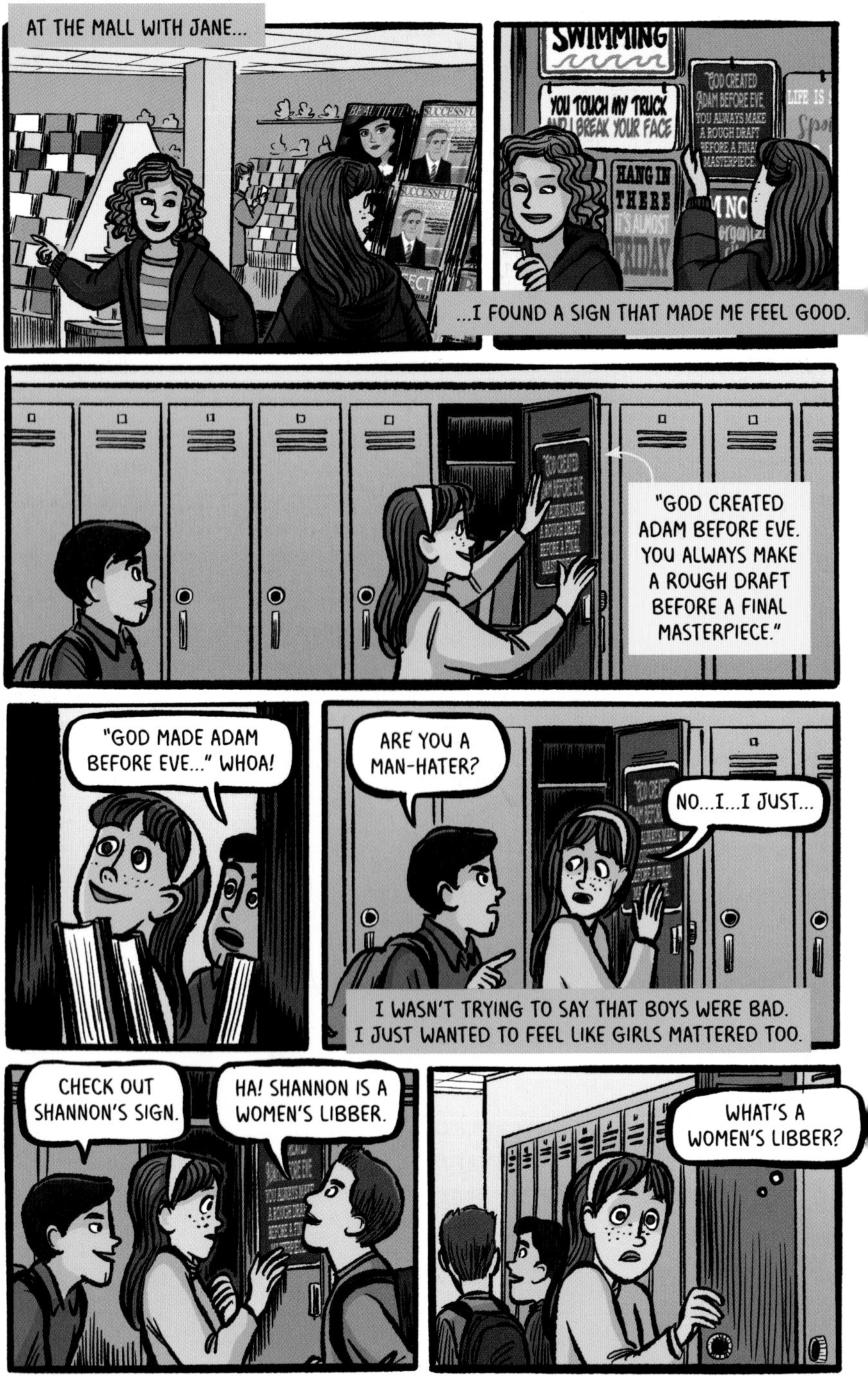
AT THE MALL WITH JANE...
BEAUTIFUL
SUCCESSFUL
SUCCESSFUL
SWIMMING
YOU TOUCH MY TRUCK AND I BREAK YOUR FACE
GOD CREATED ADAM BEFORE EVE. YOU ALWAYS MAKE A ROUGH DRAFT BEFORE A FINAL MASTERPIECE.
HANG IN THERE IT'S ALMOST FRIDAY
...I FOUND A SIGN THAT MADE ME FEEL GOOD.
"GOD CREATED ADAM BEFORE EVE. YOU ALWAYS MAKE A ROUGH DRAFT BEFORE A FINAL MASTERPIECE."
"GOD MADE ADAM BEFORE EVE..." WHOA!
ARE YOU A MAN-HATER?
NO...I...I JUST...
I WASN'T TRYING TO SAY THAT BOYS WERE BAD. I JUST WANTED TO FEEL LIKE GIRLS MATTERED TOO.
CHECK OUT SHANNON'S SIGN.
HA! SHANNON IS A WOMEN'S LIBBER.
WHAT'S A WOMEN'S LIBBER?

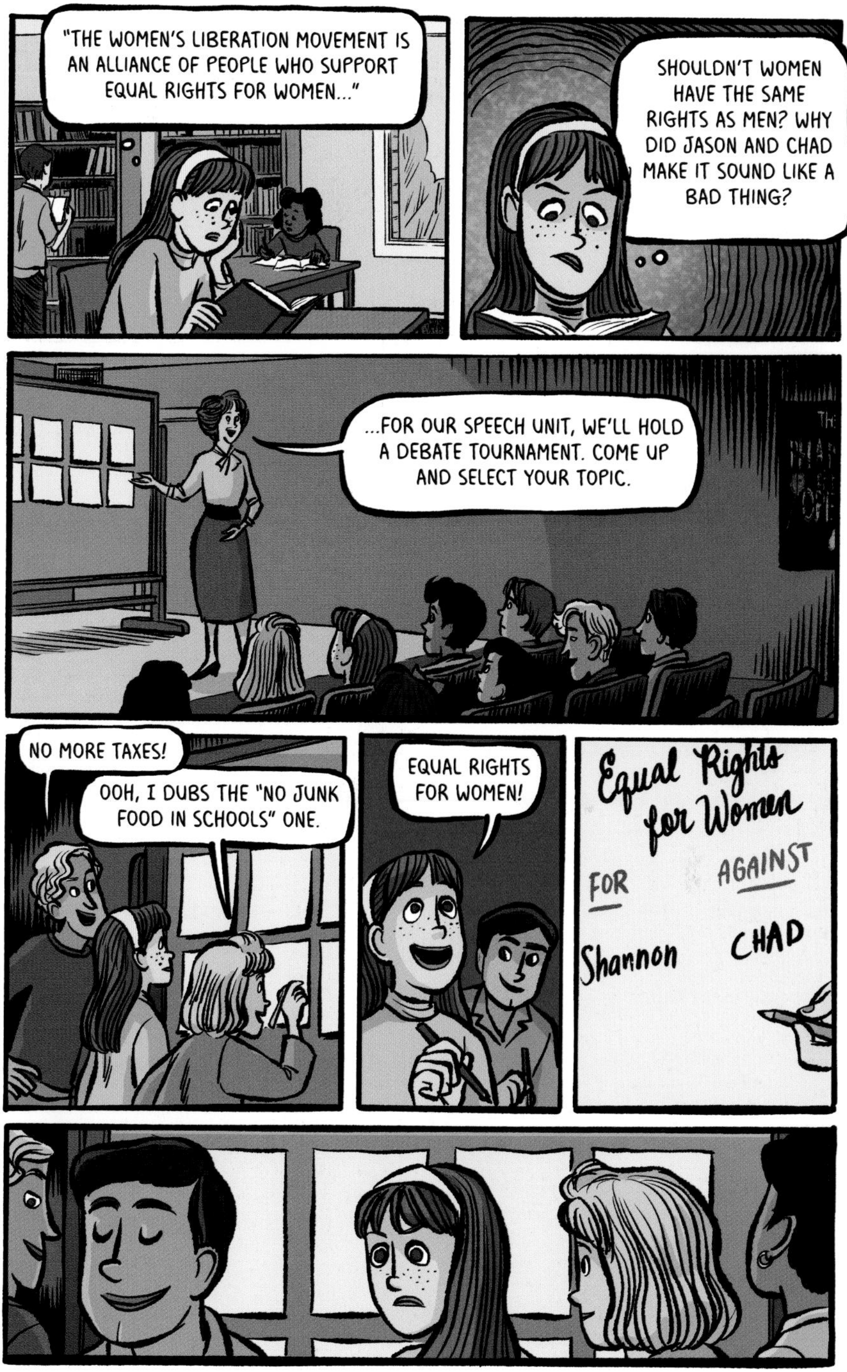
"THE WOMEN'S LIBERATION MOVEMENT IS AN ALLIANCE OF PEOPLE WHO SUPPORT EQUAL RIGHTS FOR WOMEN..."
SHOULDN'T WOMEN HAVE THE SAME RIGHTS AS MEN? WHY DID JASON AND CHAD MAKE IT SOUND LIKE A BAD THING?
...FOR OUR SPEECH UNIT, WE'LL HOLD A DEBATE TOURNAMENT. COME UP AND SELECT YOUR TOPIC.
NO MORE TAXES!
OOH, I DUBS THE "NO JUNK FOOD IN SCHOOLS" ONE.
EQUAL RIGHTS FOR WOMEN!
Equal Rights for Women
FOR
AGAINST
Shannon
CHAD

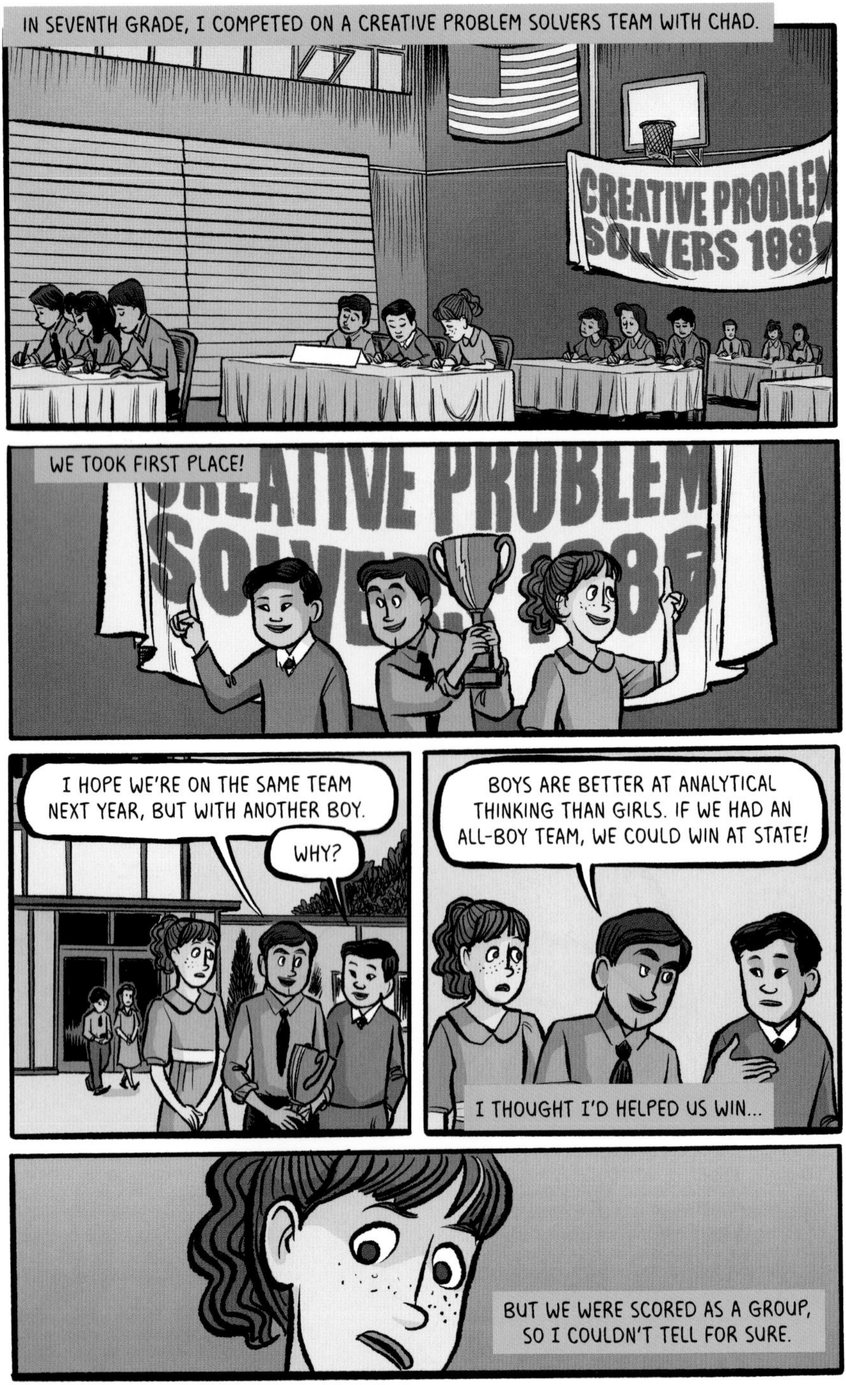
IN SEVENTH GRADE, I COMPETED ON A CREATIVE PROBLEM SOLVERS TEAM WITH CHAD.
CREATIVE PROBLEM SOLVERS 198
WE TOOK FIRST PLACE!
I HOPE WE'RE ON THE SAME TEAM NEXT YEAR, BUT WITH ANOTHER BOY.
WHY?
BOYS ARE BETTER AT ANALYTICAL THINKING THAN GIRLS. IF WE HAD AN ALL-BOY TEAM, WE COULD WIN AT STATE!
I THOUGHT I'D HELPED US WIN...
BUT WE WERE SCORED AS A GROUP, SO I COULDN'T TELL FOR SURE.

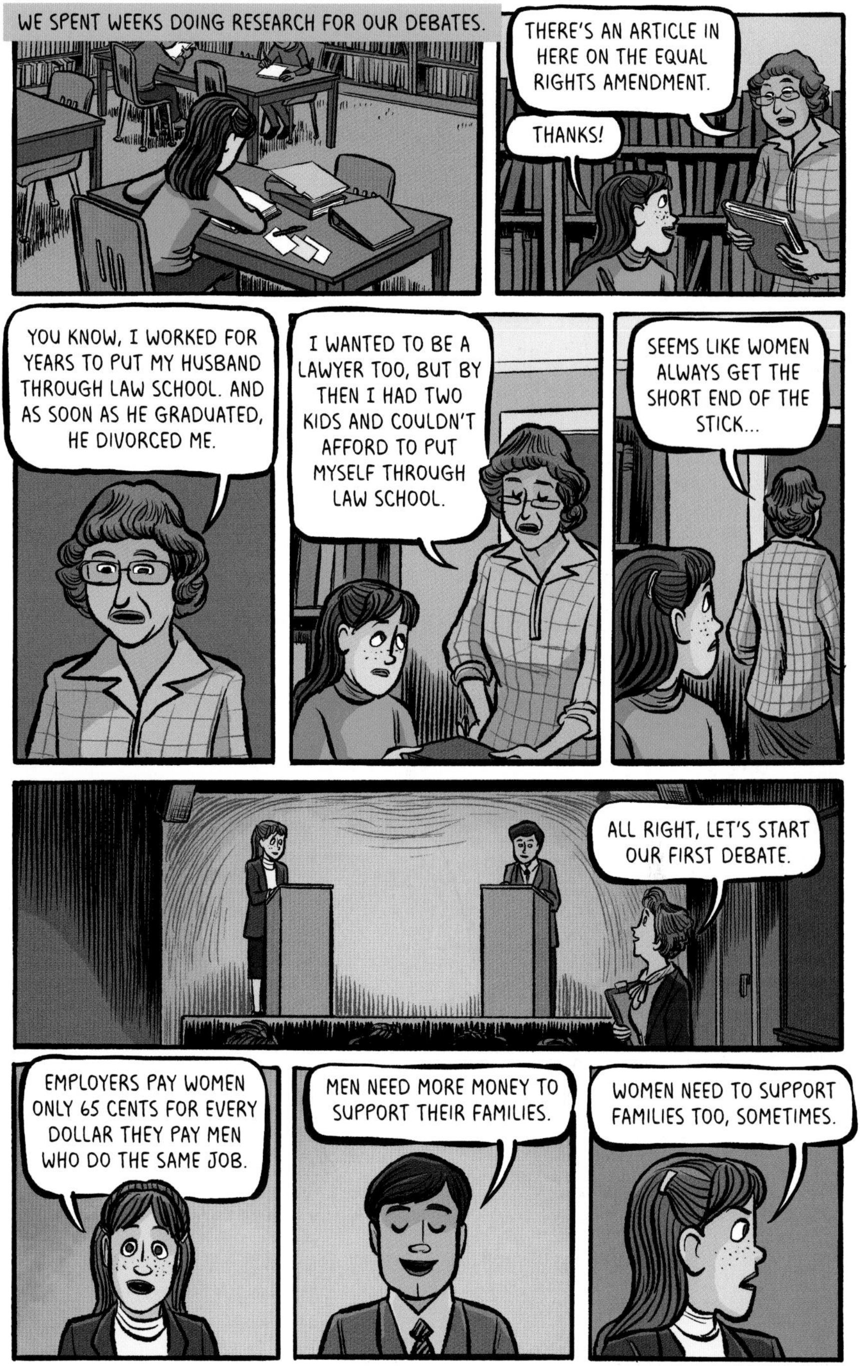
WE SPENT WEEKS DOING RESEARCH FOR OUR DEBATES.
THERE'S AN ARTICLE IN HERE ON THE EQUAL RIGHTS AMENDMENT.
THANKS!
YOU KNOW, I WORKED FOR YEARS TO PUT MY HUSBAND THROUGH LAW SCHOOL. AND AS SOON AS HE GRADUATED, HE DIVORCED ME.
I WANTED TO BE A LAWYER TOO, BUT BY THEN I HAD TWO KIDS AND COULDN'T AFFORD TO PUT MYSELF THROUGH LAW SCHOOL.
SEEMS LIKE WOMEN ALWAYS GET THE SHORT END OF THE STICK...
ALL RIGHT, LET'S START OUR FIRST DEBATE.
EMPLOYERS PAY WOMEN ONLY 65 CENTS FOR EVERY DOLLAR THEY PAY MEN WHO DO THE SAME JOB.
MEN NEED MORE MONEY TO SUPPORT THEIR FAMILIES.
WOMEN NEED TO SUPPORT FAMILIES TOO, SOMETIMES.

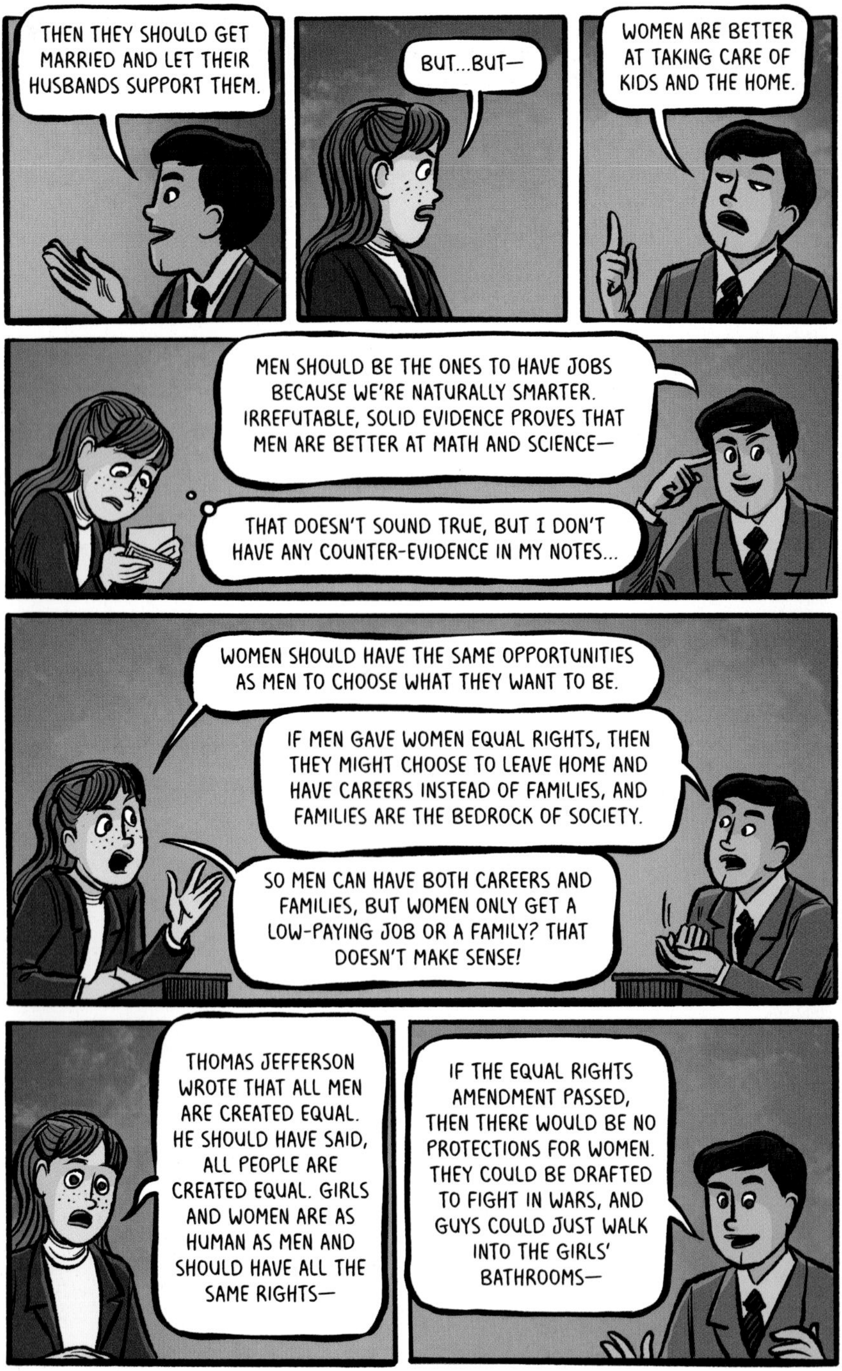
THEN THEY SHOULD GET MARRIED AND LET THEIR HUSBANDS SUPPORT THEM.
BUT...BUT—
WOMEN ARE BETTER AT TAKING CARE OF KIDS AND THE HOME.
MEN SHOULD BE THE ONES TO HAVE JOBS BECAUSE WE'RE NATURALLY SMARTER. IRREFUTABLE, SOLID EVIDENCE PROVES THAT MEN ARE BETTER AT MATH AND SCIENCE—
THAT DOESN'T SOUND TRUE, BUT I DON'T HAVE ANY COUNTER-EVIDENCE IN MY NOTES...
WOMEN SHOULD HAVE THE SAME OPPORTUNITIES AS MEN TO CHOOSE WHAT THEY WANT TO BE.
IF MEN GAVE WOMEN EQUAL RIGHTS, THEN THEY MIGHT CHOOSE TO LEAVE HOME AND HAVE CAREERS INSTEAD OF FAMILIES, AND FAMILIES ARE THE BEDROCK OF SOCIETY.
SO MEN CAN HAVE BOTH CAREERS AND FAMILIES, BUT WOMEN ONLY GET A LOW-PAYING JOB OR A FAMILY? THAT DOESN'T MAKE SENSE!
THOMAS JEFFERSON WROTE THAT ALL MEN ARE CREATED EQUAL. HE SHOULD HAVE SAID, ALL PEOPLE ARE CREATED EQUAL. GIRLS AND WOMEN ARE AS HUMAN AS MEN AND SHOULD HAVE ALL THE SAME RIGHTS—
IF THE EQUAL RIGHTS AMENDMENT PASSED, THEN THERE WOULD BE NO PROTECTIONS FOR WOMEN. THEY COULD BE DRAFTED TO FIGHT IN WARS, AND GUYS COULD JUST WALK INTO THE GIRLS' BATHROOMS—

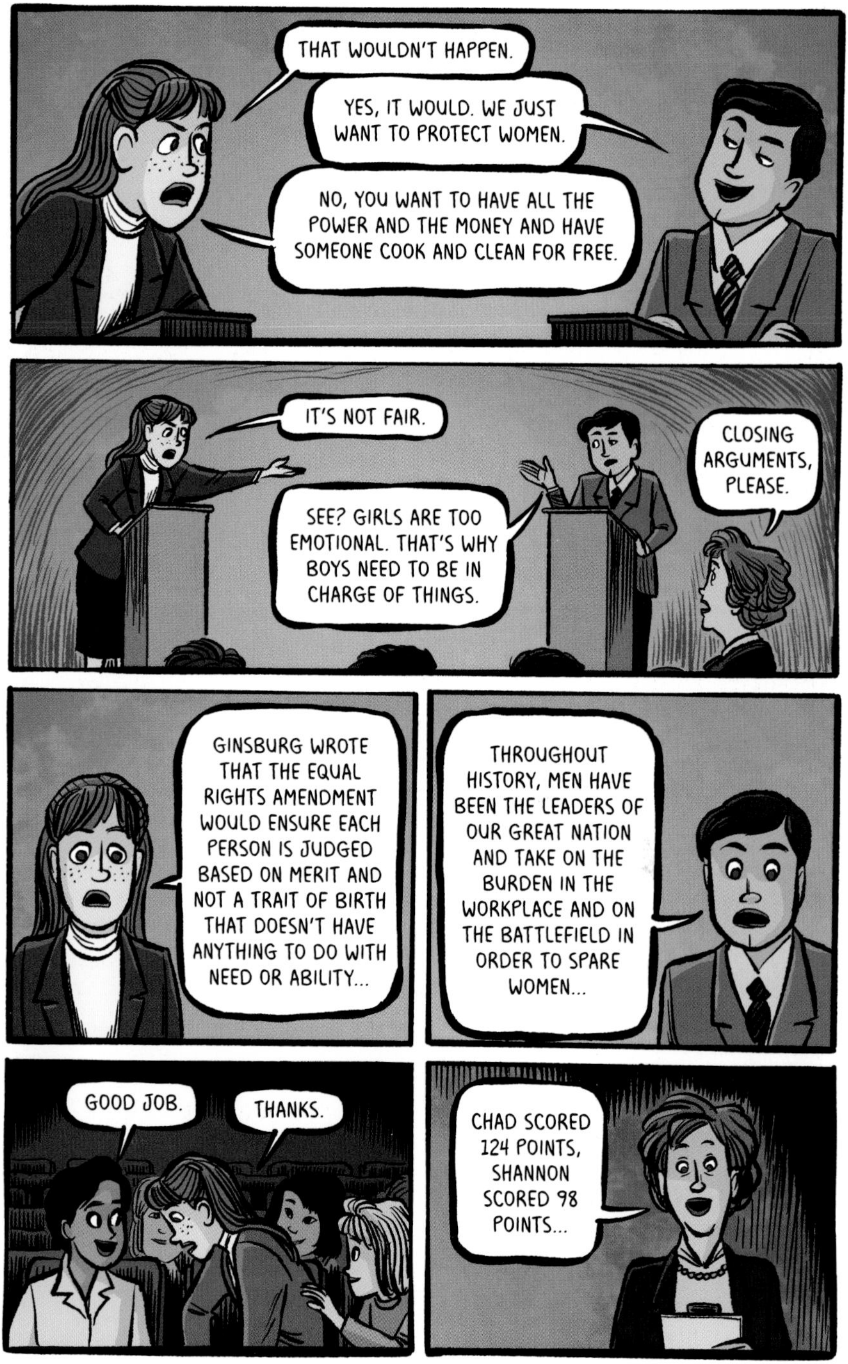
THAT WOULDN'T HAPPEN.
YES, IT WOULD. WE JUST WANT TO PROTECT WOMEN.
NO, YOU WANT TO HAVE ALL THE POWER AND THE MONEY AND HAVE SOMEONE COOK AND CLEAN FOR FREE.
IT'S NOT FAIR.
SEE? GIRLS ARE TOO EMOTIONAL. THAT'S WHY BOYS NEED TO BE IN CHARGE OF THINGS.
CLOSING ARGUMENTS, PLEASE.
GINSBURG WROTE THAT THE EQUAL RIGHTS AMENDMENT WOULD ENSURE EACH PERSON IS JUDGED BASED ON MERIT AND NOT A TRAIT OF BIRTH THAT DOESN'T HAVE ANYTHING TO DO WITH NEED OR ABILITY...
THROUGHOUT HISTORY, MEN HAVE BEEN THE LEADERS OF OUR GREAT NATION AND TAKE ON THE BURDEN IN THE WORKPLACE AND ON THE BATTLEFIELD IN ORDER TO SPARE WOMEN...
GOOD JOB.
THANKS.
CHAD SCORED 124 POINTS, SHANNON SCORED 98 POINTS...

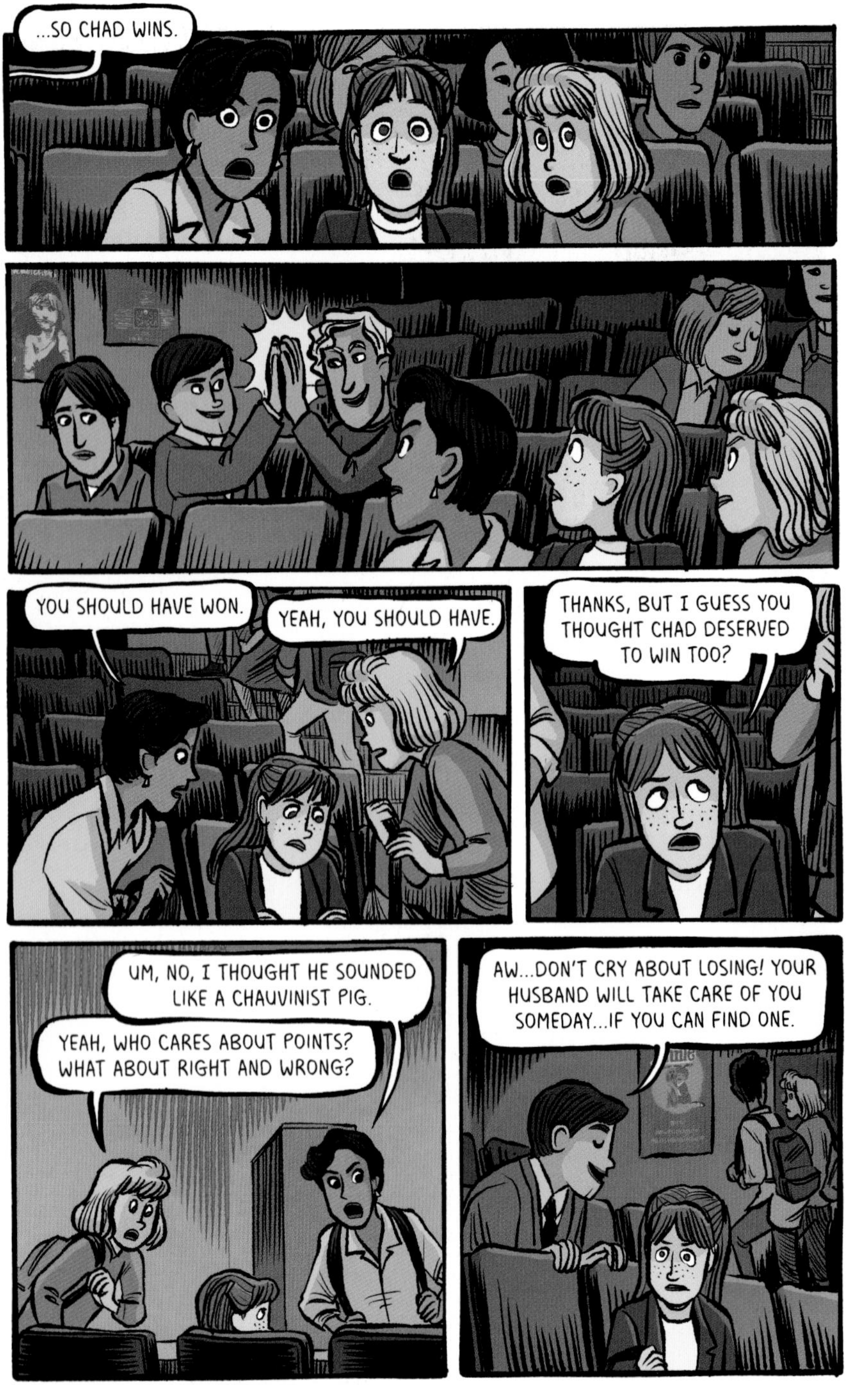
...SO CHAD WINS.
YOU SHOULD HAVE WON.
YEAH, YOU SHOULD HAVE.
THANKS, BUT I GUESS YOU THOUGHT CHAD DESERVED TO WIN TOO?
UM, NO, I THOUGHT HE SOUNDED LIKE A CHAUVINIST PIG.
YEAH, WHO CARES ABOUT POINTS? WHAT ABOUT RIGHT AND WRONG?
AW...DON'T CRY ABOUT LOSING! YOUR HUSBAND WILL TAKE CARE OF YOU SOMEDAY...IF YOU CAN FIND ONE.

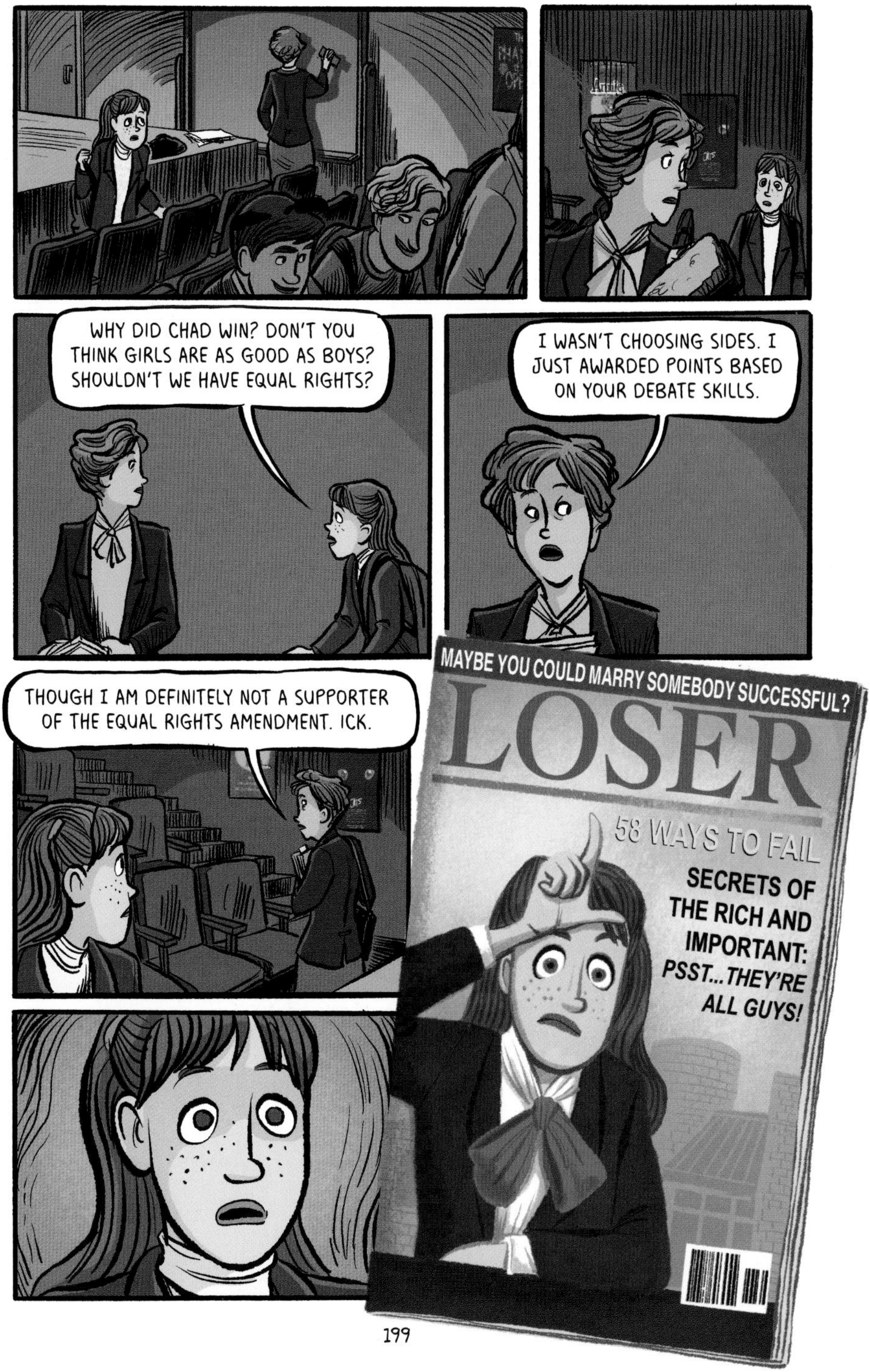
WHY DID CHAD WIN? DON'T YOU THINK GIRLS ARE AS GOOD AS BOYS? SHOULDN'T WE HAVE EQUAL RIGHTS?
I WASN'T CHOOSING SIDES. I JUST AWARDED POINTS BASED ON YOUR DEBATE SKILLS.
THOUGH I AM DEFINITELY NOT A SUPPORTER OF THE EQUAL RIGHTS AMENDMENT. ICK.
MAYBE YOU COULD MARRY SOMEBODY SUCCESSFUL?
LOSER
58 WAYS TO FAIL
SECRETS OF THE RICH AND IMPORTANT: PSST...THEY'RE ALL GUYS!

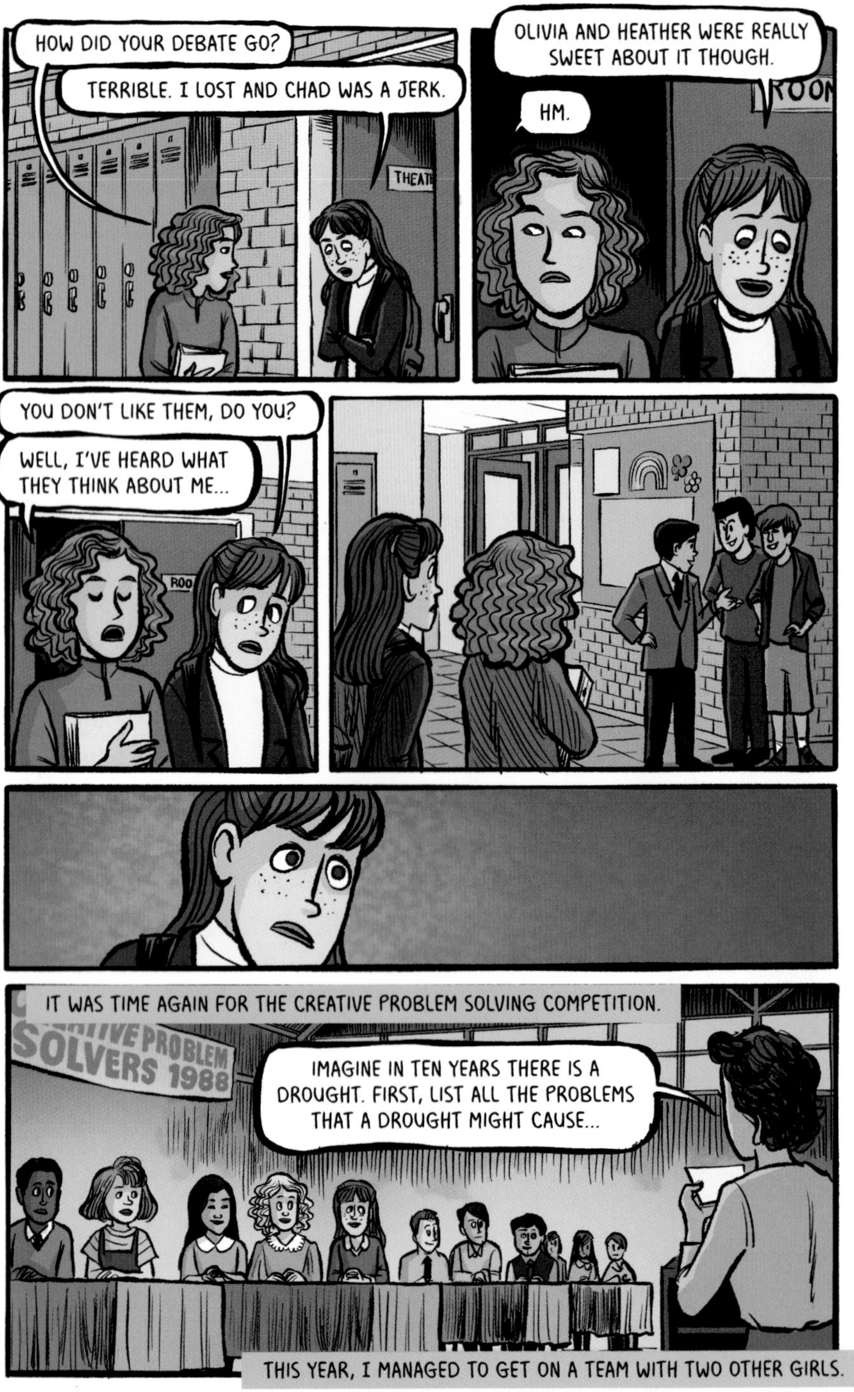
HOW DID YOUR DEBATE GO?
TERRIBLE. I LOST AND CHAD WAS A JERK.
THEATE
OLIVIA AND HEATHER WERE REALLY SWEET ABOUT IT THOUGH.
HM.
ROOM
YOU DON'T LIKE THEM, DO YOU?
WELL, I'VE HEARD WHAT THEY THINK ABOUT ME...
ROO
IT WAS TIME AGAIN FOR THE CREATIVE PROBLEM SOLVING COMPETITION.
ATIVE PROBLEM SOLVERS 1988
IMAGINE IN TEN YEARS THERE IS A DROUGHT. FIRST, LIST ALL THE PROBLEMS THAT A DROUGHT MIGHT CAUSE...
THIS YEAR, I MANAGED TO GET ON A TEAM WITH TWO OTHER GIRLS.

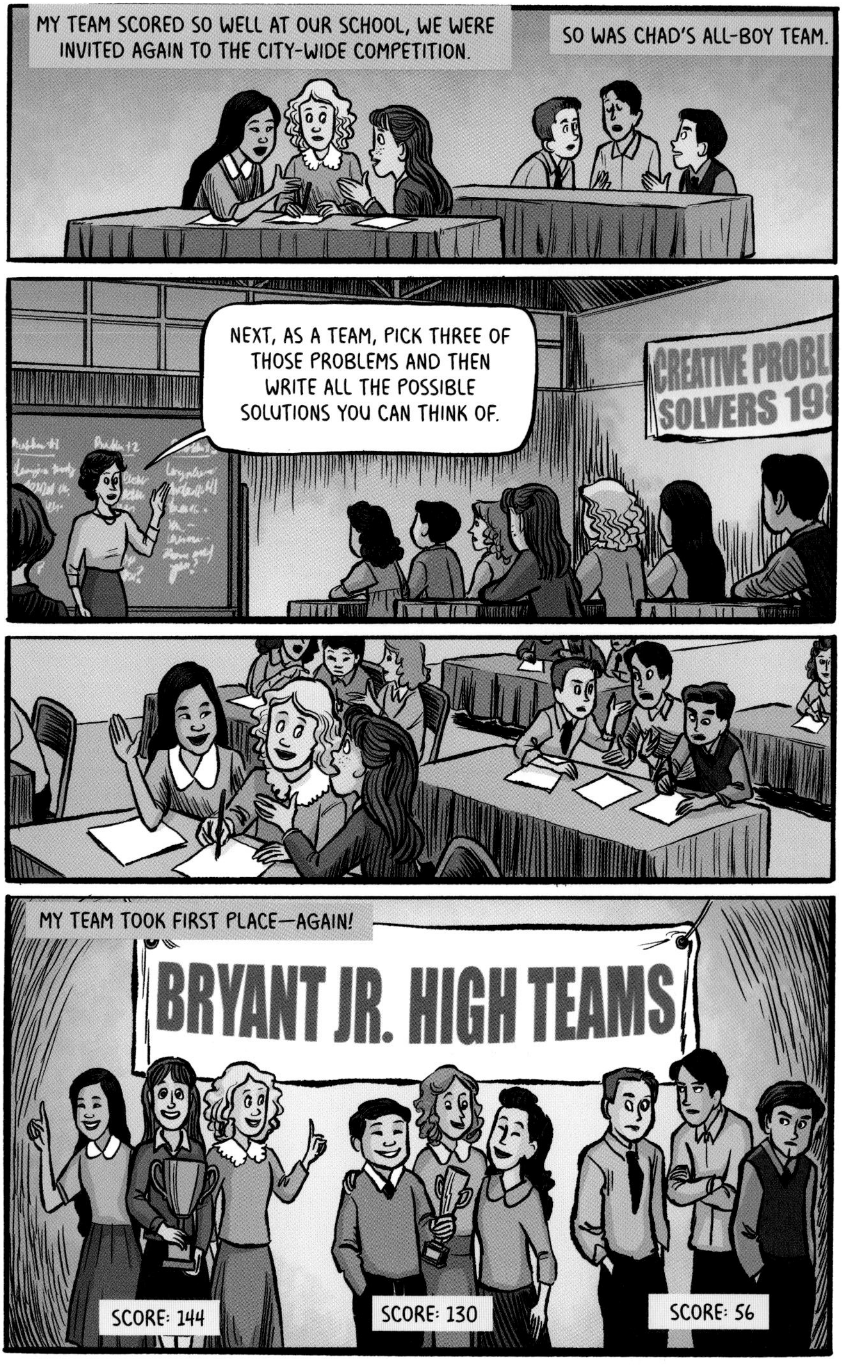
MY TEAM SCORED SO WELL AT OUR SCHOOL, WE WERE INVITED AGAIN TO THE CITY-WIDE COMPETITION.
SO WAS CHAD'S ALL-BOY TEAM.
NEXT, AS A TEAM, PICK THREE OF THOSE PROBLEMS AND THEN WRITE ALL THE POSSIBLE SOLUTIONS YOU CAN THINK OF.
CREATIVE PROBL
SOLVERS 19
MY TEAM TOOK FIRST PLACE—AGAIN!
BRYANT JR. HIGH TEAMS
SCORE: 144
SCORE: 130
SCORE: 56

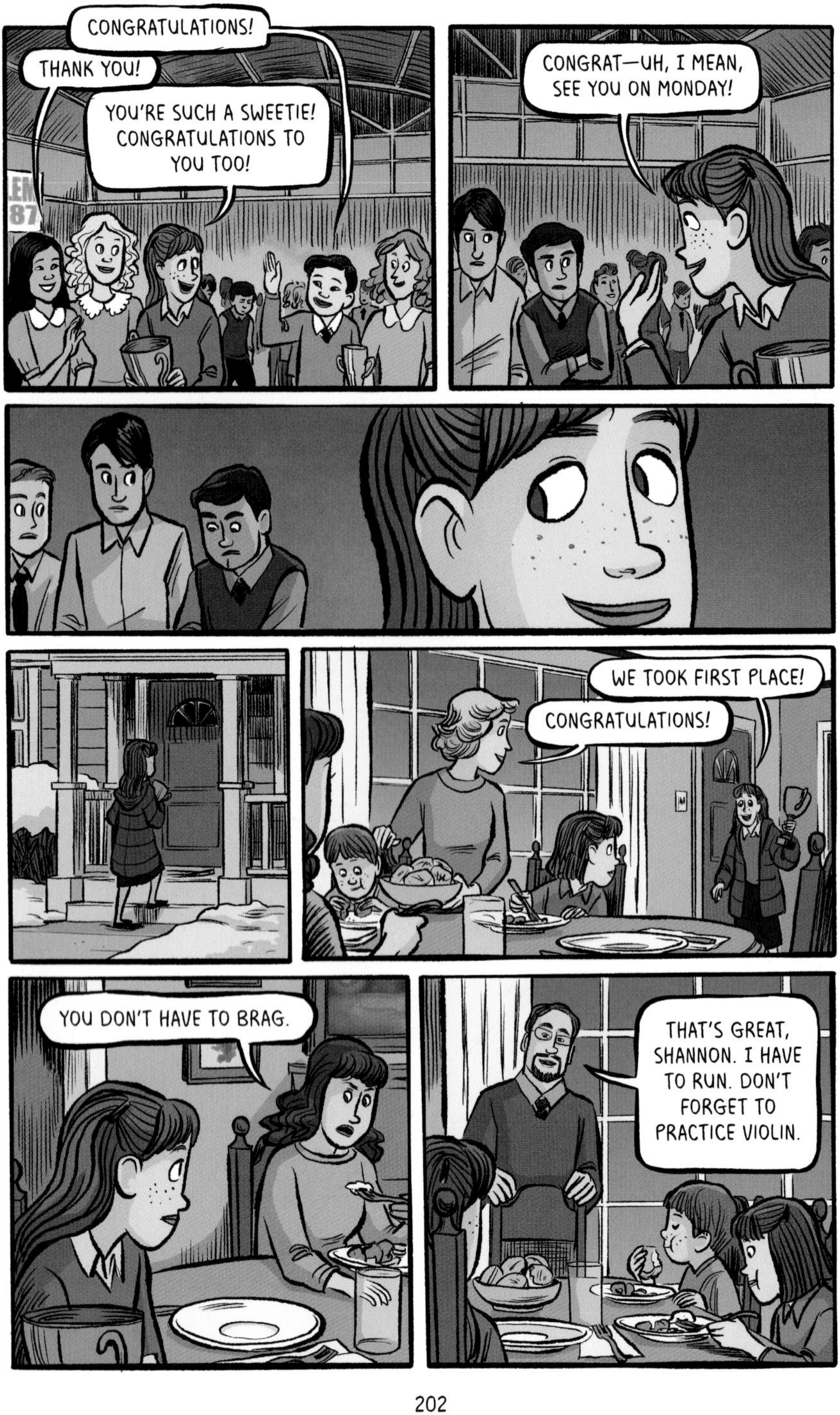
CONGRATULATIONS!
THANK YOU!
YOU'RE SUCH A SWEETIE! CONGRATULATIONS TO YOU TOO!
CONGRAT—UH, I MEAN, SEE YOU ON MONDAY!
WE TOOK FIRST PLACE!
CONGRATULATIONS!
YOU DON'T HAVE TO BRAG.
THAT'S GREAT, SHANNON. I HAVE TO RUN. DON'T FORGET TO PRACTICE VIOLIN.

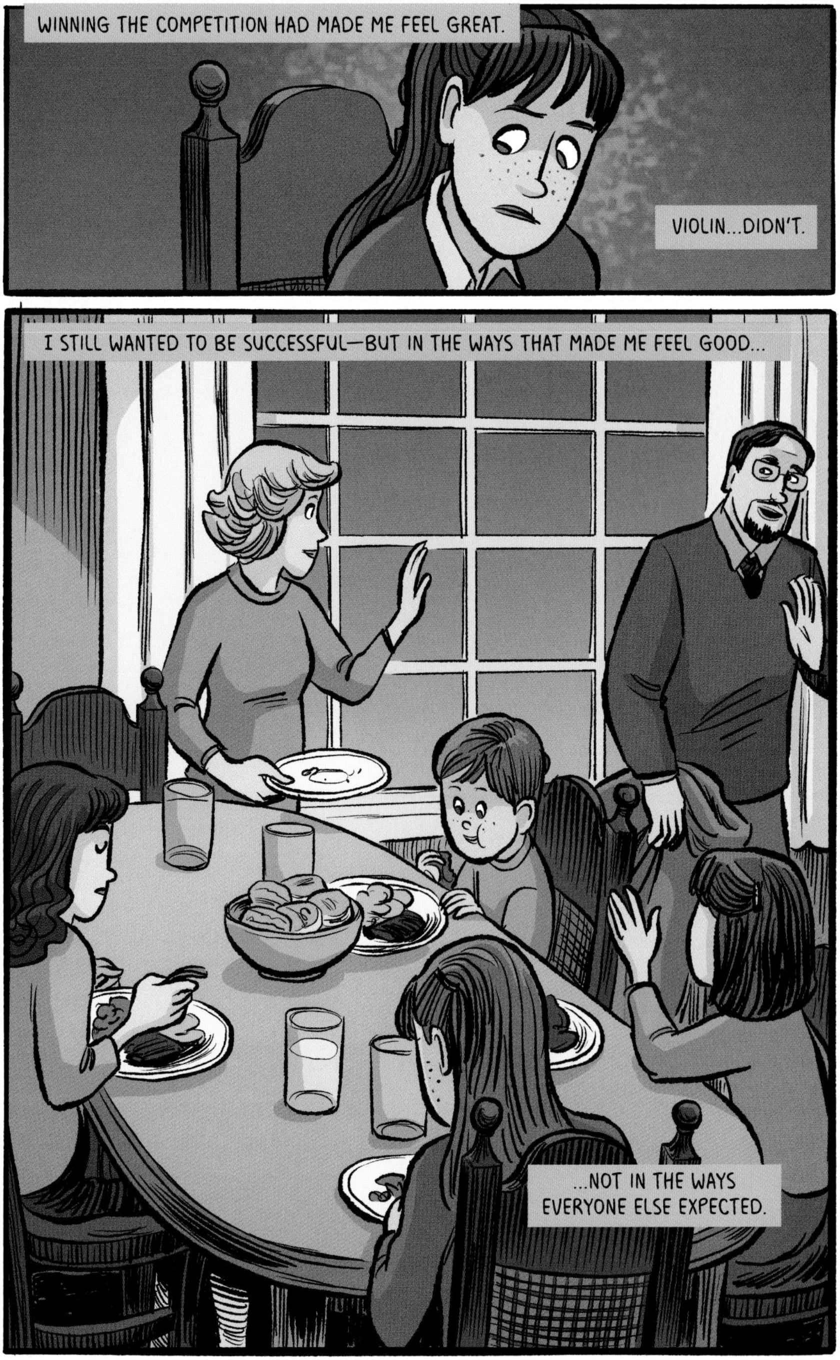
WINNING THE COMPETITION HAD MADE ME FEEL GREAT.
VIOLIN...DIDN'T.
I STILL WANTED TO BE SUCCESSFUL—BUT IN THE WAYS THAT MADE ME FEEL GOOD...
...NOT IN THE WAYS EVERYONE ELSE EXPECTED.

CHAPTER 5

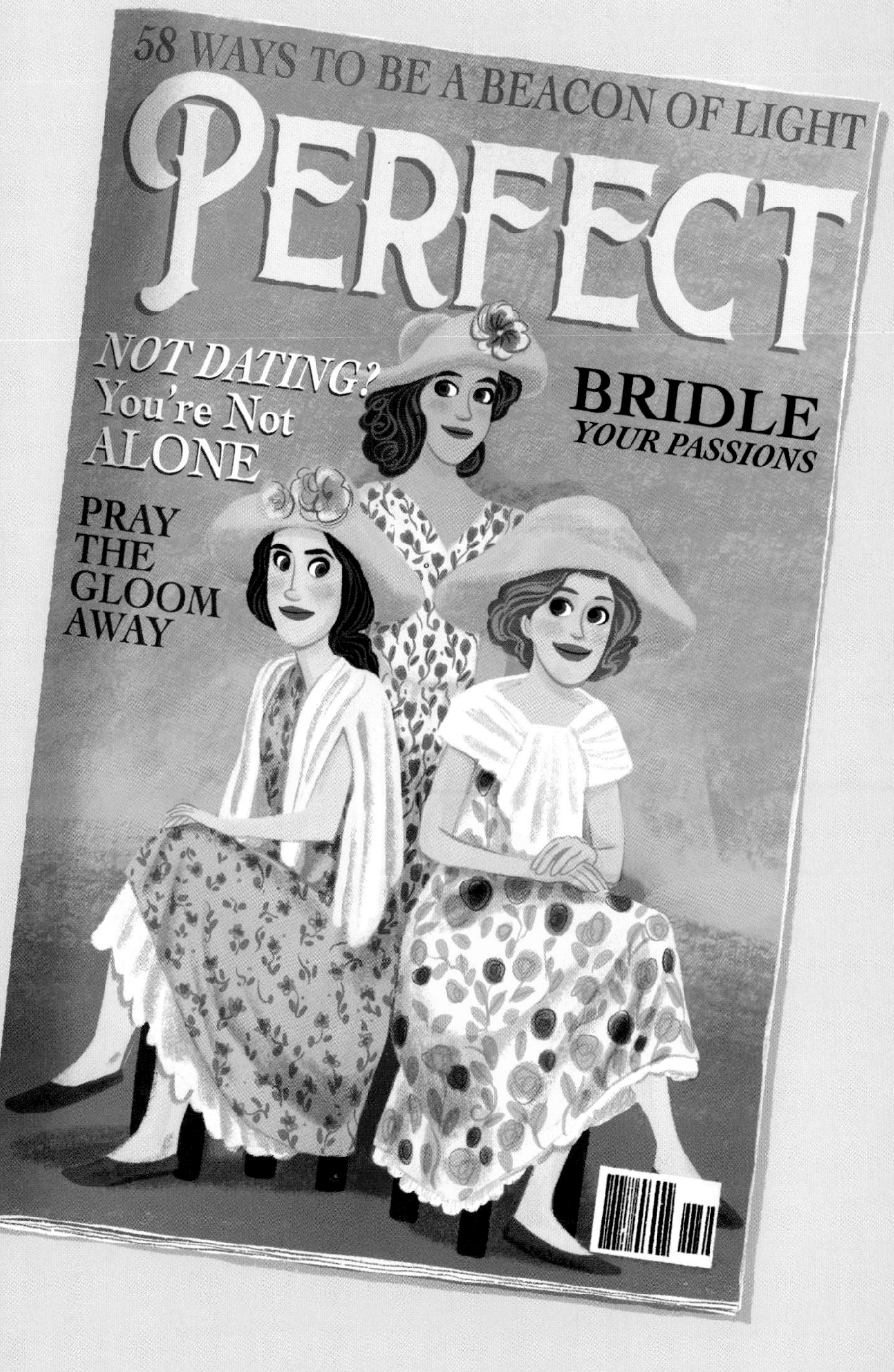
58 WAYS TO BE A BEACON OF LIGHT
PERFECT
NOT DATING? You're Not ALONE
BRIDLE YOUR PASSIONS
PRAY THE GLOOM AWAY

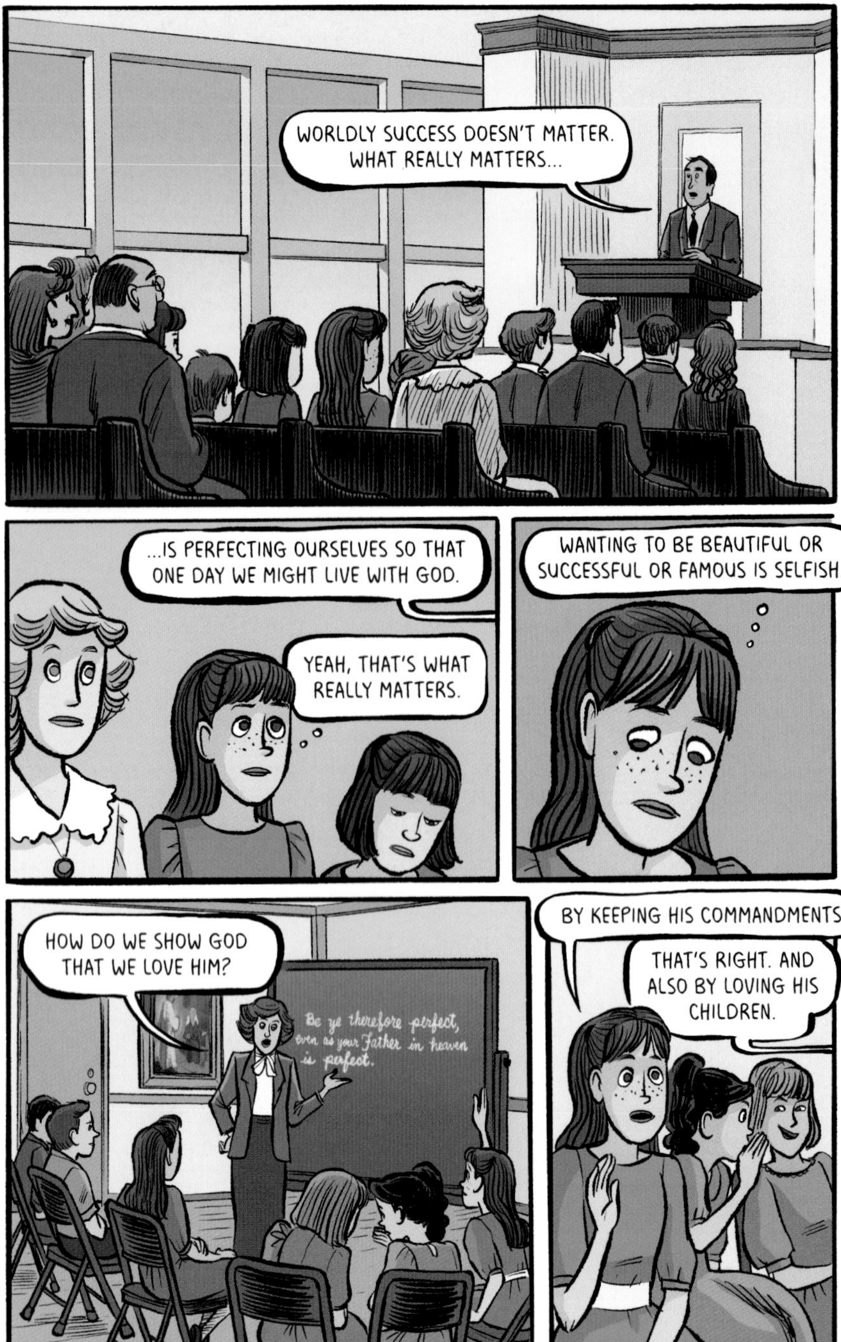
WORLDLY SUCCESS DOESN'T MATTER. WHAT REALLY MATTERS...
...IS PERFECTING OURSELVES SO THAT ONE DAY WE MIGHT LIVE WITH GOD.
YEAH, THAT'S WHAT REALLY MATTERS.
WANTING TO BE BEAUTIFUL OR SUCCESSFUL OR FAMOUS IS SELFISH.
HOW DO WE SHOW GOD THAT WE LOVE HIM?
Be ye therefore perfect, even as your Father in heaven is perfect.
BY KEEPING HIS COMMANDMENTS.
THAT'S RIGHT. AND ALSO BY LOVING HIS CHILDREN.

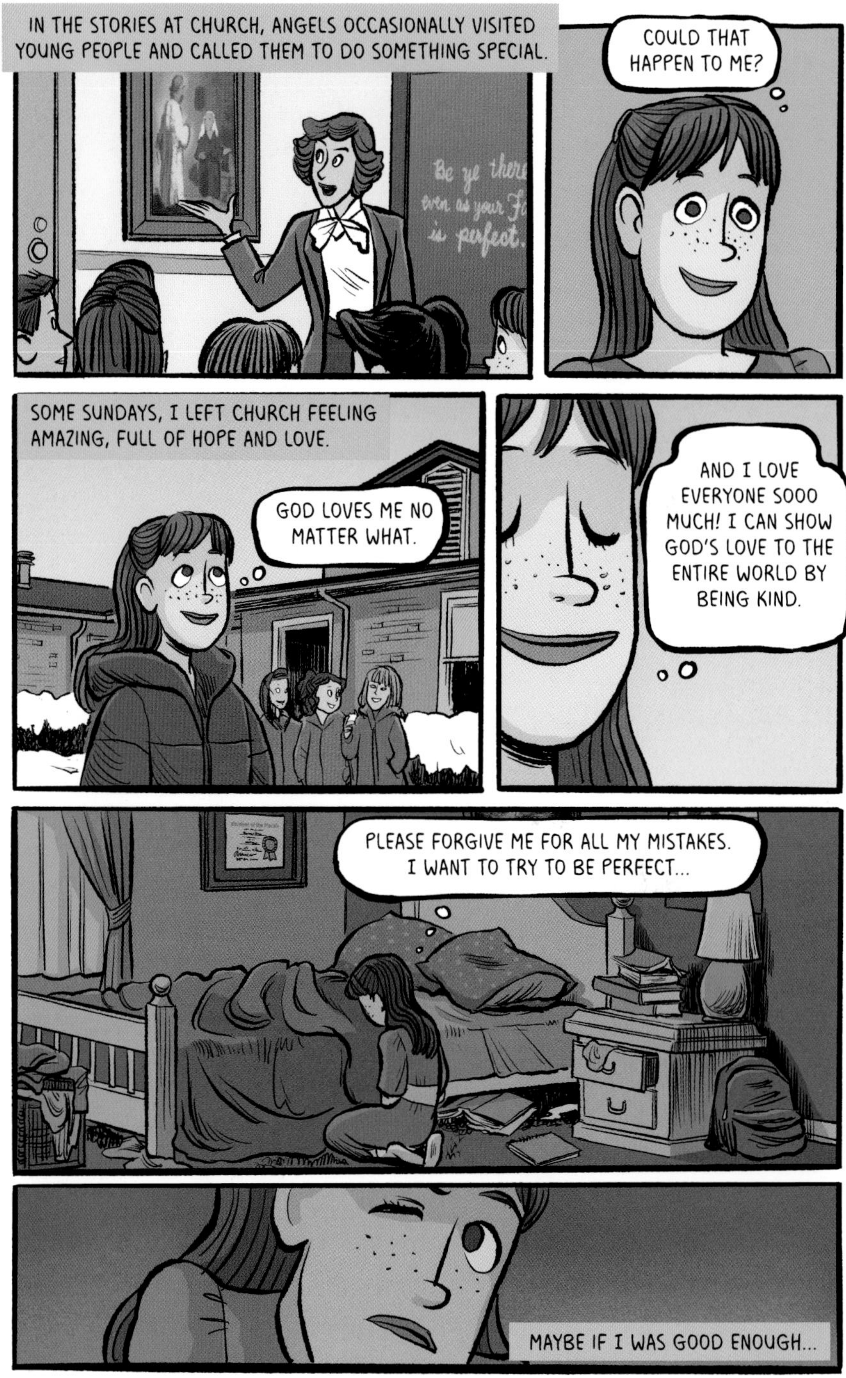
IN THE STORIES AT CHURCH, ANGELS OCCASIONALLY VISITED YOUNG PEOPLE AND CALLED THEM TO DO SOMETHING SPECIAL.
COULD THAT HAPPEN TO ME?
SOME SUNDAYS, I LEFT CHURCH FEELING AMAZING, FULL OF HOPE AND LOVE.
GOD LOVES ME NO MATTER WHAT.
AND I LOVE EVERYONE SOOO MUCH! I CAN SHOW GOD'S LOVE TO THE ENTIRE WORLD BY BEING KIND.
PLEASE FORGIVE ME FOR ALL MY MISTAKES. I WANT TO TRY TO BE PERFECT...
MAYBE IF I WAS GOOD ENOUGH...

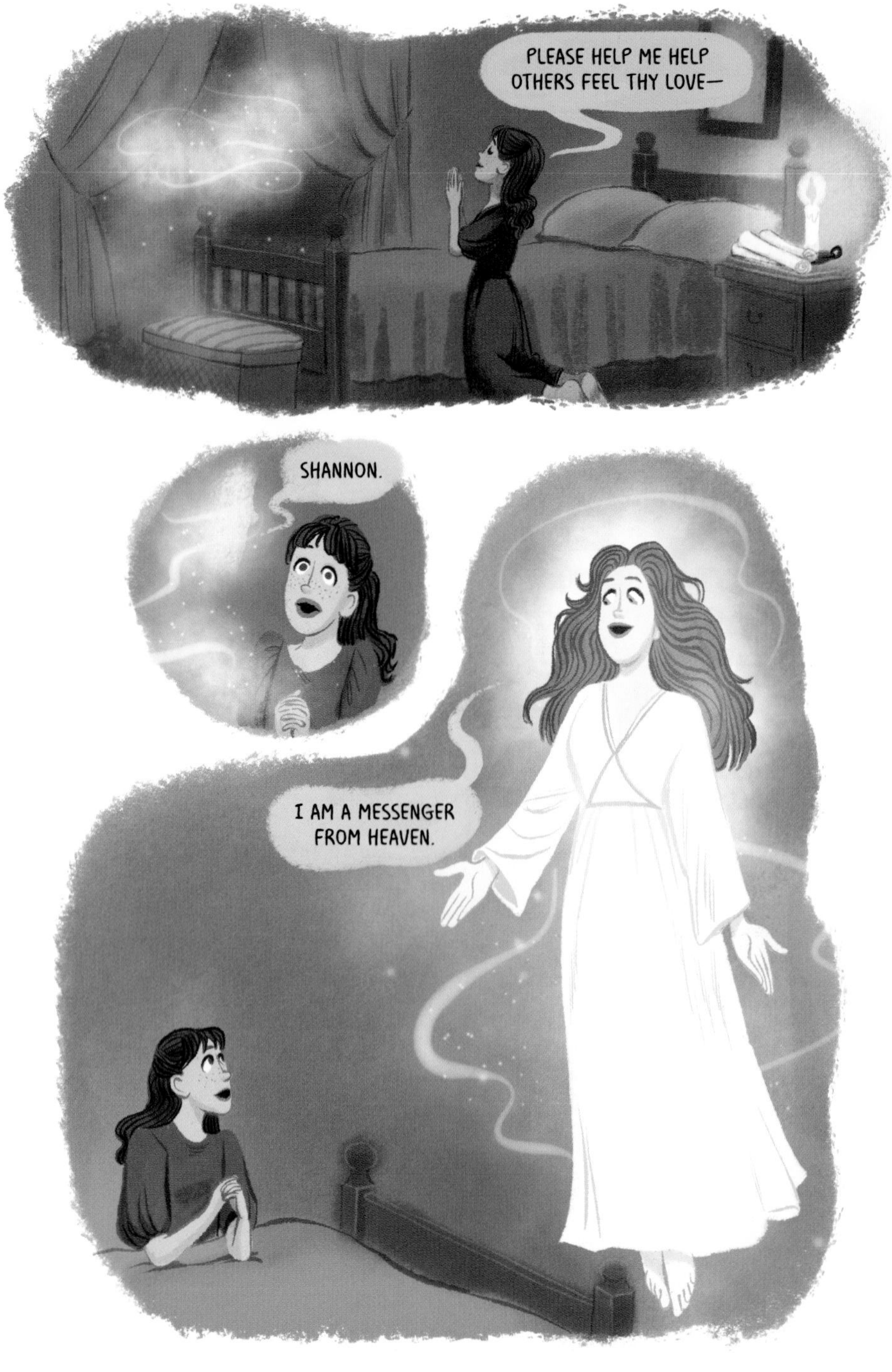
PLEASE HELP ME HELP OTHERS FEEL THY LOVE—
SHANNON.
I AM A MESSENGER FROM HEAVEN.

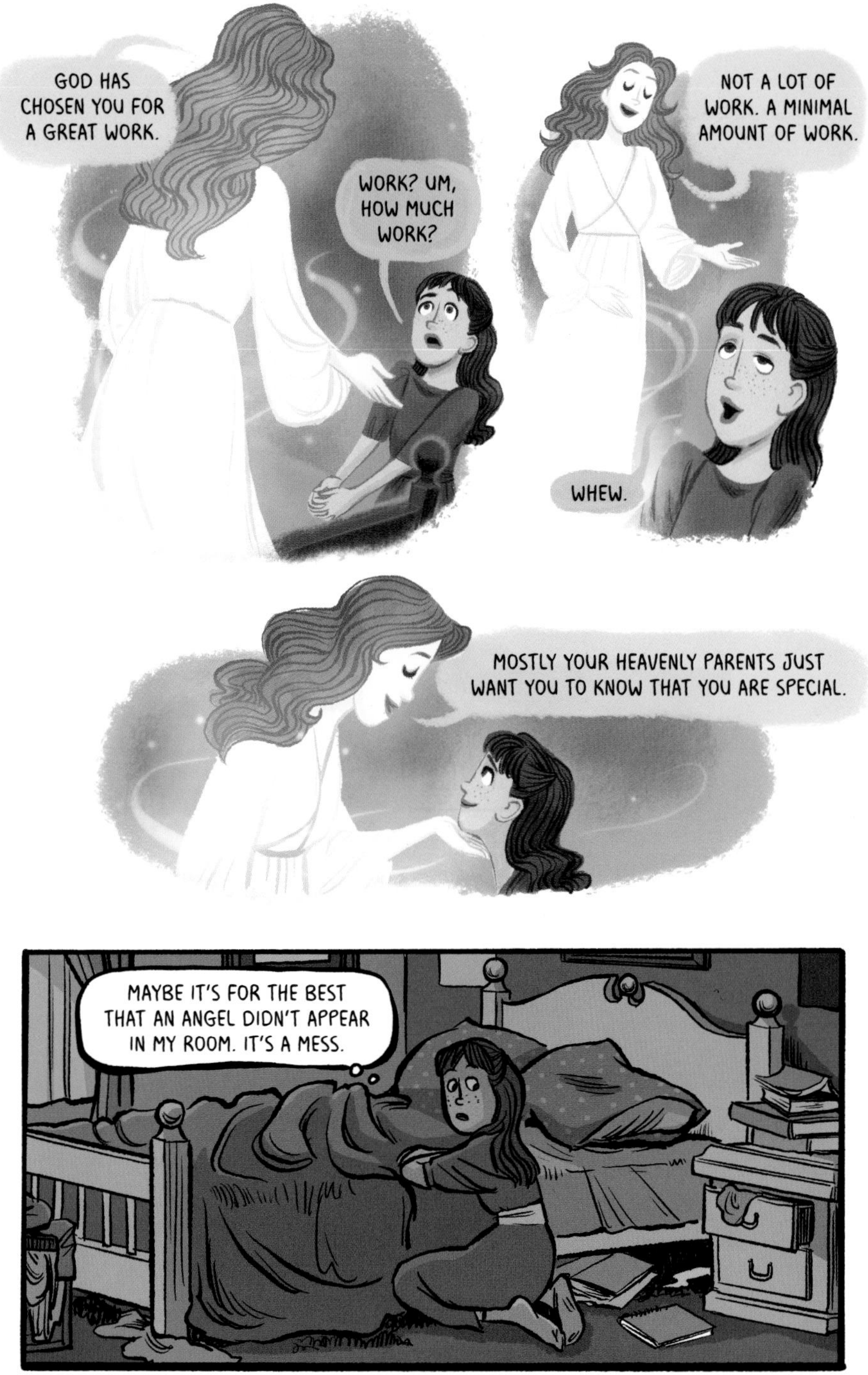
GOD HAS CHOSEN YOU FOR A GREAT WORK.
WORK? UM, HOW MUCH WORK?
NOT A LOT OF WORK. A MINIMAL AMOUNT OF WORK.
WHEW.
MOSTLY YOUR HEAVENLY PARENTS JUST WANT YOU TO KNOW THAT YOU ARE SPECIAL.
MAYBE IT'S FOR THE BEST THAT AN ANGEL DIDN'T APPEAR IN MY ROOM. IT'S A MESS.

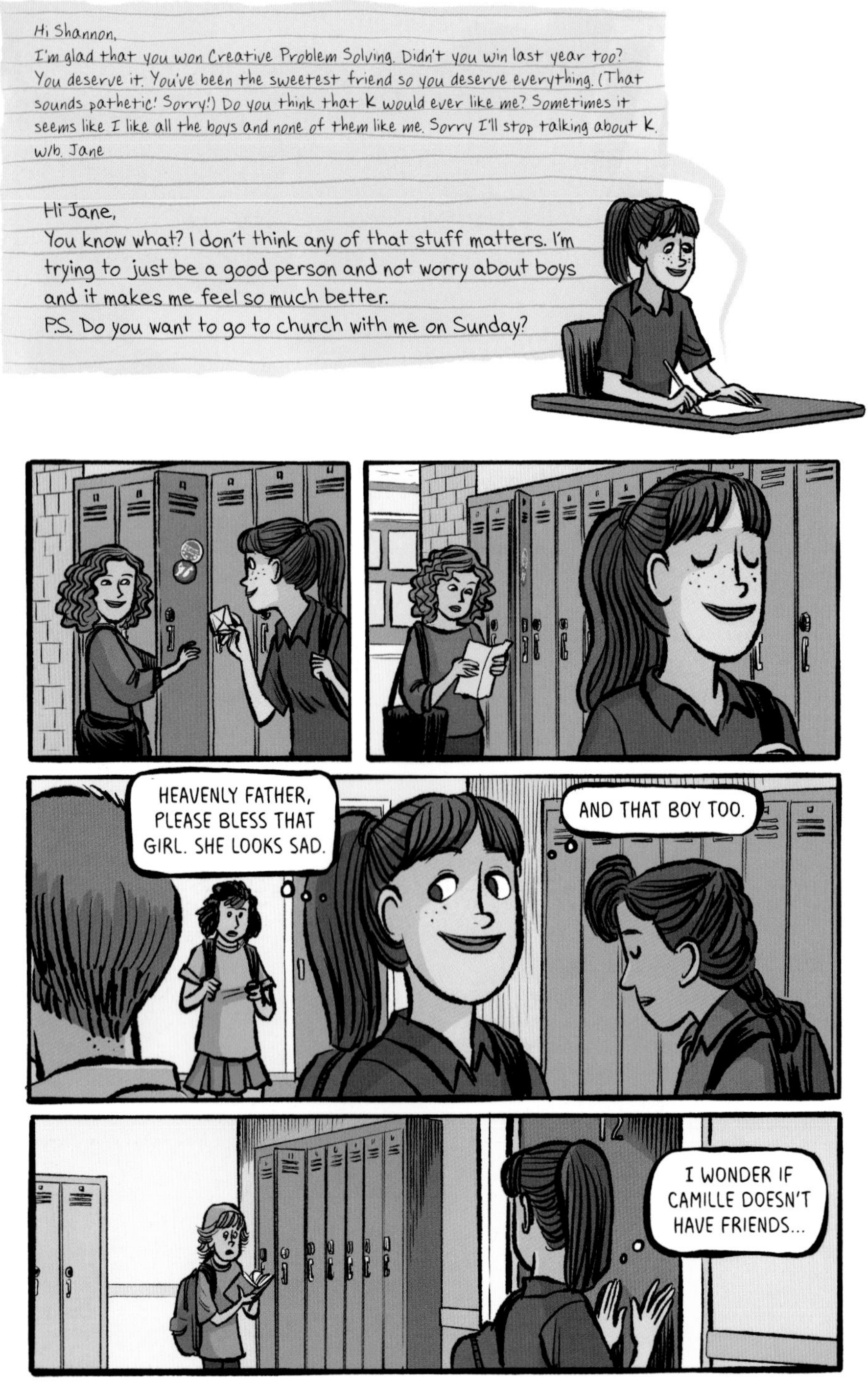
Hi Shannon,
I'm glad that you won Creative Problem Solving. Didn't you win last year too? You deserve it. You've been the sweetest friend so you deserve everything. (That sounds pathetic! Sorry!) Do you think that K would ever like me? Sometimes it seems like I like all the boys and none of them like me. Sorry I'll stop talking about K.
w/b, Jane
Hi Jane,
You know what? I don't think any of that stuff matters. I'm trying to just be a good person and not worry about boys and it makes me feel so much better.
P.S. Do you want to go to church with me on Sunday?
HEAVENLY FATHER, PLEASE BLESS THAT GIRL. SHE LOOKS SAD.
AND THAT BOY TOO.
I WONDER IF CAMILLE DOESN'T HAVE FRIENDS...

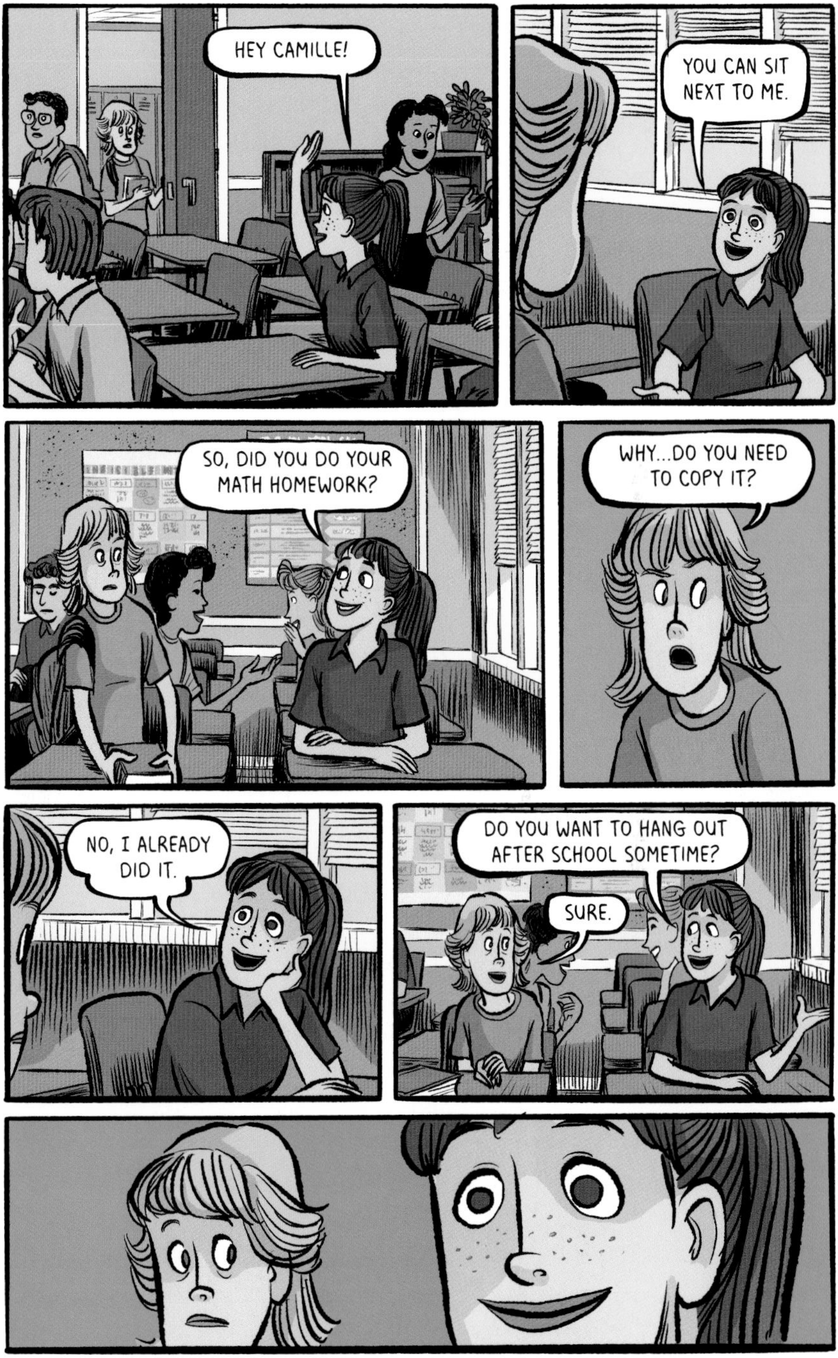
HEY CAMILLE!
YOU CAN SIT NEXT TO ME.
SO, DID YOU DO YOUR MATH HOMEWORK?
WHY...DO YOU NEED TO COPY IT?
NO, I ALREADY DID IT.
DO YOU WANT TO HANG OUT AFTER SCHOOL SOMETIME?
SURE.

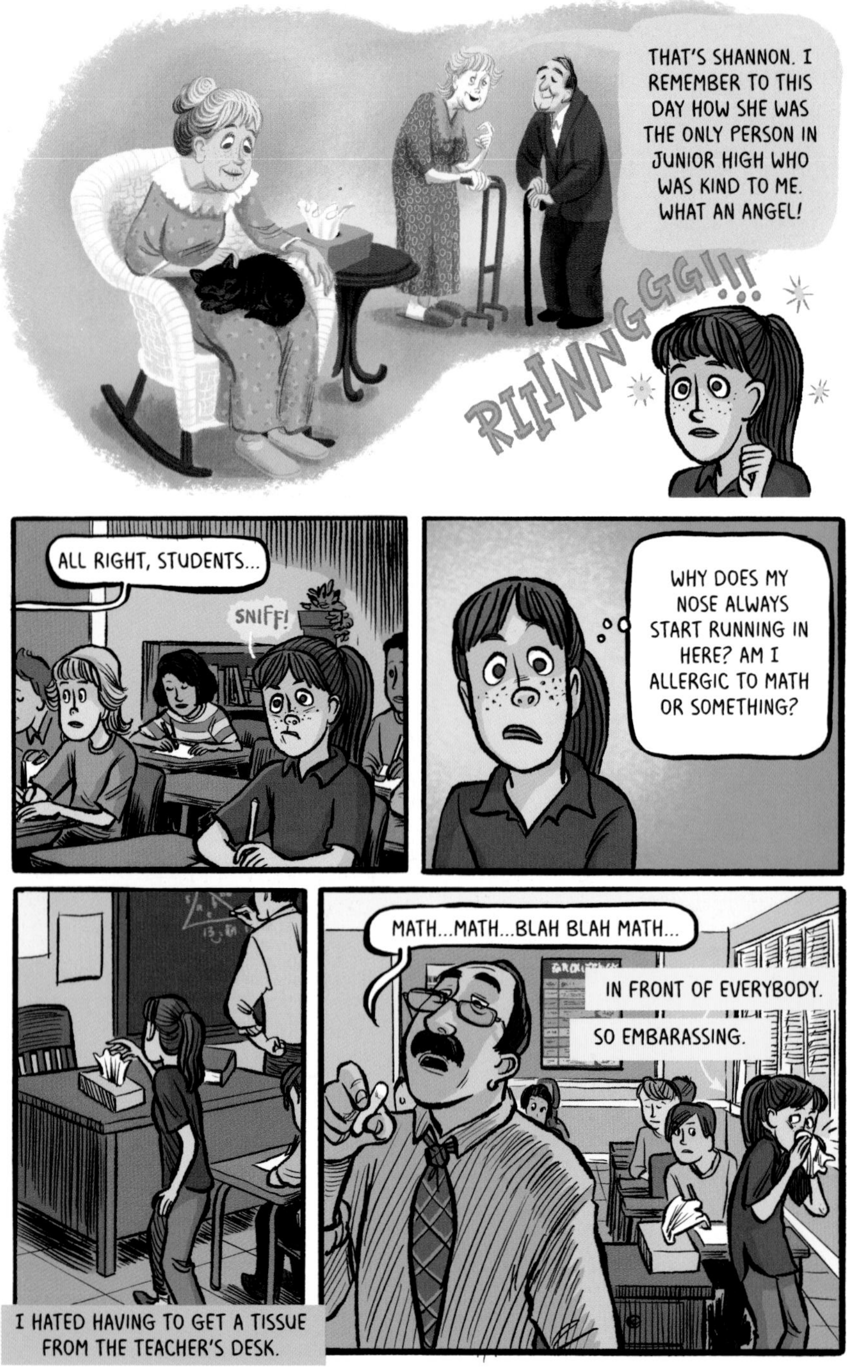
THAT'S SHANNON. I REMEMBER TO THIS DAY HOW SHE WAS THE ONLY PERSON IN JUNIOR HIGH WHO WAS KIND TO ME. WHAT AN ANGEL!
RIIINNGGG!!!
ALL RIGHT, STUDENTS...
SNIFF!
WHY DOES MY NOSE ALWAYS START RUNNING IN HERE? AM I ALLERGIC TO MATH OR SOMETHING?
I HATED HAVING TO GET A TISSUE FROM THE TEACHER'S DESK.
MATH...MATH...BLAH BLAH MATH...
IN FRONT OF EVERYBODY.
SO EMBARASSING.

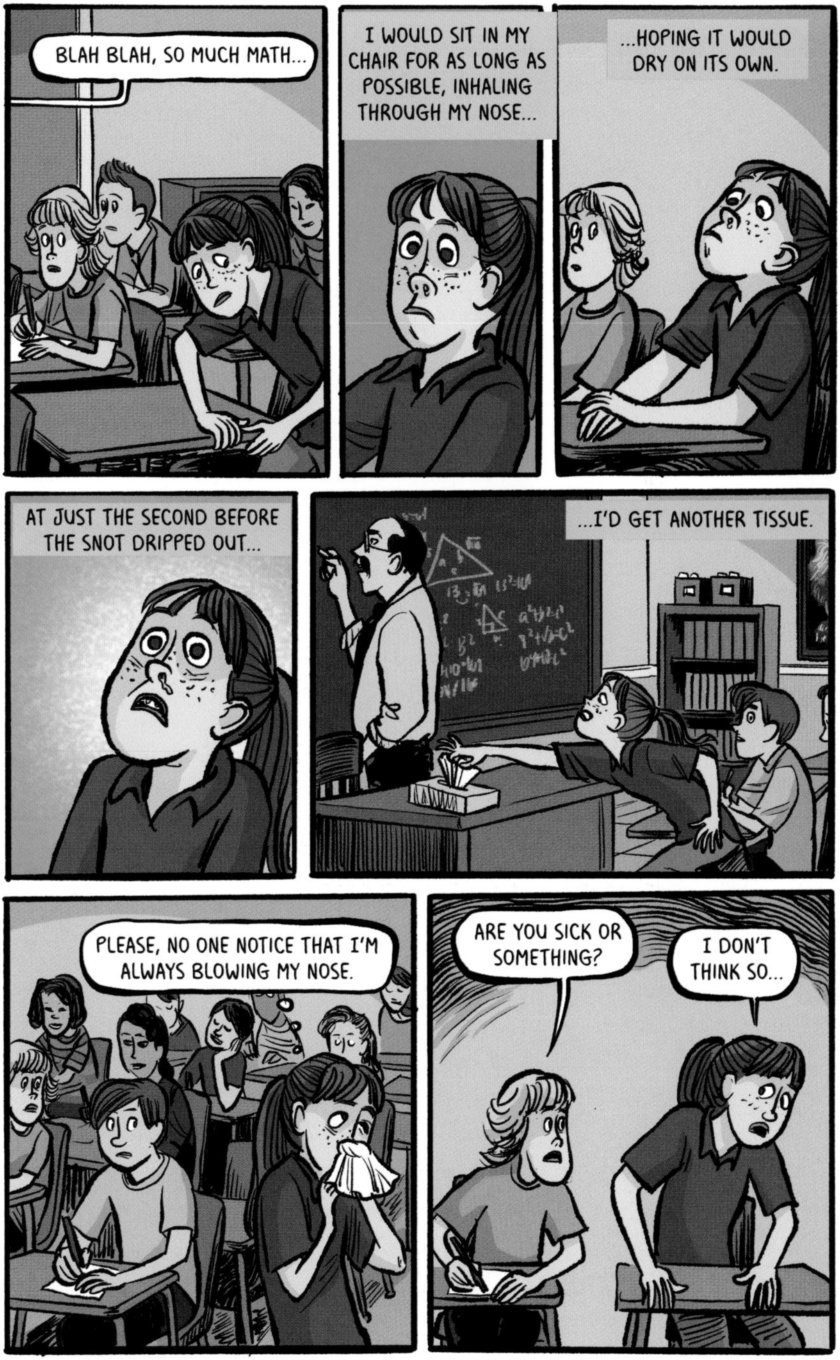
BLAH BLAH, SO MUCH MATH...
I WOULD SIT IN MY CHAIR FOR AS LONG AS POSSIBLE, INHALING THROUGH MY NOSE...
...HOPING IT WOULD DRY ON ITS OWN.
AT JUST THE SECOND BEFORE THE SNOT DRIPPED OUT...
...I'D GET ANOTHER TISSUE.
PLEASE, NO ONE NOTICE THAT I'M ALWAYS BLOWING MY NOSE.
ARE YOU SICK OR SOMETHING?
I DON'T THINK SO...

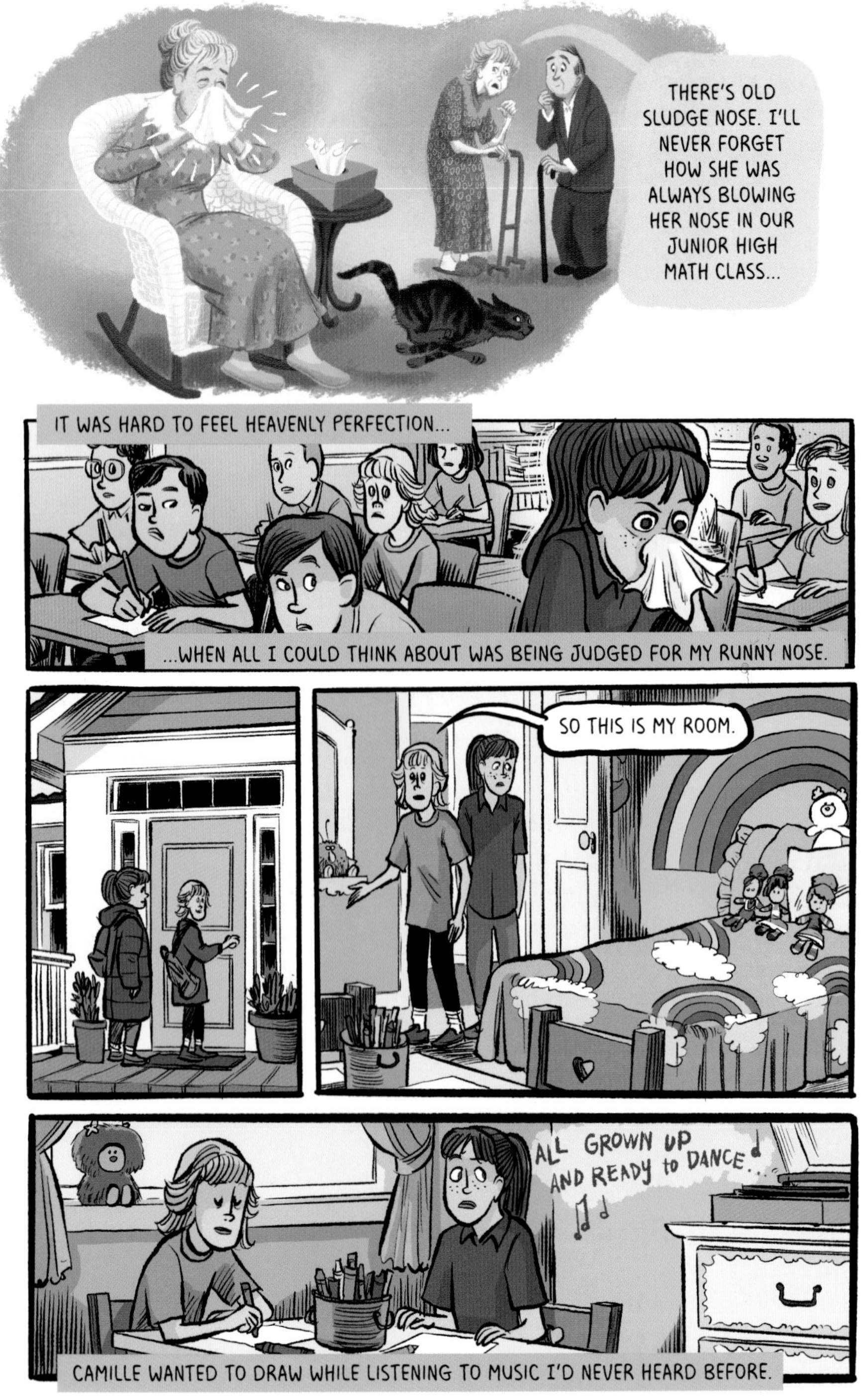
THERE'S OLD SLUDGE NOSE. I'LL NEVER FORGET HOW SHE WAS ALWAYS BLOWING HER NOSE IN OUR JUNIOR HIGH MATH CLASS...
IT WAS HARD TO FEEL HEAVENLY PERFECTION...
...WHEN ALL I COULD THINK ABOUT WAS BEING JUDGED FOR MY RUNNY NOSE.
SO THIS IS MY ROOM.
ALL GROWN UP AND READY to DANCE...
CAMILLE WANTED TO DRAW WHILE LISTENING TO MUSIC I'D NEVER HEARD BEFORE.

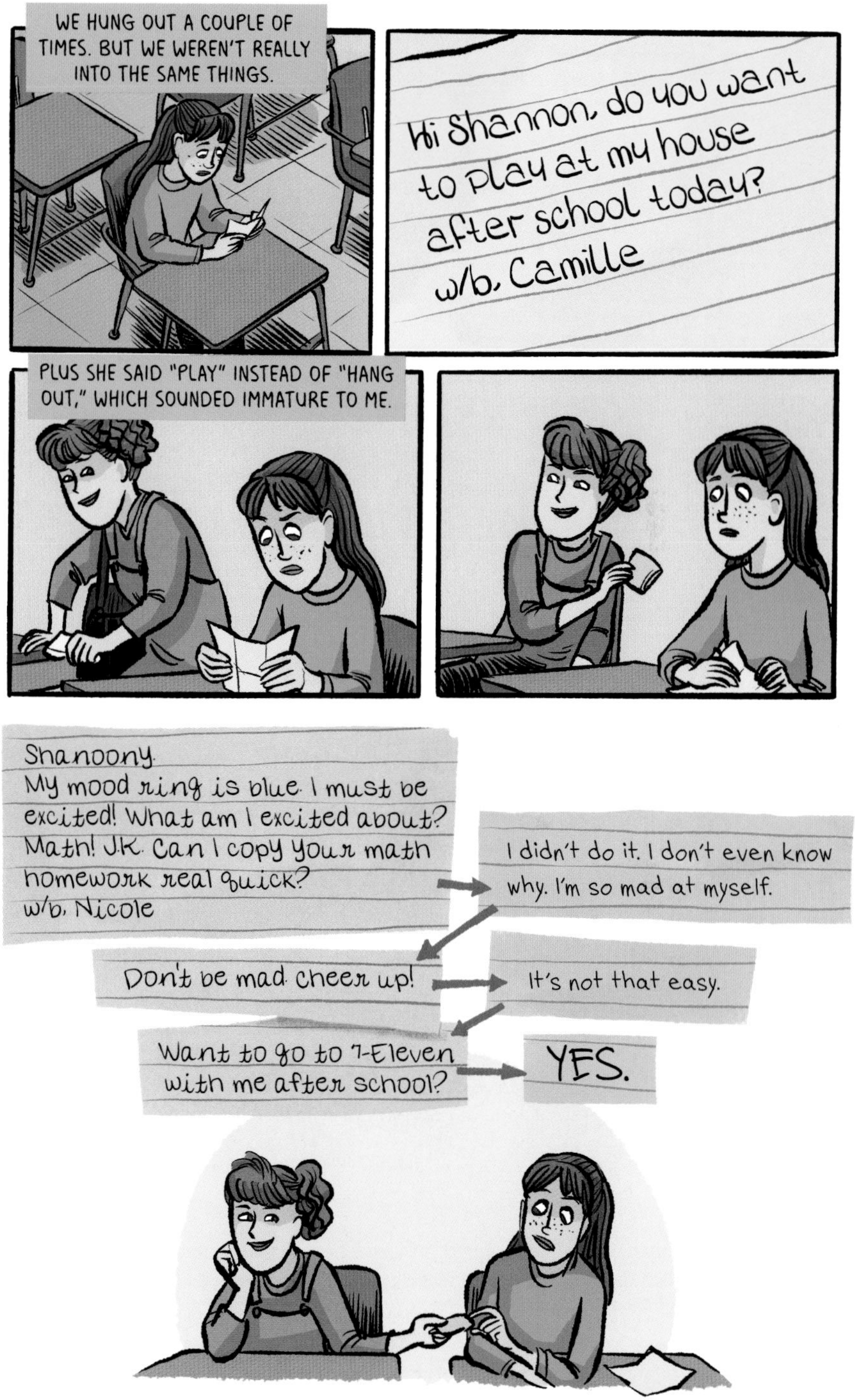
WE HUNG OUT A COUPLE OF TIMES. BUT WE WEREN'T REALLY INTO THE SAME THINGS.
Hi Shannon, do you want to play at my house after school today? w/b, Camille
PLUS SHE SAID "PLAY" INSTEAD OF "HANG OUT," WHICH SOUNDED IMMATURE TO ME.
Shanoony.
My mood ring is blue. I must be excited! What am I excited about? Math! J.K. Can I copy your math homework real quick? w/b, Nicole
I didn't do it. I don't even know why. I'm so mad at myself.
Don't be mad. cheer up!
It's not that easy.
Want to go to 7-Eleven with me after school?
YES.

I NEVER ANSWERED CAMILLE'S NOTE.

you're bad
you're bad
you're bad
you're bad
you're bad
you're bad
you're bad
you're bad
you're bad

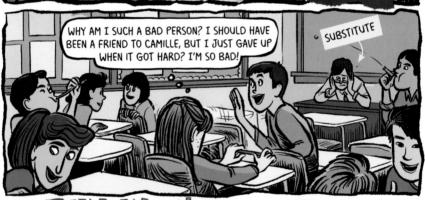

WHY AM I SUCH A BAD PERSON? I SHOULD HAVE BEEN A FRIEND TO CAMILLE, BUT I JUST GAVE UP WHEN IT GOT HARD? I'M SO BAD!

SUBSTITUTE

RIINNNGG!

ARE YOU LOST, LITTLE BOY?

MAYBE YOU COULDN'T FIND YOUR PRESCHOOL CLASS.

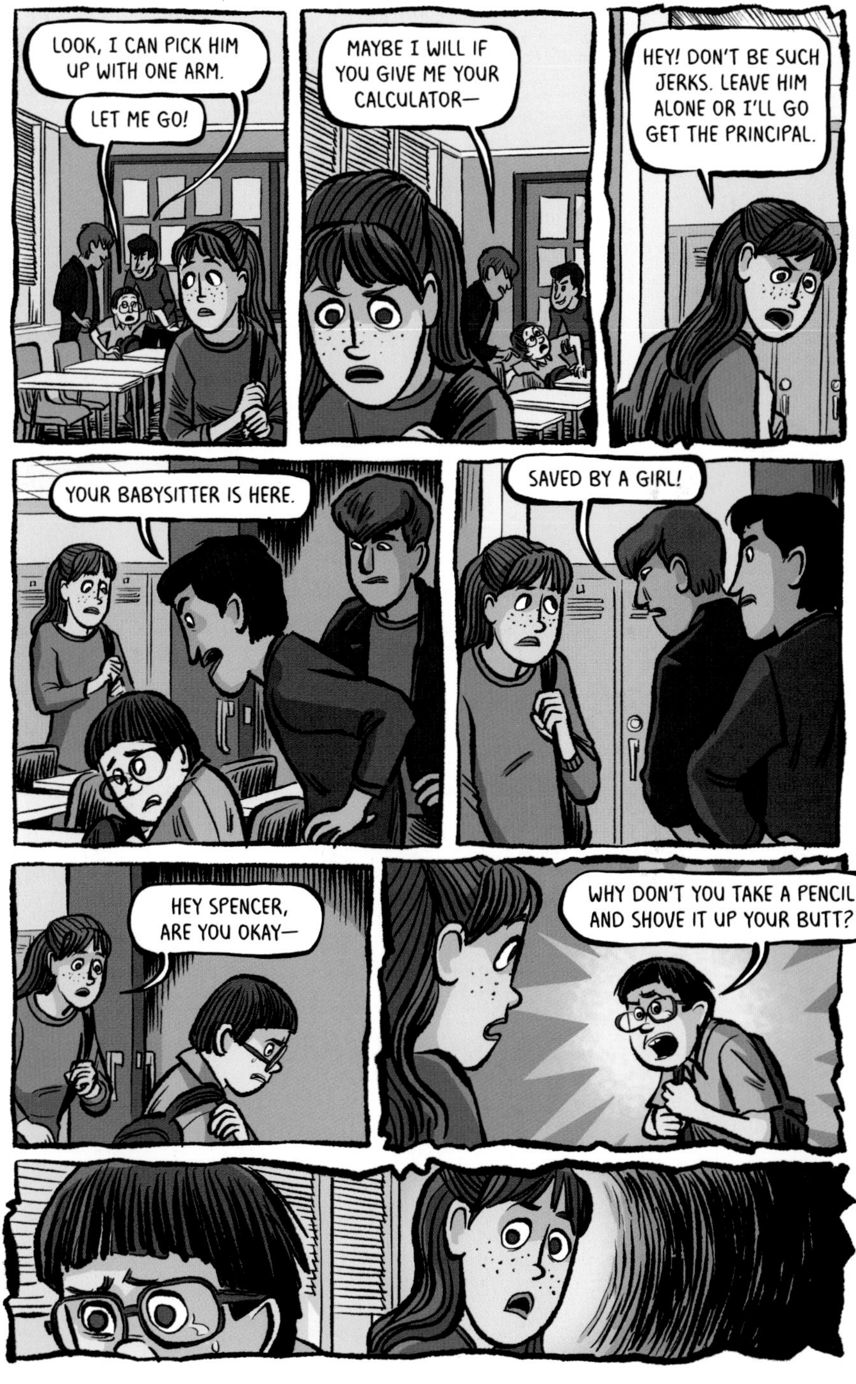
LOOK, I CAN PICK HIM UP WITH ONE ARM.
LET ME GO!
MAYBE I WILL IF YOU GIVE ME YOUR CALCULATOR—
HEY! DON'T BE SUCH JERKS. LEAVE HIM ALONE OR I'LL GO GET THE PRINCIPAL.
YOUR BABYSITTER IS HERE.
SAVED BY A GIRL!
HEY SPENCER, ARE YOU OKAY—
WHY DON'T YOU TAKE A PENCIL AND SHOVE IT UP YOUR BUTT?

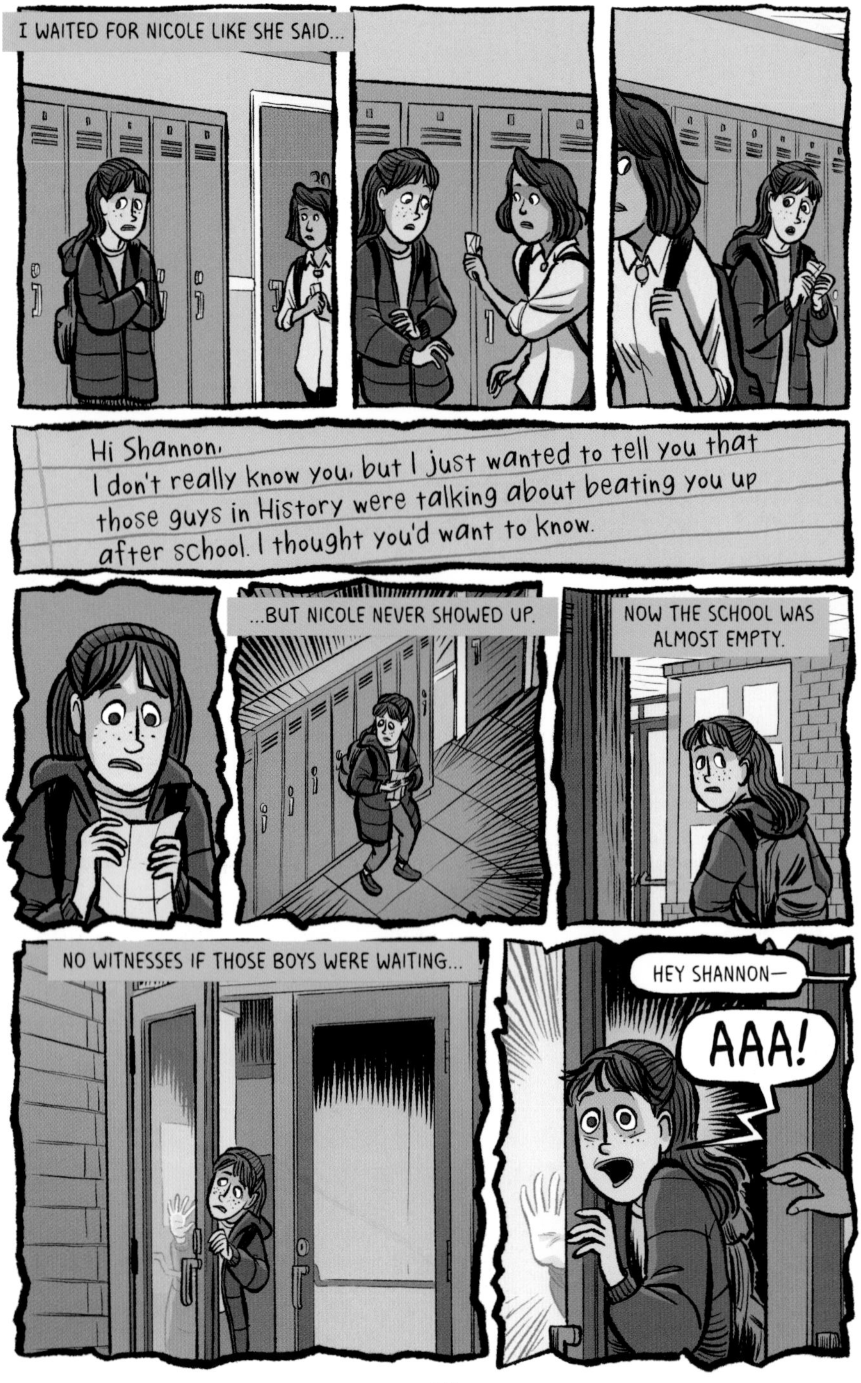

I WAITED FOR NICOLE LIKE SHE SAID...
Hi Shannon,
I don't really know you, but I just wanted to tell you that
those guys in History were talking about beating you up
after school. I thought you'd want to know.
...BUT NICOLE NEVER SHOWED UP.
NOW THE SCHOOL WAS ALMOST EMPTY.
NO WITNESSES IF THOSE BOYS WERE WAITING...
HEY SHANNON—
AAA!

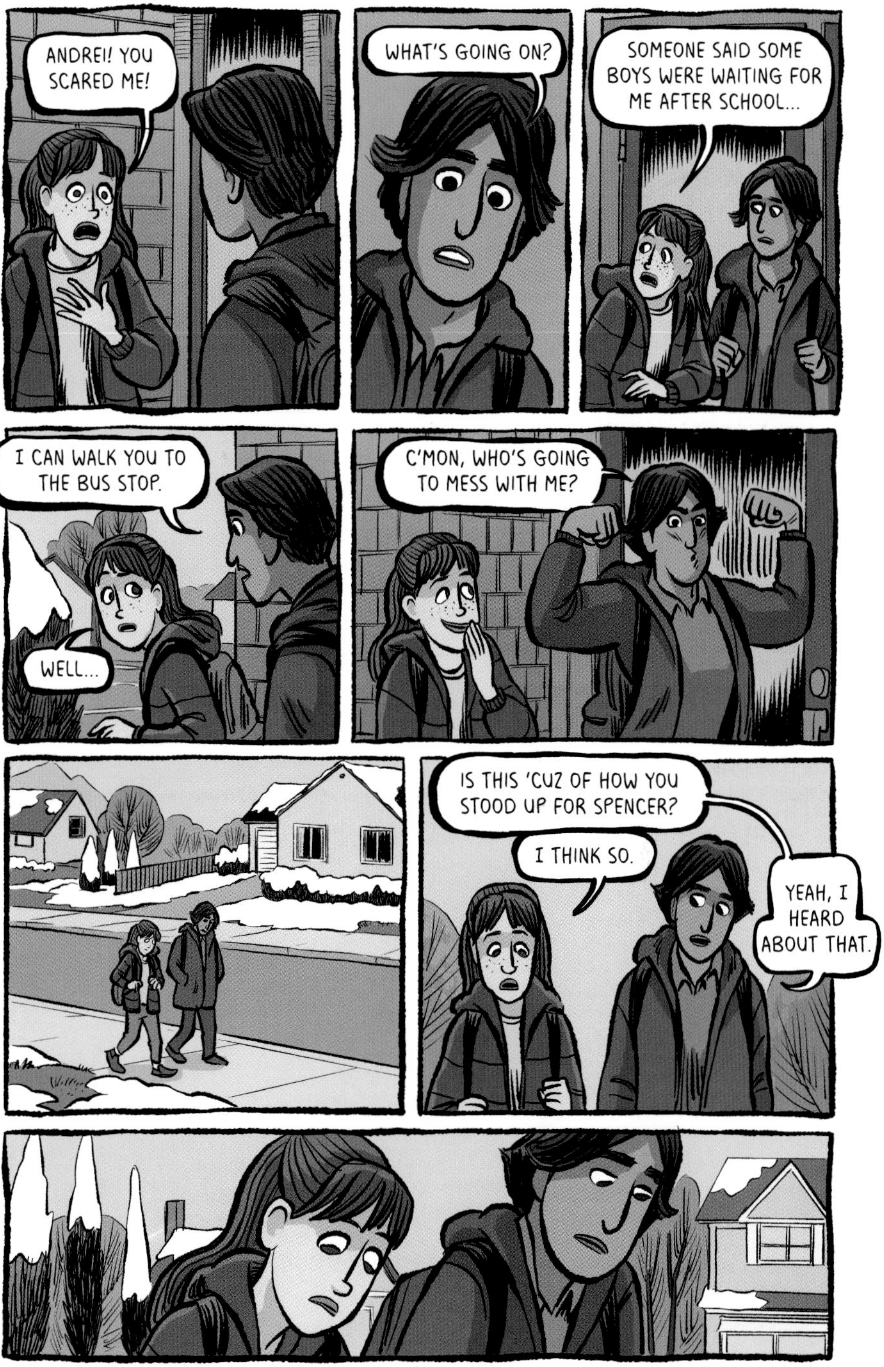
ANDREI! YOU SCARED ME!
WHAT'S GOING ON?
SOMEONE SAID SOME BOYS WERE WAITING FOR ME AFTER SCHOOL...
I CAN WALK YOU TO THE BUS STOP.
WELL...
C'MON, WHO'S GOING TO MESS WITH ME?
IS THIS 'CUZ OF HOW YOU STOOD UP FOR SPENCER?
I THINK SO.
YEAH, I HEARD ABOUT THAT.

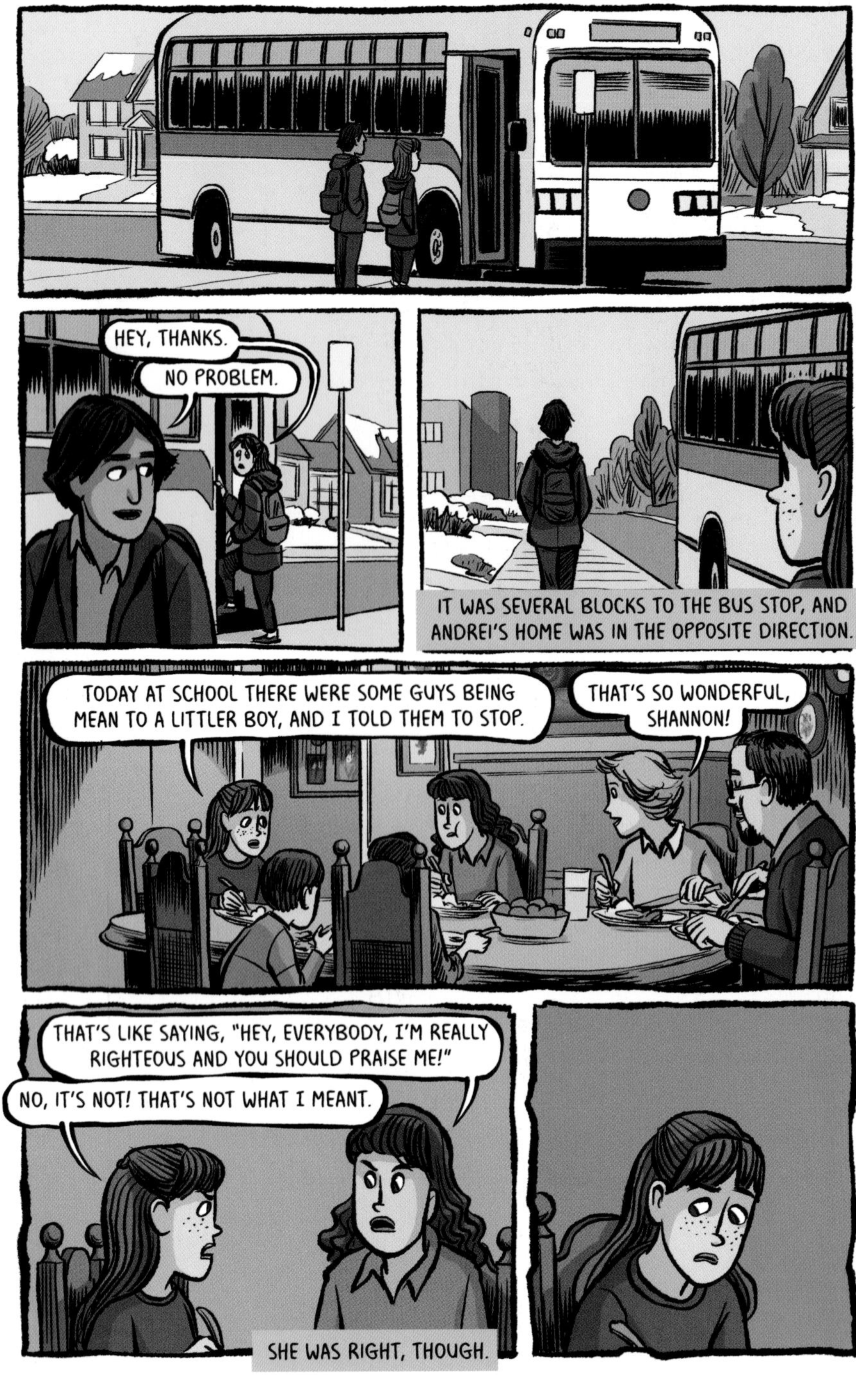
HEY, THANKS.
NO PROBLEM.
IT WAS SEVERAL BLOCKS TO THE BUS STOP, AND ANDREI'S HOME WAS IN THE OPPOSITE DIRECTION.
TODAY AT SCHOOL THERE WERE SOME GUYS BEING MEAN TO A LITTLER BOY, AND I TOLD THEM TO STOP.
THAT'S SO WONDERFUL, SHANNON!
THAT'S LIKE SAYING, "HEY, EVERYBODY, I'M REALLY RIGHTEOUS AND YOU SHOULD PRAISE ME!"
NO, IT'S NOT! THAT'S NOT WHAT I MEANT.
SHE WAS RIGHT, THOUGH.

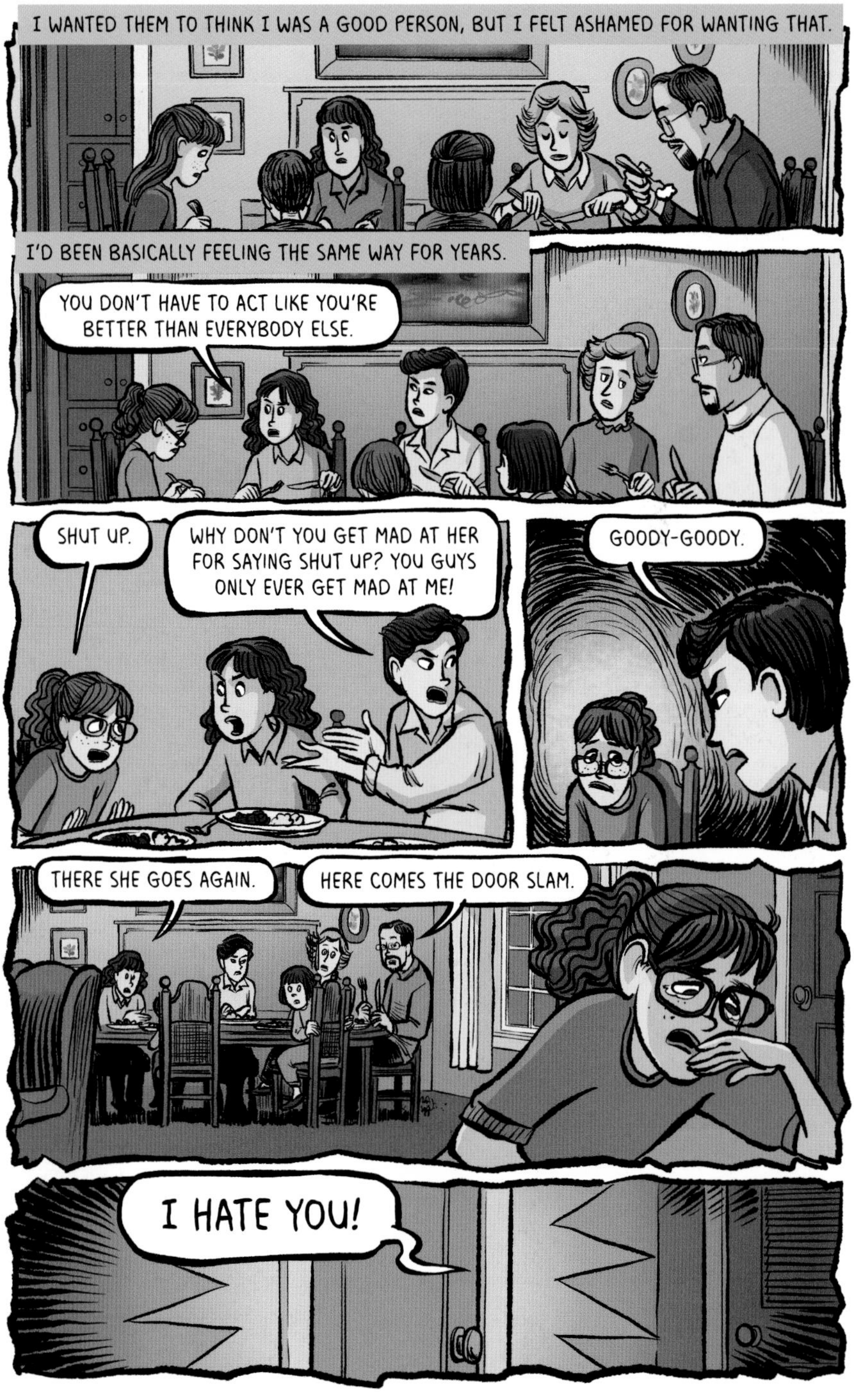
I WANTED THEM TO THINK I WAS A GOOD PERSON, BUT I FELT ASHAMED FOR WANTING THAT.
I'D BEEN BASICALLY FEELING THE SAME WAY FOR YEARS.
YOU DON'T HAVE TO ACT LIKE YOU'RE BETTER THAN EVERYBODY ELSE.
SHUT UP.
WHY DON'T YOU GET MAD AT HER FOR SAYING SHUT UP? YOU GUYS ONLY EVER GET MAD AT ME!
GOODY-GOODY.
THERE SHE GOES AGAIN.
HERE COMES THE DOOR SLAM.
I HATE YOU!

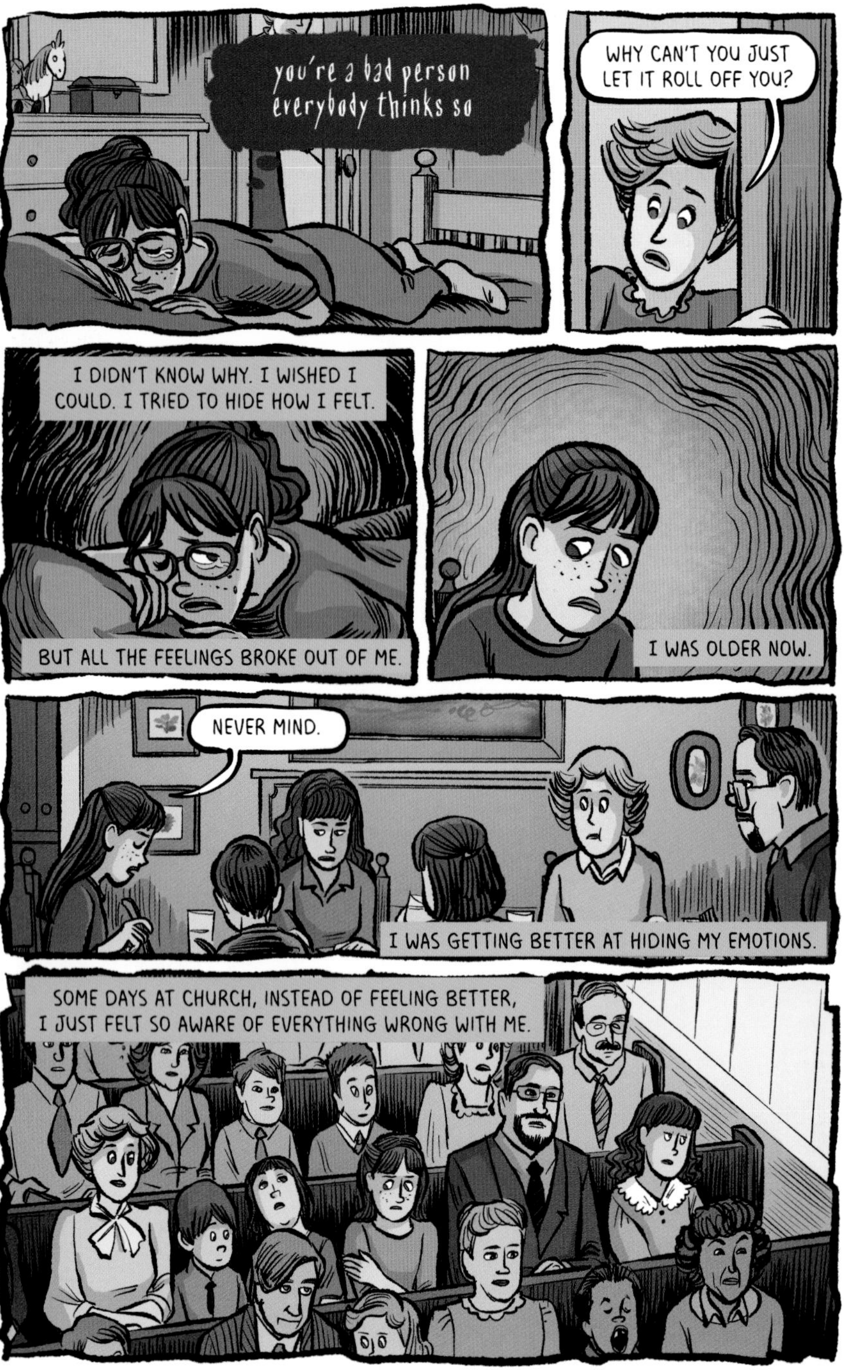
you're a bad person everybody thinks so
WHY CAN'T YOU JUST LET IT ROLL OFF YOU?
I DIDN'T KNOW WHY. I WISHED I COULD. I TRIED TO HIDE HOW I FELT.
BUT ALL THE FEELINGS BROKE OUT OF ME.
I WAS OLDER NOW.
NEVER MIND.
I WAS GETTING BETTER AT HIDING MY EMOTIONS.
SOME DAYS AT CHURCH, INSTEAD OF FEELING BETTER, I JUST FELT SO AWARE OF EVERYTHING WRONG WITH ME.

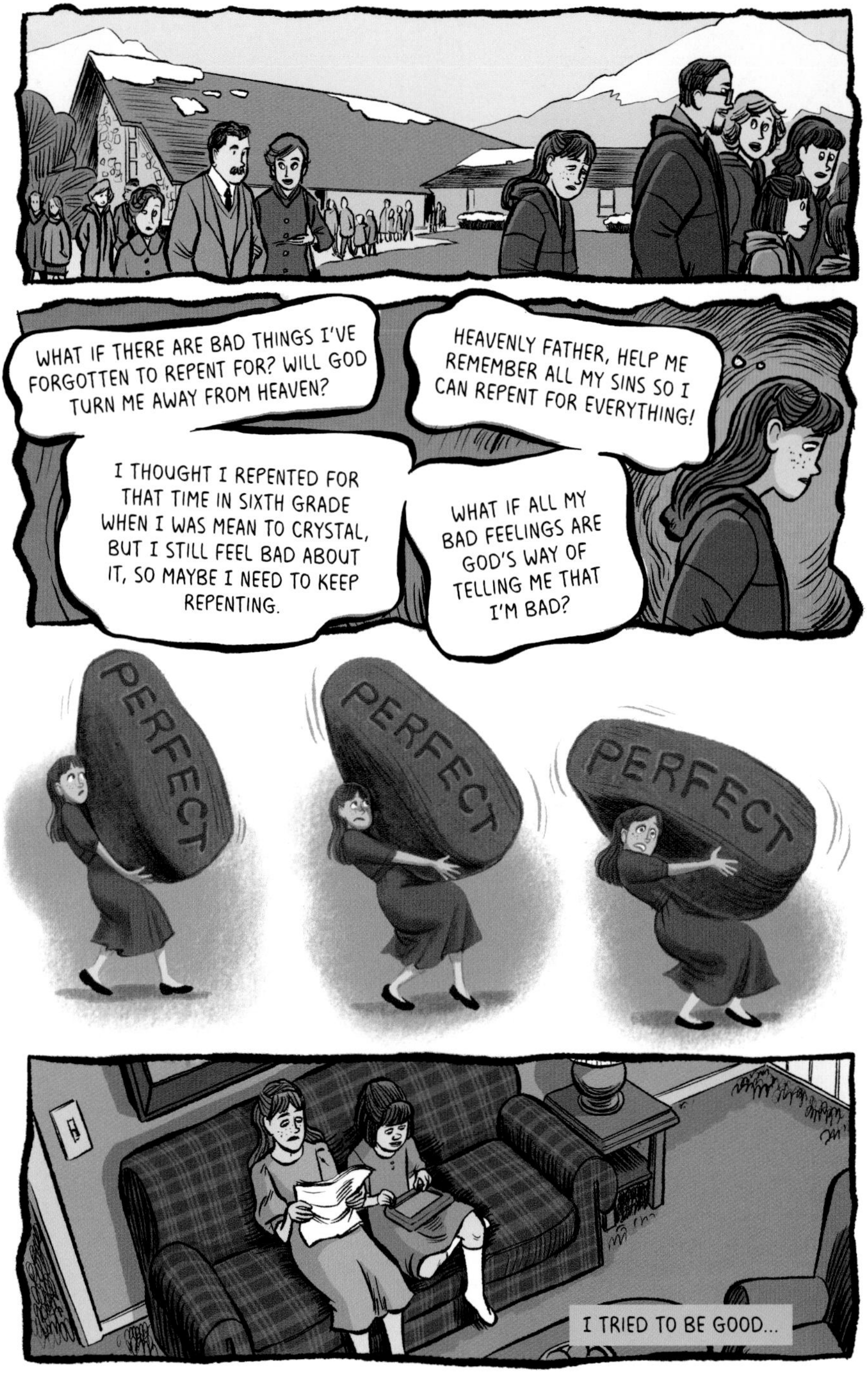
WHAT IF THERE ARE BAD THINGS I'VE FORGOTTEN TO REPENT FOR? WILL GOD TURN ME AWAY FROM HEAVEN?
HEAVENLY FATHER, HELP ME REMEMBER ALL MY SINS SO I CAN REPENT FOR EVERYTHING!
I THOUGHT I REPENTED FOR THAT TIME IN SIXTH GRADE WHEN I WAS MEAN TO CRYSTAL, BUT I STILL FEEL BAD ABOUT IT, SO MAYBE I NEED TO KEEP REPENTING.
WHAT IF ALL MY BAD FEELINGS ARE GOD'S WAY OF TELLING ME THAT I'M BAD?
PERFECT
PERFECT
PERFECT
I TRIED TO BE GOOD...

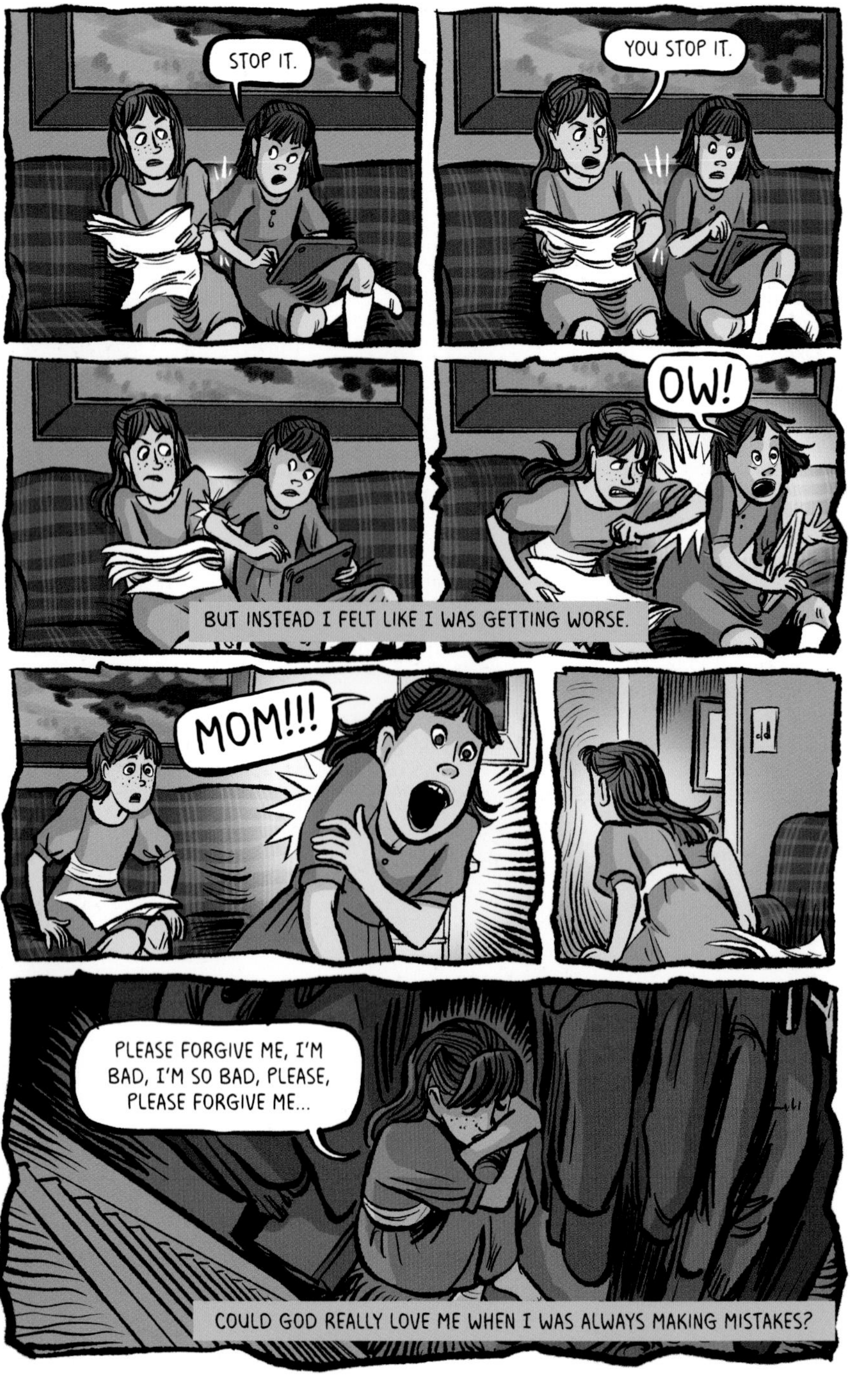

STOP IT.
YOU STOP IT.
OW!
BUT INSTEAD I FELT LIKE I WAS GETTING WORSE.
MOM!!!
PLEASE FORGIVE ME, I'M BAD, I'M SO BAD, PLEASE, PLEASE FORGIVE ME...
COULD GOD REALLY LOVE ME WHEN I WAS ALWAYS MAKING MISTAKES?

everyone is always watching you
and judging you

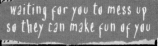
waiting for you to mess up
so they can make fun of you

MY DAD GOT A FAX MACHINE SO
MY AGENT CAN JUST FAX OVER
THE SIDES FOR MY AUDITION.

"SIDES" ARE PAGES
FROM A SCRIPT.

THE PART IS FOR THE LITTLE
SISTER IN A TV MOVIE...

Olivia thinks she's
better than you she
thinks you don't
have any talent

YOU REMIND ME
OF SOMEONE...

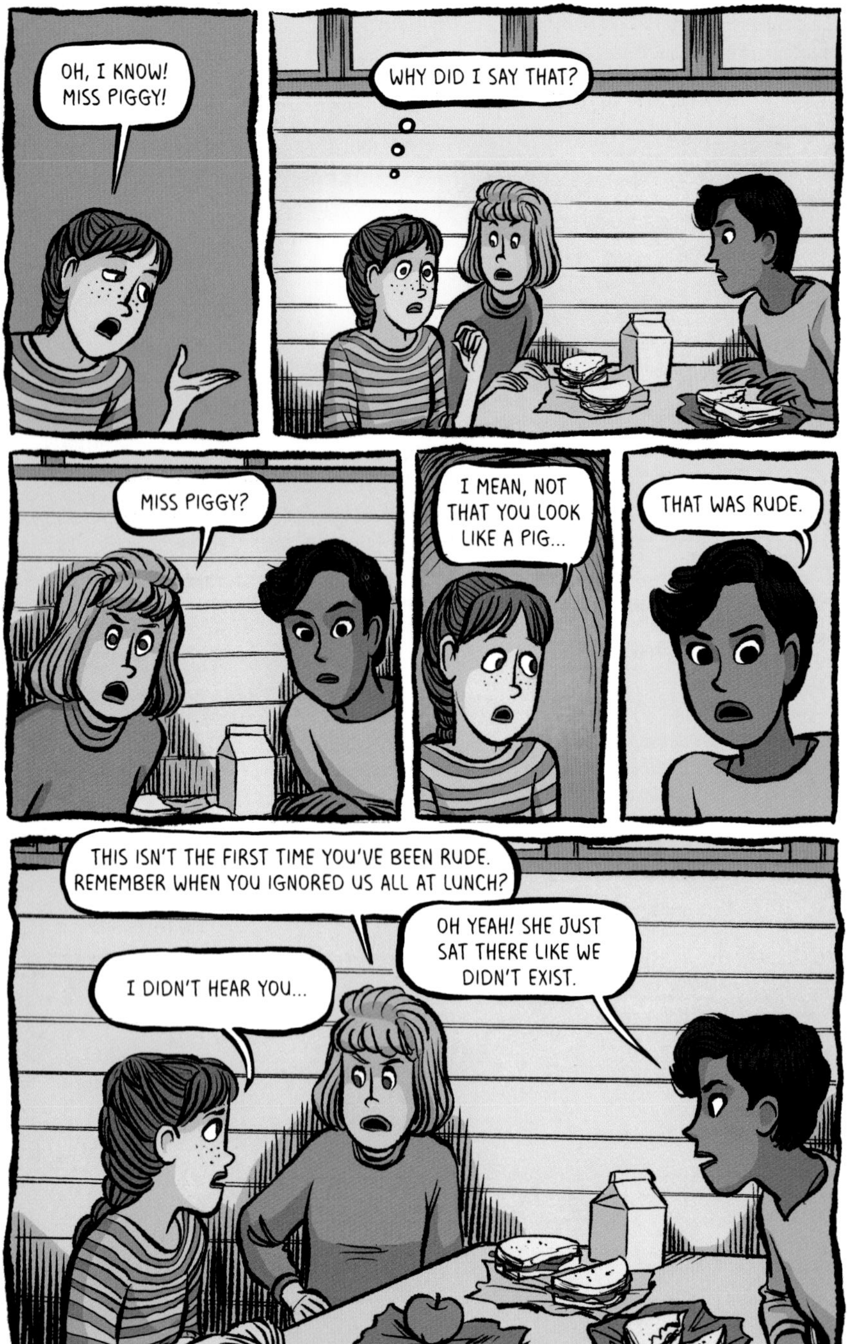
OH, I KNOW! MISS PIGGY!
WHY DID I SAY THAT?
MISS PIGGY?
I MEAN, NOT THAT YOU LOOK LIKE A PIG...
THAT WAS RUDE.
THIS ISN'T THE FIRST TIME YOU'VE BEEN RUDE. REMEMBER WHEN YOU IGNORED US ALL AT LUNCH?
OH YEAH! SHE JUST SAT THERE LIKE WE DIDN'T EXIST.
I DIDN'T HEAR YOU...

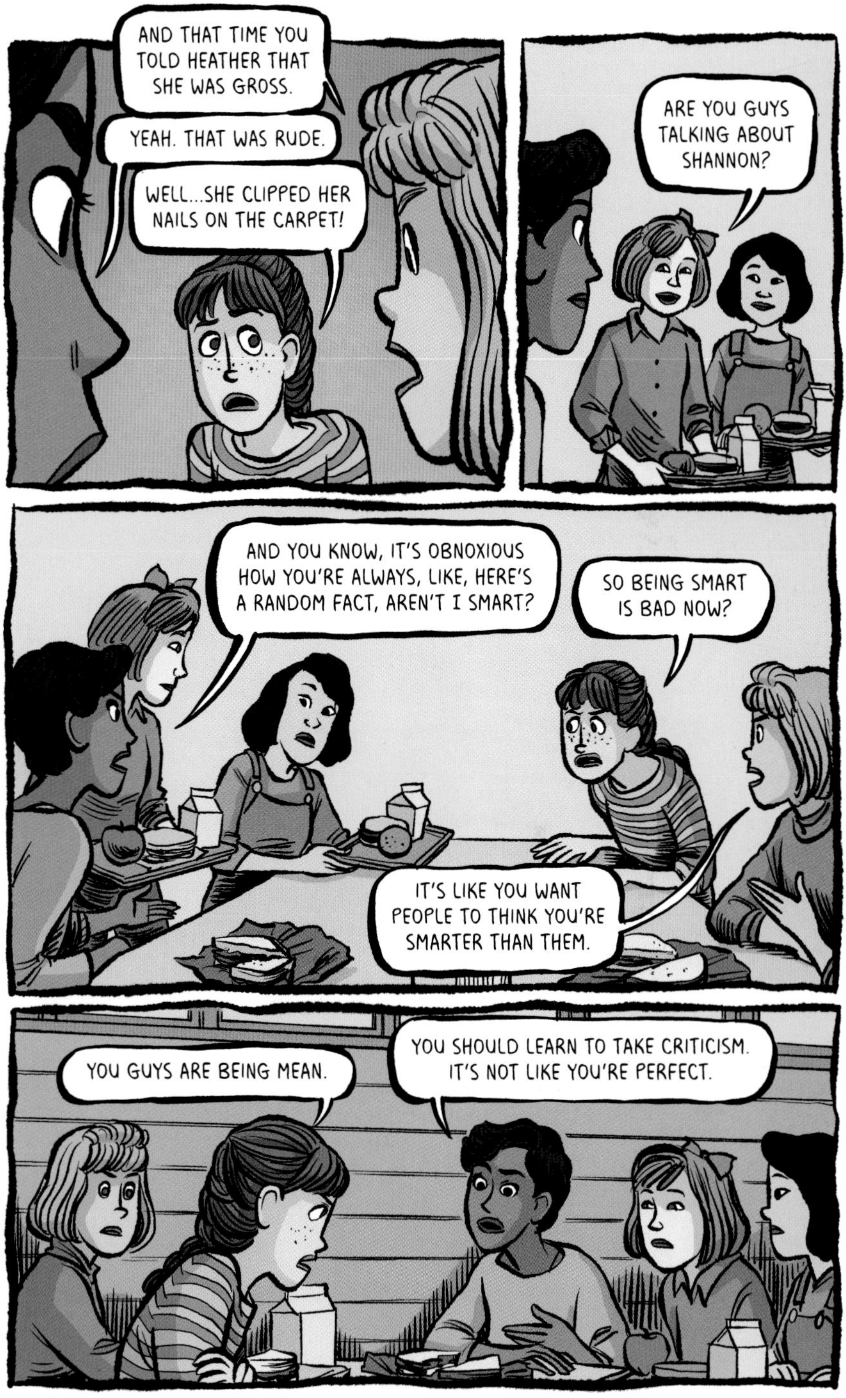
AND THAT TIME YOU TOLD HEATHER THAT SHE WAS GROSS.
YEAH. THAT WAS RUDE.
WELL...SHE CLIPPED HER NAILS ON THE CARPET!
ARE YOU GUYS TALKING ABOUT SHANNON?
AND YOU KNOW, IT'S OBNOXIOUS HOW YOU'RE ALWAYS, LIKE, HERE'S A RANDOM FACT, AREN'T I SMART?
SO BEING SMART IS BAD NOW?
IT'S LIKE YOU WANT PEOPLE TO THINK YOU'RE SMARTER THAN THEM.
YOU GUYS ARE BEING MEAN.
YOU SHOULD LEARN TO TAKE CRITICISM. IT'S NOT LIKE YOU'RE PERFECT.

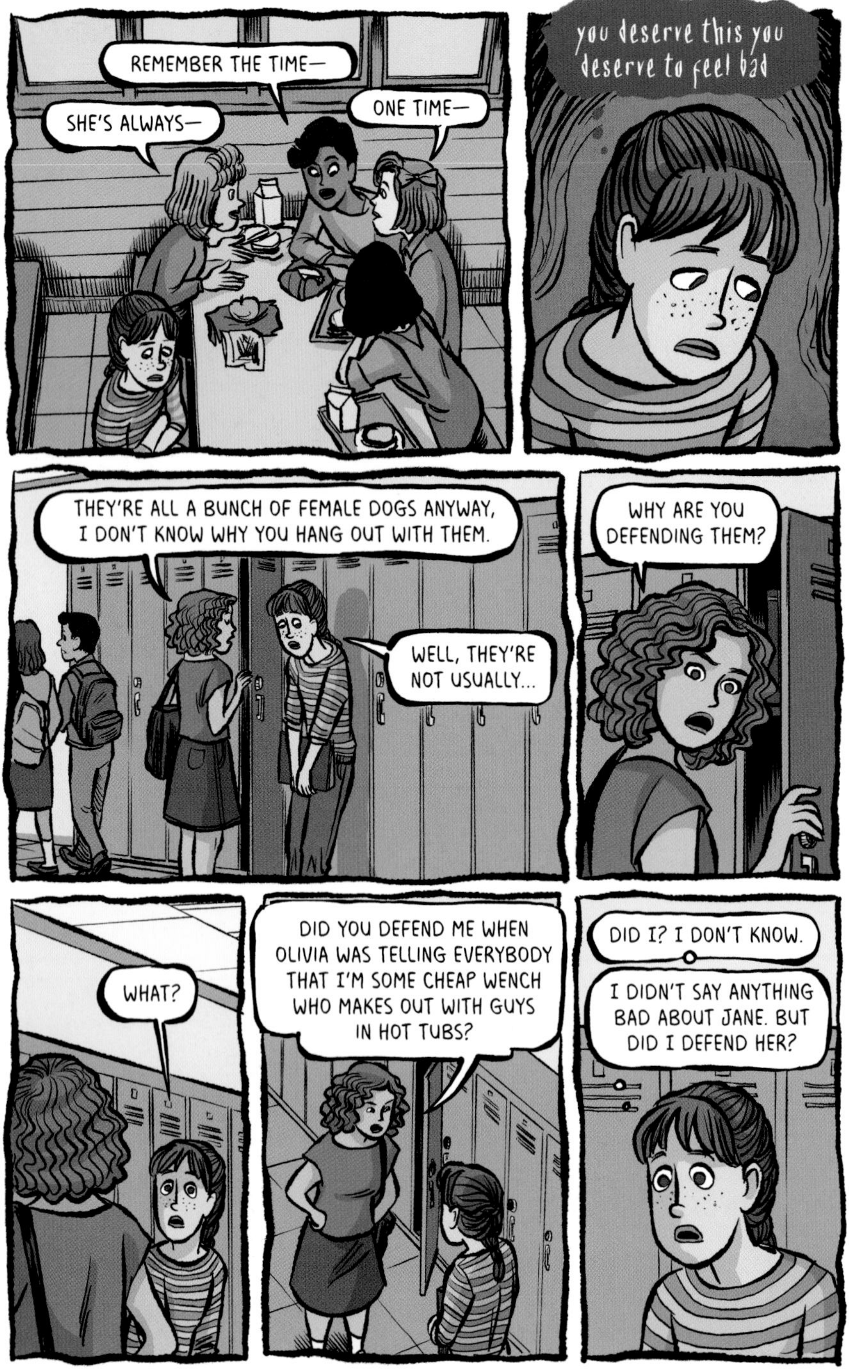

REMEMBER THE TIME—
SHE'S ALWAYS—
ONE TIME—
you deserve this you deserve to feel bad
THEY'RE ALL A BUNCH OF FEMALE DOGS ANYWAY, I DON'T KNOW WHY YOU HANG OUT WITH THEM.
WELL, THEY'RE NOT USUALLY...
WHY ARE YOU DEFENDING THEM?
WHAT?
DID YOU DEFEND ME WHEN OLIVIA WAS TELLING EVERYBODY THAT I'M SOME CHEAP WENCH WHO MAKES OUT WITH GUYS IN HOT TUBS?
DID I? I DON'T KNOW.
I DIDN'T SAY ANYTHING BAD ABOUT JANE. BUT DID I DEFEND HER?

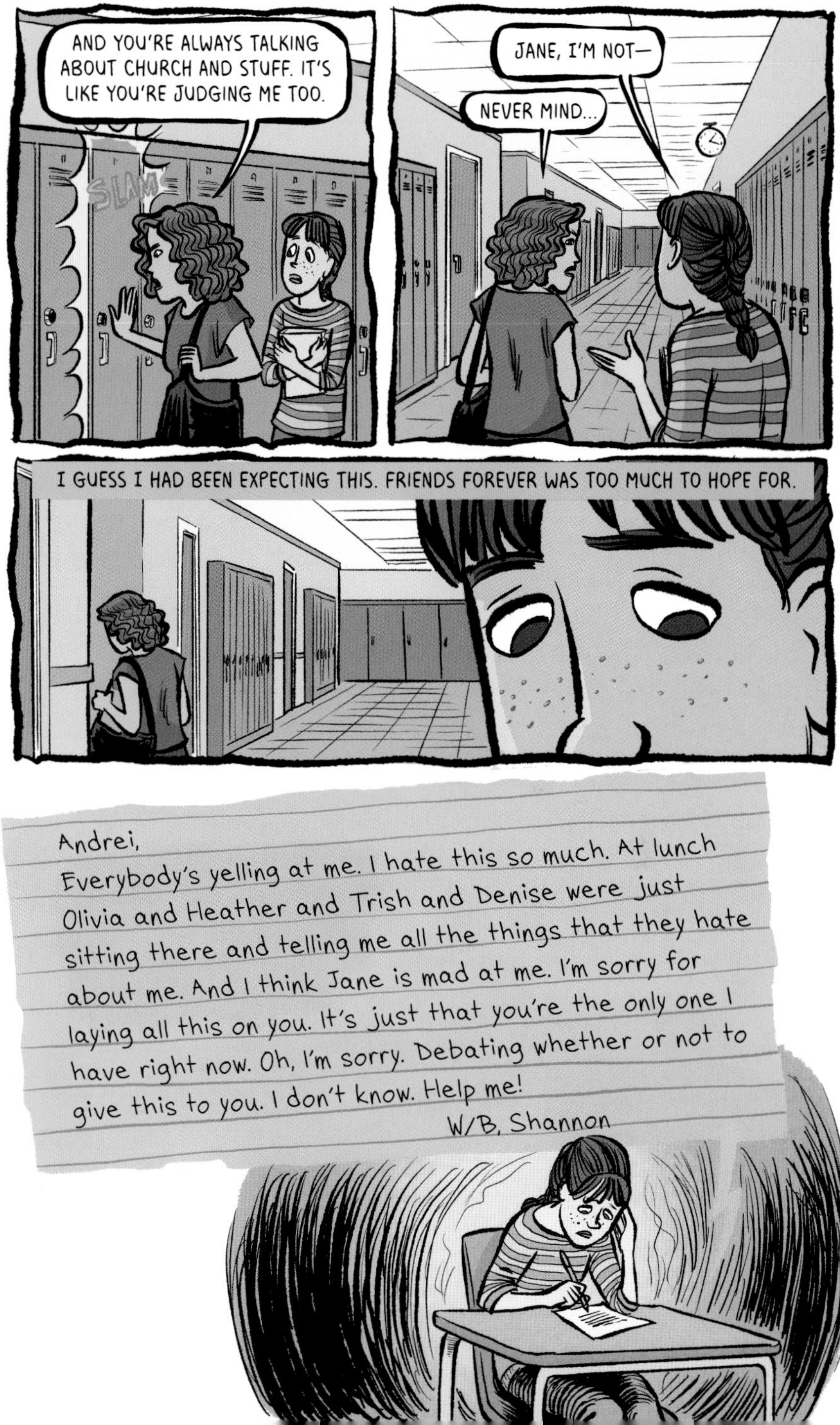
AND YOU'RE ALWAYS TALKING ABOUT CHURCH AND STUFF. IT'S LIKE YOU'RE JUDGING ME TOO.
SLAM
JANE, I'M NOT—
NEVER MIND...
I GUESS I HAD BEEN EXPECTING THIS. FRIENDS FOREVER WAS TOO MUCH TO HOPE FOR.
Andrei,
Everybody's yelling at me. I hate this so much. At lunch
Olivia and Heather and Trish and Denise were just
sitting there and telling me all the things that they hate
about me. And I think Jane is mad at me. I'm sorry for
laying all this on you. It's just that you're the only one I
have right now. Oh, I'm sorry. Debating whether or not to
give this to you. I don't know. Help me!
W/B, Shannon

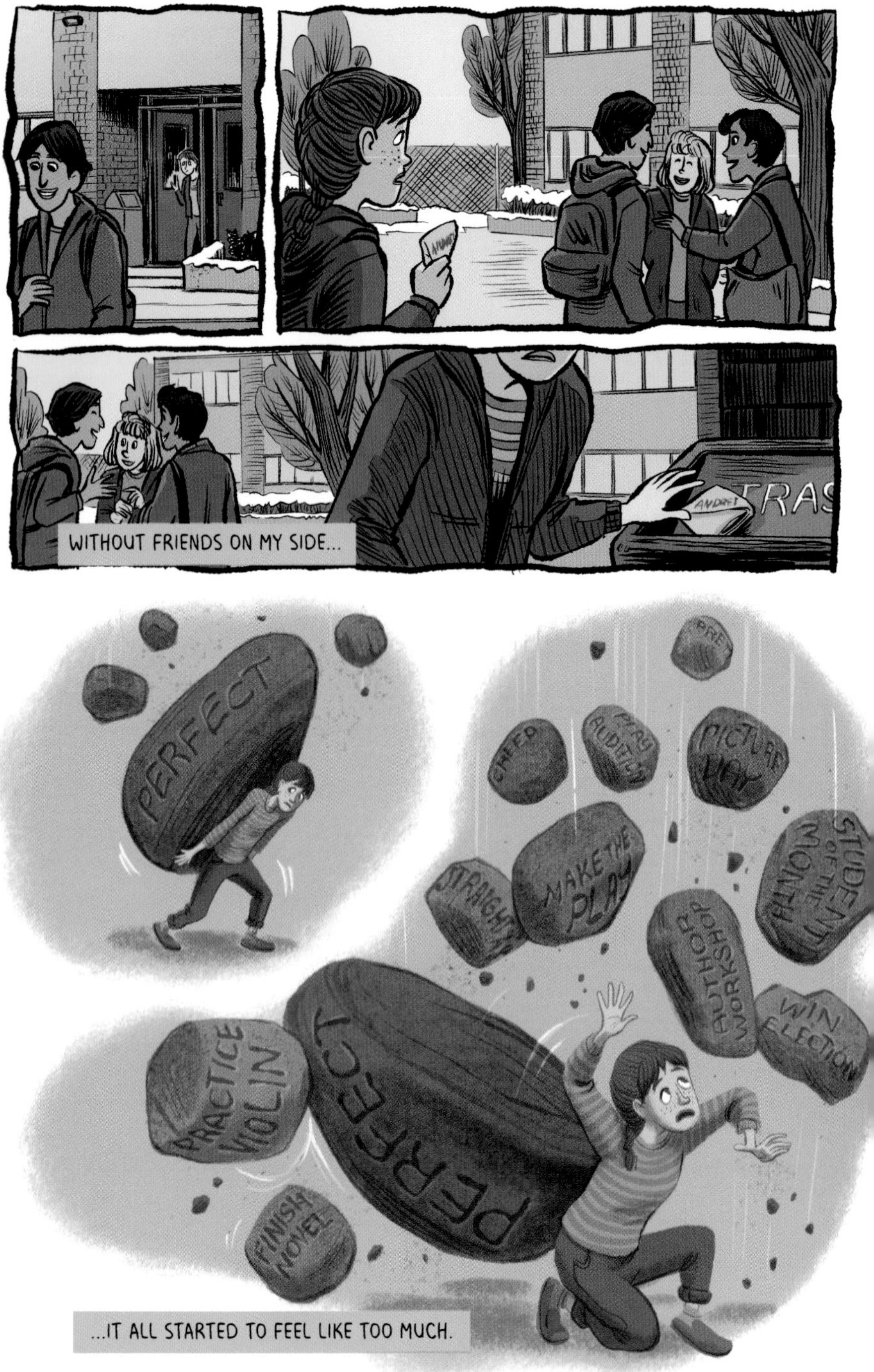
WITHOUT FRIENDS ON MY SIDE...
PERFECT
PICTURE DAY
PLAY AUDITION
MAKE THE PLAY
STUDENT OF THE MONTH
AUTHOR WORKSHOP
WIN ELECTION
PRACTICE VIOLIN
PERFECT
FINISH NOVEL
...IT ALL STARTED TO FEEL LIKE TOO MUCH.

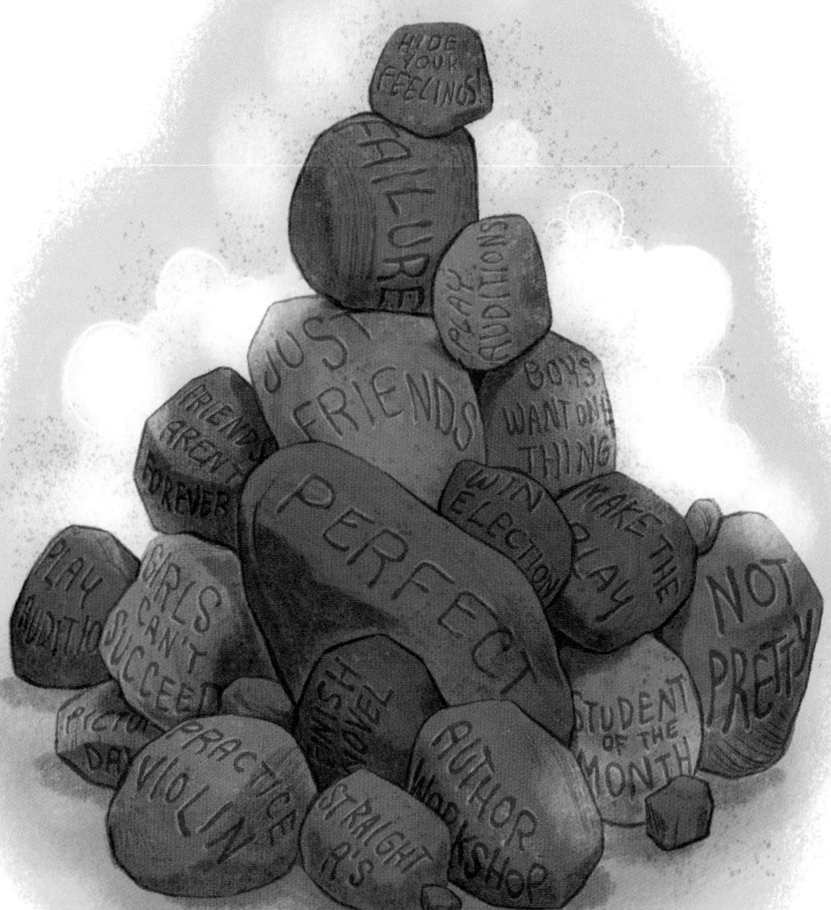

HIDE YOUR FEELINGS!
FAILURE
PLAY AUDITIONS
JUST FRIENDS
BOYS WANT ONE THING
FRIENDS AREN'T FOREVER
PERFECT
WIN ELECTION
MAKE THE PLAY
NOT PRETTY
GIRLS CAN'T SUCCEED
STUDENT OF THE MONTH
PRACTICE VIOLIN
STRAIGHT A'S

CHAPTER 6

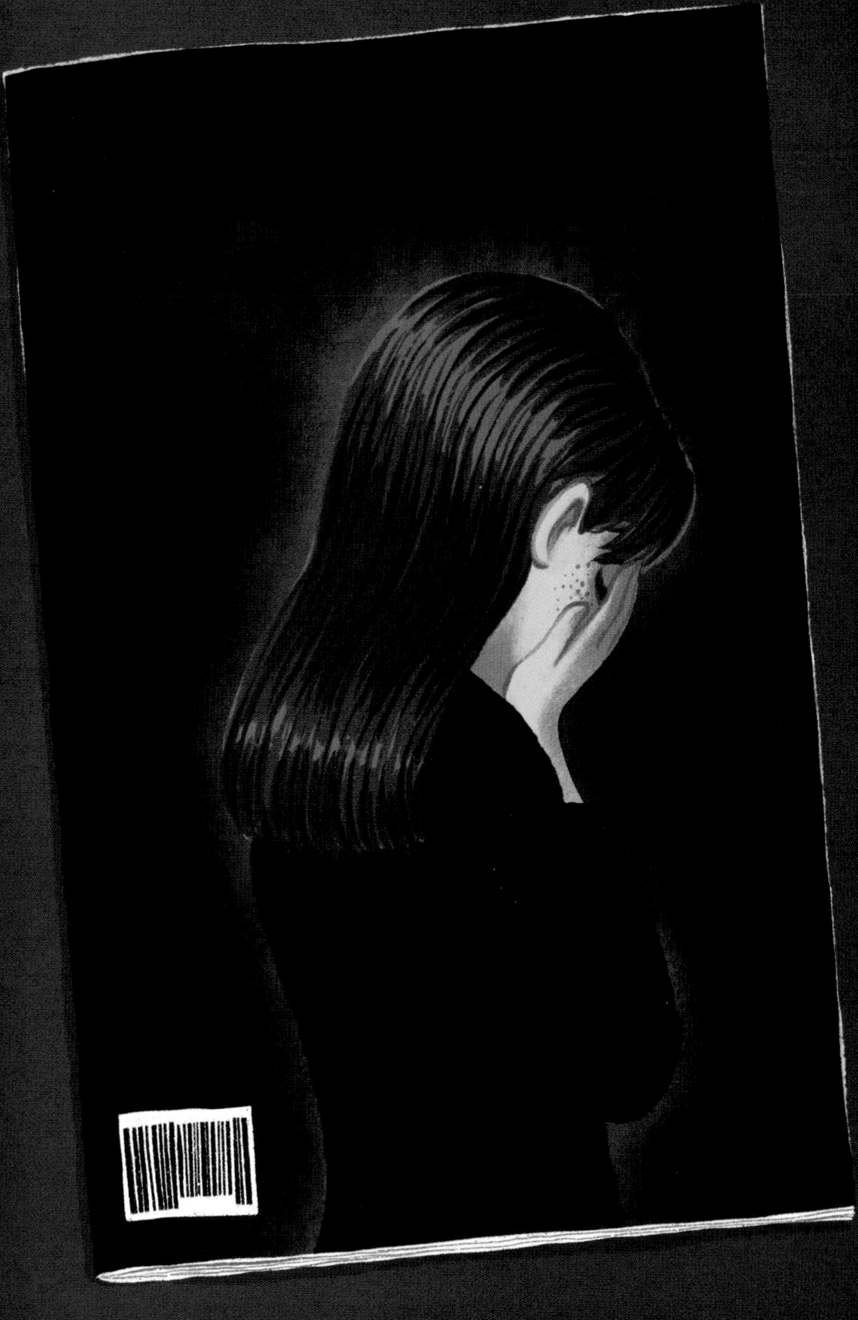

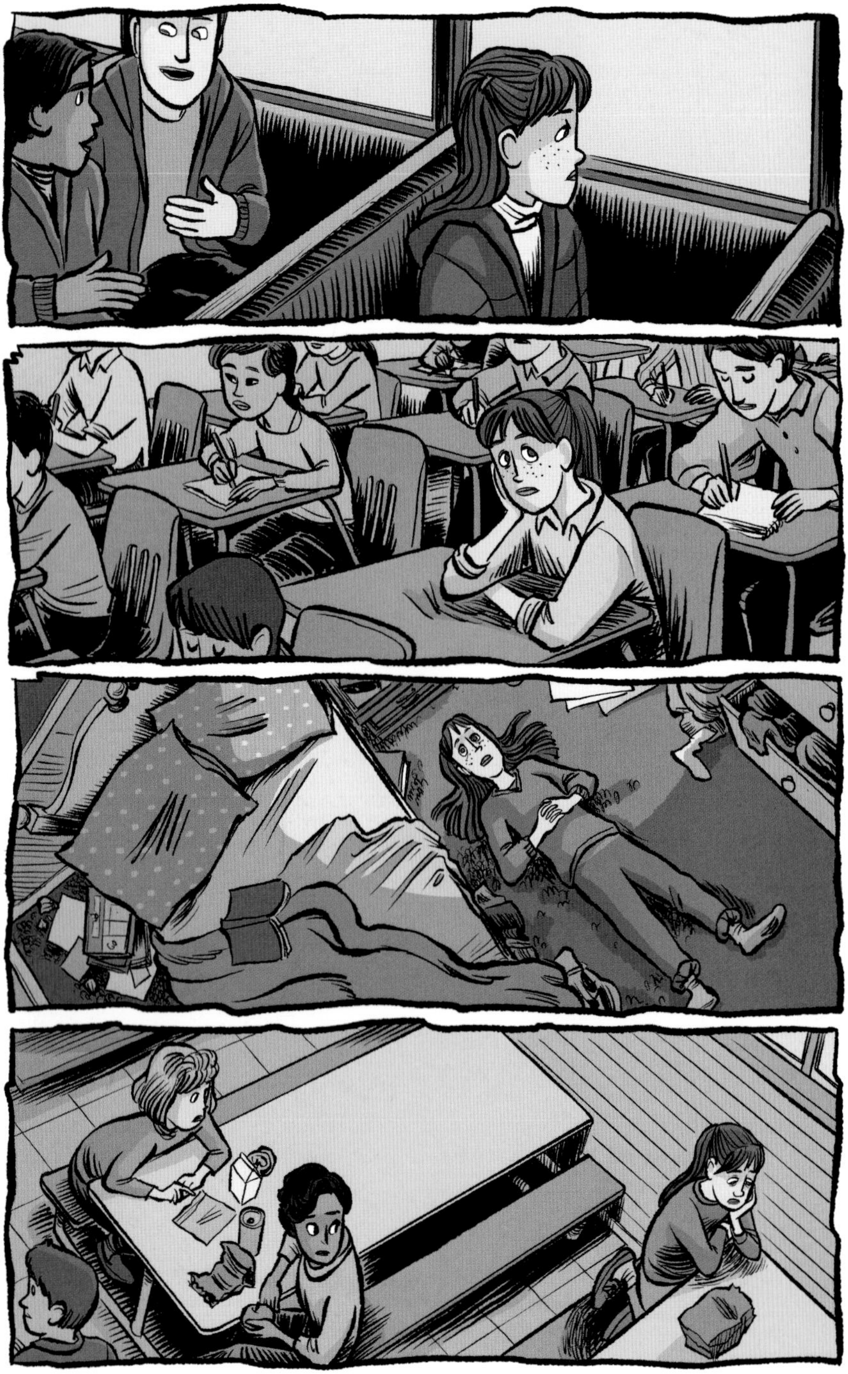

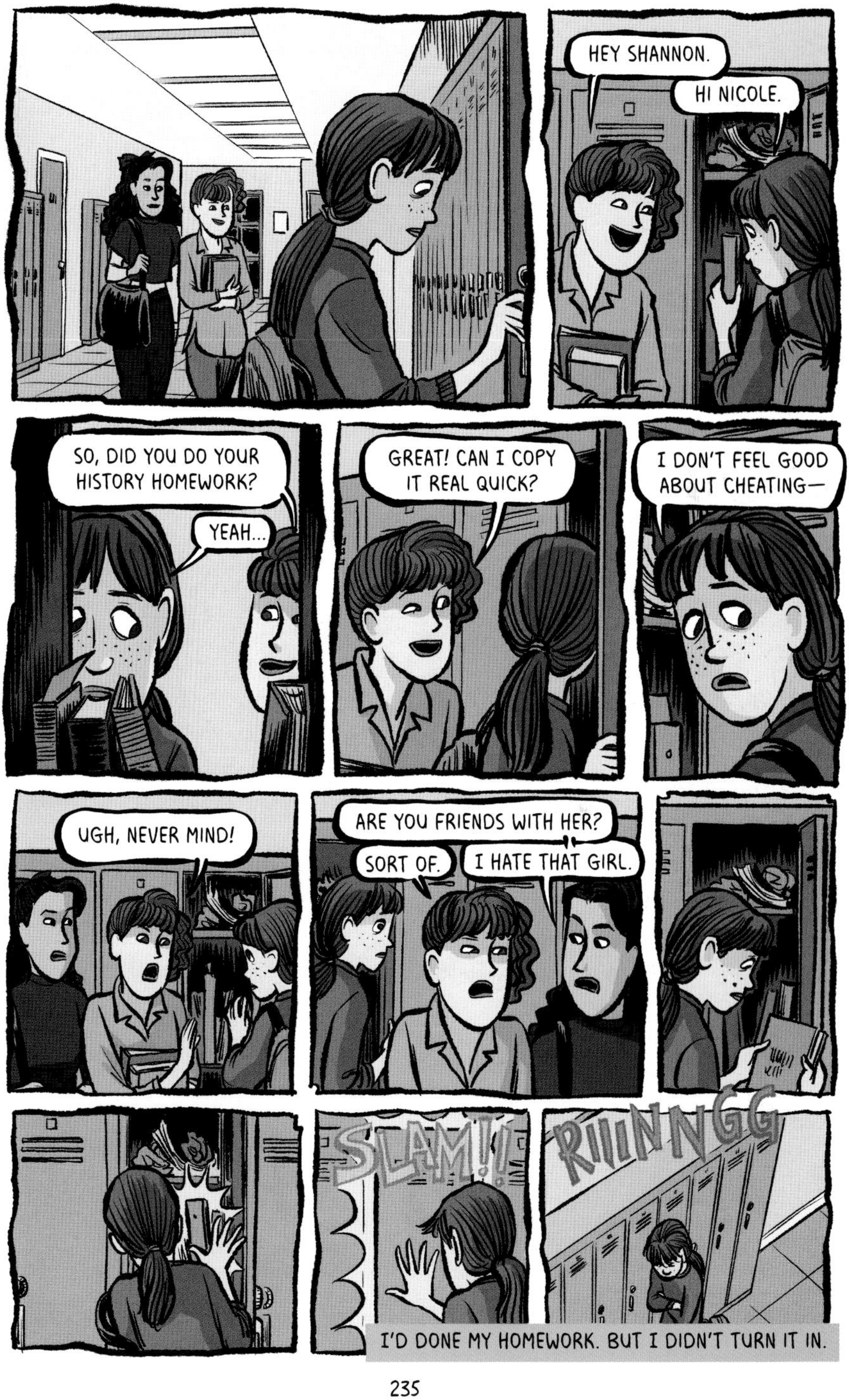
HEY SHANNON.
HI NICOLE.
SO, DID YOU DO YOUR HISTORY HOMEWORK?
YEAH...
GREAT! CAN I COPY IT REAL QUICK?
I DON'T FEEL GOOD ABOUT CHEATING—
UGH, NEVER MIND!
ARE YOU FRIENDS WITH HER?
SORT OF.
I HATE THAT GIRL.
SLAM!!
RIIINNGG
I'D DONE MY HOMEWORK. BUT I DIDN'T TURN IT IN.

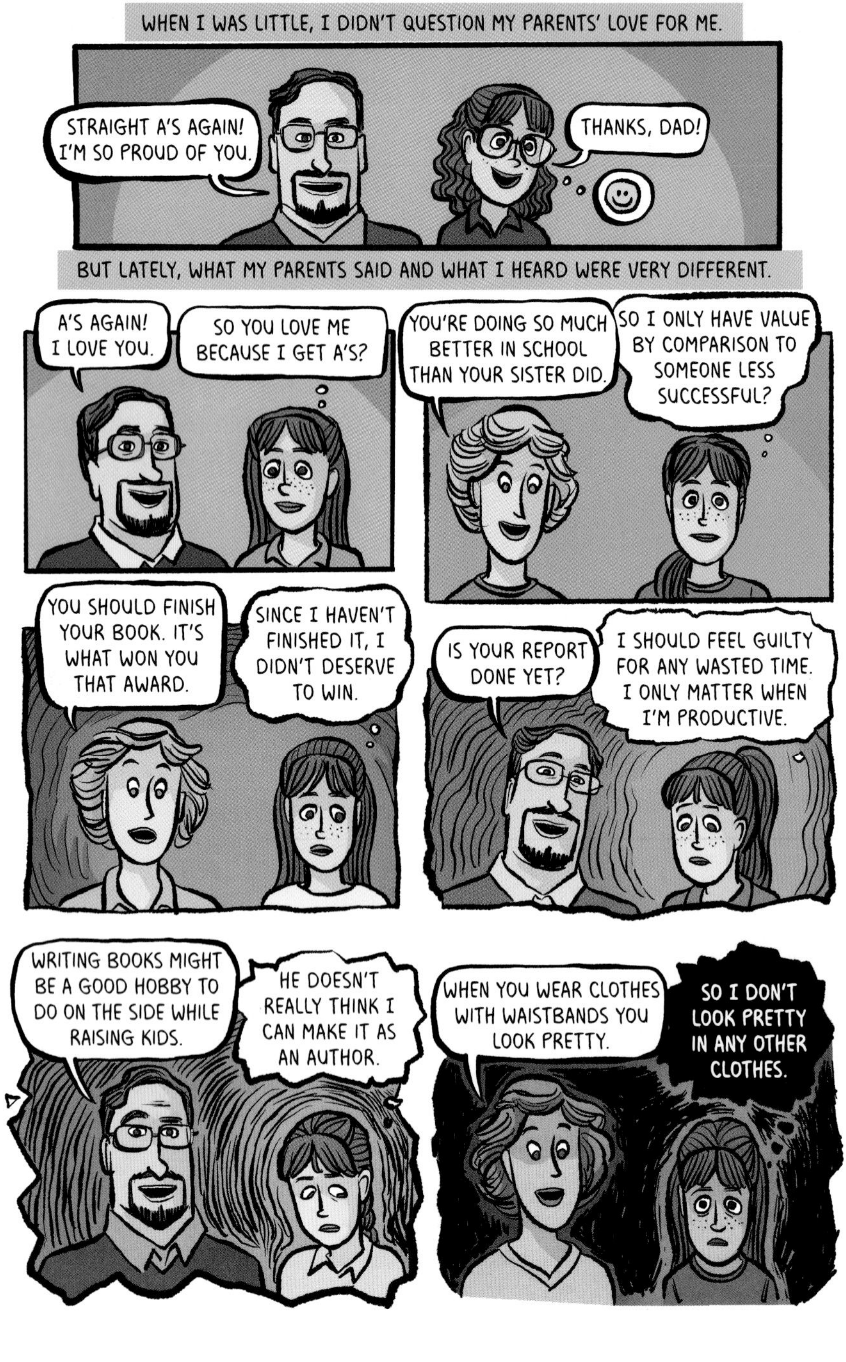
WHEN I WAS LITTLE, I DIDN'T QUESTION MY PARENTS' LOVE FOR ME.
STRAIGHT A'S AGAIN! I'M SO PROUD OF YOU.
THANKS, DAD!
BUT LATELY, WHAT MY PARENTS SAID AND WHAT I HEARD WERE VERY DIFFERENT.
A'S AGAIN! I LOVE YOU.
SO YOU LOVE ME BECAUSE I GET A'S?
YOU'RE DOING SO MUCH BETTER IN SCHOOL THAN YOUR SISTER DID.
SO I ONLY HAVE VALUE BY COMPARISON TO SOMEONE LESS SUCCESSFUL?
YOU SHOULD FINISH YOUR BOOK. IT'S WHAT WON YOU THAT AWARD.
SINCE I HAVEN'T FINISHED IT, I DIDN'T DESERVE TO WIN.
IS YOUR REPORT DONE YET?
I SHOULD FEEL GUILTY FOR ANY WASTED TIME. I ONLY MATTER WHEN I'M PRODUCTIVE.
WRITING BOOKS MIGHT BE A GOOD HOBBY TO DO ON THE SIDE WHILE RAISING KIDS.
HE DOESN'T REALLY THINK I CAN MAKE IT AS AN AUTHOR.
WHEN YOU WEAR CLOTHES WITH WAISTBANDS YOU LOOK PRETTY.
SO I DON'T LOOK PRETTY IN ANY OTHER CLOTHES.

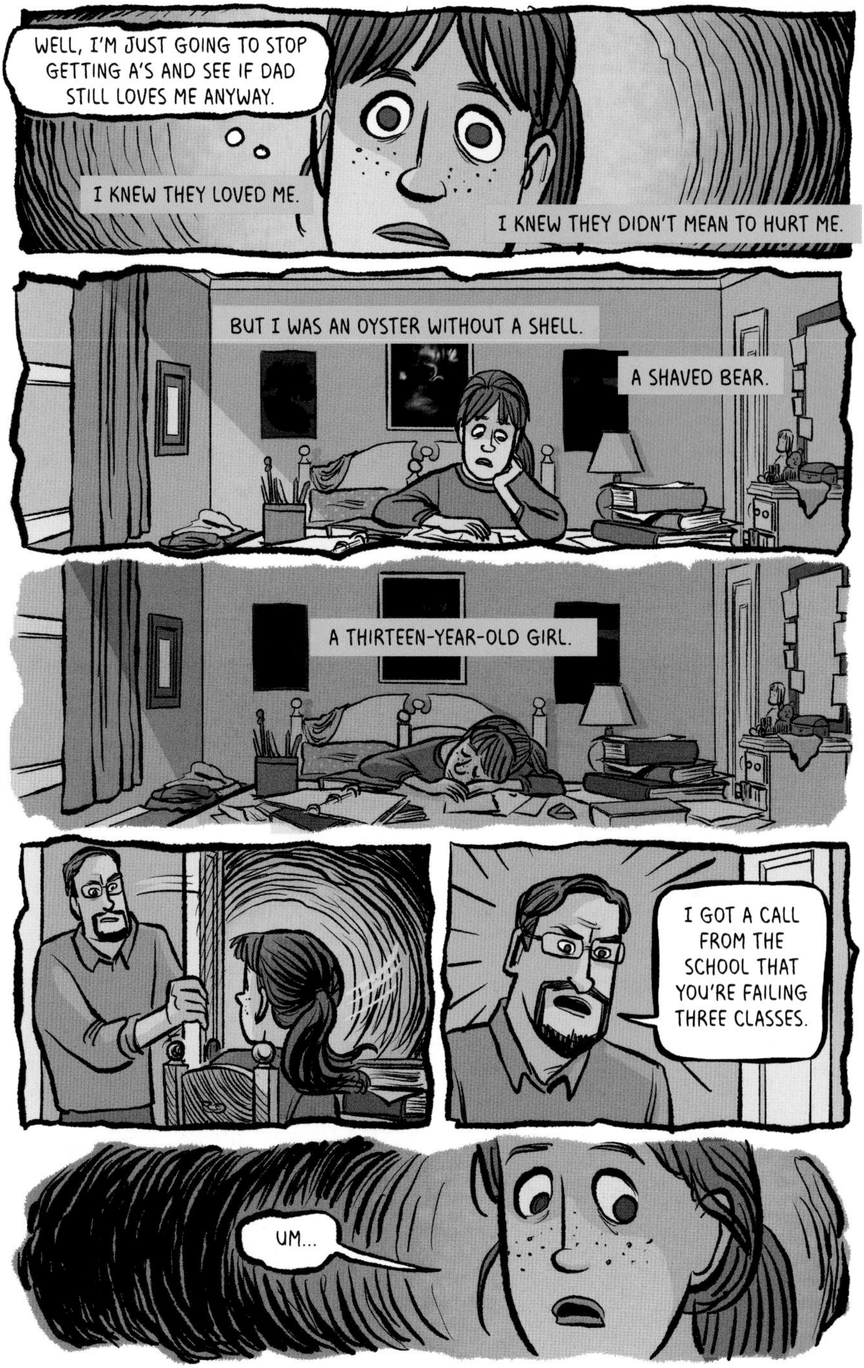
WELL, I'M JUST GOING TO STOP GETTING A'S AND SEE IF DAD STILL LOVES ME ANYWAY.
I KNEW THEY LOVED ME.
I KNEW THEY DIDN'T MEAN TO HURT ME.
BUT I WAS AN OYSTER WITHOUT A SHELL.
A SHAVED BEAR.
A THIRTEEN-YEAR-OLD GIRL.
I GOT A CALL FROM THE SCHOOL THAT YOU'RE FAILING THREE CLASSES.
UM...

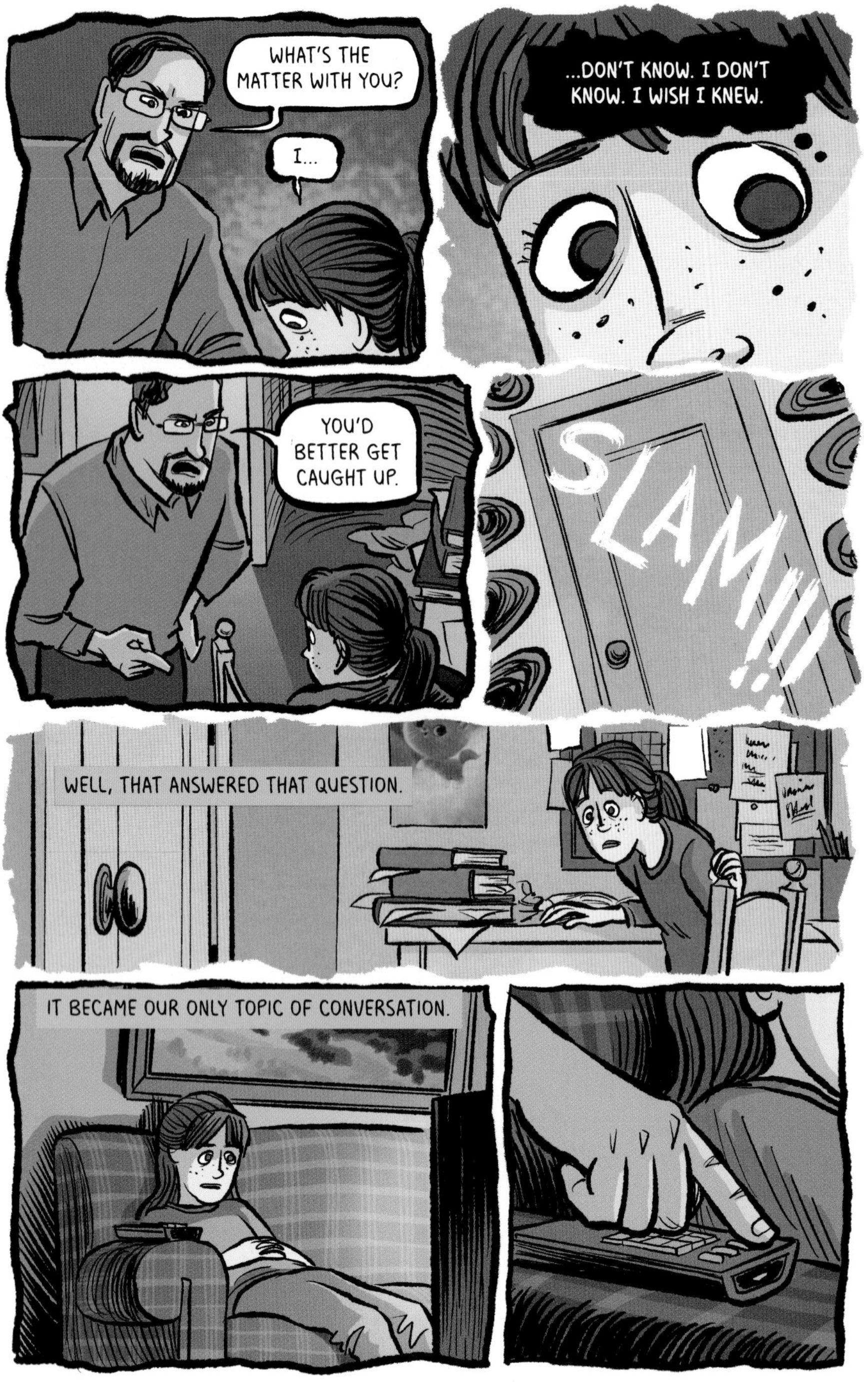
WHAT'S THE MATTER WITH YOU?
I...
...DON'T KNOW. I DON'T KNOW. I WISH I KNEW.
YOU'D BETTER GET CAUGHT UP.
SLAM!!!
WELL, THAT ANSWERED THAT QUESTION.
IT BECAME OUR ONLY TOPIC OF CONVERSATION.

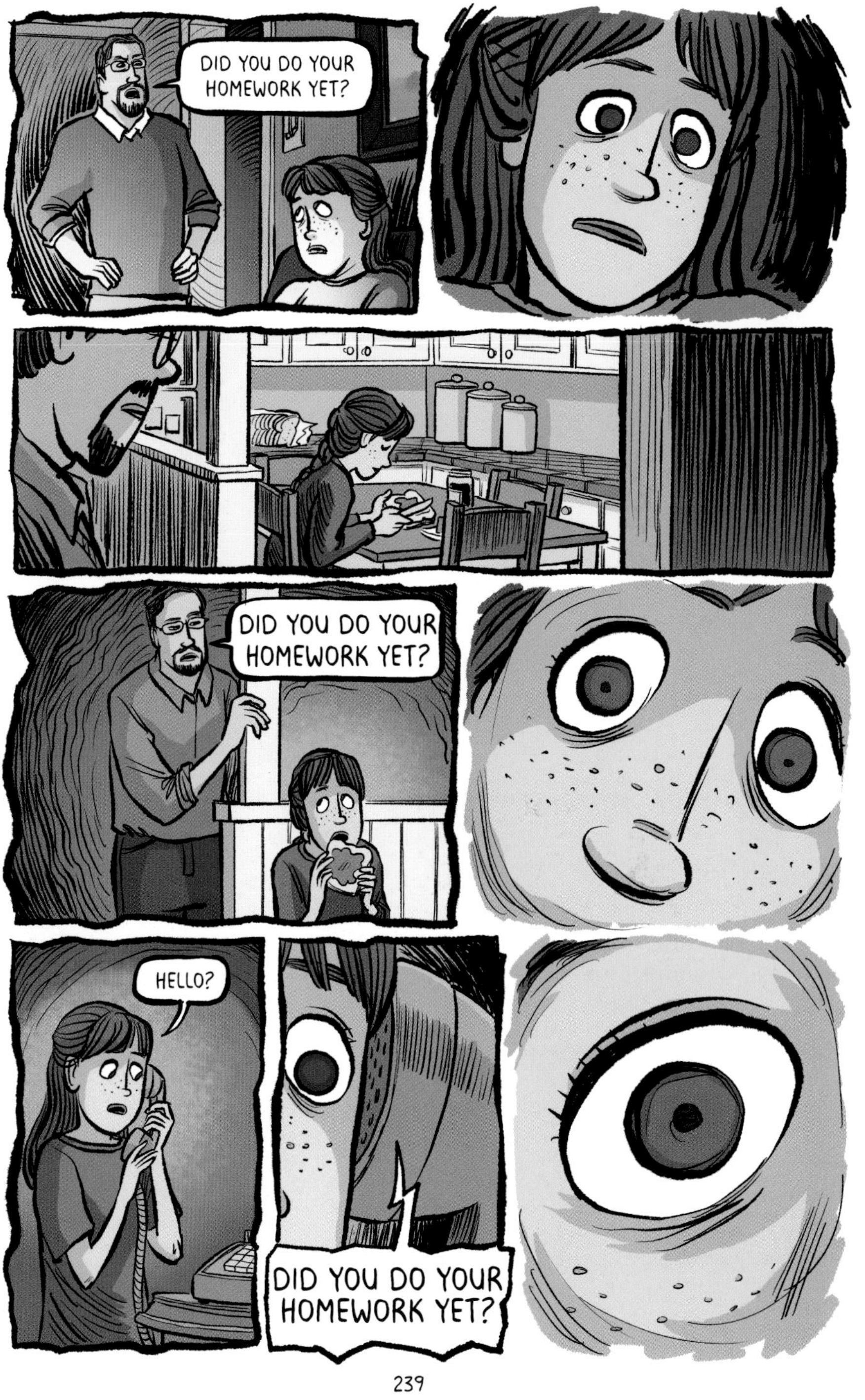
DID YOU DO YOUR HOMEWORK YET?
DID YOU DO YOUR HOMEWORK YET?
HELLO?
DID YOU DO YOUR HOMEWORK YET?

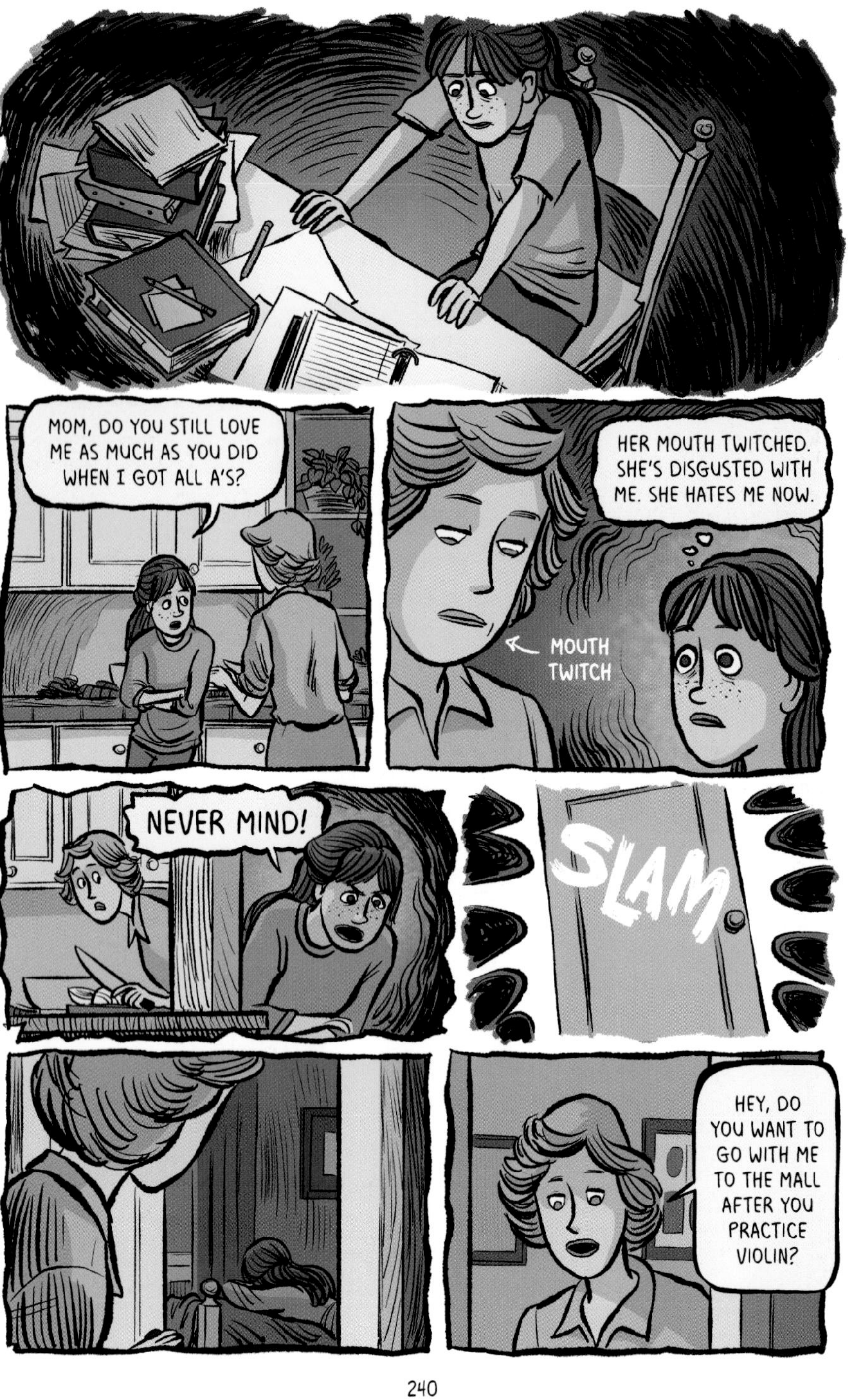
MOM, DO YOU STILL LOVE ME AS MUCH AS YOU DID WHEN I GOT ALL A'S?
HER MOUTH TWITCHED. SHE'S DISGUSTED WITH ME. SHE HATES ME NOW.
MOUTH TWITCH
NEVER MIND!
SLAM
HEY, DO YOU WANT TO GO WITH ME TO THE MALL AFTER YOU PRACTICE VIOLIN?

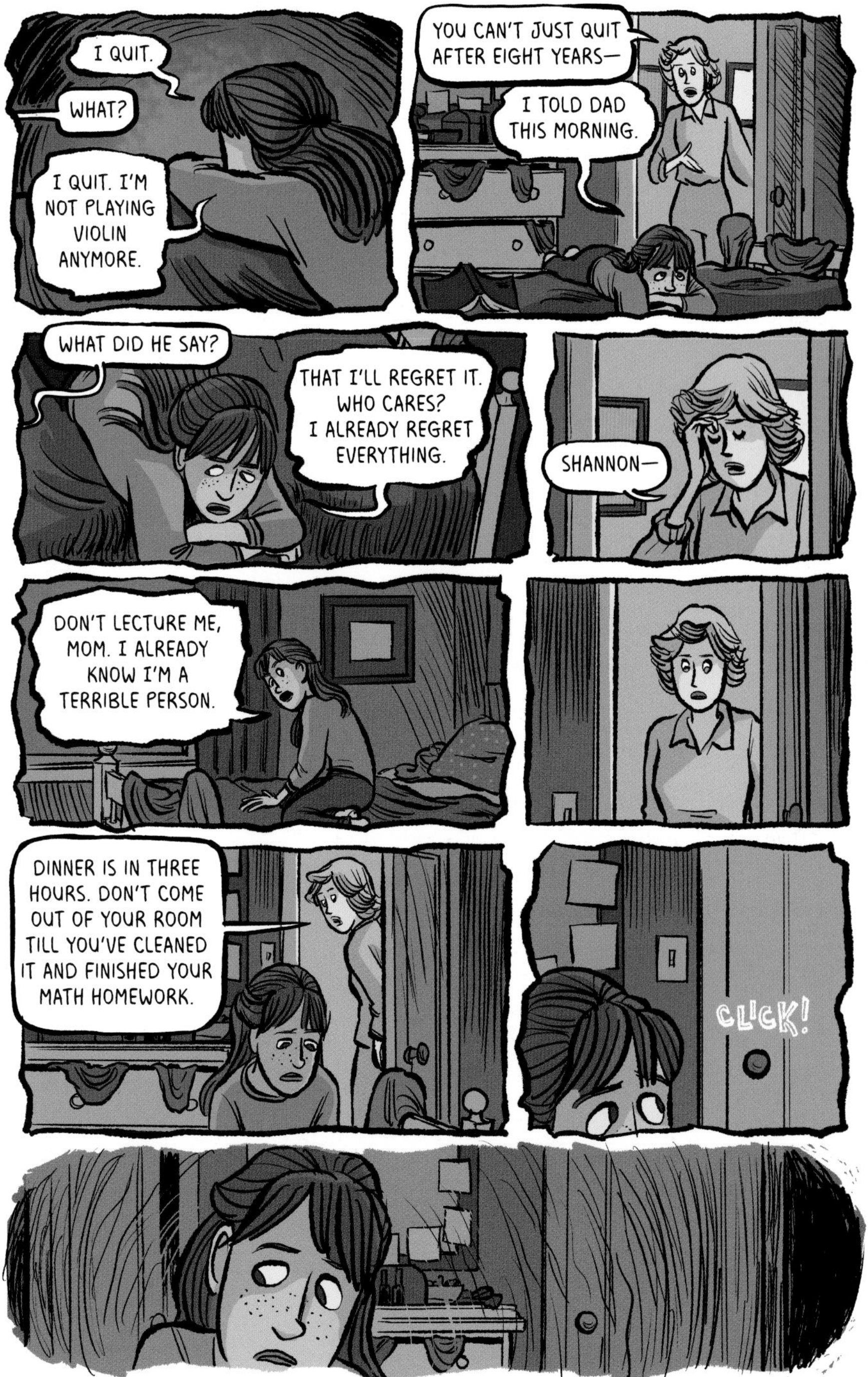
I QUIT.
WHAT?
I QUIT. I'M NOT PLAYING VIOLIN ANYMORE.
YOU CAN'T JUST QUIT AFTER EIGHT YEARS—
I TOLD DAD THIS MORNING.
WHAT DID HE SAY?
THAT I'LL REGRET IT. WHO CARES? I ALREADY REGRET EVERYTHING.
SHANNON—
DON'T LECTURE ME, MOM. I ALREADY KNOW I'M A TERRIBLE PERSON.
DINNER IS IN THREE HOURS. DON'T COME OUT OF YOUR ROOM TILL YOU'VE CLEANED IT AND FINISHED YOUR MATH HOMEWORK.
CLICK!

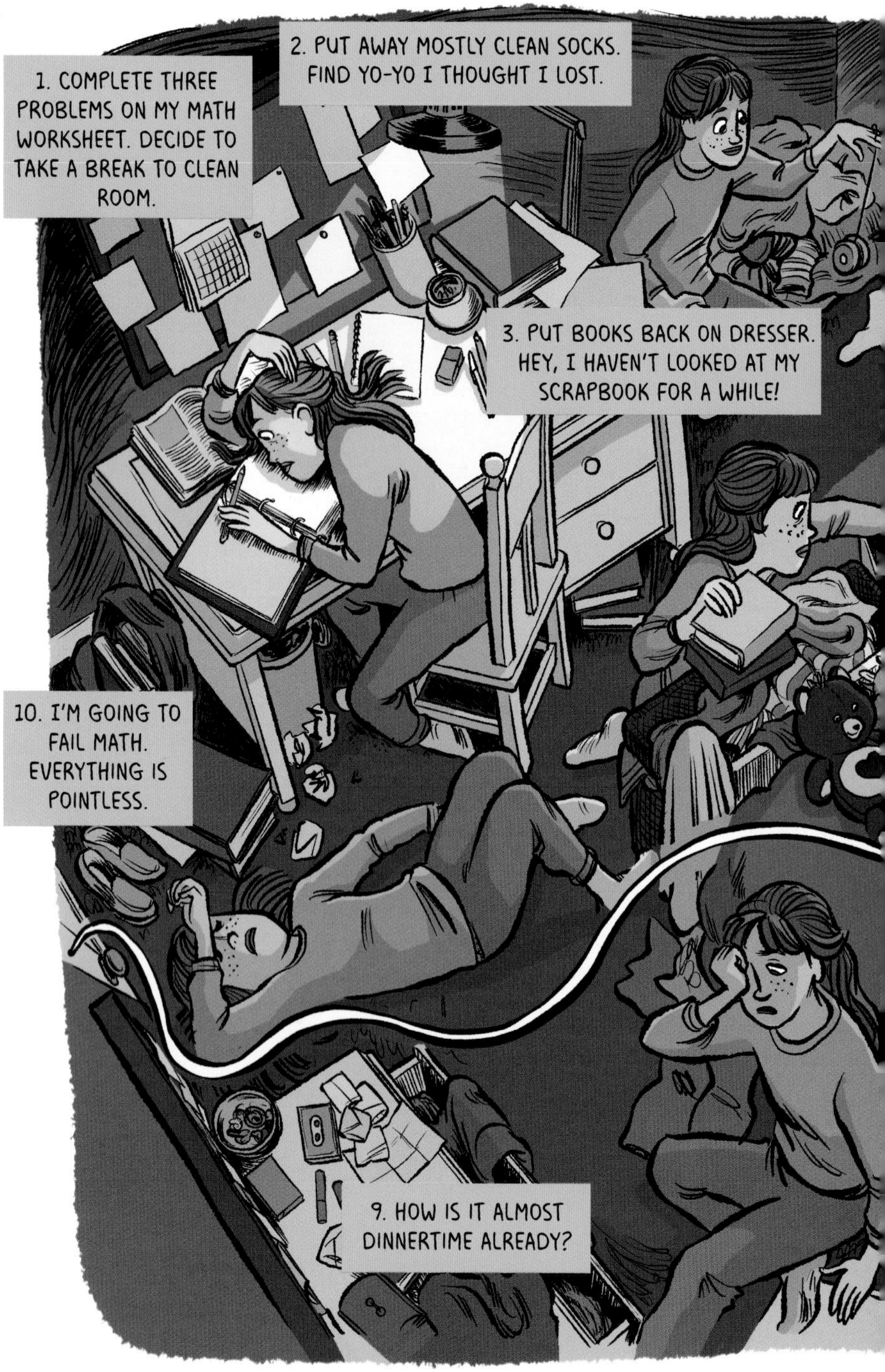
1. COMPLETE THREE PROBLEMS ON MY MATH WORKSHEET. DECIDE TO TAKE A BREAK TO CLEAN ROOM.
2. PUT AWAY MOSTLY CLEAN SOCKS. FIND YO-YO I THOUGHT I LOST.
3. PUT BOOKS BACK ON DRESSER. HEY, I HAVEN'T LOOKED AT MY SCRAPBOOK FOR A WHILE!
9. HOW IS IT ALMOST DINNERTIME ALREADY?
10. I'M GOING TO FAIL MATH. EVERYTHING IS POINTLESS.

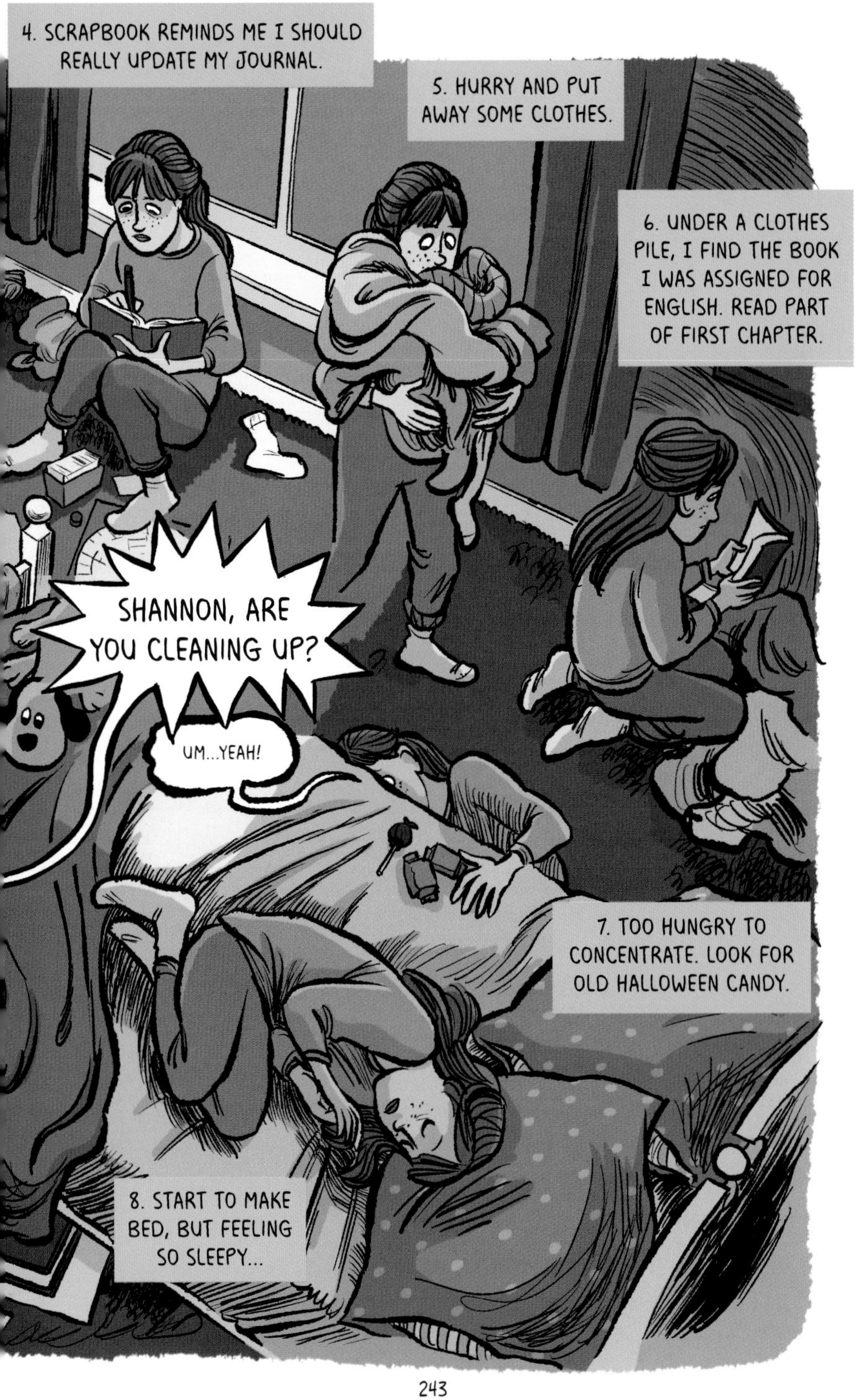
4. SCRAPBOOK REMINDS ME I SHOULD REALLY UPDATE MY JOURNAL.
5. HURRY AND PUT AWAY SOME CLOTHES.
6. UNDER A CLOTHES PILE, I FIND THE BOOK I WAS ASSIGNED FOR ENGLISH. READ PART OF FIRST CHAPTER.
SHANNON, ARE YOU CLEANING UP?
UM...YEAH!
7. TOO HUNGRY TO CONCENTRATE. LOOK FOR OLD HALLOWEEN CANDY.
8. START TO MAKE BED, BUT FEELING SO SLEEPY...

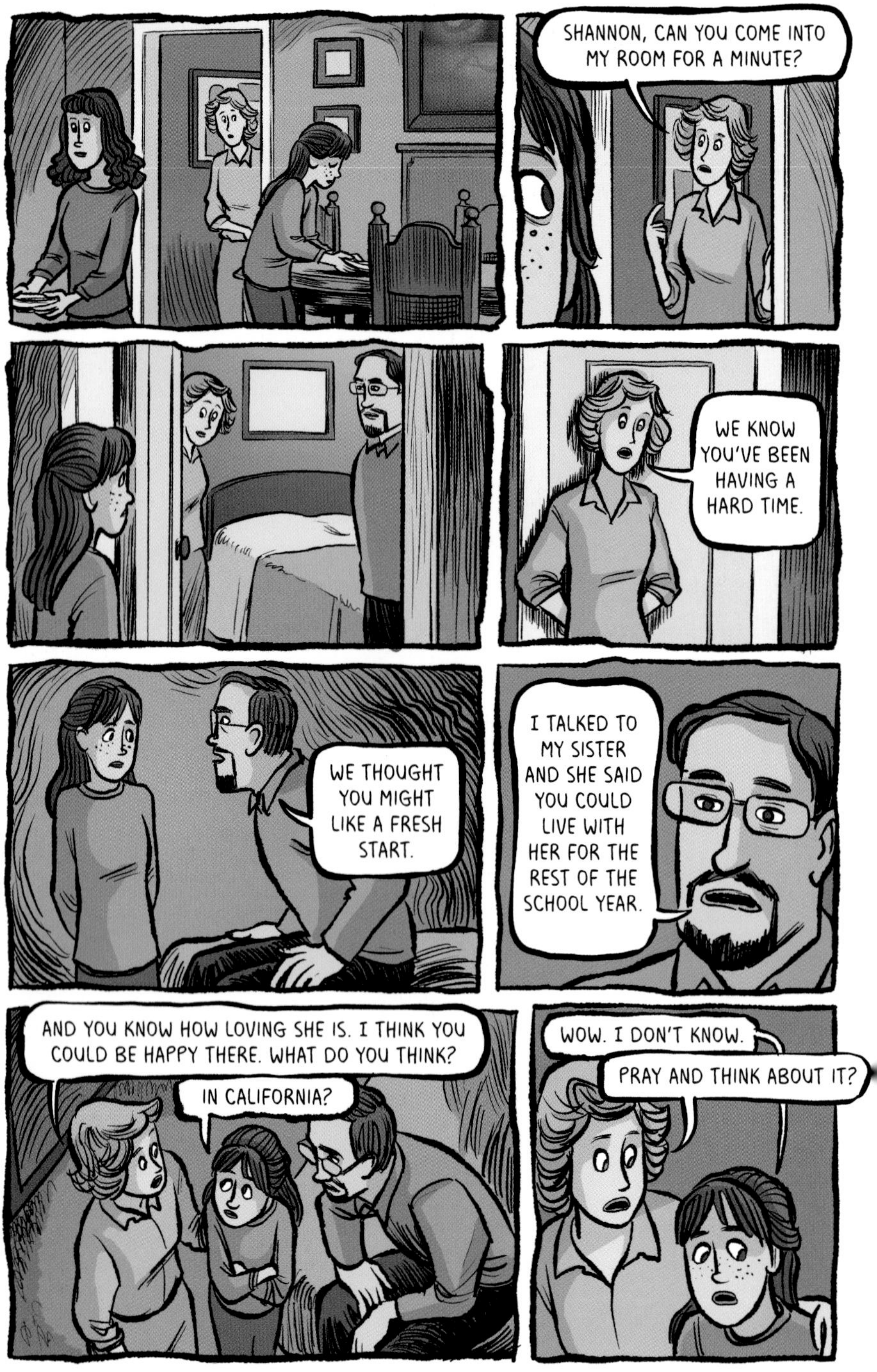
SHANNON, CAN YOU COME INTO MY ROOM FOR A MINUTE?
WE KNOW YOU'VE BEEN HAVING A HARD TIME.
WE THOUGHT YOU MIGHT LIKE A FRESH START.
I TALKED TO MY SISTER AND SHE SAID YOU COULD LIVE WITH HER FOR THE REST OF THE SCHOOL YEAR.
AND YOU KNOW HOW LOVING SHE IS. I THINK YOU COULD BE HAPPY THERE. WHAT DO YOU THINK?
IN CALIFORNIA?
WOW. I DON'T KNOW.
PRAY AND THINK ABOUT IT?

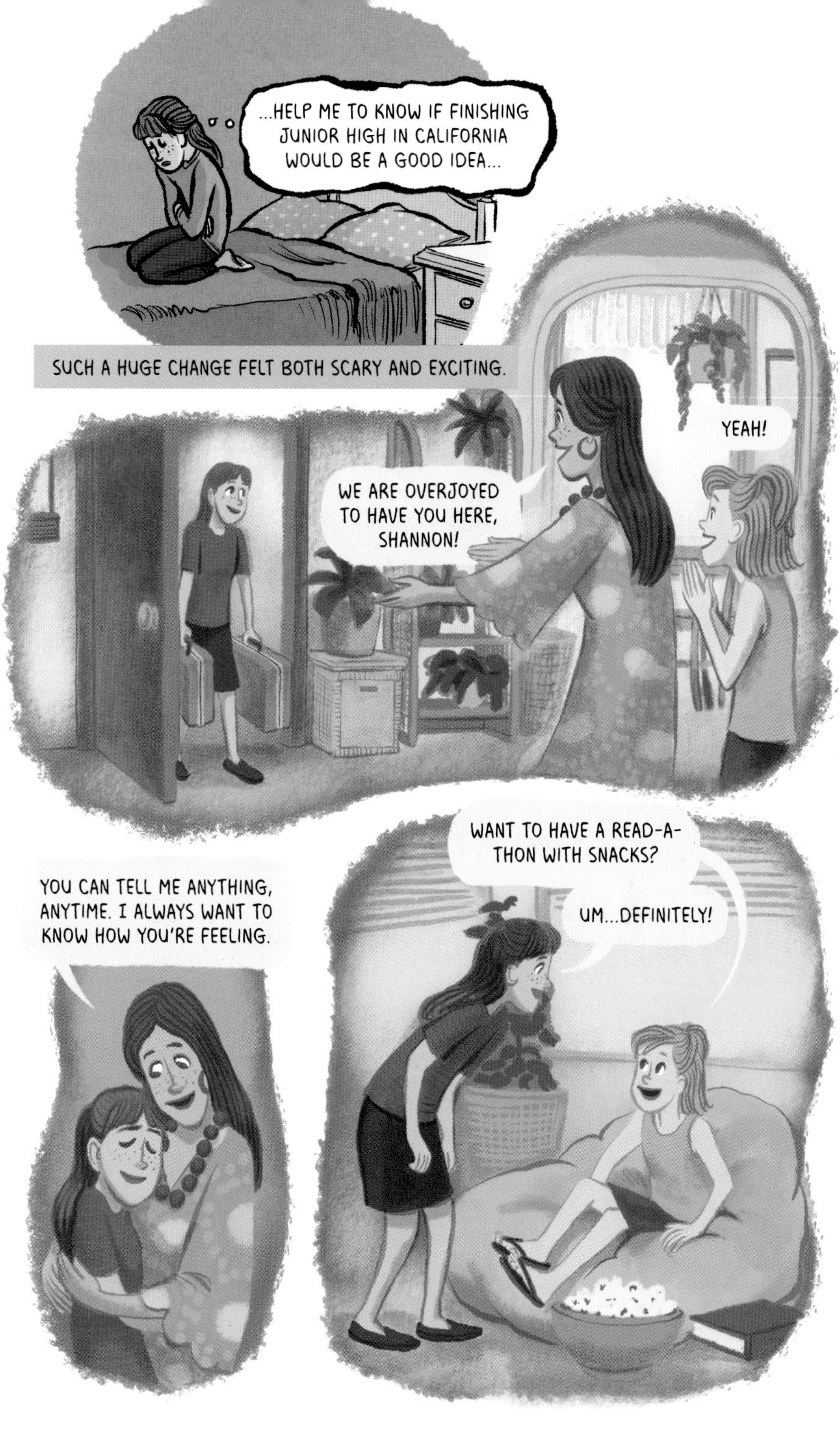
...HELP ME TO KNOW IF FINISHING JUNIOR HIGH IN CALIFORNIA WOULD BE A GOOD IDEA...
SUCH A HUGE CHANGE FELT BOTH SCARY AND EXCITING.
WE ARE OVERJOYED TO HAVE YOU HERE, SHANNON!
YEAH!
YOU CAN TELL ME ANYTHING, ANYTIME. I ALWAYS WANT TO KNOW HOW YOU'RE FEELING.
WANT TO HAVE A READ-A-THON WITH SNACKS?
UM...DEFINITELY!

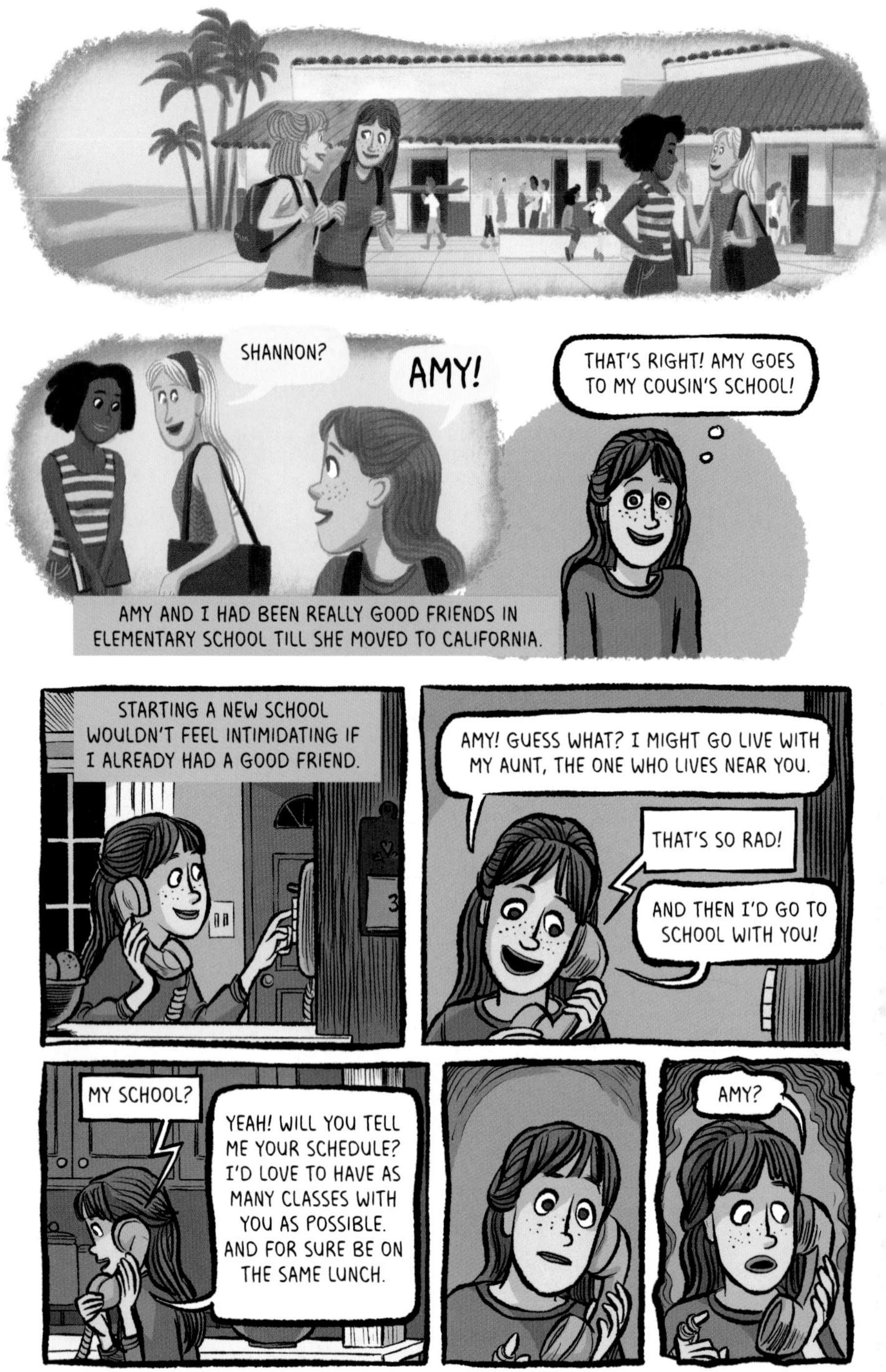
SHANNON?
AMY!
THAT'S RIGHT! AMY GOES TO MY COUSIN'S SCHOOL!
AMY AND I HAD BEEN REALLY GOOD FRIENDS IN ELEMENTARY SCHOOL TILL SHE MOVED TO CALIFORNIA.
STARTING A NEW SCHOOL WOULDN'T FEEL INTIMIDATING IF I ALREADY HAD A GOOD FRIEND.
AMY! GUESS WHAT? I MIGHT GO LIVE WITH MY AUNT, THE ONE WHO LIVES NEAR YOU.
THAT'S SO RAD!
AND THEN I'D GO TO SCHOOL WITH YOU!
MY SCHOOL?
YEAH! WILL YOU TELL ME YOUR SCHEDULE? I'D LOVE TO HAVE AS MANY CLASSES WITH YOU AS POSSIBLE. AND FOR SURE BE ON THE SAME LUNCH.
AMY?

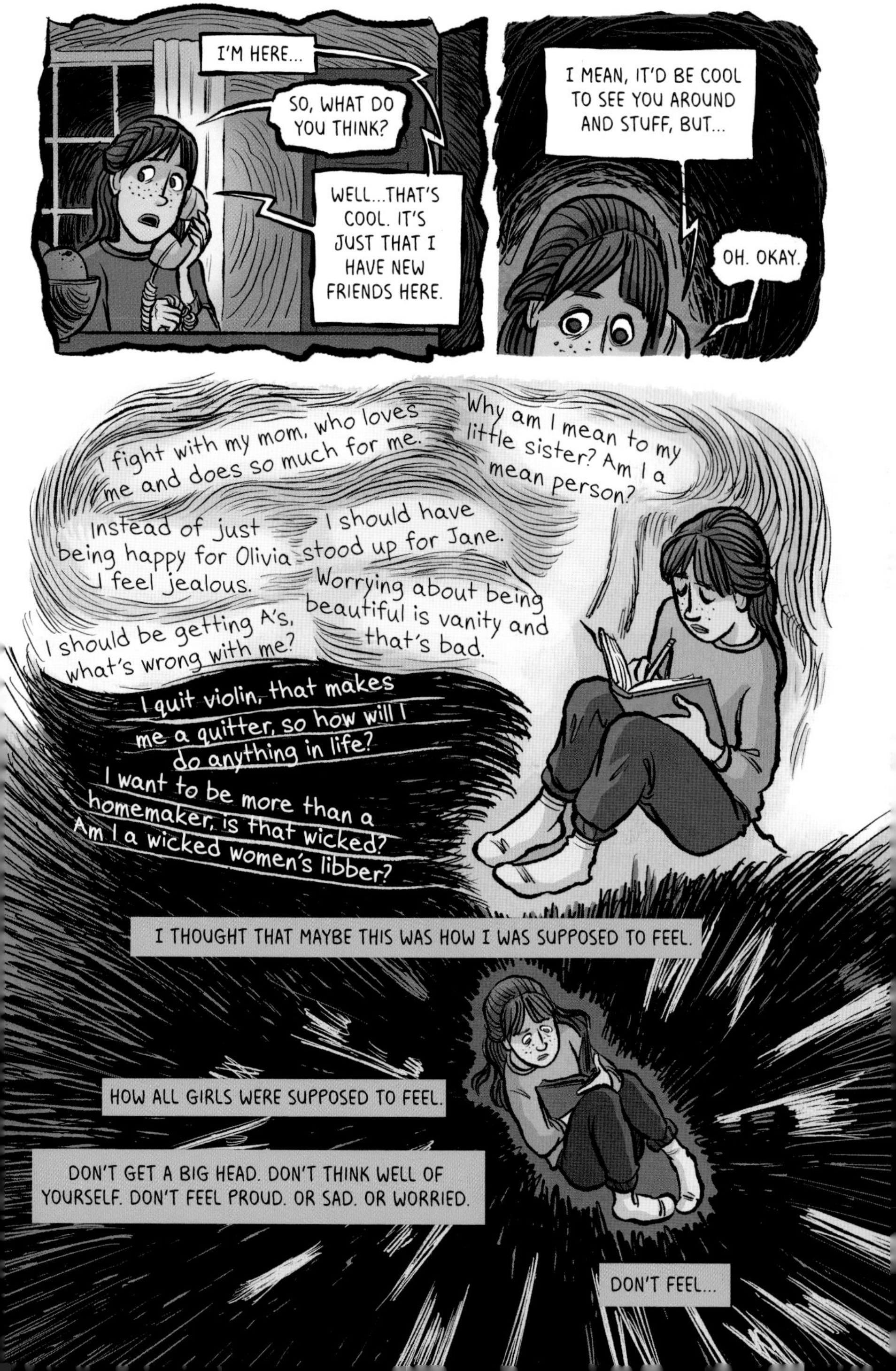

I'M HERE...
SO, WHAT DO YOU THINK?
WELL...THAT'S COOL. IT'S JUST THAT I HAVE NEW FRIENDS HERE.
I MEAN, IT'D BE COOL TO SEE YOU AROUND AND STUFF, BUT...
OH. OKAY.
I fight with my mom, who loves me and does so much for me.
Why am I mean to my little sister? Am I a mean person?
Instead of just being happy for Olivia I feel jealous.
I should have stood up for Jane.
Worrying about being beautiful is vanity and that's bad.
I should be getting A's, what's wrong with me?
I quit violin, that makes me a quitter, so how will I do anything in life?
I want to be more than a homemaker, is that wicked? Am I a wicked women's libber?
I THOUGHT THAT MAYBE THIS WAS HOW I WAS SUPPOSED TO FEEL.
HOW ALL GIRLS WERE SUPPOSED TO FEEL.
DON'T GET A BIG HEAD. DON'T THINK WELL OF YOURSELF. DON'T FEEL PROUD. OR SAD. OR WORRIED.
DON'T FEEL...

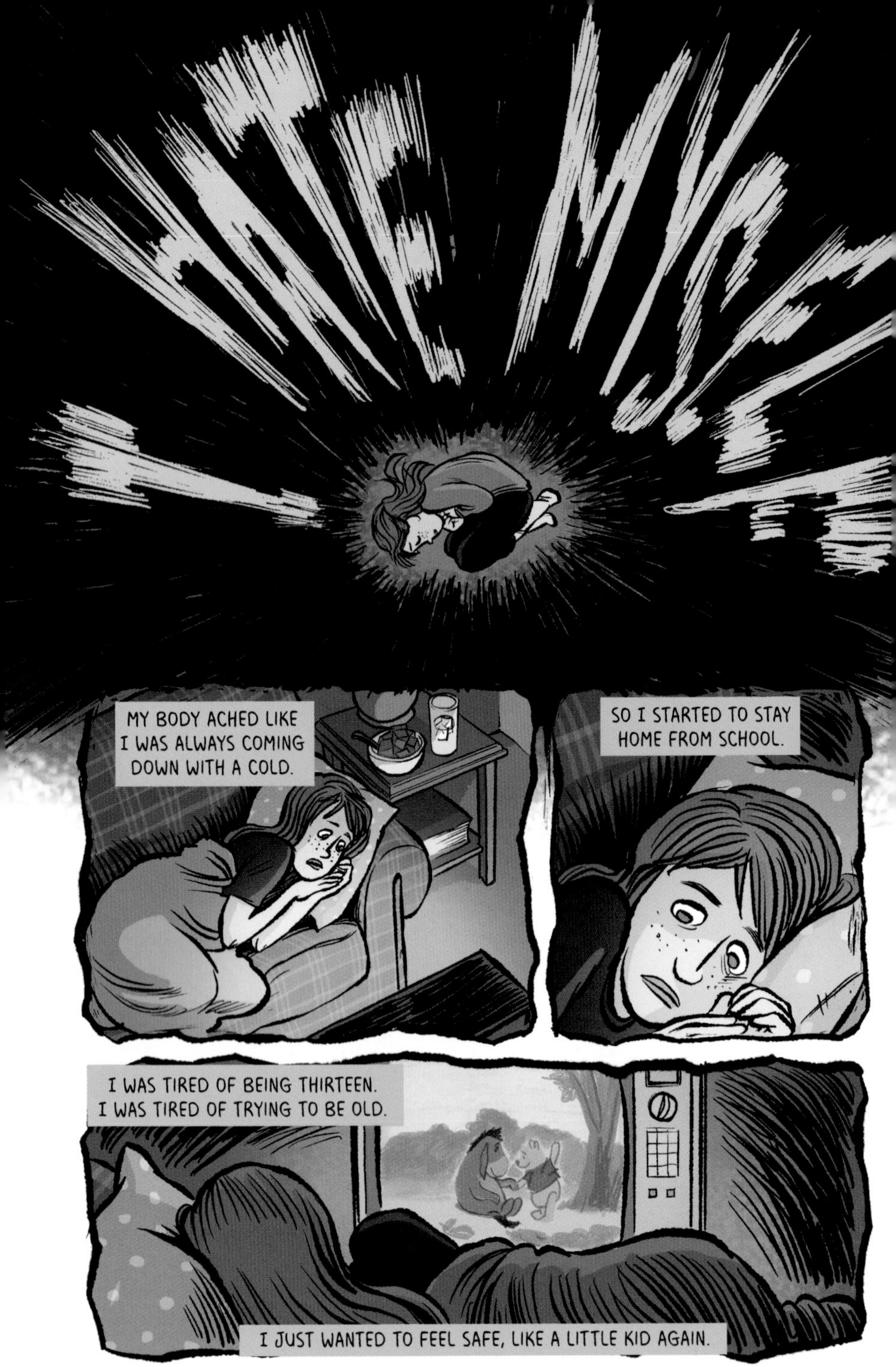
MY BODY ACHED LIKE I WAS ALWAYS COMING DOWN WITH A COLD.
SO I STARTED TO STAY HOME FROM SCHOOL.
I WAS TIRED OF BEING THIRTEEN. I WAS TIRED OF TRYING TO BE OLD.
I JUST WANTED TO FEEL SAFE, LIKE A LITTLE KID AGAIN.

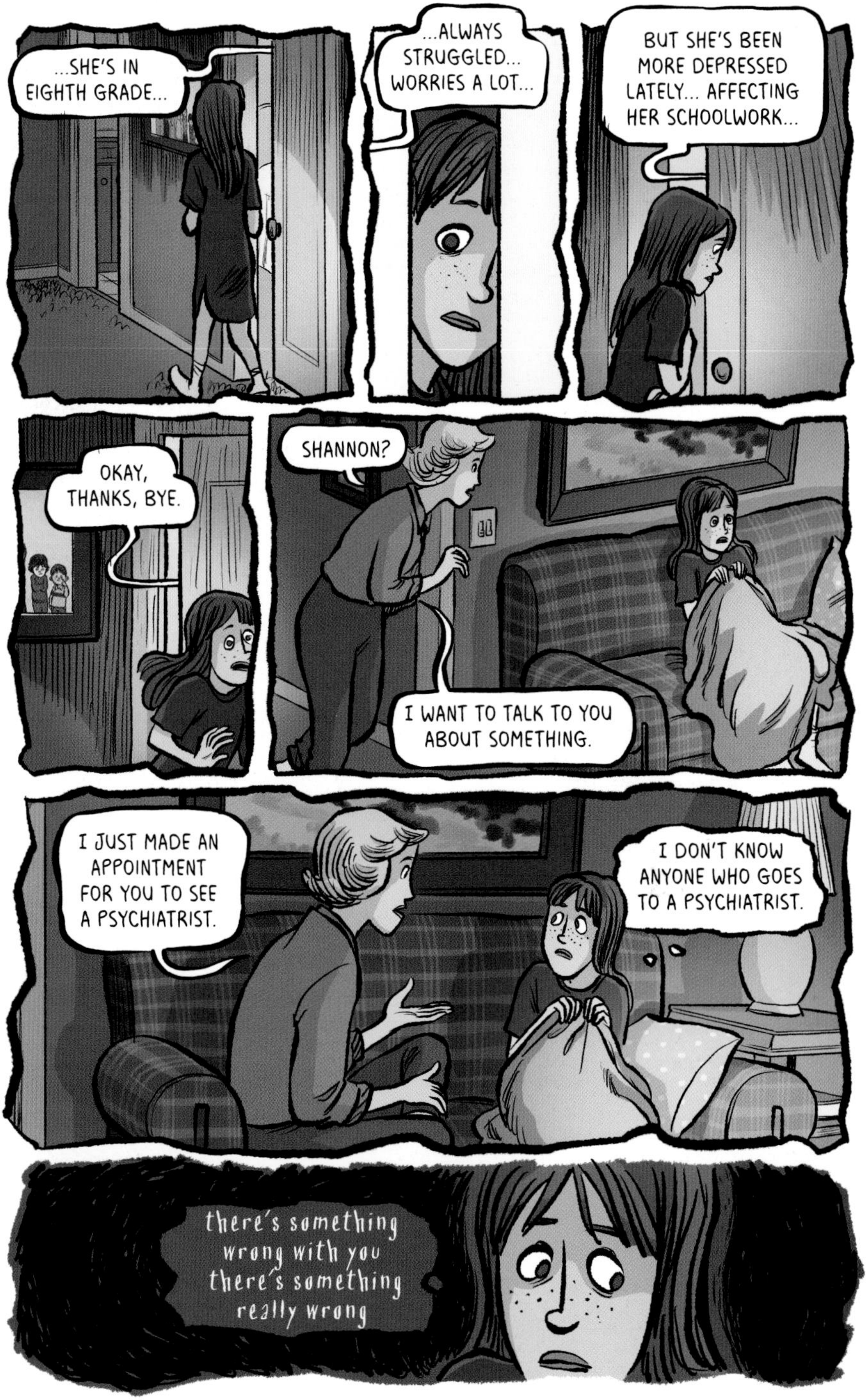
...SHE'S IN EIGHTH GRADE...
...ALWAYS STRUGGLED... WORRIES A LOT...
BUT SHE'S BEEN MORE DEPRESSED LATELY... AFFECTING HER SCHOOLWORK...
OKAY, THANKS, BYE.
SHANNON?
I WANT TO TALK TO YOU ABOUT SOMETHING.
I JUST MADE AN APPOINTMENT FOR YOU TO SEE A PSYCHIATRIST.
I DON'T KNOW ANYONE WHO GOES TO A PSYCHIATRIST.
there's something wrong with you there's something really wrong

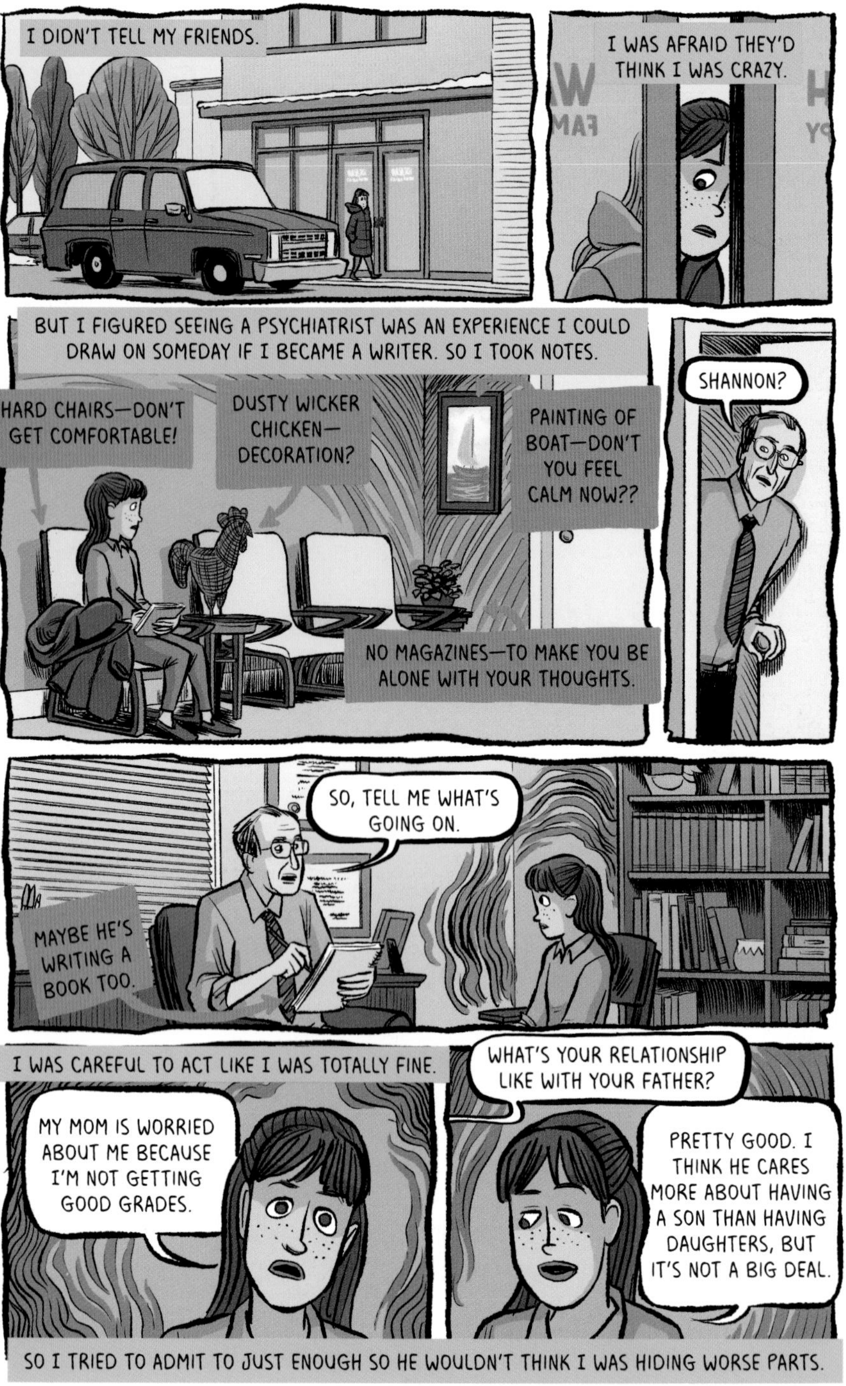
I DIDN'T TELL MY FRIENDS.
I WAS AFRAID THEY'D THINK I WAS CRAZY.
BUT I FIGURED SEEING A PSYCHIATRIST WAS AN EXPERIENCE I COULD DRAW ON SOMEDAY IF I BECAME A WRITER. SO I TOOK NOTES.
HARD CHAIRS—DON'T GET COMFORTABLE!
DUSTY WICKER CHICKEN—DECORATION?
PAINTING OF BOAT—DON'T YOU FEEL CALM NOW??
NO MAGAZINES—TO MAKE YOU BE ALONE WITH YOUR THOUGHTS.
SHANNON?
SO, TELL ME WHAT'S GOING ON.
MAYBE HE'S WRITING A BOOK TOO.
I WAS CAREFUL TO ACT LIKE I WAS TOTALLY FINE.
MY MOM IS WORRIED ABOUT ME BECAUSE I'M NOT GETTING GOOD GRADES.
WHAT'S YOUR RELATIONSHIP LIKE WITH YOUR FATHER?
PRETTY GOOD. I THINK HE CARES MORE ABOUT HAVING A SON THAN HAVING DAUGHTERS, BUT IT'S NOT A BIG DEAL.
SO I TRIED TO ADMIT TO JUST ENOUGH SO HE WOULDN'T THINK I WAS HIDING WORSE PARTS.

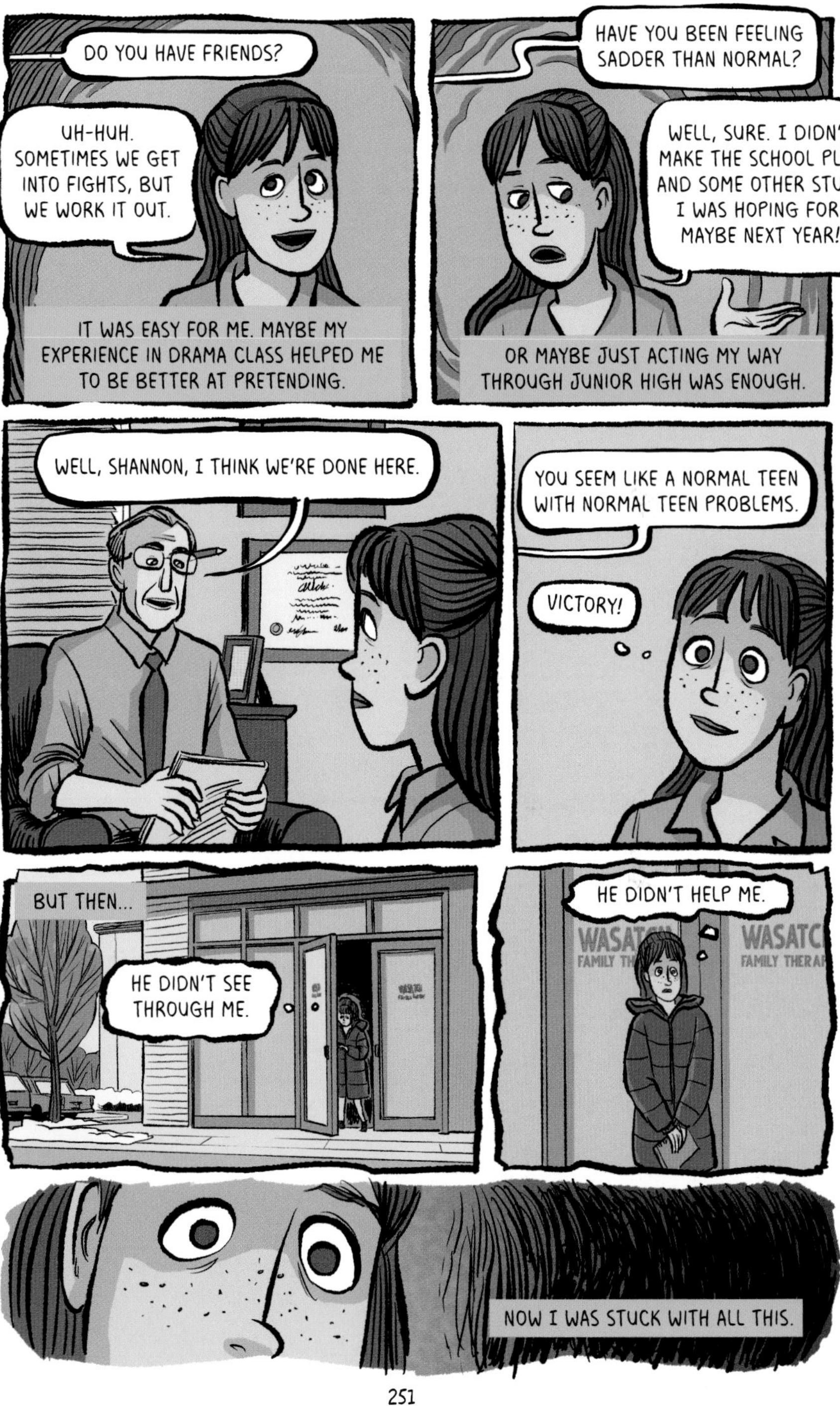
DO YOU HAVE FRIENDS?
UH-HUH. SOMETIMES WE GET INTO FIGHTS, BUT WE WORK IT OUT.
IT WAS EASY FOR ME. MAYBE MY EXPERIENCE IN DRAMA CLASS HELPED ME TO BE BETTER AT PRETENDING.
HAVE YOU BEEN FEELING SADDER THAN NORMAL?
WELL, SURE. I DIDN'T MAKE THE SCHOOL PLAY AND SOME OTHER STUFF I WAS HOPING FOR. MAYBE NEXT YEAR!
OR MAYBE JUST ACTING MY WAY THROUGH JUNIOR HIGH WAS ENOUGH.
WELL, SHANNON, I THINK WE'RE DONE HERE.
YOU SEEM LIKE A NORMAL TEEN WITH NORMAL TEEN PROBLEMS.
VICTORY!
BUT THEN...
HE DIDN'T SEE THROUGH ME.
HE DIDN'T HELP ME.
WASATC
FAMILY TH
WASATC
FAMILY THERA
NOW I WAS STUCK WITH ALL THIS.

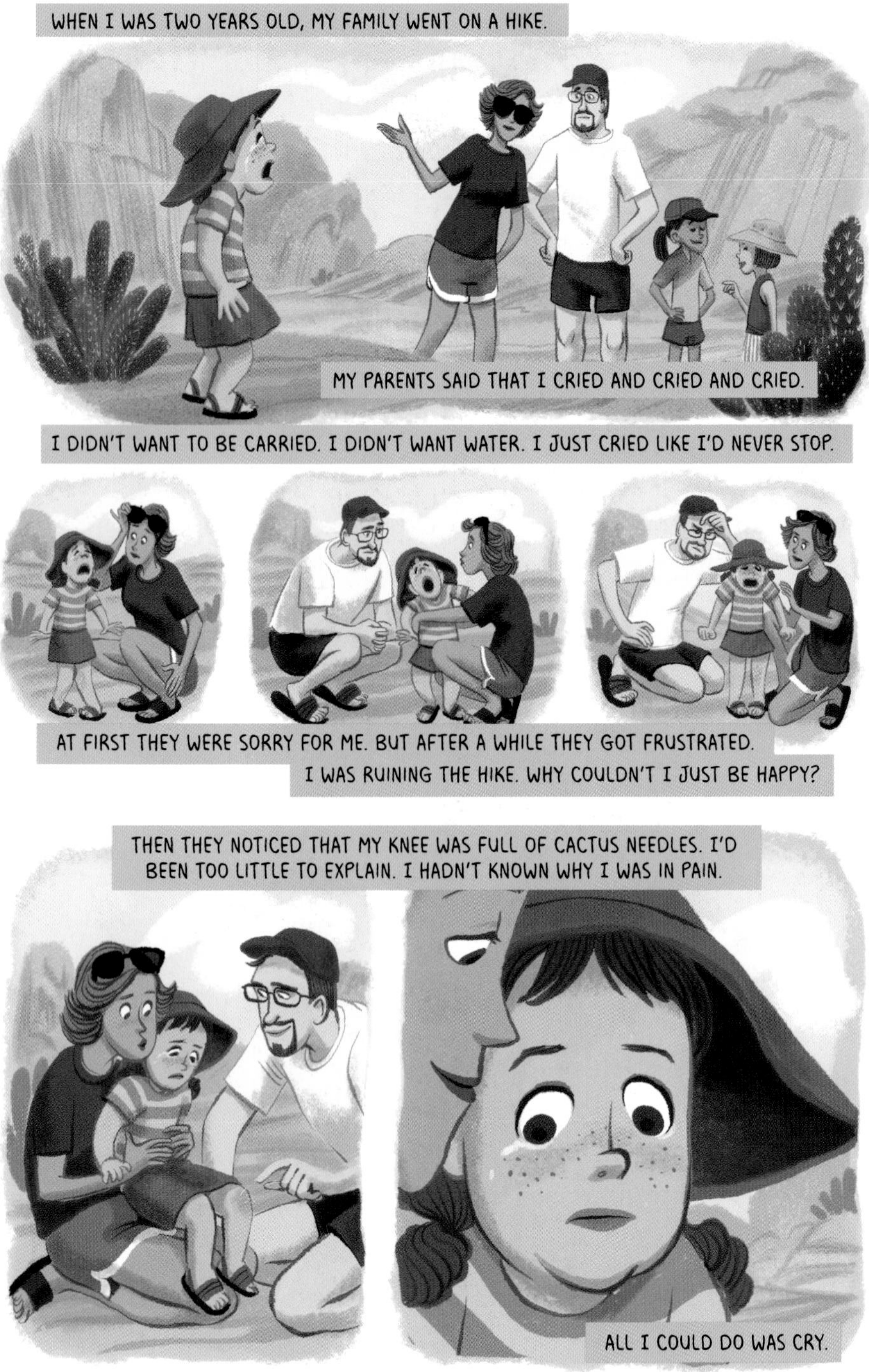
WHEN I WAS TWO YEARS OLD, MY FAMILY WENT ON A HIKE.
MY PARENTS SAID THAT I CRIED AND CRIED AND CRIED.
I DIDN'T WANT TO BE CARRIED. I DIDN'T WANT WATER. I JUST CRIED LIKE I'D NEVER STOP.
AT FIRST THEY WERE SORRY FOR ME. BUT AFTER A WHILE THEY GOT FRUSTRATED.
I WAS RUINING THE HIKE. WHY COULDN'T I JUST BE HAPPY?
THEN THEY NOTICED THAT MY KNEE WAS FULL OF CACTUS NEEDLES. I'D BEEN TOO LITTLE TO EXPLAIN. I HADN'T KNOWN WHY I WAS IN PAIN.
ALL I COULD DO WAS CRY.

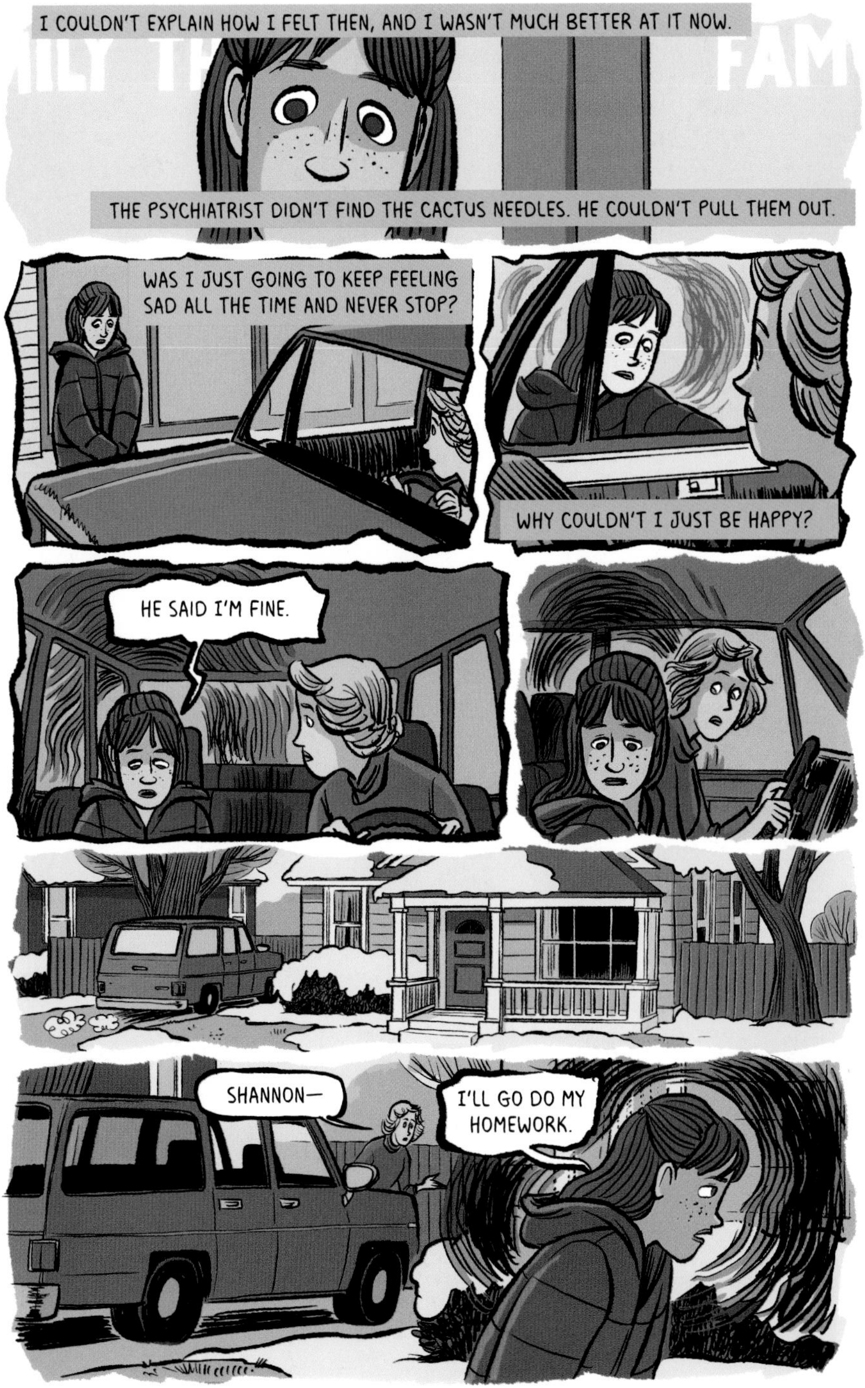
I COULDN'T EXPLAIN HOW I FELT THEN, AND I WASN'T MUCH BETTER AT IT NOW.
ILY TH
FAM
THE PSYCHIATRIST DIDN'T FIND THE CACTUS NEEDLES. HE COULDN'T PULL THEM OUT.
WAS I JUST GOING TO KEEP FEELING SAD ALL THE TIME AND NEVER STOP?
WHY COULDN'T I JUST BE HAPPY?
HE SAID I'M FINE.
SHANNON—
I'LL GO DO MY HOMEWORK.

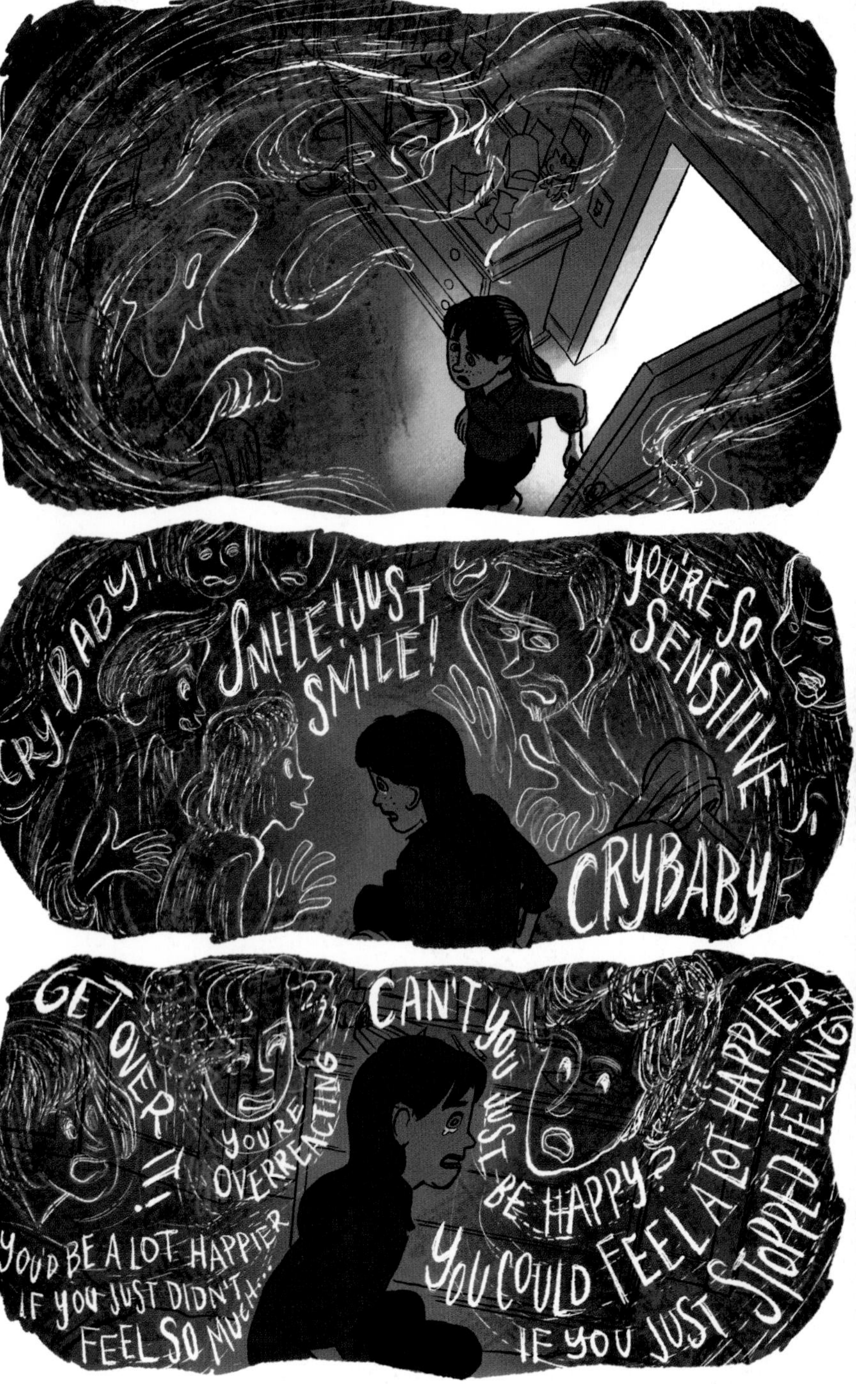
CRYBABY!!
SMILE! JUST SMILE!
YOU'RE SO SENSITIVE
CRYBABY
GET OVER IT!!
YOU'RE OVERREACTING
CAN'T YOU JUST BE HAPPY?
YOU'D BE A LOT HAPPIER IF YOU JUST DIDN'T FEEL SO MUCH...
YOU COULD FEEL A LOT HAPPIER IF YOU JUST STOPPED FEELING

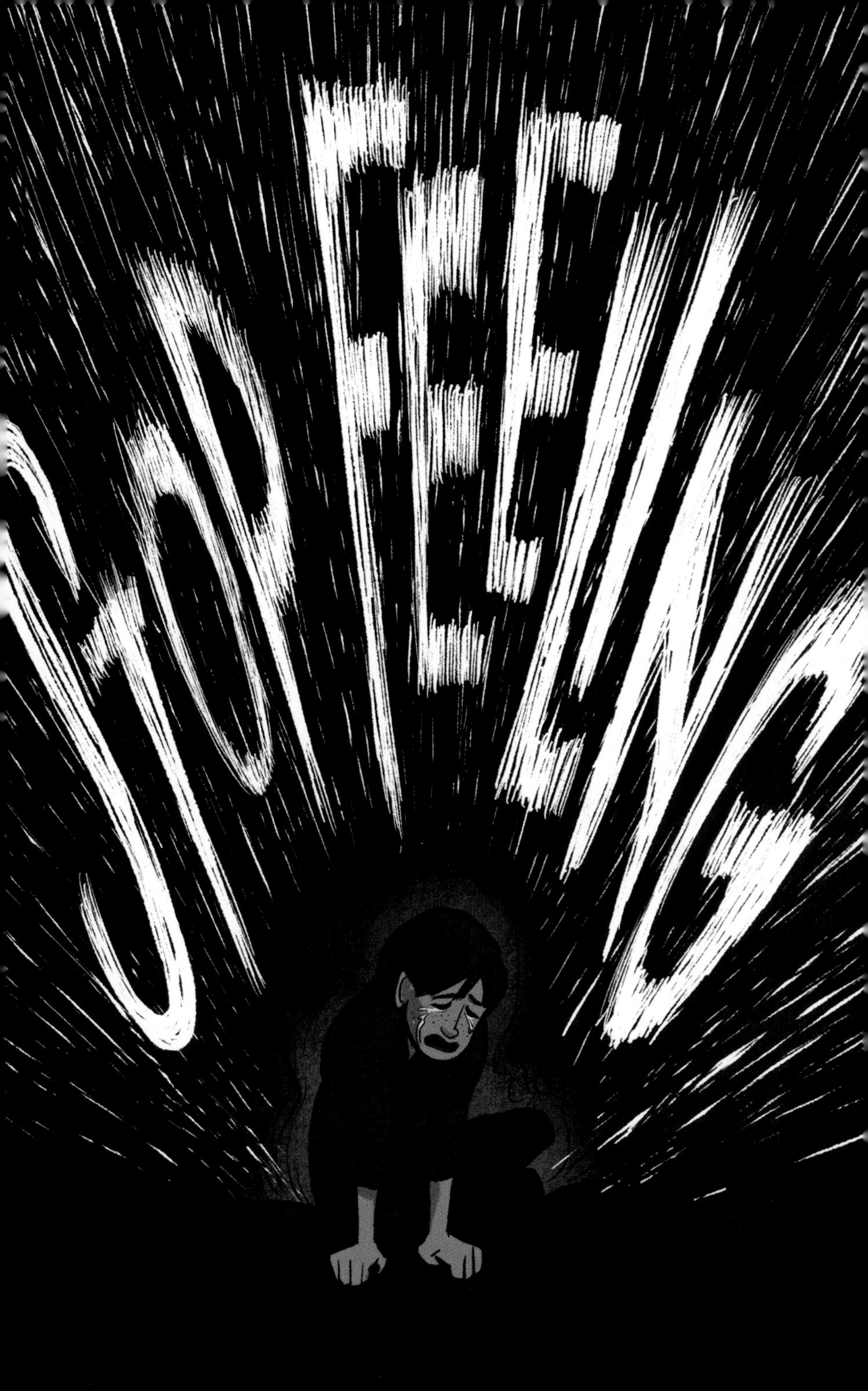

CHAPTER 7

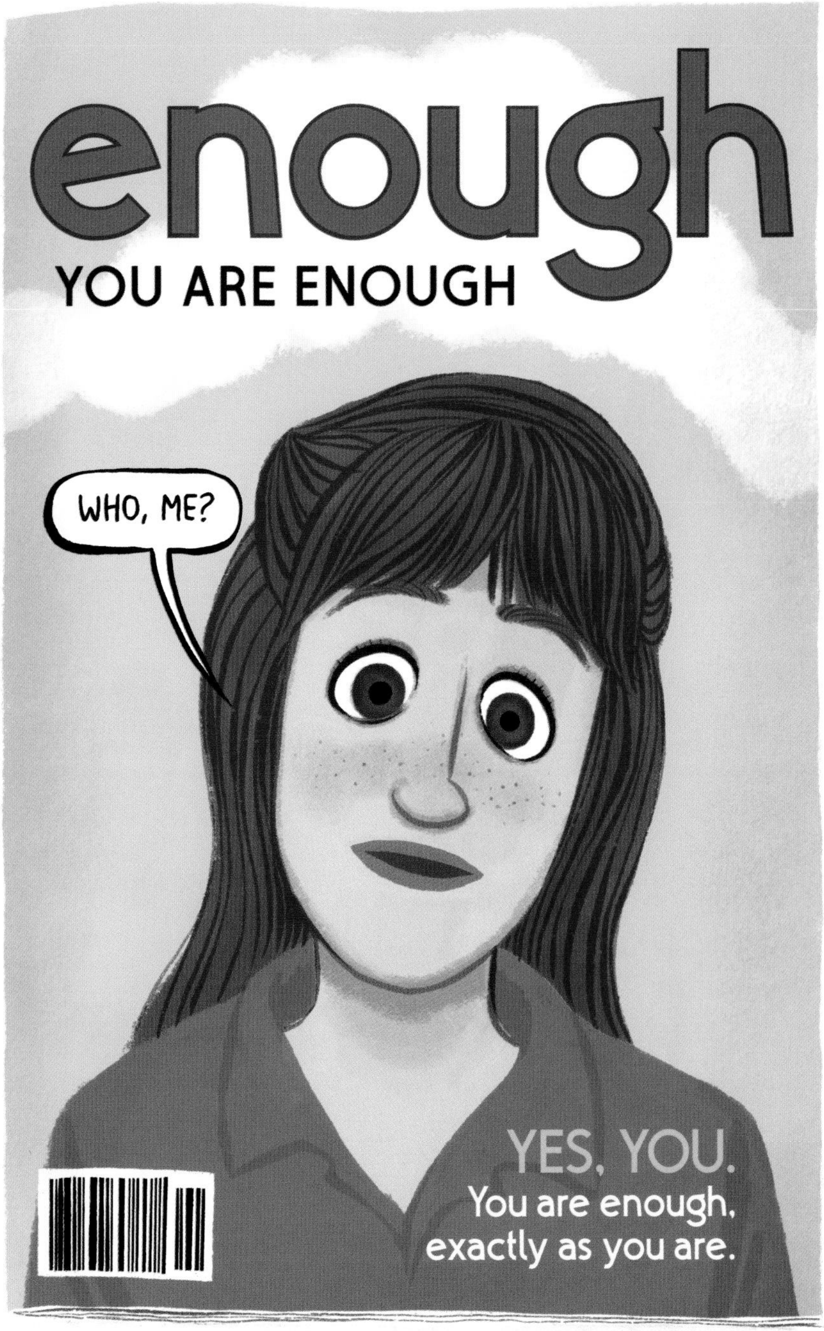
enough
YOU ARE ENOUGH
WHO, ME?
YES, YOU.
You are enough,
exactly as you are.

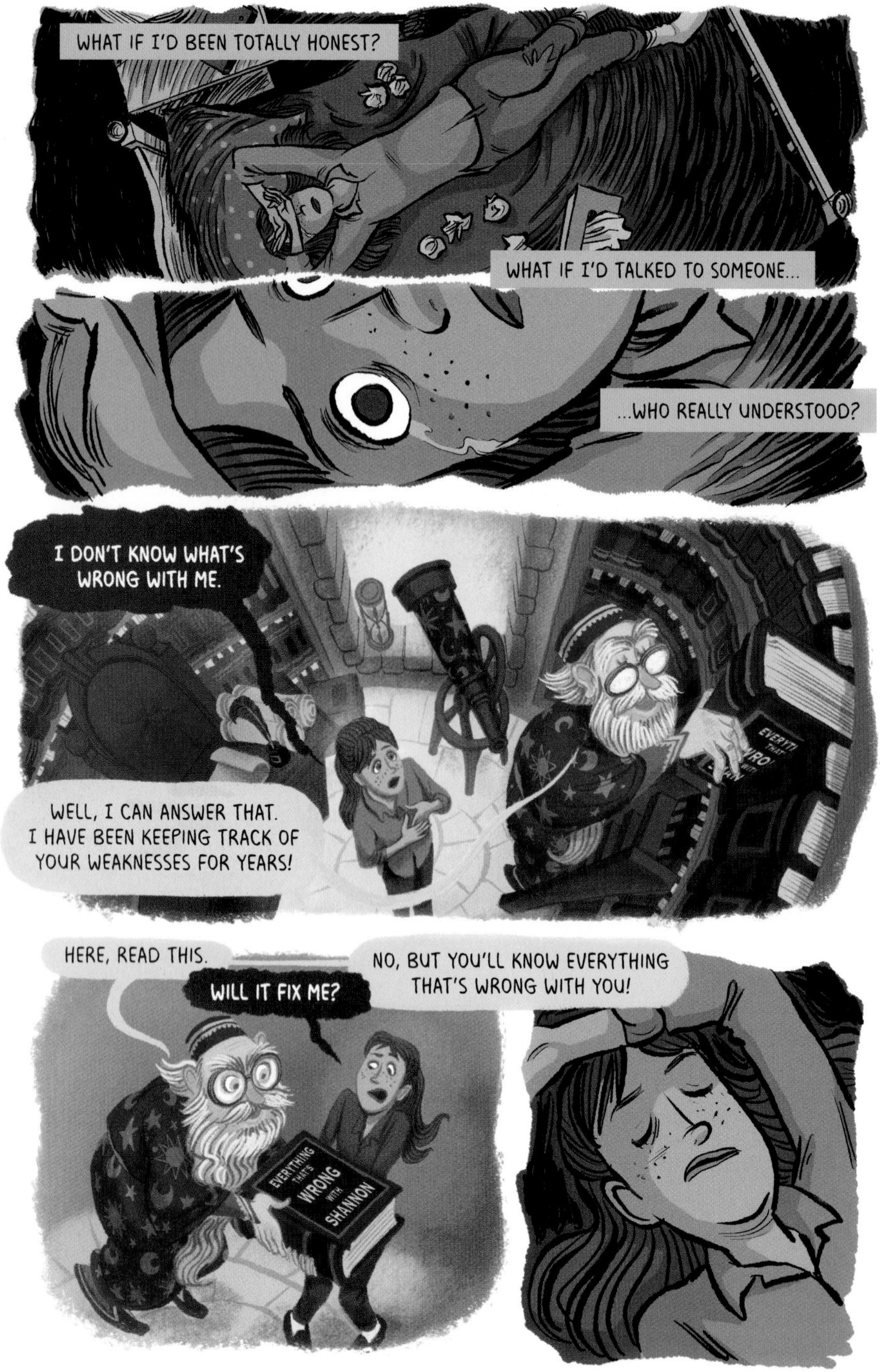
WHAT IF I'D BEEN TOTALLY HONEST?
WHAT IF I'D TALKED TO SOMEONE...
...WHO REALLY UNDERSTOOD?
I DON'T KNOW WHAT'S WRONG WITH ME.
WELL, I CAN ANSWER THAT. I HAVE BEEN KEEPING TRACK OF YOUR WEAKNESSES FOR YEARS!
HERE, READ THIS.
WILL IT FIX ME?
NO, BUT YOU'LL KNOW EVERYTHING THAT'S WRONG WITH YOU!
EVERYTHING THAT'S WRONG WITH SHANNON

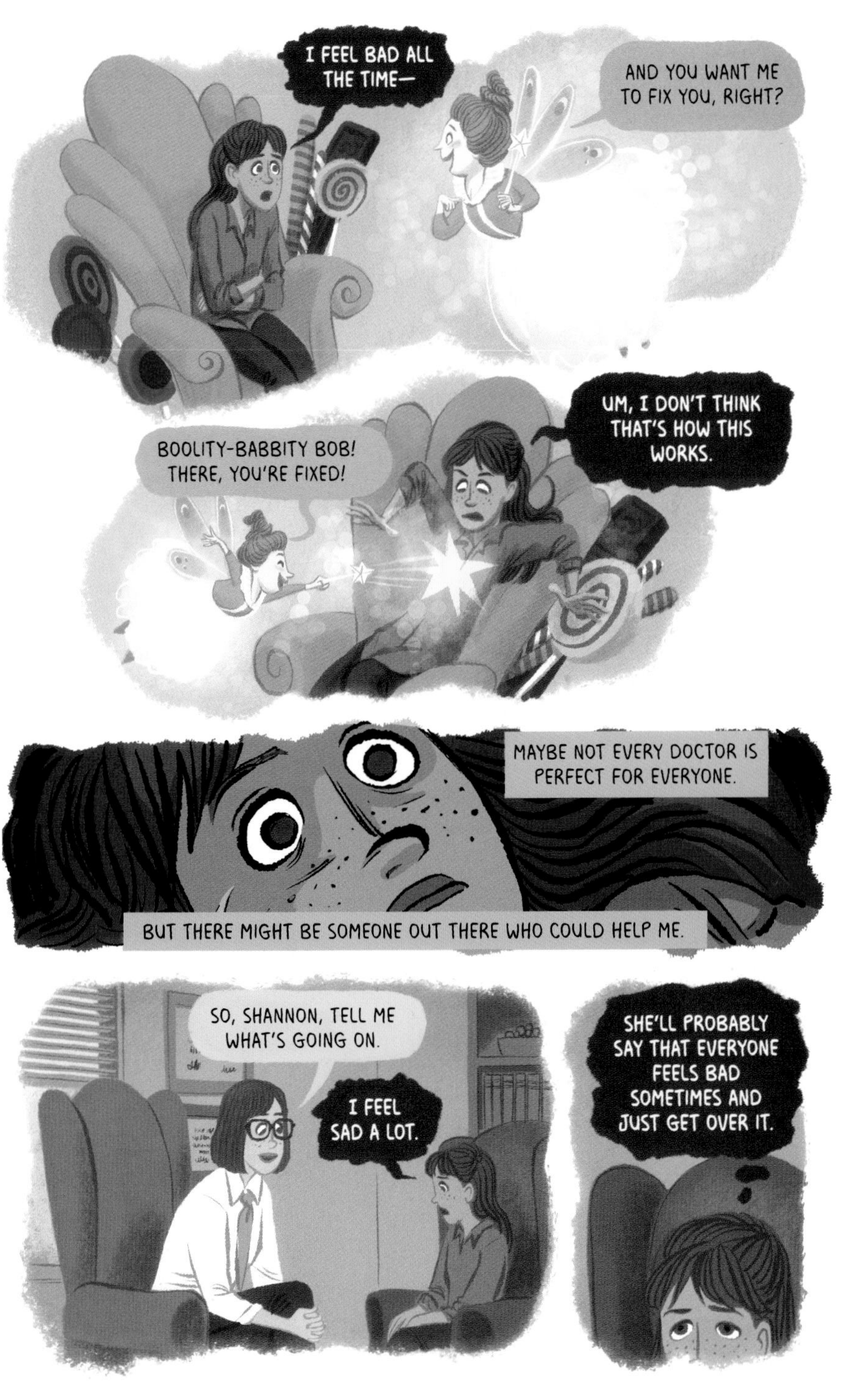
I FEEL BAD ALL THE TIME—
AND YOU WANT ME TO FIX YOU, RIGHT?
BOOLITY-BABBITY BOB! THERE, YOU'RE FIXED!
UM, I DON'T THINK THAT'S HOW THIS WORKS.
MAYBE NOT EVERY DOCTOR IS PERFECT FOR EVERYONE.
BUT THERE MIGHT BE SOMEONE OUT THERE WHO COULD HELP ME.
SO, SHANNON, TELL ME WHAT'S GOING ON.
I FEEL SAD A LOT.
SHE'LL PROBABLY SAY THAT EVERYONE FEELS BAD SOMETIMES AND JUST GET OVER IT.

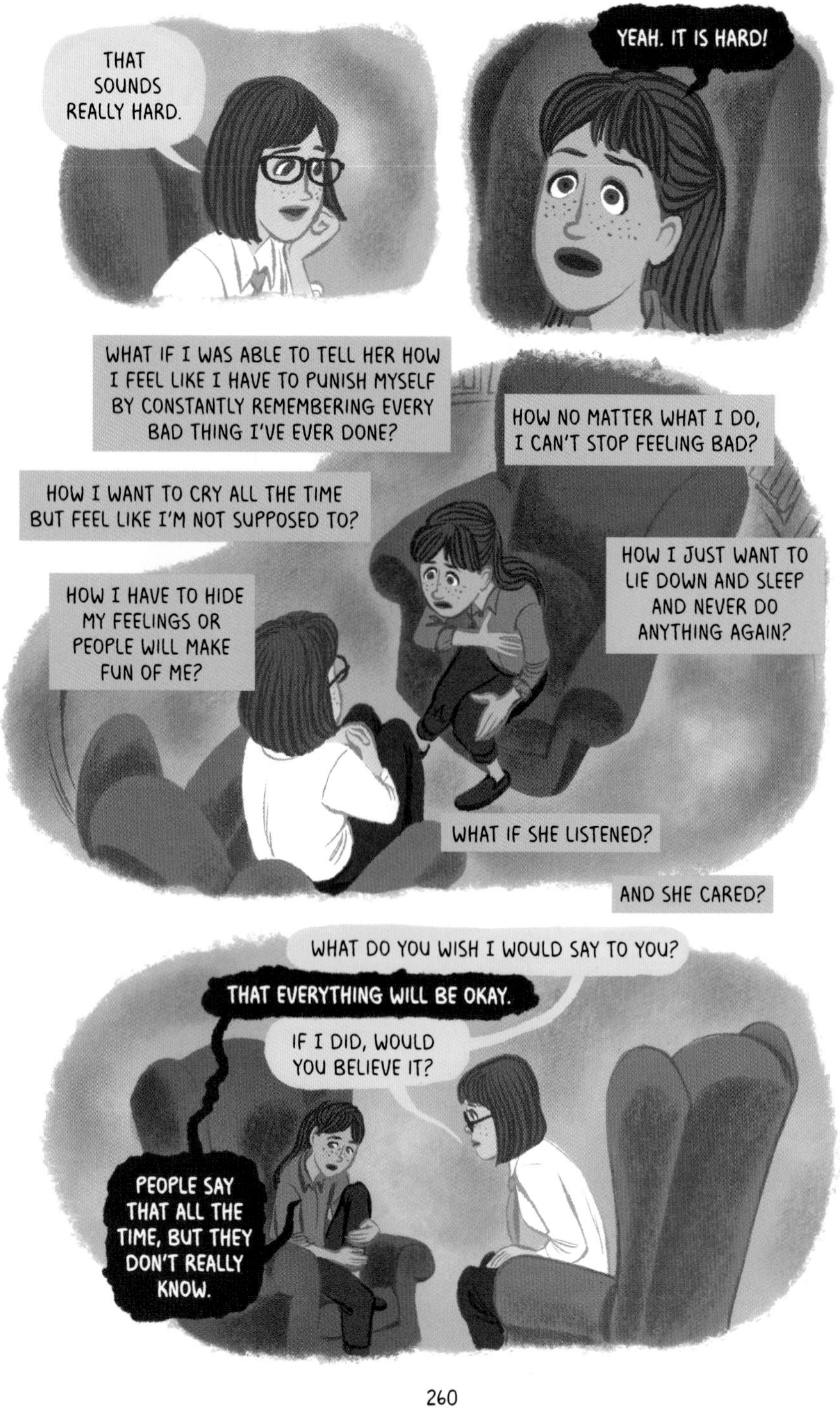
THAT SOUNDS REALLY HARD.
YEAH. IT IS HARD!
WHAT IF I WAS ABLE TO TELL HER HOW I FEEL LIKE I HAVE TO PUNISH MYSELF BY CONSTANTLY REMEMBERING EVERY BAD THING I'VE EVER DONE?
HOW NO MATTER WHAT I DO, I CAN'T STOP FEELING BAD?
HOW I WANT TO CRY ALL THE TIME BUT FEEL LIKE I'M NOT SUPPOSED TO?
HOW I JUST WANT TO LIE DOWN AND SLEEP AND NEVER DO ANYTHING AGAIN?
HOW I HAVE TO HIDE MY FEELINGS OR PEOPLE WILL MAKE FUN OF ME?
WHAT IF SHE LISTENED?
AND SHE CARED?
WHAT DO YOU WISH I WOULD SAY TO YOU?
THAT EVERYTHING WILL BE OKAY.
IF I DID, WOULD YOU BELIEVE IT?
PEOPLE SAY THAT ALL THE TIME, BUT THEY DON'T REALLY KNOW.

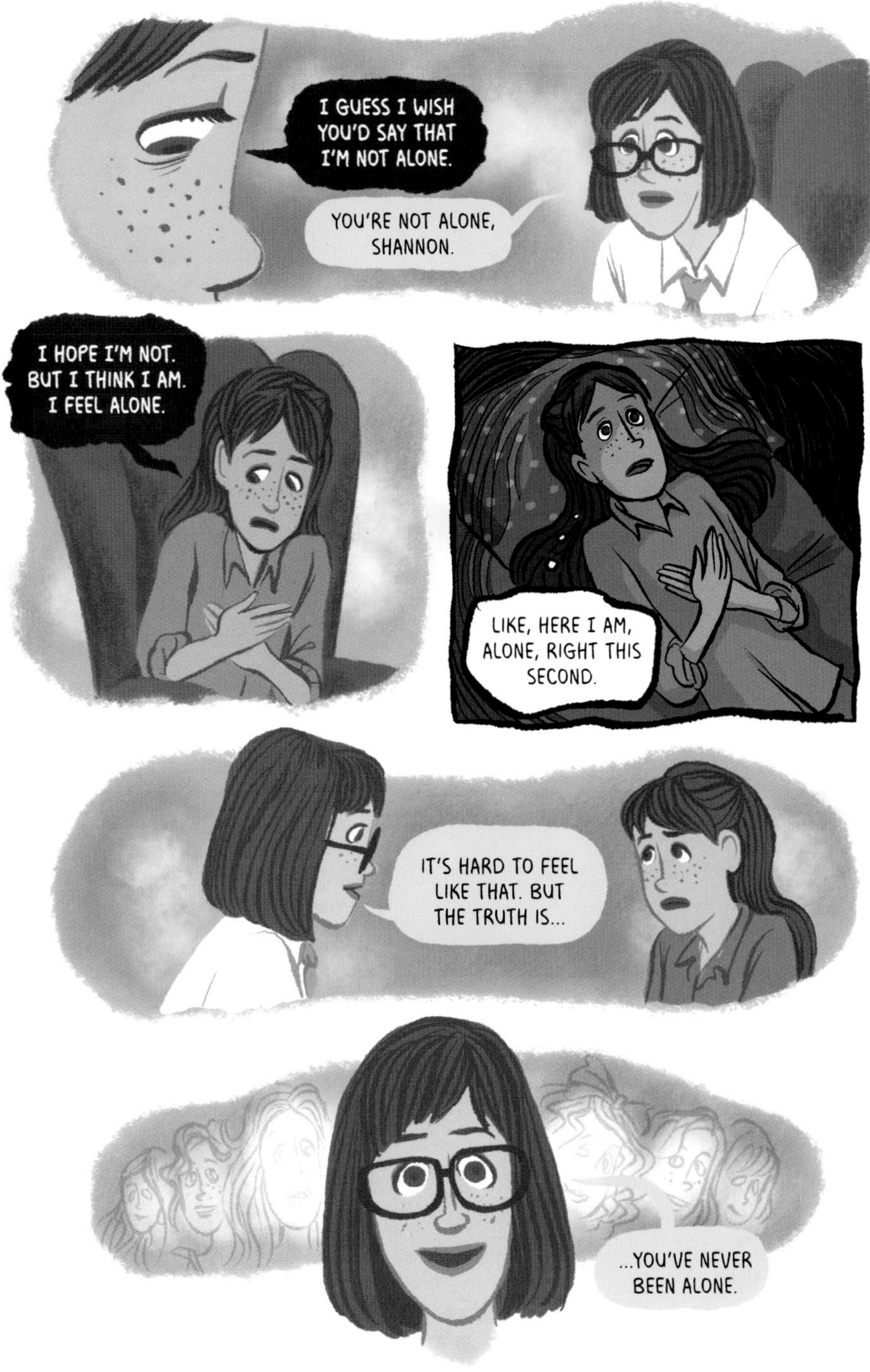
I GUESS I WISH YOU'D SAY THAT I'M NOT ALONE.
YOU'RE NOT ALONE, SHANNON.
I HOPE I'M NOT. BUT I THINK I AM. I FEEL ALONE.
LIKE, HERE I AM, ALONE, RIGHT THIS SECOND.
IT'S HARD TO FEEL LIKE THAT. BUT THE TRUTH IS...
...YOU'VE NEVER BEEN ALONE.

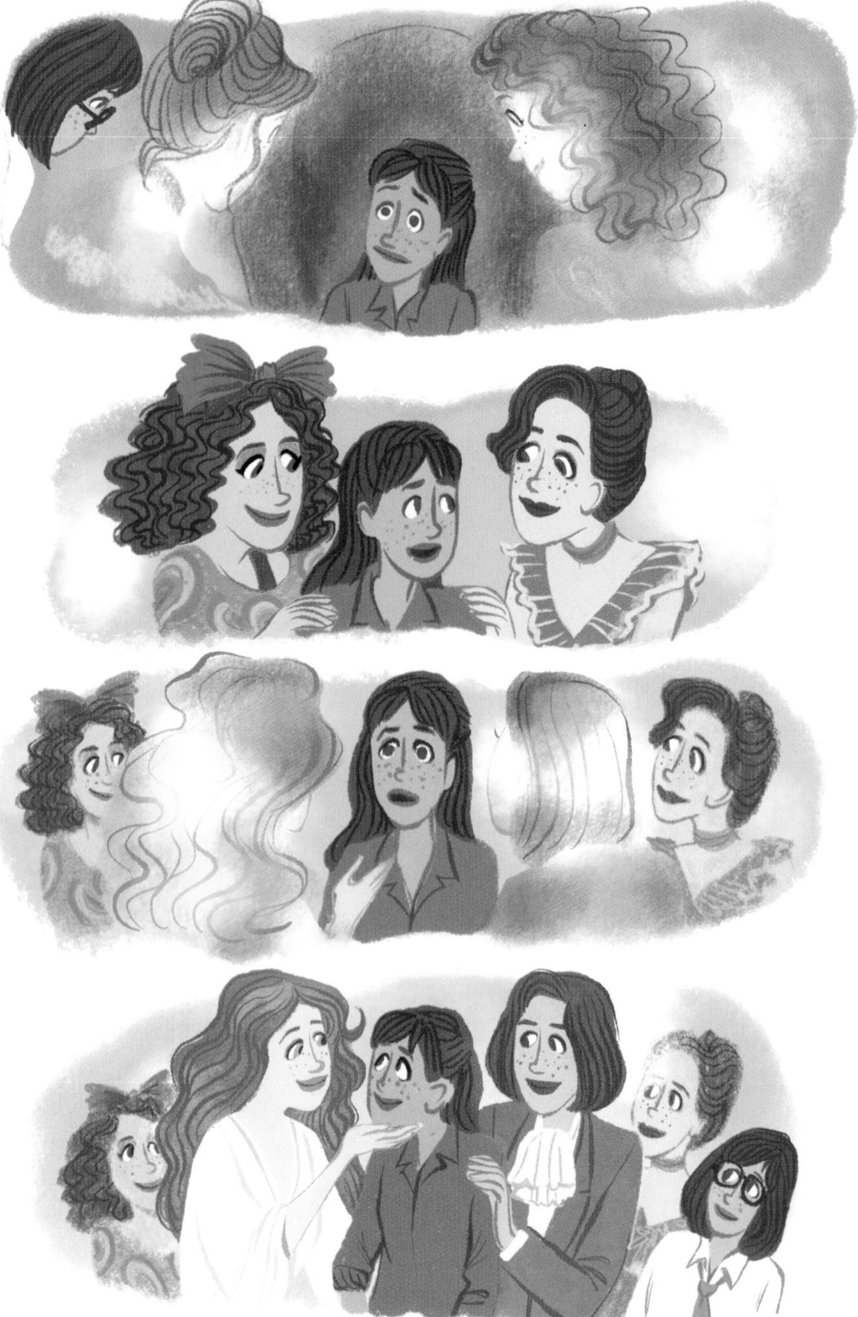

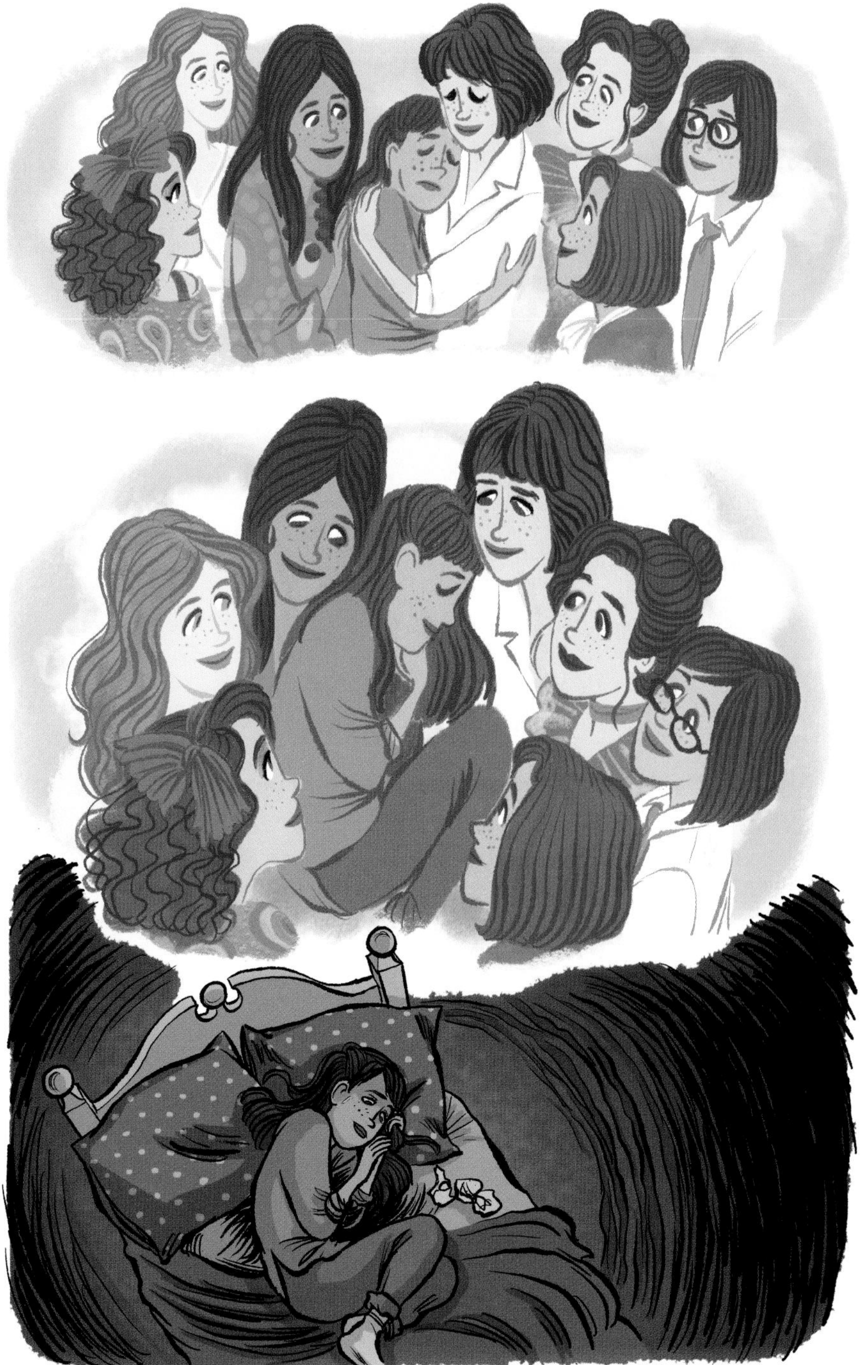

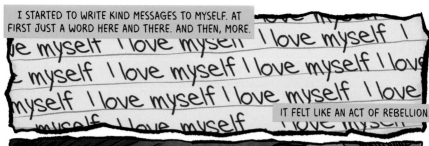

I STARTED TO WRITE KIND MESSAGES TO MYSELF. AT FIRST JUST A WORD HERE AND THERE. AND THEN, MORE.

IT FELT LIKE AN ACT OF REBELLION.

TO CHOOSE TO LOVE MYSELF EVEN IF I WASN'T SURE ANYBODY ELSE DID.

EVEN IF I WASN'T SURE I WAS WORTHY ENOUGH.

EVEN IF I WASN'T SURE THAT I ACTUALLY DID.

TO TRY TO LOVE MYSELF. THAT FELT LIKE A LOT.

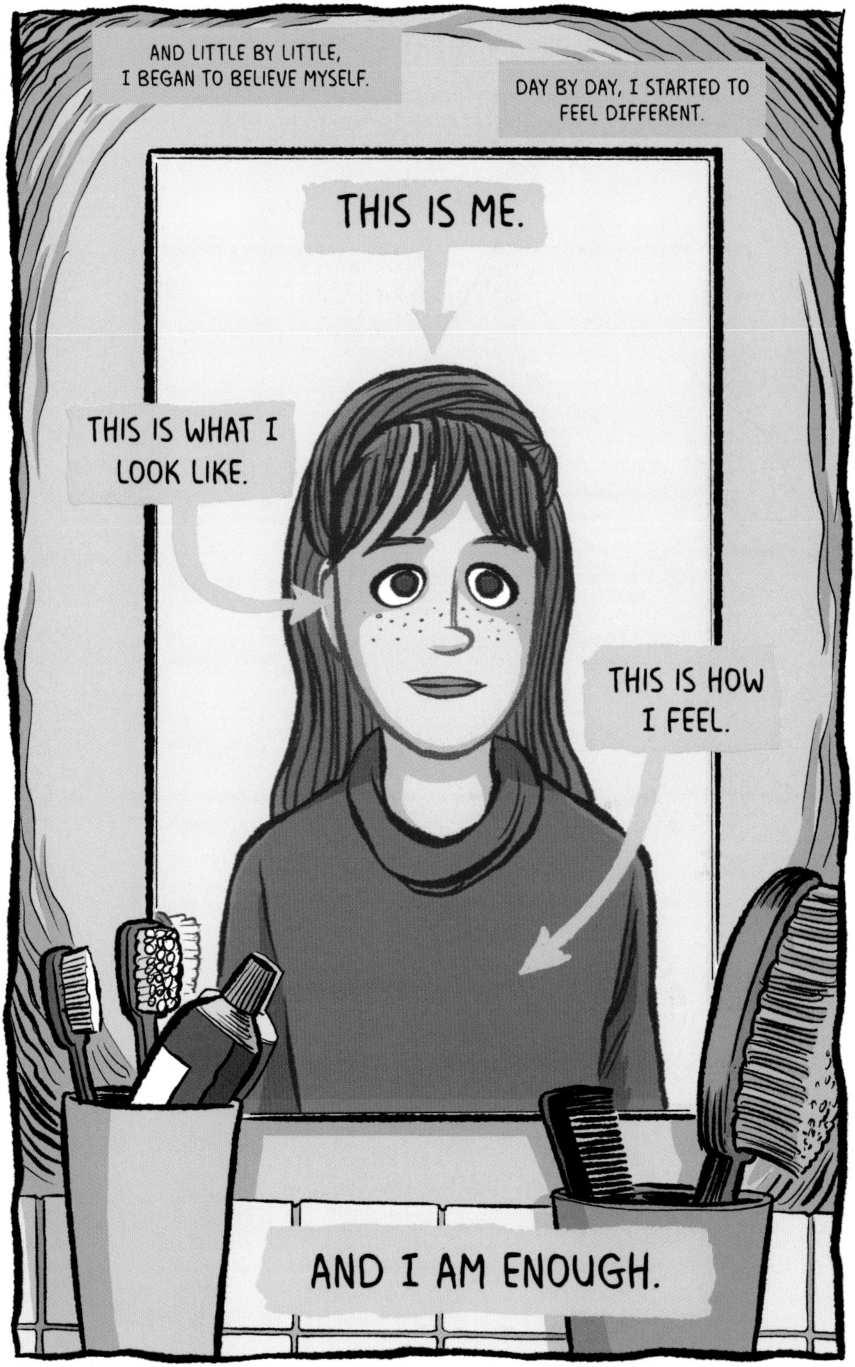
AND LITTLE BY LITTLE, I BEGAN TO BELIEVE MYSELF.
DAY BY DAY, I STARTED TO FEEL DIFFERENT.
THIS IS ME.
THIS IS WHAT I LOOK LIKE.
THIS IS HOW I FEEL.
AND I AM ENOUGH.

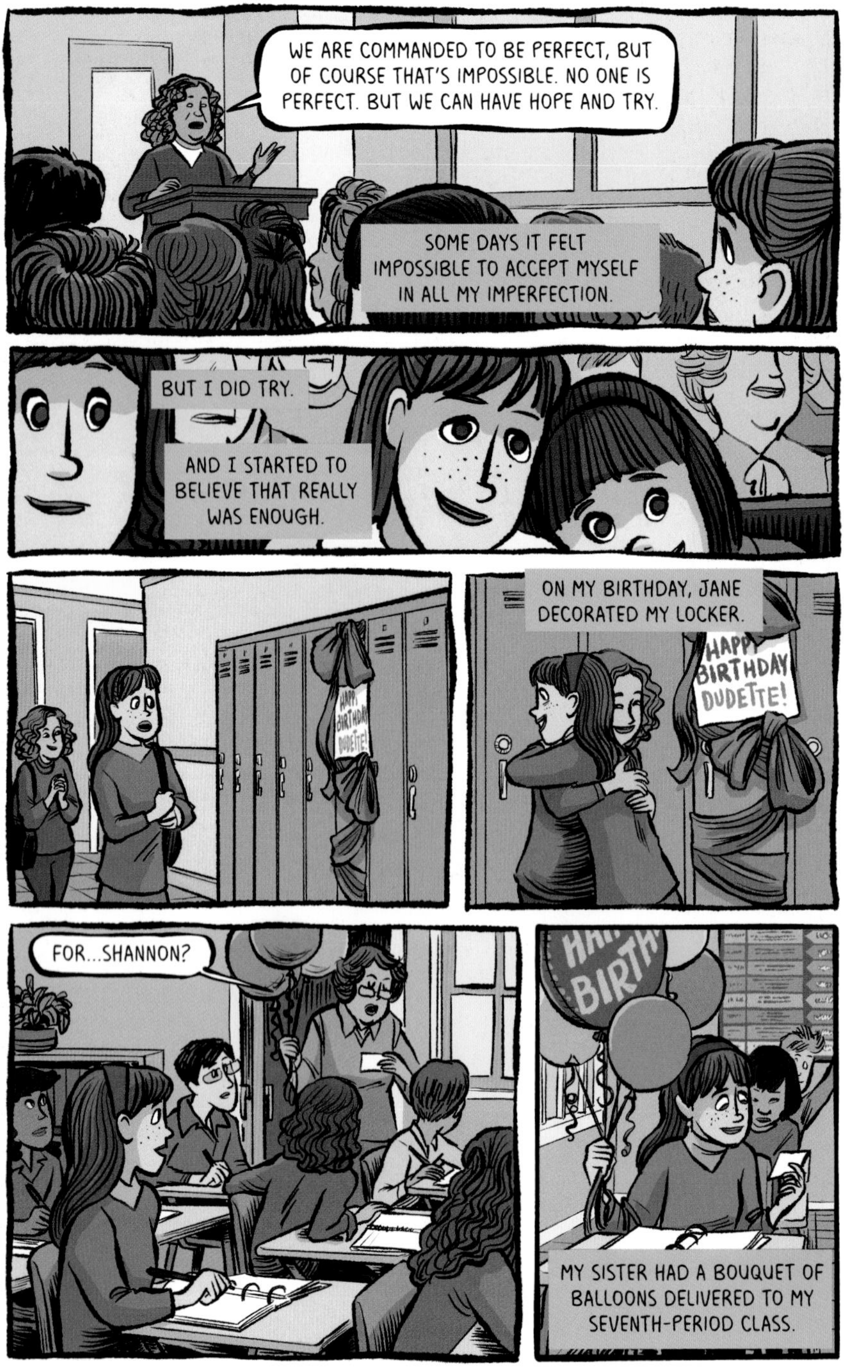
WE ARE COMMANDED TO BE PERFECT, BUT OF COURSE THAT'S IMPOSSIBLE. NO ONE IS PERFECT. BUT WE CAN HAVE HOPE AND TRY.
SOME DAYS IT FELT IMPOSSIBLE TO ACCEPT MYSELF IN ALL MY IMPERFECTION.
BUT I DID TRY.
AND I STARTED TO BELIEVE THAT REALLY WAS ENOUGH.
HAPPY BIRTHDAY DUDETTE!
ON MY BIRTHDAY, JANE DECORATED MY LOCKER.
HAPPY BIRTHDAY DUDETTE!
FOR...SHANNON?
MY SISTER HAD A BOUQUET OF BALLOONS DELIVERED TO MY SEVENTH-PERIOD CLASS.

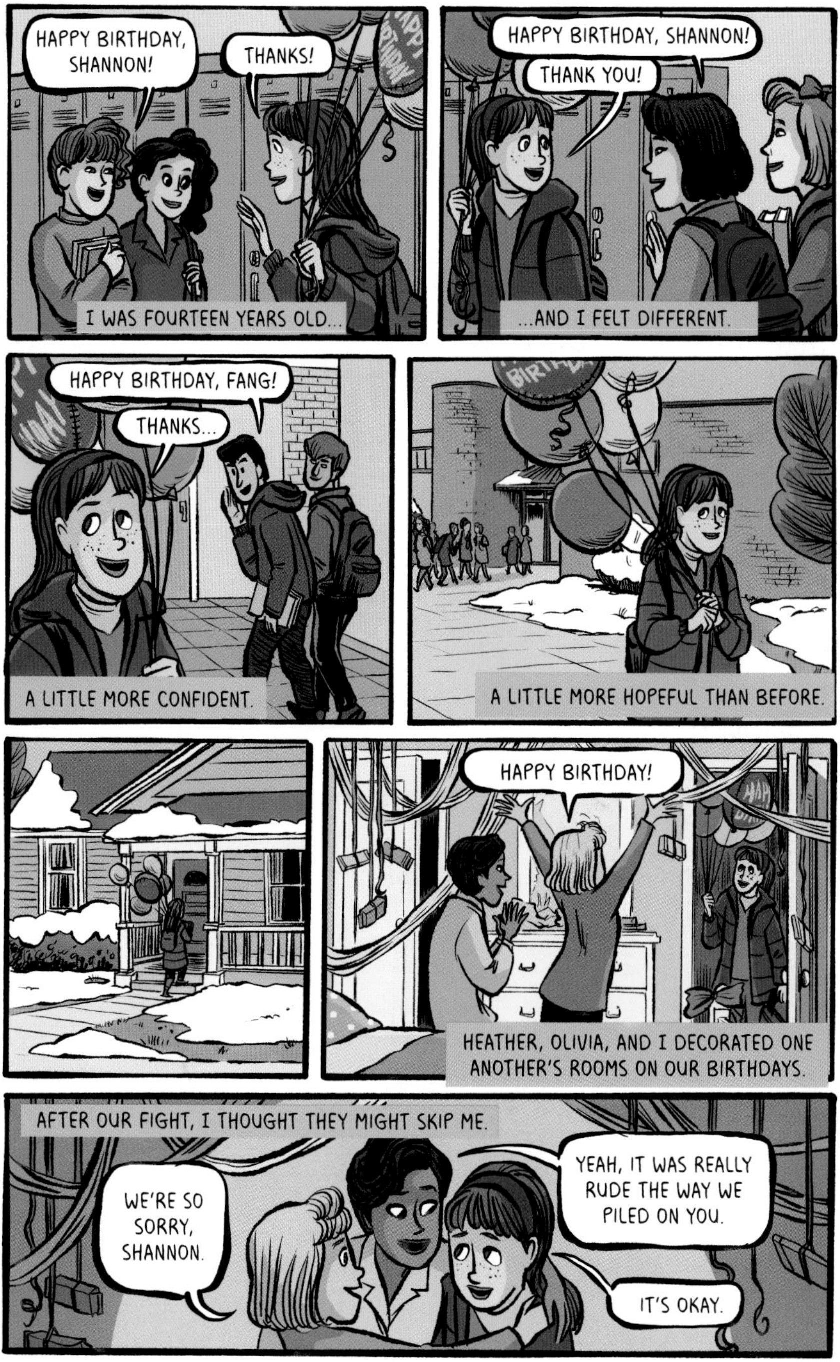
HAPPY BIRTHDAY, SHANNON!
THANKS!
I WAS FOURTEEN YEARS OLD...
HAPPY BIRTHDAY, SHANNON!
THANK YOU!
...AND I FELT DIFFERENT.
HAPPY BIRTHDAY, FANG!
THANKS...
A LITTLE MORE CONFIDENT.
A LITTLE MORE HOPEFUL THAN BEFORE.
HAPPY BIRTHDAY!
HEATHER, OLIVIA, AND I DECORATED ONE ANOTHER'S ROOMS ON OUR BIRTHDAYS.
AFTER OUR FIGHT, I THOUGHT THEY MIGHT SKIP ME.
WE'RE SO SORRY, SHANNON.
YEAH, IT WAS REALLY RUDE THE WAY WE PILED ON YOU.
IT'S OKAY.

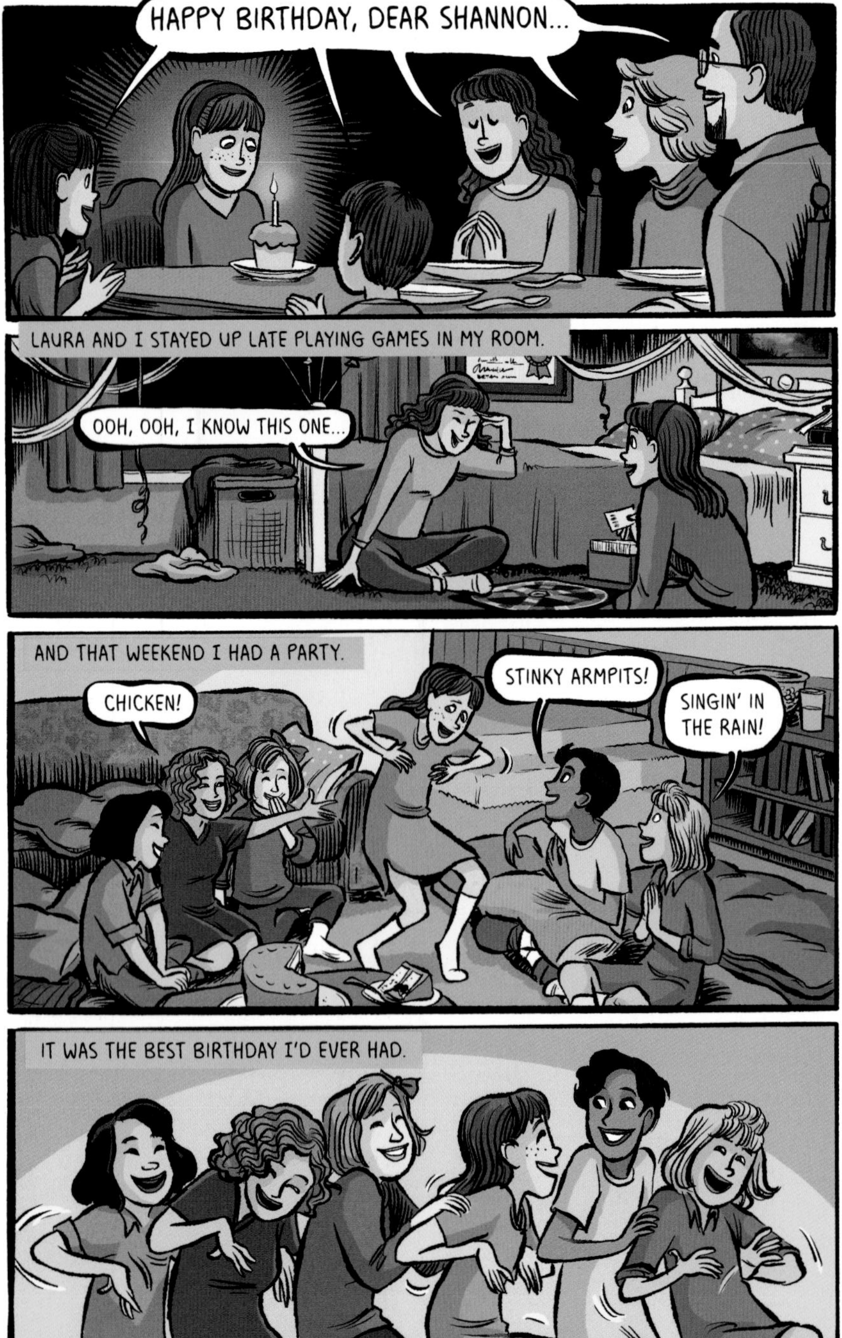
HAPPY BIRTHDAY, DEAR SHANNON...
LAURA AND I STAYED UP LATE PLAYING GAMES IN MY ROOM.
OOH, OOH, I KNOW THIS ONE...
AND THAT WEEKEND I HAD A PARTY.
CHICKEN!
STINKY ARMPITS!
SINGIN' IN THE RAIN!
IT WAS THE BEST BIRTHDAY I'D EVER HAD.

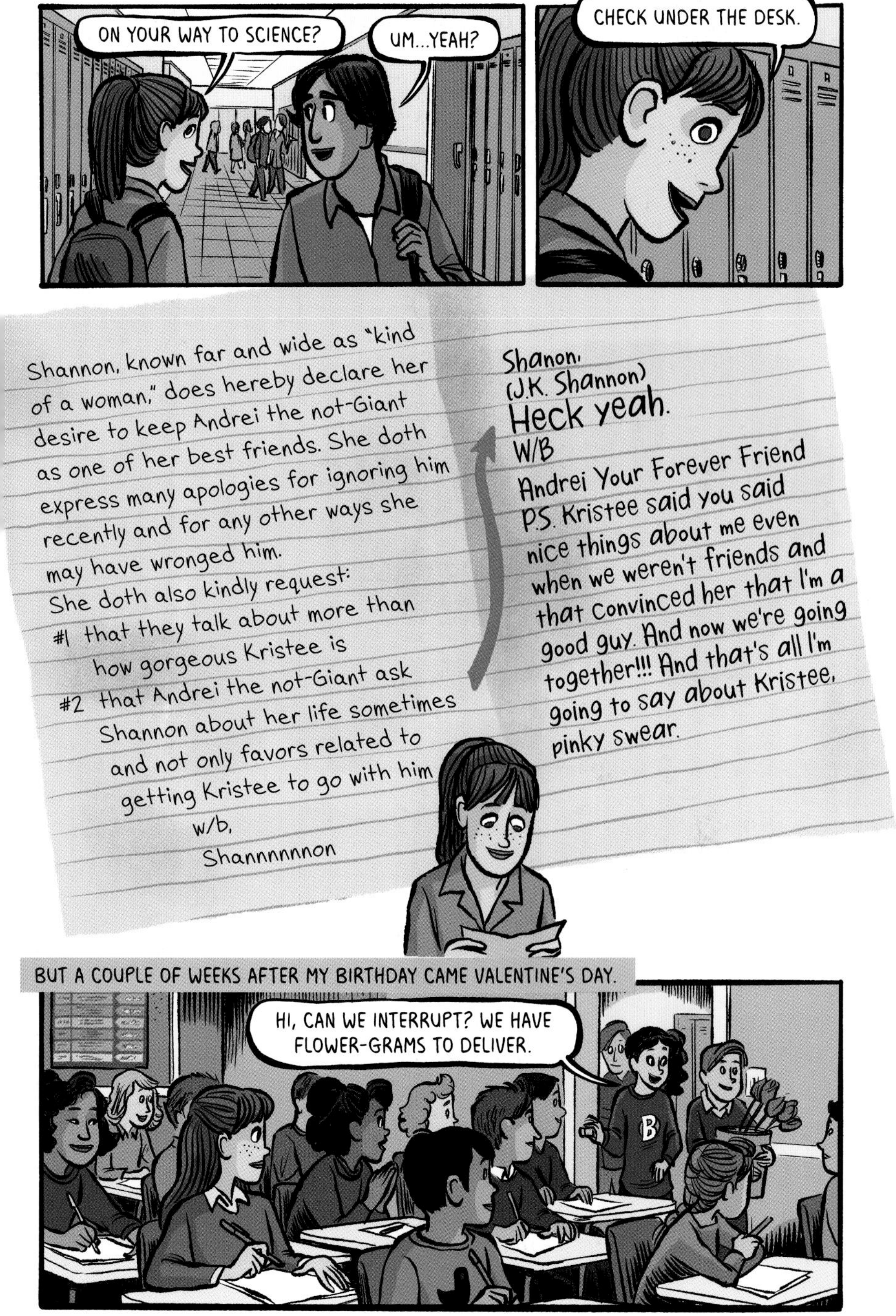
ON YOUR WAY TO SCIENCE?
UM...YEAH?
CHECK UNDER THE DESK.
Shannon, known far and wide as "kind of a woman," does hereby declare her desire to keep Andrei the not-Giant as one of her best friends. She doth express many apologies for ignoring him recently and for any other ways she may have wronged him.
She doth also kindly request:
#1 that they talk about more than how gorgeous Kristee is
#2 that Andrei the not-Giant ask Shannon about her life sometimes and not only favors related to getting Kristee to go with him
w/b,
Shannnnnnon
Shanon,
(J.K. Shannon)
Heck yeah.
W/B
Andrei Your Forever Friend
P.S. Kristee said you said nice things about me even when we weren't friends and that convinced her that I'm a good guy. And now we're going together!!! And that's all I'm going to say about Kristee, pinky swear.
BUT A COUPLE OF WEEKS AFTER MY BIRTHDAY CAME VALENTINE'S DAY.
HI, CAN WE INTERRUPT? WE HAVE FLOWER-GRAMS TO DELIVER.

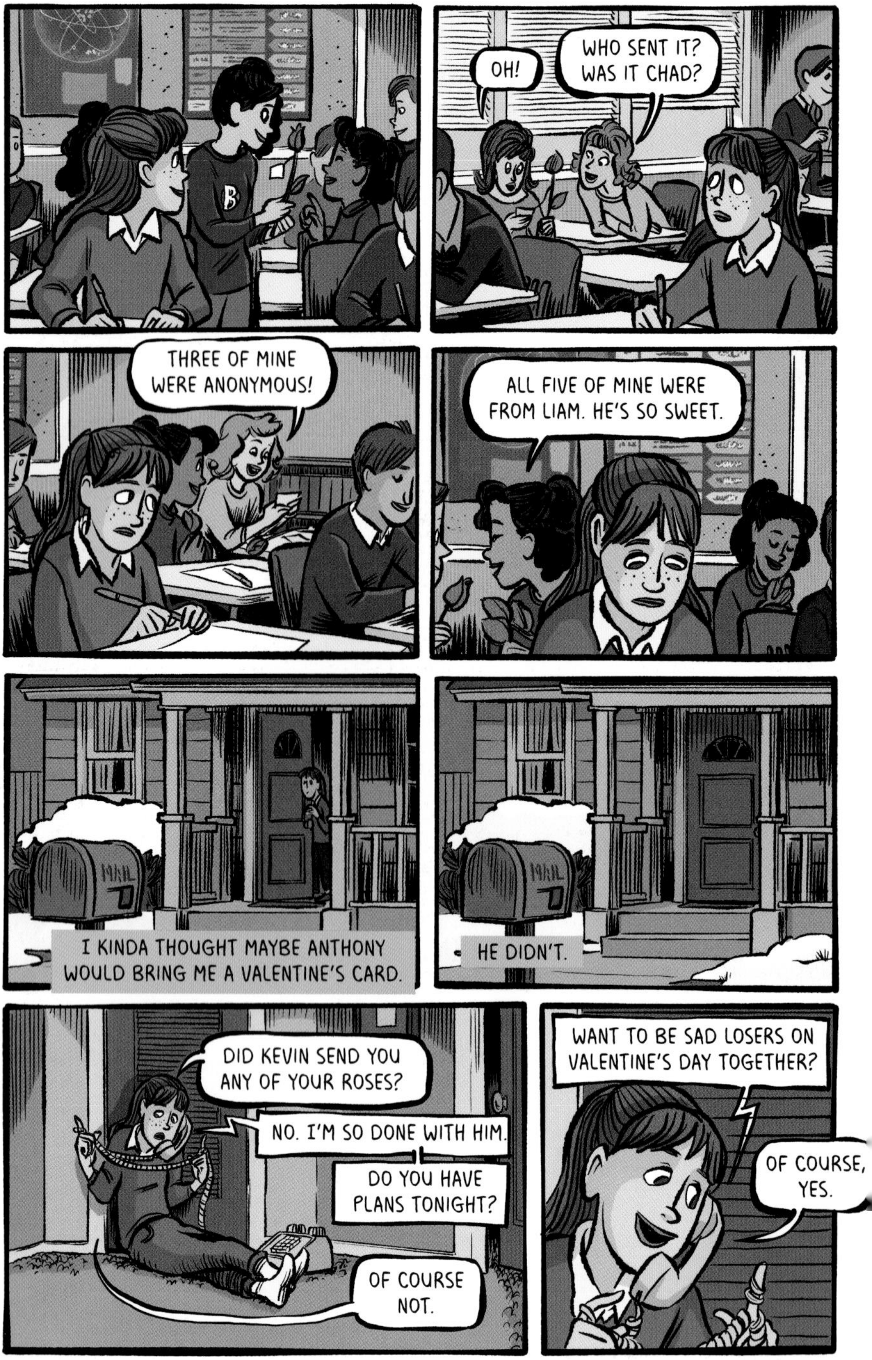
OH!
WHO SENT IT? WAS IT CHAD?
THREE OF MINE WERE ANONYMOUS!
ALL FIVE OF MINE WERE FROM LIAM. HE'S SO SWEET.
I KINDA THOUGHT MAYBE ANTHONY WOULD BRING ME A VALENTINE'S CARD.
HE DIDN'T.
DID KEVIN SEND YOU ANY OF YOUR ROSES?
NO. I'M SO DONE WITH HIM.
DO YOU HAVE PLANS TONIGHT?
OF COURSE NOT.
WANT TO BE SAD LOSERS ON VALENTINE'S DAY TOGETHER?
OF COURSE, YES.

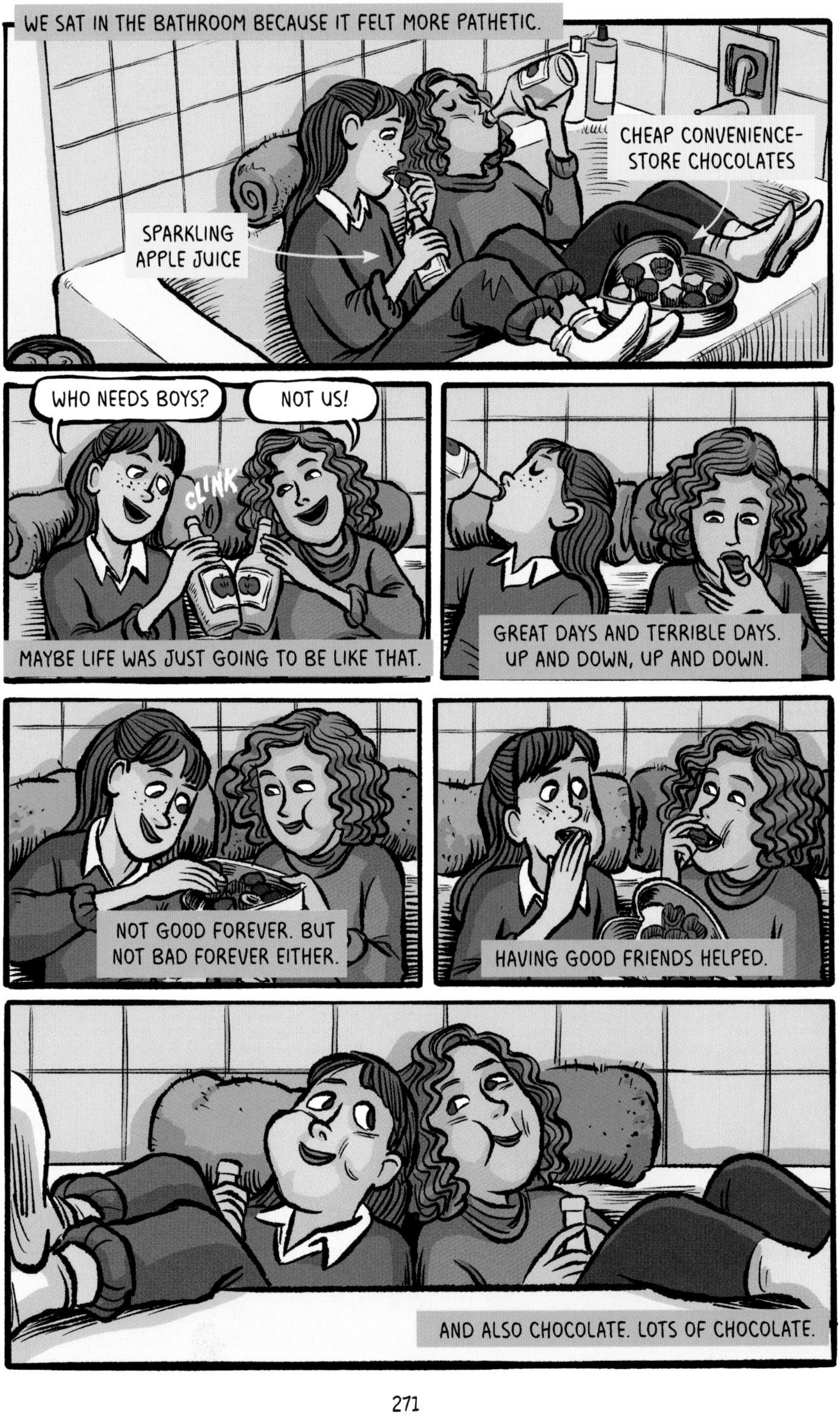
WE SAT IN THE BATHROOM BECAUSE IT FELT MORE PATHETIC.
CHEAP CONVENIENCE-STORE CHOCOLATES
SPARKLING APPLE JUICE
WHO NEEDS BOYS?
NOT US!
CLINK
MAYBE LIFE WAS JUST GOING TO BE LIKE THAT.
GREAT DAYS AND TERRIBLE DAYS. UP AND DOWN, UP AND DOWN.
NOT GOOD FOREVER. BUT NOT BAD FOREVER EITHER.
HAVING GOOD FRIENDS HELPED.
AND ALSO CHOCOLATE. LOTS OF CHOCOLATE.

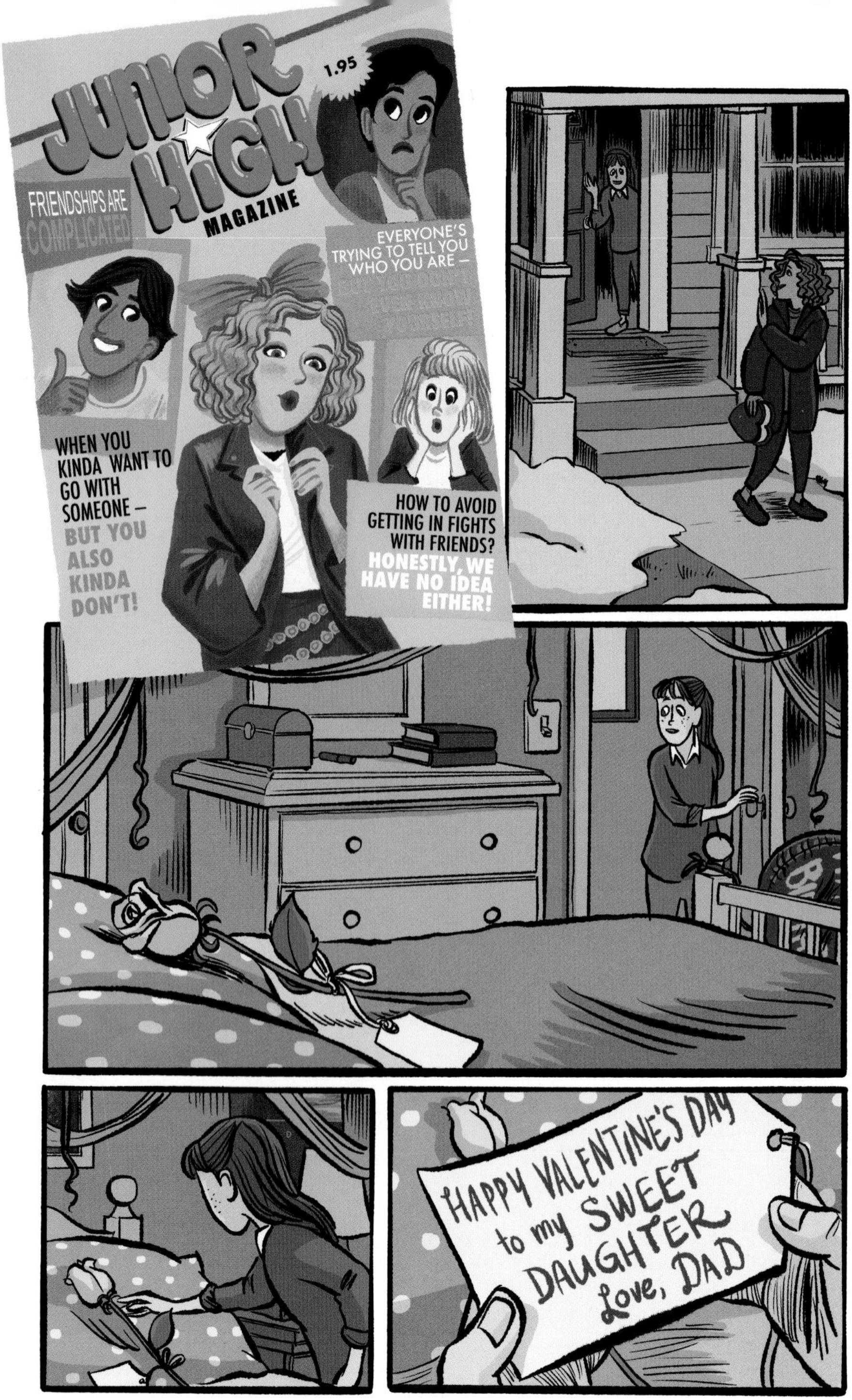
JUNIOR HIGH MAGAZINE
1.95
FRIENDSHIPS ARE COMPLICATED!
EVERYONE'S TRYING TO TELL YOU WHO YOU ARE —
WHEN YOU KINDA WANT TO GO WITH SOMEONE — BUT YOU ALSO KINDA DON'T!
HOW TO AVOID GETTING IN FIGHTS WITH FRIENDS? HONESTLY, WE HAVE NO IDEA EITHER!
HAPPY VALENTINE'S DAY to my SWEET DAUGHTER Love, DAD

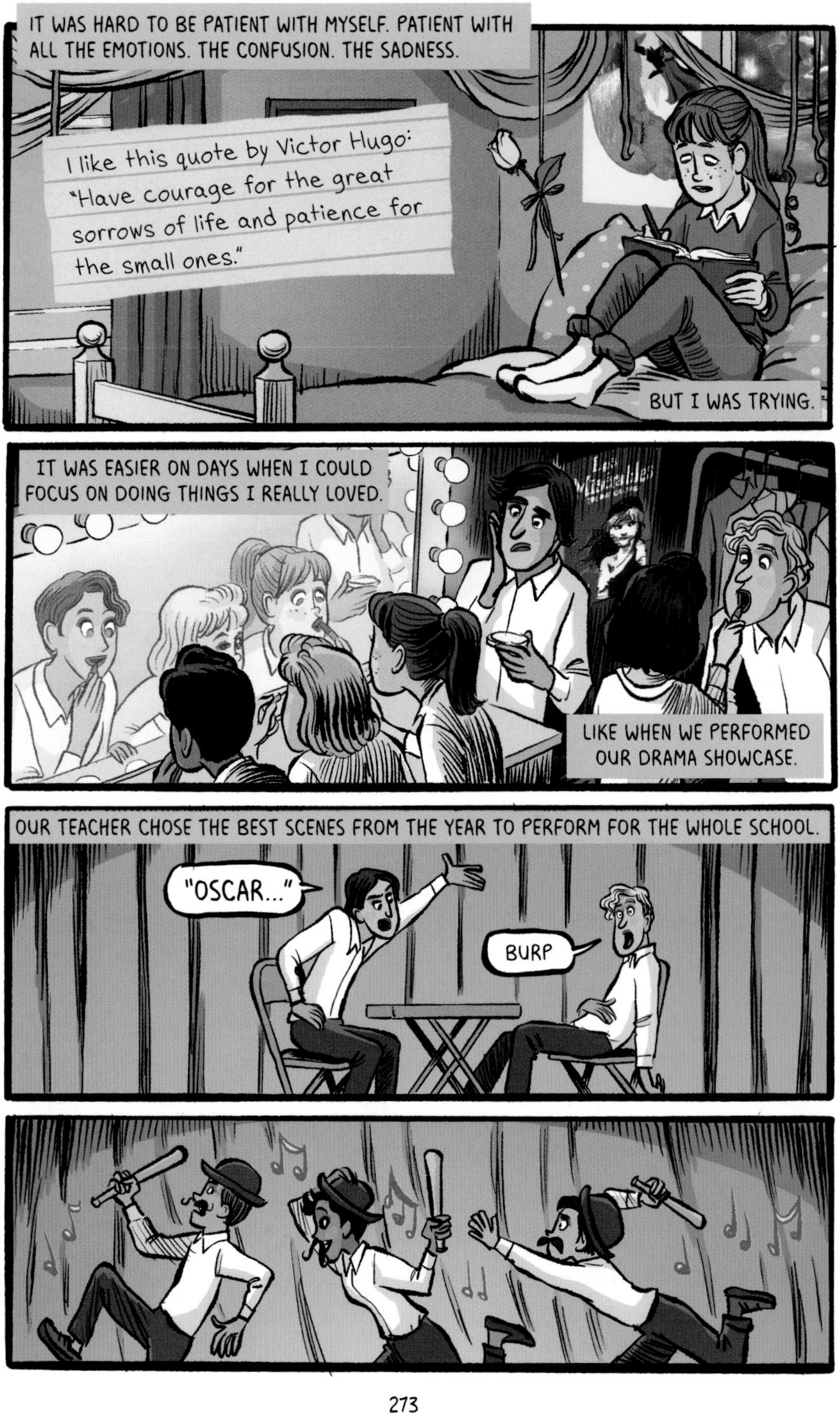
IT WAS HARD TO BE PATIENT WITH MYSELF. PATIENT WITH ALL THE EMOTIONS. THE CONFUSION. THE SADNESS.
I like this quote by Victor Hugo: "Have courage for the great sorrows of life and patience for the small ones."
BUT I WAS TRYING.
IT WAS EASIER ON DAYS WHEN I COULD FOCUS ON DOING THINGS I REALLY LOVED.
LIKE WHEN WE PERFORMED OUR DRAMA SHOWCASE.
OUR TEACHER CHOSE THE BEST SCENES FROM THE YEAR TO PERFORM FOR THE WHOLE SCHOOL.
"OSCAR..."
BURP

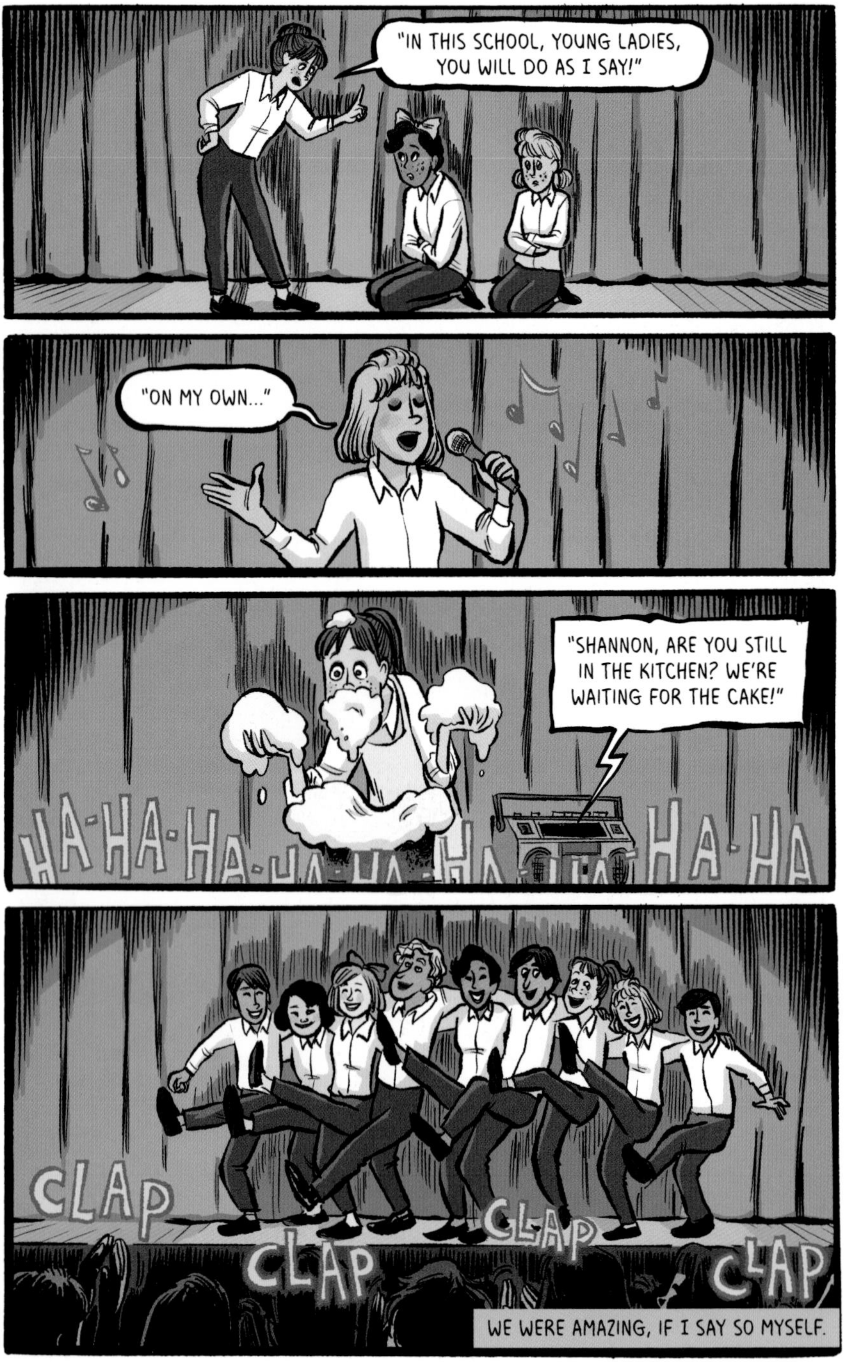
"IN THIS SCHOOL, YOUNG LADIES, YOU WILL DO AS I SAY!"
"ON MY OWN..."
"SHANNON, ARE YOU STILL IN THE KITCHEN? WE'RE WAITING FOR THE CAKE!"
HA-HA-HA-HA-HA-HA-HA-HA-HA-HA
CLAP
CLAP
CLAP
CLAP
WE WERE AMAZING, IF I SAY SO MYSELF.

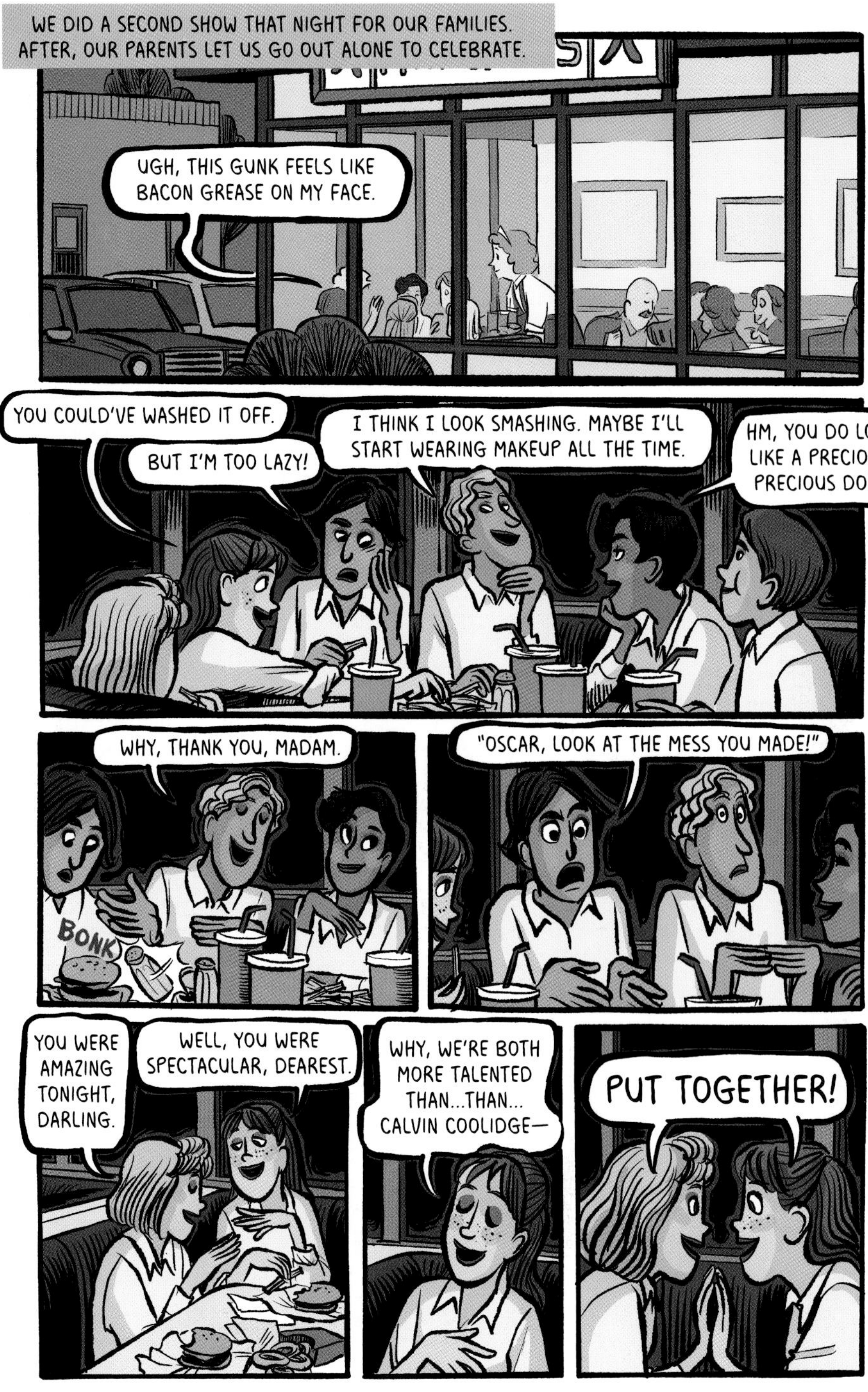
WE DID A SECOND SHOW THAT NIGHT FOR OUR FAMILIES. AFTER, OUR PARENTS LET US GO OUT ALONE TO CELEBRATE.
UGH, THIS GUNK FEELS LIKE BACON GREASE ON MY FACE.
YOU COULD'VE WASHED IT OFF.
BUT I'M TOO LAZY!
I THINK I LOOK SMASHING. MAYBE I'LL START WEARING MAKEUP ALL THE TIME.
HM, YOU DO LOOK LIKE A PRECIOUS, PRECIOUS DOLL.
WHY, THANK YOU, MADAM.
BONK
"OSCAR, LOOK AT THE MESS YOU MADE!"
YOU WERE AMAZING TONIGHT, DARLING.
WELL, YOU WERE SPECTACULAR, DEAREST.
WHY, WE'RE BOTH MORE TALENTED THAN...THAN... CALVIN COOLIDGE—
PUT TOGETHER!

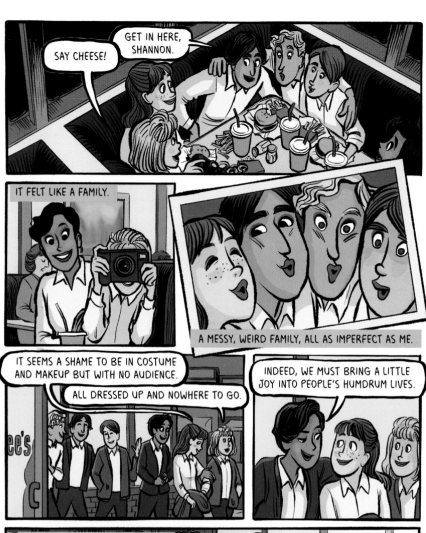

SAY CHEESE!

GET IN HERE, SHANNON.

IT FELT LIKE A FAMILY.

A MESSY, WEIRD FAMILY, ALL AS IMPERFECT AS ME.

IT SEEMS A SHAME TO BE IN COSTUME AND MAKEUP BUT WITH NO AUDIENCE.

ALL DRESSED UP AND NOWHERE TO GO.

INDEED, WE MUST BRING A LITTLE JOY INTO PEOPLE'S HUMDRUM LIVES.

SO WE DECIDED IT WAS OUR DUTY TO ENTERTAIN THE TRAFFIC.

HONK HONK

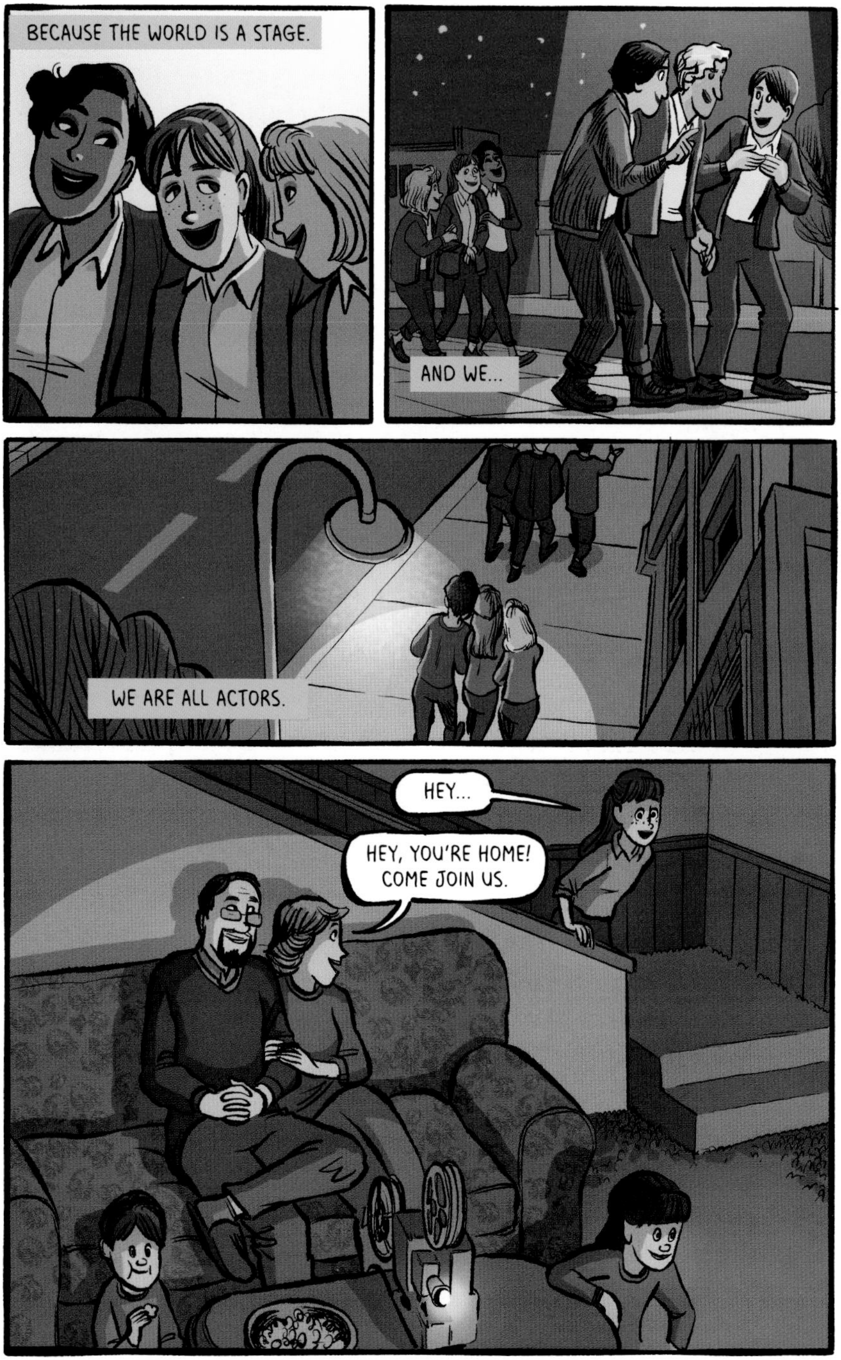
BECAUSE THE WORLD IS A STAGE.
AND WE...
WE ARE ALL ACTORS.
HEY...
HEY, YOU'RE HOME! COME JOIN US.

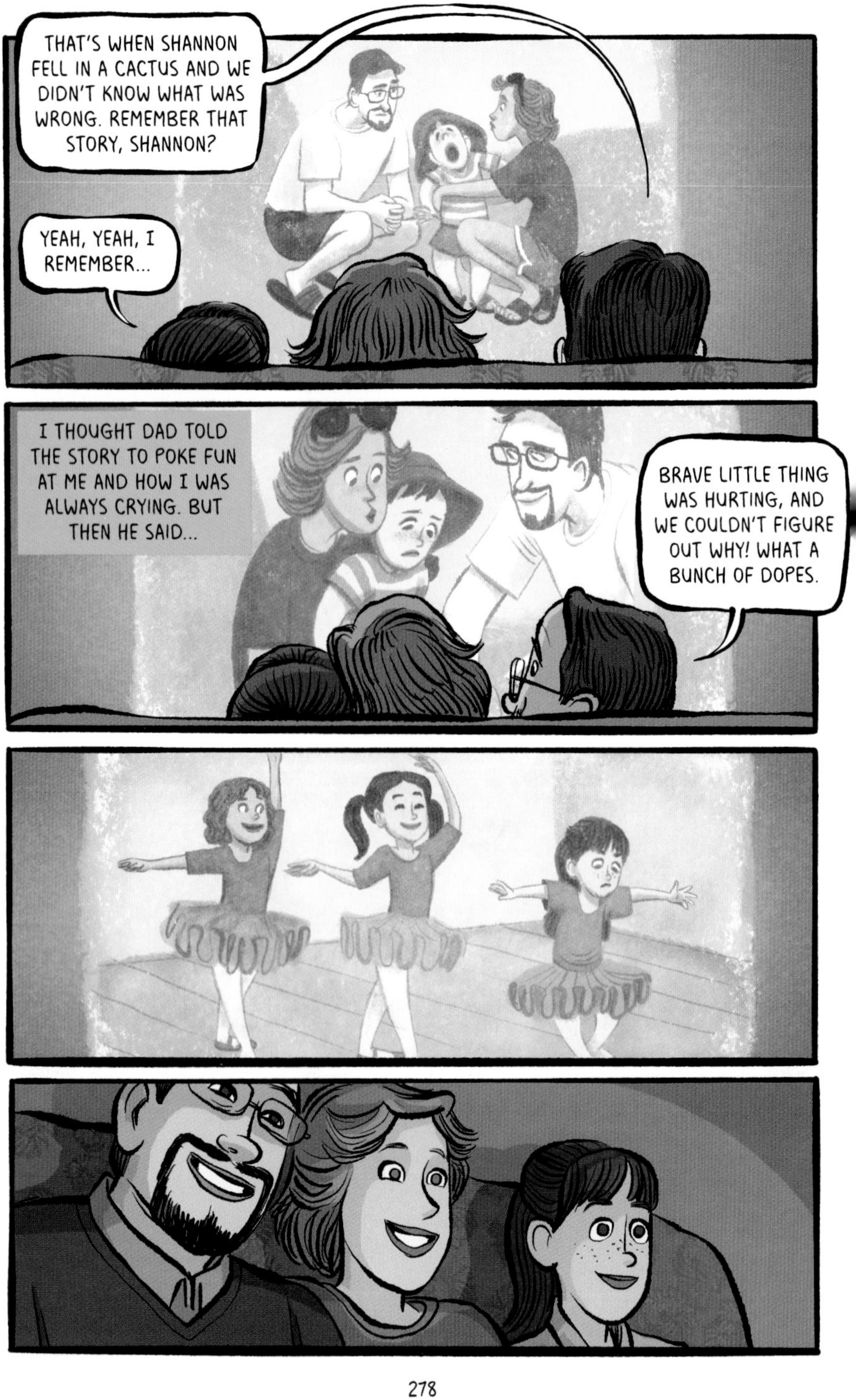
THAT'S WHEN SHANNON FELL IN A CACTUS AND WE DIDN'T KNOW WHAT WAS WRONG. REMEMBER THAT STORY, SHANNON?
YEAH, YEAH, I REMEMBER...
I THOUGHT DAD TOLD THE STORY TO POKE FUN AT ME AND HOW I WAS ALWAYS CRYING. BUT THEN HE SAID...
BRAVE LITTLE THING WAS HURTING, AND WE COULDN'T FIGURE OUT WHY! WHAT A BUNCH OF DOPES.

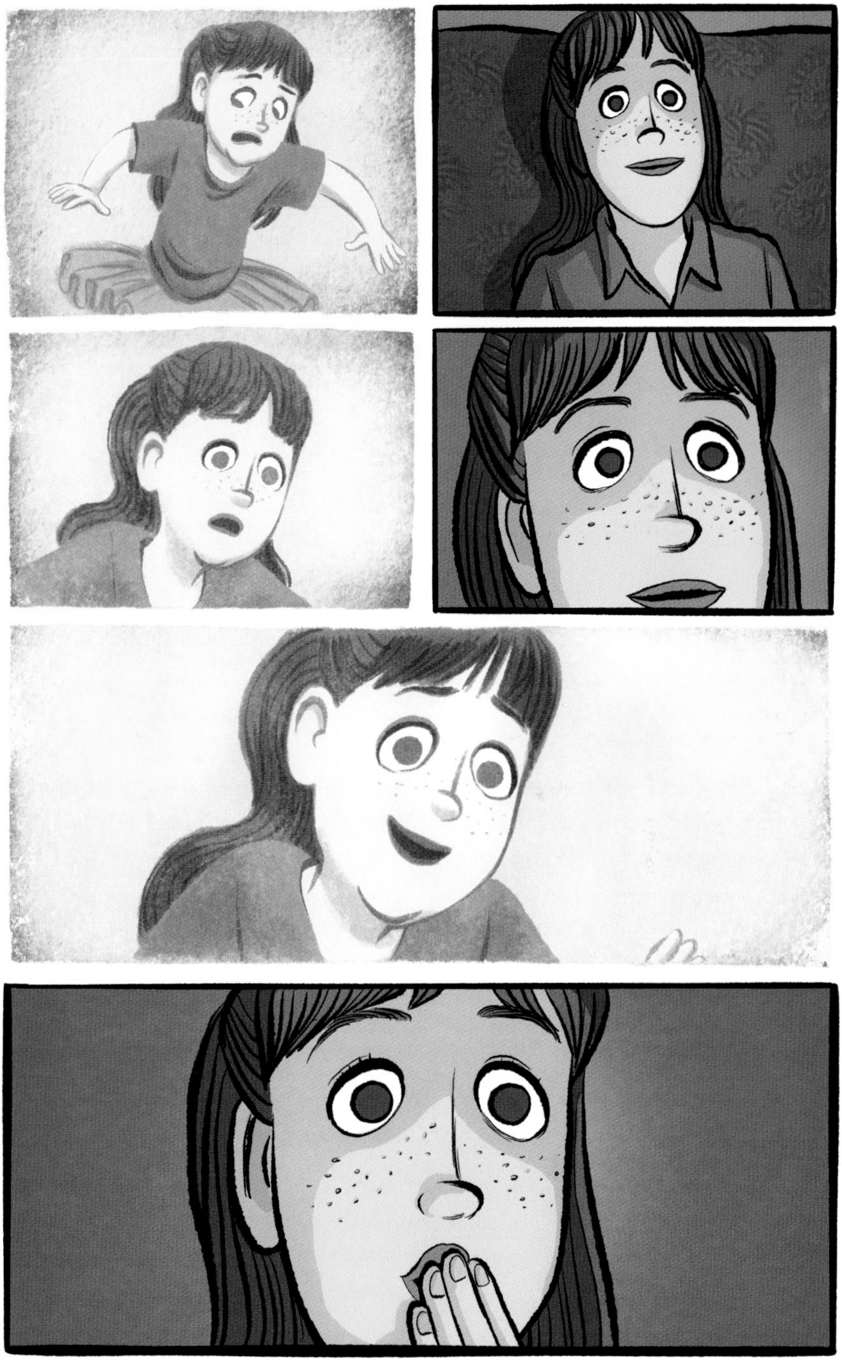

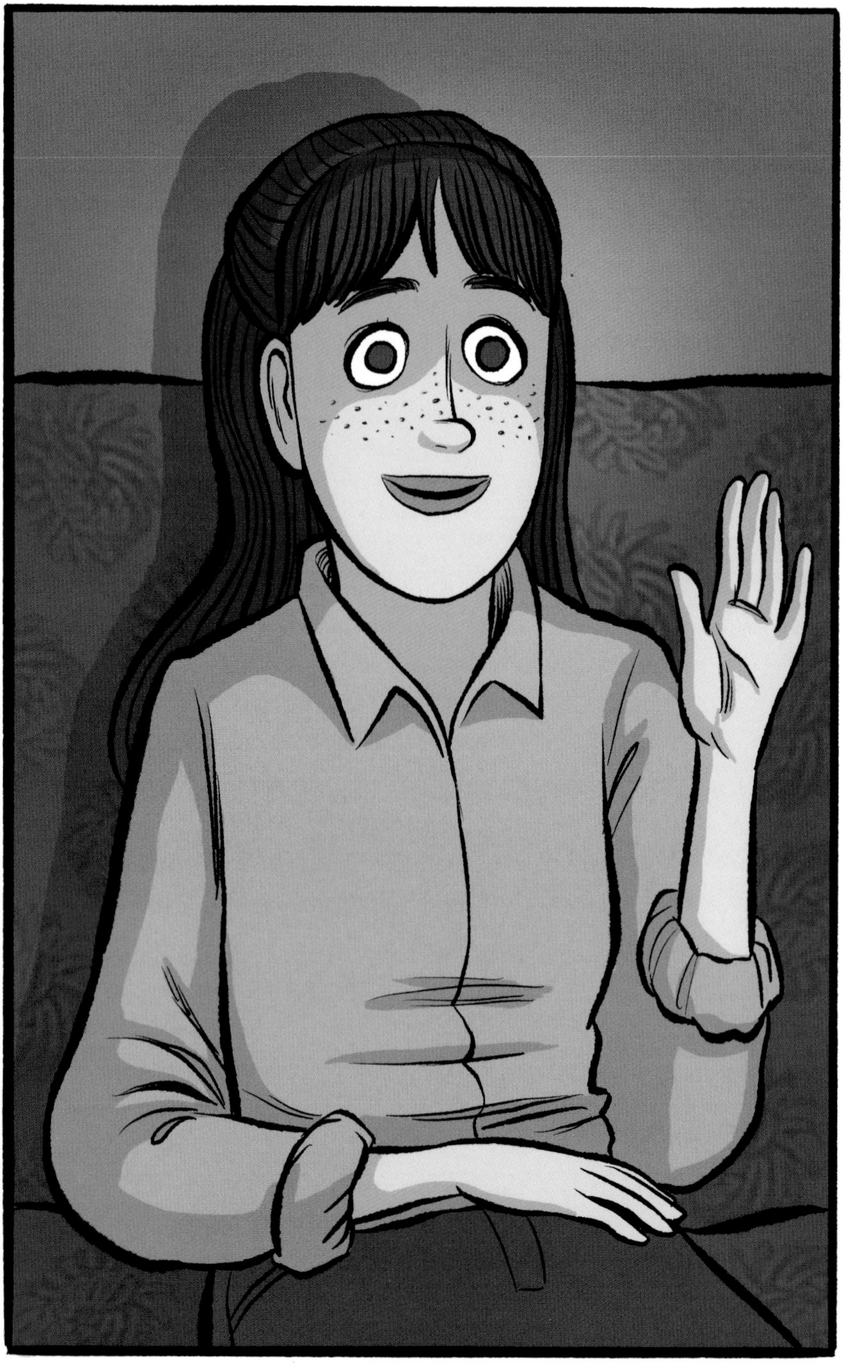

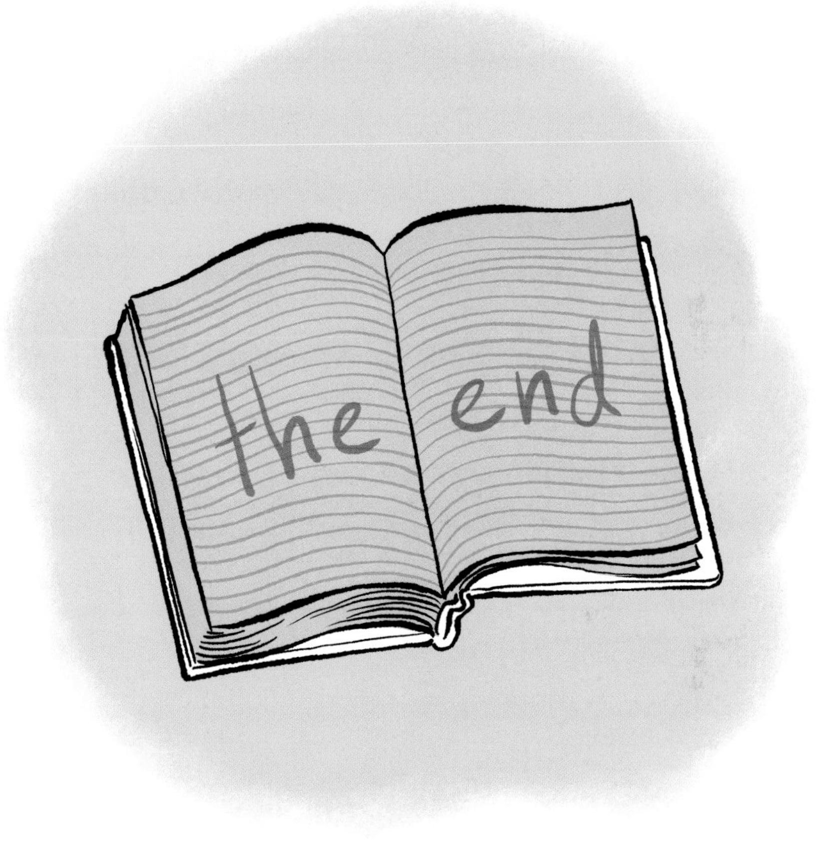
the end

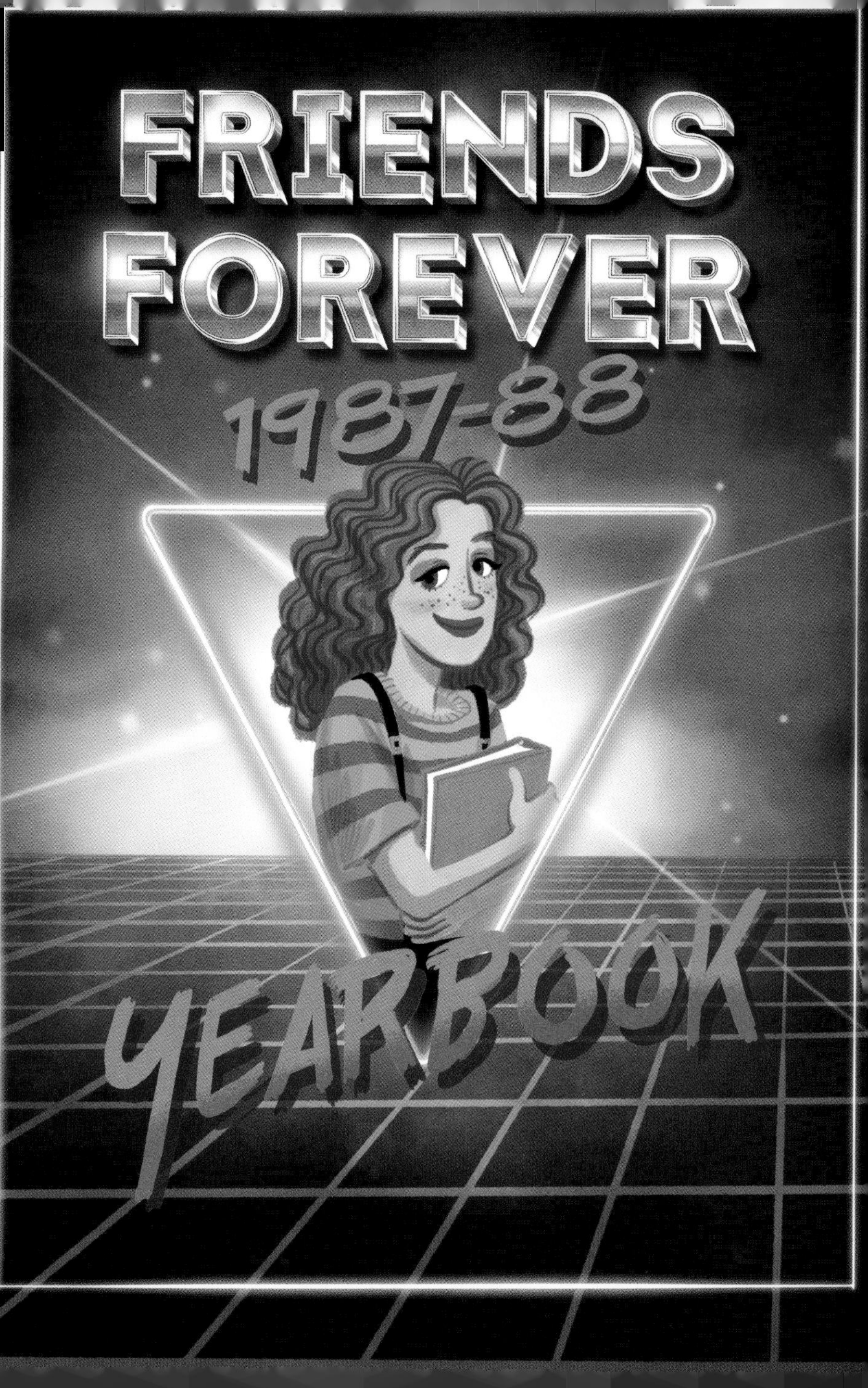
FRIENDS
FOREVER
1987-88
YEARBOOK

Hey You!

When I was growing up, adults often talked about middle school like it was some post-apocalyptic horror. But at the time, I didn't think middle school was so bad. I had fun and interesting experiences and many friends, more even than I showed in this book. I also had a lot of big emotions. At this age, our brains go through major changes, causing heightened awareness of everyone around us and unhelpful self-comparison. We're also dealing with body changes and hormone changes that can lead to emotion changes. It's a lot! I hope at the very least that this story allows you to feel compassion for thirteen-year-old Shannon and her friends—and by extension, for yourselves too. We're all going through a lot.

When I was young, I was often told, "You're too sensitive," so I spent tons of energy trying to hide and squash my feelings. Eventually I came to realize that feelings aren't a weakness. All those emotions helped me as I did theater and as I wrote stories. And they helped me as I made friends. Trying to go numb in order to avoid the bad feelings causes us to miss out on the good feelings too, and prevents us from truly connecting with people. Besides, a squashed emotion doesn't go away. It needs to be met with compassion and allowed to resolve on its own.

At age thirteen, I was living with undiagnosed anxiety disorder as well as mild obsessive compulsive disorder (OCD). It can be hard to explain OCD to those who haven't experienced it. From the outside, the thoughts and behaviors can seem odd and illogical, but inside the OCD brain, it feels very real. OCD showed itself in many different ways for me, and I often believed the overwhelming feelings and unwelcome intrusive thoughts were God's way of warning me that I was bad and needed to constantly repent. I didn't understand what was going on, so it was impossible for me to explain it to my parents or anyone else. When my support system of friends and family felt weaker, I was also more likely to sink into depression. Having access to help when young can make the path to healing much shorter. I didn't get better all at once, but I did learn and develop skills that have helped me live the kind of life I yearned for. If you have experienced anxiety, OCD, or depression, you're definitely not alone. There are many great resources, including www.adaa.org, www.dbsalliance.org, and www.nami.org.

All the stories in this book come from my memories of what really happened when I was thirteen, aided by notes my friends wrote me in eighth grade and my journal entries. But memories aren't perfect, so I'm sure there are parts that aren't exactly right. I moved events around to help the story flow, and since there's no way I could remember exactly what people said, I had to approximate the dialogue. Some of the characters are composites of a couple different people, and I changed everybody's name except my own. No memories could ever do justice to who these real and complex human beings truly are.

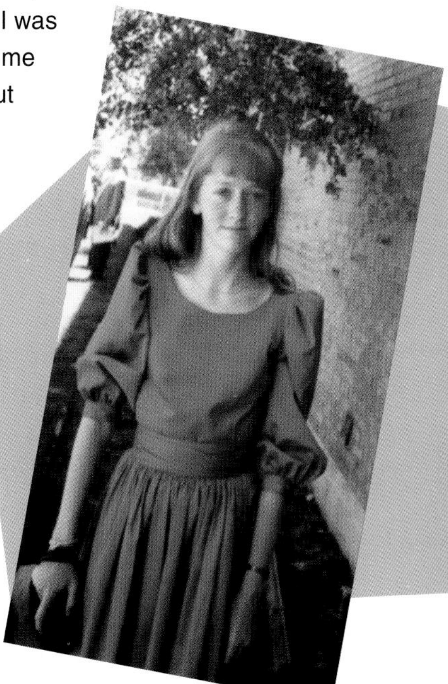

But yes, as best as I remember it, 95 percent of this stuff really did happen. For example, Andrei's movie night plays out in this book as

I described it in a journal entry (even the shocking appearance of alcohol, the first time I'd ever been offered some—and no, I didn't drink it!). Talent agents were a thing for a time with my friends, and I was scammed by a fake one. When I found out at lunch in front of all my drama friends, the surprise and humiliation was so intense that I experienced what I think now was probably "psychological shock," severe enough that I became unaware of my surroundings for several minutes.

As for that creepy fake Santa, what he did was very, very wrong. He had no right to touch me like that or say gross things. It absolutely wasn't my fault. He was an adult, I was a kid, and there was nothing I could have said or done that would have made what he did okay. As an adult now, I'm furious that a man like that was able to put on the beloved costume of Santa and meet children. I wish I'd known that I could have reported him to the security guard, our choir teacher, our parents—any trustworthy adults, and felt confident that they would have believed and protected us. I hope that every kid and teen has someone they trust who they can tell anything to.

When I was younger, sometimes adults would give girls the message that "all attention is good attention," and if a boy paid us any attention, we should be grateful. It was confusing, because I thought being liked should feel good, but the way boys sometimes treated girls felt bad. I hope your world is smarter than mine was. Hurting someone, touching them in a way they don't want, is never good attention, and it's never okay. We all deserve to be treated with love and respect.

The psychiatrist visit happened just as I wrote it here. What might have happened if I'd been able to be honest with him? Or if I'd met with someone else who'd been a better fit for me? Often it takes time to find the right person, the right diagnosis and plan, the right guidance.

There were so many things I yearned for, but ultimately what I wanted was just to feel okay. And to feel that I mattered. I wish someone helpful could have told me what I needed to know and in a way that I could have believed. Can I tell some of those things to you now? (Yes, you.)

You are beautiful.
You deserve to be seen for who you are
and loved for who you are.
You are powerful and are capable of
doing great things.
Your feelings matter.
You don't have to be perfect.
You are enough, exactly as you are.

Dealing with worries, fear, and sadness, and still getting up and doing stuff every day—that's incredibly brave.

So, there's no definitive "the end" to a true story like this, and that's really more hopeful than any tidy ending I could make up. Life moves on. Feelings change. People change. We're never stuck. There is always hope.

Your friend forever,

Shannon

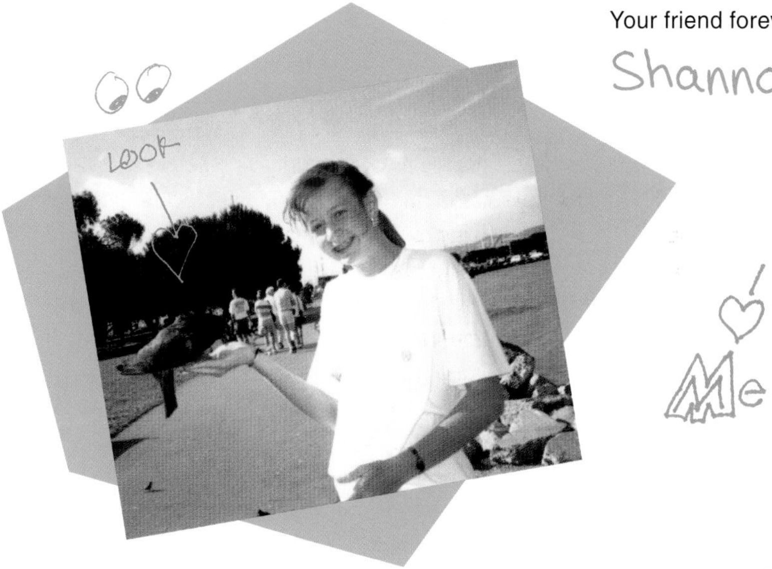
LOOK
Me

Student Life!

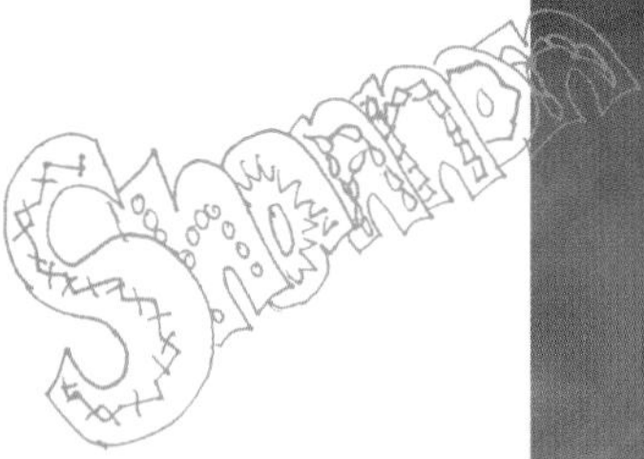
Shannon

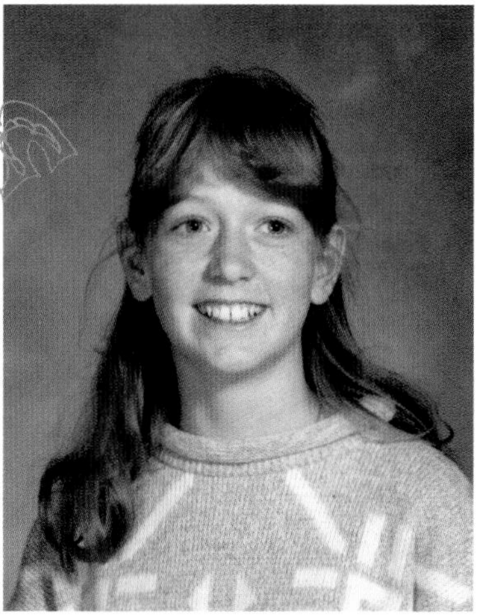

7th Grade

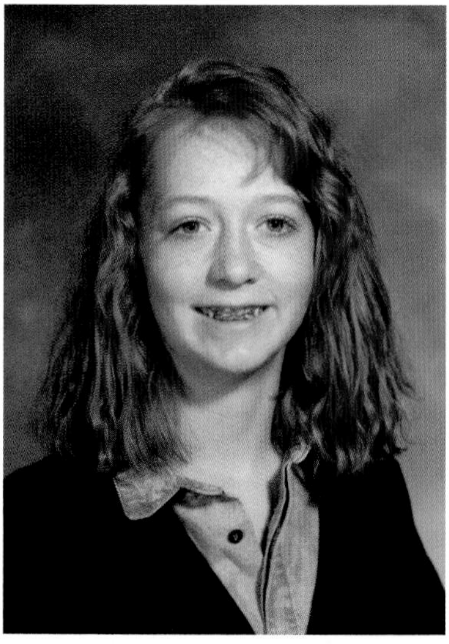

8th Grade

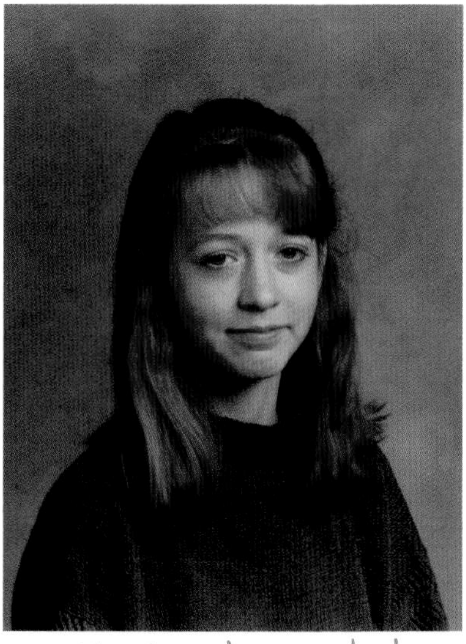

8th Grade re-take

UTA SYMPHONY
AN EVENING ON BROADWAY

Our illustrious
Student Director

This is the night after the Drama Showcase when we
performed for the traffic. All the world's a stage . . .

Eventually I got
braces on all my teeth.
No more Fang!

Art Club Rocks!

Shannon through the ages! Although we didn't meet until later in life, I feel like I've known her forever.

age 5-6   age 7-8   age 9-10   age 11-12   age 13

For the past couple of years I have had the unique challenge of illustrating someone else's life without having been there myself. How do I illustrate the first day of school if I wasn't there to see it? How do I show the pang of a first crush if I wasn't the one crushing? How do I show a first dance when I wasn't even at the dance? Combing through Shannon's brain isn't an easy thing to do, and much of it was done with fingers crossed, hoping I got it right. There were a lot of mistakes made, a lot of sketches that didn't work, a lot of ideas that didn't make the cut. And on Shannon's part, there was a lot of trust she had to put in me to hopefully get it right. It's a good thing that we're such good friends in real life!

—LeUyen Pham

ANTHONY   SHANNON   JANE   TIFFANY

1960s DANCE OUTFITS

A typical character lineup from the book. Every character has to be designed individually, including the cool clothes!

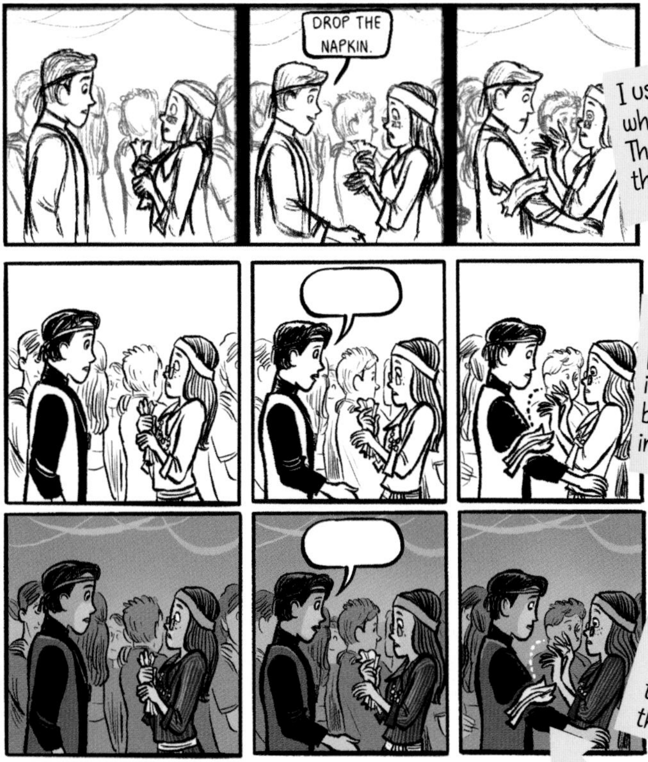
DROP THE NAPKIN.

I usually sketch the whole book out first. These are my thumbnails.

Next is the inking process. Normally I ink with a croquille, but for this book I inked it digitally.

Finally our amazing colorist Hilary comes in and adds color to the whole thing.

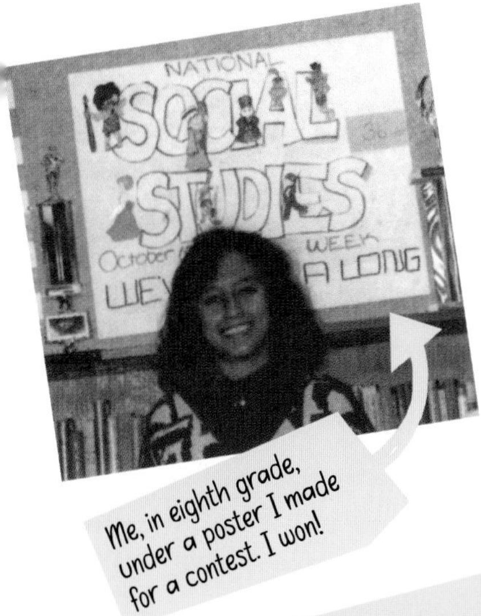
NATIONAL
SOCIAL
STUDIES
WEEK

Me, in eighth grade, under a poster I made for a contest. I won!

Dear Shannon--
I'm so happy we're friends!
I think you're SO talented. You
will definitely be famous someday.
Maybe we'll make books together!
K.I.T. &
FRIENDS 4-EVER!
♡ Ü-yEN ♡ ♡

Making History!

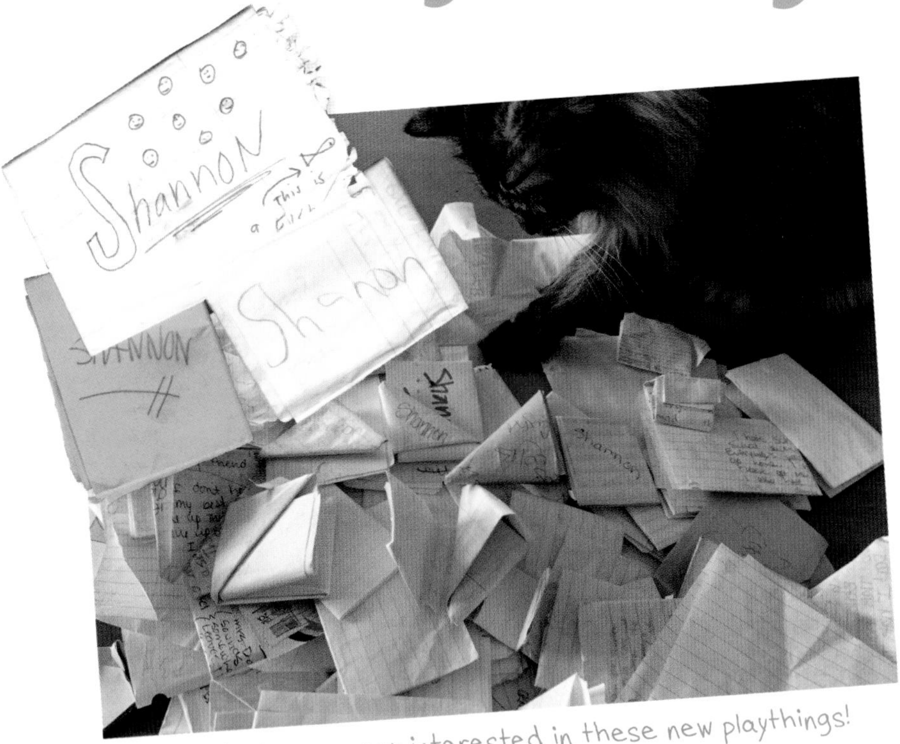
Shannon

Our cat Misty was very interested in these new playthings!

In eighth grade, I suddenly felt compelled to save the notes my friends passed me. For thirty years I stored them in a shoe box, mostly forgotten. Then when I was writing this book, I remembered—hey! Maybe I still have those notes! They proved to be invaluable as I pieced together that year and channeled the voices of my friends.

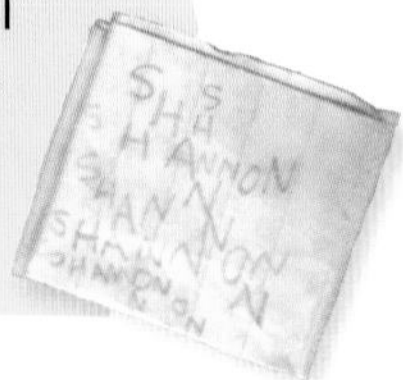

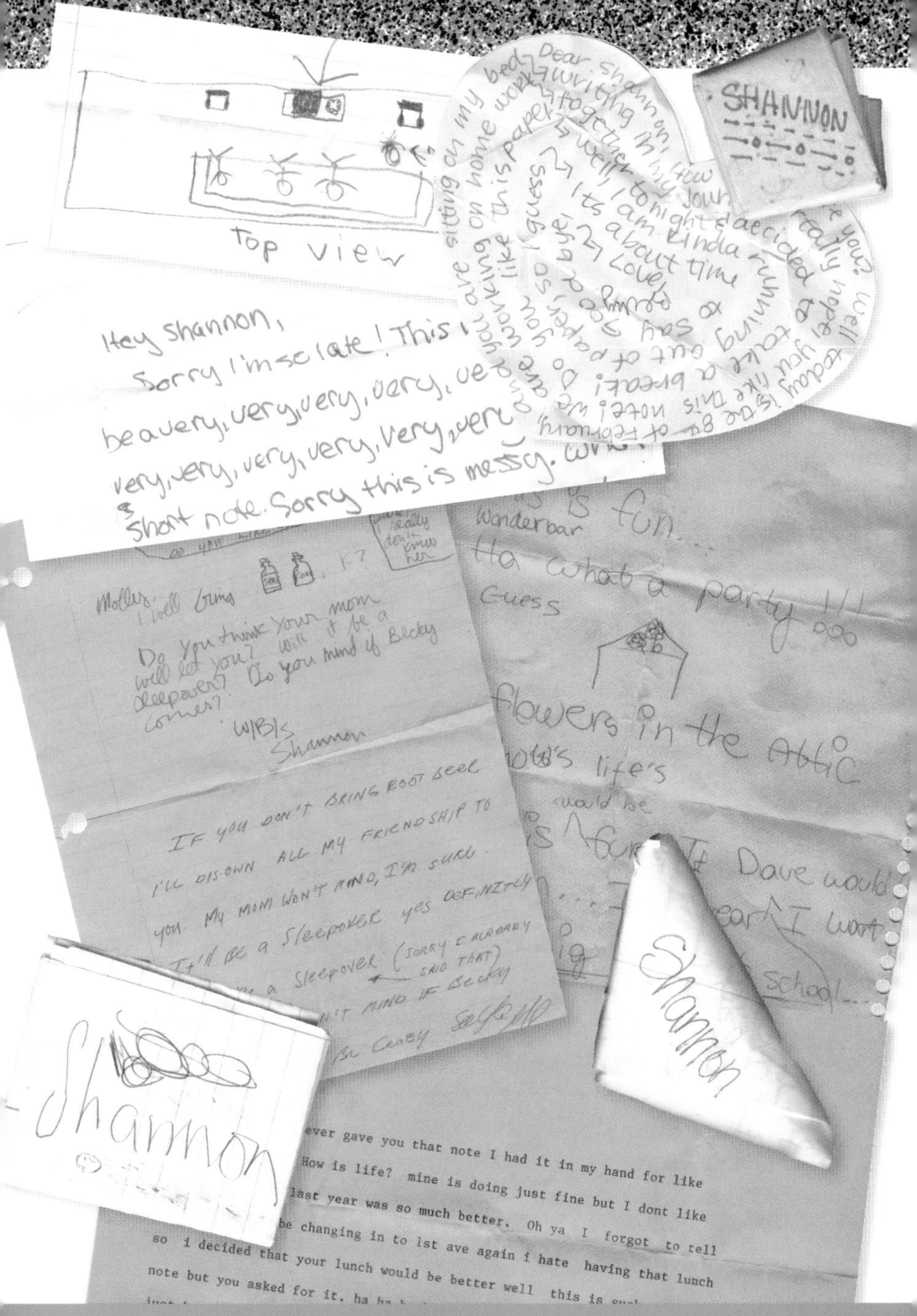
Top view
Hey Shannon,
Sorry I'm so late! This i
be a very, very, very, very, ve
very, very, very, very, Very, very
short note. Sorry this is messy.
Dear Shannon,
SHANNON
Wonderbar
is fun...
Ha what a party!!!
Guess
flowers in the Attic
life's
Dave would
I want
school...
Do you think your mom will let you? Will it be a sleepover? Do you mind if Becky comes?
W/B/S
Shannon
IF YOU DON'T BRING ROOT BEER I'LL DIS-OWN ALL MY FRIENDSHIP TO YOU. MY MOM WON'T MIND, I'M SURE. IT'LL BE A SLEEPOVER YES DEFINITLY
(SORRY I ALREADY SAID THAT)
Shannon
Shannon
ever gave you that note I had it in my hand for like
How is life? mine is doing just fine but I dont like
last year was so much better. Oh ya I forgot to tell
be changing in to 1st ave again i hate having that lunch
so i decided that your lunch would be better well this is such
note but you asked for it. ha ha

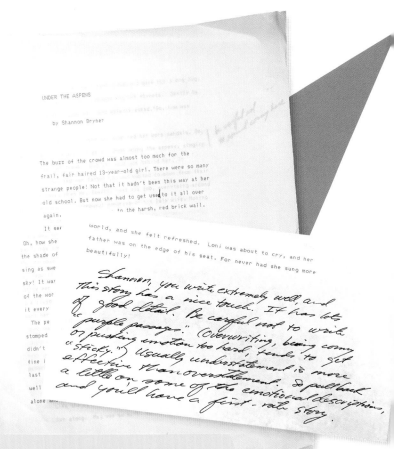

UNDER THE ASPENS

by Shannon Bryner

The buzz of the crowd was almost too much for the frail, fair haired 13-year-old girl. There were so many strange people! Not that it hadn't been this way at her old school. But now she had to get used to it all over again.

. . . in the harsh, red brick wall.

It ser   world, and she felt refreshed. Loni was about to cry, and her
Oh, how she   father was on the edge of his seat. For never had she sung more
the shade of   beautifully!

sing as swe
sky! It war
of the wor
it every
    The pe
stomped
didn't
fine i
last
well
alone a

Shannon, you write extremely well, and this story has a nice touch. It has lots of good detail. Be careful not to write "purple passages." (Overwriting, being corny or pushing emotion too hard, tends to get "sticky.") Usually understatement is more effective than overstatement. So pull back a little on some of the emotional descriptions, and you'll have a first-rate story.

In his critique of my story, the professional author who visited my eighth-grade class noted that I had an abundance of "emotional description." In life, I was working so hard to hide my big emotions, but writing stories was a place where I could let them out.

Club Rules!

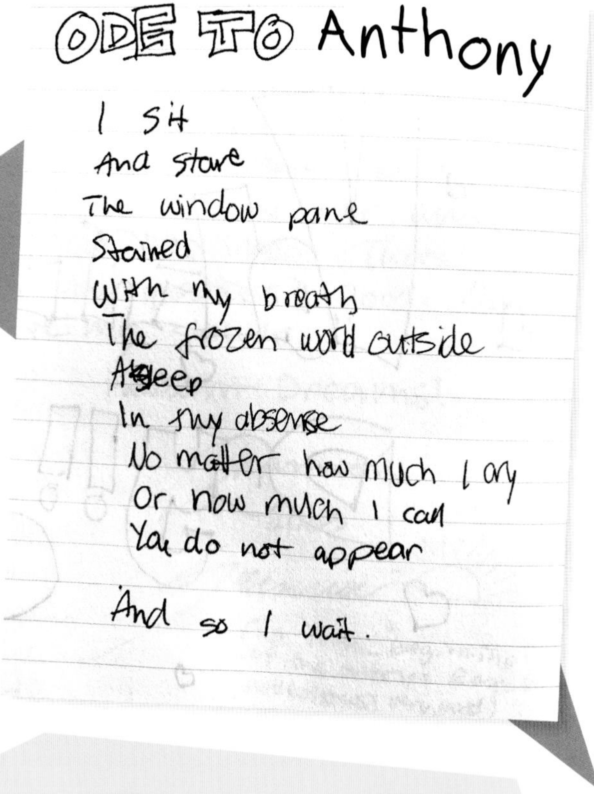

ODE TO Anthony

I sit
And stare
The window pane
Stained
With my breath
The frozen world outside
Asleep
In thy absense
No matter how much I cry
Or how much I call
You do not appear

And so I wait.

I scoured my journal entries to help me remember the truth of eighth grade. This is the actual poem I wrote in my journal after my first-ever slow dance with “Anthony.” We didn’t stay in touch, but whenever I ran into him, he was always kind and thoughtful. No wonder I wrote him an ode!

Who's Who in Junior High

Thanks to all the people who worked so hard to make this book. We love you forever!

Keep in touch!

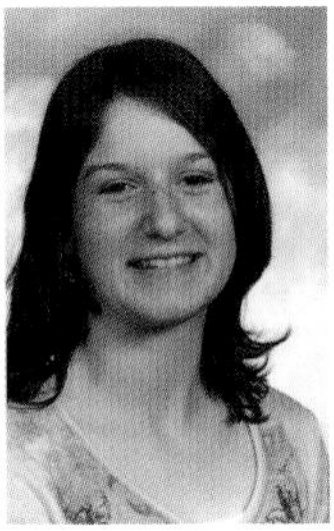

Megan Abbate,
Assistant Editor

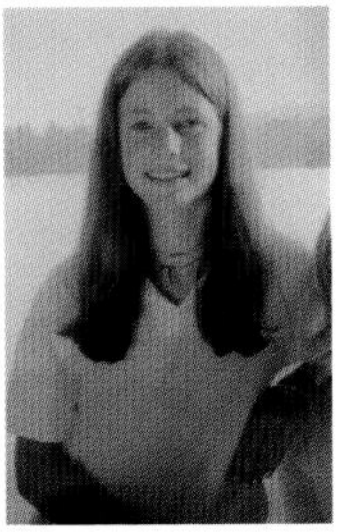

Johanna Allen,
Senior Marketing Manager

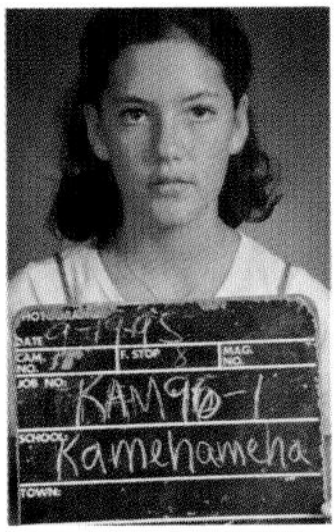
KAM96-1
Kamehameha

Starr Baer,
Associate Copy Chief

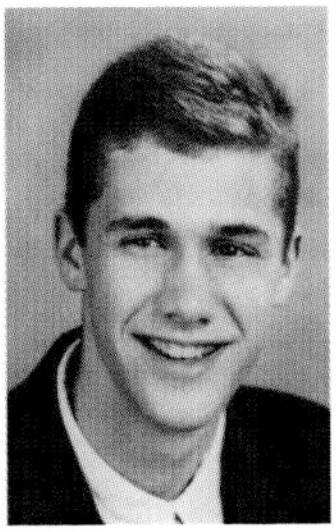

Kirk Benshoff,
Art Director

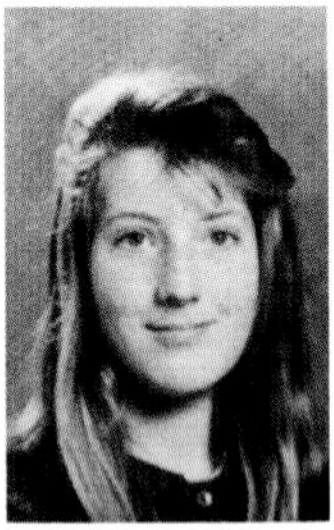

Jennifer Besser,
President of Macmillan Children's Publishing Group

Stay Sweet!

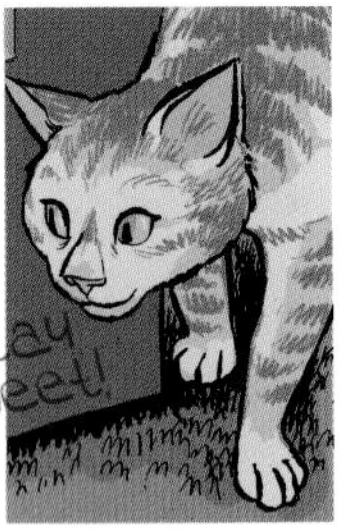

Alexa Blanco,
Senior Production Manager

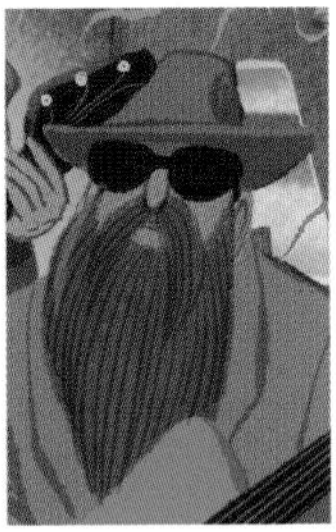

David Briggs,
Vice President of Managing & Production Editorial

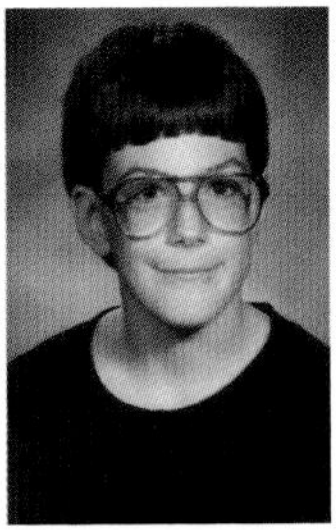

Alex Campbell,
Colorist

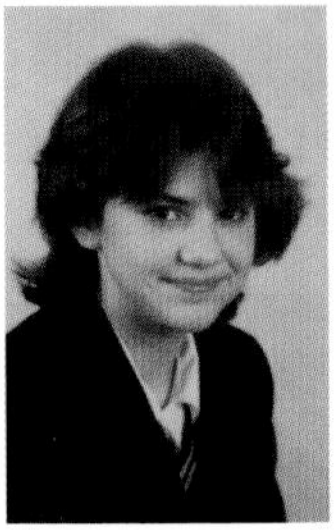

Karina Edwards,
Assistant Colorist

You're so RAD!

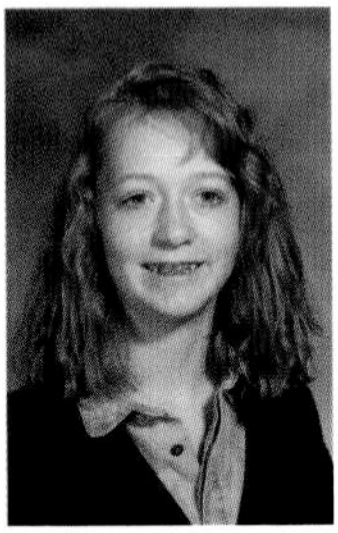

Shannon Hale,
Author

Have a tubular summer!

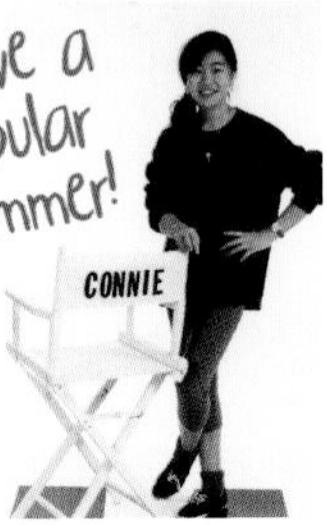
CONNIE

Connie Hsu,
Editorial Director

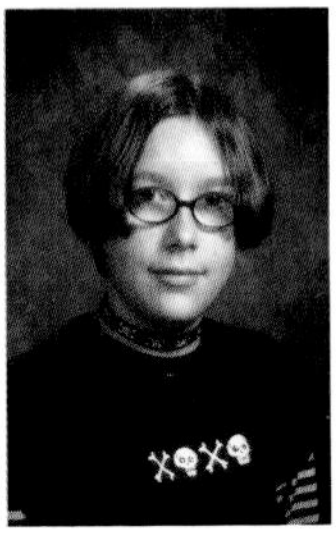

Molly Johanson,
Designer

Let's hang out this summer!

Morgan Kane,
Assistant Director of Publicity

Kristen Luby,
Marketing Manager

LeUyen Pham,
Artist

Call me!

Katie Quinn,
Marketing Manager

Dawn Ryan,
Executive Managing Editor

Mark Siegel,
Editorial &
Creative Director

Hilary Sycamore,
Colorist

Mary Van Akin,
Director of Publicity

Allison Verost,
Publishing Director

**Student of the
Month**

**Student of the
Month**

**Student of the
Month**

Never lose your awesome personality!

STAY COOL!

Have fun next year!

H.A.G.S.!

second period was a blast!

I don't know you that well but you seem nice.

All About Us!

I don't think LeUyen and I met till we were thirty, but in this picture it sure looks like we were BFFs at age thirteen! The errors of the past can be remedied through the magic of love, friendship, imagination, and photo editing...

Shannon Hale and **LeUyen Pham** are best friends who have been publishing books for young readers for two decades. They have created three bestselling series together: the graphic novel Friends series, the early chapter book Princess in Black series (with Dean Hale), and the picture book *Itty-Bitty Kitty-Corn*.

Shannon lives in Utah with her husband, four kids, and two cats, where she writes award-winning novels like *The Goose Girl*, *Book of a Thousand Days*, *Dangerous*, and the Newbery Honor book *Princess Academy*, and pens other books with her husband, Dean, including *Diana, Princess of the Amazons* (illustrated by Victoria Ying); *Rapunzel's Revenge* (illustrated by Nathan Hale); and two novels about Marvel's unbeatable Squirrel Girl.

LeUyen lives in Los Angeles with her husband, her two sons, a cat, and an orange gecko. She is the author/illustrator of the books *Big Sister, Little Sister*; *A Piece of Cake*; *The Itchy Book*; and *Outside, Inside*. She is also the illustrator of over one hundred books for kids, including *Vampirina Ballerina* by Anne Marie Pace, *Grace for President* by Kelly DiPucchio, and *The Boy Who Loved Math* by Deborah Heiligman. Her illustrations have won numerous awards, including the prestigious Caldecott Honor for *Bear Came Along* with Richard Morris.

Shannon and LeUyen plan to keep making books together for many years to come and to stay friends forever.

Dear Uyen,
You are the best artist I know, no joke!
Plus you're smart, funny, caring, and generous.
Please let's stay best friends forever—
not in a yearbook way. In a real friends way.
Xoxo, Shannon

Don't miss the start of Shannon's story!